The Library
Nazareth College of Rochester, N. Y.

NASBY IN EXILE

by

David Ross Locke

LITERATURE HOUSE / GREGG PRESS
Upper Saddle River, N. J.

Republished in 1970 by
LITERATURE HOUSE
an imprint of The Gregg Press
121 Pleasant Avenue
Upper Saddle River, N. J. 07458

Standard Book Number—8398-1158-6
Library of Congress Card—77-104516

118947

Printed in United States of America

MONT ST. MICHAEL.

NASBY IN EXILE:

OR,

SIX MONTHS OF TRAVEL

IN

England, Ireland, Scotland, France, Germany,
Switzerland and Belgium,

WITH MANY THINGS NOT OF TRAVEL.

BY

DAVID R. LOCKE,

(Petroleum V. Nasby.)

PROFUSELY ILLUSTRATED.

TOLEDO AND BOSTON:
LOCKE PUBLISHING COMPANY.
1882.

BLADE PRINTING AND PAPER CO.,
Printers and Binders,
TOLEDO, O.

PREFACE.

On the afternoon of May 14, 1881, the good ship " City of Richmond," steamed out of New York harbor with a varied assortment of passengers on board, all intent upon seeing Europe. Among these was the writer of the pages that follow.

Six of the passengers having contracted a sort of liking for each other, made a tour of six months together, that is, together most of the time.

This book is the record of their experiences, as they appeared originally in the columns of the TOLEDO BLADE.

It is not issued in compliance with any demand for it. I have no recollection that any one of the one hundred thousand regular subscribers to the TOLEDO BLADE ever asked that the letters that appeared from week to week in its columns should be gathered into book form. The volume is a purely mercantile speculation, which may or may not be successful. The publishers held that the matter was of sufficient value to go between covers, and believing that they were good judges of such things, I edited the letters, and here they are.

The ground we went over has been gone over by other writers a thousand times. We went where other tourists have gone, and what we saw others have seen. The only difference between this book and the thousands of others that have been printed describing the same scenes, is purely the difference in the eyes of the writers who saw them I saw the countries I visited with a pair of American eyes, and judged of men and things from a purely American stand-point.

I have not attempted to describe scenery, and buildings, and things of that nature, at all. That has been done by men and women more capable of such work than I am. Every library in America is full of books of that nature. But I was interested in the men and women of the countries I passed through, I was interested in their ways of living, their industries and their customs and habits, and I tried faithfully

(v)

to put upon paper what I saw, as well as the observations and com-ments of the party that traveled and observed with me.

I have a hope that the readers of these pages will lay the book down in quite as good condition, mentally and physically, as when they took it up, and that some information as to European life will result from its perusal. As I make no promises at the beginning I shall have no apologies to make at the ending.

It is only justice to say that much of the descriptive matter is the work of Mr. ROBINSON LOCKE, who was with me every minute of the time, and the intelligent reader will be perfectly safe in ascribing the best of its pages to his pen.

I can only hope that this work, as a book, will meet with the same measure of favor that the material did as newspaper sketches.

D. R. L.

Toledo, Ohio, June 29, 1882.

ILLUSTRATIONS.

No.		Page
1.	FRONTISPIECE.	
2.	The Departure	18
3.	"Shuffle Board"	22
4.	The Betting Young Man from Chicago	24
5.	"Dear, Sea-sickness is only a Feminine Weakness,"	27
6.	Lemuel Tibbitts, from Oshkosh, Writes a Letter	29
7.	Every Sin I Had Committed Came Before Me	33
8.	Off for London	35
9.	Public Buildings, London	36
10.	The Indian Policy	39
11.	The Emetic Policy	39
12.	A London Street Scene	45
13.	A London Steak	50
14.	"And is the Them Shanghais?"	53
15.	Sol. Carpenter and the Race	60
16.	Leaving for the Derby	62
17.	By the Roadside	64
18.	English Negro Minstrelsy	66
19.	The Roadside Repast	67
20.	The Betting Ring	73
21.	"D——n the Swindling Scoundrel"	74
22.	Egyptian Room, British Museum	76
23.	A Bold Briton Trying the American Custom	79
24.	A London Gin Drinking Woman	80
25.	The Poor Man is Sick	81
26.	"That Nigger is Mine"	82
27.	St. Thomas Hospital	92
28.	Interior of a Variety Hall	95
29.	The Magic Purse	98
30.	The Man who was Music Proof	100
31.	Madame Tussaud	102
32.	Wax Figures of Americans	103
33.	"Digging Corpses is all Wrong"	105
34.	Improved Process of Burke and Hare	106
35.	Isle of Wight	107
36.	The London Lawyer	110
37.	The Old English Way of Procuring a Loan	118
38.	"Beware of Fraudulent Imitations"	120
39.	The Old Temple Bar	122
40.	The Sidewalk Shoe Store	125
41.	"Sheap Clodink"	127
42.	"Dake Dot Ring"	133
43.	A Lane in Camberwell	135
44.	The Tower of London	136
45.	The Jewel Tower	140
46.	Sir Magnus' Men	142
47.	Horse Armory	144
48.	St. John's Chapel	145

(vii)

No.		Page
49.	St. Thomas' Tower	146
50.	General View of the Tower	147
51.	The Bloody Tower	148
52.	Drowning of Clarence in a Butt of Wine	149
53.	The Byward Tower from the East	150
54.	The Beauchamp Tower	151
55.	The Overworked Headsman	152
56.	The Persuasive Rack	153
57.	The Byward Tower from the West	154
58.	The Middle Tower	155
59.	The Beef Eater	156
60.	The Flint Tower	157
61.	The Traitor's Gate	158
62.	What Shall We Do with Sir Thomas?	159
63.	The Easiest Way	160
64.	The Suits Come Home	163
65.	The Candle Episode	168
66.	The Little Bill	169
67.	Getting Ready to Leave a Hotel	169
68.	The Last Straw	170
69.	The Cabman Tipped	170
70.	The Universal Demand	171
71.	The Lord Mayor's Show	173
72.	A Second Hand Debauch	175
73.	The Anniversary Ceremonies	178
74.	In the Harbor	179
75.	Isle of Wight	182
76.	The Unfinished Entries in the Diary	184
77.	Westminster Abbey	186
78.	Exterior of the Abbey	187
79.	Entrance to the Abbey	188
80.	The Poet's Corner	191
81.	Henry VII.'s Chapel	193
82.	Chapel of Edward	197
83.	Effigy Room	200
84.	The Abbey in Queen Anne's Time	201
85.	"If She Ever Miscalculates She's Gone,"	204
86.	The Death of the Trainer	206
87.	The Gorgeous Funeral Procession	207
88.	Monument to the Trainer	208
89.	The Side Show Zulu	210
90.	The Lost Finger	212
91.	On the Thames	218
92.	Sandwiches at New Haven	222
93.	Off Dieppe—Four A. M.	224
94.	"Have You Tobacco or Spirits?"	225
95.	Fisher Folk—Dieppe	227
96.	Fisher Women—Dieppe	228
07.	Fisher Boy and Child	229
98.	The Boys of Rouen	232
99.	Rouen	233
100.	The Professor Stood Before it	234
101.	Cathedral of Notre Dame	235
102.	House of Joan d' Arc	235
103.	Harbor of Rouen	236
104.	St. Ouen—Rouen	238
105.	The Showman in Paris	240
106.	Bloss' Great Moral Spectacle	241
107.	Tower of St. Pierre	242
108.	Old Houses—Rouen	242
109.	The Professor's Spectacles	245

No.		Page
110.	Old Paris	246
111.	Liberty, Fraternity, Equality	247
112.	New Paris	248
113.	The Louvre	250
114.	A Boulevard Cafe	252
115.	A Costume by Worth	253
116.	A Magazine on the Boulevard	254
117.	Mr. Thompson's Art Purchases	256
118.	The American Party Outside a Cafe	259
119.	The Avenue de L'Opera	261
120.	Cafe Concerts	262
121.	The Faro Bankeress	266
122.	French Soldiers	267
123.	Parisian Bread Carriers	269
124.	Queer—to Frenchmen	271
125.	The Porte St. Martin	272
126.	A Very Polite Frenchman	275
127.	"Merci, Monsieur!"	277
128.	Paris Underground	279
129.	Interior of the Paris Bourse	280
130.	The Arc du Carrousel	282
131.	"How Long Must I Endure This?"	285
132.	Tail Piece	286
133.	The Mother of the Gamin as She Was	288
134.	The Mother of the Gamin in the Sere and Yellow Leaf	289
135.	The Aged Stump Gatherer	290
136.	A Talk with a Gamin	294
137.	The Mabille at Night	305
138.	A Mabille Divinity	306
139.	Professionals in a Quadrille	309
140.	A Male Dancer	310
141.	The Grisette	311
142.	Meeting of Tibbitts and the Professor	314
443.	The Cafe Swell	316
144.	Tail Piece	318
145.	Beauvais Cathedral	319
146.	Struggle for the Kingship	322
147.	Of the Commune	326
148.	Tibbitts and Faro Bankeress	330
149.	Tail Piece	331
150.	Palais Royal	333
151.	Vision of the Commune	335
152.	Mother and Bonne	337
153.	The Youthful Bonne	338
154.	The Aged Bonne	338
155.	"Who Put that Ribbon in your Cap?"	345
156.	Corrective Used by Mr. Tibbitts	348
157.	The Coco Seller	349
158.	In Any of the Parks	358
159.	The No-Legged Beggar Woman	360
160.	How the French Sport Kills Game	362
161.	Fishing in the Seine	363
162.	Inside a Paris Omnibus	364
163.	The Showman Shown the Door	365
164.	The Tell Catastrophe	368
165.	Zoological Room	369
166.	Cork Harbor	370
167.	Queenstown	371
168.	Irish Woman and Daughter	375
169.	A County Cork Cabin	377
170.	Interior of Better Class Cabin	378

No.		Page
171.	Royal Irish Constabulary	379
172.	Interior of Cabin	380
173.	A Quiver Full	381
174.	Street in an Irish Village	384
175.	Blarney Castle	385
176.	Free Speech in Ireland	387
177.	In a Bog Village	389
178.	"Drop the Child!"	391
179.	Nature's Looking Glass	393
180.	Irishman of the Stage and Novel	394
181.	The Evicted Irishman	395
182.	To Market and Back	396
183.	The Real Irish Girl	397
184.	A Small but Well-to-do Farmer	398
185.	Sketches in Galway	402
186.	Affixing Notice of Eviction	406
187.	Eviction	407
188.	The Eviction we Saw	408
189.	Evicted	409
190.	Farming in County Mayo	410
191.	My Lord's Agent	413
192.	Kind of a Girl My Lord Wants	414
193.	The Woman who Paid the Poor Rate	416
194.	Conemara Women	418
195.	At Work in the Bog	420
196.	Duke Leinster's Tenants	422
197.	Tenant Farmer	424
198.	In a Discontented District	426
199.	Protecting a Gentleman Farmer	427
200.	Filling the Ditch	429
201.	Ready for Emigration	431
202.	Old but Tolerably Cheerful	433
203.	After a Wholesale Eviction	435
204.	The "Faymale Painther"	436
205.	Old and Not Cheerful	438
206.	The Proper End of Royalty	441
207.	Meath Lads at Crossakeel	443
208.	A Mayo Farmer	445
209.	Mayo Peasantry	447
210.	Inhabitants of a Bog Village	449
211.	Dublin	452
212.	They Glared Ferociously	456
213.	Bog Village	459
214.	Interior French Car	462
215.	They were Lively Children	464
216.	Geneva	466
217.	"Your Hotel is a Swindle, Sir"	474
218.	Group of Swiss Girls	480
219.	The Sweat of Other Men's Brows	481
220.	The Alpine Guide	485
221.	A Non-Professional Lady Tourist	487
222.	Young Man with Inopportune Remarks	493
223.	"Would You Oblige Me?"	495
224.	"See Me Unmask this Jew"	497
225.	Swiss Timber Village	501
226.	The Slender Bridge	503
227.	A Bit of Climbing	504
228.	Where the Maiden Leaped From	511
229.	The Chamois	513
230.	Taking the Cattle to the Mountains	513
231.	Outside the Chalet	515

No.		Page
232.	Inside the Chalet	516
233.	An Alpine Homestead	519
234.	"I Should Wake Them Cheerily"	520
235.	On the Road to Chamonix	525
236.	The Presumed Chamois Hunter	530
237.	The Fate of Two Englishmen	532
438.	A Frequent Accident	533
239.	The Mer De Glace	534
240.	A Slip Toward the Edge	535
241.	Crevasses	536
242.	The Moraine	537
243.	The Dilemma	538
244.	Rocks Polished by Old Glaciers	539
245.	The Path to the Village	548
246.	Mt. Blanc and Valley of Chamonix	550
247.	The Conscientious Barber	555
248.	The Jungfrau	557
249.	Wood Carving	559
250.	Home of the Carver	560
251.	Female Costumes	562
252.	Our Party at the Giessbach	565
253.	Peasants of East Switzerland	567
254.	Near Brienz	568
255.	Lion of Lucerne	570
256.	End of Pontius Pilate	573
257.	Lucerne Rigi-Rail	575
258.	Ditto from Kanzell	576
259.	Old Way of Ascending Rigi	578
260.	Night Ascent of Rigi	579
261.	Railway up the Rigi	581
262.	Rigi Railway	582
263.	Railway up the Mountain	583
264.	Tell's Chapel	584
265.	Tibbitts in Concert Hall	589
266.	Entrance Strasburg Cathedral	593
267.	Pig Market, Strasburg	596
268.	The Great Hall	600
269.	Tibbitts Making Plain the Point	608
270.	Front of the Kursale	612
271.	The Swimming Bath	614
272.	The Donkey Enjoyed It	616
273.	The Lichtenthal	617
274.	Promenade in Baden Baden	618
275.	Charcoal Burners, Black Forest	619
276.	Heidelberg Castle	623
277.	Heidelberg Tun	626
278.	Tibbitts and the Students	629
279.	Rhine Steamer	630
280.	Mannheim	631
281.	Tibbitts in the Cloak Room	633
282.	Mayence	639
283.	Erchenheim Tower	640
284.	Roemer	640
285.	Luther's Home	640
284.	Street on the Roemerberg	642
285.	The Jews' Street	644
286.	"Der Hind Leg of a Helty Mule"	649
287.	Cologne Cathedral	651
288.	Death of Bishop Hatto	655
289.	Legend of the Cathedral	668

CONTENTS.

PAGE

CHAPTER I.

The Departure — How the Passengers Amused Themselves — Sea-sickness—Tibbitts, of Oshkosh—The Storm........................17– 35

CHAPTER II.

London — The Englishman — A Few Statistics — The Climate — A Red-coated Romance...18– 57

CHAPTER III.

The Derby Races—Departure for the Derby—Sights and Scenes—Shows and Beggars—Betting 58– 76

CHAPTER IV.

What the Londoners Quench their Thirst with—The Kind of Liquor—Tobacco—Early Closing....................................77– 90

CHAPTER V.

How London is Amused—The London Theaters—An English Idea of a Good Time—Punch and Judy....................................91–100

CHAPTER VI.

Madame Tussaud—American Worthies...........................101–107

CHAPTER VII.

The London Lawyer—The Solicitor's Bill........................108–112

CHAPTER VIII.

English Capital—London Quacks—The London Advertiser........113–122

CHAPTER IX.

Petticoat Lane—The Home of Second-Hand—The Clothing Dealer—Diamonds—The Confiding Israelite....................... 123–134

(xii)

PAGE

CHAPTER X.

The Tower—The Royal Jewels—The Horse Armory—Interesting Relics
—The Beef-Eaters...137–160

CHAPTER XI.

Two English Nuisances—A Badly Dressed People—An English Hotel—
The English Landlord 161–172

CHAPTER XII.

Portsmouth—Nelson's Ship—In the Harbor—Tibbitts' Diary.......174–185

CHAPTER XIII.

Westminster Abbey—Seeing the Abbey—Warren Hastings—Epitaphs—
Religious Service—A Little History...........................187–202

CHAPTER XIV.

The American Showman—The Trainer's Widow–Foggerty the Zulu, 203–212

CHAPTER XV.

Richmond—The Star and Garter—Down the River 213–219

CHAPTER XVI.

Frðm London to Paris — The Custom House — Normandy—The Cathedral—On the Way to Paris 221–242

CHAPTER XVII.

A Scattering View of Paris—Drinking in Paris—Wine and Whisky —
The National Fete..243–267

CHAPTER XVIII.

Something About Parisians—French Cleanliness—The Polite French—
The Disgust of Tibbitts 268–286

CHAPTER XIX.

Parisian Gamin — Interview with a Gamin—A Contented Being...287–299

CHAPTER XX.

How Paris Amuses Itself—The Grand Opera—The Wicked Mabille—
Gardens other than the Mabille—Tibbitts and the Professor....300–318

CHAPTER XXI.

The Louvre—Art in the Louvre—The Commune...................320–331

CHAPTER XXII

The Palais-Royal—A Tale of the Commune—The Wisdom of Therese—
The Two Lovers....... 332–345

PAGE

CHAPTER XXIII.

French Drinking—The Water of Paris—The Mild Swash..........346–351

CHAPTER XXIV.

Parisian Living—The Market Woman — Parisian Washing — Female
Shop-keepers—The Career of Sam............................352–369

CHAPTER XXV.

Ireland—Cork—The Jaunting Car—Another Cabin 370–383

CHAPTER XXVI.

Bantry—How My Lord Bantry Lives—The Real and the Ideal—Several
Delusions—The Conversion of an Irish Lady.................384–401

CHAPTER XXVII.

An Irish Mass Meeting—An Eviction—Boycotting—One Landlord who
was Killed—How he was killed—Patsey's Dead..............403–518

CHAPTER XXVIII.

Some Little History—The Question of Lease—A Foiled Landlord—
Bantry Village—The Boatman and Nancy...... 419–438

CHAPTER XXIX.

England, Ireland, Scotland—Land Troubles in England—The Royal
Family—The Palace and the Workhouse—Women's Work.... 439–460

CHAPTER XXX.

Paris to Geneva—A Night on the Rail—Geneva—Affecting Anecdote—
Piracy on Lake Erie—The Irate Guest—Too Much Music...... 461–477

CHAPTER XXXI.

Switzerland—The Rhone—A Geneva Bakery—Swiss Roads—Female
Climbers—Ascent of Mont Blanc—A Useful Man at Last......478–491

CHAPTER XXXII

Chillon—Tibbitts and the Jew—On the Lake... 492–501

CHAPTER XXXIII.

From Geneva over the Alps—Mountain Climbing—Legend of the
Gorge—Martigny –A Swiss Cottage—Alpine Ascents.........502–517

CHAPTER XXXIV.

Over the Alps—Tibbitts' Idea—Dangers of Ascending Mt. Blanc...518–529

PAGE

CHAPTER XXXV.

Going up the Mountain—The Mer de Glace—The Gorge—Something
About Glaciers............ 530–545

CHAPTER XXXVI.

In Switzerland—Tibbitts' Letter—Berne and Bears—Barbers.......546–555

CHAPTER XXXVII.

Lake Thun and Beyond—Interlaken—Wood Carving—Geissbach...556–568

CHAPTER XXXVIII.

Lucerne and the Rigi—Up the Rigi—A Mountain Railway—The Rigi
Kulm—Tell's Chapel.... 569–587

CHAPTER XXXIX.

Zurich and Strasburg—Beer and Music—The Cathedral—The Wonderful Clock.......... 588–604

CHAPTER XL.

Baden-Baden—A Few Legends—Up the Mountain—To old Schloss.605–621

CHAPTER XLI.

Heidelberg—The Great Cask—The Students..... 622–630

CHAPTER XLII.

Mannheim—Opera--A Treatise on Treating.... 631–639

CHAPTER XLIII.

Frankfort-on-the-Maine—Red Tape—Jews' Street—Lovely Gardens.640–651

CHAPTER XLIV.

Down the Rhine—Bingen—Mouse Tower—Tibbitts' Romance......652–663

CHAPTER XLV.

Cologne—The Cathedral—Eleven Thousand Virgins—Home.......664–672

TO

Charles A. B. Shepard,

The "Poetical Bookseller,"

This book is dedicated (without permission)
as a
Tribute to a most Reliable Friend,
a Thorough Business Man, and
One whose steady devotion to everything right and proper,
and whose
hatred for everything mean and disreputable,
was never questioned by any one
who knew him.

NASBY IN EXILE.

CHAPTER I.

THE DEPARTURE, VOYAGE, AND LANDING.

"CAST OFF!" There was a bustle, a movement of fifty men, a rush of people to the gangways; hurried good-bys were said; another rush, assisted by the fifty men, the enormous gangways were lifted, there was a throb of steam, a mighty jar of machinery, a tremor along the line of the vast body of wood and iron, and the good ship "City of Richmond" was out at sea.

THE DEPARTURE.

I am not going to inflict upon the reader a description of the harbor of New York, or anything of the kind. The whole world knows that it is the finest in the world, and every Ameri-

2

can would believe it so, whether it is so or not. Suffice it to say that the ship got out of the harbor safely, and before nightfall was upon the broad Atlantic, out of the way of telegraph and mail facilities, and one hundred and fifty-six saloon passengers — men, women, and children — found themselves beyond the reach of daily papers, though they had everything else that pertains to civilization and luxury.

A voyage at sea is not what it was when first I sailed from — but no, I have never been abroad before, and have not, therefore, the privilege of lying about travel. That will come in time, and doubtless I shall use it as others do. But I was going to say that sailing is not what it was, as I understand it to have been. The ship of to-day is nothing more or less than a floating hotel, with some few of the conveniences omitted, and a great many conveniences that hotels on shore have not. You have your luxurious barber-shop, you have a gorgeous bar, you have hot and cold water in your room, and a table as good as the best in New York. You eat, drink, and sleep just as well, if not better, than on shore.

The sailor is no more what he used to be than the ship is. I have seen any number of sailors, and know all about them. The tight young fellow in blue jacket and shiny tarpaulin, and equally shiny belt, and white trousers, the latter enormously wide at the bottom, which trousers he was always hitching up with a very peculiar movement of the body, standing first upon one leg and then upon the other; the sailor who could fight three pirates at once and kill them all, finishing the last one by disabling his starboard eye with a chew of tobacco thrown with terrible precision; who, if an English sailor, was always a match for three Frenchmen, if an American a match for three Englishmen, and no matter of what nationality, was always ready to d—n the eyes of the man he did not like, and protect prepossessing females and oppressed children even at the risk of being hung at the yard-arm by a court-martial — this kind of a sailor is gone, and I fear forever. I know I have given a proper description of him, for I have seen hundreds of them — at the theater.

In his stead is an unpoetic being, clad in all sorts of unpoetic clothing, and no two of them alike. There is a faint

effort at uniformity in their caps, which have sometimes the
name of their ship on them, but even that not always.
In fair weather he is in appearance very like a hod
carrier, and in foul weather a New York drayman. He
does n't d—n anybody's eyes, and he does n't sing out "Belay
there," or "Avast, you lubber," or indulge in any other nautical expressions. He uses just about the language that people
on shore do, and is as dull and uninteresting a person as one
would wish not to meet.

The traditional jack tar, of whom the Dibden of the last
century sang, only remains in "Pinafore" opera, and can only
be seen when the nautical pieces of the thirty years ago are
revived. If such sailors ever existed, off the stage, they are as
extinct a race as the icthyosaurus. Steam has knocked the
poetry out of navigation, as it has out of everything else—
that is, that kind of poetry. It will doubtless have a poetry
of its own, when its gets older, but it is too new yet.

There is no holystoning the decks. On the contrary the
decks are washed with hose, and scrubbed afterward by a
patent appliance, which has nothing of the old time about it.
The lifting is done by steam, and in fact every blessed thing
about the ship is done by machinery. There is neither a ship
nor a sailor any more. There are floating hotels, and help.
The last remaining show for a ship is the masts and sails they
all have, and they seem to be more for ornament than use.

The company on board was, on the whole, monotonous.
Ocean travel is either monotonous or dangerous. Its principal
advantage over land travel is, the track is not dusty.

We had on our passenger list precisely the usual people,
and none others. There were three Jews of different types:
the strong, robust, eagle-nosed and eagle-eyed German Jew,
resident of New York, going abroad on business; the keen
French Jew, returning from a successful foray on New York
jewelers, and the Southern Jew, who, having made a fortune
in cotton, attached no value to anything else.

I like the Jews, and ten days with them did not lessen my
liking. They know something for certain; they do things,
and they do well what they do.

There was a Chicago operator in mining stocks, going

abroad to place the "Great Mastodon" in London.   There was
the smooth-chinned, side-whiskered minister, or "priest," as he
delighted in calling himself, of the Church of England, going
home, and a fiery Welsh Baptist who had been laboring in
the States for many years.

On Sunday evening the Chicago man and a Texan engaged
the English minister in a discussion on the evidences of Christianity.   It was a furious controversy, and an amusing one.
The Welsh Baptist was a more zealous Christian than the
Church of England man, and he did by far the best part of
the argument; but the priest, by look at least, resented his
interference.   Being a Baptist, he was entirely irregular, and
did not hold up his end of the argument regularly.   The
priest regarded the evangelist as a regular soldier might a
guerilla serving the same side.   The discussion embraced every
point that religionists affirm and infidels deny, commencing
with the creation and coming down to the present day, with
long excursions into the future.

A terrible disaster was the result.   The next morning the
priest met the infidel on deck, and extended his hand humbly:

"My dear sir," said he, "I have been thinking over the
matter we discussed last night.   I am convinced that you are
right, and that—"

"What!" exclaimed the infidel.   "My dear sir, I was looking for you.   Your forcible and convincing statements satisfy
me that there is truth in the Christian religion, and—"

Neither said more.   The priest had converted the infidel
to Christianity, and the infidel had converted the priest to
infidelity.   So far as the result upon the religion of the world
was concerned, it was a stand-off.

The days were devoted to all sorts of occupations.   There
were young men spooning young women, and young women
who made a business of flirtation, or what was akin to it.
One young lady who could be seen at any time in the day, in
a most bewitching attitude, reclining on a steamer chair, picturesque in all sorts of wraps, held a brief conversation with
her mother, who had hooked a widower the second day out.
The mother was skillful at looking young, and compelled her
child, therefore, to be juvenile and shy of young men.

"Helen, you were flirting with that Chicago young man, this morning!"

"Flirting! Mamma! It's too mean! You won't let me flirt. I havn't enjoyed myself a minute since we sailed. I wish you would let me alone to do as I please."

The poor child envied her mother, and with good reason, for within ten minutes she was under the wing, or arm, of the widower, looking not a minute over thirty-five.

There were old maids who found themselves objects of attention for the first time for years; there were widows who grew sentimental looking at the changing waters, especially at night when the moon and stars were out; there were married men whose wives were many leagues away, determined to have a good time once more, flirting with all sorts and conditions of women, and there were all sorts and conditions of women flirting hungrily with all sorts and conditions of men. There were speculators driving bargains with each other just the same as on land—in brief, the ship was a little world by itself, and just about the same as any other world.

In the smoking room the great and muscular American game of draw poker was played incessantly, from early in the morning, till late in the night.

A portion of the passengers, including the English dominie, played a game called "shuffle-board." Squares were marked upon the deck, which were numbered from one to seven. Then some distance from the squares a line was drawn, and what you had to do was to take an implement shaped like a crutch, and shove discs of wood at the squares. We all played it, sooner or later, for on ship-board one will get, in time, to playing pin alone in his room. The beauty about shuffle-board is, one player is as good as another, if not better, for there isn't the slightest skill to be displayed in it. Indeed, the best playing is always done at first, when the player shoots entirely at random. There is a chance that he will strike a square, then; but when one gets to calculating distances, and looking knowingly, and attempting some particular square, the chances are even that the disc goes overboard.

However, it is a good and useful game. The young ladies look well handling the clumsy cues, and the attitudes they

are compelled to take are graceful. Then as the vessel lurches
they fall naturally in your arms. By the way, it is a curious
fact and one worthy of record, that I did not see a young lady
fall into the arms of another young lady during the entire
voyage.

We had on board, as a matter of course, the betting young
man from Chicago. No steamer ever sailed that did not have
this young fellow aboard, and there is
enough of them to last the Atlantic
for a great many years. He knew
everything that everybody thinks
they know, but do not, and his delight
was to propound a query, and then
when you had answered it, to very
coolly and exasperatingly remark:—

"Bet yer bottle of wine you're
wrong."

The matter would be so simple
and one of so common repute that
immediately you accepted the wager
only to find that in some minute particular, you *were* wrong, and that the
knowing youth had won.

For instance:—

"Thompson, do you know how
many States there are in the Union?"

Now any citizen of the United
States who votes, and is eligible to
the Presidency, ought to know how
many States there are in his beloved
country without thinking, but how
many are there who can say, off-hand?
And so poor Thompson answered:—

"SHUFFLE BOARD."

"What a question! Of course I know."
"Bet ye bottle ye don't!"
"Done. There are—"

And then Thompson would find himself figuring the very
important problem as to whether Colorado had been admitted,
and Nevada, and Oregon, and he would decide that one had

and the other had n't, and finally state the number, with great
certainty that it was wrong.

The Chicago man's crowning bet occurred the last day out.
The smoking room was tolerably full, as were the occupants,
and everybody was bored, as everybody is on the last day.
The Chicago man had been silent for an hour, when suddenly
he broke out:

" Gentlemen—"

" Oh, no more bets," was the exclamation of the entire
party. " Give us a rest."

" I don't want to bet, but I can show you something
curious."

" Well ?"

" I say it and mean it. I can drink a glass of water without it's going down my throat."

"And get it into your stomach ?"

" Certainly."

" There was a silence of considerably more than a minute.
Every man in the room had been victimized by this gatherer
up of inconsidered trifles, and there was a general disposition
to get the better of him in some way if possible. Here was
the opportunity. How could a man get a glass of water into
his stomach without its going down his throat? Impossible!
And so the usual bottle of wine was wagered, and the Chicago
man proceeded to accomplish the supposed impossible feat. It
was very easily done. All he did was to stand upon his head
on the seat that runs around the room and swallow a glass of
water. It went to his stomach, but it did not go *down* his
throat. It went *up* his throat. And so his last triumph was
greater than all his previous ones, for every man in the room
had been eager to accept his wager. From that time out had
he offered to wager that he would swallow his own head he
would have got no takers.

It is astonishing how short remembrance is, and how the
knowledge of one decade is swallowed up in the increasing
volume of the next. Every one of the catches employed by
this young man to keep himself in wine and cigars were well
known ten years ago, but totally unknown now except by the
few who use them. The water going up the throat instead of

down was published years ago in a small volume called "Hocus Pocus," and it sold by the million, but nobody knows of it today. I once asked a sharper who had lived thirty years by the

THE BETTING YOUNG MAN FROM CHICAGO.

practice of one simple trick, how it happened that the whole world did not know his little game?

"There are new crops of fools coming on every year," was his answer. He was right. The stock will never run out.

There were one hundred and fifty-six saloon passengers on board, but with the exception of those mentioned, a distressing monotony prevailed among them. Never was so good a set of people ever gathered together. They were fearfully good—too good by half.

True goodness is all very well in the abstract, but there is nothing picturesque about it. It is slightly tame. Your brigand, with short green jacket and yellow breeches, with blue or green garters, and a tall hat with a feather in it, is a much more striking being than a Quaker woman. The wicked is always the startling, and, therefore, taking to the eye.

On our ship the people were all good. There wasn't a pickpocket, a card sharper, or anything of the sort to vary the monotony of life. It was a dead level of goodness, a sort of quiet mill-pond of morality, that to the lover of excitement was distressing in the extreme. The card parties were conducted decorously, and the religious services in the grand saloon were attended by nearly every passenger, and what is more they all seemed to enjoy it. Possibly it was because religious services were a novelty to the most of them.

The second day out was a very rough one. The wind freshened—I think that is the proper phrase—and a tremendously heavy sea was on. The "City of Richmond" is a very staunch ship, and behaves herself commendably in bad weather, but there is no ship that can resist the power of the enormous waves of the North Atlantic. Consequently she tossed like a cork, and, consequently, there was an amount of suffering for two days that was amusing to everybody but the sufferers.

Sea-sickness is probably the most distressing of all the maladies that do not kill. The sickness from first to last is a taste of death. The resultant vomiting is of a nature totally different from any other variety of vomiting known. The victim does not vomit—he throws up. There is a wild legend that one man in a severe fit of sea-sickness threw up his boots, but it is not credible. It is entirely safe to say, however, that one throws up everything but original sin, and he gives that a tolerable trial.

It was amusing to see those who had done the voyage before, and who had been through sea-sickness, smile upon those who were in the throes of agony. The look of superiority they took on, as much as to say, "when you have been through it as I have, you won't have it any more." And then to see these same fellows turn deadly pale, and leave their seats, and rush to their rooms and disappear from mortal view a day or so, was refreshing to those who were having their first experience.

The beauty of sea-sickness is that you may have it every voyage, which is fortunate, as having a tendency to restrain pride and keep down assumption of superiority; for when one has to suffer, one loves to see everybody else suffer.

One man aboard did not think it possible that he could be sick, and he was rather indignant that his wife should be. She, poor thing, was in the agonies of death, and he insisted, as he held her head, that she ought not to be sick, that her giving way to it was a weakness purely feminine, and he went on wondering why a woman could not—

He quit talking very quickly. The strong man who was not a woman, turned pale, the regular paleness that denotes the coming of the malady, and dropping the head he had been holding so patronizingly with no more compunction than as though it had been his pet dog's, rushed to the side of the vessel, and there paid his tribute to Neptune. The suffering wife, sick as she was, could not resist the temptation to wreak a trifle of feminine vengeance upon him. "Dear," said she, between the heaves that were rending her in several twains, "Sea-sickness is only a feminine weakness. Oh—ugh—ugh— how I wish I were a strong man!"

There is one good thing about sea-sickness, and only one: the sufferer cannot possibly have any other disease at the same time. One may have bronchitis and dyspepsia at once, but sea-sickness monopolizes the whole body. It is so all-pervading; it is such a giant of illness that there is room for nothing else when it takes possession of a human body.

During General Butler's occupancy of New Orleans a fiery Rebel Frenchman was inveighing against him in set terms.

"But you must admit," said a loyal Northerner, "that during General Butler's administration your city was free from yellow fever."

"Ze yellow fevair and General Butlair in one season? Have ze great God no maircy, zen?"

A kind Providence couldn't possibly saddle sea-sickness with any other ailment.

Was there ever a ship or a rail car, or any other place

"DEAR —, SEA-SICKNESS IS ONLY — A FEMININE WEAKNESS."

where danger is possible, that there was not present the man with a sharp nose, slightly red at the tip, whose chief delight seems to be to point out the possibilities of all sorts of disaster, and to do it in the most friendly way? I remember once going down the Hoosac Tunnel before it was finished. I went down, not because I wanted to, (indeed I would have given a farm, if I had had one, to have avoided it,) but it was the thing to do there, and must be done. So with about the feeling that accompanied John Rogers to the stake, I stepped, with others, upon the platform, and down we went. It was a most terrible descent. A hole in the ground eighteen hundred feet deep, and a platform, suspended by a single rope! In my eyes that rope was not larger or stronger than pack-thread.

"Is this safe?" I asked of the sharp-nosed man.

"Wa'all, yes, I s'pose so. It does break sometimes — did last month and killed eight men. I guess we are all right, though the rope's tollable old and yest'dy they histed out a very heavy ingine and biler, which may hev strained it. Long ways to fall — if she does break!"

Cheerful suggestion for people who were fifteen hundred feet from the bottom and couldn't possibly get off.

Another time on the Shore Line between Boston and New York, there was an old lady who had never been upon a railroad train before, and who was exceedingly nervous. Behind her sat the sharp-nosed man of that train, who answered all her questions.

"Ya'as, railroad travelin' is dangerous. Y' see they git keerless. Only a year ago, they left a draw opened, and a train run into it, and mor'n a hundred passengers wuz drownded."

"Merciful heavens!" ejaculated the old lady, in an agony of horror. "We don't go over that bridge."

"Yes we do, and we're putty nigh to it now. And the men are jest ez keerless now ez they wuz then. They git keerless. I never travel over this road ef I kin help it."

Then he went on and told her of every accident that he could remember, especially those that had occurred upon that road.

And the old lady, with her blood frozen by the horrible recitals, sat during the entire trip with her hands grasping tightly the arms of her seat, expecting momentarily to be hurled from the track and torn limb from limb, or to be plunged into the wild waters of the Sound.

We had the sharp-nosed man with us. His delight was to

are told in so good a cause. I love my mother, I do. Let's see, where was I? Oh yes."

I have just come from one at which the discussion was mostly on the progress of missions in the Far West. (*The old lady is Treasurer of a society for the conversion of the Apaches, or some other tribe.*) Just now the sailors are heaving a log, which they do to ascertain the speed the ship is making. Mr. Inman, the owner of this ship, is a very wealthy man, and he has everything of the best. He furnishes his vessel with nothing but black walnut logs to heave, while the others use pine or poplar. Captain Leitch is a very humane man, and never uses profane language to his crew. On other ships the men who go aloft are compelled to climb tarred rope ladders, but Captain Leitch has passenger elevators rigged to the masts, such as you saw in the Palmer House in Chicago, in which they sit comfortably and are hoisted up by a steam engine.

"Great heavens! You are not surely going to send that?"

"Why not? What is an old lady in silver spectacles on a farm thirty miles from any water more than a well, going to know about a steamer? I must write her something, for she persuaded the old gentleman to let me take the trip. I ain't ungrateful, I ain't. I'll give her one good letter, anyhow. Why, by the way you talk, I should suppose you never had a mother, and if you had that you didn't know how to treat her. I hate a man who don't love his mother and isn't willing to sacrifice himself for her. All I can do for her now is to write to her, and write such letters as will interest her, and the dear old girl is going to get them, if the paper and ink holds out, and they are going to be good ones, too."

I have got to be a good deal of a sailor, and if it were not for leaving you, which I couldn't do, I believe I should take one of these ships myself. I know all about starboard and port — port used to be larboard — and I can tell the stern from the bow. On a ship you don't say, "I will go down stairs," but you say, "I will go below." One would think that I had been born on the sea, and was a true child of the ocean.

Owing to my strictly temperate habits at home, and my absolute abstemiousness on the ship, I have escaped the horrors of sea sickness. As you taught me, true happiness can only be found in virtue. The wicked young man from New York has been sick half the time, as a young man who keeps a bottle in his room should be.

The nice woolen stockings you knit for me have been a great comfort, and all I regret is, I am afraid I have not enough of them to last me till I get home.

(The young villain had purchased in New York an assortment of the most picturesque hosiery procurable, which he was wearing with low cut shoes. The woolen stockings he gave to his room-steward.)

The tracts you put in my valise I have read over and over again, and have lent them since to the passengers who prefer serious reading to trashy novels and literature of that kind. What time I have had to spare for other reading, I have devoted to books of travel, so that I may see Europe intelligently.

"By the way," he stopped to say, "are the Argyle rooms in London actually closed, and is the Mabille in Paris as lively as it used to be? Great Cæsar! won't I make it lively for them!"

In another day we shall land in Liverpool, and then I shall be only five hours from London. I long to reach London, for I do so desire to hear Spurgeon, and attend the Exeter Hall meetings, as you desired me. But as we shall reach London on Tuesday, I shall be compelled to wait till the following Sunday — five long days.

Please ma, have pa send me a draft at my address at London, at once. I find the expense of travel is much greater than I supposed, and I fear I shall not have enough.

Your affectionate son,   LEMUEL.

"There," said Lemuel, as he sealed the letter, "that is what I call a good letter. The old lady will read it over and over to herself, and then she will read it to all the neighbors. It will do her a heap of good. Bye-bye. The boys are waiting for me in the smoking-room."

And stopping at the bar to take a drink — the liberality of English measure was not too great for him — he was, a minute after, absorbed in the mysteries of poker, and was "raking-in" the money of the others at a lively rate.

And the letter went to the good old mother, and probably did her good. And she, doubtless, worried the old gentleman till he sent the graceless fellow a remittance. Boys can always be sure of their mothers — would that mothers could only be half as sure of their boys.

The fourth night out we were favored with a most terrific thunder storm. I say favored, now that we are through with it, for it is a good thing to look back upon, but we esteemed it no favor at the time. A fierce storm is bad enough on land — it is a terror on water. On the land you are threatened with danger only from above — on the water you are doubly menaced. There was the marshaling of the clouds that were

arranging themselves for an attack upon us, then the terrible
darkness, then the first onslaught of the winds, that tossed the
strong ship like a cork, then the thunder that seemed like the
voice of a merciless Vengeance, and the lightnings that were
its fiery fingers; pitchy darkness, except when the lightning
illuminated the scene, and the sight it disclosed made darkness preferable, for it showed the great waves rolling one after
another, their white crests like the teeth of enormous dragons,
strong enough to crush the mass of iron against which their
fury was directed. And then the wind howl-
ing through the rigging was fearfully like
the shrieks of the monsters baffled
and robbed of their prey. It
seemed as though the entire
forces of Nature
were arrayed
intelligently
against our ship,
and for the sole
purpose of its de-
struction.

EVERY SIN I HAD COMMITTED CAME BEFORE ME LIKE ACCUSING GHOSTS.

It was far from pleasant, and it is fortunate that such displays last but a little while. In less than a second from its
beginning every sin I had ever committed, namely, the steal-
ing of a watermelon in my boyhood, and the voting of a split

3

ticket in my manhood, came vividly before me like accusing ghosts. I did remember also, once, that when a ticket-seller in a railroad station in Troy, who was very insolent and unobliging, made a mistake in my favor to the amount of thirty cents, in my anger I did not rectify it, and I debated as to whether that was a sin or not; but when I thought it over I came to the conclusion that, inasmuch as the recording angel knew how brutal the fellow was, he would blot out the record if he had to drop upon it a tear of oxalic acid.

But the good ship endured it all. The great body of iron, with its soul of steam, and muscles of steel, defied the elements and rode it out safely.

The storm hurried away to pursue and fright other vessels, and the waste of waters was once more in a sort of a light that was not lurid. Though the greatest terror was passed, the long swell which kept the ship either climbing a mountain of water or descending into its depths was anything but pleasant.

A ship at dock looks strong enough to defy all the elements, but out at sea when those elements become angry it is wonderful how frail she seems. It is man against Omnipotence.

I don't care how many times a man has been to sea, the first sight of land after a voyage is an unmixed delight. I know that, for I have crossed the Great Lakes repeatedly, and when a boy I used to "go home" via the Erie Canal, I always got up early in the morning to look at the land on either shore. A man is not a fish, and no man takes to water naturally. It is a necessity that drives him to it, the same as to labor.

Therefore the decks were crowded on the ninth morning of the voyage when the shores of Ireland were sighted. Not because it was Ireland — nobody thrilled over that — but because it was land, because it was something that did not roll and pitch, and toss and swing, but was substantial and permanent. The Mississippi Ethiopian, when discussing the difference between traveling by rail and water remarked: "Ef de cahs run off de track dah ye is — ef de boat goes to pieces, wha is 'ye?"

Ireland was there and land was there and reliable. Ireland — as land — has no machinery to get out of order, no icebergs to run into — no other steamers to collide with. I was delighted to look at her, and I venture to say that the older the sailor,

the more reassuring and delightful the sight of land:
The bold cliffs looked friendly, and the long stretches of
green on their summits were
an absolute delight. The
color was the green of grass
and trees, that had something
akin to humanity in it, not
the glittering, changing,
treacherous green of the
water we had been sailing
over and plunging through
for eight very long days.
And then to think that twenty-four hours more would release us from our friendly
prison, and that during that
twenty-four hours we should
be within a short distance of
land, was a delight.

I have at times found
fault with the Irish in
America, and I don't rank
Ireland as the greatest country under the heavens, but
that morning I felt for her a
most profound respect. Had
Ashantee been the first land
we had sighted that morn-
ing, I presume I should have
forgiven the Ashantees for
killing and eating the mis-
sionaries. After one has been
at sea, even for eight days,
land is the principal wish of

OFF FOR LONDON.

the heart. One day and night across the Channel, and we
made Liverpool. There were promises to meet in London, or
Paris, exchanges of cards, the passing the Custom House with
our baggage, the purchase of tickets, and we found ourselves
in the cars of the Midland Road and scurrying away through
Derbyshire to London.

CHAPTER II.

LONDON, AND THINGS PER-
TAINING.

THE largest city of the
world! The most mon-
strous aggregation of men,
women, children; the center
of financial, military, mental,
and moral power! The con-
trolling city of the world!
This is London!

There may be in the effete
East larger aggregations of
what, by courtesy, may be called
humanity, for in those coun-
tries the limits of cities are not properly defined, nor is the
census taken with any accuracy. But these cities exercise no
especial influence upon the world; they control nothing outside of their own countries; they reach out to nothing; they
are simply hives.

Even an American, with all his pride in his country and
her magnificent cities, feels somewhat dwarfed to find himself
in a city eight times as large as Chicago, four times as large as

New York, and his pride in wealth and power, and all that sort of thing, collapses when he realizes the fact that he is where the finances of the world are absolutely controlled ; that he is at the very center of the vastest money and military power in the world !

There is nothing greater as yet than London, and whether there ever will be is a question. I hope not. Men, women and children are all very well, but they thrive best where they have room to develop. Four millions of them together on so small a piece of ground dwarfs them. They do better on the prairies.

England is an enormous octopus, whose feelers, armed with very strong and sharp claws, embrace the world, and London, the mouth and stomach of the monster, is sucking its prey steadily and mercilessly. The animal lost one feeler which America cut off in 1776, and her grasp is weakening elsewhere, but she has enough. India contributes its life blood, China contributes, the islands of the sea contribute, and pretty much the whole world gives more or less.

England comes by her characteristics honestly. The human being we call an Englishman, half merchant and half soldier, the soldier element being purely piratical, never could have been developed out of one race. Each race has some peculiar quality which distinguishes it and marks it everywhere. The Scotchman is noted for his hardiness, thrift, and stubbornness; the Dutchman for his steadiness, boldness, and quiet daring; the Irishman for emigrating to New York and getting on the police force in a month, and so on. But the man we call an Englishman is a composite institution.

The old Saxon was a stolid fellow, with flashes of temper. He never could control things, for he was too lazy and sensual ; but he had qualities that mixed well with others. You have to have hair in plaster. But when the Dane, who was a born sea pirate, swooped down upon Britain, and the Norman, who was a born land pirate, came also, and mixed with the Saxon, there was a new creation, and that is the Englishman of to-day. He is a born trader and a born soldier, with a wisdom that the rest of the world has not. His fighting power is made subject and subordinate to his trading power.

When England wants anything she does not stop to ask

any questions as to the right or wrong of the thing—she quietly goes and takes it, that is, if she is stronger than the party she desires to capture. If the other party objects, a few armies are sent out and the country is brought to reason immediately. Your bayonet is a rare persuader.

Can a country afford to fit out costly armaments and maintain vast armies for such purposes? Certainly, if it is done on England's plan. England, after spending some millions in subjugating a country, simply assesses the cost of the operation with as many millions for interest as she thinks the subjugated party can bear without destroying it, and makes it pay. She never destroys a country entirely, for she has further use for it. She wants the inhabitants, once subjugated, to go on and labor and toil and sweat, for all time to come, to furnish her with raw material, and then to buy it back again in the shape of manufactured goods, which, as she buys cheap and sells dear, makes a very handsome profit, besides furnishing employment to her vast merchant marine in the carrying trade.

And then her merchants manage to interest a certain portion of the natives with her in plundering their neighbors, and so her rule is made tolerably safe and inexpensive. This is about the size of it. She conquers a country, and after reimbursing herself, calls a convention of native Princes and says: "Here, now, we are going to hold this country, anyhow. We are going to have the trade and the revenues, and you see we can do it. You fellows may as well have your whack in it." (These, of course, are not the exact words used, but I am writing what a New York politician would say. A ring man's words mean exactly what diplomatic language does, and they are always more to the point.) "Now you help us keep the others down, and you shall keep your own places and shall have yourselves fifty per cent. of what you can grind out of your people, and as we shall stand behind you with our power, that fifty per cent. will be more than you could possibly screw out of them alone and unaided."

The native Prince sees the point, for he is as merciless and cruel as an Englishman, and I cannot say more than that, and he assents. Immediately there is a rush of native Princes, all anxious to join in for their plunder, and England apportions to each his share, according to his importance, and in less than no time she has a native army, officered by English, to keep the people down to the proper level, and to collect taxes and protect t r a d e r s , and all that sort of thing, and London draws in the money and lives royally.

And, then, if any Prince, or people, or soldiery, or anybody else, fancy they have rights of their o w n , and question the right of the foreigner to tax them and grind them, they blow a few thousands of them from the mouths of cannon, to teach them the beauty of obedience.

It would take a wiser man than I am to determine by what right, earthly or unearthly, England holds India, but she does all the same, without a blush.

THE INDIAN POLICY.

Perhaps it is as well for the Indians. The native Princes were just as rapacious and more senseless than the English. If a native Indian should swallow a diamond, his P r i n c e would rip him opén to get it, which made him useless ever after. Johnny Bull, more politic and far seeing, would force an emetic down his throat, so that he might go on and find more diamonds to swallow. He gets the diamond all the same, and saves the subject for more profit.

THE EMETIC POLICY.

The strength of England is its fighting capacity, its mercantile capacity, and its wonderful rapacity. As was said of a noted criminal in the States, " he wouldn't steal anything he could n't lift, though he did tackle a red-hot cook-stove," so with England. The eyes of her moneyed power, and it is more than Argus-eyed, are being strained every day for new worlds to sell goods to, knowing perfectly well that when they find a field the Government will furnish muskets to occupy that field. And let no mistake be made. If the field is worth occupying it will be occupied beyond a doubt.

Ireland is an example, Scotland would be, only the Scotch, having a habit of standing together, are ugly customers to deal with, and as they and the English get along tolerably well together, there is no especial trouble between them.

Hence it is that London is so great. London is the center of this vast system of plunder and rapine, and the result of it all comes here. Here is the Court, here is the seat of Govern_ment, here is where the great nobles, no matter where their seats may be, are compelled to spend a portion of their time; they are all obliged to have town residences; here they bring their flunkies and *retinues* of servants, and they make the great city.

It is not a commercial point, as is Liverpool or New York, nor a manufacturing point, as is Manchester or Philadelphia. It is where the spoils of the present organized legal brigandage are divided, and where the surplus of the organized brigandage of past centuries is expended.

The tradesman of London would not alter the existing condition of things if he could. He believes in that shadowy myth called the Queen, not because he knows anything about her, or cares a straw for her, but simply because when she, which means the Court, is in London, trade is good. That eminent descendant of an eminent robber, Sir Giles Fitz Battle_axe, is here during the season, with all his flunkies and servitors, and the tradesmen have to supply them. As Sir Giles has vast estates in Ireland and Scotland, and the Lord knows where else, which yield him an immense revenue, Sir Giles's steward can pool his issues with his tradesman and both get rich. Sir Giles doesn't care, for he is paying all this out of rents of property, the title to which came from a King who stole the ground, and he has enough anyhow.

And then comes the foreign robberies, which he has an interest in, and those make up any waste that may happen at home. Even the cabman, who haggles with you over a shilling, is loyal to the Crown and the Church, for the Crown and the Church bring to London the people who make him his fares.

Rampant republican as I am, opposed to monarchy as I am, I am contributing several pounds per diem to the maintenance of the British throne. I am here to see royalty, and every. body that I come in contact with, from the boy who cleans my boots to the lady who rents me my rooms, sing hosannas to the system that brings me here to be plundered. When I give a shilling to a servant she doesn't thank me for it, but she goes to her garret and sings, "God Save the Queen." That amiable shadow gets all the credit for my money.

They shall give thanks to Victoria for me but very little. I will be a republican to the extent of leaving as small an amount of money in England as possible. Could there be a league of Americans formed who would refuse to pay anything, I am not sure but that royalty might be overthrown, and a republic established on its ruins.

And yet I am not certain that that would answer any good purpose. But for these advantages I don't think anybody would live in London. It was said that if the Pilgrims had landed in the Mississippi Valley, New England would never have been settled, and, therefore, it was providential that the Pilgrims were so directed. But for royalty and the profit that pertains to a Court, I doubt if London could hold population. For if there is a disagreeable — but I reserve this for a special occasion, when, less amiable than I am now, I can do the subject justice.

London has a population, in round numbers, of four millions. Without including outlying suburbs, it covers seventy-eight thousand and eighty acres, or one hundred and twenty-two square miles. The length of the streets and roads is about fifteen hundred miles, and their area nearly twelve square miles. The area of London being one hundred and twenty-two square miles, is equal to a square of about eleven miles to the side. Assuming that it is crossed by straight roads at equal intervals, there would be one hundred and thirty-six such roads, each eleven miles long and one hundred and forty-two yards apart. The sewers have a length of about two thousand miles, and are equal to one hundred and eighty-two sewers eleven miles in length, on an average of one hundred and six yards apart. At the census in 1871 there were within this area four hundred and seventeen thousand seven hundred and sixty-seven inhabited houses, containing an average of seven and eight-tenths persons to a house, exactly corresponding with the proportion in 1861. The density of population was forty-two persons to an acre, twenty-six thousand six hundred and seventy-four to a square mile. The population, estimated to the middle of the year, amounted to three million six hundred and sixty-four thousand one hundred and forty-nine.

These statistics I know to be correct, for I got them from a newspaper. I copy it entire, for the readers of this book do not take the London *Chronicle*, as a rule, and it would be too expensive to send each one a copy of it. If any false statements are made it is the *Chronicle's* fault and not mine.

The climate is, to put it mildly, fiendish. I have been in every possible section of the United States that could be reached by rail, water, or stage, and I was never in a location, excepting California, in which the citizens whereof would not remark: "Oh, yes; this would be a good country to live in if it was not for the changeable climate. The changes are too sudden and severe." One blessed result of my coming to London is to make me entirely content with the worst climate America has. Tennessee is a paradise to it, so far as climate goes, and when you have said that the subject is closed.

It rains in London with greater ease than it does in any place in the world. The sun will be shining brightly in the heavens; you look out of your window and say: "I will take a walk this morning without that accursed umbrella," and you brush your silk hat — everybody who is anybody must wear a silk hat — and you sally forth with your cane. You turn into the Strand, feeling especially cheerful in the sun, when all of a sudden the sky is overcast and you hat is ruined. You call a hansom and go back to your lodgings for your umbrella, and when you have encumbered yourself with the clumsy nuisance the sun comes out smiling, and the rain is over, only to resume operations again without the slightest possible reason.

Everybody in London carries an umbrella habitually and all the time. No man ventures out of doors without one, no matter how the sky appears. In America a fair day may be counted upon, but here there is no dependence to be placed upon anything in the form of weather. Last week (June 1) it was as hot as it ought to be the same day in Charleston, South Carolina; to-day (June 7) I came in, went out, and came in wearing an overcoat, and a tolerably heavy one at that. What the weather will be to-morrow, heaven only knows. I have experienced so many and so violent changes that I should not be surprised if it should snow. I may go skating next week upon the Serpentine.

But the Londoners don't mind it. They are used to it. From the ease with which they carry umbrellas, I am convinced that they are born with them, as George Washington was with the hatchet. A Londoner never lends his umbrella, for everybody has his own, and he never loses it. It is a part of him, as much as is his nose. The umbrella should be in the coat of arms of the royal family, and I do not know but it is.

It is a dull and heavy climate. How it affects a native I cannot tell, but an American has a disposition to sleep perpetually and forever.

In the house I am in is an American, who insisted one morning on going across the square without his umbrella. I mildly remonstrated. "It is safe," he said, "it isn't raining now, for it was a minute ago." He was right, but he came to grief for all that. It rained again in another minute.

London is a miracle of twistedness. If there is a straight street in it — that is, one that runs parallel with any other — I have not found it. The streets of Boston, it is said, were originally cow-paths. If those of London were located on the paths of cows, the cows must have been intoxicated, for there is no system nor any approach to one. They begin without cause and end without reason. There are angles, curves and stoppages, and that is all there is about it. Where a street, to answer the ends of convenience and economy, should go on,

you come squarely against a dead wall, and where a street
should naturally end, there has been constructed, at vast
expense, a continuance, and for no apparent reason. Doubtless
there is a reason, but I would give a handsome premium to
have it made manifest to me.

Like all old cities, there never was a plan. This ground
was never taken up at a dollar and a quarter an acre, as in
America, by a set of speculators, and laid out in regular
squares, and sold at so much a lot. London never was made —
it grew. The original city is a little spot, occupied mostly by
banks, but other cities grew around it, and they were joined
by all sorts of lanes and roads, which in time became occupied,
and so the inextricable jumble occurred.

The city is built entirely of brick and stone, and in the
style and convenience of its buildings, is not to be compared to
American cities. There is a terrible monotony in its architecture, and a most depressing sameness in color. All London is
dingy. Occasionally an enterprising citizen paints his house to
distinguish it from his neighbor's, but he never does it but
once. The coal consumed is bituminous, and the smoke it
produces is the thickest smoke in the world, and it hangs very
close to the earth. The paint becomes discolored in a few
months, and the aspiring citizen finds in the smoke a protest
against his vanity. His house soon drops into line with his
neighbor's, and is as dingy as before.

The streets of London are crowded to a degree that an
American can hardly conceive. Isaiah Rynders said once that
it required more intellect to cross Broadway than it did to be
a country justice. Had Isaiah stayed a week in London he
would have had the conceit taken out of him. The streets of
London, all of them, are boiling, seething masses of moving men and animals. Omnibusses, vast cumbrous machines,
loaded full inside, and with twenty people on the top, hansoms,
cabs, trucks, drays, donkey carts, pony carts, carriages, form a
never-beginning and never-ending procession, making a roar
like the waters of Niagara. He who attempts to cross a street
has to make it a regular business. It cannot be done leisurely
or in a dignified way. You narrowly escape being run down
by a hansom, only to find yourself in danger of being impaled

by the pole of an omnibus, and escaping that, a donkey cart is charging full at you, and if you escape a carriage, and a dozen dog carts, you finally find yourself on the sidewalk plump in

A LONDON STREET SCENE.

the stomach of somebody, who accepts your apology with a growl.

I shall never get over my admiration for the London driver·

How he can guide one horse, or still more wonderful, two, through this vehicular labyrinth, is a mystery that I cannot comprehend. I would as soon think of taking command of the British army, and a great deal sooner, for if I didn't stomach fighting, I could run. But they do it, and they seldom have accidents.

And while I am on the subject of driving, I may as well get through with it. The horses used in London embrace a vast variety. The draught horses are all of the Norman variety, about as large as small elephants, and magnificent in their strength. They are massive, and the loads they draw are wonderful. The trucks are enormous in size and strength, with great, broad wheels, and merchandise is piled upon them mountain high. Two of these horses, nineteen hands high, and built proportionately, with great, clumsy legs, will take an enormous load along the streets, making no fuss, and seemingly without worry.

But when one notices the condition of the streets the wonder at the loads that are drawn ceases. They are as smooth as glass. The stone pavements are evenly laid and absolutely without ruts. The wooden pavement, answering to the Nicholson, which has invariably been a failure in America, is a success here, and for a very simple reason. The contractors are compelled to do their work honestly. There is no shoddy in the pavements of London. They are all as sound as the Bank of England. They don't lay down some pine boards in the mud, and then stand rotten blocks on end upon them, as we do in America, but there is a solid foundation of broken stone and such matter laid down first, and this is filled with sand, and then the blocks, all good timber, are placed upon that in a proper way, the whole resulting in a road-bed as solid as stone itself, and smooth and noiseless, making a roadway over which any load can be drawn without injury to either beast or vehicle, and one which will be good long after the makers are dust. The vehicles are made so strong as they are, not for fear of the roads, but to hold the enormous weights that the roads make possible.

Sometime we of America will get to doing things in a permanent way. It will be, however, after all the present race of contractors are worth several millions each. I presume in the ancient days there were rings in London. If so I can understand the uses for the beheading blocks exhibited at the Tower.

All the vehicles used in the city are massive and solid. You see none of the flimsy spider-web wheels and light airy bodies in carriages that we affect in America. The wheels of a cab to carry four people are quite three inches thick, and the bodies are correspondingly clumsy. Like their owners, they are very solid.

But the hansom is the peculiar vehicle. The four-wheeler is a sort of a sober-going cab, the one you would expect the mother of a family or a respectable widow lady to use. The driver sits in front, as a driver should, and the entire concern is closed except as you may desire to have air by letting down eminently respectable windows in the side. But the hansom is quite another thing. The occupant is in a low seat, while his driver sits above him on a perch and the reins go over the occupant's head. Next to swindling his customer out of a sixpence on his fare, the chief ambition of the driver of a hansom is to run down a foot passenger, and in this ambition his horse shares fully, if he does not exceed him. The horses used in these piratical vehicles are generally broken-down hunters, who, too slow to longer hunt the wily fox, and harnessed in the ignoble hansom, have transferred their hunting instincts to men. When the "jarvey," as he is called here, fixes his eagle eye upon a citizen whom he proposes to run down, the horse knows it as if by instinct, and they come charging down upon him at a pace something as did the French cuirassiers at Waterloo. And if the intended victim escapes, the driver gnashes his teeth in rage, and the sympathizing horse drops his head and moves on a walk till the sight of another countryman or stranger rouses his ambition. It is said that when a driver succeeds in running down a foot passenger the injured man is the one who is arrested.

The shops of London are of two kinds—the gorgeous modern and the respectable ancient. The modern are of the most gorgeous kind. They are not as in New York, immense show windows with a door between; but there is an immense show

window in the middle, with a small passage on the side. When
a London tradesman wants a show window he wants it all
show. It is very like the piety of some men I know. He
doesn't care how small the opening is to get into the place, for
he knows if he attracts a customer by the display of his goods
in the window, he, the said customer, will manage somehow to
get inside. The point is to corral the customer. Once in, his
bones can be picked at leisure.

The modern shops are as gorgeously fitted up inside as out.
They have silver plated rails, magnificently decorated counters
and show-cases, even more than the New York stores have.

Then there is the eminently respectable shops which despise
these gorgeous ones about the same as an old noble, descended
from one of the first robbers, looks down upon a Knight of
day before yesterday. These are the shops that have over
their doors "Established in 1692." They would no more put
in a plate glass window than they would forge a note. They
revel in their dustiness, and are proud of their darkness and
inconvenience. They wouldn't sweep out the premises if they
could help it, and the very cob-webs are sacred as being so
many silent witnesses to the antiquity of the house.

"The house, sir, of Smithers & Co., was established by
Samuel Smithers on this very spot in 1692, and business has
been done under that name, and by his successors, ever since,
except an interval of two months, which was occasioned by a
fire — from the outside. The house of Samuel Smithers & Co.
could never have originated a fire upon their own premises.
The business is conducted with more system. We have never
had a protested paper and never asked an accommodation."

This is what the present head of the house will say to you.
He has as much pride in the house as the Queen has in her
Queenship, and with infinitely more reason. He would not
allow a new pane of glass to be put in, and he wouldn't change
a thing about the premises for the world. He prides himself
on the inconveniences of a hundred years ago, and would die
sooner than to use a modern notion in the business.

But the Smitherses are good people with whom to do business. Among the other old-fashioned customs they preserve is
that of honesty. They keep good goods, no shoddy ; they

have a fair price, and you might as well undertake to tear down Westminster Abbey with a hair-pin as to induce any variation therefrom. They want your trade — every Englishman wants trade — but they prefer their system to trade. You buy, if you buy of them, on their terms. But you know what you get, and that is worth something.

This affection for the old is general. It is a fact that one eating house, noted for its chops and steaks, and ales and wines, which had been in existence no one knows how many years, and had its regular succession of patrons, who came in at regular hours, and ate and drank the same things, and read the same newspapers till death claimed them, fell, by reason of death, into the hands of young men. These young fellows were somewhat progressive, and they determined to bring the old place abreast with modern ideas. And so they swept out the cob-webs, painted the interior, decorated it in bright colors, put in new tables, swept and cleaned things, and replaced the old floor with modern tiles, and made it one of the most handsome places in London.

The effect was fatal. The old *habitues* of the place came, looked inside, ran out to see if they had not made a mistake as to the number, and finding they were right as to locality, sighed and turned sadly away. They could not eat in any such place, and they went and found some other antiquated den, whose proprietor was sensible enough not to tear down sacred cob-webs, and put in fresh floors.

The old patronage was lost forever, and the proprietors were compelled to build up an entirely new business, the cost of which nearly put them into bankruptcy.

All travelers lie. I am going to try to be an exception to this rule, and shall, to the best of my ability, cling to the truth as a shipwrecked mariner does to a spar. I shall try to conquer the tendency to lie that overcome every man who gets a hundred miles away from home. But I presume I shall fail; and so when I get home and say that living is cheaper and better in London than it is anywhere in America, please say to me, " You are lying ! " You will do the correct thing.

No doubt when there I shall say to Smith or Thompson, "My boy, what you want to do is to go abroad. You want to

4

see London. And as for the expense, what is it? Your passage across is only one hundred dollars — ten days — and that
is but ten dollars a day. And then you can live so much
cheaper in London than you can in New York that it is really
cheaper to go abroad than it is to stay at home."

I presume I shall say this when I get home, for I know the
tendency of the traveler to lie. I have traveled all over North
America, and I confess, with shame mantling my cheek, that
I have at times added some feet to the height of mountains

A LONDON STEAK.

and to the width of rivers, and to the number of Indians, and
once I did invent an exploit which never happened, and I have
narrated incidents which never occurred. It is such a temptation to be a hero when you know you can never be successfully
disputed.

While I am yet young in foreign travel, and capable of an
approximation to truth, I wish to say that London is not only
not a cheap place to live, but an exceedingly dear one.

"Just think of it," said a travel-wise New Yorker, in New

York, to me, "just think of a steak for a shilling! Here you pay twice that!"

So we do, but when you pay fifty cents for a steak in New York, you get a steak, and you get with it bread and butter *ad libitum* — you get pickles, and sauces, and potatoes, and all that sort of thing. Your fifty cent steak, with the accompaniments it carries, makes you a meal, and a good one.

In London your steak is twenty-five cents, but it is only a sample. After eating it you want some steak. Then you pay six cents for potatoes, two cents for what they call a bread — you always have more and there is a charge for each individual slice — you pay two cents for each tiny pat of butter, you are compelled to struggle for a napkin, and if you ask for ice to cool the infernal insipid water, you pay two cents for that, and you get just enough to aggravate you. And, then, when you are through, the smirking mass of stupidity and inefficiency they call a waiter wants and expects a sixpence, which is twelve and one-half cents more.

Where is your cheapness now? If you have a square, appetite-satisfying, strength-giving meal, it has cost you twice as much as it would in New York, with the difference that in New York it would be decently cooked, decently served, and done with a sort of breadth that makes it a luxury to eat, while here it is so hampered about with extras and charges for minute things — things which in America are free to everybody — that eating is reduced to a mere commercial basis and has no comfort in it.

The hotels are simply infamous in their charges. You agree to pay so much per day for your rooms, and it looks tolerably cheap, but you discover your mistake at the close of the first week, when you come to settle your bill. Though you have never touched your bell and have never seen the face of a servant, you are charged so much a day for "attendance," you are charged for light, for fires. If you have ordered a bit of anything, no matter how infinitesimal, it is there, and these charges make up a bill larger than your room rent.

There is no use in remonstrating, nor in threatening to leave. You know, and the landlord knows a great deal better, that no matter where you go it will be the same, and so submitting to the inevitable, you draw a draft for more money, and settle down to be cheated in peace.

The lodging houses are quite as bad, only of course in a smaller way. Your accommodations are less, and the swindle less, but the proportion is very carefully observed.

Clothing is somewhat cheaper than in America, but nevertheless let me warn the intending comer against buying it here. You may buy cloths, if you choose, and pay duty on them and take them home, but never let a London tailor or dressmaker profane your person, be you man or woman. The Creator never made either for a London tailor to mar. He has too much respect for His handiwork. I have been here now two weeks, and have yet to see a native Englishman or a tailor-spoiled American who was well-dressed. The English tailor has no more idea of style than a pig has of the revised Testament. You can tell an American a square off by the cut of his coat, and an American woman by the very hang of her dress. The English tailor looks at you wisely, and takes a measurement or two, and puts his shears into the cloth. The result is a sort of a square abortion, loose where it should be close, close where it should be wide, long where it should be short and short where it should be long, and the poor victim takes it and is miserable till time releases him from it.

The majority of English women are dowdies, and by the way they have immense feet and hands. They are excellent wives, mothers and sisters, but their extremities are something frightful. They do have delightful complexions though, and are as bright and good as they can be.

Speaking of the feet of English women reminds me of Captain McFadden, of Pittsburgh. The dear old Captain — he is dead and gone now these many a year — in addition to being one of the best river men that Pittsburgh could boast of, was also,— think of it,— a poultry fancier. When the fancy for Shanghais broke out the Captain joined in it, as he did in everything in the fowl way, and he paid cheerfully twenty-five dollars for a half-dozen eggs of the famous breed, which he immediately put under a hen that was in a setting mood. But Captain McFadden had a son who was without reverence either for his father or poultry. Young Jim McFadden went and bought a half-dozen duck's eggs and removed the Shanghais and put the duck's eggs under the hen, the said hen not knowing or caring whether she was hatching the common

"JIM, MY BOY, AND IS THEM THE SHANGHAIS? LUK AT THEIR FUTS!
HEVENS, JIM."

duck or the royal Shanghai. In time its labors were accomplished and Captain McFadden was viewing the resultant ducklings, with Jim laughing in his sleeve as he looked on.

"Jim, me boy, and is them the Shanghais? Luk at their futs! Hevens, Jim, luk at their futs. All h—l wouldn't uptrup em."

I can't imagine anything that would "up-trup" an English woman. But as small feet and hands are not essential to salvation I forgive them this. They can't help it. I presume they would if they could, but they are so kindly, so hospitable, so bright and pleasing generally, that I shut my eyes gladly to their feet, and their bad taste in dress, and accept it all without a word.

Still I wish they could pare down their feet. Then an English woman would be the simple perfection of nature's most perfect work. I can't help thinking, however, that when your hostess's shoe is — but never mind. Their kindliness and their cheery laughs and their never failing good humor are admirable substitutes for small feet. Feet are not the whole of life.

You see soldiers about London. They are as common as mosquitos in New Jersey, and to me just about as offensive. They are everywhere. Go where you will, you see a tall fellow in a blue or scarlet, or some other colored uniform, with an absurd little cap on his head, to which is attached a leather strap which comes down to his lower lip, to keep the absurd little cap in place. He has sometimes a sword hanging to him, and sometimes not, but he is a soldier all the same. England has need of a great many soldiers. In London they are used as a sort of show, as walking advertisements of the power and strength of the Government, and to make the picture of royalty complete.

As soldiers don't cost much here, it is a luxury royalty can afford a great deal of. The ordinary soldier gets twenty-five cents a day, and his rations, and after twenty-one years service, if rum and beer and bullets — the two first are the most dangerous — have not finished him, he becomes a pensioner, which means he puts on a red coat and eats three times a day in a sort of hospital, all the rest of his life.

The army is recruited largely from Ireland and the poorer districts of England and Scotland. It is about the last thing an Englishman or Irishman does, but various causes keep the ranks full without conscription. Women are the best recruiting officers the Queen has. It is the regular thing for a young fellow who has been jilted to go and enlist. He thinks he will make the girl feel badly. But it doesn't. She rather prides herself upon the number of young fellows she has given the army, and when the time comes to marry and settle down, she goes and marries, and laughs at them all.

Poverty is another very active and efficient recruiting sergeant. A young fellow comes down to "Lunnon" to seek his fortune, equipped with a few pounds and his mother's blessing. He finds London quite different from what he expected. He discovers it to be a very hard and cruel place, with more mouths than bread, and more hands than work. He lives as closely as he can, but, as meagerly as he lives, his pounds melt into shillings and his shillings into pence. And finally, when his last penny is gone, and hunger is upon him, he takes the Queen's shilling, and the next thing his mother hears of him, he is fighting the Boers in South Africa. And once a soldier, always a soldier. The life unfits a man for any other, and when he has once worn a uniform, he never wears anything else.

As I said, women are the best recruiting sergeants. I got into a conversation with one very handsome young fellow who had been in the service only a year, who told me his little story. He is the son of a small farmer in Scotland somewhere, with an unpronounceable name, where it doesn't matter. He had been in love with a pretty daughter of a widow near by from the time he was a boy, and the girl professed to be, and doubtless was, in love with him, but as she grew up she made the discovery that she was very handsome (what woman does not?), and she found that that beauty attracted others beside poor Jamie. Other swains in the neighborhood laid siege to her, and she, exulting in her power over the young fellows, and being unquestionably the belle of the neighborhood, made it very uncomfortable for her real lover, to whom she was betrothed.

Sore were the conflicts between them. The girl delighted in annoying him, for she was as wilful and cruel as she was beautiful. She would dance with the others, and she would flirt with them to the point of driving the poor man mad, and then, just at the nick of time, she had a trick of coming back to him, and for a time being as sweet as possible, and so for several years she kept him alternating between the seventh heaven of happiness, and the lowest depths of a hell upon earth.

There was one fellow in the neighborhood as much smitten with her as Jamie, who was determined to marry her, whether or no. He was a well-to-do young man, who had a farm of his own, and being quite as good-looking and more enterprising than Jamie, was a most dangerous rival to the hapless youth. Jennie had dismissed all the others, but with the perversity that seems to be an infallible accompaniment to beauty, she persisted in receiving the attention of this man.

Finally it came to a head. Jamie insisted that she should not see him any more, and he insisted upon it with an earnestness that affected the girl, and she made a solemn promise that she never would see him again.

It so happened that the very next day after this promise was asked and given, Jamie was to leave for Glasgow on business, and he started early the next morning. He hadn't got to the railroad station before his mind misgave him. Something worried him. He had slept all the night comfortably on her promise, but something told him that she did not intend to keep it, and that something preyed upon him to the degree that instead of proceeding on his journey he turned about and walked back.

She knew that he was going to be· gone a week, and the other man knew it also. If she intended to play him false, this was her opportunity, and he would know for certain, and set his mind at ease.

Poor devil! It would have been better had he proceeded on his journey. For if he had known anything he would have known that if a woman wanted to deceive him, watching her would amount to nothing. The devil is very lavish of opportunities, that being all that he has to do, and simple human nature is certain to avail itself of them; but Jamie was not a philosopher, or a very bright man. He was a simple Scotch lad, frightfully in love with a wilful and perverse beauty.

But he did go back, and he concealed himself near her cottage, where he could watch unobserved, hoping, in a desperate sort of way, that he had made a fool of himself, but rather certain that he had not.

And sure enough, along toward evening his rival made his appearance sauntering down the road, and sure enough he had no sooner appeared in the road than Jennie, as if by accident, appeared, and the two talked across the little gate in front, very earnestly, she in a mixed sort of way.

And Jamie, full of rage at what he believed to be a betrayal, and desperate on general principles, sallied out and attacked his man, and after a fearful struggle left him almost dead on the ground, and despite Jennie's tearful assertions that she had seen him only to tell him that he must not follow her any more, as she would henceforth and forever have nothing whatever to do with him, Jamie, who didn't believe a word of it, announced his intention of enlisting, and started off toward the station again.

Jennie followed him, for it appears the girl's story was true, and she, coquette as she was, did love him, but she arrived too late. He had taken the fatal plunge, and was in the Queen's uniform.

"And Jennie?" I asked.

Jennie was in London in service. She would not stay at home after he left, and she came to town where she could see him at times, and things were so arranged between them that when his term should expire they were to marry and go back and settle down upon the old place and be happy for evermore.

If his regiment should be ordered upon foreign duty, she would manage somehow to accompany him. Anyhow, she was entirely cured of flirting, rightly concluding that one true man is enough for one woman, and he was equally soundly cured of jealousy, though it must be admitted that he had sufficient cause therefor.

And so ends a red-coated romance.

CHAPTER III.

THE DERBY RACES, WITH SOME OTHER THINGS.

Horse-racing in America is not considered the most exciting, or, for that matter, the most reputable business in the
world. A horsey man, except in New York, is not looked
upon with much favor, being, as a rule, and I suppose justly,
regarded as a modified and somewhat toned down black-leg.

I never ventured money upon but one race. I shall never
forget it, for it was my first and last experience.

It was many years ago, ere time had whitened my locks,
and had set the seal of age in my face in the form of wrinkles.
It is needless to say I was as immature mentally as physically,
or what is to follow would not have occurred.

There was a horseman in the county in Ohio in which I
was living named Carpenter — Sol. Carpenter. Every horseman's given name is abbreviated, the same as a negro minstrel's.
Carpenter was the possessor of many horses which he used in
racing, but he had one, "Nero," which commanded the confidence of all the sporting men for miles around. In a mile race
he had never been beaten, and there were wild rumors, which
obtained credence, that he had won a four-mile race in Kentucky (which at that time was the starting point for all the
running horses), and that Sol. was holding him back for some
great master-stroke of turf business.

Presently there appeared in Greenfield — Sol. lived in Plymouth — a horse named "Calico," which the owner intimated
could *lay out* "Nero," without any particular trouble or worry.
Carpenter laughed. the man to scorn — his name was Pete
Scobey — and promptly challenged him for a mile dash, two
best in three.

(58)

Scobey accepted the challenge and the date was fixed. There was the wildest possible excitement in Plymouth. Greenfield did not share in it as there were no horsemen there, the village consisting of one Presbyterian Church, a dry goods store, and a blacksmith shop. But Plymouth absolutely boiled. Carpenter poured oil upon the fire by confidentially assuring everybody that "Nero" could get away with "Calico" without the slightest trouble; that he knew "Calico" like a book, and knew exactly what he could do, and if the people of Plymouth were wise, they would impoverish Greenfield, or rather the Norwalk parties, who were to back "Calico."

His advice was taken. Every man in Plymouth who could raise a dollar went to that race at Greenfield and staked his money on "Nero," on Carpenter's assurance as well as their own confidence. There was nobody doing much betting on "Calico," except Mr. Scobey and one or two others, and they held off at first, which gave Plymouth more confidence. So eager were we to despoil the adverse faction that we gave great odds, all of which Mr. Scobey and his confreres took, finally, with a calm confidence that should have taught us better. But it didn't. I remember that I wagered every dollar I had with me, and some more that Mr. Carpenter kindly lent me, taking my note, and in addition to this a sixteen-dollar silver watch.

The first heat was won by "Nero," easily, and Mr. Carpenter winked to Plymouth to make another assault upon the purses of Greenfield. We did it. We gave even greater odds than before, which Mr. Scobey required, as he admitted that his chances were very slim.

"But," he remarked, "I will bet one to ten on anything."

To our surprise the second heat was won by "Calico," by just about a head. Then Mr. Scobey offered to take even bets, and he would have got a great many but for the fact that Plymouth had staked her entire wealth already.

The next and decisive heat was run. It was closely contested. Each horse seemingly did his best, and the jockeys seemed to ride properly. Alas for Plymouth! "Calico" won, as he did the second heat, by just a head.

The indignation of Mr. Carpenter knew no bounds. He

grasped his jockey by the neck and pulled him from the horse, and accused him of giving away the race, and he stormed about the track very like a madman.

"Pete," he said finally, "Nero kin beat that cart horse of yours ez easy ez winkin. I'll run yoo two weeks from to-day

SOL CARPENTER AND THE GREENFIELD RACE.

at Plymouth for two hundred dollars a side, and I'll hev a rider that won't sell out to yoo."

"Jest ez you please, Mr. Carpenter. It's easy enough to charge up a poor horse to the account of a rider. Here's the boodle."

And so another race was arranged, and Mr. Carpenter went

among us and assured that his own son should ride the next time, and there would be no trouble about it.

We consulted all the next week, and Mr. Scobey was approached on the subject. Mr. Scobey assured us that he know "Nero," and knew his own horse. "Nero" was good for a long race, but for a dash of a mile "Calico" could get away with him every time. We shared Mr. Scobey's opinion, and to Mr. Carpenter's disgust, Plymouth wagered all the money it could raise upon "Calico." It requires but few words to state the result. "Calico" won the first heat easily, and "Nero" won the other two just as easily, and Plymouth was again bankrupt.

And then one of the riders who was disappointed in his share of the plunder, came to the front and made known what, if we had not been an entire menagerie of asses, we might have known in advance, that Mr. Carpenter and Mr. Scobey were in partnership, and that "Calico" was a horse hired from Cleveland for the occasion, and that it was a very ingenious scheme put up by Mr. Carpenter to victimize his neighbors, and that out of the speculation the two had made a very nice lot of money.

I don't pretend to say that this has anything to do with the Derby, but it illustrates the morals of the turf so well that I could not help putting it upon paper. Racing is about the same thing everywhere, except upon Epsom Downs. These races are conducted fairly, for they are under the patronage of men to whom the honor of owning a winning horse is more than any amount of money that can possibly be won. The English noblemen want this honor, and they spend fabulous amounts of money to attain it. I won't say that the Duke of Wellington would have exchanged Waterloo for the Derby, but I do say that if after Waterloo he could have had a horse capable of taking the prize, he would have died better satisfied with himself.

Thirty Americans were in the party that, on the morning of the first of June, left the American Exchange at Charing Cross for Epsom Downs. It was a very jolly party, and none of the accompaniments were forgotten. An Englishman does nothing without a great plenty of eating and drinking, and so the inside of one of the immense omnibusses —"breaks" they call them — was filled with great hampers of lunch, and wine, and things of that nature.

As early as it was all the avenues leading to the Downs were literally packed with conveyances, to say nothing of the

LEAVING FOR THE DERBY.

railroad trains which passed in quick succession, and such a motley procession! There were lords and ladies, merchants and clerks, prostitutes and gamblers, workingmen and beggars, sewing-girls and bar-maids,— in fact every sort and condition of people, who had for one day thrown care to the winds and were on pleasure bent.

The roads swarmed with vehicles, and there was as much of a surprise in the variety as in the number. There was My Lord in his dog cart, or, if a family man, in his gorgeous carriage, which does not differ materially from the American open barouche, save in the accommodations for the everlasting flunkies behind, without which no English establishment is complete. Then came the swarm of hansoms — which is a two-wheeled vehicle, with a calash top to it, carrying the driver on a high perch behind — the army of omnibusses, the tops covered with chaffing people, and the inside full of more sober ones, and add to these every variety of vehicle to which an animal can be attached, that would carry a human being, and you have some faint idea of the appearance of the roads leading to Epsom Downs on the 1st of June, A. D. 1881.

It was rather amusing than otherwise to note two kinds of vehicles and the people they hauled. They have in London a little pony, not much larger than a good-sized Newfoundland dog, extensively used by costermongers and that class of tradesmen to deliver goods. A half of these in London were at the Derby, hitched to a two-wheeled cart of twice their size, and seven heavy men and women would be packed therein, and this little mite bowled them along at a good pace, without being worried. There were literally thousands of them upon the roads, the pony pulling his heavy load, and seeming to enjoy the sport as much as those he was hauling. He was having a holiday, and his holiday was much like a human one, very hard work.

The donkey is another English institution. He is not as large as the pony, but what enormous loads he will pull, and what a slight amount of food he requires. He will breakfast on a tin tomato can, and relish a circus poster for dinner. He is a patient little brute, and bears his loads as meekly as the English laborer does his, and in just about the same way.

As we leave the city the crowd of vehicles and pedestrians becomes denser and denser. At the point where all the streets out of the city meet the throng becomes more than immense, it is terrific The drivers of the vehicles, skillful as they are, have difficulty in guiding their teams, whether it be the pretentious four-in-hand, or the humble donkey-cart, through the mass, though they did it, and without an accident.

And now the fun begins; that is, the English fun. Troops of fantastics, with false faces, spring up, the Lord knows from where, or for what purpose, unless it be to blow piercing horns

and beat toy drums for their own amusement. On one side just over a hedge, an admiring party are witnessing a boxing match between two yokels, who are giving and taking real blows in dead earnest, while just beyond is a Punch and Judy show, which always has been popular in England, and will be to the end of time. All along the dusty road are men over come with liquor, sleeping the sleep that only the drunkard knows, with faces up-
turned to the hot sun.
They are perfectly
safe, and will not be
disturbed. Every Eng-
lishman of the lower
class knows all about
it, and as for robbery,
all that he has on him
could n't be pawned
for a penny. Next to
the boxing match was
a street preacher of
some denomination,
armed with his testa-
ment and hymn-book,
"holding forth" to a

BY THE ROAD-SIDE.

throng constantly coming and going. I didn't hear this one, for we were too much on pleasure bent to stop for a sermon, be it ever so good or our need for it ever so great. But I did hear one on the grounds, and a curious sermon it was. There was no Miss Nancying about that preacher. He did not attempt to win his hearers by depicting the delights of a heaven for piety on this earth, not any. He knew his hearers too well. The lower grade Englishman might try to be good to escape a hell, but no one ever conceived a heaven that would win him. His idea of a heaven is a pot-house, with plenty of beer, and bread and cheese, and nothing to do. And so the preacher sang the hymn:—

> "My thoughts on awful subjects roll,
> Damnation and the dead,"

In which his audience joined, some devoutly and some jeeringly.

And he pictured hell in such lurid colors as to frighten the most hardened. He had no fancy for a hell, such as American clergymen talk about, which consists merely in being deprived of the company of angels and all that sort of thing, but he had a substantial, real hell, with actual fire and brimstone and real devils with red hot pitch-forks, toasting and gridling sinners, and rivers of fire, and perpetual torments of this cheerful kind, forever and forever. That was the kind of a hell he had.

It had its effect. One man who stood listening, with his wife, said to her as they turned away :

"Weel, Jenny, 'ell is a hawful thing, I don't knaw but what I'll turn around and do better, hafter to-morrow."

And the wife assenting to this proposition they went to the nearest beer place and buried their countenances and their consciences, or their fright rather, in pots of beer that would swamp the most seasoned American, and a few moments after were dancing like mad in a booth constructed for the purpose.

Except there be a special dispensation this party will never repent, and if there be such a hell as the preacher described they will find it. Their to-morrow for becoming good, like everybody else's, will never come. The negro who, when asked why, in view of the punishment that must follow his sinful life, he would continue in his evil courses, replied :—

"Boss, de great comfort and 'scurity I has, is in a deff-bed 'pentance."

"But suppose you die too suddenly to repent ?"

"Boss, I alluz keeps myseff ready for 'pentance."

The road down is lined with public houses, little quaint inns in which nobody sleeps, but which are devoted exclusively to the selling of beer and spirits. At each of these half the vehicles stopped, and the scenes about them were curious, if not altogether enjoyable. The only business done inside was the drawing and drinking of beer, and outside—heaven help an American—negro minstrelsy. Imagine three cockneys burnt corked, and dressed in trowsers striped in imitation of the American flag, with long blue striped coats and red vests, one playing the banjo, another the concertina, and the third doing the silver sand clog, with that peculiar soul-depressing, spirit-quenching expression that all clog dancers wear habitu-

5

ally.   A clog dance on a stage in a hall is sufficiently depressing to send a middle-aged man home to make his will, but

ENGLISH NEGRO MINSTRELSY.

imagine it done by an Englishman on a board outside an inn,
on a hot day, so hot that the perspiration streaming down his

face washed the burnt cork out in streaks, and then when this doleful performance was finally accomplished, think of a negro melody sung in the genuine cockney dialect, and accepted as a correct representation of the American African. By the way, in a first-class music hall I heard an English minstrel use the word "nothink," and misplace his h's as fluently as the most accomplished shopman. But the un-enlightened Englishman who had never heard the rich, mellow tones of the genuine African didn't know any better, and so it was as well. People who love minstrelsy deserve nothing better.

By this time it was noon, and the sun was blazing hot. But the sun doesn't mean as much on English roads as it does on American. England is some centuries old, and the roads are bordered on either side with immense trees, the hedges afford a grateful shade, and he who cannot find a delightful seat upon the soft grass is very hard to please. Exactly at noon the thousands of humble folk, the pony and donkey-cart people, stopped and unharnessed their diminutive power, and permitted it to crop the grass, while they unloaded those wonderful hampers, and spread them upon the grass and ate and drank. There was the boiled ham, the great masses

THE ROADSIDE REPAST.

of very bad bread made from the cheapest and worst American flour, the pot of mustard, and the inevitable bottle of beer. They sat under the delicious shade, men, women and children, and ate and drank and chaffed, and seemed to be enjoying themselves.

I think they all did enjoy themselves, except the women.

The children got more to eat than they did other days, so they were satisfied; the men, great hulking fellows, gorged themselves, and were pleased because they were full of beer, but the poor women had the children to care for, and that ought to have been enough to have destroyed all the pleasure there was in it to them.   For be it understood, no English laborer's wife ever leaves her children at home on holiday occasions. There are two reasons for this.   One is there is nobody to leave them with, and the other is there is a vague idea that it is a part of a child's education to know all about beer and public houses from its very beginning.   Therefore, almost every woman on that road to the Derby, had from one to four children with her, the youngest very frequently being at the very tender age of a month.   The husbands always permit the mother to assume the entire charge of the youngsters, and the wives accept the situation uncomplainingly.   They carry the "brats," as the fathers delicately style their offspring, and the small woman with a healthy baby in her arms, keeping three others in tow, under a hot sun, must have an amusing time of it.   But they seem to like it, and I don't know as it is any of my business.   Only I am rejoiced that the venerable Miss Susan B. Anthony don't know how the lower-grade Englishman treats his wife.   Could she see what I have seen she would start upon another lecturing tour, as ancient as she is.

One peculiarity strikes an American — everything has its price, which is rigorously exacted.   Everything is fenced up and the slightest accommodation has to be paid for. Do you want a glass of water?   It is given you, and you drink and set the glass down.   Immediately the man or woman who handed it to you remarks quietly, but with a tone that admits of no question: "Penny, sir!"   You pay it, for it is the custom of the country,   It isn't for the water, but for the handing it to you.   At every gate stands a man who asks for his penny as he opens it, and he gets it.   It got to that point with me, that when I felt a breeze striking my face and I got a breath of fresh air, I instinctively turned around to see to whom I should give the inevitable penny.   Air is the only thing that is not charged for, and if there were any way of fencing that in and selling it, it would be done immediately. I remonstrated mildly at paying for a very simple service, for which in no country I was ever in would a fee be demanded, but I was silenced instantly.

"It helps me make a day's wages, sir, and it won't break you, sir," was the very prompt answer.

I never dared to object again, but whenever I asked a question I offered the penny, and I did not find any one too proud to take it.

Finally we reached the Downs. Epsom Downs is an immense field, the property of the Earl of Derby, whose seat, "The Oaks," is about two miles distant. The "Derby" is only one of many races, but out of compliment to the Earl, it is counted the chief event of the racing season. The importance given to it may be inferred from the fact that it is really a, national holiday, that business is almost entirely suspended, and that Parliament adjourns to attend it.

I am not going to write a description of the race, for one very good reason. I didn't see it. I could do it, but I am too honest, and beside I have no idea that it would interest anybody. One race is just the same as another. The horses all start, and run the course, and come in. One horse wins, and a dozen lose; as in the American game of keno, one man exclaims "Keno!" and forty-nine utter a profane word. A quarter-race in Kentucky is precisely the same as the Derby, except that one is witnessed by a hundred men in jeans, and the other by some hundreds of thousands in all sorts of clothing. At all events I was too busy studying the people to pay any attention to the horses. Possibly I made a mistake, the horse may be the nobler animal of the two. I should like to get the opinion of the horse on that point.

The sight of the field was indescribable. There were people by the hundred thousand. The railroads brought down one hundred and twenty-five thousand, and nobody goes to the "Darby" by train if he can help it. Many prefer to walk the sixteen miles to going by rail. These either haven't the money to pay their fares, or shrink from giving money to railroads so long as there is beer to be had. The grand stand, an immense three-story structure, was black with people, and as far as the eye could reach there was nothing but people. And, as it is in America, the people were there for everything except to see the races, which is proper. For if there be anything under

heaven that is exasperating it is a horse race, unless it be a
regatta.   Except as an excuse for something else, I never could
see why people went to either.   To sit or stand for an hour
under a hot sun, while a lot of jockeys are undertaking to
swindle each other, simply to see a field of horses run or trot
for a minute or two, or a parcel of boats start and come to the
finish, always did seem to me to be the very acme of absurdity.
But when you have thirty jolly fellows with you, who make
good talk, a wild profusion of lunch, and oceans of wine, it is
quite another thing, that is if you like lunch, wine, and talk.

The principal race this year, and the one on which the
interest centered, was between " Peregrine," the English favorite, and "Iroquois," the American horse.   There were others
in the field, but these two absorbed the entire attention of the
throng.   It was a national matter, and a vast amount of money
was lost and won on the event.   As is known, "Iroquois" won
the race by a very small majority, and the American eagle
screamed with delight, and the British lion hung its head.
The English felt more humiliated than they did when they lost
the Colonies, and Archer, the English jockey who rode "Iroquois" to victory, was considered a very unpatriotic man.   The
English found one consolation: "Well, you know, the blarsted
Yankee 'oss couldn't 'ave won the 'eat if a Hinglish jockey
hadn't ridden 'im."   This was the remark that I heard everywhere.

The enthusiasm of the Americans knew no bounds.   The
glorious victory was made the reason for a fresh assault upon
the lunch and wine, and a number of American parties had
provided themselves with American flags, which they immediately pulled from their hiding places and flung to the breeze.
And then as the emblem of freedom displayed itself upon
English soil, it became immediately necessary to drink to the
flag, which was done with that promptness which has ever
distinguished the genuine American.   Parties of Americans
would   arm themselves with champagne bottles, and   pass
to the carriages displaying the flag, and insist upon the occupants partaking with them in honor of the victory and the flag,
and when one would get the address of the other, they would
find the one was from Kalamazoo and the other from Oshkosh,
and the coincidence was so striking that they would drink

again. By that time a New Yorker would appear, and "Why, you are from New York! Open another bottle!" and so on.

It was a glorious day, but for all that anybody saw of the race, it struck me that it would have done just as well to have taken the lunch and the wine to any other field outside of London, and become patriotically intoxicated.

The country people and the laborers of London enjoyed the races about as the Americans did. For their amusement there were shows and games on the ground by the hundred. There were penny theaters; there were shooting galleries, and the cocoanut game. A dozen or more pegs are driven into the ground, and on each is placed a cocoanut. The man who hungers after cocoanuts and amusement pays a penny, for which he has the privilege of throwing a wooden ball at the row of pegs. If he hits a peg the nut drops off and he is entitled to it, with the resultant colic. There were hundreds and hundreds of tents, inside of which were cheap shows, precisely such as we see at State fairs and outside of circuses. As I gazed upon the enormous pictures of fat women, and bearded women, and Circassian beauties with enormous masses of hair, and the wonderful snakes, and the groups of genuine Zulu chiefs, and heard the inspiring tones of the hand organ, accompanied with the bass drum, and heard the man at the door imploring the people not to lose the great chance of their lives, and saw the young fellow with his girl, torn by the perplexing conundrum as to which was the better investment, the show or more beer, I fancied for a moment that I was at home. But I was not. I was three thousand miles from home, but I was seeing exactly what I should have seen had I been there. Human nature is about the same everywhere. Certainly, there is no difference in the side-showmen or the people from whom he earns his living.

Beggars and gipsies, so-called (there was no doubt about the genuineness of the beggars), were as thick as leaves in Vallambrosa. Stout men who could have wrestled with the primeval forests were begging for half-pence; women, with bloated faces, on every inch of which was written "gin" in unmistakable characters, carrying wretched babies, beset you at every turn; and hideous hags, with unmistakable Irish brogue, thronged about the carriages with: "My pretty gentlemon,

will ye cross the palm ov the poor gipsy, and let her till yer
forchoon? Och, and I kin till ye the shtyle ov the shwate lady
ye'll marry, and the number ov childher ye'll hev, an bring ye
gud luck."

The absurdity of addressing me as a "pretty gintlemon,"
and of proposing to tell me the sweet lady I'd marry! I, a
married man this quarter of a century and the father of a
family! That old lady got nothing from me. But the good-
natured fellows in the carriage did throw her pennies, which
she took with the regular "God bless yez," and I have no
doubt that in the course of the day she picked up a very pretty
sum, enough at all events to keep her full of gin during the
night.

The gipsies proper were on the ground in force, and a curious folk they are. The women were telling fortunes, and a
vast number of customers they secured from the shop and servant girls on the ground, to all of whom she promised speedy
marriages, no husband being under the degree of a Duke, and
all of them very handsome and very rich men. The girls paid
their pennies and sixpences with great alacrity, and went home
to dream of their good luck, as they had a score of times before.
The investment was doubtless a good one. They were satisfied
with themselves for a while, at least, and when happiness
can be had for a penny, why should any one be miserable?

The men were hiring donkeys, saddled and bridled, for the
boys and girls to ride. To ride a donkey a certain fixed distance costs a penny, and among English children it is famous
fun. And as the gipsy owner lives out of doors and steals all
his food and the subsistence of his animals, and the animals
themselves, it was great fun for him. Albeit, as he steals
everything he uses and always proposes to, and never intends
to reform and start a bank, I don't see what he wants of pennies. Were they philosophical they wouldn't let donkeys, but
would lie down in the shade till hunger compelled them to
steal something to eat, and enjoy themselves all the time.

As I said the races on this course are fairly conducted, and
the best horse, or the best jockey, actually wins. But there is
as much rascality here as on an American course, and I can't
say more than that. Under the grand stand is the "betting
ring," in which the book-makers stand. These are flashy gen-

tlemen, with tall hats of painful newness, and diamonds of unearthly size and luster, which gives one a comforting assurance of solvency. These men take bets at the market rates. Thus, the betting that morning was three to one on "Peregrine." Now in America the betting ring is under the control of the association owning the track; but it is not so here, as any number of Americans discovered. They had faith in "Iroquois," and "laid" their money on him freely. One gentleman of my acquaintance deposited ninety pounds sterling with a book-maker, and was consequently entitled to two hundred and seventy pounds sterling, as his horse won. In great glee he hied himself to the ring, after the race, to collect his win-

nings. He hied himself back to the carriage sadly. Had "Peregrine" won the race the book-maker would, unquestionably, have been there and received the gentleman smilingly; but as "Iroquois" won, he folded his tent, like the Arab, and as silently stole away None of them were to be found. Smarting under the sense of wrong, the American told his story to the party on the way home, and he was pitied or laughed at, according to the temper of his listener, quite a number laughing at more than pitying him One gentleman laughed at him fearfully, but before we had got half way home, he broke out with "D—n the swindling scoundrel."

THE BETTING RING.

"To what swindling scoundrel do you refer?"

"That blank, blank, swindling devil of a book-maker!"

"Oh! oh! you were taken in, were you?" joyously exclaimed victim No. 1.

"Of course, I was, thirty pounds sterling!"

"And you were laughing at me."

And then one after another confessed to have been bitten the same way, and upon getting all the confessions in, it was discovered that one carriage had deposited to the credit of a set of London sharks three hundred pounds sterling, or fifteen hundred dollars.

I lost nothing, for I do not bet upon horses now, for reasons stated at the beginning of this epistle, which shows that perfect safety is only found in complete virtue.

One peculiarity of the event was the absence of fighting. During the entire day I did not see a fight or anything that

"D—N THE SWINDLING SCOUNDREL."

approached it. Gather three hundred thousand people together in one field in America, and fill them with our whisky, or even beer, and there would be processions of broken heads, and funerals in plenty the next day. There is no question as to the Englishman's fighting qualities, but he does not fight on his holidays. There were "d—n his eyes," in plenty, and any quantity of talk, but no actual combats, except the boxing matches, and they were all in good humor. Why? I can't tell. Possibly it is because the beer they drink tends to peace, and possibly it is because they find vent for their combativeness in whipping their wives at home. But they don't fight on race courses.

The mass commenced melting away at about four o'clock in the afternoon, and the grounds were entirely deserted, except by the showmen and those who have money to make during the entire racing season. They live in their tents.

The scene on the road back was slightly different from the morning. The people on the way out started to get drunk, and a vast majority succeeded. The road was lined with prostrate forms of men and women. The English women of the lower order drink as much as their husbands and brothers. You see them in the public houses standing at the bars with their husbands or lovers, pouring down huge measures of beer, and it is a toss which can drink the most, or which enjoys it the most keenly. It is certain that the woman gets drunk with more facility than the man, she being the weaker, if not the smaller vessel. And understand, these women are not dis-reputable ; they are hard-working wives and daughters of respectable laboring people, mechanics and the like. It is their notion of a day's pleasure.

Possibly they are not to be blamed. The life of a London workingman or woman is not a pleasant one; their pay is very small, and beer is very cheap, and for the time they are happy.

But the next morning! Dickens and all other English writers, have given most charming descriptions of the delights of a night's drinking, but why, oh why, have none of them ever described the repentance of the next morning? That would have done the world some good.

And so we rode on through masses of people, two-thirds of them at that stage of intoxication where the idea of enjoy-ment is noise and horse-play, shouting, cheering, singing, yell-ing, waving handkerchiefs, and all without the faintest idea of the object of either, till we struck the lights of the city. Then the masses separated, and we finally reached our homes, tired, half-pleased and half-disgusted. The Derby was over.

No American, unless he be a sporting man, ever goes to the Derby twice. It is necessary to go once to see it, but once is quite enough. It is a sight to see three hundred thousand people in one mass, but it is not a pleasant thing to realize the

fact that two-thirds or more of the number are under the influence of liquor, and that they did it deliberately, and went
there with no other idea. It rather lessens one's confidence in
the future of the race, and leads one to the increasing of his
donations to the home missionary societies. But it has always
been so in England, and probably always will be. And then
if the English workingman didn't get drunk at the Derby he
doubtless would find some other place for it, and as he gets a
day's pure air and sunshine, it is perhaps, as well. If any
good can be drawn from it, let us hunt it persistently.

EGYPTIAN ROOM, BRITISH MUSEUM.

CHAPTER IV.

SPEAKING within bounds, I should say that one-half of England is engaged in manufacturing beer for the other half. Possibly it takes two-thirds of the entire population to make beer enough for the other third, but I think an equal division would be about the thing. The British public is very drouthy.

One is astounded at the amount of drinking that is done here. Go where you will, turn whichever way you choose, the inevitable "public," or the "pub" as they say between drinks, stares you in the face. And on the streets almost every other vehicle you see is a vast, massive, clumsy truck, loaded either with full kegs for the publics, or taking away empty ones.

The British public house is not the same thing as the American. Except in a few instances you see none of the glass and mahogany palaces of New York, you see none of the flashy bars with plate glass, silver rails, elegant glass-ware, and the gorgeous bar-tender with diamonds as large as hickory nuts.

The London public house is a dingy affair, the dingier the better, with barrels piled upon barrels, and cob-webs as plenty as liquor. There is a wild superstition prevalent that age has something to do with the quality of liquor, and therefore, every place devoted to the sale or handling of the stuff, assumes as much of a Methuselean appearance as possible. You are to have a party of friends at your lodgings, we will say. You must have at least two kinds of liquor to entertain them withal, for no Englishman does anything without moistening his clay, and his clay is of a variety that absorbs a great deal of moisture. You pay for it and the man sends home the bottles.

Now an American liquor dealer would carefully wipe the
bottles, and they would be delivered at your house as clean
and tidy as a laundried shirt, but not so here. They are sent
with dust on them, and with cobwebs on them, and to brush
off the dust would be sacrilege. That dust is a sort of patent
—a testimonial to its age, and consequently a guarantee of its
excellence.

I mortally offended one liquor dealer by asking him to
show me his machine for dusting bottles, and also would he
kindly explain to me his process for cob-webbing them, and
was it expensive to keep spiders? The man actually resented
it — was angry about it. Singular how sensitive the Islanders
can be about trifles like that! To keep spiders for the manufacture of cobwebs would be more enterprising than to buy
cobwebs, and no American would dust bottles by hand, when
a very simple machine could be devised for the purpose.

The British landlord don't set the bottle before his customer as his brother does in free and enlightened America.
Now at home,— as I have been told by those who frequent
bar-rooms — the barkeeper sets before his customer a bottle of
the liquor he prefers, and the drouthy man helps himself to
such quantity as he deems sufficient for the purpose desired.
If he is fixing himself for a common riot, he takes a certain
quantity ; if for a murder, more or less, according to how
aggravated the crime is to be. A man would take more to
fit himself to kill his wife than he would for his mother-in-law,
and the wife-killing draught is at the same price as the mother-
in-law annihilator.

But over here the bar-maid measures your liquor. You
may have three penn'orth, four penn'orth or six penn'orth.
It is measured out to you and handed to you, and you swallow
it and go away.

I remonstrated with one proprietor as to the absurdity of
the custom, and the meanness of it.

"I will show you the reason for it," he said, quietly. Just
then a bold Briton came in and the landlord directed the maid
behind the bar to set down a bottle. The astonished customer
was invited to help himself, after the American custom. He
was an astonished Briton, but he managed to express his grati-

fication at the innovation. Seizing the bottle he poured out
an ordinary dinner tumbler full, and, looking grieved because
the glass was no larger, drank it off without a wink.

A BOLD BRITON TRYING THE AMERICAN CUSTOM.

I could easily see why the British landlord measures the
liquor to the British public. Two such customers on the American plan would bankrupt a very opulent proprietor.

The quality of liquor used by the better classes is perhaps
a trifle better than that consumed in America, at least so I
have been informed by those who use liquors. A vast quantity
of brandy is imported from France, and it is so cheap there
that it doubtless approximates to purity. The whiskies drank
are entirely Scotch and Irish, the English making none whatever. Wines are consumed in great quantities, and there is no

question as to the purity of the cheaper grades, which is to say they are undoubtedly the pure juice of the grape. The duty on wines is so small that there is no inducement, as in America, for the manufacture of bogus varieties

But the liquors consumed in London by the lower classes are probably the most execrable and vile that the ingenuity of the haters of mankind ever invented. The brandy they drink is liquid lightning—chain lightning—which goes crashing through the system, breaking down and destroying every pulsation towards anything good. The gin—well, their gin is the very acme, the absolute summit, of vileness. There is a quarrel in every gill of it, a wife-beating in every pint, and a murder in every quart. A smell of a glass of it nearly drove me to criminal recklessness.

A LONDON GIN DRINKING WOMAN.

And yet they all drink it, and especially the women. The most disgusting sight the world can produce is a London gin drinking woman standing at a bar, waiting feverishly for her "drain," with unkempt hair, a small but intensely dirty shawl, with stockingless feet, and shoes down at the heel, with eyes rheumy and watery, that twinkle with gin light out from the obscurity of gin-swelled flesh, with a face on which the scorching fingers of a depraved appetite have set red lines, as ineffaceable as though they had been placed there by red-hot iron, every one of which is the unavailing protest of a long-outraged stomach.

There she stands, a blotch upon the face of nature and a satire upon womanhood. It is difficult to realize that this bloated mass was once a fair young girl, and had a mother who loved her, and it is equally difficult to comprehend how any power, even that of Nature, could ever make use of it. But the elements are kindly to man. When they have done their work, sweet flowers may grow out of this putridity.

In America this sort of being exists, but it is herded somewhere out of sight. It does not stand at the bars in the best streets to offend the eyes of decent people. But it is everywhere here. It is in the Strand and on Piccadilly and Regent street.

The average Englishman of the lower, and even the middle classes, dearly loves to booze. Drunkenness is not the result either of conviviality or desperation as it is in other countries. It is the one thing longed for and set deliberately about.

Rare John Leech, illustrated it in his picture in *Punch*, years ago. A man

THE POOR MAN IS SICK.

was lying very drunk at the foot of a lamp-post. A benevolent old lady of the Exeter Hall school seeing him, called a cabman. "The poor man is sick," quoth the kindly dame, "why don't you help him?" "Sick, is he," replied cabby, "sick! don't I vish I 'ad just 'arf of vot ails him?" The cabby spoke the honest sentiment of his heart. The Londoner of his class loves it for the effect it has upon him,

6

and as he accomplishes his design with English gin, he
carries with him a breath that suggests the tomb of a not very
ancient king, a breath which has a density, a center, as one
might say.

At twelve o'clock, Saturday night, he would fight a rattle-
snake and give the snake the first bite. Were a venomous
snake to bite such an Englishman the man would never know

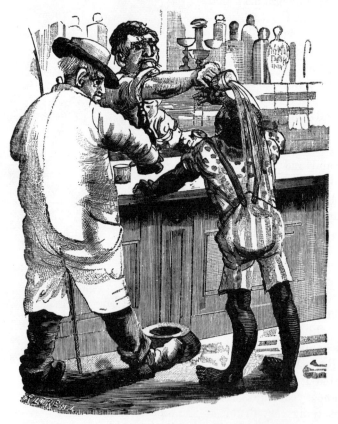

"THAT NIGGER IS MINE, AND WORTH FIFTEEN HUNDRED DOLLARS."

it, for alcohol is a sure cure for reptilian poison, but the poor
snake would wriggle faintly away to some secluded spot and
die sadly. This is why, I presume, I have seen no rattlesnakes
in London; they cannot safely prosecute the business for

which they were created. They are similarly worried, I believe, in West Virginia.

To drink this vile stuff successfully one would want his stomach glass-lined and backed up with fire-brick. I never would attempt it except as the man did in Kentucky. He walked into a bar, and distrusting the quality of the whisky, called up a negro and gave him a glass before drinking his own. The landlord, divining his purpose, knocked the glass out of the negro's hand. "No you don't!" said the Boniface, "that nigger is mine, and worth fifteen hundred dollars. Get an Irishman to try it on."

And while I am about it I may say that alcoholization is not confined to the lower order by any means. Almost every body drinks something beside water. The tradesman who can afford it has claret at his table, and during the day his "drains" of brandy are very frequent. The gentry and nobility drink more costly wines and better brandy, but liquor is everywhere. Nothing is done without the accompanying drink; it is universal and in all places. The climate prevents the injury that would visit the same man in America, but it hurts. If the English could only live as temperately as the Americans they would be the greatest race of people on earth.

The exclusiveness of the English is manifest in their vices as in their virtues. Every bar is divided in the front by partitions, one for each class. Over the one designated as "the private bar," you get precisely the same liquors as at the others, but you pay more for it, because laborers and the like are not admitted. One compartment exacts four pence, the next three pence, and the last and lowest two pence. But all are served out of the same wood.

But very few men are employed behind English bars, women filling those places. The London bar-maid is an institution to be studied. To begin with she must be pretty, for being pretty is a part of her qualifications. As her feet cannot be seen, owing to her standing behind the bar, she *is* generally pretty. Then they are required to dress well, and all in one establishment dress their hair alike. In one place the maids part their hair on one side, in another on the other, and in a third in the middle. They are alike in each shop.

They are required to make themselves pleasant to customers, for each one is expected to influence an amount of trade to the house. They are exceedingly free and easy damsels, without being positively indelicate, and there isn't a cabman in the city who is so much a master of chaff as they are. They will wink and leer at you in the most free way possible, they will talk to the very verge of indelicacy if they think it will please you, and if they form another judgment of your tastes they will be as sedate as priests. These bar-maids were all born a great while ago, and have improved all their time.

They are not only expected to be pretty, but they must have the power of extracting drinks for themselves from the young or old fellows who delight to chaff with them. If the young fellow who is enjoying the delight of her conversation is not sufficiently prompt, the warning eye of the landlord or landlady intimates that she has wasted enough time upon him, and she simply asks him, when he has ordered a drink for him self, if he won't treat her, and he always does. Per conse-quence by eleven at night the gentle maids are in a condition highly satisfactory to the house, for their drunkenness repre-sents so much money in his till. He who serves the British public with drink would utilize the very soul of an employe to make money, man or woman.

As a rule the wife of the landlord of a popular drinking place takes personal charge of the bar, and she is a thousand times more cruel and grasping than her husband. When a woman does unsex herself, she can give a man points in wick-edness that he never dreamed of. These wives are as eager to have liquor paid for for themselves as bar-maids, and the sharp eye they keep upon the girls to see that they swallow enough to make the business profitable is something wonderful.

They are invariably dressed very richly, with elaborate coiffures, and sparkling with diamonds. As the British young man prefers blonde hair to any other, the landladies are mostly of that persuasion. If they were born brunettes there are arts by which they can be changed, and besides wigs are very cheap in this country.

The British woman drinks as much as the British man, and possibly more. I am not speaking of the low, degraded woman, but of the respectability. It is nothing singular to see women, respectable women, sitting in bars with their husbands and lovers, and the amount of stout and "brandy cold," they make away with is something wonderful.

I was through the wonderful park at Richmond the other day. It was a holiday, and all London was out of the city in the parks. All the little roadside inns were filled with the populace, women and children being largely in the majority; and there was never a woman, no matter if she had a child at the breast, who did not have a monster pot of pewter filled either with porter or ale. And they gave it to their little children as freely as an American mother would milk.

The drinking house in London is, as a rule, especially for drinking. There are no free lunches, no nibbling bits, free on any bar. Nothing but liquids are sold. An American speculator conceived the brilliant idea of starting a bar with the addition of the American free lunch, with which to attract trade. It did attract altogether too much. In twenty minutes the lunch, which should have lasted all day, was gone, and the British public was indignant that it was not renewed. They pronounced the proprietor a swindle, and the speculation was a disastrous failure.

At some of the bars an attempt is made to take the curse off the liquor traffic by making some pretence of selling eatables. But the British public knows this is a sham, and resents it by never buying any comestibles at the counter. The British public scorns eating in such a place, and insists upon drinks. Indeed, the British public won't eat at all as long as it can drink.

What they generally have in these places under glass covers, are curiously indigestible meat pies, sandwiches, cheese, cakes and buns. Sometimes at railway stations a hungry Briton buys and partakes of these things, but not often, and never without his glass of something to wash it down. This is the time I forgive him for drinking. It is necessary.

The sandwich is made either of ham or beef, and may be said to be the universal cold refreshment. It is about four inches long by two wide, and is a miracle of thinness. It is the thinnest thing on earth. I have often purchased them, not to eat, but to admire this quality. How bread and meat can be cut so thin, especially bread, is one of the mysteries that never will be solved till I penetrate a public kitchen and see the operation. It is an art I suppose, and the professor of it gets, I presume, a very high salary. He ought to. The bread is stringy enough and the meat tough enough to be cut as thin as might be desired, but the puzzle is how any one can acquire the skill to cut it, that way. But they do it. The English sandwich is more an object of interest to me than the obelisk, and is just about as digestible. I would as soon undertake to eat the one as the other.

The meat pie is made of hashed beef, the fat being put in liberally, enclosed in a wrapper of dough, and all baked together, in some sort of way. I could procure and write out the process, but being a true American and loving the American people I will not. It is utterly indigestible. I ate one at eleven P. M. one night, and woke up in the morning feeling as though I had swallowed the plaster bust of the infant Samuel at prayer that stood on my mantel. The pie is a trifle worse than the sandwich. The cheese cake may be dismissed with the simple remark that it is a trifle worse than the meat pie. The bun is a stand-off as to the others. Altogether they make a frightful stomachic quartet. But the British public, who know nothing of our hash and other luxuries, are content with them, and I don't know as I shall undertake to reform them in this particular. I pity them, but there are so many things to reform here that I shall not attempt any movement in that direction. Life is very short.

The Englishman takes his liquor straight, or neat, as they call it. Mixed drinks are entirely unknown. The sherry cobbler, the mint julep, the fragrant cock-tail, are never heard of in regular English bars, but the drouthy man who drinks, and they all do, takes either brandy or Scotch or Irish whisky, raw from a barrel, and swallows his portion and walks away satisfied. One woman in a famous drinking place was taught by an American to make cock-tails, and the fame of the mixture drew all the Americans to this particular place. The proprietor was sore displeased at this trade, and raised the price two pence above what was regular, to keep it away. It took too much of the girl's time to compound the mixture.

Drinking does not have the effect upon an Englishman that it does upon an American. The Englishman is a more stolid and phlegmatic man anyhow, and the climate is less exciting. There is not the exhilaration in the atmosphere that there is in America, and the moist humidity that you exist in is very favorable to the consumption of alcoholic drinks. I had got so before I had been here a week, that I think I could have endured a glass of brandy and water. I did not do it, but I say I could have done it.

The prices of liquors average quite as high as in America, and tobacco and everything made of it, is much higher and the quality is vile. A decent cigar, or one counted decent here, costs twenty-five cents, it being of the grade that in New York sells for ten cents.

No tobacco is chewed except by sailors, and the Englishman, very properly, considers it a disgusting habit, only to be practiced by very low people. In consequence of the high price of tobacco, pipes and cigarettes are very generally used. The Englishman of the better class smokes his pipe upon the street, the same as an American does his cigar. He prefers a pipe to a cigar, possibly because it is better, and possibly because it is cheaper. Your Englishman loves dearly to get the value of his money, and he generally does it.

The lover of drink in America, especially our German fellow citizens, are emphatic in their denunciation of the liquor laws of the United States. They ought to live in England a little while to appreciate the privileges they have at home. Hartford, Connecticut, is, I believe, a paradise to those who live there. One old lady who was born and had always lived in Hartford, came to die — an impertinence of Nature, as all Hartford people firmly believe. People should die in other places, but not in Hartford. But this old lady had come to death, and her minister was consoling her.

"I trust, Mrs. Thompson, ' he said, professionally, " that you are prepared to die ? "

"I am," was her answer ; "I owe no pew rent."

" And are you content with the change ? "

"Well, on the whole, yes. Heaven is no doubt a very nice place, but I shall greatly miss my Hartford privileges."

There is no especial moral to this story, except that if our German population were compelled to endure English law they would greatly miss their American privileges. While you can get all the drink you want during the day, you must either have it at home or go without it after twelve o'clock at night.

In London no liquor can be procured after twelve o'clock at night. Every bar, big or little, is closed, and this law is not evaded, for the risk is too great. A man's license would be taken from him immediately, and without remedy.

Persons are not licensed to sell liquor in England — it is the premises that are licensed. The Board having it in charge license one public house in a district, basing it upon the supposed necessity, and these premises hold this license till deprived of it by violation of law. If you desire to sell liquor you cannot go and rent a room and open your bar; you are compelled to buy the lease of a place which carries the license with it. Consequently a licensed place is a valuable piece of property. One at the corner of St. Martin's street and Orange, a dingy building in a dingy neighborhood, was bought by an American to be used as an American bar, and he paid twenty-five thousand dollars bonus for the lease. The annual rental of the place is fifteen hundred dollars, and the lease for which he paid the bonus has forty-five years to run. For any other business the bonus would have been next to nothing in that neighborhood.

Sunday is an especially drouthy day in London. All the bars are closed till one o'clock P. M., and are then open but an hour. Then they are closed till six, and are permitted to keep open from that hour till eleven. And let it be remembered that law in England is law. You cannot laugh at it as you do in America. There is no evasion of this law attempted. The publics are required to be closed and they are closed. There are no side-doors, as in New York — there is no selling on the sly — they are closed. The only exception is at the railroad stations. The refreshment bars there are permitted to be kept open as long as trains arrive or depart, for the British Government recognizes the necessity of an Englishman having his grog till the prescribed hour for his getting into his bed. The thirsty soul who pants for beer after twelve goes to Charing Cross station, and buys a ticket to the first station out, which is "tuppence ha'penny," or five cents. Then he walks into the bar, and being a "traveler," can buy, drink and pay for all the stimulants he desires, till the last train has arrived or departed for the night. His ticket he puts into his pocket, to be used when he desires.

The night trade in liquor is something enormous. A landlord in the Haymarket, whose lease is about expiring, is now paying one thousand dollars a year rent, and the proprietors have notified him that his renewal will cost him just five times that sum. He told me that he should not renew, but that he would gladly if he were allowed to keep open till half-past twelve, a half hour after the regular time. That half hour each day would more than make the difference in rent.

A walk along Piccadilly after twelve explains this difference. The street, from end to end, is crowded with prostitutes, and drunken rakes who think they are having a good time, but they are not. They walk up and down, chaffing with these poor unfortunates. They take them into the publics, and pay for their drinks, all of which the landlord not only approves of but encourages. And the English prostitute can drink as heartily and just as long as any man alive. She has just as drouthy a system, and it takes just as much to fill it. And there they sit, and chaff, and booze, till the clock strikes twelve and the place is closed. The landlord turns off the gas and puts up his shutters, cursing the law that compels him to close just as his harvest begins.

As there are literally tens of thousands of these women walking the street, and as ninety per cent. of them are drunk at ten, with a carrying capacity of continuing to drink every minute as long as anybody will pay for it, and as there is an equal number of men prowling the streets whose highest idea of amusement is to pay for it, the importance of an extra half hour after midnight may be appreciated.

But it is of no use. Law is law in England, and whether the citizen likes it or not, he is compelled to obey it in letter and spirit. Were a public house to be open a minute after the hour, a policeman would walk in and close it for him, and the next day the nearest magistrate would revoke his license, and he could never get one again. No proprietor would rent him a place, for the license is too valuable to be risked by a violator of law.

There are a few bars in London that make a specialty of American drinks, which are very curious. The names they palm off as American are very funny to an American, because they are never heard of over there. None of my readers ever go into bars, except for curiosity, but just imagine this list of drinks:

"Copper-cooler," "Pick-me-up," "Our Swizzle," "Maiden's Blush," "Bosom-caresser," "Corpse-reviver," "Flash-of-Light ning," and so on.

And these names are actually believed by Englishmen to be genuinely American, and in common use in the States.

Ice is about the scarcest thing in England, and cannot be had at the majority of bars. At some of the very best it will be furnished, if very forcibly asked for, but then in too small quantities to be satisfactory to an American, who is accustomed to taking his drinks ice cold. The frozen reminiscence of Winter is rather expensive here, and, besides that, the Englishman very rightly considers it unhealthy. The water is drank in its natural temperature, and it is really wonderful how soon one becomes accustomed to it.

The prices of strong beverages run about the same as in the United States. Brandy is three pence, six cents of our Bird of Freedom money, and when the amount is considered, your three pence buys about the same as twelve and one-half cents in New York. Malt liquors are about the same. The glass is a trifle smaller, and the regular price at the small publics is two pence, an equivalent, quantity considered, of five cents.

The quality of malt liquors is a long way below the American article, and America, singular as it may seem, drinks better English ale than the Englishman does. The ale made here for home consumption is vile stuff, while that made for export is infinitely better. The Englishman eats what he cannot sell.

To get at these facts concerning drinking has cost me an inconceivable amount of wear and tear of feeling, which sacrifice I trust my readers will appreciate.

CHAPTER V.

To pass from rum to amusement is a very easy and natural transition, for unfortunately the people who drink are, as a rule, those who need and will have amusement. Having done with liquor forever, I am glad to get to a subject not quite so disagreeable.

London supports forty theaters proper; that is, forty theaters devoted entirely to dramatic or operatic representations, and several hundred places of amusement of all kinds, which may be classed as variety shows.

The regular theaters are a long way beyond those in America. I dislike to acknowledge this, but candor and fairness compels it. I cannot tell a lie, even for national pride. My hatchet is bright — it has never been used much. The London theaters will not compare with those of any of the large American cities in point of size, or convenience of access. They are generally situated in out of the way places, and the halls and entrances are as shabby as anything can be, but when you are once in nothing can be more delightful. There is a softness in the appointments, a perfection in the furnishing, a good taste generally that America has not. We are splendid, but it must be confessed, rather garish and loud.

The character of the performances excels the style of the theaters. Their pieces are put upon the stage with an attention to detail, and with a strength of cast which we at home never see, even in the best.

I witnessed a piece at the St. James, the time of which was the First Charles. In a drawing-room scene musical instru-

(91)

ST. THOMAS HOSPITAL AND HOUSES OF PARLIAMENT.

ments were necessary. In America it would have been nothing singular had a Chickering piano been used, and a parlor set in reps. Imagine the delight of seeing a drawing-room furnished with furniture of the period, with an old harpsichord, such as the ladies of the time used, with the ancient zittern, and the gorgeous harp, with the chairs and couches precisely as they were in the country house of the time. The costumes were not mere guess work — they were designed and constructed by a professional costumer, who made studies from pictures, and put upon the stage men and women of King Charles' day. This was a delight, in and of itself, that paid one for his time and expenditure, even if he cared nothing for the play.

And then the acting. If there is any one thing in the way of amusements that is utterly and fiendishly detestable, it is the acting of the usual child. The mother or father who trains the ten year old phenomenon to play children's parts, takes it as far away from childhood as he can possibly, and the child does not play a child at all. He does, or tries to do, *Hamlet*, in children's clothes. But nothing of the sort is permitted in London. The child plays the child, and does it as it should be done. It was a comfort to see two children on the floor in one scene, playing at the game of " See-saw, Margery Daw," and doing it exactly as children would do in real life, instead of mouthing the lines like an old-style actor in " Macbeth."

And all the way down there was the same perfection in the acting as in the setting of the piece. There was not one star and twenty "sticks," as is the rule over the water, but the servant who merely said, "My lord, the carriage waits," did that bit just as well as the hero or heroine of the piece.

The Englishman is a very thorough sort of a man, and wants what he has done well, according to his notion of what well is.

The places of amusement, other than the regular theaters, are of as great variety as they are vast in number. The prevailing attraction is, of course, the regular variety theater, which does not differ materially from its brother in America. It is singular that the stock attraction at the variety theater is the negro minstrel act. Minstrelsy originated in America forty years ago, but it has as firm a hold upon England as it has upon America, and a trifle firmer. No programme is complete without it, and no part of the performances are so heartily enjoyed.

But their minstrelsy would drive an American negro crazy. It is sufficient for a London audience to have a performer black his face and hands, and put on a long-tailed coat, and striped trowsers, and sing negro songs. The rich, mellow accent of the American African, the rollicking humor, the funny grotesqueness, all that is wanting. At any music hall you shall hear the songs popular in America sung by a cockney with all the cockney peculiarities of speech, even to the misplacing of the h's.

The leg business is even more common and more indecent than in America, and variety performance is more highly flavored generally. Magic and athletic performances are greatly in favor, albeit fine vocalism and instrumental perform ance of a very high character must be interspersed.

These variety performances are attended by all classes. The respectable mechanic and his family, the professional man and his family, the thief, pickpocket, and prostitute, are all mingled in one common mass, the only division being the prices in different parts of the house. And here, as everywhere, drinking goes on incessantly and forever. Waiters move about through the audience, taking orders for beverages, and men and women drink and guzzle, and men smoke during the entire performance. No matter what else stops, the flow of beer never does. It is very like Time in this particular, constantly moving.

The life of a variety actor is a very busy one after eight at night. If he has any popularity at all he has engagements at three and even four theaters. He sings one song and responds to three *encores*, then throwing himself into a cab he is driven to another and to another, the time of his appearance at each being fixed to a minute.

Singular as it may seem, the wretches who sing the most idiotic songs, of the "champagne Charley" kind, compositions so utterly and entirely stupid that one wonders that any audi-

ence would endure them for a minute, are the most popular.
They sing them in extravagant evening costumes, in the most
doleful and melancholy way, and call themselves "comiques."
One of them, probably the nearest approach to an idiot of any
man on the English stage, makes from two hundred to three
hundred dollars a week, and is in demand all the time.

INTERIOR OF A VARIETY HALL.

But they have a good time at these theaters. To hear a
woman sing a slang song dressed — or rather undressed — is
not calculated to inflict much wear and tear upon the mind,
and as all the performances are of the alleged humorous order
there is abundant room for chaff and talk of like cheerful

nature, which is further aided and promoted by the consumption
of beer.   The parties seem to enjoy it, and I presume they do.

The low Londoner has very brutal tastes.   His greatest
delight is a prize fight; a dog fight comes next in his estima-
tion; a rat pit is satisfactory in default of anything more
bloody; a cock-fight will answer as an appetizer; and a horse
race is pleasing, though that shades up into something too
near respectability for him.

A dog fight in London is a sight that is worth seeing just
once, if studies of *in*human nature are what you want.   The
arena is always behind a "sporting public," on whose tables
in the parlor you shall always find the flash and sporting
papers of the metropolis, and the walls of which are decorated
with engravings of prize fights, portraits of famous dogs, and
highly colored lithographs of noted horse encounters.

Gathered around the arena will be a hundred or more of
"the fancy," who were to me anything but fancy.   They are
the broad-jawed, soap-locked, sturdy brutes, of the Bill Sykes
type, beer-bloated and gin-inflamed, who subsist by practices
which, if not absolutely criminal, come as close to it as possible.

The dogs are of the English bull variety, those plucky, tenacious brutes who will die rather than yield, or even make any
manifestation of pain.

At the signal the brute dogs are let loose upon each other,
the human dogs about expressing the keenest possible delight
at any especial and exceedingly bloody performance.   The
highest pleasure is attained, and the wildest enthusiasm is
evoked, when one dog gets the shoulder or jaw of the other
in his iron jaws, and holds it there, while the other literally
eats him up.   Then wagers are laid as to which will hold out
the longest, and every movement is watched with the keenest
solicitude, and when the bloody drama ends in the death of
one or both, and the wagers are settled, the conversation flows
naturally into a dog channel, and the victories and defeats of
past years are discussed, much as soldiers discuss their achievements.

Dogs of this breed, of approved courage and strength, are
of great value, and large sums of money are hazarded upon
their performances.   The aristocratic dog fanciers can have a

private match made for them at any time for from one to five pounds.

Of course there are any quantity of aquariums and menageries, and institutions of a supposed usefully scientific nature, which are largely attended, but the variety theater, or music hall, as it is called, is the stock amusement of the Londoner. He can drink to better advantage in them than anywhere else, and that, after all, is the principal business of his life.

The street amusements are beyond any possibility of enumeration or description. You will not walk a dozen blocks without seeing the very absurd and very brutal Punch and Judy, which has delighted England for centuries, and seems to be immortal. One would naturally suppose that when a boy had laughed at two wooden figures manipulated by a man inside of a box, knocking each other on the head, with squeaks and idiotic dialogue, every day up to his twenty-first year, would naturally pass it by ever afterward, but it is not so. I have seen venerable men, who were doubtless bank presidents or clergymen, or something of the eminently respectable kind, stop in front of a Punch and Judy show, and laugh as heartily at the ancient performance as they did when they were boys in roundabouts. And they would stand out the performance, and at its conclusion give the performer their two pence, and go away as if they had been amused.

There never has been any change in Punch and Judy from the time it was brought to England from Italy. The fun is now, as then, in Punch knocking Judy on the head with his stick, and the shrieks of Judy with an expression on her face of enjoyment. That is all there is of it, and all there ever has been. And singular as it may seem, it is the first amusement of an English boy, and it delights him till he dies. He enjoyed it at eight, and just the same at eighty. No doubt he has a vague idea that he will find a Punch and Judy show in heaven when he reaches it.

But Punch and Judy shows are not all the amusements of the great city. Garden hose not being common, owing to the fewness of gardens and the limited use of water, the hand organ flourishes in all its native ferocity, the grinders being, as over the water, Italian noblemen with their wives. And

7

they are just as dirty and grimy here as there. The mixed brass and string banditti perambulate the streets making the day and early night hideous, and in the side streets where the policeman is infrequent the street juggler plies his vocation.

One, for instance, has a common purse with four shillings. He places the four shillings in the purse, the country yokel sees them placed therein, and he chinks the purse. So far as the

THE MAGIC PURSE.

countrymen's eyes and ears go there can be no doubt as to the fact of the four shillings being in the purse. Then the fakir offers to sell the purse to the countryman for sixpence, which, were the shillings actually inside, would certainly be a bargain. The countryman pays the sixpence, and straightway opens the purse, but he does not find the sixpence therein. It is as empty as his head. He finds that he has paid sixpence for a purse dear at a penny, and he retires amid the jeers of the populace.

As the clever juggler only finds a few victims each day, and as from each he makes only ten cents, I don't see how he expects to ever retire from business and live upon his hard earned capital. The skill, knowledge of human nature, and hard work necessary to the successful prosecution of this little swindle would make him rich, with half the wear and tear. But such men would rather work a day to swindle somebody out of sixpence than to earn a dollar by honest work in a quarter of the time. That is why I shall never go into the business of juggling with four shillings and a penny purse. It is disreputable, and then it does n't pay.

Couples of negro minstrels are a common sight on the streets, one armed with a banjo, and another with a concertina, that he plays with an atrocious disregard of time and tune, which under a despotism would consign him to a block. They roam from house to house and play, as they call it. The helpless family, worried to the very verge of madness, throw them sixpence, and they move on. They stand and play till they get their sixpence. The race is not as it was in Jem Bagg's day. He played the clarionet. "Ven the man tosses me a sixpence," was his remark, and says 'Now, my good man, move hon,' I gently says to him, says I, 'I never moves hon for a sixpence. I knows the vally of peace and and quietness too much for that, and then, hif 'e doesn't throw me another sixpence, I tips him my corkscrew hovertoor, and that halways fetches 'im.'"

In this degenerate day either the street musicians have forgotten their "corkscrew overtoors," or they are satisfied with less money. A sixpence moves them on now certainly, but woe be to you if you are short the sixpence.

Next door to me lives a deaf man who is a bachelor. It is his delight to have the musicians come to this house. He sits in the doorway, and they play and play, and he assumes an

ecstatic expression, and they wonder why he doesn't order
them to "move on," but he doesn't.   It amuses him and they
play, till, lost in amazement at his powerful endurance, they

THE MAN WHO WAS MUSIC PROOF.

put up their instruments sadly and move on of their own
accord. I get very little amusement out of him now. The
majority of the fiends have found him out.

CHAPTER VI.

MADAME TUSSAUD.

ONE of the stock sights in London which every foreigner as well as every man, woman and child from the country who goes to London, does with great regularity, is Madame Tussaud's Museum. It is known the world over and is as regular a thing to see as the Tower.

A great many years ago, some time since the flood, a Swiss woman named Tussaud, who had studied art in Paris, took the brilliant notion into her wise head that money was better than fame, and instead of spoiling marble she commenced doing some very good things in wax. She brought her figures to London and opened a museum, which she added to and enlarged as men and women became of sufficient interest to attract attention, until she got pretty much everybody of whom the world ever heard.

She died many years ago, but the collection was continued by her family, three generations of which have waxed rich and gone to join those whom they put so well in wax in life.

This wonderful museum, which actually deserves all the attention it gets, is filled with really excellent figures of the entire line of English Kings, dressed in the costumes of the period in which they lived, including arms, although court dresses generally adorn them. As the Tussaud family were, and are, artists, these figures are not the limp, misshapen, grinning effigies usually exhibited, but are in size, stature, color and general grouping, perfect.

I cannot say that the effigies of King Edward and Richard, and those other ancient marauders, are correct, for I never

saw them in life. They died many years ago. But all you
have to do is what Dicken's Marchioness did with the orange
peel wine: "Make believe very hard," and they will do. The
faces were modeled from portraits, and their dresses were
made from actual costumes preserved in the curious reposi-

MADAME TUSSAUD.

tories of which London is full. The visitor gets some notion of
what the subjects were like, and that ought to be and is satisfactory.

You see, standing or sitting, marvelous likenesses of all the
great soldiers and statesmen of England, but heavens! how
our poor Americans have been abused! Washington is about
as like our Washington as he is like an Ohio River coal boat

captain. Ex-President Grant has good cause for action for libel, for such a face as they have put upon him could not have been on a third corporal of the poorest company in the very worst North Carolina regiment, and President Hayes and Garfield have been similarly treated. That of Franklin is a tolerable likeness of the maker of infernal maxims, but there was a malicious design evident on the part of the artists to dwarf the Americans, as I fancy there was to enlarge and exaggerate the Englishmen.

The groups are something wonderful. The Lying-in-State of the Czar, a recent addition, is a miracle of naturalness and awful beauty, as is the death of Pope Pius; and they are so

WAX FIGURES OF AMERICANS.

natural that one cannot help feeling that he is in the presence of actual death, and not a counterfeit presentment.

The Museum contains, among other curiosities that are of interest, the identical coach used by Napoleon at the battle of Waterloo, with a vast number of other relics of the great Corsican. From the number of Napoleonic relics I fancy that the Madame was at heart a French woman, though she was making her money from the English.

Great halls are filled with correct statuary in wax of the world's great, or notorious men, all of which have to be "done," as a matter of course.

But the great point, and one which no visitor ever fails to visit is the "Chamber of Horrors." You pay a sixpence extra — there is always sixpence extra in England — and you are introduced to the most cheerful assemblage of monsters that the world has ever produced.

If there ever was a murder committed of an especially atrocious description, one done under peculiarly horrifying and terrible circumstances, here is a wax figure of the murderer, and, if possible, of the victim.

There is the original guillotine which made the acquaintance of so many necks during the various French revolutions. There is the identical scaffold which was devised by a man condemned to be hung, and on which he suffered, with forty-eight others afterward, before it was retired, and there are ropes and delightful articles of that nature with which criminals have suffered, and in such numbers that we come to the conclusion that the principal business of the English and French is to kill somebody and get hung for it.

The two criminals in which I took the liveliest interest were Messrs. Burke and Hare, of Edinburgh, Scotland. These gentlemen had a contract with the medical university of Edinburgh, to furnish the students with corpses for dissection, which they did by resurrecting them from various church-yards.

Mr. Burke, who was evidently the leader in the enterprise, remarked one night to Mr. Hare,— that is, I presume he did:

"Why go out this dark and rainy night and dig in the damp earth for corpses? Digging corpses is all wrong. If the friends of the deceased should ever discover that a corpse had been abstracted it would occasion the most profound feeling. We should have more respect for the survivors than to raise their dead, and then, in the interest of science, we should give the students fresher bodies for dissection. I am inflexibly opposed to digging any more."

"But how shall we get the corpses?" asked the obtuse Mr. Hare.

"It is far easier," replied Mr. Burke, "to knock a man on the head than it is to dig him up, and, in addition to the other

"DIGGING CORPSES IS ALL WRONG."

reasons I have mentioned, a sand-bag or a club is cheaper than a spade."

And Mr. Hare coinciding with Mr. Burke, they went out that night and killed a man, and they kept going out and killing men till thirty had disappeared. The authorities finally got upon their track, when Mr. Hare turned States' evidence and hung Mr. Burke, and he went peacefully into some other business.

It is needless to add that a careful study of the faces of the

THE IMPROVED PROCESS OF MESSRS. BURKE AND HARE.

two men would not lead one to purposely encounter them in a dark alley after twelve at night. Nothing earthly could be so villainous.

A little incident that occurred the day I explored the Museum illustrates the perfection of the modeling and draping the figures. There were in the party a gentleman and lady from Pennsylvania, the former being a devotee of the alleged science of phrenology, and rather fond of discussing the subject.

A female figure was standing on the floor, which attracted his attention. This was in the Chamber of Horrors.

"I want to call your attention," he said to his wife, "to this illustration of the truth of phrenology. Could there be modeled a more vicious face? Notice the development back of the ears, showing the head to be all animal, and the pinched forehead and the general insignificance of the front head as compared with the development of the back portion. There is murder in every line of that face. Let me see who it is."

"Thank you," exclaimed the figure as it moved away. It was a very estimable American lady whom the phrenologist had mistaken for a wax figure.

OSBORN HOUSE, ISLE OF WIGHT.

CHAPTER VII.

THE LONDON LAWYER.

LONDON is probably the most expensive place to do business in the world. Its business men are conservative, so conservative that they would not for the world part their hair in any way differing from their fathers, nor would they adopt a modern convenience unless it were absolutely necessary to the maintenance of English supremacy, and they would sigh as they parted with an old nuisance for a modern delight. Their professions have all got into ruts from which you can no more move them than you can the Pyramids, and their practices are so established that they may and do do as they please, without regard to the notions of any body.

An American resident in London bargained for a house, and the lease had to be transferred. Now in any country where a common school exists almost anybody can assign a lease, but not so here. A solicitor had to be employed, and afterward a contract long enough to cover a sheet of legal paper had to be drawn up. It was a very plain matter — forty words would have been sufficient. But a solicitor must be employed nevertheless. How much do you suppose it cost Mr. Foote to have this trifle of work done? As a matter of instruction to the American people and for the benefit of American lawyers, who are too modest in their charges, and I am now convinced that the majority of them are, I make a partial copy of the solicitor's bill, as it is a more interesting document than anything that I can write. Here it is:

(108)

W. M. FOOTE, ESQ ,
>> *To* BLANK, BLANK, Solicitor.
>> *Re* Star of the West.
>> Prior to Yourself.

	£.	s.	p
Clerk attending at Messrs. Ingram's (Vendor's Solicitors), for draft proposed contract		6	8
Procuring and considering and found same objectionable		6	8
Instructions for contract		6	8
Drawing same, folios twenty	1	11	1
Engrossing in two parts		1	8
Writing Messrs. Ingram with one part		3	6
Writing Mr. Challer for schedule of fixtures to answer to contract		3	6
Same as to appointment for Monday		3	6
Drawing telegram and attending to forward and paid		7	8
Attending you, and then at Messrs, Ingram, engaged a considerable time going through deed and documents, etc., and settling contracts and signing	3		0
Writing your hereon, fully		6	8
Instructions for registration on title		6	8
Drawing same		12	0
Engrossing		4	0
Attending to deliver		6	8
Replying to your letter		3	6
Attending appointing conference		6	8
Engrossing papers, leases and covenants	1	10	0
Attending Dr. Thomson therewith		6	8
Fee to him and clerk	1	3	6
Paid conference fee	1	6	0
Attending conference and cab hire		13	4
Perusing his opinion	1	0	0
Writing you with copy Dr. Thomson's opinion		6	8
Making copy of schedule and fixtures		5	6
Waiting uopn Messrs, Ingram with same		3	6
Perusing abstract	2	10	6
Writing with appointment to examine deeds with abstract		3	6
Attending examining deeds with abstract, self and clerk	2	2	0
Attending searching liquidation proceedings of Arthur Coleman and paid		14	4

As this remarkable document extends over four and a half pages of foolscap paper I will not give it all. However, there are some other charges worthy of going upon record. For instance this item:

A replying to your letter		3	6

And this:

	£.	s.	p
Attending you long conference, and you left cheque for purchase money	13	4	0
Writing you fully		3	6
Attending appointing conference		3	6

The entire bill footed up forty-two pounds, fourteen shillings and ten pence, which, reduced to bird of freedom money amounts to about two hundred and twenty-five dollars.

And all this for transferring a lease from one party to another, about which operation there couldn't be the slightest trouble, except as the two attorneys made it.

Doubtless the Messrs. Ingram and Dr. Thomson, whatever he had to do with it, put in a similar bill against their clients, so both sides had a very good thing of it.

But this was not all there was of it. It was necessary that Mr. Foote should have a little article of agreement with Mr. Welch, his manager, not that there was any especial need for

THE LONDON LAWYER.

it, but as a mere matter of form, as we say when we want a sure thing on somebody. The same attorney was employed to do this, in fact he suggested it and did it before this bill was presented.

The bill for this service is precisely like the other. There are items for "attendance," for "preparing telegrams," for "waiting, self and clerk," for "instructions," and so on, the amount charged for preparing an article of agreement being eight pounds sterling.

The attorney's fees for the whole of this trifling piece of business footed up exactly seventy-two pounds sterling, or three hundred and sixty dollars.

"What do these items mean?" I asked Mr. Foote.

"Well, the items for attendance mean that I went to his office and told him in three minutes' time what I wanted, and he made minutes with a pencil."

"The clerk?"

"Oh, they never go anywhere without a clerk. His business is to carry a green bag with nothing in it, and look like an umpire. All the writing of letters, for which he relentlessly charged three shillings and sixpence each, was totally unnecessary, as they related to matters of which I fully informed him at the beginning. But he was the most industrious letter writer I ever saw. And I would answer his letters like an idiot, and he charged for replying to mine, and then he would write again and charge for that, and so on. And when he couldn't decently write another letter, he would telegraph me and charge for that, and — well, if I had taken two leases I shouldn't have been through till this time.

"Did you pay it?"

"Pay it? Of course I did. To have resisted would have been ruin. He would have sued me, and I should have had to have employed another attorney, and the case would have gone into the courts, after about a thousand instructions, conferences, letters, and telegrams, and clerks, and all that, from him — the same as this — and it would have dragged along, with more clerks, and letters, and telegrams, till the crack o' doom. Instead of bills of four pages I should have had bills of forty, and then there would have been money to be paid on account, and bail, and the Lord only knows what. A law suit in London means ruin to everybody but the lawyers and officers of the court. And in the end I should have been compelled to pay it, for the courts take care of the attorneys.

And, after all, he only made the regular charges that every London lawyer does. Indeed, as he omitted twice to charge three and six pence for bidding me good morning, I don't know but that he is rather liberal than otherwise. I think," said Mr. Foote, reflectively, "that three times he shook my hand, and I find no charge for that. On the whole, he is a tolerable fair lawyer to do business with."

"Tell me all about him."

"He is one of say twenty thousand lawyers in London who get a case like this, occasionally. He occupies "chambers," as they call their offices, and keeps a clerk, as they all have to, to ever expect any business, as a lawyer without a clerk would have no standing. The clerk spends most of his time eating ham sandwiches, having nothing else to do, except when his employer gets a man like myself on a string, on which occasion he follows him about carrying a bag which is supposed to contain papers of great moment. My lease was all that was in that bag for a month or more. He lives well all the time, for no matter how poor he may be, or how little business he has, he must live well for the sake of appearance. Finally he does get the management of a good estate, and is fixed for life. An Englishman reposes confidence in his solicitor, and would no more think of disputing a charge made by him than he would of heading a rebellion. They are doubtless a very nice lot, but the less you have to do with them the better. A little of them go a long way. Dispute his bill, not I. I don't want to make England a permanent residence, for I hope to get back to America some time, and a law suit would keep me here all my life, provided I had money enough to pay fees and costs. They'll hold on you as long as you've a penny."

That Mr. Foote did not exaggerate, I know. Had I supposed he had been exaggerating I should not have written this. But I copied this bill from the original, which was receipted by the attorney, who, doubtless, sighed as he wrote his name, that some mistake had not occurred which made litigation necessary.

CHAPTER VIII.

SOME NOTES AS TO THE INVESTMENT OF ENGLISH CAPITAL, AND
ALSO BRITISH PATENT MEDICINES.

IT is a very common remark that Americans love to be
humbugged. Perhaps they do, but their English cousins can
give them points in this desire. The ease with which adven-
turers and bogus schemers get their claws into English money-
bags, is something astounding. Perhaps it is because the
nation has so much money that it don't know what to do with
it, or possibly because the Englishman is naturally credulous,
but it is a fact that London is the paradise of the sharper, and
the pleasant pasture for the bogus speculator.

There are several reasons for it. Interest is very low in
England, and for the man who desires to live "like a gentleman" the temptation to increase the rate is very strong.
Then again there is an immense amount of capital lying idle
and seeking investment, and the man who has just enough
money at three per cent. to live upon very closely, is always
anxious to increase his income by making, it six. Every man
who has just money enough to drink beer, has an insatiable
thirst for champagne. And the Englishman who has a
strong sense of mercantile honor, naturally has more faith
than the inhabitant of a country where the standard of honor
is lower, and men are, by habit, more cautious of believing.

The papers of London are filled with prospectuses of companies organized for developing something in all parts of the
world, and these prospectuses are so written that they would
deceive the very elect.

The principal point at the beginning is to get a board with
a great many lords, dukes, esquires, and all that sort of thing,
on it, the average Englishman not seeming to realize that

8 (113)

there are a good many of these gentry who are as impecunious as anybody else, and who would do a piece of roguery for enough to live upon comfortably upon the continent, as readily as the commonest sharper in the world. The baronet has a stomach to fill and a back to cover the same as the costermonger. In this, all humanity stands upon an equality.

Before me. lies a repectable paper, its pages filled with glowing advertisements of projected companies. The first is for the "Acquiring and further developing the well-known so-and-so gold mine," in Venezuela.

It begins with the Board of Directors, not one of whom is less in degree than an Esquire, and several "Sirs" figure in it. Then comes the bankers — nothing in London is complete without a banker — then solicitors, then brokers. After this elaborate outfit, all of which looks as solvent and sound as the Bank of England, comes a glowing prospectus.

Nothing can be finer than this prospectus. "The property proposed to be acquired consists of six hundred and fifty-nine acres, which contain the most of the noted Venezuela gold mines. The vein has been traced on the surface for a distance of one thousand nine hundred feet," and so on. Then comes a very complete table showing the profit that *has been* made mining in Venezuela, and after this a statement from "Mr. George Atwood, A. M. Inst., C. E., F. G. S., etc., etc.,"— it would not be complete without all these initials, even to the etc., the etc., showing that as learned as is stated there is more behind him,— who makes a statement as to the probable profits of the enterprise, all of which are as good as anybody could desire. The estimated profits are set down at twenty per cent. on the investment.

The capital wanted is two million five hundred thousand dollars, in shares of five dollars each. You are asked to pay the moderate sum of sixty-two cents on application, which is modest enough, and the balance of the five dollars you pay as the work goes on.

What could be better than this? Here is a man with some money bearing three per cent., and here is a proposition to give him twenty per cent. There are "Honorables," and "Sirs," and "Esquires" on the board, and Mr. Atwood, F. R.

S., and all the rest of it, shows that twenty per cent. has been made in Venezuela. Why should not the man convert some of his beggarly three per cents. into cash and take a shy at it, as Wall street would say, and set up his carriage on the profits? True, he don't know one of the Sirs or Honorables, and Atwood, F. R. S., etc., is quite as unknown to him. But then the advertisements! They cover half a page in each paper in London, and that costs an immense sum, and were there not something in it how could they make that vast expenditure?

He takes it, never dreaming that the speculators who pay for these advertisements, do it for the purpose of catching just such gudgeons as he is, knowing, for they know human nature, that the modest announcements that are made for really solid investments, would not catch him at all.

There are projected companies for supplying London with fish, all with boards of directors, and all promising from ten to twenty per cent. profit, not one of them with less than two million five hundred thousand dollars capital, in shares of five dollars each. Now there is no city in the world so well supplied with fish as London, in fact the supply is far beyond the demand, and there is no city which has cheaper sea food. There being innumerable private firms in the business, and there being fish markets everywhere, it would be supposed that a man of fair intelligence would question the possibility of any new company being able to compete in the business profitably But, as in the mining companies, the array of names, and the deliciously worded prospectus, are hooks that never fail to catch. It is not the fish in the sea that these fellows are after.

These are only specimen bricks. There are companies for the development of iron mines, of tin mines, of copper mines, and all other kinds of mines in England, Spain, Algeria, India, and everywhere under the sun, companies proposing to buy vast tracts of land in Iowa, Minnesota, Wisconsin, Colorado, New Mexico, and everywhere else, each with its board of noblemen, its bankers and solicitors.

The American sharpers who have mines in Colorado and Nevada have reaped a rich harvest. The city is full of them.

You shall see about the place where Americans most do con-
gregate, sharp faced fellows, dressed very seedily, whose trowsers are chewed off at the heel, and whose coats bear unmistaka-
kable evidence of having passed through the renovator's hands
a great many times, and would again if their proprietors only
had the one-and-nine pence necessary, or had another to wear
while it was being done, the said coats buttoned very closely
to the throat, so closely that a cheap scarf conceals the condition of the shirt beneath, if happily there be one, standing
listlessly, as if waiting for some one who will never come.

They know you to be an American at once, and one intro-
duces himself, claiming to have seen you in the States :

"What are you doing here?" is your first inquiry.

"Oh, I have been here a year. I came over to place a
mine I own in Nevada."

"How are you getting on?"

"Splendid! I just sold the half of it for five hundred thous-
and dollars. I ought to have got more for it, but I am tired
of waiting, and want to get home, and so I let it go. Five
hundred thousand dollars is a good sum, and then I retain a
half interest in it. It will make me all the money I shall ever
want. By the way have you met any of the nobility? No?
I shall be glad to introduce you to the Duke of Buccleugh.
I am going down to his country seat to-morrow. He is interested with me, and he's a devilish clever fellow."

You plead a prior engagement if you are wise, but you
have not seen the last of your American friend who has just
sold the half of a mine for five hundred thousand dollars. Oh,
no! For the next day he will be waiting for you, and he will
volunteer to go about with you in so persistent a way that you
cannot refuse without being brutally blunt, and after taking
you to all sorts of show places which are open to anybody, and
which you want no guide for, he will establish himself in such
a way as to make you feel, whether or no, that he has some
claim upon you.

Then comes the final stroke. As you part with him, he
will take you one side, and then this :

"By the way, I am waiting for the final drawing of papers
to complete the sale, when I get my money. I have been here

so long that I have exhausted my ready money, and my remittances did not come by the last steamer, but they must come by the next, which will be Saturday. Would you mind lending me five pounds till Saturday?"

You have but little pocket-money, you say.

"An order on the American Exchange will do as well."

You never give orders.

He lowers his want, till, finally, when he gets down to five shillings you give it to him, glad to be rid of him so cheaply.

Nevertheless this fellow will finally sell his mine, or his alleged mine. All he has to do is to wait long enough, and he will find some credulous Englishman who will bite at the naked hook, and put his name and influence to it, and it will be done. Then he will go home and establish himself in good style, and be a prominent man.

But what becomes of the English investors? Echo answers. It is a conundrum that goes echoing down the ages, and will only be answered in that period of the next world when everything shall be made plain. The poor widow who put her little pittance in the hands of these sharks doubtless started a private school, if she was qualified for it, or made use of her one accomplishment, painting, music or what not, to earn a miserable existence. The poor clerk who was saving to purchase a home of his own, went back to his lodgings and put his nose freshly upon the grindstone, and the young tradesman went into bankruptcy, his shop passed out of his hands, and he served where he had once commanded. And the shark, if an English one, shelters himself behind his assumed name, or goes to the Continent, and lives in luxury all his days

Inasmuch as these things have been going on ever since the South Sea bubble it would seem that people would get wiser, and know better than to put their all in such wild-cat schemes. But bear this in mind, the loser never admits that he lost in so stupid a way and his fellows are never fully informed about it, and besides there are children born every day, a certain percentage of them with sharp teeth, and the rest with fat. The teeth find the fat, the shark finds the gudgeon invariably. That's his business. When I read these prospectuses I find myself getting up a great deal of respect for the old barons who, when they wanted money, seized a rich Jew and starved him awhile in a dungeon, and if

THE OLD ENGLISH WAY OF PROCURING A LOAN.

that gentle treatment did not suffice to extract the requisite cash, pulled out his teeth, one by one, till he disgorged. In those days a venerable Jew whose teeth were all gone was as fortunate as the man caught by the Indians who was bald and wore a wig—he saved his scalp.

These ancient robbers did not add grandiloquent lying to theft. It was with them a simple taking of what they wanted without circumlocution. It was highway robbery to picking pockets, and was certainly the preferable of the two.

Were I an Emperor, with absolute power, I should immediately discharge the honest soldier, who would work for a living were he out of the service, and draft in the army all these fellows. And the regiments composed of them should lead every forlorn hope, charge every battery, and do all the dangerous and fatiguing work that soldiers have to do. A country could afford to lose a great many battles to rid itself of these worse than thieves.

Do you remember Dickens' Montagu Tigg in Martin Chuzzlewit? I used to think it an overdrawn picture, but it is not. It is as correct a portrait as was ever limned.

America has been deemed the paradise of the quack, but before England she must pale her ineffectual fires. Next to beer, patent medicines stare you in the face everywhere. The walls fairly shine with the advertisements of remedies for every disease known to the faculty, and when that supply runs out the ingenious proprietor invents a stock of new ailments that never did exist, and inasmuch as the least of them are six syllabled ones, it is to be hoped never will.

There are medicines for the liver, for the kidneys, for the lungs, for the feet, for the head, for the ears, for the eyes, for the scalp, for the hair, and for every part and parcel of the human body, and for every animal that man has subjugated and brought subservient to his will. There are certificates from Lords, and Dukes, and Honorables, as to the efficiency of Hobson's Vermifuge, though with these it is always a tenant's child that was cured, the scions of noble houses being of too blue blood to ever have so vulgar a complaint. In case of gout, or any genuinely aristocratic ailment, they are not so particular.

The advertisement of every remedy ends with the announcement:—

"As there are unprincipled parties in the kingdom who seize upon every article of known merit, to imitate the same, the purchasers of Hobson's remedies are respectfully requested to particularly observe the label on the bottles. The name of "Hobson" is printed on the steel engraving, on the face of the bottle, fourteen hundred and sixty-three times, and without this none are genuine. Beware of fraudulent imitations."

And the British dame will stand at the counter and count the wearying repetition, much to the disgust of the shopman, who, knowing that the remedy is only three days old, and that there are no imitations, and never will be, wants her to take her bottle of the stuff and move on and make room for another victim.

"BEWARE OF FRAUDULENT IMITATIONS."

Their ingenuity in advertising is as good as that of their trans-Atlantic brethren. You see vast vans driven slowly up and down the streets, built up twenty feet with canvass, showing an emaciated mortal, with scarcely an hour of life in him, with the legend underneath, "Before taking Gobson's Elixir," and the same party dressed, and walking the streets with the physical perfection of a prize fighter, and underneath, "After taking Gobson's Elixir." Transparencies at night flash forth the miraculous virtues of "Hopkins' Saline Draught," and there isn't an inch of dead wall anywhere that has not its burden of announcements. Long processions of ragged men the most of them too old and weak to do anything else, march along the sidewalks sandwiched between two boards, each one bearing testimony to the virtues of some wonderful compound, there being enough of them to weary the eye and make one wish he could go somewhere where advertising was impossible.

One of these human sandwiches remarked to me that the boards were a little uncomfortable in the Summer, but the two made a mighty good overcoat in the Winter.

And as if there was not enough of it already, an enterprising Yankee is here with a steam whale, ninety feet long, spouting water sixty feet high, the machinery and crew concealed in the boat on which it rests, which is to ply up and down the beautiful Thames, bearing upon either side the announcement of a liver pill. The proprietor gives him ten thousand dollars for the use of it for the season, and bears all the expenses of running it. It is very like a whale, and as it attracts much attention will doubtless pay a handsome profit to the man by whom it has been engaged.

The papers are full of such advertising, the only difference between England and America being that the advertisements here are more elegantly written, and couched in really superior English which ours are not, always. The English shoemaker who turns doctor, employs the best literary talent at command to write his announcements, and he pays more liberally than the magazines do the same men. Many a London writer, struggling for fame and a place in literature, makes a handsome addition to his slender income by going into the service of these patent medicine vendors.

Nearly all of them succeed. The British public are a medicine-taking people by nature. There are not many diseases upon the island naturally, but the inhabitants create a very large number by their habits. The universal use of beer — and vile stuff it is — is not conducive to general health, and the Englishman is about the heartiest eater on the globe. He is more than hearty — he verges very closely upon the gluttonous. Consequently he needs medicines, and the manufacturers adapt themselves to the market. There are more than a thousand "after dinner pills," warranted to correct all the effect of "over-indulgence at the table," which means that it will do something toward keeping up a man who eats about four times what he ought to, and drinks enough every year to drive an American or Frenchman into delirium tremens.

The market for these goods is world-wide, and enormous fortunes are amassed. I must say, however, that the trade is not in the best repute. Many brewers have been knighted, but no patent medicine man. In the matter of ennobling people the line must be drawn somewhere. Dickens' barber drew it at the baker — the English draw it at the brewer.

THE OLD TEMPLE BAR.

CHAPTER IX.

THERE is no Petticoat Lane any more, some finnicky board having very foolishly changed the good old name to Middlesex street. There was something suggestive in the name "Petticoat Lane," for it indicated with great accuracy the business carried on there, but there is nothing suggestive about Middlesex street. It might as well have been called Wellington street, or Wesley street, or Washington street. I hate these changes. A street is a street, and calling it an avenue don't make it so. Why not Petticoat Lane? By any other name it smells as strong. It *is* Petticoat Lane and always will be Petticoat Lane, and despite the edict of the board, the Londoner calls it by that title and always will.

Petticoat Lane is a long, tortuous narrow street, properly a lane, (about the width of an ordinary alley in an American city,) in the heart of the city proper. It is probably the dirtiest spot on the globe. If there is a dirtier I do not wish to see it—or, more especially, to smell it. It is the very acme of filth, the incarnation of dirt, and the very top, the peaked point of the summit of rottenness.

A friend of mine who had lost the sense of smell was condoled with on his misfortune.

"Don't pity me," he said, "please don't. It is a blessing, and not a misfortune. In this imperfect world there are more bad smells than perfumes. If I am deprived of one delight I escape a dozen inflictions. If I can't enjoy the rose, I, at least, dodge the tan yard."

Precisely so another friend who had his right leg torn off in a threshing machine during the war, reveled in his cork leg, because, having but one flesh and blood foot, he only took half the chances of ordinary mortals of taking cold from wet feet.

So does philosophy turn misfortunes into blessings. To carry out the idea I suppose the more troubles happen to a man the happier he should be. Would that I could take life that way, but I can't. Unfortunately the day I was in Petticoat Lane my sense of smell was unusually acute, at least so it seemed to me.

Philosophers of this school should spend a great deal of their time in Petticoat Lane, for in that savory locality all the senses one needs are his eyes and ears. A loss of smell there would be a blessing.

It is the especial street belonging to the Jews. Not the Jews we have in America, the bright, busy, active men, who have left their impress upon every spot they have touched, who have done so much to make America what it is—not the well-dressed, well-housed leader in business and everything else he puts his hands to, but the old kind of Jew, the Jew of Poland, with the long beard and long coat, very like the gaberdine we see in pictures and on the stage, the Jew of Shakespeare, the Jew who will trade in anything, and live in a way that no other race or section of a race on earth can live. There is a denser population in Petticoat Lane, I verily believe, than anywhere else on the globe, outside of China, and it is all Hebrew.

You should go Sunday morning, which is their especial day, and get there about ten o'clock, to see it in all its glory. All places for selling liquor in London are closed part of the day Sunday, except in this street; but here they are all open and in full blast. Whether there is a special exception made by law, or whether there is a tacit winking at the violation by the authorities because of the religion of the people, I do not know; but it is a fact that in this street the beer shops are open all day and a thriving business they do.

It is the busiest place I ever saw. The streets are crowded, not the sidewalks only, but the streets, to the very center. You see no horse-drawn vehicles — it is all people. Barrows and carts drawn by people, men or women, are the only vehicles. There would be no room for any other. The fiery steed attached to a hansom, which shares its driver's noble ambition to run down a foot passenger, would be tamed in Petticoat

Lane. The number of opportunities to run down people would embarrass, and, finally, subdue him.

What do all these people do? It would be easier to answer

THE SIDEWALK SHOE-STORE.

the question, What don't they do? They do everything. If there is an article on earth — that is, a second-hand article,— that is not bought and sold in Petticoat Lane on Sunday morn-

ing, I have not seen it.   You can buy anything you want there,
provided you want it second-hand, from a knitting needle to a
ship's anchor.   There is nothing in the street that is not second-
hand, except the people.   They all bear the stamp of origi-
nality, every one of them.   They are born traders.   If a pair
of Petticoat Lane Jew twins in a cradle don't trade teething
rings, and attempt to swindle each other, the father and mother
drop tears of sorrow over them, and as soon as they are old
enough, take them out of the place and apprentice them to a
trade.   Without this manifestation they would not be considered good enough for Petticoat Lane.   Very few have, however, been so apprenticed.

Here is a hideous old woman on the sidewalk with her stock
in trade under her eye, and a sharp eye it is, arranged along
the curb.   What is it?   A few dozen or more pairs of boots
and shoes, in all stages of dilapidation, carefully polished, and
made to look as respectable as possible, any pair of which (by
the way, they are not always mates,) you shall buy, if you
desire, at any price ranging from a penny to a shilling.   No
matter what the ancient dame gets for them, she has made a
profit.   She picked them up on the streets, save a few that she
may have borrowed when the owner was not looking.   What
anybody wants of these remnants, these ghosts of foot wear, I
can't conceive.   But she sells them.   The trade is consum-
mated easily after the chaffering is over with.   The purchaser
pays the woman, and sheds the worse ones he has on, and puts
on his acquisition, and wends his way.   Probably in an hour
he would be glad to trade back, but it is too late.

Next to her stands a cart, which is a portable hardware
store.   There are hinges, nails, all second-hand, carpenter's
tools, axes, locks, keys, and all sorts of iron-mongery, and he
sells, too.   Somebody wants these goods, and he gets his price.
As these things are collected as were the boots, the vender is
happy at every pennyworth he sells.

Here is a clothing merchant with his stock laid conveniently
on the sidewalk.   It is a motley mass, and his method of disposing of it is precisely the same as that of the second-hand
clothing dealer the world over.   I don't know as these dealers
rise to the sublime height of the New York Chatham street

Jew, who claimed that a villainous green coat was made for
General Grant, but that he wouldn't have it because the velvet
on the collar was too fine for his taste, but they approach it.
He has everything that one can conceive of. There are
flunkeys' uniforms, sailors' jackets, worn-out dress coats that

"SHEAP CLODINK!"

once figured in the best society, but they decayed, and went
down and down through all the grades of society, till they
finally landed in Petticoat Lane, where they will be sold for a
shilling, and the purchaser will tear the tails off as useless
encumbrances that give no warmth and are simply in the way,
and comfortable jackets will be made of them.

Under this head I might ring in *Hamlet's* soliloquy about
the dust of great men stopping cracks, and preach a very
pretty sermon on the mutability of human affairs, but I won't.

Petticoat Lane is not exactly the place for philosophizing, nor will it be for me till I get its smell out of my nostrils. Visiting Petticoat Lane is very much like eating onions — you carry the taste with you a long time, which is a blessing — for those who like onions. The onion is an economical vegetable at any price. It may come high to begin with, but it lasts a long time.

I saw General's uniforms, American sack-coats, trowsers that may have graced the legs of royalty, and a great many that had not, there not being many of the royalty. There were French blouses, police uniforms, Irish knee-breeches, everything. One coat I saw sold for a penny, the vender originally asking two shillings for it.

Next to this merchant was a man who had an assortment of sewing machines — Wheeler & Wilson, Wilcox & Gibbs, the Domestic, Singer — all the American machines were represented, and he sold them, too. People come there to buy these things. They went as low as three dollars, and as high as five. One bloated aristocrat, who was particular as to appearances, actually paid seven dollars for a Wheeler & Wilson, and was not above carrying it off himself.

In Petticoat Lane they don't have wagons to deliver your purchases as they do in Regent street and elsewhere, nor do they sell on time. You buy, and pay for what you buy, and to prevent mistakes you pay for your goods just before you get them. It's a habit they have.

The furniture stores — all on the sidewalk — are curiosities. It would delight a gatherer-up of unconsidered trifles to see one of them. I did not notice a whole piece of furniture in the lot. There was either a leg gone, or two legs, or the top, or the side, something must be gone. But the dealer didn't mind that. "You see, ma teer, all you hef to do ish to get dot leg put on, and its shoost ash goot as new, efery bit." Bureaus with missing drawers, tables with three legs where four were essential, chairs with the top, bottom and legs gone; in short, everything that was broken and condemned as useless by everybody finds its last resting-place here. Surely there can be no lower depth for the disabled.

As I gazed in wonder upon some of the articles I saw, and

noticed how little of the original article could be sold, I bethought myself of the cooper who was brought a bung hole, with the request that he build a barrel about it.

The street vendors of eatables formed no small portion of the traffic that was going on incessantly. You can get a slice of roast beef with greens (greens is what these people call cabbage, and, by the way, they call a lemonade a "lemon squash"), for a penny, and you shall see it cut from the joint, otherwise you wouldn't know what it was. True the plate on which the satisfying food was placed had been merely dipped in cold water, and true it was that the two hundred pound woman who served it had never washed her hands since the day she was married, but that did not matter. The dish was taken and devoured, the ceremony of paying before getting it being religiously observed. There were shrimps, and snails, and lettuce salads, and moldy fruit, and everything else that the British public eats, all on the street, which is convenient, to say the least.

Sharpers were not wanting to complete this variegated scene. The thimble-rigger was there, his game being confined to a penny, so as to harmonize with the general cheapness of the locality, and, to keep it in perfect accord, his little portable table, and his thimbles were second-hand. There were street acrobats, nigger minstrels, hand organs, hurdy-gurdys, street singers, and the inevitable street brass band, made up of four sad-looking men who appeared as though there was nothing in life for them, and that they were playing in expiation of some great crime, and were compelled to play on forever. How these people live I never could make out. During the whole day I never saw a penny given them, except one which one of our party threw them. They took it up with an expression of the most intense surprise, as though it was an astounding and unlooked-for occurrence, and immediately stopped playing, and made for the nearest cook stand and invested the whole of it in a plate of beef and greens, which was divided among the four. I was about to throw them another penny, but was checked by our guide. He protested against pampering them. I understood him. The American Indian will consume a month's provisions in a single day's feast, and starve the other

9

twenty-nine. Had I given them another penny they would
have had another plate of beef on the spot, and then gone
hungry a week. As we intended to come again next Sunday
for their own good I reserved the penny for that occasion.

Understand it is not Jews who are the purchasers of these
wrecks of goods, these reminiscences of furniture and the like;
they are the sellers. The purchasers are the British public
proper, who come here for bargains. They get them—
perhaps.

The question is, where do all these things come from? If
there are more than one in the Jewish family, and whether
there is or not depends upon the age, for they marry very
young, and have children as rapidly as possible, all but one of
them roam through the country incessantly, buying, bartering
for and picking up all the stuff, which, after bought or picked
up, is brought here and fixed as far as the skill and ingenuity
of the purchaser and the rottenness of the material will
permit. Then it is sold, at no matter what price. The motto
in Petticoat Lane is, " no reasonable offer refused."

It is not, however, only the second-hand that Petticoat
Lane deals in. You see moving among the crowd here and
there quite another class of Israelites from those who are
vending dilapidated clothing and broken furniture. They
are well dressed men, with coats buttoned up very closely.
Their raven locks are surmounted with tall hats, and their
boots cleaned as carefully as any swell's in London. They are
all distinctively Hebrew, there being no exception to this rule.

Across the way is a beer-shop, kept by a Hebrew, the
bar-maids and all being Hebrew. On the one side of the bar
is a small dining room; back of that a kitchen, and from the
bar-room is a flight of stairs. Follow your guide, who in this
instance was an American Hebrew, and you find yourself in a
low room just the size of the bar below, and a curious scene
presents itself. These rooms, and there are scores of them in
Petticoat Lane, contain on an average any number of millions
of pounds that you choose to say. I could say that there
were a hundred millions of wealth in each one, and perhaps
wouldn't be very much out of the way, but as I desire to be
accurate, I will not. If there is anything I detest, it is exag-

geration. I hope to distinguish myself by being the first tourist who adhered strictly to the naked truth.

These rooms are diamond marts. In them all the diamonds that deck out royalty and the wives of patent medicine men, gamblers, negro minstrels, and other people who are not royal, are first handled. To these dingy dens in the very heart of the worst quarter of the worst city in the world, comes the diamond merchant, and here he meets the broker who deals with the manufacturer in the city. Here all the diamonds of London are first bought and sold.

One looks at it with amazement. Enter a young Jew with the preternaturally sharp features that distinguish the race. All the merchants, and there may be a dozen, each sitting at his little table, hail him, and all in the language that the new comer speaks the best. The Hebrew speaks all languages, and all of them well. (Facts crowd upon me so fast that it is difficult to keep to my subject.) The young fellow unbuttons his coat, and then the top buttons of his vest, and takes from an inner pocket a long leather pocket-book, which he opens carefully. There are disclosed a dozen papers folded like an apothecary's package, and he opens them. Your eyes dance as you see the contents. Diamonds! I never dreamed there were so many in the world. Each paper contains a handful of all sizes and qualities, cut and uncut, of all colors and shades known to the diamond, and the ancient Jews at the tables take these papers and examine critically the different sparklers, going over the lot as the Western farmer would his cattle. With a little steel instrument he separates this one from his fellows and puts it under a glass, and screws his eye into the stone, and then little tiny scales, which would turn under the weight of a sunbeam, are brought into requisition, and then would come more chaffering and bargaining than would suffice to buy and sell an empire.

This young fellow does not own these precious stones. He is a broker. The diamond is first brought to light in Brazil, India, or the Cape of Good Hope. From the original producer it passes into the hands of the resident buyer, who consigns it to the broker to sell, and he does it on commission the same as

the elevator men handle wheat. The buyer in Petticoat Lane
either cuts and sets it himself, or re-sells it to the fashionable
jeweler, as he can make the most profit. Trust them for
doing that. It is something the London Hebrew understands
long before he cuts his teeth.

But is is not alone diamonds you find in these rooms. On
the various tables may be seen jewelry of every possible
description, and all sorts of goods, from a tooth-pick up.
You can buy a watch or a jack-knife, a button-hook or a
diamond bracelet. Especially is the variety of curious old
jewelry very extensive. You find there rings and brooches set
with all sorts of stones, of every period in the world's history,
which makes it the resort of the wealthy collectors of the
ancient and curious. Here is a brooch, said to have been
worn by Queen Anne, and another by one of the mistresses
of Louis XVIII., of France. The seller says it was, and if he
happens to be mistaken, what difference does it make so that
you believe it? It is just as good to you as though the history
was accurate. One should not be particular in such matters,
though I saw enough brooches that were once the property of
an English Queen to have set up a very large jewelry store,
and were they all genuine it explains the high taxes in
England, and justifies all the rebellions the country has
suffered. But it is all well enough. The goods are actually
quaint and beautiful. It is darkly hinted that these Jews
have factories where jewelry once worn by royalty is manufactured by the bushel, and I should not wonder thereat.
For, you see, a brooch of modern style, worth say fifty
pounds, is worth one hundred pounds if it were once Queen
Anne's. "Dose goots, ma tear sir, vat ish anshent, and hef
historical associations, are wort any money. At one hundred
pounts it ish a bargain."

As the price doubles because of historical features it pays
very nicely to manufacture the old styles, and tarnish the gold,
and make antiques. But possibly this is a weak invention of
the Gentiles who do not deal in antiques.

One would suppose that it would be rather hazardous to
carry about so much wealth in a paper. What is to prevent

the Jew at the table who has a paper before him containing, say, two hundred diamonds, from secreting one or two? The broker hands a paper to one, and another to another, and divides his time between them, and to take a stone would be as easy as lying.

Possibly it would be hazardous among Gentiles, but not so among these Jews. There is an unwritten code among them which makes the property as safe in their hands as though one diamond were shown at a time. There is absolute honor among them, which was never yet known to be tarnished. It is absolute and perfect.

One venerable Jew was very anxious to sell me a ring, the price of which he fixed at one hundred and twenty dollars, "and no abatement." (When

"DAKE DOT RING."

a Jew diamond merchant says "no abatement," that settles it. There is none.

"Dake dot ring, put him in your bocket, go to any scheweler in Rechent street, and oof you can get him vor dwice de monish I will give him to you."

"What!" was my reply, "do you say that I, a perfect

stranger to you, may carry off a ring worth forty pounds?
Suppose I shouldn't come back with it?"

"Ach, ma tear sir, Philip (my American friend) vouldn't
pring nobody here vot vould do such a ting. Dake der ring,
ma tear sir, and see about him. It ish a bargain."

Philip or any one of the guild would be allowed to carry
away a king's ransom.

Would, oh would, that the other people of the world were
equally honest and upright. Still, I wouldn't advise any one
to depend upon their word in a purchase. They have two
kinds of morality. A trade with them is a battle royal, in
which each tries to get the better of the other, but the word
once passed is never broken.

The merchant sits all day at his table, his meals, always a
cut of beef and greens, with a pewter of bitter beer, being
brought to him from the kitchen below. He sits and eats,
never permitting, however, his eating and drinking to interfere with his business. He would put down his pot of beer to
continue a trade any time, something I know a great many
Americans would not do.

Petticoat Lane is one of the curiosities of London, and the
day was well spent. It is a world by itself — a foreign nation
preserving its religion and customs intact, injected into the
very heart of London.

A LANE IN CAMBERWELL.

(135)

THE TOWER OF LONDON

WHITE TOWER

BYWARD TOWER

STAIRCASE WHITE TOWER

PASSAGE IN BLOODY TOWER

ST. JOHN'S CHAPEL

JANE

BLOODY TOWER

BELL TOWER

BOWYER TOWER

TRAITORS GATE

W. H. PRIOR, del.

BYWARD TOWER

CHAPTER X.

To visit the Tower is to draw aside the curtain that separates the past from the present. It is to go back a thousand years, and commune with those who have long ages been dust, and of whom only a memory remains. Once in the Tower, one seems to be with them, to see them, and to feel their influence as though they were living, moving beings, and not historical ghosts.

The vast structure, now in the heart of the great city, though once on its borders, is as much out of place in this day and age of the world, as a soldier would be in any of the suits of armor within its walls. It is war in the midst of peace, it is a fortress surrounded by traffic, it is lawless force against law, it is simply an incongruity, and only valuable and interesting as showing what was, in comparison with what is.

It was built originally as a stronghold, to keep the fiery and oft-times rebellious citizens of London in check, and was afterward occupied alternately, or at the same time, as a prison or palace. Many a terrible drama has been enacted within the ancient walls, many a broken heart has wasted away within the solid stone in its gloomy dungeons, and many a noble head has parted company with its body, under its cold shadow, and there is any quantity of "human interest," as the dramatists say, connected with it. There is a strong flavor of murder all through it, there is cruelty written upon every stone, and treachery and death on every inch of the cold, paved floors.

If a king desired to put quietly out of the way a dangerous rival, or if he lusted after a woman, or wanted anything that was especially unlawful and damnable, he could not have been better fixed for the business than with this fortress, provided he had a sufficient number of servitors to do his bidding faithfully. And that sort of material was very plenty, in those days, for kings who had the means of rewarding them. The devil himself could not have fitted up a better arrangement if he had given his whole mind to the matter, and his ability in this direction is unquestioned.

There are dungeons where an unfortunate's cries could never be heard; there are cells so strong that escape was simply impossible, even without the watchful care of the soldiery with which it was filled, and in short over each of its gates might well be written, "Who enters here leaves hope behind." It is a wonderful but an intensely disagreeable place.

These old places are not the most cheerful in the world, but still I like them. A ride behind a tandem team through the green lanes of Hampstead, with the beautiful hedges on either hand, and the quaint old houses with their steep red-tiled roofs, and their low rooms and curious little windows that look more like eyes than windows, the broad fields, grass green, (grass is greener in England than America,) with the beautiful sleek cattle feeding peacefully, is a more pleasant thing, for it is a singular as well as delightful mixture of to-day and yesterday. The fields and cattle are of to-day, the houses are of a long ago yesterday, but there is added what the Tower has not, the sun, which is of yesterday, to-day, and to-morrow, shining down, and lighting up the quiet glories that surround you. This is not depressing. The houses fit the atmosphere — in good sooth I cannot imagine such houses in any other atmosphere, and certainly the atmosphere would not be complete without the houses. Everything adapts itself to everything else. A pale face would be as much out of place in an American rum shop as a strawberry patch in an alkaline desert. Rum requires something lurid — the quiet, soft, hazy English atmosphere exactly fits the soft brown and the subdued red that almost narrowly escapes being a brown of the houses.

But in the Tower you have nothing that is soft, nothing that is pleasant, nothing one would like to have about him.

The Tower is a good thing for a world to see, so that it can know what to avoid.

Two teachers of elocution were in great rivalry. One gave an exhibition with his pupils.

"Where are your classes to-day?" asked a friend of the other one.

"Gone to Mr. Blank's exhibition."

"Do you permit your pupils to attend your rival's exhibition?"

"Certainly. I want them to learn what to avoid."

No light ever penetrates its gloomy walls. There are but two colors — the blackened wood painted by time, and the cold gray of the stones. All the color indicates cruelty — the very stones typify the character of the men who put them together, and their successors who used them. It is the cruelest appearing place on the face of the earth, now that the French Bastile is gone, and I doubt if a Frenchman could possibly construct a place so grimly severe, so unutterably merciless as the Tower. He would have had some fancy about it — it would have been lighted up somehow.

The Tower is so severe that a picture of a beheading, or of a torture, would be cheerful by contrast and improve it.

I would suggest now, that to enliven the old place a bit, and save a man from giving way too much to the depression that governs the spot, that a fresco be painted representing the burning of John Rogers at the stake, or the disemboweling of the Waldenses, or some cheerful historical picture of that kind. Should the artist select pictures from Fox's Book of Martyrs, that one where the soldiers are crowding people off a precipice so that they fall upon iron spikes about four feet long, would impart a cheerful tone to the surroundings in the Tower and make one feel more kindly toward his race.

As it is, he who enters and stays awhile becomes a convert to the doctrine of Total Depravity. He gets blood-thirsty himself, and feels like snatching up some one of the million weapons that are stored there and killing somebody. The articles preserved with so much care are all suggestive of blood. It is a Moloch of a place; but one must see it, all the same.

The most cheerful place in the great structure is the jewel room, or tower, as it is called. It isn't very much of a room, but there is a great deal in it which is of interest. Here are kept the regalia appertaining to the throne. In glass cases very carefully guarded are all the crowns of the royal family,

THE JEWEL TOWER.

and the scepters and things which they display on state occasions, and a rare lot they are.

The prevailing impression among those not used to royalty is that the King and Queen and the rest of their "royal nibses," as an American would irrevelantly say, go about dressed in velvet robes, covered with jewels, with crowns upon their heads; that when the Queen goes to bed at night she removes the crown, or a dozen maids of honor do it for her, and that she resumes it the first thing in the morning, before she comes down to breakfast. A moment's reflection will show any one the impossibility of anything of the kind. A crown would be no protection for the head, and velvet robes would be exceedingly warm in summer, and not warm enough in winter; and besides were the Queen to wear a crown with some millions of dollars' worth of precious stones in it, some enterprising footpad would have it in no time, and then what would she do? For these reasons, which ought to be satisfactory to any reflective mind, the crowns and articles of like nature are kept in the tower, and are only worn on state occasions, when the public want a free show.

At all other times the Queen dresses like any other lady, with a regular dress, and bustles, and all that sort of thing, and a bonnet, and she dresses frightfully plain, so all the milliners and modistes say, too plain for their trade; for Victoria, to a certain extent, sets the fashion, which the court follows.

But in these cases you shall see the Queen's crown, a cap of purple velvet enclosed in hoops of silver, surmounted by a ball and cross, and glittering with actual diamonds. In the center is an immense sapphire, and in front is a famous heart-shaped ruby, said to have been worn by the Black Prince. I don't know the value of this article, or where he stole it, but if Victoria gets hard-up and wants to raise money, I presume the Jews in Petticoat Lane would advance a million or two on it, and take their chances. Queens have done this before now, and all the crown jewels in Europe have been in the hands of the Israelites at different times; but I rather think Victoria will worry through. She has an income of many thousands of pounds a year, and is very economical. If I remember aright, she sent the starving Irish a thousand pounds, which was about her income for an hour. And then an admiring Parliament, to make it good to her, voted her thirty thousand pounds sterling, which the people accepted without a murmur. She finds profit in liberality.

Then there is St. Edward's Crown, the Prince of Wales's, the ancient Queen's Crown, the Queen's Diadem, that of Charles the Second, and a dozen or two others, with scepters and rods, and all sorts of things which are carried before, or behind, or on one side or the other, of Kings and Queens, on occasions of great solemnity, when the people are to be impressed with a sense of the importance of these individuals to the world at large. The famous Koihnoor, stolen from an East India Prince, some years since, is there — in glass, which is a swindle.

We wanted, and expected, when we paid our sixpence, to see the genuine article, not a base imitation. It is as it is at side-shows at a circus, you are allured inside by a picture of a vast giraffe, nipping boughs from trees, and when you have paid and are in, you are shown a stuffed giraffe, who can no more

SIR MAGNUS' MEN.

eat boughs from tall trees than he could preach a funeral ser-mon. Possibly we should have demanded our money back, but we didn't.

From the jewel room you pass on to an infinity of towers, all through long halls, how long I can't say, filled with all sorts of armor and weapons. Horses are set up and figures placed upon them, dressed in the identical armor worn by the old kings and nobles, who, in their day, rode about the country clad in iron fish scales, with a half ton of iron, more or less, on their heads, engaged in the (to them) delightful occupation of burning each other's castles and killing the occupants. They did not require a "cause," or anything of the sort. If Sir Hugh Bloody-bones wanted the wife or daughter of Sir Magnus Blunderbore, he simply donned his iron, picked up his lance, called together the inferior cut-throats who followed and lived upon him, and went for it. Sir Magnus, if not surprised and murdered in cold blood, and he was generally not, for those old ruffians slept upon their arms, harried the country for supplies, shut the clumsy gates of his castle, and stood the siege. If the castle was carried, all within were put to death, except such of Sir Magnus' cut-throats who were willing to join Sir Hugh, the women were carried off, and so on. The survivors were willing, always, to join the victor. The successful Knight would say, "Now look here, you fellows, Sir Magnus is dead. I slew him, and you can't get provisions from him any more, while with me there will always be plenty of prog. I shall keep you busy, for there are other castles to storm, and I am not very particular with my men."

And they would all "take service," as they called it, with the successful robber, and go right on as usual. They would take anything.

It was a cheerful life these ancient murderers lived, though the people who supported them didn't find it so pleasant.

The Horse Armory, so called because the figures in it are mostly equestrian, is one hundred and fifty feet in length by thirty-four in width. There sits a Knight of the time of Henry VI., in complete armor, lance and all, just as he appeared when he started out to kill somebody and steal his effects. The armor, understand, is not a *fac-simile*, it is the genuine thing, actually worn by the marauder of that time. Then come Knights of the time of Edward III. and Edward IV., both on their horses and armored from top to bottom. How any man could carry such a load of iron and sit upon a horse, and how any horse could carry such a mass of iron, with his own, for the horses were armored also, passes my comprehension.

Imagine a man in July, with the thermometer at ninety-five
in the shade, with a steel pot on his head, covering his face
entirely, with little holes to admit air, with a breast-plate of
boiler-iron, and a similar one on his back, with his arms and
hands guarded with iron, and his legs and feet likewise, with
swords and battle-axes, and daggers hung to him, and a lance

HORSE ARMORY.

fourteen feet in length, to handle, doing battle. Yet they wore
all this, and in Palestine, and in every other hot country in the
world.

Woe to the Knight who was unhorsed with all this pot-
metal on him. He couldn't rise under the load, and the other
one could prod him to death at his leisure, and enjoy himself
at it as long as he pleased.

Next to this is the figure of that wonderful old Mormon, Henry VIII. The armor on this figure is the most curious and valuable in the collection. It was presented to him on the occasion of his marriage to Catherine, his No. —, —. I forget what her number was—and he wore it at many a tournament. This King, it will be remembered, had a way of getting rid of wives that was far superior to Indiana divorce courts. Whenever he saw a woman that he thought he wanted, and he had an eye for women, he merely accused his wife of being unfaithful to him, and had a court which always brought her in guilty, and her head was chopped off without ceremony, and he married his new flame, only to accuse her and bring her before the court and chop her head off

ST. JOHN'S CHAPEL.

in her turn. He finished eight in this way. It was the Pope's opposition to one of these little arrangements that brought about the divorce of England from the Church of Rome, and was the beginning of the Protestant movement. But for Henry's terrible liking for women and his peremptory and decisive way of divorcing wives, I probably to-day should have been a Catholic! What great events spring from trifling causes.

All the way down the long hall are equestrian figures, all

10

armed in the identical armor worn by the men whose names
they bear, and between the figures are the arms of the
various periods of English history since men took to killing

ST. THOMAS'S TOWER.

each other as a
trade. In this
and adjoin-
ing halls are
grouped very
artistically the
arms of every
country of the
globe, and of
all ages and
times. There
are guns of
every possible
kind, most of
them of very
rare workman-
ship, for the
mechanics of
those old days
put more work
upon arms
than upon any-

thing else, and swords and daggers, and battle-axes, and various
devices for knocking out brains.

By the way, the revolver is popularly supposed to be an
American invention, but it is not. There are a score of revolvers here that were made almost as soon as gunpowder was
invented and came into use. The very one from which Colonel
Colt got the idea of a repeating arm is here, and it is identical
in construction with that which now graces the thighs of so
many Americans, and which has done so much for the glory of
our happy country. They were not very much used, however,
as, owing to the imperfect means of firing the loads, all the
barrels were liable to go off at once, invariably killing the
shooter without materially damaging the shootee. The invention of the percussion cap made the revolver practicable, and

Colonel Colt's widow is living in great luxury upon an idea taken by her husband from the Tower of London, the work of some humble mechanic hundreds of years ago. I doubt not that if she could find the heirs of that mechanic she would pension them. But they were doubtless all killed in the wars of the day, and so it probably would not be worth her while to try to seek them out.

GENERAL VIEW OF THE TOWER

To enumerate everything that is curious in the way of arms and armor in this hall would be to make a catalogue. It takes more than a day to merely see (not study) this collection, and then one has his mind overloaded.

The different buildings that make up what is known collectively as the Tower, have all histories, and all bloody ones. There is nothing but blood connected with it. In the White Tower, Sir Walter Raleigh was confined, and near his den is that once occupied by Rudstone, Culpepper, and Sir Thomas Wyat, who were all beheaded on Tower Hill. The Council Room was used by the Kings when they wanted to give some sort of show of law for a murder, and in this the Council sat when Richard III. ordered Lord Hastings to instant execution.

The Bloody Tower (that would be the proper name for all of them) was where Richard III. was supposed to have murdered the two children of Edward IV., his brother, on which event Shakespeare founded his play of that name. Some English historians have endeavored to show that Richard was no such a man as Shakespeare represents. Instead of being a hump backed, distorted villain, such as we see upon the stage,

THE BLOODY TOWER.

they insist that he was the handsomest man of his time; that he did not even try to murder the Princes, and, moreover, that he was one of the most humane, politic Kings England ever had, and during his short reign of nine months, instituted material reforms, and did more to promote the welfare of England than any King who had preceded or followed him. Also, they deny the story of his drowning his brother Clarence in a butt of Malmsey wine, and likewise his murder of King Henry.

Probably these historians are right. Since it has been shown that General Jackson did not fight his men behind a breastwork of cotton bales, a delusion that grew up with me, and since it has been demonstrated that there is no maelstrom on the coast of Norway, that takes down ships and whales into its terrible vortex, as shown in the ancient geographies of thirty years ago, I have lost faith in everything. When I want romance I read history, and when I hunger for history I read novels. But whether he was a good man or a bad,

Shakespeare has fixed his flint for all time.   The essayist may essay, and facts may be piled up mountain high in his favor, but Richard will always appear to us as Shakespeare painted him, a hump-backed, withered-legged man with a villainous

THE PRESUMED DROWNING OF CLARENCE IN A BUTT OF WINE.

face, killing Princes, stabbing Kings and drowning brothers in wine.   Still, I don't suppose Richard cares now what is said of him.   If he killed the Princes, they, dying young and before they could be Kings, and consequently comparatively pure, he will never meet them. If he did not, and is with them, they have had ample time to arrange their little differences. The opinion of the world makes little difference to Richard, wherever he is. Nevertheless, as I wish to stand well with the world hereafter, I shall try not to get the ill-will of the poets whose works are likely to live. Richard's reputation should be a warning.

THE BYWARD TOWER.
(From the East.)

The bloody record contin ues. Devereux Tower is where the brilliant Essex was confined till he was "privately behead ed." The Byward Tower is where Duke Clarence is said to have been drowned in the wine, which was a great waste of wine, though it was a delicate compliment to the Duke, who was fond of it. It was probably distributed among the soldiers who did the job. In the Brick Tower Lady Jane Grey was immured, and in the Martin Tower Anne Boleyn, one of Henry VIII.'s wives, was confined, till she was beheaded, as well as "several unhappy gentlemen" who were foolish enough to stand up for her, who also had their heads chopped off. The word "unhappy" is not misused in their case. In the Salt Tower is shown an inscription made by a gentleman who was accused of using enchantments "to the hurt of Sir W. St. Lowe and my ladye," who also found himself short a head one fine morning. It was a comfortable time to live when "Sir W. St. Lowe," a court favorite, could accuse a man he owed money to of being a wizard, and then ordering him beheaded. It was easier to pay debts in those days than going through bankruptcy is now.

There were so many murders committed in the Beauchamp Tower that in the guide books it is counted worthy of a chapter by itself, not only because of the number, but because of the peculiarly atrocious quality of them. The other murderers were mere apprentices at the business compared with those who had the Beauchamp tower in charge. They were artists, and knew all about it. They gave their whole mind to it. Marmaduke Neville with fifty others who believed in Mary, Queen of Scots, were confined in this tower,

THE BEAUCHAMP TOWER.

and they were all beheaded in one day. Likewise Mr. William Tyrrell, who had some differences with the government; then the Earl Arundel was beheaded from this interesting old slaughter house for aspiring to the hand of Mary Queen of Scots. It appears that a man couldn't safely make love in those days. But as he was tried for his religion—not for love —he was not beheaded, but was mercifully permitted to "languish in prison" till he died. It is probable that his jailors did not feed him on porter-house steaks.

The Earl of Warwick and the three brothers Dudley were

here. The Duke, the eldest of the three, was beheaded, and the others mercifully starved to death. A gentleman named Gyfford was put to the rack in the Tower, and finally consenting to answer the questions put to him—your rack was a rare persuader—was probably dismissed. But doubtless the headsman got him. Dr. Stohr, who refused to deny his religion—he was a Catholic—was imprisoned here, and was released only to suffer a cruel death at Tyburn. Being a Catholic, and

THE OVERWORKED HEADSMAN—FIFTY IN ONE DAY.

murdered by Protestants, we may draw from his history the useful lesson that persecution was not, strictly speaking, confined to the Catholic church, as is popularly supposed. The Protestants, when in power, knew the uses of the rack, and thumbscrew, and stake, just as well as the Catholics, and they were just as handy with them.

The Brothers Poole wanted Mary to be the Queen, and they went the long road from here.

But the list is too long for these pages.

That you may be perfectly sure of the accuracy of these things, the identical headsman's block is carefully preserved, with the ax he used and the mask he wore when engaged in his delightful duty. The ax is shaped very like a butcher's cleaver, and the mask is about the most fiendish face that a devilish ingenuity could devise. Ugly and devilish as it is, it was probably an improvement on the face it concealed. You are shown

THE PERSUASIVE RACK.

the thumbscrew and rack. The thumbscrew would extort a confession from a dead man; and the rack — well, that is something inconceivably devilish. You are laid in a box; ropes on windlasses are tied to your ankles and wrists; then the windlasses are turned, inch by inch, till your joints are dislocated.

After enduring the rack and answering questions the way they desired,—for a man in that apparatus would say anything for a moment's respite—you are hurried to the block for fear you may recant as soon as you get out of it. Then what was said in the rack was put upon record as a testimony on which to rack and behead other people. Those were the "good old days of merrie England."

During the reign of Edward III. six hundred Jews were imprisoned in the dungeons of the tower for "adulterating the

THE BYWARD TOWER.
[From the West.]

coin of the realm." The trouble with these Jews was they had too much of the coin of the realm, and Edward too little. The chronicler goes on to say that so strong was the prejudice of the King against these people that he banished the race from England, but, with the thrift that distinguished the Kings of that day, he compelled them to leave behind them their immense wealth, which he gobbled, and their libraries, which, as he couldn't read he had no use for, went to the monasteries. I suppose he sold them by the pound to the monks who could read. King Edward has a counterpart in the English landlord of to-day. He allows no foreigner to take any money out of the kingdom. It is curious how national traits show in people through ages. England has no more

Barons to take things by the strong hand, but she has hotel-keepers. Their processes are different, but the result is the same. They have no racks now, but they have beds — the thumb-screw is gone forever, but bills are yet made out.

In those days it was not enough to be a heretic or disturber to gain admission to this portal to the tomb; it was only necessary to be suspected, and when a man in favor wanted to get his enemy out of the way, it was very easy to suspect. Talent, usefulness to the State—nothing was proof against it. Cromwell, one of the most brilliant men of his day, Secretary to the still greater Wolsey, on a most frivolous charge, was seized and beheaded. He was becoming too powerful to suit the favorites. Women suffered the same as men, and exalted station went for nothing. Sir Walter Raleigh was beheaded to

THE MIDDLE TOWER
(From the East.)

please the Spaniards, one of whose Princesses the King desired to marry.

A large part of the vast building is now used as a great National armory. Stored within its walls are ninety thousand rifles of the latest and most approved patterns, all in perfect order, even to the oiling, and ready for use at a moment's notice England is always ready for war. It would be a quick nation that could catch her napping. These murderous weapons looked cheerfully by comparison with the barbarous tools the old English used. After looking at the battle-axes, and flails, and lances, it would seem to be a comfort to be merely shot to

THE BEEF EATER.

death with a Martini Henry rifle. One could feel some sort of comfort in going out *via* a decent rifle ball.

The guards of the Tower are the famous "Beef Eaters,"

and are all habited in the uniform of the Yeomen of the Guard of the time of Henry VII., who instituted the corps. The present yeomen are all old soldiers, who have distinguished themselves, and a very pleasant time they have of it. They don't have to drag women to the block by the hair of their heads any more, but spend most of their time standing around listlessly and eating ham sandwiches, which is certainly better than their ancient employment. There is nothing cruel in an English ham sandwich but its indigestibility, and that only concerns the eater. It is a matter entirely between him and his stomach, and does not concern me at all.

The ancient kings did not have as good a time as one would think, for every now and then a baron would raise a rebellion, or a knight would shoot a vicious arrow at him, or the House of Com-

THE FLINT TOWER.

mons would rise, and protest with arms in their hands against his abuses. But their followers, these fellows whose armors are before me this minute, they did have a good time. Their masters found it to their own interest to feed them well, and their little acts of oppression on their own account were winked at. And so they lived a jolly life, their bodies pampered with food, their noses in a constant blush for the liquor they consumed, and with the pick of the daughters of the peasantry, who were helpless against them. It was no small thing to be a stout man-at-arms in those days, and in the service of a powerful Lord. Fighting was really and literally meat and drink to them, and they actually liked it.

Suspected men of unusual importance were always conveyed to the Tower by water, in barges gorgeous to a degree. Hence there is a water gate called "Traitor's Gate," which is worth

THE TRAITOR'S GATE.

seeing, when one considers how many great men have passed through it to their death. For a commitment to the Tower was equivalent to death. If a man was accused of treason, or witchcraft, or anything else, and the party against him was strong enough to send him to the Tower, that ended it. Or if a King desired to get rid of anybody, man or woman, it was easy enough to have a charge brought, a commitment to the Tower followed, and the dispatch was easy enough. The Tower was a slaughter pen where those obnoxious to a King or his favorites could be butchered without uncomfortable publicity, and, if necessary with some color of law. As if the favorite should say :

"Your majesty, what shall we do with Sir Thomas Buster? Behead him?"

" Oh, bother, what's the use of going to that worry. A knife under his fifth rib will do as well."

And accordingly the next morning, just before his breakfast was served, a low-browed ruffian would go to his cell, and Sir Thomas would get the knife under his ribs, and a hole would be dug, and that was the last of him. They generally stabbed them at seven in the morning, to save the expenses of the last breakfast. He might as well go into the hereafter on an empty stomach, and it was that much saved to the King's treasury. They had a good notion of economy in some directions. Or a hasty trial might be had, and the illustrious prisoner might be led to the block and have his head chopped off. Anyhow it amounted to the same thing. Sir Thomas was bound to die in one way or another.

WHAT SHALL WE DO WITH SIR THOMAS BUSTER?

I have a profound respect for the murdered of the Tower, but not a particle for their sacred butchers, the Kings and Queens of that day. To have been murdered in the Tower, no matter by what means or in what way, was a certificate of good character that should have lasted till to-day. By chance, they might occasionally kill a bad man, but as a rule the victims were men who incurred the displeasure of the powers that were by opposing infamy; by making some sort of a stand, no matter how weak, for something good. I should liked to have had time to get flowers to drop on the spots where they were supposed to be interred, and I would have done it to some extent, only no one knows where these spots are. A flower dropped anywhere within the Tower would fall on some one's grave, but you might possibly decorate the wrong man. I didn't do it, and I don't suppose the illustrious deceased would care much about it anyhow. If I cared anything about what posterity should say about me after I had gone hence, I shouldn't

THE EASIEST WAY.

want anything better than to have been butchered in the Tower. That is a better patent of nobility than any that King or Kaiser can confer. Whoso died there, died in a good cause, no matter what it was. The victim must have been good, for the kingly butcher was always bad.

CHAPTER XI.

WITH that propensity for lying on the part of traveled men and women to which I have had occasion to refer, the intending tourist is warned by all who have crossed the water to take as little clothing as possible, for the reason that "you can get any clothes you want in London at half the money, and then you have the style, you know." What infernal spirit seizes traveled people and compels such terrible falsification, I cannot conceive.

Quality considered, clothing is no cheaper in London than in New York. Which is to say, if you are so lost to all sense of what is due yourself and the world as to wear such clothes as the Londoner does, you can get them quite as cheaply in New York as in London, and even if you want bad clothes the style will be better. Should the American tailor try ever so hard to make a badly-fitting garment, his conscience, his taste, his everything, would rebel against doing such work as the English tailor considers quite good enough for anybody.

You can get at a fairly fashionable shop in London a suit of black or blue, frock coat, trowsers and vest, for five pounds, which looks very cheap to one who has been in the habit of paying sixty-five dollars for the same clothing in New York or Boston.

But just wait till you get the clothes and the idea of cheapness goes like dew under a July sun. All there is cheap in the transaction is the suit. The material is very cheap, cheap to the point of flimsiness, and the making — heaven help you — it is thrown together. There are no stays to the pockets, no reinforcing to the seat, no leather on the inside of the bottoms of the trowsers, and the linings of the coat and vest, or waist-

11   (161)

coat, as these semi-barbarians call it, are of the cheapest and flimsiest material that a devilish ingenuity can weave. The suit cannot possibly wear a month and look decent.

But the worst is yet to come. You try it on. We will suppose the coat to be a single-breasted frock. You are immediately astonished at the liberality of your tailor in the matter of cloth, for when you draw the lapels together you find yourself able to button the right hand one on the left hand shoulder.

"Too much cloth in front," you remark.

"I thought you wanted an easy fit!" the villain answers without a blush.

"So I did, but I did not want all the cloth in your shop."

Then comes an animated discussion. You insist that it never has been your habit to go about in a sack, that you prefer not to appear habited in a bag. The tailor stands off a foot or two, and admits that while it is perhaps "a trifle easy," it is still a proper garment and quite in the mode. But if you prefer he will alter it. Prefer! why it will fit Daniel Lambert. It is twice too large for you and of course it must be altered. Then he takes French chalk, and makes a lot of marks on it and you leave it. In a few days he sends it to you altered. You put it on, and commence swearing if you are a profane man, and objurgating, if you are not. I objurgated. For the trowsers hang about your legs like bags, the waistcoat climbs up the back of your neck to the ears, the coat is loose where it should fit closely, it is tight where it should be easy, the skirts hang about you awkwardly, it is angular, stiff and awkward, and yet it comes so near to being a garment that you are compelled to take it, especially, as, following the advice of the infernal tourist who said to you to take only one suit with you, you must have it at once. And so you put it on, and go out into the street, feeling as though you were an object to be stared at, and blighted. You bear not only the burden of physical discomfort, for a misfit is always uncomfortable, but have the consciousness that you are badly dressed, and that every bad point in your physical make-up, is made still more conspicuous by the lack of skill in a tailor.

The only comfort you have is that everybody else is just as badly apparelled. Your American friends know at a glance that it is not your fault, but that you have passed under the blighting shears of an English tailor, and your English friends are all in the same fix. But then they enjoy bad clothes, never having had any other.

There were four Americans in one house in London who each ordered a suit of clothes of one tailor at one time. The four suits came home Saturday evening, and were all tried on Sunday morning. One was tall and slender, another short and

THE SUITS COME HOME.

stout, the third was dumpy, and the fourth was medium in height and breadth.

No. 1 rushed into my room. "Look here," he exclaimed "there is a mistake somewhere. These clothes must be yours. They were never made for me."

No. 2 entered. "These d——d trowsers must be yours. They were never made for me."

And in a minute No. 3 came in with the same exclamation. An examination of the addresses on the wrapping paper showed, however, that each had received the clothes intended for him, notwithstanding that each suit would have better fitted some other man. And then I soothed them by explaining that the English tailor makes all clothes alike; that he goes upon the supposition that every man should be so high, and so broad, and that measurement is a mere form gone through with as a professional fraud, the same as a lawyer looks the wisest when he knows the least; and that to make any fuss about it would result in nothing, and the only thing to do was to take them, pay for them, and wear them while in England. They were no worse off than everybody else, and that they should be philosophical and content. One remarked, with a great deal of truth, that all the philosophy in the world wouldn't make a six foot man look well in a pair of trowsers constructed for a five foot sixer, and another that he knew of no philosophy that would support one under the trying affliction of a coat that bagged on the shoulders and in the back, and that had no more shape to it than a bean sack.

That is where they were wrong. That is what philosophy is made for. England has given the world its greatest philosophers, her philosophers being made necessary by her tailors, the same as every country that cherishes an especially poisonous serpent, also grows a particularly powerful antidote, and the snake and antidote grow together.

The women dress a trifle worse than the men — their dressmakers are a trifle worse than their tailors. If an English woman would only buy her gowns ready made, it would be better, for there would be a chance — only a slight one, it is true, but yet a chance — of her getting a fit; but she will not. She goes to the most expensive modiste, "to get something good," and then all hope of a prettily dressed woman is gone, and gone forever.

You can tell an American or French woman as far as you can see one. The neatly fitting dress, so neatly fitting as to make you almost think the woman had been melted and poured into it, the dress of which an American girl said, that when she got into it she felt as if she had been born again; the neat little shoe; the grace with which the dress is carried, and the grace of the woman who carries it; all contrast terribly with the angular gown, the shawl badly hung, and awkwardly worn, the ugly shoe and the large foot it covers, and the square, steady, grenadier-like step of the English woman.

No matter how expensive the material, or how costly the garments, no matter how much Nature has done for the Englishwomen, (and they are, as a rule, magnificent specimens of womankind,) they can't dress, and consequently lose half their attractiveness. They have strength, but they sadly lack grace.

It is all well enough for me, for I prefer badly fitting clothes, desiring to keep down to the ordinary level, and not be made too conspicuous; but it is hard upon those less favored, and who need to reinforce nature by art.

But always bear this in mind. When you come abroad bring with you all the clothes you think you will need, unless, indeed, you come flying light in the matter of baggage for convenience of transit. If that is your idea it is well, but if you come expecting to furnish yourself in England at a less price, or to get superior styles, you will be the worst deceived man or woman in the world. Quality considered, there is nothing cheaper than in America, and, as for style, it is a Parisian dandy to a Hottentot. The English tailor is the most detestable cloth-butcher on the globe. So unutterably bad is he that I cannot ascribe his miracles of misfits to lack of mechanical skill, or general imbecility; there must be underlying his work a fiendish purpose and determination. The English tailor or dressmaker must be a misanthropic individual who has a spite against the human race, and they must have a vengeance to wreak which they accomplish in this way.

I don't wish it to be understood that all English men and women are badly dressed. I have seen some most charming toilettes, but on inquiry I found that they were well-to-do people who could afford to go to Paris to get their clothes, or those who had just returned from New York.

If you desire to be well dressed in London, take your clothes with you. This is the parting advice of a sufferer and victim. I have paid for my experience—I give it to my readers gratis. That is what I am here for, and I shall discharge my duty regardless of consequences.

The next principal nuisance you meet in England is the
system of "tipping." "Tipping," be it known, is gratuities
given to servants, or whomsoever does anything for you which,
in any other enlightened country on the face of the globe, is
considered an act of courtesy, or a matter of right.

It commences the moment you leave the dock at New
York. You have paid a very large sum for your passage,
enough to entitle you to every comfort that money can buy.
But there sets upon you immediately a horde of blood-suckers
who never let go, till, gorged, they drop off at Liverpool.
There is a sovereign to the man who makes your bed; there is
the chamber-maid, there is the table steward, the smoking-room
steward, the deck steward; there are collections for asylums
in Liverpool; there are collections for the man who attends to
the purser's room, where a select few are treated to a little
refreshment at five in the afternoon; there are fees for showing the machinery of the vessel; there are tips for the Lord
only knows what. The only thing free about the vessel is the
water outside, and could a scheme be devised for making you
pay for a sight of that it would be put into operation at once.

Then there is the English hotel. The landlord measures
you as you come in. He inventories you. He says "this man
will stand six pounds, or eight may be. That will leave him
enough to get back to London, with a cab fare to take him to
his lodgings." And so when he makes his bill he manages to
make it to the exact amount of what he thinks you have about
your person, irrespective of what accommodation you have
received. In paying this enormous bill should you display more
money than he supposed you carried, he gnashes his teeth and
howls with rage. But he very seldom gnashes or howls. He
is a very skillful person, and knows intuitively to a half-sover-
eign how much you will, or rather can, bleed.

You contract for your room for so much a day — and the
sum is always a round one — and it is explained to you that you
may order your meals from a bill of fare, the price of each dish
being set down opposite its name. Very good, you say to yourself, I know now what I am to pay, and you fall to work. Do
you? Not much. There stands a waiter, who makes a frantic
effort to appear like a man, but only succeeds in getting to
where Darwin commenced the human race. But he rubs his

hands, and smirks, and smiles, and brings you your orders, and still smiles and smiles, and would be a villain were there enough of him. He does all he can in this direction, however.

When you are through, you rise and prepare to get out. The waiter stops you with an obsequious smile in which there is much determination, and remarks, "the waiter.!" You are made to understand that he expects a shilling. You give it to him. Getting to your room you want a pitcher of water. A servant brings it, and waits till you give him a six pence. You take a drink—if you do drink—I know this from seeing other victims—you pay for the drink, and the servant who brings it to you expects and manages to get three pence. The boy who cleans your boots wants six pence, the chambermaid who sweeps your room wants a shilling, the boy who goes down to see if you have any letters wants six pence, and after paying for all this you get your bill. Understand you have already paid exorbitant prices for each and every bit of service you have received, but nevertheless, there in your bill is an item, "attendance four days, eight shillings." You pay it without a murmur, externally; and hope you are done with it. Not so. As you leave the hotel, there stands the entire retinue of servants, the boots, the chambermaid, the bar-man, the bell-boy, all with their hands extended, and every one expecting a parting shower of small coin. You pay it. There is no other way to do.

You see how it is. You pay the servants for the performance of every possible duty when they perform it; you then pay the landlord for the duties already paid for, and then as you leave the house you pay the servants over again. Three times for the same service, and that whether any service has been rendered or not.

You get into your cab and drive to the station. The legal fare is one and six pence. The cabby expects six pence in addition, for himself, the porter who shows you what car to get into, with the uniform of the company on his back, expects four pence for that, the other porter who takes your valise to the car-door, must be feed, and so on, and so on forever and forever.

I tried conclusions with a hotel clerk in a city in England, but I shall never do it again. There is no use. You might as

well submit first as last. You may struggle, but they have you
as certainly as their ancestors and prototypes, the old Barons,
had the Jews.

I went to bed at night with two candles on the mantel. It
was bright moonlight, and as I had read my regular chapter in
the Revised Testament in the office, I had no occasion for light.
I simply wanted to get into bed, therefore I didn't light the
candles, at all.

THE CANDLE EPISODE.

The next morning I
found in my bill a charge
for two candles, two shillings. I protested.

"I used no candles," I
said.

"But they were there,"
was the cool reply. "Perhaps you used matches —
it is all the same."

"But I didn't use
matches, and if I did, I
had my own."

"We do everything for
the comfort of the guests
of the house. There were
candles and matches for
you."

He never blushed but
took the two shillings as
coolly as possible, receipted
the bill and said "Thank
you," and hoped if I ever
visited the place again I would call upon them.

I presume I shall. It does n't make any difference where
you go, it is all the same; and if you are to be swindled, it is
preferable to have it done by somebody you have a slight
acquaintance with.

It reminded me of the man who built a tavern in Indiana.
A traveler stopped with him one night, and the next morning
asked for his bill.

"Twelve hundred and fifty dollars," said the landlord, promptly.

"Twelve hundred and fifty dollars for one day! It is outrageous!"

"It is a little high," said the landlord, "but I'll tell you how it is. I opened this house exactly a year ago yesterday. I expected to make a thousand dollars the first year, and you are the first customer I have had. I ought to charge you a little more to cover insurance, but I like you, and don't want to be hard on you. Twelve hundred and fifty dollars will do."

The English landlord likewise makes out

THE LITTLE BILL.

his bill with the calm confidence that he will never see his guest again. He seldom does — if the guest can help it.

I have orated much against the American hotel clerk and his diamond pin and cool insolence, but I shall never do it again. He is a babe in arms as compared with his English brother.

The system of feeing goes into everything and every-

GETTING READY TO LEAVE A HOTEL.

where. You are begrudged a breath of fresh air, unless you are willing to tip somebody, and I suppose a tip would be required for a snore, if a servant could possibly get into your room.

In fact, you cannot go anywhere in London without the everlasting and eternal tip, except the British Museum. That is the single and sole exception. There, on certain days, there

THE LAST STRAW.

is no admission fee, and you pay nothing for having your cane and umbrella cared for. But everywhere else you pay an admission fee, you pay a swindler for taking your cane, and you pay the guide for giving you an entirely unintelligible

THE CABMAN TIPPED.

account of what is to be seen. Even Westminster Abbey, the most sacred spot in England, has its regular system of tips. It is not as it was in the Temple of Jerusalem, in the time of our Savior. There were money changers there — here the vergers give no change. They keep all you give them. Consequently they are not liable to be scourged out.

In the restaurants there is a charge on the bills for attendance, but nevertheless you are expected to tip the man who waits upon you. By the way, these waiters get no pay for their services; they pay the proprietors a bonus for their places.

The hackney coach driver gets about two shillings a day from the proprietors of his vehicles, and makes his money from his customers. The man who drove us down to the Derby expected, and did not expect in vain, for he demanded it directly,

THE UNIVERSAL DEMAND.

two shillings each from his twelve passengers, notwithstanding the fact that we had paid twelve dollars and fifty cents each for our passage.

It runs through everything. I will not say that the Queen herself divides with her servants the tips they receive, for I do not know. I will not make statements rashly. But I presume she does. I do not see how so important a source of revenue should escape her notice, or be neglected. I shall not offer her sixpence when I inspect any of her palaces, nor do I say she

would take it from me. But so firmly fixed is the infernal
system, so much is it a part of English life, that I verily believe
it would wrench the amiable old lady's heart not to take it, and
I also believe that she would so manage that I should not get
away with it in my possession.

Oh! my countrymen! It is my duty to warn you against
a great impending danger. The system of tipping is, gradually
but surely, getting its rapacious fingers upon your vitals. It
has its clammy grasp upon your sleeping cars; it is gradually
working into hotels, and everywhere else. Strangle the monster in its infancy. Declare war upon it at once, and fight it to
the death. Refuse to pay the sleeping car porter for what you
have already paid the corporation of which he is an excrescence.
Refuse sternly to fee the servant at a hotel, the porter who
handles your trunk, and the man who waits on you at table.
When he says to you, "My wages are small, and I must have
fees," say to him, kindly but firmly, "Either make the proprietor pay you proper wages or quit his employ. If you cannot
plow or hammer stone, go out quietly and die for the good of
the many. It is not necessary that you should wear a swallow-
tailed coat, and make more for trivial services than the average
menhanic does for a hard day's work. We will none of it."

And so shall you rid yourself of the most infernal nuisance
that afflicts England, the one petty worriment that makes the
life of the tourist unhappy. We can endure a giant monopoly,
but these small tyrannies are unbearable.

THE LORD MAYOR'S SHOW — ON THE THAMES.

CHAPTER XII.

WAY down upon the Southern coast of England is an old town of more than ordinary interest. Everybody is familiar with that great depot for England's naval and military forces — Portsmouth.

The run down from London is one of delight, that is it would be were it not for the fact that the stolid Briton will not keep pace with the times, and introduce upon his railroads modern carriages, in which a traveler may ride with some degree of comfort. He refuses to abandon the ancient compartment carriage, which is the most abominable arrangement conceivable. The cars, as we would call them, are about half the size of the ordinary American passenger coaches, but instead of being large, roomy and convenient, they are exactly the reverse. They are divided into compartments, each one of which will hold ten persons, five on each side, facing each other.

After booking your place, instead of buying your ticket — although really you do buy a ticket — you take your seat in one of these compartments, in which are nine other persons. Thereupon the guard, about like our brakeman, locks the door, and you are a prisoner until the next station is reached.

There are absolutely no conveniences. You are simply compelled to sit bolt upright, in a close, stuffy room, in company with nine other persons whom you do n't know, and do n't care to know. You can't walk from one end of the car to the other, because there is no aisle, as in our cars. You can do nothing but sit there and think what reforms you would inaugurate were you only a Board of Directors on one of the roads.

(174)

It is possibly a finicky sort of a person who would object to
trifles light as air; but there be breaths that are not as light
as air, and they are no trifles. You travel second or third
class, and there shall be nine sturdy Englishmen smoking short
pipes, or villainous cigars, with their breaths ornamented with
every variety of very bad liquor that the combined genius of
the liquor compounders of all nations can produce. Likewise
there are feet innocent of baths. If you happen to have an

end seat you may let
down the window and
get fresh air, but heaven
help you if you are in
the middle. You in-
hale the fumes till a
state approaching in-
toxication ensues, but
you must sit there all
the same, for there is
no escape. Such a de-
bauch may be cheap;
but I never did like any-
thing second-hand —
second hand intoxi-
cation least of all. I

A SECOND HAND DEBAUCH.

vastly prefer original sin. And then imagine the pleasure of
traveling in such company as one must necessarily be thrown
into by this system. The terrible tragedy on the Brighton
road recently, gives a good idea of some of its beauties. A
well-to-do merchant living in the country had been to London
to make some sales of land, and was spotted by an impecunious wretch, who had previously known him. The merchant,
whose name was Gold, left London on the afternoon train, and
was alone in one of these compartments, securely locked with
the villain, whose name was Lefroy. It seems from the facts
of the case, as gathered by the police, that while between two
stations Lefroy attacked Gold. There was a violent struggle,
during the course of which Lefroy killed Gold, rifled the body
and threw it out of the window, as it was found by the road
side. When the guard unlocked the compartment at the next

station Lefroy invented some flimsy story about some mysterious shooting, to account for the presence of the blood, and actually made his escape. It is comforting to know that afterward Lefroy was caught, tried and hung. England does hang murderers.

How utterly impossible such a tragedy would have been in an American car. But here the victim had absolutely no way of calling for or obtaining assistance. The two were alone, locked in the compartment, and the cries of the wretched man as he realized his danger, were drowned by the noise of the train thundering along at sixty miles an hour.

But to return to Portsmouth. The scenery from London is charming. The train rushes along, after leaving the fog and smoke of London in the rear, through the garden land of England. The fields are all cultivated, the farm houses, ancient and peculiar, have an air of solidity and comfort, and an occasional castle lends variety to the scene and makes the picture perfect.

The towns through which the road passes are, of course, all very old. They abound in red-tiled houses of antique pattern, narrow streets, that at the end of the village lose themselves in beautiful lanes, fringed on either side with long rows of stately trees that shade the close-cut hawthorne hedges. But over all these is an air of age. Everything is finished. Everything is complete. We have visited so many old towns, and inspected so many old buildings, that it would be a positive relief to see a brand new house, painted white, with green shutters, whose gable roof glistens in the sunlight with its new pine shingles. But, alas! that cannot be. Here everything is old and purely English.

Portsmouth was reached after a delightful run of two and a half hours, and soon after we were snugly quartered in the queerest hostelry imaginable, our comfortable room overlooking an arm of the sea, upon which were all manner of craft, from the diminutive dory to the massive merchantman.

Portsmouth is, and always has been, one of England's strongest points. Situated in a most commanding position it has been an invaluable factor in her matter of defenses. Only five or six miles away, the Isle of Wight runs for miles parallel with the coast, forming a narrow passage through which the vessels for a foreign nation, if they intended to make a hostile landing in that neighborhood, must pass. Spithead, the famous place of entry and departure of vessels, is just off Portsmouth, and is guarded, as is the passage, by two immense stone forts, built at no end of labor and money, directly in the channel, effectually protecting that entrance. And then to make things more secure, there is a series of three forts on the Isle of Wight, while Portsmouth, to speak within bounds, is made up almost entirely of forts.

At first one wonders why England finds it necessary to keep these forts, and the heavy force of soldiers required to garrison them. At Portsmouth is one of the largest, if not the largest, dock yard in the world, upon the safety of which the fate of the nation's navy depends, and if that point, strong as it is, and affording such excellent opportunities for the protection of the southern coast, were to fall into the hands of an enemy, it would open all England to it. And your English are great Generals. In time of peace they prepare for war, and keep all things in readiness for any emergency, no matter how sudden or how severe.

The harbor is a beautiful one and full of interest. Of course there is the inevitable waterman, with his tarpaulin hat and tight fitting "Jersey," who beseeches "Y'r hon'r," to let him row you about. And of course he carries his point.

The very first thing he does, before you can admire the strange species of ships that are on every hand, is to row you directly to Lord Nelson's flag ship, the "Victory," on which the gallant sailor died, at the battle of Trafalgar. But one is not sorry at that, for Nelson's character was one that compelled the admiration of every one who had ever studied him and his glorious achievements. With what a thrill, then, one stands upon the very deck upon which he trod during one the most brilliant sea fights in the annals of history, to go upon the gun decks where he commanded his gallant sailors. With what feeling of sadness one stands on the spot where he stood when the deadly leaden ball of a French sharpshooter gave him his death wound, and with uncovered head bows before the spot where the soul of the greatest, bravest sailor the world

12

ever knew, winged its way amid the smoke and horror of battle
to the peaceful haven of the great hereafter.

THE ANNIVERSARY CEREMONIES — "HERE NELSON FELL."

The anniversary of the battle is celebrated regularly, and
the old ship is once each year made radiant with flowers.   A

beautiful wreath is always placed upon the spot on the deck where the hero fell.

It does not seem possible that the great, clumsy-looking vessels that were used in those days could even be navigated, to say nothing of fighting with them. The "Victory," which is only one of a half dozen of the same kind now laid up — put on the retired list — in Portsmouth Harbor, is a huge floating castle, and required, when in commission, one thousand men to operate her. She is fifty-eight feet from the main

IN THE HARBOR.

deck to the hold, though she seems, with her four decks above the water line, to be even higher than that. Comparing her with the long, narrow iron-clad of to-day, it requires a considerable stretch of imagination to realize that she had once been really in service, and no slight service, either.

A two hours' trip around the harbor is one of constantly increasing interest. There are ships and ships. Here are immense men-of-war, full rigged and ready for a cruise, alongside of which is a trim yacht flying the pennant of the Royal

Yacht Squadron. Here a hugh merchantman, with a cargo from Bombay, perhaps. Beyond, a great white steamer, larger than the transatlantic passenger steamship, that takes England's soldiers, these same red-coated fellows we see strutting about here with their diminutive caps jauntily perched over their left ear, out to India to help keep the natives quiet and subdued. Right here is the Queen's private yacht, the "Albert and Mary," a vessel of large dimensions, and fitted up in the most exquisite manner. This is the ship the Queen takes her little excursions in, and occasionally sends it across the channel to bring over some distinguished personage whom she wishes to honor.

Near this palatial steamer, as though to make the contrast all the greater, is an old man-of-war, built years ago, and found now to be of no use, either for the purpose for which it was originally built, or for the carrying trade. So it lies there a worn-out monument of the past, gradually yielding to the ravages of time.

But the great point of interest in Portsmouth is the dock-yards, the finest in the world. A thorough survey of it would take three or four days, but a stroll of four or five hours gives one a fair idea of what it is. Here the mammoth vessels belonging to England's naval equipment are taken for repairs, and the dry docks, of which no description is sufficient to convey a definite idea of their size and general appearance, are constantly filled with them. These docks are magnificent specimens of masonry, some of them being acres in extent, and built in the most solid, substantial manner. In the great buildings fronting on the water are vessels of all sizes and descriptions, in course of construction, some ready to launch, and others in the first stage of the work.

Just now the workmen are engaged in putting the finishing touches on a great iron-clad turret-ship, of which England is very proud. And well she may be, for the "Inflexible" is really a wonderful vessel with her two turrets bearing each two guns of eighty tons weight. The turrets, made of heavy iron plates, are made to revolve by machinery, so that the guns may be fired in any direction. The loading and cleaning is all done by ingeniously arranged machinery, worked by hydraulic pressure. In fact, all over the ship steam power is used wherever it is possible, and in some instances where it seems almost impossible. She is built entirely of iron, and seems impregnable. As one gazes upon her monstrous proportions, her terrible facilities for dealing death and destruction, there comes involuntarily the wish that there may never be an occasion when her loud-mouthed and frightfully effective services may be required.

Impregnable as she seems to be, English mechanics are busy inventing guns to pierce her. That is going on all the time. They construct a vessel which will resist any gun they have, and then construct a gun which will pierce the vessel. Where it will end the Lord only knows. In England the irresistible is always meeting the immovable, and vice versa.

In Portsmouth, more than in any place in England, the policy of England is manifest. Portsmouth is one vast fort, and every other man you see on her streets is a soldier. You come upon vast fortifications everywhere, long lines of earth works stretch in every direction on the coast, commanding every approach to the city, and vast stores of ammunition are piled away safe and secure but ready for use at a moment's notice. Portsmouth is a watch dog for that part of the island, and it would be a daring foe that would attack her. It gives you a very good idea of England's strength, and of her power of defense. But heaven help the people who have to foot the bills for all this.

After a day spent in the midst of all these places suggestive of war with its terrible sequences, it was a pleasure, in the evening, when the light sea breeze tempered the heat that had been so oppressive, to stroll down to the "Old Fort," as it is called, though it bears but faint resemblance now, to an effective fortification. Its heavy stone abutments that were once crowned with cannon, are now covered with moss; the cannons have been taken away, and in their stead are rustic seats around which happy children laugh and play, while their nurses sit talking of their red coated favorites in the adjoining barracks. There is just now an air of peace and harmony, of war days done away with, that is only disturbed by the occasional sight of a sentry who paces his beat in front of the barracks. It is

peace now, but the sentry shows how insecure the peace.
England must be always ready for war. But standing upon a
parapet, overlooking the sea, one forgets for the time the fact
that he is in the very midst of that oppressive power, the

UNDER CLIFF—ISLE OF WIGHT.

strong arm of the soldier, and gives himself up to kindlier
thoughts, brought up by the marvelous beauties of the scene
spread out before him like the mystic picture painted by fairy
hands. The sea, over which the last rays of the sinking sun

dance and shimmer, is just rippled with a light breeze that sends the graceful little yachts skimming merrily over its surface. The misty outlines of the Isle of Wight, half hidden by a delicate purple haze, gradually fade from sight as the sun sinks lower and lower, and throws a broad path of golden light along the bright blue water. As it sinks into the sea, a great globe of brilliant red, a stately ship, with graceful masts rising high in air, cuts the path of golden light, and for an instant is clearly outlined against the glowing orb. Every mast, every rope, even, can be seen clearly and distinctly against the beautiful background. For an instant every outline is tinged with gold, then it passes slowly on, the sun sinks beneath the waves, and then comes the soft twilight, when one "sinks into reveries and dreams."

This reverie and dream business is all very well for awhile, but it cannot last, and the awakening is not pleasant. The good old town of Portsmouth, with its historical memories, the beautiful harbor filled with so much that is interesting, must be left for others to enjoy while we go back to London and resume the routine of sight seeing — that is, to draw it mildly, becoming just a trifle tiresome. One can have too much of even London.

*　*　*　*　*　*　*　*　*　*

On our return to London we met our old steamer friend, Tibbitts's Lemuel, of Oshkosh. He had been traveling in the North of England, and tiring of the smaller cities and the country, had returned to London to " do it." He was rather puffy in the cheeks and rather bleary about the eyes, which showed a season of not altogether strict adherence to the precepts of Father Matthew. He was overjoyed at seeing us, as men always are at seeing anybody of whom they want something. He was in trouble.

" Look here," said Lemuel, " you are a good fellow, now, and I know you will help me out. You see I came over for improvement and experience, and to enlarge my mind, and all that sort of thing, and the old gentleman insisted that I should keep a diary, and note down *my* impressions of scenery, and industries, and modes of living, and all that, and send it to him regularly, and I *must* do it, or he will cut off the supplies, and bring me home."

"Well, that is easy enough. You have done it? You have kept a diary?"

"Yes, a sort of a diary. You see there were four of us in the party, devilish good fellows, one from Chicago, and two from New York, and we went to a lot of places, and saw a great deal, and I wrote in my memorandum book every day, but it was certainly the last thing I did before going to bed, about four o'clock in the morning, or a little later. What the old gentleman wanted was not only an account of all this rot, but *my* impression of the places, to develop me. You understand?"

THE UNFINISHED ENTRIES IN THE DIARY.

"Yes; and a good idea it is. Did you write down your impressions of the places you visited?"

"Well, yes; but I am afraid they won't satisfy father. He is mighty particular, and awful sharp."

"Will you let me see your memorandum book?"

He handed it to me, and these are some of the entries, which were, no doubt, written at four in the morning, the last thing before getting into bed; and they were, unquestionably, *his* impressions. I select a few at random, these few being excellent samples of the whole lot:—

Leeds—Manufacturing city—Beer very bad—Scotch whisky tolerable, though I never liked it cold.

Birmingham—Manufacturing city—Beer bad—Not equal to our lager—No good beer in England—Stout rather better—Went in on stout.

Manchester—Good bottle beer—Draft beer bad—All draft—(This sentence was not finished, probably for reasons. He explained that that night he slept in his boots.)

Sheffield—Manufacturing city—found some genuine American bourbon, and went for it—It was refreshing, as a reminder at home—Don't know about the beer—There's no place like home.

Nottingham—Don't know what the people do—a great many of them—Beer bad as usual—Guinness' stout in bottles fairish—Wish—

(Another unfinished sentence, explained as before.)

And so on. I told Lemuel that it certainly would not do to send these impressions to his father, as evidently he observed only one side of English life; that he had taken his observations through a glass darkly, but that I really hadn't the time to write up a set for him, especially as I had not visited those places myself.

"But what am I to do?"

Advising him to procure a good guide-book, and remain sober for a week, and get to work, we parted.

There are a great many Lemuels getting similar impressions of Europe—a great many; I may say altogether too many.

WESTMINSTER ABBEY — INTERIOR.

CHAPTER XIII.

SOMETIME in the sixth century a Saxon King, named Sebert, founded an Abbey, where Westminster now stands. It is another of the regular show places of London, and possibly the most interesting, unless it be the Tower. It has been

EXTERIOR OF WESTMINSTER ABBEY.

rebuilt a dozen or more times, and is really the most beautiful building in London of its class.

The Abbey is three hundred and seventy-five feet in length,

(187)

by two hundred in width, and its height from the pavement to the foot of the lantern is one hundred and forty feet. I know this, for I got it from the guide-book.

There is nothing in England, in the way of architecture,

more striking or grand. The beautiful is not always the grand, or the grand the beautiful. Westminster Abbey is both. The old architects might not have been able to have built the Capitol at Washington, and they certainly could not have built the Court House in New York, and made it cost more than the Houses of Parliament, for they were not that kind of architects; they mostly died poor and did not wear diamonds, but they managed to erect a building that is worth the passage across the Atlantic to see.

On entering the Abbey you run the gauntlet of a dozen or more fellows who have the privilege of selling guide-books. They will not take "No!" for an answer, but manage

THE ENTRANCE TO THE ABBEY.

somehow to compel the gratuity. They are Potiphar's wives with designs upon your pockets, and you have to choose between yielding to them, like Joseph, or leaving some portion of your garments in their grasp. You always shed the six-pence. Then you wander about through the magnificent structure, reading tablets on which are inscribed the virtues of all sorts of men, till happily remembering that kings and queens were buried in the building, you ask whereabouts they may be lying. Some one gives the information, the party is made up, and you place yourself under the charge of what they call a verger, a beery old fellow, with a face that blazes like a comet, with some sort of a black gown over his shoulders, who conducts you to the gate of a chapel, at which stands another beery old fellow, with a like face and a similar gown on his shoulders, who deliberately asks you for sixpence apiece, which being paid, you pass in, very like you would in a circus. Then the beery old fellow commences in a sing-song, monotonous way, his descriptions:—

"The first on the left is the tomb of Queen Eleanor, who died in the year of our Lord," and so on. He intones his service just about as those officiating in the other services do, only he goes on without making a stop or punctuating a sentence. He guides you from one room to another without the slightest pause, and when he gets through he and the one at the gate, who takes the money, go out and drink beer till another party is formed.

But it is a very cheap show, and I am under obligations to the Church of England for the delight. In fact, it is a big shilling's worth—for a drinking man. One blast from the fiery orifice in the volcanic face of the verger is enough to save anybody sixpence in beer, and as for the book, why you have it, and it is worth the money. Thus, you see, you have the show of the building and the dead Kings thrown in. I was not sure that we should not have given the Dean a shilling or two, and I felt like offering it to him, but, unfortunately, I was out of silver.

It is not the magnificence and grandeur of the structure, or its sacredness as a place of religious worship, that give Westminster Abbey its interest to the average tourist. It is the burial place of the great dead of England, and its walls contain the dust of more great men than any building in the world.

Of course I did not enthuse a particle over the tombs of the old Kings, those ancient robbers, whose titles came from force and were perpetuated by fraud, thirteen of whom are buried here, and fourteen Queens, commencing with Sebert, the Saxon, and ending with George, the Second. They may sleep anywhere without exciting a thrill in me, for not one of them ever did the world any good, or added one to the list of achievements that really make men's names worth remembering.

I do not like kings, and if we must have them, I much prefer them dead. Safe in an abbey, they are not making wars upon each other, and besides, a dead king can be kept much more cheaply than a living one. I pay sixpence willingly to see where a dead king lies. When I remember that they must die, I always feel encouraged.

But England has buried here those who made her glory on the field, the wave, and in the Senate and closet, and it is England's glory that she does this. England has never let a great achievement go unnoted, or unremembered. In the floors and on the walls of this great church, are tablets, commemorating not only Generals and Admirals, but Captains and Lieutenants, who aided in repulsing the foes of the country, or extending its possessions, and the private soldier or common sailor receives his meed of praise, the same as his officer.

In this, England is wise, as she is in most things. In this faithful remembrance, the youth of England have a constant incentive to great deeds and meritorious acts.

Speaking of monuments and commemorative structures, how many has the United States? One was attempted to the memory of Washington, of the general form and style of a Scotch claymore, set on end, hilt downward, and it was placed in the mud, on the banks of the Potomac, where it has been surely and certainly sinking these thirty years at least, and is not yet half finished.

Occasionally, some enterprising woman, who wants a house, or to pay off a mortgage, or something of the kind, organizes a Washington Monument Association, and collects money for the purpose of completing it. But it never amounts to anything. The lady and the managers collect a great deal of money, but no stones are added to the monument, and there stands, or rather, is sinking, a monument, not to Washington, but to the inefficient management of the citizens of the country he freed, and their indifference to the fame of their best and greatest men.

England does not do this. There is never a name in English history that is not carefully preserved in the Abbey, and it is not permitted to wear out and fade. When time has meddled with it the chisel is brought into requisition, and it is restored.

If one wishes to thoroughly and completely appreciate the worthlessness of human reputation, he should walk through these walls and over these floors. While the fame of the heroes, poets and statesmen have been

POETS' CORNER — WESTMINSTER ABBEY.

carefully cared for, the nobodies buried here and hereabouts, and there are thousands of them, have been permitted to fade out mercilessly. Sir Toby Belch, we will say, or Sir Toby Anybody Else, who was so circumstanced that he received the honor of being buried in the Abbey or the grounds adjacent, lies here under a slab, on which is a long inscription. The slab is here; but alas! where is the inscription? The iron-nailed shoes of generations have as completely obliterated it as though a chisel had been used for the purpose.

But not so the actually great. The slab that covers the remains of Dickens has flowers placed upon it every day, and the inscriptions to the memory of Shakespeare, Byron, Handel, Haydn, Macaulay, Sheridan, Garrick, Rare Ben Johnson, and others, who made English literature, and the innumerable warriors by land and sea who have extended English possessions and defended England's greatness, are kept as distinct and as bright as the day they were erected.

One singular thing is that there are no bad men buried in the Abbey; that is, if you may believe the marble inscriptions. Marble is a bad material to tell lies upon, because of the limited space that can be used. Were there more room there would be more lies, I suppose, but the English have managed it tolerably well.

There was Warren Hastings, for instance, Governor-General of India, who in his day was held up as a monster of cruelty, and a model of rapacity and oppression. Even the English Parliament and the East India Company were forced to protest against his extreme cruelty to the East Indians. Nevertheless Hastings has a bust in the Abbey, and an inscription on it, in which he is given every virtue under the sun. He is extolled as being all that was merciful, just, kind, good, and wise, and if there is a virtue that is not ascribed to him, the man who wrote it forgot it. As a matter of curiosity I copied the epitaph, and here it is:—

SACRED TO THE MEMORY OF

THE RIGHT HONORABLE WARREN HASTINGS,

Governor-General of Bengal,

Member of His Majesty's Most Honorable Privy Council, L. L. D., F. R. S.

Descended from the elder branch of the Ancient and Noble Family of Huntingdon.

Selected for his eminent talents and integrity, he was appointed by Parliament, in 1773, the first Governor-General of India, to which high office he was thrice re-appointed by the same authority. Of a most event-

ful period, he restored the affairs of the East India Company from the
deepest distress to the highest prosperity, and rescued their possessions
from a combination of the most powerful enemies ever leagued against
them. In the wisdom of his counsels and the energy of his measures, he
found unexhausted resources, and successfully sustained a long, varied,
and multiplied war with France, Mysore, and the Mahratta States, whose
power he humbled, and concluded an honorable peace; for which and for
his distinguished services he received the thanks of the East India Company, sanctioned by the Board of Control. The Kingdom of Bengal, the
seat of his government, he ruled with a mild and equitable sway, preserved
it from invasion, and while he secured to its inhabitants the enjoyment of
their customs, laws and religion, and the blessings of peace, was rewarded
by their affection and gratitude ; nor was he more distinguished by the
highest qualities of a statesman and a patriot, than by the exercise of every
Christian virtue. He lived for many years in dignified retirement, beloved
and revered by all who knew him, at his seat of Daylesford, in the county
of Worcester, where he died in peace, in the 86th year of his age, August
22, in the year of our Lord 1818.

HENRY VII.'S CHAPEL—WESTMINSTER ABBEY.

Pretty good, this,
for a man who was
the terror of the East,
and who was publicly
branded in Parliament
as the most audacious,
corrupt and cruel
tyrant that ever seized
anything that armed
force could lay its
hands upon. But as
England reaped the
benefit of a portion, at
least, of his wicked-
ness, England manu-
factures a record for
him and permits it to
stand among its other
heroes, for the admira-
tion of future genera-
tions.

I can imagine the
ghost of Hastings, as
he hovers over this
tablet and reads it. He must have smiled a spirit smile.
However, it is probably as correct as other history, marble or

13

written upon paper.   The inhabitants of the other world must
be amused as they read what is said of them in this.   A great
many of them must feel as the horse thief did when he wept
after the speech of his counsel in his defense.

"What are you sobbing so for?" asked the counsel.

"I never knew before what a good man I am," was the
reply.

There are hundreds buried in the Abbey who have no
especial claim to the honor, that is so far as to deeds that
survive the ages gone.   They enjoyed what we of to-day
would term a mere local reputation, and all that remains of
them is what the marble says.   The inscriptions are all in the
same strain, and are curious specimens of obituary literature.
For instance this : —

TO THE MEMORY OF

JAMES BARTLEMAN,

formerly a chorister and lay clerk of Westminster Abbey,
and Gentleman of His Majesty's Royal Chapel.

Educated by Dr. Cooke,
He caught all the taste and science of that great master,
Which he augmented and adorned.
With the peculiar powers of his native genius,
He possessed qualities which are seldom united ;
A lively enthusiasm, with an exact judgment,
And exhibited a perfect model
Of a correct style and a commanding voice;
Simple and powerful, tender and dignified ;
Solemn, chaste and purely English.

His social and domestic virtues
Corresponded with these rare endowments ;
Affectionate and liberal, sincere and open-hearted,
He was not less beloved by his family and friends,
Than admired by all for his pre-eminence
In his profession.

He was born 19 Septr. 1769.   Died 15 April, 1821.
And was buried in this cloister,
Near his Beloved Master.

" Solemn, chaste and purely English " is very good.   What
could Mr. Bartleman ask more ?

On the monument of Admiral Sir Wondesley Shovel the inscription reads :—

"He was deservedly beloved by his country, and esteemed, though dreaded, by the enemy, who had often experienced his conduct and courage. Being shipwrecked on the rocks of Scilly, in his voyage from Toulon, Oct. 22, 1707, at night, in the 57th year of his age, his fate was lamented by all, but especially by the seafaring part of the nation, to whom he was a generous patron and a worthy example. His body was flung on the shore, and buried with others on the sand ; but being soon after taken up, was placed under this monument, which his royal mistress had caused to be erected to commemorate his steady loyalty and extraordinary virtues."

Mr. William Lawrence, who was a prebendary, gets this poetical effusion :—

With dilligence and trust most exemplary
Did William Lawrence serve a prebendary,
And for his paines now past before not lost
Gained this remembrance at his Master's cost.
O read these lines again: you seldom finde
A servant faithful to a master kind.
Short hand he wrote, his flowre in prime did fade
And hasty death short hand of him hath made.
Well couth he numbers, and well measured land,
Thus doth he now that ground whereon you stand,
Wherein he lies so geometrical ;
Art maketh some, but this will nature all."
    Obit Dec. 23, 1621.
    Æstatus bud 29.

As a specimen of old English, this can hardly be excelled :—

Ander neath Lyeth
The Bodyes of 3 sonns
of Mr. Christopher Chapman,
Richard Christopher and
Peter Peter dyed the 11th
of September, 1672.
Richard dyed the 1th of
February, 1672, and
Christopher Chapman,
M. of Artes, dyed the 25
of March, 1675.

The next is a memorial to an authoress, who was the most popular of her day, and whose pieces were the delight of

London. To-day, she is only remembered by book-worms and antiquaries :—

> MRS. APHRA BEHN,
>
> Dyed April 16,
> A. D. 1689.
> Here lies a proof that Wit can never be
> Defence enough against Mortality.

This lady was the authoress of many dramatic pieces — all as dead as their author.

The Wesley family are represented in this :—

> NUTTY, SUSANNA,
> URSULA, SAMUEL,
> WESLEY.
>
> 1725, 1726, 1727, 1731.
> Infant children of
> *Samuel Wesley,*
> Brother of John Wesley.

The British merchant was honored, as well as the British soldier :—

> SACRED TO THE MEMORY OF
>
> JONAS HANWAY,
>
> who departed this life September 5, 1786, aged 74,
> but whose name liveth, and will ever live,
> whilst active Piety shall distinguish
> *The Christian.*
> Integrity and Truth shall recommend
> *The British Merchant.*
> And universal Kindness shall characterize
> *The Citizen of the World.*
> The helpless *Infant* natur'd thro' his care:
> The friendless *Prostitute* sheltered and reformed;
> The hopeless *Youth* rescu'd from Misery and Rum,
> And trained to serve and to defend his country,
> Uniting in one common strain of gratitude,
> Bear testimony to their Benefactors' virtues—
> *This* was the *Friend* and *Father* of the Poor.

The wandering about among the tombs of so many illustrious dead, and the reading of so many fulsome epitaphs — albeit I know they were not altogether deserved — produced an impression, a feeling of solemnity, that no other one place in all England could conjure up. It was in vain that Tibbitts tried to make fun out of some of the quaint inscriptions. It could not be done, and in a very short time the youth succumbed to the influence of the mighty memory, and became a subdued and quiet admirer of the solemn grandeur of the place.

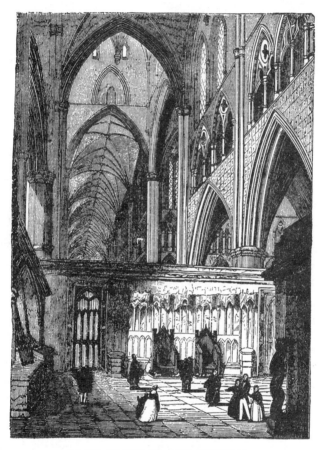

CHAPEL OF EDWARD, THE CONFESSOR.

Three is the hour that religious services are held in the large nave. More out of curiosity, perhaps, than anything else, we determined to remain during the service. As we sat there looking over into the Poets' Corner, the deep silence of the majestic building, growing more and more profound, there came trooping through the mind constantly changing pictures

suggested by the memories awakened by the vivid recollections
of the once great in literature and art, science and warfare,
who are still alive in the hearts of all English-speaking people,
although their bodies have been lying for years beneath the
massive pillars and superb arches of Westminster.

As the eye wanders upwards along the walls, covered with
tablets and rare pieces of sculpture, and seeks to unravel the
intricacies of the fretted roof, just discernible through the
dim light, the great organ peals forth the wondrous strains of
the Processional.

At that instant, as though to lend a new and greater
impressiveness to the scene, the clouds, which had been lowering all the afternoon, suddenly breaking with a glorious burst
of sunshine, that comes streaming in through the tall, graceful
windows, beautiful with their colored designs, lights up the
Abbey even to its darkest recess with a light, soft, and mellow,
which only intensifies the mystic feeling of reverence and joy
combined. And then the boy choristers, with their fresh,
innocent faces, sing in wondrous tones the Gregorian chant.
Nothing more is needed; everything is complete. You are
lost in a rapturous reverie, the mind is cleansed of all things
earthly, and wanders unchecked and unfettered through the
boundless realms of purity. One sits almost entranced; his
very being filled with the wondrous power of the place.
Gradually it dawns upon him that there is a discord somewhere, that something has occurred to mar the perfection of
the whole. For an instant he rebels against the thought, and
strives to believe that he still dreams. But the inspiration has
fled. The music, which a moment before caused the tears to
fill his eyes, has lost itself in the far-away cornices of the high
columns, and in its stead there is the dull, monotonous chant-
ing of a priest, who is intoning the service in a tired sort of
way, as though he thought that, having done the same thing
every afternoon for forty years, it was time for him to retire
upon a pension, and enjoy the quiet of a pleasant home, where
there was no absolute necessity of going through the ritual
every afternoon at three o'clock.

The awakening was not a pleasant one, and so we left the
Abbey, disappointed, as though we had been given the promise

of something wonderful and then been denied it. The service, no matter how beautiful in and of itself, is not in keeping with the grandeur of the place. There is lacking, to an American, that sense of power and majesty in it that the massive building, glorying in its wondrous architectural beauties, demands. The clergymen had an aimlessness that was simply tiresome, and as they drawled out the words, it seemed as though they did not care whether it produced an effect upon the worshippers or not. But it did produce an effect. Not the one to be desired, perhaps, but an effect after all, for the greater number of them quietly left the place, and reached the open air with a sigh of relief, as if they had escaped from some very depressing, dispiriting place.

In America religion and religious services mean something more than form, and the ministers, no matter of what denomination, or in what sort of a building, throw something of life and fervor into their services. They act and talk as though they had souls to save, and that the responsibility of the souls of their congregations were upon them. This was not of that kind. The priests went through the service as though, having offered the bread of life to their people, it was for them to take it or let it alone, as they chose. Indeed, when one was a little slow, as though he had been up the night before, the other would look at him reproachfully, as if to say, "Look here; why don't you hurry up and get through with this, and let us get home. I don't want my dinner to spoil," and the boys in the choir, though they sang like angels, did it, not as if they knew or cared anything about it, but as a mere matter of business, looking from one to another, and then upon the congregation. Whatever the effect upon the people, their beautiful music had no more effect upon them than as if they had been so many oysters.

These people would not do for a Western camp-meeting, or even for a fashionable revival in an Eastern church. But they have their uses.

One room in the Abbey is devoted to the effigies in wax of seven Kings and Queens, but few people visit it. They can see a more extensive collection of murderers at Madam Tussaud's for the same money, and they go there

The cloisters, as they are called, form a not uninteresting portion of the Abbey, they being the former places of residence of the monks of the establishment. In the various walks, with their quaintly carved pillars, and moss-covered

EFFIGY ROOM — WESTMINSTER ABBEY.

arches, are buried many distinguished personages, most of whom belonged to the Abbey.

Another point of interest is the " Chapter House," a circular room, of large dimensions, which was built in 1250 by Henry III., on the site of the earlier Chapter House belonging to the Abbey, founded by Edward the Confessor. It was the chamber in which the abbot and monks, in the time of the ancient monastery held their " Chapter," or meeting for discussion and business. The stone seats upon which the abbot and the monks sat are still preserved.

In 1265, when the House of Commons came into existence, it first sat in Westminster Hall with the House of Lords; but the two bodies having parted, the Commons held its meetings

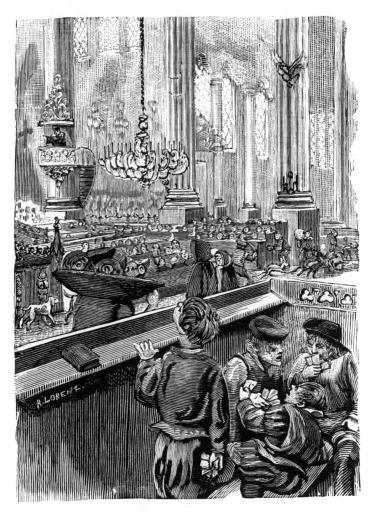

THE ABBEY IN QUEEN ANNE'S TIME.

in the Chapter House for nearly three hundred years. The last Parliament known to have sat here was that which assembled on the last day of the reign of King Henry VIII. After

that the House passed into the possession of the Crown, and
from 1547, when the House of Commons was transferred to
Westminster Palace, until 1863, it was used as the depository
of public records, and was very much disfigured. In 1865 its
restoration was begun, and it now presents the same appearance it did in years gone by, save where the finger of Father
Time has been laid rather heavily upon its once fair paintings
and graceful proportions.

It does not appear that the nave and cloisters, though the
last resting places of so many eminent persons, were treated
with due respect in the reign of Queen Anne. At all events,
the following occurs in the Acts of the Dean and Chapter,
under date of May 6, 1710.

"Whereas, several butchers and other persons have of late, especially on
market days, carried meat and other burdens through the church, and that
in time of Divine service, to the great scandal and offence of all sober-
minded persons; and, whereas, divers disorderly beggars are daily walking
and begging in the Abbey and cloisters, and do fill the same with nastiness,
whereby great offense is caused to all persons going through the church
and cloisters ; and, whereas many idle boys come into the cloister daily,
and there play at cards and other games, for money, and are often heard
to curse and swear, Charles Baldwin is appointed beadel to restrain this,
and to complain of offenders, if necessary, to a justice of the peace."

The Abbey is the especial pride of England, and well it
may be. It is a delight in and of itself, and would be were it
empty. But filled, as it is, with the enduring monuments of
its glory, it possesses a double interest. Every American visits
it, and every American should, for those who built it and those
who sleep under its wonderful roof, are of the same blood
and kin. America shares in England's glory, if not in her
shame. But then, we have some sins to answer for, and an
Englishman may not blush in the presence of his cousin across
the water.

CHAPTER XIV.

SOME ACCOUNT OF AN AMERICAN SHOWMAN, WITH A LITTLE INSIGHT INTO THE SHOW BUSINESS.

RIGHT in the heart of London—if London may be said to have any heart—is a tavern kept by an American, which is the headquarters of American "professionals," as showmen delight to call themselves. You can never go there without meeting managers, nigger minstrels, song-and-dance-men, unappreciated actors, and all sorts of people who prefer living from hand to mouth and wearing no shirts, in this way, than to making a fortune in any regular business. I go there frequently from sheer loneliness, and to hear the kindly American language spoken; and, besides, a man alone is generally in bad company, for the heart of man is deceitful and desperately wicked. Any company that is fair to middling is better than none at all. Even a hostler can tell you something you don't know. You may excel him in the philosophy of finance, but when it comes to horses you are nowhere.

I met one circus manager who is over here, as he expressed it, to "secure talent," and he proved a delight. He was short and very thick, and wore a sack coat, of rough material, and a little mastiff followed him about constantly. His hat and necktie were something too utterly gorgeous for description, his face was of a peculiarly puffy purple, and his nose blazed like a comet. And he would sit and talk of his business by the hour, keeping before him all the time a glass of British brandy and water, which he pronounced "goodish." You could be sure he was a showman as far as you could see him. My first interview with him was something like this :—

"I shall have the biggest list of genooine attractions that ever was taken across the Atlantic, and if I don't astonish the showmen of our great country, as well as the people, I'm a sinner. I have got a baby elephant, and a genooine Babulus, capchered by Stanley in the interior of Africa, at a great loss of life, and I am after a performer sich as the world never seen. She does an act on the trapeze that is so risky, that sooner or later she *must* be killed. There ain't any doubt about it. I have seen her. She runs up a rope like a squirrel, and jumps from a horizontal bar, twenty feet, catching hold of

IF SHE EVER MISCALCULATES BY A HAIR'S BREADTH, SHE'S A GONER, SURE.

her pardner's hands, and then plunges down from his body head-fust, at the frightful altitood of seventy feet, catchin' a rope twenty feet from the ground. If the lights are ever wrong by a half inch, or if she ever miscalculates a hair's breadth, she is a goner, sure."

And the enthusiastic old gentleman rubbed his hands in glee, as though the death of a performer was a consummation most devoutly to be wished.

"Do people enjoy such perilous feats?"

"Enjoy em! Enjoy em! Why, bless your innocent soul, a feat ain't nothin'—won't dror a cent onless it's morally certain that the performer will break his neck. This woman I'm after draws crowds every night, because she *must* kill herself. The trick is so dangerous that men make bets every night she will miss her lucky, and be carried out a corpse. I'm a goin' to have that woman, no matter what the salary is. She does this trapeze act, and then goes on in the first part of the minstrel entertainment after the big show. Oh, she's got talent into her."

"But if the performance is so hazardous, and she should be killed, would it not entail a heavy loss upon you?"

"Killed! Loss! Where was you born? My child, there never was a feat so dangerous that there ain't a thousand waitin' to attempt it, and they'll do it. When Mamselle Zhoubert gits killed, as she will, I'll hev to hold a lev-vee to decide atwixt the dozen who will want to take her place. I'll select one of 'em, give her a French name—yoo can't get on in the perfesh with a English name—and she'll go on and do it, and do it jist as well. And then wat an advertisement it is! This will be about the size of it:—

"The management begs to state that since the untimely death of Mademoiselle Zhoubert, at Cincinnati, it was doubtful if another lady competent to fill her place could be found. The feat was so difficult, so dangerous, and required such arduous training and such wonderful nerve, that it was feared that this leading attraction of the World's Aggregation would have to be omitted. There was only one other such artiste in the world — Mademoiselle Blanche, but she was engaged at the Cirque Imperial, Paris. The management knows no such word as fail, and a commissioner was dispatched at once to Paris, with unlimited powers to treat for this stellar attraction, this acme of talent. At an expense which would bankrupt any other establishment, conducted by narrow-minded managers who advertise more and perform less, she was secured and is now with us. Mademoiselle Blanche not only performs the original feat of the sincerely mourned Zhoubert, but adds to it one so much more dangerous as to make hers seem insignificant and commonplace. Mademoiselle Blanche will appear at each and every performance, all reports to the contrary notwithstanding."

"That'll fetch 'em."

"Dangerous feats! why, I run a whole season on a lion that had once eaten a keeper. The people come in crowds, expecting every day to see him make a breakfast of his trainer."

"Was he actually dangerous?"

"Dangerous! He et another trainer, and then I lost him.
His widder was actilly in love with her husband, and she swore
the animal shood be killed, and the people sided with her, and
as the broot was gettin' old, and the killin' made a sensation,

THE DEATH OF THE TRAINER.

I did it.   But I made all there was out of it.   I insisted that the
husband should have a gorgeous funeral.   The woman kicked
at the idea of a funeral, for she sed there was nothing to
berry, as the lion had eaten her husband.   But ain't the dear
departed inside the lion?   If we berry the lion, don't we berry
the dear deceast?   Cert.   And we hed it, and it was gorgeous
We hed a percession, with all our wagons in it — the regelar
street parade—only all the riders hed black scarfs on 'em, and
the wagons and hosses and elephants and sich was draped in
black (mourning goods is cheap,), and the band played a dead

march. The widder was in an open carriage, in full mournin'
with a white handkerchief, with a black border, to her eyes

THE GORGEOUS FUNERAL PROCESSION.

lookin' on his minatoor. There wasn't no minatoor, but she
held a case jist the same. That nite the canvass coodent hold
the people, and we run on that two weeks to splendid biz. In
two weeks, the woman got over her grief and went into the
lion trainin' line herself, ez 'Senorita Aguardiente, the Lion
Queen.' I give her some old lions to practis on, and in less than
a month she could do jest as well as the old man. She was a
good woman, too. She rid in the grand entree, and rid in the
'Halt in the Desert,' did the bar'l act, rid a good pad act, and
is now practisin' bare-back. She juggles tollable, and does a
society sketch song and dance in a side-show. When I git
talent I pay it and keep it. My treasurer changes the names
of my people every season, so as to have always fresh attractions. Oh, I know my biz. But that wuzn't all I made out uv
that afflictin' event. I went and hed a moniment made and
sot up over his grave. This is the vig., inscription and all:

HERE LIES
The Body of the Famous Fero-
cious Lion,
EMPEROR,
which contains the body of
SENOR SERONIMO CASTILLO
The Celebrated "Lion King,"
for many years connected with
BLOSS'S
Stupendous and Unapproachable
International Aggregation,
The Best Circus and Most Wonderful Collection of Wild
Beasts and Natural Curi-
osities in the World!
SENOR CASTILLO
was devoured by the ferocious
animal while exhibiting him
under the spacious tents of the
International Aggregation,
in St. Louis, August 10, 1871.
He was a worthy man, a talented
performer, and died cheerfully
in the discharge of his duty.
His place in the Great International Aggregation is more
than filled by
SENOR TOMASO CREVADO,
of the Royal Menagerie, Madrid,
who daily enters the den of a
still more ferocious Lion
than Emperor, at the
RISK OF HIS LIFE!

R. LORENZ. CHI.

And on the back uv the monument, I had this:—

"His sorrowing widow still does her unapproachable act of Equitation and Prestidigitation, in the Great International Aggregation, with which her devoured husband was so long connected, and may be seen at each and every exhibition.

"While mourning the loss of our friend, the Great Aggregation travels as usual, and exhibits without regard to weather, twice each day. Lion Kings may die, but the Great International Aggregation is immortal."

"The widder insisted on hevin a Scriptural quotashen on the moniment, and it took me a good while lookin up suthin approprit. I know more about circus than I do about Bible, but when I set out to do a thing I do it. Ez the two hed lived together and died together, ez the lion et him for cert, it struck me that this wuz about the racket, and I put it on the base:—

They were lovely and pleasant in their lives, and in death they were not divided.— 2d Sam. 1:23.

"I had the monument did in galvanized iron, and it will stand there for forty years, and every visitor to that cemetery will know suthin about the Great International. I wrote it modest, for I didn't want it to look too much like an advertisement, though, of course, I wanted to get all I could out of the afflictin event."

Ordering another brandy cold, the pleasant old gentleman murmured more reminiscences. He had always had a penchant for wild Indian troupes, and, since the Zulu war, for Zulus, and he flowed on about them:—

"Foggarty," said he, "was the best Zulu I ever had, and I have had a hundred of 'em. He laid over the lot. He entered into the spirit of the thing, and did the bizniss conscientiously. When he came outside with a iron girdle about him, and a pizen spear, he lept in dead earnest, he did. He made it mighty lively for the keeper to hold him, and he howled so like a savage that he skeered the wimin and gals to a degree that they couldn't help goin' in to see him. Foggarty was a great man, and hed talent. He was the best Modoc Chief I ever had. O'Finnegan cood lay over him on the green corn dance, and possibly drest the best, but Foggarty's war-whoop was suthin' sublime. We hed him one season as Scar-Faced Charley, and the next as Shack-Nasty Jim, and he did himself proud in

14

both. And then, there wan't no dam nonsense about him. He
wood peel out of his Injun clothes, and go and clean the lamps,
and help pack, or do anything. Before the doors opened, he'd

THE SIDE-SHOW ZULU.

do canvasman, and howl at the door, and at the door he'd play
the bass drum or grind the organ with cheerfulness. In the
street parade of the big show, he was, for five years, our

Washington, The Father of his Country, standing on a revolvin' pedestal. Then, jist as soon as he got his dinner, he'd help get up the canvas, and then skin into the Zulu rig, and after that, he'd peddle lemonade, or do anything to make himself yooseful. But a woman spiled him. Wimin spile a great many good men. We hed a woman, Biddy McCarty, wich was doin' the Circassian lady, with hair to her heels, you know 'em, and sometimes the bearded lady. Likewise, she was a Chinese knife thrower, and Foggarty yoosed to do the Chinaman she throwed her knives at. Well, Foggarty, seein' that she was an Irish gal, and he an Irishman, coodent no more help fallin' in love with her than fire kin help burnin' tow. He got it into his head that ef he could marry a gal with so much talent, he might, some day, have a side-show of his own. And then, as time rolled on, and they hed kids, he cood train 'em up to the family business, and do things cheap. He wanted to be a Bearded family, or a Zulu family, or a Jap family, or suthin, and so he married Biddy, and they went double. Biddy hed a will of her own, and besides she would git drunk. Rum spiles more talent in the perfesh than anything else. She had a trick of beating Foggarty, and she led him the devil's own life. It was at Leroy, New York. She had bin on as the Bearded Woman, and as the Circassian Lady, and hed sold all the photographs she cood, and hed changed to go on as the Chinese Knife Thrower, from Hang Fo. Foggarty hed changed to a Chinaman — Lu Fu, the Wizard — when I diskivered that Biddy hed bin drinkin'. I warned Foggarty to look out, for she was ugly, but he laughed, and said she wouldn't hurt him, and went on. You hev seen that act. Foggarty stands agin a board with his arms spread out, and the China woman throws knives all around him. She puts 'em between his fingers, and clost to his neck and between his legs. Biddy could throw a knife within a hair of where she wanted it to go. She hed talent, as I sed. But that day she was ugly. She and Foggarty hed hed it hot, and when she came in twistin' her queue, I knowd suthin was goin' to happen. She throwd six or eight knives all right, and then one went, whiz! It took off Foggarty's second finger on his right hand, as clean as a butcher's cleaver could do it. And Biddy fired the rest of the knives at him and rushed out, yellin', 'Be gorra, Mike

Foggarty, and ye'll bate me over the head with a tent pin agin, will ye? Ye'll hev one finger less to do it wid, onyhow.' Most men would hev abandoned the perfesh with that finger off, but while it was bein' dressed Mike whispered to me, 'Put it on the bills that the Zulu Chief lost the finger by a English saber, at the battle of — where was the battle?' I hev Foggarty yet, but Biddy broke his heart and he aint as good as he was. She run away with the cannibal from the Friendly Islands, who cood do the tight-rope and fire-eatin', and they are doin' hall shows and the variety business together.

THE LOST FINGER.

He taught her to do a song and dance, as well as fire-eatin', and she is now 'M'lle Lulu Delmayne.' They do society sketches, too. Foggarty is jest as willin' as ever, but the blow was too much for him. He goes with us next season as a Zulu, and also lecters the sacred Burmese cattle, and has a part in the wild perarie scene, and fires the calliope. He can't do Washington any more, for he has rheumatiz, and can't stand an hour with his right hand in a military coat. He's practisin' to be a lion tamer, but I don't bleeve it'll do. He may git to play the snake, but that is about as high as he'll ever git in the perfesh."

The next day the old gentleman departed for the continent.

CHAPTER XV.

RICHMOND.

Four weeks in London! Twenty-eight days of incessant sight-seeing. A series of continual surprises day after day, from early in the morning until late at night; a constant succession of new things of interest crowded and forced upon one, until at length the senses weary, the mind refuses to take in any more, and imperatively cries out for a change, for rest. The body is exhausted. The dull, dense atmosphere is enervating. A night's sleep gives no refreshment. One rises in the morning by sheer force of will power, with a feeling that it would be a delight, pure and simple, to go back to bed and sleep five or six hours longer, and when he does finally dress and go out on the street, he has no more ambition, nor inclination to do anything, or go anywhere, or see anything, than as if there were nothing to do, nowhere to go, nor anything to see. But that is what he is here for, and from force of habit he goes on the everlasting treadmill of sight-seeing, until the very name of London is odious, and its never-ending throng of people, hurrying along in the pursuit of pleasure or business, that, at first, was such a novel and interesting study, becomes distasteful to a degree, and he wishes he were home again or in some vast wilderness, or — anywhere, away from the narrow, crowded streets of high wall, and old-fashioned buildings, that stifle all his energies and tire his very nature.

So it seemed — so it really was — after four weeks' stay in London, when one forenoon a trip down to Richmond, twelve miles away, was suggested. The suggestion was acted upon with alacrity, and half-an-hour's ride produced a change such as one sees in the transformation scenes of a pantomime. Vanished the dull, heavy air; gone all the queer old buildings, with

their still queerer old people; hushed the noise and bustle of
the streets, with their never-ceasing turmoil of struggling
humanity and ever-rolling 'ansoms, and instead a bright blue
sky with a glorious flood of sunlight, its fierceness tempered by
a gentle breeze, cool and delicious, that was breathing through
the grand old oaks, and stirred with gentle ripple the placid
bosom of the Thames, which wanders like a ribbon of silver
through the wonderful meadows and dales of the beautiful
country that makes Richmond seem like a paradise.

The first feeling was one of relief — that the terrors of London had been left far behind; and there was light and air and
happiness again. Then this gave way to exultation. The pure
air intoxicated, the green trees, the velvety turf, the warbling
of the birds, after four long, dreary weeks in London, caused
the heart to throb with new life, the blood to course through
the veins with new strength, and there came an almost irresistible desire to throw up one's hands and shout for very gladness.
It was almost too good to be real, and once in a while one really
stopped to think whether or not he would suddenly awaken
and find himself in dingy, smoky London.

But no. It was all real. The pure air was there, the
sunlight, the breeze, the green turf, the magnificent trees,
centuries old. All, all were there, and the day was to be one
of unalloyed pleasure and happiness. God made the country
— man made the town.

In all truth Richmond is a most charming place. Only
twelve miles from the metropolis, and in reality one of its
many suburbs, it nestles among the hills, and looks off upon a
broad expanse of field and meadow and forest, as though there
were no such place as London in existence. It is not a commercial city, although of course it has its quota of shops. It
is a residence city — or, as they call it, town — for, although it
has a population of one hundred thousand, there is no cathedral, so it cannot aspire to the dignity of being a city. The
town is made up in great part of families whose members do
business "in the city," and they live in quiet elegance in
beautiful homes. That is the ideal suburban existence.

But aside from the quaint beauty of the town itself, its
chiefest perfection is in its environs. A few minutes' walk

from the heart of the town is that famous hostelry, known the world over, "The Star and Garter," where, in olden times, royalty disported itself under its moss-covered roof, in grand entertainments lasting for days at a time. For generations it was the resort of nobles, and then, when they tired of it, the people, imitating them as far as they were able, took it up and basked in the mellow light of its former grandeur, which has long since departed, it having become unfashionable.

Gay old times these noble roysterers used to have in this beautiful spot. The wines of the South, actually cobwebbed and dusty, flowed like water, and the most delicious food, brought from the forests and seas of all climes, graced the board. It was no trouble to them. They had no occasion to count expense as the people who go there now have to. For they had their tenants working for them at home, and they had their armies and fleets bringing them wealth from everywhere, and they could afford to eat, drink and be merry, and they did it all.

To be a King in those days was a very comfortable thing, except when some sturdy commoner, like Cromwell, tired of all this, and cut off a head. Opposed as I am to royalty and nobility and all that sort of thing, had I lived in those days I should very much liked to have been even a Duke. It was n't a bad situation, at all.

It is no wonder that the Star and Garter was a great favorite, and is yet in its way, for it is most beautifully situated. Standing in its broad verandas there is a rural panorama spread out that is simply superb. Near at hand is the Park, filled with gnarled old trees, under whose branches hundreds of years ago haughty ladies and imperious lords indulged in courtly pleasures, or engaged in intrigues where the nobles amused themselves in hunting the wild deer that ranged across its commons; where the flower of the youth of the country met in fierce tournaments, with all the pride and pomp of the time. Just below the cliff is the Thames, placid and serene, that winds in and out the wooded lands in graceful curves, while beyond, rising not boldly and grandly, but none the less beautiful, are green hills, dotted here and there with clumps of beautiful oaks and pines; dales and valleys that give us a view miles in extent. Over all this picture, to which no pen can do justice, is that marvelous atmospheric effect that can only be found in an English woodland scene. Not a mist, and yet a delicate haze, soft and subdued, that tones down the broad effects and gives the whole a perfection that is enchanting. One can stand, as before a magnificent painting, gazing for hours upon the scene and find new features every instant.

And then the long walk through the Park, itself a marvel of the picturesque. Along winding paths, over rustic hedges, resting here under the cooling shade of a huge chestnut, whose branches cover a vast extent of ground, stopping anon to admire the graceful deer that gaze timidly and yet curiously at the passer-by, as though wondering why he should trespass upon their domain. For a whole hour there was a continual revelation of natural beauties, and then suddenly the old town of Kingston was entered.

Here the streets were narrow, the houses low and old-fashioned, and the people quiet-going English, who have lived in the same place where their fathers lived before them, and their's before them.

Passing the cattle market, which is about the only live business of Kingston, a large square stone, surrounded by an iron railing, attracts attention. Examination shows it to be the identical stone upon which sat the ancient Saxon Kings when they were crowned. There was nothing particularly peculiar about the stone, but of course it would not have done to have gone by without at least casting a glance at the relic of so long ago. Possibly the proper thing to do was to uncover and drop a tear as the memories of the glorious scenes thereon enacted went trooping through the mind. Possibly it would have been the thing to sit on the queer old stone and imagine the space around filled with warlike chiefs and outlandishly arrayed ladies of the Court, and indulge in a day dream of the times when such things occurred. Possibly this may have been the thing to do, but it wasn't done, and for good reasons, too. Even if one had had the inclination to act in such an orthodox, sight-seeing manner, which is much doubted, there was a high iron railing, with sharp pointed iron palings, that would have effectually kept the greatest enthusiast outside the sacred enclosure.

Passing on through the town, the long walk begins to tell upon one's powers of endurance, so a rest is taken at "Bond's." Who has not heard of Bond's, the great resort of boating parties on the Thames? It is noted all over England, and its fame has spread even to America. A pleasant Summer garden, with trees and plants and flowers, gravelly walks and rustic arbors, on a high terrace, at the bottom of which the limpid stream glides smoothly along, while beyond, as far as the eye can reach, is the beautiful scenery that seems almost like fairyland. What better place can be imagined for a lunch — a biscuit and a bit of cheese, washed down with a pint of refreshing "shandygaff." One could drink the bad beer of the country here. It is truly delightful. And then a quiet smoke, the light clouds curling upward in an atmosphere as pure and clear as the air of life; while all that is poetic in one's nature is appealed to by the beauty of the scene, the sense of delicious comfort, and the faint music of distant boating parties, who, singing as they row, make a harmony that intensifies the pleasure of the hour, and makes one almost wish that this most perfect day might go on forever.

But still a greater treat is in store. A ride back to Richmond on the water, rowed by a brawny waterman, who does, as a matter of business, exactly the same thing that so many of the "swells," who are seen skimming past in their graceful single sculls, are doing for pleasure.

"Why," said I to the waterman, "do you make us pay for doing what those men do for nothing?"

"Ah!" was his reply, "'spose they 'ad to!"

Philosophic waterman! Whether any given exercise is pleasure or pain depends very much whether one "has to." The London jarvey drives a four in hand for one pound a week, and Lord Tom Noddy does precisely the same thing for the fun of it. One has to, and the other has n't, and there's the difference.

By this time the river is full of pleasure crafts. Here comes an eight-oared shell, whizzing along at a rattling pace, the little cockswain urging the crew on to still greater efforts as

he skilfully guides the long, slender boat through the multitude
of pleasure barges and skiffs. Over there is a trim craft gliding
along lazily, a pair of brawny arms just moving the oars, while
a pair of honest, manly eyes are speaking in unmistakable
language to a fair-haired girl who is reclining in the stern, idly
tossing the tassels to the rudder strings, as if she did n't care
about what was being said, even though the swift glances from

ON THE THAMES.

under her broad brimmed hat, and the mantling crimson on
her cheek, tell an entirely different tale.

Just beyond is a boat, large and roomy, in which five young
ladies are enjoying the pleasure of the hour. While four of
them pull strong and gracefully, the fifth steers the rapidly
moving lapstreak with a skill and precision that shows a master
hand. These English girls may be laughed at by their more

delicate American cousins, but in the matter of health and strength, they are the ones to laugh. They believe in plenty of exercise in the open air, and they take it; as, for example, these girls, beautiful as a picture, who row as perfectly and in as good "form" as though they had always been on the water. See the perfection of their development, the ruddy glow of health in their cheeks, the merry sparkle of the eye, the gladness in their hearty laugh, and then talk about the usefulness of outdoor exercise.

Every stroke of the oar as the boat speeds merrily down the river, reveals a new picture, each one as perfect in its completeness as that which preceded it.

On the left bank are the country seats of gentlemen of means. They are for the most part odd looking old places, with their angular towers and turrets, and bowed windows long and narrow. The lawns sloping gradually from the house down to the water's edge are perfectly smooth, and ornamented with clustering chestnuts and laburnums, elms and lindens, and the green foliaged birch, while the green hedges, wonderfully well kept, add to the general effect of the scene. The river winds in and out among all the charming places, for seven miles, and the town of Richmond is seen far off in the distance.

As the river makes a sudden bend there appears still another picture, the masterpiece of the series that has delighted the senses for the last two hours. There on the bluff stands the picturesque "Star and Garter," with its background of foliage. Just below is a portion of an old stone bridge across the Thames, while to the left the beautiful landscape stretches away to the distant hills, whose summits are lost in the purple haze of the closing day. It is a sight never to be forgotten; one that will linger ever upon the memory as a revelation of the absolutely beautiful in Nature.

CHAPTER XVI.

GOOD-BYE for the present to London. Good-bye to its smoke, its fogs, its predatory hackmen, its bad water, its worse beer, its still worse gin. Good-bye to its eternal rains, its never-ending badly-dressed men and worse dressed women. Good-bye to very bad bread. Good-bye to the greatest collection of shams and realities, goodness and cruelty in the world. Seven weeks in London and its environs is all that an American can endure, who ever expects to get back to his own country. Were fate to have a spite at him, and condemn him to make his residence there forever, he would settle down as a man does in a penitentiary and do the best he could, but for one who has a hope of returning to a country that was made after the Maker had had some experience in making countries, a longer stay in London than seven weeks would be too much. Seven weeks of biliousness and depression — seven weeks of exasperation and discomfort, seven weeks of extortion and tipping, seven weeks in an English suit of clothes, is all that an average American can endure.

And so good-bye to London till we renew our strength and can tackle it again. It is not exhausted, nor could it be in a year. It is a brute among cities, but it is a mastodon. It is a very large and variegated animal.

To the south lies France — La Belle France — and thither we go. Our landlady would hold us if she could, and gives expression to many reasons why we should stay in London: It is very warm in Paris; it is very disagreeable crossing the channel; Paris is unhealthy. At this time of the year Paris is crowded, and it is probable that we will not be able to get apartments such as would be suitable. It is not the season in

(220)

Paris, and we had better go there later, and so on and so forth. You see the season in London is waning, and the good lady will have difficulty in filling her rooms. It is delicately hinted that if a slight deduction in rent (we have been paying three prices) would be an object, etc. But it all avails nothing. We should go to Paris if we should be compelled to sleep under a bridge and eat in a market. It is not so much to get to Paris as it is to get out of London, and raise our spirits to something like their normal condition. And so, when the good woman finds there is no holding us, she makes out our bill vindictively, racking her imagination to find items to insert, and weeping, no doubt, after our departure, over items that she might have inserted, but, in the hurry, forgot. The cabman, knowing by the station he was driving us to that we were going, managed to charge an extra shilling, and at the lunch counter at the station we paid an extra penny for the everlasting ham sandwich, which was to be the last. And when the last tip was paid, and the last extortion submitted to, we were finally locked in our villainous compartment, and were off. London, or the fog that covered it, faded from our sight, we saw the sun, and were scurrying through the green fields and the real delights of rural England.

From Victoria Station to New Haven is not the most interesting trip that can be imagined, although there are picturesque towns, waving fields of grass, with an occasional bit of woods, that relieve the journey of some of its unpleasant features, and make it rather enjoyable. But by the time one has gone through miles and miles of such scenery, the towns become monotonous, each succeeding field of grain waves just as the one before it did, the woods, miniature forests, are just alike, and, leaning back in the corner of the compartment, the time is spent in dozing until eleven o'clock, when the train rushes into the station at New Haven, and we struggle through the dimly lighted passages to the dock, where lies the steamer that is to take us across that bugbear of all tourists, the English Channel.

And then we have the satisfaction of learning that the tide is not in, and the steamer will not leave for two hours and a half. It is a dark, windy night, and there is no way to spend

the time save by pacing up and down the narrow confines of
the deck, watching the enormous cranes loading huge packages
of merchandize into the vessel's hold; or taking a stroll along
the dock, regardless of the momentary danger of stumbling
over an unseen cable and pitching headlong into the water.

There is one other way of passing the time. Whenever a
tourist can find nothing else to do, he eats. There is in the
station at New Haven the inevitable lunch counter, with the

SANDWICHES AT NEW HAVEN.

orthodox ham sandwich and bitter beer. To this everybody
was attracted as by a magnet. There is no escaping it. No
body was hungry; but it seems to be a law of Nature that
you must eat ham sandwiches while you wait at railroad
stations. And in obedience to this law, a cart-load of the
sandwiches were devoured and paid for

The New Haven sandwich is very like its London brother,
only it is a trifle thicker. The cutter is not as expert as the

London professional, but he makes it just as indigestible. It is a trifle worse, because it is a trifle larger.

But time goes on, no matter how slowly it seems to move, and the tide comes in, although its rise cannot be seen, and so, just before one o'clock the warning whistle was given, the passengers took their places, the great wheels began to revolve, and we slowly steamed out past the breakwater into the channel.

The necessity for making the boat's landing so far away from the deep water cannot be understood. But so it is. Instead of running the track down to the dock and establishing the station there, where there would be no occasion to wait for the tide, the steamer goes up an arm of the sea about an eighth of a mile, and has to stay there until the water is deep enough to allow the passage to be made.

Once out upon the channel, the fresh breeze blows away all the wicked thoughts the two hours' detention had engendered, and as the moon breaks through the clouds, dimming the fast disappearing lights on shore, we give ourselves up to pleasant reverie. There is the memory of all that has occurred during an exceedingly busy seven weeks in London, and the anticipation of experiences new and strange that are to fill in the next two or three months. And as we sit on deck smoking and dreaming, until, our last cigar having gone out, and the chill air made us shiver, we go below only to find fresh cause for growling at the English, and things English.

Instead of commodious, airy staterooms in which we can go regularly to bed and enjoy a good night's rest, there is nothing but a series of bunks, upholstered in a cheap red plush, on which the weary traveler may stretch himself, and, putting a blanket over him, get such rest as he can from such scanty accommodations. And this, too, for the first-class passenger.

At four o'clock every one was turned out, for Dieppe was in sight. Such a sorry looking lot of passengers I never saw. Most of them had caught a severe cold, and all of them looked uncomfortable and cross, as though they really had not enjoyed the luxurious quarters furnished by the enterprising manager of that line.

The view from the steamer's deck was beautiful. The sun, about half an hour high, made the water sparkle as the light off-shore breeze rippled its surface. The channel, which had behaved wonderfully well, was dotted with fishing smacks from Dieppe, while here and there a steamer, trailing a long

OFF DIEPPE—FOUR A. M.

cloud of smoke behind, sailed along utterly indifferent to the smaller craft that had to tack with each phase of the ever-varying wind. Just ahead of us, half hidden by chalky cliffs, could be seen a part of the town, while to the right, huge white cliffs arose and stretched away almost as far as the eye could reach, the straight white sides rising abruptly from the water, reflecting the rays of the sun, and shining with dazzling whiteness. On the left, high up on the hills, were stately mansions, pretty villas, cool looking parks and pleasant drives. It was indeed a beautiful sight, and we were gazing on it with rapture when a bell sounded, the paddle wheel stopped revolving, and we drifted slowly on.

"The tide does not serve, and we will have to cruise about here for two or three hours."

So said one of the seamen when asked why the steamer had been stopped.

It was pleasant. We enjoyed it. We fairly reveled in it.

We were hungry, it's true, but what was hunger to the delight of waiting three hours in an abominable steamer? We were cold and tired. But what of that? We could gaze on white cliffs and talk pleasant things to each other for three hours!

When the tide did serve, and we were landed, which happened about six o'clock Sunday morning, we went through the Custom House, our countenances expressing such Christian resignation as must have indicated our character to the officials, for they never opened our baggage at all. They simply said: "Avez vous tabac ou liquers?" (observe how well we are

HAVE YOU TOBACCO OR SPIRITS?

getting on in French), and as we murmured "No," aloud, and to ourselves, "but we wish we had," they waved us on, and we were all right.

Adjoining the Custom House is a coffee room, and we entered. The repast spread out for us was just a trifle the worst that was ever seen. It was worse than anything in London, and more than that cannot be said.

15

I suppose it is all right, and for the best. I suppose that taking us out of London at six o'clock P. M., and waiting two and a half hours in New Haven for the tide, and two hours in Dieppe harbor also, for the tide, is unavoidable. But if I ever get a chance I shall ask the manager of the line these questions:

1. Do you know the hour at which the tide comes in at New Haven?

2. Do you know the hour the tide serves to enter Dieppe?

3. If so, why not give us the five and a half hours that were consumed in useless waiting at New Haven and Dieppe, in London?

4. Has your company any interest in the ham sandwich and beer counter in New Haven? and is this delay in that most uninteresting place for the purpose of compelling the waiting passengers to leave a few more shillings in England?

And I shall demand specific answers to these queries. The taste of the New Haven sandwiches is yet in my mouth.

Dieppe is a pleasant little city of perhaps twenty thousand population, devoted to the carving of ivory, fishing, and swindling tourists, the latter pursuit being evidently the most prosperous. The fisher people are a picturesque lot as to costume, and are hardy withal, men, women and children. They are bold sailors, and what they do not know about water and its contents is not worth knowing.

Bad as the English trains are, in France, where there is the same system, it was even worse, for we were a little shaky in our French. However, we put on a cheerful countenance, and said "*Oui*" to everything, and made believe we knew all about it, and let the guard put us where he pleased, and were soon humming along through the outskirts of Dieppe. We were just beginning to enjoy the prospect of rural scenery, when, without a note of warning, we plunged into a tunnel, which seemed to last forever, though it was only a mile long.

Emerging from this, it was seen that an immense mountain had been pierced, and we were at once in the fertile valleys of picturesque Normandy. As the train hurried along there was a constant succession of pictures that would drive a poet or painter into raptures.

The broad valleys, the hills and dales, were intersected by smooth white roads that wound around side hills, through forests and then far away over a long, level stretch, through queer little towns, the existence of which was never dreamed

FISHER FOLK — DIEPPE.

of by the outside world. All along these well-kept wagon-ways were lined on either side by closely trimmed hedges, shaded by tall and stately Lombardy poplars, that stood grim and erect as though they were the guardians of the country.

Here and there between the quaint little villages, with their one main street running their entire length, were the high, narrow houses of the peasants, with thatched roofs and queer little windows. Around them, neatly piled, were bundles of fagots, carefully done up and stored away for winter use.

They are a frugal people, these Normans, and waste absolutely
nothing.

Although it is Sunday morning, and we are sad because
circumstances will not allow us to attend divine worship, it

FISHER WOMEN—DIEPPE.

seems to make no difference with the people here, for in every
field are seen women, with their high peaked bonnets, busily
engaged in raking fragrant hay into huge piles, which the men,

arrayed in the traditional blue blouse and overalls, are loading upon wagons for carriage to the barns.

FISHER BOY AND CHILD — DIEPPE.

These men and women are well built, sturdy people, who

have thrived well upon the pure air that comes down from the mountains above. In the olden time the men were noted for their stature and strength, and furnished the French army with its best troops; and they are to-day fine specimens of physical manhood.

I don't know why it is, but there is something irresistibly fascinating in an old castle, or the ruins of what once was a great stronghold. After passing Malaunay and getting well out into the country, we came to a series of hills stretching way back from the railroad. There was a dense forest near the summit of the highest part, upon the top of which, half hidden by the trees, was part of a castle, a bit of wall and a huge round tower, all that remained of what was, in the early history of the country, a castle that was utterly impregnable. As the train wound round the base of the hill, a better view of it was obtained, and then came the longing to plunge through the forest, clamber up the steep hillside and wander through the old ruins, hunting for trap-doors and deep, dark dungeons, where noble knights had been confined for years and years, while fair ladies pined away and died because they came not back to them. This pleasant reverie might have gone on indefinitely, even after the romantic spot had been left far behind, had not the other passengers in the compartment began preparing to alight at the next station, Rouen.

We determined to stop over one train at Rouen, to see not only a French city, but the old statue of the French heroine, Joan of Arc, who was there burned at the stake, and the famous cathedral therein. Tibbitts, Lemuel, was of the party, and a Professor in a western college likewise.

The Professor was calmly enthusiastic, and Tibbitts was unutterably miserable. He could not speak a word of French, and it puzzled him to even order a drink. And then the wine! He did not like wine, and French brandy was not to his taste. He managed to make them understand, however, what he wanted, and managed to get it a minute after he landed from the cars.

It was Sunday, but the shops were all open, and newsboys were crying their papers upon the streets. Their announcements were very long, and Tibbitts stood and heard one of them clear through.

"Listen to the little villain," he exclaimed. "I don't believe a d—d word of it." And Mr. Tibbitts preached a short sermon anent the exaggerations common to newsboys, recounting the number of times he had been induced by their false representation to purchase papers in America. He considered himself too old to be taken in by a French newsboy. "Newsboys are the same in Rouen as in Oshkosh," he said.

After a light lunch in an arbor in a delicious garden back of a café, we started to see Rouen, its cathedral and the statue of Joan, and what else was to be seen. We urged Tibbitts to accompany us. He concluded to do it, though he protested it was far more pleasant to sit in that arbor, even though it was beastly wine he was drinking instead of the delicious whisky of Oshkosh, than it was tramping around in search of antiquities.

We came to a narrow street, one of the kind only to be seen in French cities. The entire space from wall to wall could not have been twelve feet, and on either hand were curious houses, seven stories high, entered by dark, narrow tunnels rather than passages, but with flowers at every window, clear to the queer, quaint top, which was continued after it had reached what should have been its summit. The professor stopped before one of these dark passages, and observed a parcel of illy dressed but marvelously clean children — there are no dirty children in France — playing some game.

"It is wonderful!" said the Professor, in an ecstacy; "here are we, of the new West, standing on ground in a street through which, may be, the soldiers of old France marched. Here are we within sight of the place where Joan of Arc was burned, on ground pressed by the feet of Charlemagne. In this house, perchance, were born heroes; within these walls for hundreds of years have been born children who have grown to manhood, and died. These children, playing in this gutter, were born in this historic city, and —— "

"And they all speak French," interrupted Tibbitts, "which I can't, but, thank Heaven, I can lay all over 'em in English. Look here, Professor, don't give us any more rot about this being old. We are just as old in Oshkosh as they are in Rouen. When the old Norman warriors were cruising about

loaded down with pot-metal, killing each other, the Indians of
America were doing the same thing among themselves, only
they were clothed more sensibly. A breech clout was a

THE BOYS OF ROUEN.

thundering sight more comfortable in the summer than steel
armor, and I do n't know that killing a man with a lance was
any more deserving of adoration than killing one with a bow
and arrow. The point to it all is killing the man. Antiquity!

What do you know about it? Here is a lot of stone that has been piled up a thousand years or more. How do you know but what the Indians are older than the Gauls? I hold that

ROUEN.

they are. The Gauls built a cathedral that is standing yet. I defy you to go anywhere in Wisconsin and find such a cathedral standing. What does that prove? Why! that the ancient Indians built their cathedrals so much farther back than the Gauls that they have all disappeared. Nothing can resist the iron tooth of time. Now I think that this cathedral is rather modern than otherwise. [By this time we were in front of the cathedral.] It is tolerably ancient, but if you want to visit a really old country, go to Wisconsin. That is so old that everything of this kind has disappeared entirely."

We left the cathedral, and after infinite trouble, owing to

the fact that the average citizen of Rouen is sadly deficient in English, found the statue of Joan of Arc. The Professor stood before it in an ecstatic mood; Tibbitts, profoundly disgusted.

THE PROFESSOR STOOD BEFORE IT IN AN ECSTATIC MOOD.

"Who was Joan of Arc, anyway?" said he. "A dreamy sort of a girl who thought she had a mission. There were no lecture courses in France in that day, and no lecture bureaus. Had there been such a vent for her inspiration she would have been an Anna Dickinson No. 1. She would have gone about France lecturing for anywhere from one hundred and fifty to three hundred and fifty dollars a night, and would have made a pile of money, and bought a place in fee simple for her father, and got a lot of money in bonds; that's what she would have done. But there were no such facilities for genius at that time, and so she put on armor, and led soldiers, and won victories, and finally was burned at the stake for a witch. I don't see anything special to craze over in Joan. I'm going back to the café and put in the time before the train leaves in literary pursuits. I'll write a letter to my mother. It's a thousand pities that we did n't go straight on to Paris, instead of stopping in this infernal old hole. We might have got there in time to go to the Mabille to-night. But it will be too late by the time we get there."

And Tibbitts left us and returned to the café and we went on. There is nothing in Rouen that is not interesting. Sunday as it was, the sidewalks in front of the numberless cafés were occupied with chairs, the white-aproned waiters flitting hither and thither, serving their customers with the light wines of the country; the market was in full blast, and business was going on the same as any other day. There is no Sunday in France, that is as Americans understand the day.

Due honor having been done to Joan of Arc, we entered a narrow, crooked thoroughfare, spanned by an old arch, built hundreds of years ago to mark the spot where a peasant named Rouen built the first house, erected

CATHEDRAL OF NOTRE DAME—ROUEN.

on the site that was destined to play such an important part in the subsequent history of the country.

The one great sight of Rouen, however, is the Cathedral of Notre Dame, which is one of the grandest Gothic edifices in Normandy. It dates back to 1207, and is a magnificent building. It is impossible to describe the grandeur of the structure, with its finely carved figures, its symmetrical proportions, its graceful spires and lofty towers. The interior is very fine, the high columns of white marble supporting the roof, which is formed of a succession of arches. Adjoining the high altar is the *Chapelle du Christ*, containing an ancient, mutilated figure in limestone of Richard Cœur

HOUSE OF JEAN D'ARC—ROUEN.

de Leon, discovered in 1838. His heart, which was interred in the choir, was found at the same time, and is now preserved in the museum.

St. Maclou and St. Ouen are two fine churches of the florid
Gothic style, the latter said to be one of the most beautiful in

HARBOR OF ROUEN.

existence. It was founded in 1318, and completed toward the
close of the fifteenth century.

Throughout the entire city the prevailing style of architecture is Gothic—the Palais de Justice being in late Gothic, and

is a very handsome building. The residences, for the most part, are large and beautiful, surrounded by well-kept lawns and adorned with flower beds and fountains.

Rouen is a very important cotton manufacturing place, and is one of the principal depots for the wines of Bordeaux. It is a commercial center, too, the Seine affording a good harbor for large ocean steamers, most of which are in the Mediterranean trade.

When we returned we found Tibbitts sitting in the arbor, with a pile of manuscript before him, and we asked what he had been doing.

"I promised the old gentleman," he said, "to learn the languages of the countries I passed through, and I shall do it. I shall learn French, some afternoon when I get time. And he requested me to practice writing things for general improvement. As I am in France I have written mother a letter, and I have enclosed in it a part of a chapter of a story, into which I have jerked a lot of French to show her that I have not wasted my time. Here it is, and I think it's devilish good!"

This was Tibbitts' part of a chapter of a story:—

"Precisely at the stroke of seven the Count was upon the ground, and the clock had not ceased to sound the hour before the Marquis appeared. Both threw off their outer clothing, and stood in their shirts, sword in hand."

"It's an account of a French Duel," explained Tibbitts.

"*Fromage!*" hissed the Count, between his clenched teeth.

"*Fromage Gratin!*" echoed the Marquis.

The swords crossed with an angry clang.

It was a supreme moment. The two men glared at each other, each fearing to hazard a movement. Finally, tired of inaction, the Count took the offensive. His rapier flashed like lightning. With an adroit *mouton*, he well nigh succeeded in breaking his enemy's guard, indeed he would have done it but for the skill with which a *marrons glacé* was interposed.

Both pause a moment for breath. Breath is necessary to a duelist. The Marquis was the first assailant. He delivered a fierce *cotellette de veau*, which had stretched many a tall fellow on the sod, followed by a *mayonnaise*, of which few are the master, but gnashed his teeth to find himself stopped by a *poulet a la Paris.* They paused again.

"I see you have advantaged by practice with Vol au Vent," said the Marquis. (Vol au Vent was the most celebrated swordsman of Paris.) "He taught you the lunge — I invented the parry. We will resume."

They eyed each other closely.

"This time I will finish him," said the Count to himself.

Using the *pomme de terre* as a feint, he threw himself with all his force into a *patè*, and would have ended the contest then

ST. OUEN — ROUEN.

and there, but that the Marquis avoided the thrust by a *poisson.*

"Ah! ha!" said the Marquis, "I have had other masters than Vol au Vent! Didst never hear of Vol au Vent's younger brother!"

"*A La Carte!*" hissed the Marquis.

"*Table D'Hote!*" was the determined reply, and again the swords crossed.

It was over in a moment. The Marquis, springing lightly back made a rapid advance. His rapier made a motion that was as quick as the stroke of a cobra. It was as fatal. A lightning-like *potage*, to which the Count opposed a *patisserie* in vain, and he fell to the ground lifeless, the thirsty sand drinking up his blood.

"*Haricot!*" said the Marquis, as he wiped his sword as cooly as though blood had never stained it, and walked deliberately away.

"In the name of all that's good what *is* all this about?" exclaimed the Professor. "Why, Tibbitts, all this French you have taken from this bill of fare here. *Pomme de Terre*, means simply potato, and *Poisson* is fish, *Mouton* is mutton, and *Fromage* is cheese. You are not going to send this to your mother?"

"Ain't I though! The good old girl don't read French, and this will do just as well as any I ever saw in anybody's novel. It shows that I have not neglected my opportunities. Send it? You bet!"

And he did fold it, and put it into an envelope, and after several frantic endeavors he made the boy understand that he wanted a postage stamp, and in the box it went.

And now that I come to think of it, I am not sure but that Tibbitts was right. If French phrases must be used in English writing, why not take them from a bill of fare? So far as the general public goes they would do just as well. I have no doubt but his French will pass muster, twelve miles back of Oshkosh.

Leaving Rouen with its rich mediæval architecture, its quaint streets and lovely parks, we cross the Seine and are whirling along at a rapid rate towards Paris, the center of the gay world. As we approach the metropolis several beautiful cities are passed, the principal one being Poissy, a town of fifty thousand inhabitants, which was the birth place of St. Louis, who frequently styled himself "Louis de Poissy."

At Asnieres, the Seine is crossed for the last time, and in a few minutes Cluney is reached, and away over to the right may be seen the tomb of Napoleon, its gilt dome sparkling in the sunlight. Here we pass the fortifications and in another brief interval are in the station at Rue St. Lazarre, and before us with all its beauty is Paris.

In Paris the first American I met was Bloss, my circus friend. He had succeeded in getting his "wonder" in Germany, and in Switzerland he had purchased two bears, which he had with him.

THE SHOWMAN IN PARIS.

"They are probably the greatest wonders of the nineteenth century," he remarked. "Garsong, two cognacs, lo. I am pretty well up in French. I hev got so sence I hev bin here that I kin order my drinks without any trouble, and that's the main pint. Them bears are something inscrutable. They kin waltz on their hind legs; they kin fire pistols, and will work in splendid with my Injuns. But what is more wonderful, they kin ride a horse, ef the pad is made big enuff. And that's where I'm goin' to fetch the public. To yootilize bears I'm goin' to present a grand scriptooral spectacle. The public want moral amoosement, and the public is goin' to hev it now till they can't rest. Them bears is what is goin' to do it. I shel present the unparalleled spectacle uv Elijah and the bears eatin the children, all on hosses. Come to think of it, wuz it Elijah, or Elisha? I've forgotten, and must read it up afore I git it on the bills. When yoo hev a scriptooral spectacle yoo want be very akerit on the bills.

"It will be the gorgusest thing ever seen. Elijah — Foggarty kin ride well enough to do Elijah, and I got a dozen kids in the company, mostly tumblin', wich will anser for the children. Elijah, perfectly bald-headed, will ride in on a black hoss to slow moosic, a sort uv Scriptural waltz ez it were. The kids will ride in on spotted ponies and shout, all in chorus, "Go up bald head!" Then the two bears — they ain't she bears, but that's no difference — will come in on white hosses, and chase the children. Then the band will play furious moosic, jist ez they do at the finish of a tumblin act, and the bears will each snatch a kid off his pony by the belt and ride out.

"But the children were eaten by the bears?"

"Cert. But suthin must be left to the imagginashen. Realism is all well enough, but it kin be carried too fur. The children will all rush out and the eatin will be supposed to have taken place outside. I can't afford to feed them bears on children every afternoon and evenin'. It would draw, no doubt, but I couldn't afford sich a luxury. But the spectacle will

BLOSS' GREAT MORAL EQUESTRIAN SPECTACLE.

draw. It will fetch the religious people. They disapprove of the circus, as a rool, but they will all come to see a great moral lesson, illustrated. To see this great moral lesson, they will come early so as to get good seats, and when it is over they won't go till the show is out. To accommodate their prejoo-disses and give 'em the hull show I shel hev it put on the last thing, for once in they won't leave till they see the moral spectacle. To see this they'll shock theirselves with Madem-oiselle Blanche on the tight rope, in tights. You've got to have a moral show, and these bears will lay over anything on

16

the road, becoz it's not only moral, but it's actilly scriptooral. I'm after a lot uv attracshens here. There's a sword swallerer

that I think I kin git, and I know uv a lot uv the loveliest anacondas that ever went under a canvas."

The old gentleman by this time had consumed a half dozen brandies and water, and was becoming incoherent. The waiter knew him so well that whenever his glass was empty he filled it without orders, all of which he approved, as it saved wrenching himself with French. "Bong Garsong," he remarked as he went off into a doze.

TOWER OF ST. PIERRE—CAEN.

OLD HOUSES—ROUEN.

CHAPTER XVII.

WHEN an enlightened public sentiment drove the pirates from the high seas, and compelled them to seek other methods of supplying themselves with means for the enjoyment of luxury, I am convinced that every one of them came to Europe, and went into the hotel business. A few of them might have got hotels in America, but the vast majority came here. I did come across one at the Gorge de Triente, in Switzerland, who might not have been a pirate, or, if he was, he was either a mild one, or, being now very old, is endeavoring to patch up his old body for heaven. I am inclined to the belief that he was a pirate, but not of the sentimental order who shed human gore for the love of it; that when his schooner, the "Mary Jane," captured a prize, he only killed such of her crew as were necessary, in the action, and after the vessel had surrendered he did not make the survivors walk the plank for the amusement of his men, but mercifully set them adrift in an open boat, without water or provisions. That's the kind of pirate he was. And since he has been a landlord, he does not take every dollar you have — he leaves you enough to get to the next bank, where your letter of credit is available. I shall always remember this landlord. He is an ornament to his sex.

But the first hotel we encountered in Paris had for a landlord one who must have commanded the long, low, black schooner, "The Terror of the Seas," who never spared a prisoner, or gave quarter to anybody, but who hove overboard for the sharks every human being he captured, without reference to age, sex, or previous condition of servitude. Indeed, I think that after he was driven from the seas, he took a shy at

(243)

highway robbery before taking his hotel in Paris, thus fitting himself thoroughly for his profession.

" Ze room will be ten francs, messieurs," was the remark of the polite villain who showed us our apartments.

" *We, we*," we cheerfully replied, for the room was worth it. We said "*we, we*," that the gentleman might know that we understood French, and that he need not unnecessarily strand himself upon the rocks of the English language.

But the next morning! The bill was made out, and as we glanced at it we forgave the English landlords — every one of them. Apartment ten francs, candles, or "bougies," as the barbarous French call them, two and one-half francs; attendance (we had not seen a servant), two and a half francs each, five francs. Then there were charges for liquors enough for Bloss, the American showman, not a particle of which had been ordered or had been brought to our room, and so on.

We expostulated, but when we commenced that, the clerk began to talk in French, and as all the French we had between us was "*we, we*," he had rather the advantage. In reply to some question he appeared to be asking, we said, "*we, we*," whereupon he dropped back into English promptly, and said that inasmuch as we admitted that the bill was right, why did n't we pay it? That "*we, we*" was our ruin.

> " A little knowledge is a dangerous thing;
> Drink deep or taste not the Pierian spring."

Were we over with it? By no means. As we were ready to file down the stairs there came to our various rooms more porters than we ever supposed lived, each of whom seized a piece of baggage, when one might well have carried it all. We discovered, finally, what that meant. Those who did not carry baggage stood grinning in the passages, with their hands extended, and those who did expected each a franc. As we had passed the concierge, who had certainly been no earthly use to us, his hand was extended, and to crown the whole and have it lack nothing, a chambermaid came running to me with a handkerchief which " Monsieur had left in his room," and out went her hand. The brazen hussy had abstracted it from my valise, and held it till the last moment, that she might have some excuse for a gratuity.

Tibbitts and the others shed silver freely, but the Professor did not. Entrenched behind his spectacles he did not catch the eye of one of them, and he stalked majestically through the lot, turning neither to the right nor the left till he was safely ensconced in his fiacre. That pair of spectacles saved him at least their cost that day. I shall wear them hereafter.

THE PROFESSOR'S SPECTACLES.

They are good for this purpose, and then one behind this wall of glass can look another man in the eye steadily when he is enlarging on facts. Spectacles have uses beside aiding the vision.

We paid everybody and everything, and departed sadly. No matter how joyously you enter a French hotel, you walk out to the music, mentally, of the Dead March in Saul. But what are you going to do about it? You cannot sleep in the streets, and you must eat, and the pirates have you in an iron grip, and they realize the strength and impregnability of their position.

Paris is another octopus, differing from London only in the quality and style of its feelers. London has been built up by main strength, that being its characteristic. Paris has as many feelers as London, and they are perhaps as strong and far-reaching; but they are wrapped in velvet. It is a rather pleasant thing to be devoured by the French octopus. He does not rend you limb from limb, like the English one, but he holds you just as firmly, and sucks your life blood in so delightful a way, that you rather like the operation.

Paris is the city of luxury. No matter where you go, nor among what class of people, you see but two things — a vast population catering to sensualism, and another vast population paying the price for it.

The difference between London and Paris is shown even in its proprietary medicines. In London the walls groan, or

would if they could, under announcements of liver medicines; in Paris the walls of corresponding conspicuousness are covered with advertisements of articles for the hair and complexion. A French woman will get on with almost any kind of a liver, but she must have hair to her heels, and a complexion that is faultless. No matter what kind of underclothing she has on, or no matter if she hasn't any, the outside must be dressed in elegance and taste. Paris lives largely for the eye.

OLD PARIS.

The city is made up of two distinct parts — the old and new. Old Paris, the Paris of Sue, and Dumas, and Victor Hugo, still exists, and its people are precisely the same as when these authors wrote of them. You leave the most splendid streets in the world, wide, and paved like floors, with enormous rows of palatial structures on either hand, as modern as modern can be, and in fifteen minutes you are in narrow, crooked alleys, with the quaint old houses on either hand, six and seven stories in height, with all sorts of gables, all sorts of deformities in the matter of walls; with the quaintest and most curious passages, and paved with the boulders which the Parisian of twenty or thirty years since found so useful in constructing barricades when they had their regular monthly revolution. And you see the same men and women who fought behind these barricades, and who will do it again — the wine shop politicians, who believe in "liberty, fraternity and equality" to-day, and accept an empire to-morrow for a change. A Parisian cannot endure monotony, even in a government.

Possibly he accepts imperialism, now and then, just for the pleasure of overturning it.

"LIBERTY, FRATERNITY, EQUALITY."

But the new Paris is quite another thing. All Paris was, not many years ago, like the portions of the Latin Quarter

and the Faubourg St. Antoine, but the Third Napoleon
intended to be Emperor all his life, and these crooked streets
were not good for Imperial artillery, and the pavements were
easily torn up for barricades. So he called to himself Baron
Haussman, the prefect of the Seine, and said, "We will recon-
struct Paris." The Baron, thoroughly devoted to the Emperor,
and himself, called about him the best talent in the world, and
the work was begun.

But be it understood that the Baron and the Emperor did
not go about this work carelessly. The Baron, whose ances-

NEW PARIS—BOULEVARD DES ITALIENS.

tors were Israelites, had all the thrift of that remarkable race,
and Napoleon was not much behind him. Whenever they
decided upon tearing down the whole quarter and a score of
crooked streets, and constructing a boulevard wider than the
widest street in New York, they had an agent who, before the
design was made public, went and purchased the entire property at the market rate. Then came the necessary legal steps
for the condemnation of the property, and the payment there-

for by the city. The new owner was allowed twenty or thirty times for it above what he paid, and vast sums were by this simple process turned into the Emperor's private exchequer and added to the already vast estate of the astute Baron.

The Emperor used his share of the plunder in amusing the Parisians, but the Baron's share is still in his family.

There are Tweeds in every country, but these were greater than our great peculator. The Emperor Napoleon and Baron Haussman were just as much greater than Tweed as France is greater than the single city of New York. But then their opportunities were greater. Had Tweed had a chance he might have risen to the front rank.

It is perhaps as well for Paris that it had an Emperor, and possibly it would have been better for the United States had she had a King in her earlier days. For a republic will never do toward the beautifying a city or country what an Emperor will. I helped to elect a member of Congress once, who, finding that a single door in the Capitol at Washington cost twenty thousand dollars, exclaimed against the extravagance of the country. "Why," said he, "a good two inch pine plank door, painted white, with three coats of paint, can be had in Upper Sandusky for eight dollars, and it would do just as well as this infernal bronze thing covered all over with figures."

Had Paris been governed by a Congress, the honorable gentlemen from Normandy, and Savoy, and other out-lying districts, would never have paid for the wonderfully beautiful boulevards that make Paris the most beautiful city in the world. The old alleys were good enough for their fathers, and why not for the present generation?

But the will of a single man did it, and the memory of that man is still worshiped in Paris. Dead though he be, he wields power in Paris to-day, and had not his son been so reckless in Africa, the chances are a hundred to one that he would to-day be occupying his father's throne.

New Paris is made up of beautiful wide boulevards, some of them two hundred feet wide, with sidewalks at least thirty feet wide on either side, and lined with shops and cafés, the shops devoted almost entirely to the sale of articles of luxury.

The cafés are very peculiar. Paris lives, as much as possi-

ble, out of doors, for Paris desires to see and be seen. Therefore, in front of every café, under tasteful awnings, are chairs
and little white sheet iron tables; there sits Paris, drinking its
drinks and eating its light repasts, from early morning till very
late at night.

To an American it is a most peculiar sight. No matter
where you go, in old Paris or new, it is the same, except in the
grade of the people. In old Paris you see blue blouses and calico dresses at these tables, and in new Paris broadcloth and silk, but the tables are there on the sidewalk, and the people sitting by them, the same in one as in the other, and very jolly they are.

Paris is the most temperate city on

THE LOUVRE FROM THE RUE DE RIVOLI.

the globe. There is as great a quantity of liquids consumed
as in London, and perhaps more, but it is a different kind.
The Frenchman drinks the light wines of the country, or
curious compounds of stuff that are as innocent as milk, so
far as intoxication goes. He has syrups something like those
the American druggist uses in his alleged soda water, and he
either mixes that with pure water and makes his heart glad,

or, if he is particular about it, he mixes it with Seltzer water from the gushing syphon. There are vast varieties of these syrups, but they are all alike except in the matter of flavor.

Occasionally one rushes to the extreme of dissipation and stupefies himself with German lager beer, but as a rule it is either wine or these syrups.

Of course there are French drunkards. The brain-annihilating absinthe obtains here, and a seductive fluid it is. It is the most innocent tasting stuff in the world, and does not affect one immediately. And so the ignorant stranger, on his first introduction to it, takes dose after dose of it, and goes home wondering why people are so mortally in dread of absinthe. In the still watches of the night he becomes convinced that he has been taking something, and the next morning he, or his friends, are entirely sure of it. For in the morning he is drunk, drunk clear through, and he generally manages to stay so for some days. Tibbitts, whose experience I am relating, said it was much cheaper than Oshkosh whisky, for one night's sitting at absinthe lasted him a week. There is a vast quantity of absinthe consumed in Paris, but it is done quietly and in great moderation. An American or foreigner who likes it drinks it immoderately, and pays the penalty of his folly. The Frenchman knows exactly how much is safe for him, and very rarely exceeds his limit.

I have seen but one drunken man in Paris, and he was either an Englishman, or an American who had been long enough in London to get spoiled. He spoke English, and from the style of his clothes I should take him for an Englishman, but there was an especial wobble in his step that proclaimed the American. I have seen the same a great many times in my beloved country.

Drunkenness is impossible on these innocent liquids. The wine of the country is consumed everywhere and in large quantities, and its use by all ages and sexes is unrestricted.

It is on every table for breakfast and dinner, and is everywhere the substitute for tea and coffee. Containing as it does a very small proportion of alcohol, and as that is diluted fully a half with water, it cannot be a very dangerous beverage. At all events, the French — men, women, and children, — drink it in great quantities at all hours, and intoxication does not ensue. Outdoor sitting is made possible by the harmlessness of

GLACES
ET
SORBETS.

A BOULEVARD CAFÉ—OUTSIDE.

their accustomed drinks. The climate of New York is well adapted to this sort of thing, but were Broadway lined with these cafés, with the public sitting at the small tables, how long would it be before a gang of ruffians, filled with the frightful whisky of the country, would swoop down upon them and scatter tables and people. A gang from the Bowery, filled with the fighting whisky of America, or the soul-searing brandy of the British land, turned loose upon the Boulevard des Italiens, or any other boulevard in Paris, would occasion as much terror

A COSTUME BY WORTH — THAT COSTS.

as a Communist insurrection. But with the light wines of France, and the quiet pleasure-seeking and pleasure-enjoying disposition of the Parisian, everything is as quiet and orderly as could be desired.

There cannot be in city life any sight so bewilderingly gor-

geous or so delightful as the boulevards, either by day or night.
The streets are lined with beautiful trees, and then the shops
and cafés are exquisitely beautiful, as are their contents.   As I
said, the shops are almost entirely devoted to the sale of articles
of luxury, for the Frenchman, acute being that he is, discovered
thousands of years ago, that a profit of five hundred per cent.
may be made upon articles of fancy; while the dealer in things
essential, which may not be dispensed with — articles of prime
necessity — obtains a beggarly ten or twenty.   He learned centuries since that Madame will pay any price for a hat that
pleases her taste, and do it without question, while she will

A MAGAZINE ON THE BOULEVARD.

haggle an hour over the price of twenty pounds of sugar or a
cut of beef.   He who deals in necessities must find his reward
in the consciousness of honesty.   His customers will not let
him be anything else.

You shall see shop windows filled with jewels that might
well hang about the neck of royalty — indeed, so costly that
only he or she who has an empire to tax can afford them —
shops devoted to the sale of pipes, the price of which, some of
them, go up into thousands of francs; galleries of pictures,
magazines of bronzes, and all kinds and descriptions of statu-

ary, and the thousands upon thousands of costly nothings with which rich people adorn their homes. Artistic paper hangings ornamental work in leathers, and every other material; shops for the sale of everything that is ornamental in women's wear, and, in a word, everything that delights the eye, but which humanity, but for its vanity and longing for the beautiful, could do without as well as not.

And an enormous trade these caterers to the non-useful carry on. The whole world comes to Paris for these things, and they bring their money with them for this purpose and expect to spend it.

Woe to the American man or woman, who ventures into these shops. The shopman knows the moment he enters that the coming victim who is rushing upon his doom is an American; he knows that he has so much money to leave with him, and no matter how much knowledge he affects, that he is as ignorant of the real value of his wares as a babe unborn.

What should the citizen of Terre Haute, Ind., know of the value of bronzes? Nothing, whatever. But he has just made a good speculation in pork, and he has built him a two-story house, with a Mansard roof on it, and has furnished it gorgeously with upholstered chairs, and on his floors he has laid Brussels carpets, and his wife and he are taking their first visit "abroad." Mrs. Thompson is determined to astonish her female friends and excite their envy with some "statoos" from "Paree," and she is going to do it. The pair look critically through the assortment. They object to the Venus of Milo, because the arms are lacking, and are surprised that an imperfect sort of second-hand work of art of that kind can't be had at a reduced price. The price of a picture takes their breath away, and Mr. Thompson suggests that a few pairs of chromos can be had a great deal cheaper, and he thinks they will make a better show than the paintings that are shown them. Perhaps he is right, when the paintings that are shown him are critically considered. But Mrs. T. will have none of the chromo business. She will have some works of art from "Paree," and Mr. T., fired with ambition, assents, and the "works of art" are bought and paid for at anywhere from four to ten times their value, and they retire with them grieved and yet satisfied — grieved at the hole the purchase has made in their pocket-book, and satisfied to think what a sensation the purchase will make when they are displayed in their home in the West. Thompson anticipates the pleasure of calling the attention of his guests to these wonders, and remarking casually, as though he were a regular patron of art, "Oh, them! They are a few little things I bought in Paree, the last time I was over. They are nothing. I only paid four thousand francs for the pair. I shall buy more when I go over again. I really hadn't time to look around."

And then Mrs. T. must have a Parisian watch, and some jewelry, and the dealer sells them to her at a very large advance over what a Parisian would pay, and when they are gone, loaded with their absurd purchases, he falls upon his knees and prays for good crops in America, and a more plentiful rush of visitors. They are his wheat fields.

MR. THOMPSON'S ART PURCHASES.

The difference between the English and French is admirably illustrated by two incidents somewhat similar in nature. It was our fortune to be in London on the occasion of the celebration of the Queen's birthday, a time that is always made a general holiday by all classes. Business was suspended, and every one gave himself up to pleasure — the kind of amusement that the Londoner considers pleasure. The bands were out, the military paraded, and all the parks were filled with people in holiday attire.

As the afternoon wore on it became apparent that there was some agency at work aside from devotion to royalty. There was a boisterousness that savored of strong beer and still stronger gin. The crowd of men and women who thronged the Strand and Regent.street, and Piccadilly, laughed and shouted, not with the merry ring of pure pleasure, but with the maudlin utterances of semi-drunkenness.

In the evening there was a grand illumination of the government buildings, the clubs and the prominent business houses. The streets were thronged with people — men, women, and children — all elbowing their way along, eager to see all that was to be seen, and willing to give no one an opportunity they themselves could not enjoy. It was a motley crowd, composed of all classes. The well-dressed shopman was jostled by the rag-picker; and ragged, homeless girls, arm in arm, shoved aside the elderly matron, who had come out with her children to see the illuminations. There were all classes and conditions of people, and they raved and tore about more like escaped lunatics than the staid, sober Britons they pride themselves upon being.

A walk down Pall Mall was almost worth one's life. On this thoroughfare are located the principal clubs of London, and as they were rather brilliantly lighted with gas jets arranged in fanciful designs, the crowd flocked there to see them. The street was actually packed from curb to curb, so that locomotion was difficult. The illuminations were not on a scale grand enough to merit all this outpouring of people, this great hub-bub, this drunkenness and gin-incited hilarity. For the most part the designs were simply the English coat of arms, with the letters " V. R." on each side, the whole being done in plain gas jets. Occasionally some thriving shop-keeper, who had made a little something from the Royal family, would branch out a little more extensively, and use tiny glass shades of different colors, over his gas. But it was dreary beyond measure. The streets were dark and gloomy, the air was close, and the so-called illuminations were so very, very meager that they made the general effect only more dismal.

Yet the people surged up and down the streets, hurrahing and shouting for the Queen, for the Prince of Wales, for the

17

Royal family, for themselves, for anybody they could think of. The public houses were open long after other places of business were closed, and there was a constant stream of thirsty people gliding from behind the half-closed doors out upon the street to yell until another dram became necessary. The customers were not limited to the sterner sex by any manner of means. There were crowds of young girls ranging from fourteen to twenty, poor working girls, who had saved all of their scant earnings they could in anticipation of this holiday, who boldly pushed their way with a coarse laugh, through the crowd of men and, standing at the bar, would call for and drink their bitter beer, or ale, or stout, or gin, even, with all the effrontery of an old toper. And old women there were too, who would quietly glide into the compartments marked "private bar," and there drink their brandy or Irish whisky. Throughout it all there seemed to be a dogged determination to become intoxicated, just as though there could be no pleasure, the Queen's birthday could not be celebrated properly, unless every one filled himself up with ardent spirits.

As it grew later, the crowds increased both in size and disorder. Notwithstanding the fact that most of the illuminations had been extinguished, the masses had had a taste, and they wanted more. They became momentarily ruder and more boisterous. As the time approached for the closing of the publics, the crowd received fresh installments of the worse class of women, and then drunken women tried to do worse than the drunken men, and they succeeded. A woman thoroughly under the influence of liquor is something simply terrible to see, and here we saw it. On that night the air rang with their ribald jokes and coarse songs, as they jostled each other in their unsteady walk.

This, it must be remembered, is not a scene that occurred down in Cheapside, or in the Seven Dials, or the streets down near the river. No, indeed. Pall Mall, one of the most aristocratic streets in London, Regent street, the Broadway of London, Piccadilly, the Haymarket, these were the scenes of this frightful display, and evidently nothing was thought of it. The police made no arrests, and did not seem to know that there was anything occurring that was not perfectly allowable and justifiable. So the wild debauch went on all night, and it was not until the gray light made its appearance in the east that the city quieted down and the streets no longer echoed with the maudlin cries of the host of people who celebrated

THE AMERICAN PARTY OUTSIDE A CAFÉ ON THE BOULEVARD.

in their own peculiar style the anniversary of their Queen's birthday.

How entirely different was the grand National fête of France on the 14th of July. This, too, is made a day for general rejoicing and merry-making, and the French people get out of it all that is to be had. For days before, active preparations for the event are made, flags and streamers of the colored bunting are put up all over the city, elaborate designs in gas jets are prepared; fountains erected; electric lights put up; in a word, everything is done that can in the slightest way add to the brilliancy of the beautiful city, whose white buildings make it bright and cheerful at all times.

On the night of the 13th it was apparent that something was about to occur, for the streets, the broad, brilliantly lighted boulevards, were crowded with people, all of them full of life and animation. The great stores, with their glass fronts, were literally ablaze with lights; the gaily decorated cafés with their inviting tables on the broad sidewalks, were filled with people sipping wine, or coffee, and discussing with the animation and vivacity that a Frenchman only possesses, the attractions of the morrow. All along the principal boulevards electric lights were suspended high in the air, while in the Place de Concorde, and out the Champs Elysées, were thousands of brilliant clusters of gas jets, making the night seem day. The crowds swayed hither and thither with one impulse, to see everything, yet there was no departure from decorum. Everybody was happy. But it was the happiness that comes of a sense of pleasure, from bright and beautiful surroundings, and the knowledge that every one else is happy. There was no sign of drunkenness; there was no rowdyism; there was nothing suggestive even of offensiveness. Everybody was gay and merry. There were songs and hearty peals of laughter, but it was pure and wholesome, something that one could participate in with all his heart.

The morning of the 14th dawned with a bright, clear sky, and the sun came up with a serenity that augured well for the fête. During the night, while all Paris slept, busy workmen put the finishing touches on the decorations, and when all business suspended, Paris turned out to see itself, there was a general murmur of approval at the beautiful sights displayed everywhere. The houses along the streets were almost hidden by flags and banners and streamers; the statues were decorated; high staffs that were not visible the day before, now floated long streamers; the parks and gardens were in holiday attire. Paris was arrayed in gorgeous dress, and every one went in for a day of rare pleasure.

At all the theaters, including the Grand Opera, free performances were given during the afternoon, and there were all sorts of entertainments provided by the government for the amusement of the populace. In various quarters of the city

THE AVENUE DE L' OPÉRA.
From the Loggia of the Opera House.

platforms were erected, and all during that warm afternoon the working classes danced to the music of superb orchestras, which were furnished to them without money and without cost.

But when evening came the fête was seen to its best advantage. As it grew dark the whole city blazed with light. There were millions of lanterns of every possible color, hanging from every point that could hold a support. Electric lights flashed from every corner, and gas jets blazed everywhere. The Boulevard des Italiens, from the Madelaine to the Bastille, was as light as though a noonday sun were pouring down upon it. And so with the other large thoroughfares, while the different *quartiers* had illuminations of their own, each of which was wonderfully brilliant.

The one particular place that eclipsed all others was the two mile stretch from the Tuileries to the Arch of Triumph, and then on to the Bois de Boulogne. The straight promenade through the Tuileries garden was lined on either side with a high trestle work, literally covered with fanciful designs wrought in gas, while high arches of brilliant flame intersected it at regular intervals.

The Place de Concorde was a marvel of beauty. All around the immense square were hung festoons of gas jets, while all the statues of the different cities of France that

CAFÉ CONCERTS — CHAMPS ELYSÉES.

ornament each corner, were thrown into bold relief by brilliant lights on the limpid water of the fountain in the center; different colored lights were thrown during the evening, the effect being wondrously beautiful.

Standing in the center of the place, and looking towards the arch, the sight was simply marvelous. Nowhere in the world but in Paris could such a thing be seen. The broad avenue, Champs Elysées, rising with a gentle slope, was lined its whole distance on both sides with a stream of light, that drooped gracefully from cluster to cluster, all the way out, as far as the eye could reach. Then the concert cafés which abound on either side, made unusual displays, swinging lines of light from tree to tree and café to café, till the effect was dazzling, and one really had to stop to realize that he was here on earth and not in some fairy land.

The Bois de Boulogne, always beautiful, with its charming lakes, long winding drives, its parks, tiny brooks and pictur-esque café, was unusually brilliant that night. On the shores of the lake large set pieces of fire works were diplayed, while bands of music in odd looking gondolas blazing with colored fires, furnished exquisite music. The paths and carriage-ways were lined with small set pieces, which, together with the con-stantly burning colored fires, produced an effect that was grandly weird. All Paris was one blaze of light. And all night long the people of Paris and all France were on the streets enjoying the rare sight. After nine o'clock carriages were compelled to keep off the principal boulevards and streets, so densely were they packed with people. The Champs Elysées from ten o'clock was one surging mass of people — men, women and children — returning from the Bois. From curb to curb was one solid mass of humanity, and such a jolly good-natured crowd was never seen before. They sang patriotic songs, and laughed and joked, and had a good time generally. Now and then there would come down the street a small procession of students, wearing grotesque caps, each student bearing a Chi-nese lantern. They sang funny songs, and chaffed those that passed. But there was not a single display of temper. Every-body took everything in good part, and every one was super-latively happy.

During all that long day and still longer night, not a single case of drunkenness did I see, and during that time I was in a great many different places, and would have seen it had there been any. There was fun and frolic on every side. But it was the overflow of exuberant spirits, and not the outgrowth of too much wine and beer and liquor. In no city in England, nor, I am afraid, in America, could there be so gigantic a celebration, so much fun and hilarity, with so little drunkenness and so few disturbances. Verily, the French, insincere and superficial as

they are, know how to get the most enjoyment out of life.
They have all the fun the Anglo-Saxon has, without the subsequent horror.

Foreign travel is of a vast amount of use to a great many
people. Coming from Dieppe to Paris there were seated in our
compartment two ladies with their husbands, who were in
New York, bankers, one regular and the other faro, and both
with loads of money. The wife of the faro banker was
arrayed in the most gorgeous and fearfully expensive apparel,
with a No. 6 foot in a No. 4 shoe. The other lady *was* a lady,
and she really desired to see something of the country she was
traveling through. The faro bankeress talked to her from
Dieppe to St. Lazarre station, and this was about what she
said:—

"You never saw anything so perfectly lovely as the children's ball last year at the Academy of Music. My little girl,
Lulu, you saw her at the school — she goes to the same school
with your Minnie, only Lulu isn't studying anything but
French and geography now. I want her to get to be perfect
in French, because it will be such a comfort to travel with her,
and see things, and not be entirely dependent upon your
maid — we have a maid with us, but, of course, we have her
travel third-class — not for the difference in the expense, for
we don't have to economize — but you know it won't do to
have your servants too close to you; they get to presuming
upon their privileges, and you must make them know their
place. Oh, how I wish we had a monarchy or something of
the kind in America, so that we could be divided up into
classes, and not be compelled to mix with the lower orders."

[I may as well remark here that this fine lady was originally a McFadden; that she came to America in the steerage,
and was a chambermaid in a boarding-house, where she first
met her husband, who was a brisk young bar-tender, who
finally got a bar of his own, which gradually blossomed into
a faro bank. The maid was a thoroughly educated and refined
young lady, who was compelled by poverty to take a position
of this kind.]

"Well, Monsieur Bigwig, the dancing teacher, you know
of him. He was a Russian or a Prussian, or one of them

people. Why, he has taught the children of all the kings in Europe — the little princesses; but he came to America and has three schools in New York and one in Brooklyn, and he is perfectly splendid. Dodworth isn't nothing beside him for giving dancing lessons. Monsieur was a great friend of Lulu's, and showed her a great deal of attention, and paid her a great many compliments. When a new pupil came in he used to take Lulu and dance with her to show the new one the step, Lulu danced so prettily, and was altogether too sweet for anything. And at his ball he had one tableau of four little girls representing Spring, Autumn, Summer, and Winter, and he came to my house and gave me the choice of characters for dear Lulu. I remember he came to the house to do it, because he took dinner with us that day, and my husband lent him fifty dollars. Well, I selected ' Winter' for Lulu, for I could dress her warmer in that character than in any of the others, and the dear child is delicate; she is so spirituelle, and I had for her a costume which was altogether too sweet for anything. She had on a dress —"

" Oh heavens! do look at that beautiful valley," exclaimed the unwilling listener.

There was a valley spread out before us, so entirely perfect in its soft loveliness that it was worth a voyage across the Atlantic to see it. The faro bankeress glanced out of the window, and with the remark, " It's altogether too lovely for anything," went on without a moment's pause :—

" I had a dress made of a white material that represented ice, with little balls of white down to represent snow balls all over it, and furs, the edges trimmed with down, and a little crown upon her head, with points like icicles, and the same things tacked onto the bottom of her outer skirt, and her hair powdered so as to be like snow, and she was the Ice Queen, and had a retinoo of ice men, twelve little boys with ice axes, and she was drawn in on a sled by two boys dressed like reindeers, and in front of the reindeers was two little boys dressed like bears, and it was altogether too sweet for anything. I don't know how the other little girls were dressed, but everybody looked at Lulu; and then, after they four had made the circuit of the Academy (it was all floored over), they formed in the center and danced a dance which Monsieur had arranged for them, and Lulu danced too sweet for anything. Everybody said to me that she was the sweetest little girl in the ball. Where did you get that lace? I got some in Paris last year; we go abroad every year; we are tired of Saratoga;

we have been going there so long that it is an old story, and then you have to meet all sorts of people there, and I don't like it. I don't suppose it is just right, but I do wish we could have a monarchy, so that the better classes could be

THE FARO BANKERESS ADMIRING THE VILLAGE.

more select. That lace was altogether the sweetest thing I ever saw, and it cost less than half it would in New York, and then—"

"What a delightful village this is, and how quaint! Do look at it!" This from the actual lady.

There was the same quick sweep of the head by the lady of laces, with the regular remark: "Yes; it's altogether too sweet for anything," and she resumed:—

"Now when we get to Paris I do so want you to go with me. I can show you where you can get laces and everything for half you pay in New York. And hosiery! Well now. I always buy five dozen pairs of silk stockings in Paris. And gloves! You can get kid gloves in Paris for almost nothing, and all you have to do not to pay duties is to put them on once and swear they have been worn. I always spend my last day in Paris putting on and off gloves. And children's clothes! Let me see; you have a little boy, and so have I. Is yours in pants yet, or is he in kilts? Mine is in pants, but I

hated to take him out of kilts; he was altogether too sweet
for anything in them. With a broad white collar, and lace
about his wrists, and little black shoes, and red stockings, with
a Highland cap and feather in it, just like a Highland chieftain
and —"

At this point the train stopped at a station, and our party
got into another compartment. I pitied the lady who had to
stay, but self-preservation is the first law of nature. I should
not like to be with her on a steamboat, where escape would be
impossible. Travel does her a power of good. But heavens!
how many like her are strewing their gabble all over the continent!

CHAPTER XVIII.

PARIS covers an area of thirty square miles, has five hundred and thirty miles of public streets, and has a resident population of nearly two millions, all engaged in trading in articles of luxury for the rest of the world. It supports about one hundred and fifteen thousand paupers. Its religion is a very mild form of Catholicism tinged with infidelity, or infidelity flavored with Catholicism, as you choose. Which flavor predominates in the average Parisian I have not been able to determine. I should say Catholicism Sunday forenoon, and infidelity the remainder of the week. At all events, the cafés are always crowded, while the churches never are, except by strangers, who go religiously and devoutly thither — to see the buildings and the decorations. The Parisian generally puts off going to church till next Sunday, and goes this Sunday to the country instead. One-fourth of the births are illegitimate, which is doing very well for Paris.

The city consumes annually eighty-six millions gallons of wine, and three millions five hundred thousand gallons of spirits; the latter going very largely into the seasoned stomachs of foreigners, the French themselves being altogether too acute to use anything of the kind. However, they are very willing to sell it, and welcome the Englishman or American with hospitable hands to drunkards' graves — if they have the money to pay for it — with great politeness and suavity.

I have not yet been in any country which did not extend a hearty welcome to any stranger with money.

About ninety-five millions of gallons of water per day

come from the water-works, which is mostly used in keeping the streets clean. I have not yet seen a Frenchman who ever used any as a beverage or on his person. For economy he

PARISIAN BREAD CARRIER.

mixes some of it with his wine, and his ablutions may require a pint or such matter a day, but that is all the use he has for water.

The very first thing that strikes an American in Paris with

astonishment is the meagreness of the water supply in the houses. You look for the faucets which supply your room with hot and cold water, as at home, but you don't find them. A chambermaid pours out about two quarts in a diminutive pitcher, and that is expected to last you for purposes of ablution twenty-four hours. And this with the Seine running directly through the center of the city. The houses are from five to seven stories high, but all the water used in them, for all purposes, is carted up to the top by men. My landlord told me it was cheaper to have it so carried than to put plumbing in his house, and pay the water-tax, "and we don't use much of it, anyway," he remarked, and he was right. Still, accustomed as I have always been to the use of a great deal of it, it took me some time to fall into their ways. Pure water is a very good thing to have plenty of, but it's all a matter of habit, I suppose. A man can get to be a Frenchman, in time, if he tries hard enough. Nothing is impossible, where there's a will and a stubborn purpose. But to keep oneself clean with a pint, or thereabouts, of water per day looks rather difficult to a novice.

John Leech was very fond of illustrating this peculiarity of the French people, in *Punch*, years ago. When the first English Exposition was in progress in London, the city was overrun with French. One picture he made was of two elegantly dressed young Frenchmen, standing in front of an ordinary wash-stand, on which was the usual pitcher, wash-bowl, soap-dish, etc., and underneath was this conversation:—

Alphonse — What is this?

Henri — I do not know. It is queer!

The good Leech doubtless exaggerated, as all satirists do, but he had sufficient foundation for his skit.

But whatever may be the condition of the French, man or woman, interiorally, the outside is as delightfully clean as could be desired. The blouse of the workman is outwardly as fresh and clean as the coat of the swell on the boulevards, and the said swell would sooner lie down and die than to wear soiled linen or uncleaned boots. The women, high and low, are invariably neat and tidy in appearance — immaculately so.

The chambermaid, who cares for your room; the washer-woman who brings you your linen; equally with my lady in her drawing room or in her carriage, is neat-ness itself, and not only that, but elegance itself. Condition is no excuse for outward slovenliness in Paris. The servants in the house always have white about the throat and wrist, and it *is* white. And then their dresses are made with some degree of taste, and are worn in such a way as to make the cheapest and most common goods attrac-tive. With the same

QUEER — TO FRENCHMEN.

eye to appearance, and with the devotion to comfort that is a part of French nature, the streets of Paris are the best kept in the world. I do not wonder that the Frenchman, con-demned by business or other considerations to live in New York, considers himself a sort of Napoleon, after Waterloo, and New York his St. Helena. The streets of London are kept clean; the dirt from the throngs of horses and vehicles is carefully removed, and it is done thoroughly, but not so much because of cleanliness as for want of manure. The streets of Paris are kept absolutely clean, simply for comfort and appearance. The neatly polished boots of Monsieur and Madame must not be soiled on crossings, nor must the skirts of its women be made unwearable by dragging through dust and filth. The streets of New York would send a French woman to a mad-house — they are nasty enough to send any one there compelled to wade through them.

There are no people in the world who are so delightfully polite as the Parisians. I might say the French, but Paris is

France, and it is the same all over the country. It is a delight
to be swindled by a French shopkeeper, man or woman, they
do it so neatly and with such infinite grace.   There is so much

THE PORTE ST. MARTIN.

patience, so much suavity, such a general oiling of the rough
places, and such a delightful smoothing out of creases.   It is
Monsieur who is the obliged party if you come into his place.
He feels the honor that you have conferred upon him, and he

makes you feel that he feels it. True, you pay for all this politeness, and pay for it at very high rates, but it is, like all high-priced commodities, very pleasant.

He never wearies of showing you goods; your atrocious French is laboriously translated, and if you buy a franc's worth Monsieur seems as much delighted as though you had beggared yourself by taking his whole stock. And if you have taken an hour of his time and purchased nothing, he seems to be even more pleased. Indeed, his politeness on occasions that to an English or American tradesman would be depressing, is even more marked. He bows and smiles, not grimaces, as has been vainly written, but a most gracious bow and a most delightful smile, which, if not genuine, is a most natural substitute for it, and he modestly hopes that if Monsieur or Madame desires anything in his line that they will give him the preference. Possibly he says " *sacre* " to himself after you are on the sidewalk, and possibly he launches all sorts of curses after you, but you don't know it, and so it doesn't hurt you. Go back within five minutes and you will find him with the same smile, ready and willing to go through the same operation over again.

Tibbitts tried to worry one of them, and for once succeeded. He stopped the party promenading with him on the Boulevard des Italiens, at a jeweler's, who displayed in his window the legend, "English spoken." The "English spoken" in the shops is good enough, as a rule, to explain the nature and quality of the goods, and that is all. Further than this, the English-speaking salesman has no more idea of English than he has of Ashantee. Tibbitts marched in boldly, and the English-speaking man appeared. He was a very well-preserved, bald-headed man of fifty, and at him Tibbitts went.

" Do you speak English ? "

" Oui — yees, Monsieur."

Tibbitts grasped his hand enthusiastically.

" It 's refreshing to meet one in a strange land who can speak one's own language."

" Yees, Monsieur."

" Well, what I want to know is, is the Chicago & North-western Railroad cutting rates the same as the other roads,

18

and do they cut for Western-bound passengers the same as for
Eastern, and have you the remotest idea that the cutting will
be kept up till September when I return, and does the Pullman
Sleeping Car Company cut the same as the railroad companies ? "

" Eh, Monsieur ? Zeese watches —"

" You don't quite understand me. You see the Pullman
Sleeping Car Company is quite distinct from the railroad
companies, and one may cut rates without the other. See ?
Now what I want to know is — "

The bewildered Frenchman who spoke English stared in a
wild sort of way, but his politeness did not desert him.

" Ees eet ze watch, ze diamond, ze —"

" Not yet. What I want to know is, who is this Lapham
and Miller who have been elected to fill the vacancies occasioned by the resignations of Platt and Conkling, and is
Miller going to be a tail to Lapham's kite, or are they both
square, bang-up men, and —"

" Will Monsieur look at ze goods ? "

" No, no! Is the Chicago & Northwestern in this row ? "

By this time the Frenchman was out of patience.

" Monsieur, talks — wat you call 'im — gibberish. I 'ave
not ze time to waste. Eef it ees ze watch —"

" Sir," replies Tibbitts, severely, " when you announce
' English spoken,' you should speak English, or at least understand it. Good morning, or, as you don't understand the
plainest English, *bong-swoir*."

He had succeeded this time, and should have rested on his
laurels. But Tibbittses, alas, always overdo what they undertake. He had extracted so much amusement from his first
experiment that he tried it over again the next day. He
entered a similar place and commenced the same thing.

" What I want to know, is the Chicago & Northwestern in
the railroad war, and do you suppose the cutting of rates will
continue till September, when I return, and —"

" Indeed I cannot tell you, sir. It is something I do not
keep the run of. You had better apply at the American
Exchange, or the *Herald* office."

This in the best and clearest American English. Poor Tibbitts had fallen upon a bright American who was turning his knowledge of French to account by serving as a salesman in Paris. He smiled a ghastly smile as he bowed himself out of the place. Bad marksmen who by chance hit the bull's eye, should be very modest and refuse to shoot again. Even Napoleon, great as he was, fought one battle too many.

Politeness with the French is a matter of education as well as nature. The French child is taught that lesson from the beginning of its existence, and it is made a part of its life. It is the one thing that is never forgotten and lack of it is never forgiven. A shipwrecked Frenchman who could not get into a boat, as he was disappearing under the waves, raised his hat, and with such a bow as he could make under the circumstances, said, "Adieu, Mesdames; Adieu, Messieurs," and went to the fishes. I doubt not that it really occurred, for I have seen ladies splashed by a cab on a rainy day, smile politely at the driver. A race that has women of that

A VERY POLITE FRENCHMAN.

degree of politeness can never be anything but polite. When such exasperation as splashed skirts and stockings will not ruffle them, nothing will.

The children are delightful in this particular. French children do not go about clamoring for the best places and sulking if they do not get them, and talking in a rude, boisterous way. They do not take favors and attentions as a matter of course and unacknowledged. The slightest attention shown them is acknowledged by the sweetest kind of a bow — not the dancing-master's bow, but a genuine one — and the invariable "Merci, Monsieur!" or Madame, or Mademoiselle, as the case may be.

I was in a compartment with a little French boy of twelve,

the precise age at which American children, as a rule, deserve
killing for their rudeness and general disagreeableness. He
was dressed faultlessly, but his clothes were not the chief
charm. I sat between him and the open window, and he was
eating pears. Now an American boy of that age would either
have dropped the cores upon the floor, or tossed them out of
the window without a word to anybody. But this small
gentleman every time, with a "permit me, Monsieur," said in
the most pleasant way, rose and came to the window and
dropped them out, and then, "Merci, Monsieur," as he quietly
took his seat. It was a delight. I am sorry to say that such
small boys do not travel on American railroad trains to any
alarming extent. Would they were more frequent.

And when in his seat, if an elderly person or any one else
came in, he was the very first to rise and offer his place if it
were in the slightest degree more comfortable than the one
vacant, and the good nature in which he insisted upon the new
comer taking it was something "altogether too sweet for
anything," as the faro bankeress would say.

And this boy was no exception. He was not a show boy,
out posing before the great American republic, or such of it as
happened to be in France at the time, but he was a sample, a
perfect type of the regulation French child. I have seen just
as much politeness in the ragged waifs in the Faubourg St.
Antoine, where the child never saw the blue sky more than
the little patches that could be seen over the tops of seven-
storied houses, as I ever did in the Champs Elysees. One
Sunday at St. Cloud, where the ragged children of poverty
are taken by their mothers for air and light, it was a delight
to fill the pockets with sweets to give them. They had no
money to buy, and the little human rats looked longingly at
the riches of the candy stands, and a sou's worth made the
difference between perfect happiness and half-pleasure. You
gave them the sou's worth, and what a glad smile came to the
lips, and accompanied with it was the delicious half bow and
half courtesy, and invariable "Merci, Monsieur." One little
tot, who could not speak, filled her tiny mouth with the
unheard of delicacies she had received, and, too young to say
"_Merci_," put up her lips to be kissed.

Tibbitts gave some confectionery to her elder sister, a young girl of eighteen, but she merely said "Merci, Monsieur," and that was all. She took the candy, but declined to kiss him, much to Tibbitts' disgust.

Oh, ye thoughtless, heedless mothers of America, would that you could all see these children and take lessons from their mothers. There is a difference in people, and a still

"MERCI, MONSIEUR."

greater difference in children. Our American Congress could well afford a commission of ladies to learn the secret of training children, and a school for mothers should be established in every city for their preparation for this important duty. It would pay better than any monetary conference.

The French family is an unknown quantity. Monsieur, the husband and father, spends his time at his café according to his quality, while Madame the wife receives her friends, or admirers, if she be not too old to have them, in her drawing-room. There are no homes in France, as the English and Americans understand the word. It would drive a Frenchman crazy if, when business hours are over, he should be compelled to eat his dinner and afterward go up stairs, sit with his wife and children quietly till bed-time, and then retire in good order. Likewise would it be distasteful to the French wife. She may be in love — in fact, she always is — but not with her husband.

A Frenchman once, who was too fond of the softer sex, pledged himself to avoid women. Later he was asked if he had kept his pledge. "Certainly, or rather partially. I have religiously avoided Madame; I can keep that pledge always, so far as she is concerned."

He meets his wife with, "Good evening, Madame. I trust you have had a pleasant day."

"Merci, Monsieur; very pleasant."

He does not ask her whether she has been driving out with the children, or with a lover; in fact, he does not care. He knows she has a lover, but that is nothing to him so long as he himself sees nothing wrong.

And after dinner he bids her "Good evening," and goes to his favorite café, where he, and other similar husbands, save the country over innumerable bottles of wine, and when the cafés are shut, and there is no other earthly place to visit, he goes home and retires to his room, only to meet Madame the next morning at breakfast.

This is not singular. The French girl is kept by her mother under the strictest possible guardianship till she is of the age to marry. She might as well be in a prison, for she is never out from under the sharp eye of her mother, or aunt, or in default of these, a governess. Her life, when she gets to be about fourteen, and begins to know something of what life really is, and wants to enjoy it, is most intolerable.

She is married in due time, but she has very little to do with it. A husband is selected for her, and she accepts him scarcely knowing or hardly caring who it is she is to wed, for she wants that liberty which in France comes with marriage, and marriage only. She knows that a wife may do that which a maiden may not — that matrimony means in France what it does not in any other country — almost absolute freedom. Once married, the mother washes her hands of her, considering that she has discharged her whole duty by her child.

The whole idea of French matrimony from the girl's standpoint is well illustrated in the picture of the French carica-

PARIS UNDERGROUND — MAKING THE TOUR OF THE SEWERS.

turist. Two girls are discussing the approaching marriage of one of them. The bargained-for girl exclaims lugubriously, "But I love Henri!" "Very good, my child," replies her elder and wiser friend, "you *love* Henri; then *marry* Alphonse."

Her marrying Alphonse made love for Henri possible. It was all there in one small picture and two lines of print, but a page of small type could not explain the situation more clearly.

Marriages are arranged by the parents of the parties, and an exceedingly curious performance it is. The girl's parents actually buy her a husband. The two old cats who have one

INTERIOR OF THE PARIS BOURSE.

a son and the other a daughter, meet like two gray-headed diplomatists, and there ensues a series of negotiations that would put to shame traders in anything else. The girl has to have a *dot*, which is to say, a dowry, and the son must have money or property settled upon him. The mother of the girl proposes to give her one hundred thousand francs as the *dot*. The mother of the son insists that it is not enough, and enlarges upon the perfections of the young man. He is educated, he is polished, he is handsome, he is amiable. He isn't a brute who would make a wife miserable; not he. Clearly one hundred thousand francs is not enough for such a paragon. The mother of the girl strikes in. The girl is the handsomest in Paris, and has had every advantage. She is a lady, and would make a desirable addition to the house of any man in Paris; but finally she names one hundred and ten thousand francs.

It will not do. "*Mon dieu!*" exclaims the mother, "you must remember I have three other daughters to provide for, and the estate is not large. If I give one hundred and ten thousand francs to one, what will become of the others? There is reason in all things, even in marrying off a daughter!"

And thus they haggle and haggle, just as though they were trading horses, until finally it is fixed. The happy pair are permitted to see each other; so much is settled upon the young man and so much upon the girl, and they are married, and by the laws of France and the sanction of the holy church, are man and wife. They are man and wife legally but in no other sense.

Of course there can be nothing of love, or affection, or even esteem in such marriages. Monsieur wants Madame to be handsome and accomplished, precisely as he wants a handsome horse — it pleases his eye and gratifies his tastes — but the main point after all is the *dot*. He has that additional income to live upon. Madame desires Monsieur to be likewise prepossessing, for she wants the world to believe that she married something beside the title of Madame, though all the world knows better.

Each wants the other to be amiable, for even living separate, as they do, they are necessarily under one roof, and bad temper on either side would make things uncomfortable. Above all, they want no jealousy or inquisitiveness. Each wants to be let alone; each desires to follow the bent of his or her inclination, undisturbed and unmolested. And they get up, doubtless, some sort of an esteem for each other, which may in time ripen into something like what outside

barbarians call love. But that occurs, probably, after one of
them is dead, provided the survivor is too old to marry again.
It looks well for a widow of fifty or sixty to revere the
memory of her dear departed, and they generally do it, no
matter on what terms they lived.

Of course they have children born to them, for there must
be heirs to the estate. Madame loves them very much, or

THE ARC DU CARROUSEL.

appears to, but she sees very little of them. She puts them
out to nurse at once. Children are tiresome and wearying to
a woman whose day is divided into so much for dressing, so
much for riding, so much for eating, and so much for balls or
opera. She sees them and admires them. and when they are
old enough, marries them off. The father is pleased to see that
Henri is growing into a fine boy, or Marie into a fine girl,
but he has his business and pleasures to attend to, and besides,
there is invariably some woman, somewhere in Paris, that he
does love, and she has children also. And so the children
grow up, Monsieuring their father and Madaming their mother
till they escape from under the paternal and maternal charge,
only to go and do the same things for themselves.

Curious notions "our lively neighbors, the Gauls," as Mr. Micawber says, have of domestic life. There is no such thing in Paris.

This among the upper classes. Jean and Jeannette, the baker and the milliner, are not so particular about the *dot*, and for a very good reason — neither of them or their parents have a sou to give more than the wedding clothes and a holiday, with an extra bottle of wine on the occasion of the wedding. They dispense with the *dot*, and, in very many cases, with the legal and religous ceremonies, which are considered necessary among other classes, and among all classes in other countries. Having nothing else to marry for, they marry for love, and very good husbands and wives they make. True, Jean goes to his café every night, to save the country in his way, and Jeannette expects him to, but as they do not inhabit large houses they are naturally brought closer together, and, consequently, are more in sympathy with each other. Jean, with two francs a day, even with the help of Jeannette, who may earn quite as much, cannot afford the luxury of separate rooms or separate beds. One answers them both, and not infrequently they have not that one.

But with their cheap wine and their very cheap bread, and, above all, their careless, happy-go-lucky dispositions, they manage to get along very comfortably. So long as they can work, and they do work, both of them, they live very well; and when sickness or old age comes there are excellent hospitals to go to, and after that — why, the church has fixed their hereafter, and so everything is smooth with them.

Poverty has its uses, though, desirable as it is, I find I can get on with a very little of it. I firmly believe that in time I could accustom myself to riches, and really enjoy myself. But it may never be.

Madame, the faro bankeress, is at the same hotel with us, and is getting on famously in French. This morning at breakfast — she calls it " dejuner " — much to the waiter's astonishment, she ordered " café o' lay — *with milk*," and at dinner, "*frozen* champagne glace," never knowing, poor woman, that *café au lait* means, simply, coffee with milk, and *champagne glacé* is simply chilled champagne. But it did nobody else any harm except the waiter, and it pleased her. She remarked to the other lady that she was sure she would have no trouble in getting along — which she would not, as the waiter, being an Englishman, could understand even her English, except when she plunged too much into French.

"Have you been to the Louvre?" asked the other lady, or *the* lady, to be accurate.

"Oh, no, not yet. I have no doubt it is altogether too sweet for anything, but I have not had time. I dote on art. But I have found a new place where you can get such lovely laces, for almost nothing, and another where silk hosiery can be had for less than half what you have to pay in New York. And I bought such a lovely dress for Lulu, a pearl silk, with such a lovely waist, and an embroidered front, with roses embroidered in the skirt. It is just like the one she wore at the children's ball, at Mrs. Thompson's, last Winter, which cost me more than twice what this one did and wasn't half so nice. But Lulu looked altogether too sweet for anything in that, though, and everybody at the ball was in perfect rapture over her. And then I bought a sweet suit for little Alfred, my youngest child, nine years old. It is such a perfectly sweet little pair of pants with a waist that buttons on just lovely, and with red stockings and purple shoes he will be altogether too sweet for anything. They will fit, for I have the measure of both the children with me. I have found out that when one travels to see nature and things, one ought always to be prepared. That's why I brought their measure with me."

At this point the husband of the other lady, who could not help hearing all this, as he had for many weary days, told me an anecdote like this:—

"A young man with a very bad voice, but who firmly and steadfastly believed that in the article of voice he was the superior of Brignoli, engaged a teacher to give him lessons. When asked how he liked his teacher his reply was that he was a good master, but he was altogether too religious for him.

"How too religious?"

"Why, while I am practicing, he walks up and down the room wringing his hands and praying."

"What is his prayer? What does he pray about?"

"I can't exactly say, but I caught the words, 'Heavenly Father! how long must I endure this?' There was doubtless something the matter with him."

There was no necessity for him to point to the moral of this, for the stream of gabble flowed on in a smooth and continuous flow, finding no rocks of thought to give it picturesqueness, or no impediment of fact to make it pause. It was simply the wagging of a tongue that was hung on a swivel in the middle — a tongue which would wag so long as the lungs furnished breath and the muscles that moved it held out. Inasmuch as she has pleasant rooms and likes the hotel, and will not move, we are going to find another. But probably we shall find another just like her at the new place. They are the people who delight in travel and are everywhere.

"HOW LONG MUST I ENDURE THIS?"

Tibbitts has made the acquaintance of a wholesale liquor dealer, who is going to "do" Switzerland, and Tibbitts has determined to join him.

"Why join a wholesale liquor dealer?"

"With an eye solely to the future. In the coming years what may happen to me? Will it not be handy to drop into his place, and, after remarking about the weather, say, 'Thompson, do you remember it was just five years ago to-day that we climbed Mont Blanc? And do you remember when you gave out at the foot of the first glacier how I pulled you up?' Or, 'What day of the month is this? 16th? Yes; exactly six years ago to-day we were skimming over the

Brunig Pass, on our way to Lucerne.' Then he can't do less than to ask me to take something. And then we will sit and sit, talking over our European experiences and drinking his liquor. I shall live very near his place, so as to have it handy. It is a provision for a doubtful future. You are altogether too careless about such things. You haven't common prudence. A man who in his youth do'n't lay up provision for his old age is very reckless indeed. I count the association with this delightful man as good as half my living all my life. I shall try to strike a merchant tailor after I have fixed myself in this man's memory, and after that, if I stay long enough, a boot and shoe man. The past is safe; the present I am satisfied with. What I want now is an assured future. Then I am heeled."

CHAPTER XIX.

PARIS has one institution possessed by no other city in the world — the genuine street Arab. London has, heaven knows, enough homeless waifs, born the Lord only knows where, and brought up the Lord only knows how; but the London article is no more like the Parisian than chalk is like cheese. The New York street boy comes nearer it — New York is more like Paris than any other city — but even the New York Arab is not to be compared with the Parisian. He stands alone, a miracle of impudence, good nature, self-possession and resource.

Where he was born he never knows and never cares. He don't carry his pedigree in his pocket, not simply because he has no pocket, but because he don't care a straw about it. It doesn't concern him. He would not give a sou to be the son of the late Emperor. Birth and blood concern him very little. What his mind is running on, chiefly, is where and how to get a crust of black bread, a draught of very cheap wine, and a dry, warm place to sleep.

His mother was, and is, a seamstress, or a house servant, or woman of all work, or a shop girl. His father — well, it is doubtful if the mother could give any very definite information on that subject. She may have been a true daughter of Paris, or she may have come from the delicious valleys of Normandy or Brittany, or the mountains of Switzerland, with her heavy shoes, her quaint bodice, and her long, braided hair hanging down her shapely back. She got work, she wrought in a clothing warehouse, or she went behind a counter; then came the balls in the Latin quarter (it is a part of the nature of the girls of this country to love lights

(287)

and glitter and dancing, and the like); then appeared the
student with his half-polished brigandage, and then began the
life of a grisette. They lived together till the student was
called home, and he went back to his native country to marry
and settle down into respectable citizenship, forgetting entirely
the poor little girl he left be-
hind, and the wee baby she
had borne him.

THE MOTHER OF THE GAMIN—AS SHE WAS.

But whoever his father might
have been he never saw him that
he remembers, and he has a
very indistinct idea of what a
father is.

The uncertainty of father-
hood in Paris is illustrated by
the grisette who was walking
with her little boy. A funeral
procession was passing:—

"Who is it that is dead?"
asked the boy of his mother.

"I do not know, but take off
your hat, my child. It may be
your father!"

It was not unlikely. I don't
think this ever happened, however, for in France, every one
removes his hat while a funeral
passes. They are polite to the
dead as to the living. Besides
this, the boy had no hat to
remove.

He knows his mother, how-
ever, very well; he remembers
a pale, worn woman, who always gave him the largest half of
the scant bread, and assuaged her hunger by seeing him eat,
and who managed somehow to keep the rags that hung about
him clean, and had hidden somewhere, a neat and tidy suit of
clothes which were worn only on fête days, and when they
went to church. No matter about the father, since every boy

knows who his mother is, and he knows likewise that whatever may happen to her, he is sure of all she can possibly do for him, even to the last, the supreme sacrifice.

They lived together in a garret, somewhere, or a cellar. With these people it is always one extreme or another,— they never have the middle of anything.

Somehow she managed to make the little den they existed in rather pleasant, and he had a tolerably happy life. Only the mother was compelled to leave him very much alone, for there was the black bread to earn, and no matter how miserable their apartment, there was something to pay for rent. He was left, always, with a score of others just like him, with an old woman who had once gone through the same experience, and who, unable now to do other work, earned her few sous a day caring for children that were short a father, and whose mothers were skirmishing on the outside borders of existence

THE MOTHER OF THE GAMIN IN THE SERE AND YELLOW LEAF.

for enough to keep body and soul together. This was all very well till the little legs were strong enough to walk, and the old woman could no longer control him. Armed with the preter-

19

natural sharpness that always accompanies poverty, he took to
the streets, and, in the old times when begging was permitted,
he was a beggar. Now he is anything. He scorns regular
work, he is a hawk, who picks up his living here, there and
everywhere. He may be on the boulevards, and a handker-

THE AGED PICKER-UP OF CIGAR STUMPS.

chief may be dropped; the apple-women, sharp as they are,
find in him a most competent brigand. There are cigar-stumps
to be picked up, and they are worth something an ounce to be

worked over into smoking tobacco. Everywhere in the great
city there are unconsidered trifles, but an unconsidered trifle is
everything to a boy who has no use for clothing, and to whom
a crust of bread is enough for a day.

Finally, at the mature age of eight, or thereabouts, he leaves
his mother; or, rather, some night he does not come home.
He has found a dry place under an arch to sleep, or a hole in
the docks, and he has associated with him other boys of the
same breed; now he is an independent citizen.

His mother knows the way of the world, and she goes
right on, sure that her child is living, and, in his way, well.

He occasionally goes to see her, till she moves some time
suddenly, and is lost to him in the great desert.

He probably never sees her again. If she gets on well and
keeps her health she dies finally in a hospital — if not, a plunge
in the Seine ends her struggles with a very hard world. Not
infrequently his last look at her is taken in the Morgue.

While he is a boy he leads a very independent and happy
life. He toils not, neither does he spin; he does not dine at
the Maison Doree; nor does he drink champagne or burgundy.
He drinks wine when he can get it, and water from the public
fountain when he cannot. He eats black bread when he has a
sou to buy it with; lacking the sou, there are always opportunities to steal an apple, and failing in that, there are apple
cores to be picked up on the streets.

As for clothing, very little does him; very little, but where
he obtains that little, I have never been able to ascertain. He
gets it, though, somehow, each article in the suit coming from
a different source, and all just strong enough to hold together.
A picturesque vagabond it makes of him.

His conversation is something wonderful. There isn't a
slang phrase in French that he has not, and as the mothers
are of all nations, he has made piratical excursions into other
languages, and has the worst of them all. He can swear very
well in English, not the unctuous, brutal oaths of the American
or Englishman, for even a Parisian gamin has taste, but
English oaths lose none of their strength in him. He ornaments them, but not to the degree of weakening.

No Frenchman would ever think of chaffing a gamin twice, for he knows by bitter experience that the gamin always gets the best of it, and the first and last time he tried it he retired with everybody laughing but himself and the boy. He did not laugh, because the boy had routed him, horse, foot and dragoon—the boy did not, because to have laughed would have been undignified, and lessened the effect of his wordy victory. He professed to sympathize with his victim, which was adding insult to injury.

In this matter of talk the very cabmen are afraid of him, and the policemen dread him. It is his delight to catch a policeman or a soldier in a position where he cannot move, and to cover him with not exactly abuse, but what the English call chaff. He makes the poor fellow ridiculous; he sets a crowd laughing at him, and does it in perfect safety, too, for the official cannot leave his post to capture and punish him, and if he could it would do no good. The urchin is as slippery as an eel, and as fleet as an antelope. He can slip through the crowd and be a safe distance long before the encumbered man has made up his mind to go for him.

These boys make up no small portion of every mob that has devastated Paris for centuries, and popular risings are altogether too common for comfort in that excitable city. In all the revolutions these little fellows have handled muskets and pikes, and made much of them. The gamin was foremost in the mob that leveled the Bastille to the ground, and when that monument of irresponsible tyranny was in ruins the dead bodies of hundreds of them were found underneath them, and the living bodies of hundreds of others waved their crownless hats over the smoking debris. There never has been a barricade erected that had not gamins behind it, boys of fourteen, fighting as coolly and steadily as grizzled veterans of sixty.

They knew not what they were fighting for, nor cared. They only felt it was the people against the recognized authorities, and that was enough. The Parisian gamin hates the authorities, for his chief idea is that the name means a prison, police, and everything else that a brigand in a small way don't like. He loves commotion, for commotion signifies excitement, and excitement is as necessary to him as bread itself. He will stand behind a barricade and load and fire as long as the oldest man, and, firing with a musket, he is as good as a giant.

There are theaters which he patronizes regularly, for next to a revolution he loves the theater. Where he procures the money for admission, small as it is, heaven only knows; but he gets it somehow, for he is there nearly every night. If he cannot get in at the beginning, he hangs about the entrances, waiting for some good-natured man, who does not care to see the performance out, to give him his check, or he wheedles a good natured doorman into letting him pass. And once in, there is no adult in the audience who is so critical an auditor. He knows all about the drama, all about the music, and all about everything connected with it. He applauds at the right place, and if there be the slightest fault of omission or commission in the representation, his hiss is the first and the most distinct and deadly.

The Parisian actor dreads the gamin almost as much as he does the newspaper critics. They have made and unmade many an aspirant for public favor.

I gave a sou to one for the privilege of a minute's conversation. (I had a friend to translate — a street boy would not understand my French.)

"Where were you born?"

There was a comprehensive wave of the hand which took in all Paris. He might have been born all over the vast city.

"How do you live?"

There was an expressive shrug of the shoulders that meant anything you chose.

"What are you intending to do when you are older?"

Another expressive shrug, as if to say "Who knows?" (These French boys can talk more with their arms and shoulders than other people can with their tongues.)

But when he saw the sou in hand he had expression enough all over him for a dozen boys. He took it with the invariable " Merci, Monsieur," and darting away, in a minute re-appeared with a loaf of black bread, and was as willing to be communicative as you desired.

All that could be gathered from him was that his mother

was a washerwoman, his father the Lord only knew, and he had been living on the streets as long as he could remember anything. That was all. That was his beginning—his end was in the hands of fate; possibly one thing, and possibly another, but, one thing or another, he had bread enough to last him twenty-four hours, and he was more happy than many a man in a palace.

A TALK WITH A GAMIN.

They are ubiquitous, and all alike. Their being all alike is what makes them ubiquitous. You see him on the boulevards — you dive down from those dizzy heights of splendor, from the broad glare of that magnificence, to the poverty-made twilight of the Latin quarter, or the Cimmerian gloom of the Faubourg St. Antoine, and you see him.

Just the same. He wears the same reminiscence of a hat, the same remnants of trowsers, the same shirt with holes torn in it in the same places, the flag of distress floats from the same quarter, if, indeed, the shirt is long enough to boast a lower end, and the bare feet in the summer, and the dilapidated shoes in the winter, are the same. It is not the same boy, but it is the boy cast in the same mold, and with all the others, subject to the same conditions, and consequently exactly like as peas.

Nature makes men in molds. Noblemen's sons have something in their make-up besides their clothes, and so have the children of poverty. A pallet in a garret, or, more usually, the bare floor; a crust, or the core of an apple at rare and uncertain intervals, are as certain to produce one typical face and a typical body as luxurious beds and rich food do another.

The Parisian gamins are alike wherever you see them, for

they all come from one stock, and are all brought up in one way. So nearly are they alike that the old saying might well be reversed.   Instead of its being "It's a wise child that knows its own father," it should read "It's a wise mother that knows her own child." With these waifs, a child's knowing, or even guessing, at its own father, would be an idea utterly chimerical.

Yet they are good-natured, and even kind to each other. There are girl vagabonds and girl waifs as well as boy waifs. The boys are wonderfully good to the little homeless girls who are too Arab-like to go to the retreats provided for them by the Government. If the boy has a warm place under a bridge or over a lime kiln, he gives it up to the wandering female rat, with as much chivalry as any grand Seigneur could display, and he shares with her the result of his predatory excursions, even going a trifle more hungry himself that she may not entirely starve.   They are always hungry — it is only a question of how hungry they may be.

What becomes of them? I don't know.   Sometimes they get into other ways and grow into respectable citizens.   Occasionally one of them is sufficiently tamed to learn a trade, if some citizen picks him up and cares for him, and now and then a street boy or girl drifts, by accident, into a profession and becomes eminent.   The great French actress, Rachel, was a street girl, whose only fortune was her guitar, and whose living was made by singing in front of cafés.   By hook or crook she got upon the stage, and once there her genius made her way for her.   The Frenchman cares nothing for birth or position in the matter of genius.   He wants good singing and good acting, and he cares not whether the singer or actor comes from the gutter or the palace.   If from the gutter, the genius which delights him removes the slime, and he does it even greater honor than as though it had been pushed by more favorable circumstances.

Rachel not only made a world-wide fame, but she raised her family, all of whom were as poor and low down as herself, to the very heights of French grandeur.   One of the Felix girls — that is their name — is now the wealthy and prosperous manufacturer of a face powder, which is the delight of the

upper classes. With the shrewdness of the Israelite, she did
not go into groceries or such trifles. She knew the French
people too well. She invented a face powder and hair restora-
tive, and waxed rich. She will marry her daughters to
noblemen, and possibly Kings may spring from a line that
once was delighted with a sou thrown into the gutter for
them to scramble for.

One of the great chocolate manufacturers, whose name is
known wherever there is civilization, who counts his residences
by the dozen, and his wealth by millions, was a gamin till
he was eighteen.

Some of them, like Rachel, from their intense love of the
drama, get to be actors, when they are old enough. Some of
them become rag-pickers, or work into other employments of
a semi-vagabondizing nature; some of them become thieves,
and take in all the range of crime from picking a pocket to
committing murder, and numbers of them go into the army
and navy.

But these instances are comparatively rare. The gamin
grows, as a rule, into a vagabond, the vagabond into a criminal, and the criminal either ends at the guillotine or in the
prison hospital. A lucky chance may graft something better
on them, or a revolution may afford them opportunities for
distinction in a military way, but those so promoted are excep-
tions. The rule is quite the other way.

In New York these human rats sell newspapers, clean
boots, and do things of that nature, nominally. The genuine
Parisian gamin might do this, for there are papers cried and
sold on the street, though the most of this trade is transacted
in picturesque little buildings called "Kiosques." But he will
have none of it. Should he labor or do anything approaching
labor, he would lose caste with his fellows, and become to them
a social pariah.

One important specimen of the kind, nine years old, and
weighing, perhaps, fifty pounds, saw a former member of the
fraternity, who had seceded, passing with packages to deliver,
neatly dressed, and with a general air of being well cared for,
and comfortably fed and housed.

The ragamuffin looked upon him with an expression of

contempt never equalled off the stage, and he called the attention of a score of his ragged comrades to the seceder:—

"Look at him! just look at him! He has got to be a
baker's boy! Poor devil! Poor devil! He has clothes, he
has a cap on his head, and shoes on his feet. He sits at a
table with the maid, and eats three times a day, and has a
bed to sleep in! He will never more be one of us! He is
ruined! Poor devil! Why can't everybody have spirit?
Bah! A bed to sleep in, and regular meals!"

And the mob of ragamuffins jeered and hooted at him
as he passed, and the boy himself looked as though he had
been a traitor to his class, and as if he had half a mind to
confiscate the bread he was carrying and return to his former
fellows.

The young bundle of rags felt all that he said. To him
this desertion from a life of vagabondage was a betrayal, as it
were, and he felt, actually, a supreme pity for the gamin who
could be anything else for so small a consideration as a comfortable life. To him the liberty of the streets was better than
any house that required regularity. He would not have dined
at the Grand Hotel if it required his coming at regular hours,

And after venting his opinion he went out in search of
something to eat, and if he found that something he was
happy — if not it was a shrug of the shoulders, and to sleep an
hour or two sooner. They have a trick of making a dinner
upon an hour or two of sleep, and an enjoyable breakfast by
not waking up till dinner time. It is an economical way of
living, but not conducive to increase of flesh. How long they
can stand it has never been determined, for, not regarding the
interests of science, they always manage to find a crust, or a
bone, or something, just as the experiment is getting to be
interesting. None of them have ever been willing to die in the
interest of science. They are largely devoted to themselves.

The gamin of Paris is deserving of more credit than the
gamin of New York, for he has nothing especially cheerful
before him. When he ceases to be a vagabond boy he becomes
a vagabond man, except in the rare cases I have mentioned,
and ends his career, as vagabond men do, the world over.

In New York the ending is quite different — indeed the

vagabond boy has better opportunities than the good boy.
For in New York he loafs about gin mills, and he has the
advantages of free lunches, an institution unknown in Paris,
and the good old ladies get up excursions for him, and give
him sandwiches and ice cream, in the hopes of reaching his
better nature through the medium of his stomach, they firmly
believing there is a better nature, and as it has never been
seen it must be in the stomach. In time he grows up and gets
as far along as to have that blessed boon of the ballot, and
becomes useful to the politicians, who transfer him from the
front of the bar to the back of it, and he has a gin mill of his
own, and controls votes, and "hez inflooence in my warrud."

When his "inflooence" is sufficient, he boldly demands
office for himself and becomes a School Commissioner, or an
Alderman, and finally goes to the Legislature and waxes enormously rich, and his wife — for this sort of a fellow marries
when he gets off the streets and has a gin mill of his own —
wears diamonds and has a carriage.

It was Teddy McShane, and Mickey O'Finnegan, two of
this class, who got into the Board of Aldermen of New York.
Alderman McShane had heard of gondolas and wanted a few
in the little lakes in the park, for, of course, had his motion
prevailed he would have got his commission from the builder
thereof. And so he spoke :—

"Misther Prisidint — We cannot be too liberal in ornamintin' our parruks. A parruk is for the paple, and they
should be ornamintid. To this ind, I move ye sorr, that
twinty gondolas be purchast for the lakes in Cintril Parruk
to-wanst."

Alderman McFinnegan, who saw a job in this, decided to
oppose it till McShane should come to him and propose a
divide. And so he said :—

"Misther Prisidint — No man in New Yorrick will go
furdther in ornamintin' the city than mesilf; but the paple's
money musht not be squandered. Why buy twinty gondolas,
to-wanst? Why not buy two — a male and a faymale, and
breed thim ourselves?"

The Parisian gamin can do nothing of this kind — indeed,
it is impossible in Paris, and he would not want to do it if it
were possible. He does not care for money; he does not long

for houses and lands or a fixed habitation. If he had the best house in Paris, with silken beds and all that sort of thing, the second night he would steal away and sleep comfortably under an arch, or in one of his accustomed places. He is very like one of the chiefs of the Onondaga Indians, who was persuaded to build him a house in the civilized fashion. He slept in it one night and the next morning broke every pane of glass out of the windows. That night he slumbered with the rain and sleet pouring in upon him, and was happy. That was something like.

The Parisian gamin, grown to be a man, could not sit still long enough to make an efficient Alderman, and he would not give a turn of his hand for all the money that could be made out of the position. He can be happy with rags and a crust, and what is money to such a being? He understands better than any philosopher, that riches consist in not how much you have, as how little you can get on with. If rags and apple cores suffice, why more?

And so he does n't go about speculating in stocks, and getting "politikle inflooence," as his counterpart in New York does, but he is content with what he finds himself. No one ever heard of a Parisian grown-up gamin attempting to control railroads, or build steamships, or anything of the sort. He dies as he lived, and is always happy. Possibly he is the wise man. Who shall say?

But he is a part and parcel of French civilization — a natural outgrowth of French habits and customs. Without the gamin, Paris would not be Paris. Bad as he may be, he is always like Artemus Ward's kangaroo, "an amoosin' little cuss," a perpetual mystery, an everlasting study, and something that no other city in the world possesses. He can live on less and get more happiness out of it than any other human being on earth; but he could not exist out of Paris. He had rather be in prison in Paris than to have a palace anywhere else. He belongs to that atmosphere, to those surroundings, and can exist nowhere else in the world. He is a savage in the midst of the highest civilization, a drone in a hive of industry, and hungry in the midst of plenty. He is everything that he should not be. Nevertheless, I rather like him, to say the least. He is picturesque.

CHAPTER XX.

THE average Parisian thinks of but two things — how to get the wherewith to amuse himself, and how to get the most amusement out of that wherewith. I doubt if he ever thinks of any hereafter beyond to-night. His religion is admirably adapted to his nature. He is either a Catholic or an infidel. If a Catholic, a few minutes at the end suffices to fix him for the next world; if an infidel, death is annihilation, and therefore he proposes to have as much enjoyment as possible out of the present.

Paris would not be a good place for a series of revival meetings. The Parisian would jeer at the exhorters, and say, " Go to ! "

Paris supports seventy theaters, good, bad, and indifferent. It is not fair to use the words " bad and indifferent," with reference to the quality of acting, for there is no bad acting in Paris. It is as to the quality and material of the representations. They have all kinds, from the gorgeous Italian opera down to the small and cheap affairs in which burlesque comic opera of the funniest, and melodrama of the most lurid character is performed, for the especial delectation of the lower classes.

The theaters devoted to the melodrama are of the most melodramatic kind. There can be no crime too horrible for representation, and the situations cannot be too intense, or the plot too complicated. French life, like French cooking, must have any quantity of pepper in it.

About the least thrilling situation that would be considered good in these theaters would be the chopping up of the villain's grandmother, and the roasting alive of a parcel of illegit mate children, to hide the consequences of a "damning crime." There is always any quantity of blowing up of towers, of stabbings and shootings and bludgeonings, and all that sort of thing. There are secret passages in ancient castles, and paid cut-throats, and blue lights, and heroines with hair hanging down their backs, and everything pertaining to what in America is known as the "blood and thunder drama."

One that I saw reminded me of an incident that happened at home many years ago. In a village in which I was residing, there came the usual strolling company of players of the olden time, the sad-faced men and wan women, who knew by actual walking all the various roads in the United States, to whom a good house would be a novelty that would make them uncomfortable. They had played to empty benches so long that they could not do well if living people occupied the seats.

I was fond of the drama, and the variety that we had there was better than none at all ; so that I always patronized the strolling companies, attended invariably by a German physician who was quite as fond as myself of theatrical representations, and who, like myself, preferred a half loaf to no bread. We went together that night.

The play on the occasion was that cheerful drama from the French, "La Tour de Nesle." The plot is variegated, to say the least. Margaret of Burgundy is afflicted with a desire for lovers, and she has a tower in which she receives them and holds her orgies. It is a pleasant thing to be invited to sup with the fair Margaret, while the supper lasts, but the pleasure doesn't hold out. It is not continuous. For when you have bidden her good-evening, and get your hat on, you come across a trap door on which you step, and you go down several hundred feet, and alight on spikes situated conveniently in a bed of quick-lime, and your friends never know what has become of you; and if your life is insured there is always trouble about that, for there can be no proof of your death. Margaret loved amusement, but, for reasons, she desired no living witnesses of her escapades.

She fell in love once with a captain in the French army, one Buridan, and invited him to one of her little receptions.

The disappearance of so many of her gallants had made the youth in the neighborhood rather wary of her, and Buridan was advised not to go, and good reason was given. An intimate friend of his had disappeared mysteriously a little while before, and the last that was ever heard of him was when he entered the tower.

Hearing of this, Buridan determined to go anyhow, and find out whether this friend had really dropped out of the way, *via* the tower. He went and supped with the fair Margaret, with whom he fell in love in the regular French fashion. For reasons of her own, Margaret did not want him to take the regular walk over the trap-door, but desired to let him out another way. All would have been well had not Buridan discovered, inopportunely, that his friend had been in the same room, and had stepped on and gone through the trap, and that the lime had finished him. Margaret confessed it, whereupon Buridan drew his sword and killed her to avenge his friend. Before Margaret passed out she informed Buridan that he was her son! Buridan then immediately killed somebody else, and that one, before dying, stabbed another, and so on, till the entire company, fifteen in all, were piled upon the stage like cord-wood, which ended the play, there being no living actors to continue it.

My friend, the German physician, rose and remarked :

"My frendt, dere ish shoost one ding lacking to make dish blay gomplete. Der beople on der stage ish all deadt. De first violin shood now stab der second violin mit his bow, and gommit soocide mit himself by schwallowing his fiddle. Dot wood endt de entire gompany."

As we were leaving the hall a young man named Smith, who was always blatting about art, and music, and the drama, and such things, having been in New York once, seized the doctor and said, "Was it not a good performance? There is power in this company. Have you anything better in Germany?"

The doctor looked at him pityingly.

"My tear young man, you are not to plame. I pity you. When de Almighty rained common sense, de Schmidt family all shtood unter umbrellas."

"La Tour de Nesle," as lurid as is its plot, would be mild meat for the frequenters of the minor theaters of Paris. They would insist upon seeing the actual trap-door, and the lovers of Margaret falling through it, and I am not sure but what they would demand real spikes and lime.

You pay enormous prices in the one class and next to nothing at the other; but in both the standard of performance is a very high one, and is rigidly maintained. The Parisian, gamin or marquis, will have no bad music or acting. He may tolerate adulteration in his food, but none in his amusements.

It was always the policy of the French government to see that the people were sufficiently amused, and also to do every thing possible to attract strangers to the gay capital. Therefore, the theaters are the most gorgeous in the world, and as it would be impossible to maintain them from the admission receipts, the deficiencies are made up from the public treasury. The Grand Opera receives from the government nearly two hundred thousand dollars per year, and a number of other theaters receive like support, the entire amount thus paid aggregating something over six hundred thousand dollars per year. The citizen who may never see the inside of the Opera House is content with this, for it attracts to Paris the foreign sheep whose fleece is his living. Without the Opera the rich American would not come to Paris, and then what would trade be? The Parisian shopkeeper pays that tax willingly; and they pay their artists well, so as to have and keep the best. Any eminent tenor has a salary of twenty to twenty-five thousand dollars per annum; and other talent in propor. tion. It is not a bad thing to be a tenor in Paris. The salary is very comfortable.

In addition to the regular theaters there are numberless open-air concerts and variety performances in gardens, the spectators sitting on benches on the sand, the stage only being covered. These are always brilliantly lighted, and most artist-ically and profusely ornamented, and as attractive to the Parisian as to the stranger.

There is no entrance fee to these places. You wonder at the liberality of the proprietor, and say to yourself, if you could only find a hotel with similar views, you would immediately remove to Paris, and make it a permanent residence. But once inside, you find a pang in store for you. The free entrance is merely to evade some ordinance or other, and you are required to purchase refreshments, and no matter what it is, an ice or a glass of beer, the price is the same, three francs, or sixty cents, which makes really a high admission, even for Paris. It is the same as though a landlord should make no charge for his rooms, but compel you to pay two dollars for the privilege of getting into bed. Nowhere can something be had for nothing, and the more liberal it is at the beginning, the dearer it is at the ending.

But the chief delight of the middle and lower class of Parisians is the ball at night. There are scores and scores of gardens in every part of the city, immense enclosures, with a magnificent orchestra in the center, in which the Parisian dances and dances, seemingly never tiring. He stops now and then for a glass of wine, or the non-exhilarating syrup with which he lights his soul and ruins his stomach, if he has soul and stomach, but he seems to regret even this loss of time. The women are even more intoxicated with the dance than the men. A man may stop a minute and be easy, but the women chafe under the pauses in the music, and are impatient to be in motion.

There are gardens for the very poor, where the admission is a sou, or such a matter, for the men, and nothing for the women. The grounds outside are rather diminutive, and the ornamentation somewhat scanty, but the dancing floor is there and the orchestra likewise, and the blouses and calico enjoy themselves as thoroughly as the broadcloth and silk that frequent the higher priced places.

The Jardin Mabille, near the Champs Elysées, is the best known in Paris. It has world-wide celebrity, and no foreigner, no matter of what nation, ever leaves Paris without paying it, at least, one visit. It is a wondrously beautiful place, gorgeously illuminated with colored lights, and full to excess of trees, shrubbery, flowers and everything else that is beautiful. There are long walks, tortuous labyrinths, tables everywhere under trees, and it is filled with all sorts of attractions to take money from the visitor.

The foreigner goes there to see the peculiar dancing, of which he or she has heard so much. The whole world knows of the can-can, and the whole world has heard of the frightfully immodest exposure of person visible at these bac

THE MABILLE AT NIGHT.

chanalian orgies. I doubt if a youth ever left his native home in America that his mother did not exact a promise from him that he would not visit this horrible Mabille, which promise he gave, with, "Why, mother, do you suppose I would go to such a place? Never!" And then he went there the first time he was in Paris. He wasted no time.

Inasmuch as the Mabille has, ere these pages will be printed, gone the way of the world (the ground has been sold, and is to be used for legitimate business purposes), some little account of it is proper, even though it is like embalming a fly in precious ointment.

Mabille was established in 1840 by an old and not very popular dancing master named Mabille, by virtue of his age known as Père (Father) Mabille. He purchased or leased a piece of ground on the Allée des Veuves and the Champs Ely-

20

sees, and built thereon a dance house. Originally it was a
dingy structure and the admission, male and female, was only

ten sous. It pros-
pered, for it was
the resort of the
doubtful classes
who always pay.

The sons of
Père Mabille
took the money
the old gentle-
man had saved,
and enlarged it.
They substituted
gas for oil; they
enlarged and

A MABILLE DIVINITY AND THE IDIOT WHO PAYS.

decorated the grounds; they planted shrubbery and introduced
decorations; they had better music, and made it the resort of
the better, that is, richer class of the *demi-monde*, the wild
Bohemians and that enormous class in Paris who live from
hour to hour like butterflies.

Then commenced its prosperity. It became the fashion
among all classes. The rich and aristocratic went there to get
the dissipation that more correct amusements would not afford
them; the foreigners flocked thither in droves, for the Jardin
Mabille was one phase of Parisian life which must be seen, and
every girl who wanted to display her charms and graces in a
way to excite attention, chose Mabille as the stage upon which
to make her essay.

Enter a girl from the Provinces of any peculiar type of
beauty, any especial beauty of face and figure, with the wit
and boldness for the venture. She danced at the Mabille.
Some rich or notorious debauchee picked her up at once, and
made her the fashion. He gave her carriages, costumes, palaces. Poets, who are never so divine as when a responsible
spendthrift inspires them, sang the beauties of the new sensation, and all Paris talked of her. Of course she did not dance
at Mabille after she had made her conquest — Mabille was her
opportunity.

They lived their brief existence, they were attired like the butterfly while they lived but, alas! they died as does the butterfly.

Originally it was the resort of the middle class of Parisians, who worked for their living, clerks, students, and that class, and grisettes, and the women who skirted the edges of decency. The dances that made the place famous were born of the natural extravagance of feeling that possesses these classes of Frenchmen, and they were done with an abandon which their paid imitators never rivaled. It was grotesque, wild and suggestive, but it was genuine. If Finette flung herself into a position that procured applause, Marie would excel her or die in the attempt. These people, forty years ago, did the grotesque because it pleased them to do it — the paid dancers last summer were mere imitations, and bad ones at that.

The proprietors encouraged this kind of thing, for in it was their profit. And they engaged other women, not beautiful enough to become sensations, but accommodating enough to stay in the place nights, who were ready to endure the attentions of any man who had francs enough in his pocket to afford it, and who, for their society, would pay ten prices for refreshments ; they getting their percentage regularly in the morning.

We saw them by the hundred, each one with some wealthy idiot attached to her, spending his money supposing that he was seeing "life." He was, the dirty end of it, and he was paying roundly for it.

Who went to Mabille? Everybody. Thirty years ago, Harriet Beecher Stowe visited it, and described it as follows :

We entered by an avenue of poplars and other trees and shrubs, so illuminated by jets of gas sprinkled among the foliage as to give it the effect of enchantment. We found flower-beds laid out in every conceivable form, with diminutive jets of gas so distributed as to imitate flowers of the softest tints and the most perfect shape. In the centre there is a circle of pillars, on the top of each of which is a pot of flowers with gas jets, and between them an arch of gas jets. In the midst of this is another circle, forming a pavilion for musicians, also brilliantly illuminated, and containing a large cotillion band of the most finished performers. Around this you find thousands of gentlemen and ladies strolling, singly, in pairs, or in groups. While the musicians repose they loiter, sauntering round, or recline on seats. But now a lively waltz strikes the ear. In an instant twenty or thirty couples are whirling along, floating like thistles in the wind, around the central pavilion. Their feet scarce touch the smooth-trodden earth. Round and round, in a vortex of life, beauty and brilliancy they go, a whirlwind of delight, eyes sparkling, cheeks flushing, and gauzy draperies floating by, while the crowds outside gather in a ring and watch the giddy revel. There are countless forms of symmetry and grace, faces of wondrous beauty; there, too, are feats of agility and elasticity quite aerial. One lithe and active dancer grasped his fair partner by the waist; she was dressed in red, was small, elastic, agile, and went by like the wind, and in the course of a very few seconds he would give her a whirl and a lift, sending her spinning through the air, around himself as an axis, full four feet from the ground. It is a scene perfectly unearthly, or rather perfectly Parisian, and just as earthly as possible; yet a scene where earthliness is worked up into a style of sublimation the most exquisite conceivable. Aside from the impropriety inherent in the very nature of waltzing, there was not a word, look or gesture of immorality or impropriety The dresses were all decent, and if there was a vice it was vice masked under the guise of polite propriety.

It was different in the Summer of 1881. The dancers were professionals; the poor, painted, broken down danseuses of the minor theaters, and the male dancers were professionals, or semi-professionals, who came every night and went through the same dreary performance.

Now it is no more. It existed forty years; poets have raved over its habitues; women who made their *debut* on the treacherous surface of Parisian life, survive only in their rhymes, and the visitor to Paris next season will find in its place imposing structures devoted to trade. It is well. The more trade and the less Mabille the better for the world.

But the American youth who thought to have a bacchanalian orgie was terribly disappointed, for there is nothing bacchanalian about it. All he saw was the entire dancing platform occupied by waltzers, who waltzed just as everybody does in good society, nothing more or less. Only after each waltz comes the terribly immoral can-can, and the eyes of the young American, or English, man or woman glitter with expected enjoyment. Alas! they do not get it. The can-can is simply a quadrille danced by two or more couples; there is no prompter, no set figure as I could see, and nothing about it singular except the extravagant poses of the dancers. They advance and retreat, not with the dignified walk-through that the English speaking races affect, but more like Comanche

Indians.   The male being who dances, always with his hat on, will indulge in the most terrific leaps; he will twist his body into every possible shape that the human body is capable of, and will do more grotesque work than any pantomimist on any stage.   He twirls, he twists, he leaps, he dances on one foot, and then on the other.   He throws his body into the air in all sorts of shapes; he squats, he lolls his tongue out of his mouth, he makes play with his hat, he puts it back on his head, either at the back or over his eyes; he springs and knocks his feet together; all without system or design, but always  in time with the music.   It is not the poetry, it is the delirium tremens, of motion.   It is such a dance as one might expect to see in a lunatic asylum containing only incurables.

PROFESSIONALS IN A QUADRILLE AT THE MABILLE.

As an exhibition of absurd posturing, it is always a success; as a specimen of dancing, as we understand dancing, it is anything else.   But for just once it is amusing.   As between seeing it every night and serving an equal time in the penitentiary, I would unhesitatingly choose the penitentiary.   The human body is a thing of joy when naturally carried, but you do not want too much of it in the can-can.

The women are, it must be confessed, a trifle freer.   They will kick a bystander's hat from his head, and in some of the movements there is a very free exhibition of leg; that is to say, if the leg be shapely.   I noticed that the ladies whose general contour suggested pipe-stemmy support were as modest about their displays as though they had been nuns, and I fancied I could detect a shade of anguish pass over their faces as they observed the shapely proportions of their more favored sisters.

But be it known that the especial dancers, those who do these extraordinary leaps and contortions, are such by profession, who get so much per night, the same as at any other theater.   This style of dancing was always in favor in Paris among the people, and the proprietor of the place, finding that it attracted strangers, reduced it to a system. He hires a certain number of dancers, the same as he does his orchestra, and these set the fashion for the citizens who indulge in terpsichorean gymnastics.

You can easily detect the professionals. They come on the floor at regular intervals and do their dreary performance coolly and in a purely professional way, without any more emotion than they would manifest in combing their hair.

I do not know what it might have been in other days, but at present writing it is about the tamest place I know of. I overheard this conversation between two young ladies one morning : —

"Mary, dear, where did you go last evening? I could not find you."

"Ah, don't tell anybody, but Mamie, and Charlie, and I, went to the Mabille."

"Is it good?"

"Good! It is nothing. *It is the most shockingly moral place I ever saw. Why, anybody can go there.*"

Mary dear had expected to be shocked, but she was not.

A MALE DANCER AT JARDIN BULLIER.

Possibly the world never saw so much of her lower limbs as it did of the ladies dancing at the Mabille, but I will venture to say that she, herself, under the eyes of her prudish mamma at home, had more than made that up by display from the neck downward, a great many times.

It is not altogether pleasant for young Americans of the gentler sex to visit Mabille, no matter how good their escort. There are too many draw-backs to the pleasure, and it is being continually marred. I noticed one party, a young lady and gentleman who were perpetually troubled; they would be observing something that interested them, when very suddenly the girl would exclaim, "Charley, this way! quick! There comes Sadie Mercer, and I would not have her see me here for anything. Sammy Burton is with her!"

They rose and darted down a path-way, only to turn and meet another party whom they knew, and so on. The most of the evening was spent in vain endeavors to keep their acquaintances from knowing they were there, and their friends were similarly employed.

There was no occasion for all this effort. Everybody goes to the Mabille, once at least, because everybody must. But it isn't worth the time, however.

At the *Jardin Bullier*, in the Latin quarter, there is wilder dancing and more freedom than the Mabille. It is the resort of the students and the

THE GRISETTE WHO PREFERS THE JARDIN BULLIER.

grisettes proper, and the spectacle is genuine. There are no professionals there, and the dancing is done by those who have paid for it, and do it for the pleasure they find in it. The high-kicking girl kicks as a colt does, because she enjoys it, and not in the languid way of the paid dancers. The brigandish youth who can contort the wildest is cheered on to renewed exertions, and the grisette who can kick the highest or do the most grotesque things is applauded to the echo. And when in these extravaganzas one slips upon the waxed floor, and falls, what a shout goes up from the excited spectators! She cares nothing for it—slips are common on these floors. She laughs more heartily than the rest, and rises and resumes her place.

The French quadrille is like American hash—a mystery. There is no earthly system in it. Like volunteer soldiers, each one operates upon his own hook. They forward and back with the most sublime disregard of everybody else; they combine in the one dance the American quadrille, the German and French waltz, the Spanish fandango, the galop, the polka, and every other dance known to ancient and modern times. The only reason that they do not incorporate other dances into their alleged quadrille, is because they do not know any more. They put in all they have heard of, and one would be unreasonable to expect more of them.

But they have a good time, and, as the French world goes, an innocent one. There is perhaps more freedom in gesture than would be considered proper in England or America, but there is no drunkenness, and the utmost decorum is observed. Such a thing would be impossible with the fighting whisky of America, or face-bruising brandy of England. Get together a thousand of the lower classes in either of those excessively moral countries, and the affair would break up in a row in an hour. There would be knock-downs and dragging-outs without number; there would be bruised heads and mashed faces, and the broken nose brigade would be largely recruited.

The Frenchman does not get drunk. He drinks his light wine to the point of exhileration, and that is all. The student of art, or law, or medicine, who finds his enjoyment at these places, keeps as sober as a judge, and a great deal more sober than a great many judges in America I wot of. He looks to be capable of any enormity, but he is the most inoffensive being on earth. Indulging in the wildest vagaries — dressed in the most rakish and brigandish costume, he is scrupulously polite and intensely considerate. He could not be more so were the grisettes his sisters, and the spectators his father, mother and aunts.

One evening at the *Jardin Bullier* one young fellow, utterly and entirely brainless, evidently the fop of his quarter, appeared dressed, to his taste, gorgeously. He wore a pearl gray suit; the bottoms of his trowsers were so absurdly wide that they covered his boot; his coat sleeves were so wide that they made a fair match for his trowsers; his cuffs (with a showy sham button) came down to his knuckles; his shirt collar was cut half way down his breast, and his hat was the most painful in shine that I had ever seen. He was, in short, gotten up regardless of expense, and entirely for effect.

This young fellow offered some slight indignity to a girl with whom he was dancing. Very promptly she cried out, and in an instant the dancing was suspended. "Put him out!" cried those near them, who comprehended the matter. "Put him out! Put him out!" was echoed from one side to the other of the vast hall, and a rush of excited Frenchmen was made toward that part of the room. The fellow attempted some sort of an explanation, but it was of no avail. Out he went, guilty or not. In that place everybody must be like Cæsar's wife — above suspicion. Out he went, and the dancing was resumed with redoubled fury. A duty discharged, they might abandon themselves to pleasure with increased zest. All the difference was those who had yelled "Put him out" the loudest, kicked a trifle higher than before, and went crab-like sideways with more extraordinary contortions.

Tibbitts and the Professor had an awkward experience the first night they were in Paris. The Professor had received a letter from Tibbitts' father requesting him to look after the young man, and see that he attended to legitimate matters and be not carried away with the frivolities of Parisian life, which destroy so many inexperienced youth. In fact, he gave the Professor authority in the matter, and made him a sort of a guardian over him.

After dinner the Professor showed Tibbitts the letter and assumed control at once.

"To-night, Lemuel, I have to meet the American delegates to the International Science Congress, and I cannot be with you. But I must exact a promise from you that you will not go to any of those public balls, such as the Mabille. I have no objection to your visiting the Opera, for I understand the building itself is a study, and it is perhaps well that you should

hear and enjoy the music of the masters.   This is as far as I
can permit you to go.   You promise?"

"Certainly," replied Tibbitts, "though it is not necessary.
Without a promise I should not go to those wicked places."

THE MEETING OF TIBBITTS AND THE PROFESSOR.

Scene the second: The Jardin Mabille — music, lights, gaily
dressed women, little tables, wine, and all that sort of thing.

Tibbitts dancing furiously with a lady in silken attire, and
striving in vain to do the high, grotesque dancing of the
Parisian.   The music ceases and Tibbitts leads his partner to
a table.   In his excitement he does not at once notice that at
the table exactly in front of him is seated the Professor, who,
inasmuch as he was holding an interesting conversation with a
lady who spoke English somewhat, did not notice Tibbitts till
their eyes met.

Tibbitts is a young man of great presence of mind.   He

was equal to this emergency. The Professor regarded him a moment, and said: —

"Lemuel!"

Lemuel stared at him and replied: —

"Are you addressing me, sir?"

"Certainly I am."

"You are mistaken in the person, sir. I do not know you. My name is not Lemuel, it is Smith. Smith, of Hartford, Connecticut. May I ask your name, and why you address me, a perfect stranger? Do I resemble any friend of yours? Am I like any grandson you have? If so, could you, for the sake of the resemblance, lend me a hundred francs?"

"Lemuel, this is trifling. What are you doing here?"

It suddenly occurred to Lemuel that he had the Professor in as close a corner as the Professor had him, and he replied:—

"Professor, what are *you* doing here?"

"Lemuel, I was fearful that you would break your promise to me, and I came here to be sure that *you* were not here."

"Professor, I was fearful that *you* might accidentally stray hither after the meeting of the Social Science sharps was over, and I came here to see that no harm came to you."

"Lemuel, we are, I perceive, both innocent of any harmful intention, but as our action might be misconstrued at home, it would be as well if no mention is made of this unfortunate matter."

Lemuel coughed slightly and appeared wrapped in thought a moment. Finally he spoke: —

"I do not know but that I am permitting my good nature to get the better of my duty, but I will not make mention of your escapade. But I wish it distinctly understood that this must not be repeated, and that you go home at once. You ought to be ashamed of yourself. It is no place for you. You, a teacher, an instructor of youth, a man of sixty, one whose duty it is to form the morals of American youth, one to whose care is entrusted inexperienced youth, to be seen in such a place and in such a company. It is too much, and would not sound well in the West. For shame. As I said, it must not be repeated. Go. I now see why you were so willing that I should go to the Opera, and why you exacted of me a promise that I should not come here. You intended to come here by yourself, and did not want me to be a witness to your shame. But go! I forgive you! I forgive you."

The Professor went, and as soon as he was safely away, Lemuel took the seat he had vacated, and was presently engaged in a very pleasant conversation with the lady who spoke English somewhat.

The Professor's guardianship will not be of much use to the pleasure-seeking youth. Professors have curiosity, which they generally gratify, in one way or another. Poor humanity!

THE CAFÉ SWELL.

The café is the Frenchman's especial resort, however. They are everywhere and of all classes, and from six to twelve at night are full. The regular Frenchman sees his friends here; business is transacted here; the political questions of the day are discussed, and here nations are made and unmade. In foul weather the inside is crowded; in fair, the little tables on the sidewalk under the beautiful trees are all occupied. And these little tables outside afford never-failing pleasure, to any one, native or foreign. There is a constant ebb and flow of humanity along the streets; there the costumes of all nations and the manners and customs of the world are reproduced for your benefit. Americans, English, Germans, Turks, Tunisians, West Indians, Carribeans, Russians, and Polanders. If there is a nation on earth that is not represented in the Boulevard des Italiens or any of the principal streets, any fine night, I do not know of it.

And here sits the Parisian, hour after hour, watching this human kaleidoscope, and thanking heaven that he is a Frenchman, and above all a Parisian.

The electric lights shine through the foliage of the trees, making figures of rare beauty upon the faultless sidewalks; there is the constant procession of vehicles more beautiful under this light than at noonday; opposite him are the brilliantly lighted shops with their wealth of beauty in the windows, and all around him is bustle, stir, and life. There is nothing dull or stagnant on the streets of Paris at night. The Parisian will not have it that way. The glitter may be very thin, but he will have the glitter. He lives upon it.

Paris by day is beautiful — Paris by night is superb.

The faro bankeress is getting ready to go home. She has well nigh done Europe, which is to say, she has explored every shop in Paris and London. She may go through Switzerland and Germany with us, but we hope not. We are praying that she will go home from Paris, and she can't start any too quick. That she is making preparations for a start, she confesses. She is afraid of sea voyages; she has a mortal dread of water; she remarks that she always lives very correctly a week or so before she sails. She says her prayers regularly, attends church every service, and does nothing wrong that she knows of. She will not go to an Opera on Sunday; she declined to go to the Mabille at all; nor will she even play cards any day. This for ten days before sailing.

" And after you land safely in New York? "

" O, I ain't on the water then, and it don't differ so much."

Which is very like a negro I once knew in Bucyrus, Ohio. He was very religious, of the African kind of religion, and was the loudest and most muscular man at a prayer meeting for many a mile around. A gentleman who had a piece of work to do that was not entirely legal offered Sam two dollars to do it for him.

" Massa Perkins, dis ting doesn't adzackly squar wid my perfeshn, an' it's decidedly wicked. It's suthin' a perfessin' Christian shouldn't do, nohow. But two dollahs is a mi'ty heap ob money foh de ole man, and ain't picked up ebery day. I'll chance it. Bress de Lawd! It's a sin, but I can 'pent. Bress de Lawd, I can 'pent.

> " While de lamp holds out to bun,
> De vilest sinnah may retun."

" Bress de Lawd foh de deff-bed 'pentance. Dat is de great
t'ing. Yoo can 'pent on a dying bed."

" But, Sam," said Perkins, " I don't want you to do anything that grinds against your conscience. A death bed
repentance is all very well, but suppose you die too suddenly
to repent ? "

" It's a risk, Massa Perkins, but I'll chance it. Two dol
lahs is a great deal ob money foh de ole man. It's a mi'ty
sudden deff dat'll ketch me onpropared. And come to t'ink
ob it, to be ontirely safe, I'll 'pent — jist ez soon ez I git de
two dollahs."

Our faro bankeress had the same kind of religion. Land
her safe in New York, and she was easy as to her sins. It was
only against the dangers of navigation that she wanted to be
insured.

BEAUVAIS CATHEDRAL.

CHAPTER XXI.

Paris, the magnificent, has thousands of structures that are worth a voyage across the Atlantic to see, but there is in all that wonderful city no one that is so utterly bewildering in its magnificence as the massive pile, the Louvre, one of the largest as well as grandest places in the world. Its long galleries and beautiful salons, with hundreds of winds and turns, form a labyrinth in which, without a guide, one may almost be lost.

It required a great deal of time to build the Louvre, as its completion was being continually retarded. But through all the years and the changes in the styles of architecture, a general oneness of plan was maintained, and the noble structure, though constructed piece-meal, is consistent and symmetrical.

It is admirably located near the banks of the Seine, and with the Tuileries, occupies forty acres of ground. It is of a quadrilateral form, enclosing an immense square. Approaching it from the Place du Royale, its imposing front challenges attention and then invites study. Admiration is excited by the solidity, as well as symmetry of the pile, and this is increased by its elaborate ornamentation.

Such buildings are impossible in this day and age of the world. Private means are not sufficient. An American railroad magnate might do something in this direction, but when the idea of expending even a few paltry millions upon a residence for himself comes to him, he puts it off till after he has attempted a corner in some stock or another, which generally makes a lame duck of him, and he is glad to retire to the humble mansion which he always has — in his wife's name.

Modern governments cannot do it, for they haven't the facilities of the ancient Kings for this kind of work. All that

(320)

the old French Kings had to do when they wanted a palace of this kind was to call upon the workmen of the nation, with spears, and set them about it, and feed them upon black bread and very sour and cheap wine, and take possession of the stone quarries and the lumber mills, and put it up. The painters and sculptors and the makers of the furnishings they were compelled to pay, but that was nothing. An extra tax on everything the people lived upon was levied and collected with great vigor and much certainty, and so without any bother or worry the King had a new palace, with fountains, and trees, and flowers, and pictures, and statuary, and all that sort of thing, in the most gorgeous style. A French King, a few hundred years ago, had what an American would not unjustly style a soft thing of it. It was a good situation to hold, and I don't wonder that Nobles fought to be Kings, and Kings struggled to be Emperors. Everybody wants power.

And this reminds me of a little incident that happened in my own beloved America, illustrative of this principle. In a certain county in the good State of Ohio was, and is, a township called Cranberry, inhabited largely by Germans and those of German descent. These Germans, without exception, adhered to one political party, and all voted one way, and their devotion to their party was such that it was considered an unpardonable sin to "scratch" a ticket, or in any way run counter to the action of their convention. In politics they were as regular as a horse in a bark-mill.

One man, always the stoutest and best one physically, of the party, stood at the polls, and every one of his organization as he came to vote was expected to show his ticket to this recognized King, that it might be made certain that no one scratched or acted unorthodox. This man was by right entitled to a county office, and held one as long as he could maintain his position at home.

One Peter Feltzer had been King of Cranberry for a great many years, and by virtue of his position had been successively Commissioner, Treasurer, Representative, and, in fact, had gone up and down the ladder of earthly glory a great many times, and was waxing as full of glory and honors as he was of years.

21

There was a young man named Meyer, who had an idea
that he wanted to hold a county office, and live at the county
seat, and spend his time in drinking beer, at good pay, and he
knew there was but one road to this summit of human bliss,
and that was over Feltzer's body. So one election day he

THE STRUGGLE FOR THE KINGSHIP.

presented himself at the polls, and ignoring Feltzer, offered a
folded ballot.

"Mike, show me dot dicket!" exclaimed Feltzer.

"Yoo shust go mit hell!" was Meyer's answer.

Feltzer divined the meaning of this revolt at once. He
knew that this was a challenge to mortal combat, and that
the prize of the victor was the crown. Meyer was a splendid
young man, built like a bull, and only thirty. Feltzer had

been, in his day, more than a match for him; but alas, he was sixty, and had been enervated by the soft allurements of official position. However, he determined not to die without a struggle, and so laying off their coats, at it they went. Meyer had no easy contract. Feltzer was fighting for life, and the contest was long and severe. Youth finally triumphed, and Feltzer, after half an hour of rolling in the mud, admitted defeat. Meyer sprang gaily to his feet, and seizing Feltzer's hickory club exclaimed to the bystanders, "Now, yoo men vat vants to vote will shust show *me* your dickets!"

They accepted their new ruler the same as the French do, and he was elected to an office the ensuing Fall, and ever since, for aught I know. He held it, anyhow, till some younger man deposed him.

This has nothing to do with the Louvre, except as showing that humanity is the same everywhere. If any other moral can be got out of it I have no objection.

All over the Louvre are statues of men who are famous in French history — those who have achieved fame in art, science, literature or war. They are here, and in stone that will last for ages; longer, probably, than the memory of the acts that placed them there.

On the north side of the Place Napoleon there is a wonderful Corinthian colonnade, over the columns of which are heroic statues of eighty-six celebrated men, and on the balustrade are sixty-five allegorical groups, wonderful in design and execution, and so, all the way around the enormous building, story after story is burdened with works of art. Wondrous works, artistically bestowed, always profuse, but never overdone. Every column, every window-cap, even the ledges just under the projection of the roof, bear the impress of genius. There are statues, medallions, large groups illustrating important events in the history of France, exquisitely carved by master hands, on all four sides of the exterior, all symmetrical in design and faultless in proportion.

The interior is in keeping with the exterior. The noble pile is a fit repository for what it contains. The one hundred and forty salons into which the Louvre is divided are marvels of artistic beauty. Intended for the abode of royalty, it was

royally constructed. The kingly builders did not spare the
sweat or blood of their subjects. They set out to have a royal
palaise, and they did not allow the miseries of a few millions
of their people to stand in the way of its achievement.

The most beautiful of them all is the Galerie d' Apollon,
the ornamentation of which, in beauty of design and skill
in execution, is marvelous. It is of itself a study. The
vaulted ceiling is filled with paintings by Le Brun, one of the
greatest of the French masters. The cornices and corners
are ornamented with beautiful designs in gilt, elaborately
wrought, and on the walls are portraits of French artists in
gobelin tapestry, making it one of the finest collections of this
kind of work extant. There is a perfection in the drawing
that is remarkable, and the coloring is exquisite, the various
shades and tints blending with a nicety that makes one almost
feel that they were done by artists with brush and paint.

Tapestry, as a rule, has small degree of expression in face
and feature, but in these every feature is faithfully reproduced,
and the whole figure is strikingly life-like.

This room has a history. It was originally built by Henry
IV., and was burned in 1661. During the reign of Louis
XIV. the work of reconstruction was begun, Le Brun furnishing the designs. His death in 1690 put a stop to the work,
and for a century and a half it stood in an unfinished condition. In 1848 work was resumed, and in three years it was
finished as it now stands.

There are scores of other rooms of quite as much interest.
In all, the frescoes and wall paintings are incomparable, and
though the galleries aggregate over a mile and a half in length,
in no place is there a barren spot. The great masters, through
all these ages, gave to it their best years and their best work,
and so long as the Louvre remains these rooms will be monuments of their genius.

The Louvre is inseparable from the history of France. In
all the upheavals, the tearings down and overturnings, it has
been a central figure. It was from the Louvre on that dreadful night in August, 1572, that Charles IX. fired the shot that
was the signal for the horrible massacre of St. Bartholomew,
which ended in the indiscriminate slaughter of the Huguenots,

and from that time on to the present it has been the stage on which tragedies have been enacted. It figured in the terrible days of the Commune, in 1871, and but for an almost Providential interference, would have passed into history as a memory.

The Louvre has always been the especial object of the hatréd of the Parisian mob, and no wonder. Every stone laid was so much bread taken from the mouths of French workingmen; every stroke of a chisel, every inch of the wonderful pile, was a robbery of himself of whatever it cost. It was the habitation of a nobility, supported in luxury at the expense of the French people.

It is all well enough to talk of reason, but there is no reason in a revolution. The Parisian whose wife and family were living in garrets and cellars, eating black bread and drinking sour wine, could not be reasoned with when he caught glimpses of the luxurious salons in which the few took their pleasure. He could not be expected to have much reason when he got a smell of the delicacies of the royal table, and thought of the scant fare on which he was compelled to subsist. His garret and thin pallet did not contrast well with the gorgeous apartments and silken couches of his royal masters, nor did the offal with which he was fed compare pleasantly with the wild profusion of dainties which they rioted upon.

It was nightingale tongues *versus* offal — it was poverty in the extreme *versus* prodigal waste.

And then the arrogance of these tyrants! They held the commoners as an inferior race, as another creation, much as the Southern planter used to hold his slaves.

One of the ancient nobility replied to a demand from the workingmen for better food: "The animals! Let them eat grass!" It is no wonder, a few months later, when this silken lord was beheaded, that the mob carried his head upon a pike with a tuft of grass in his set jaws.

It is no wonder that when the mob, starved and frozen to a point where death was preferable to life, wrested the power from the nobility and controlled Paris, that it should blindly destroy everything that symbolized royalty, everything that smacked of class rule.

True, the Commune should not have destroyed fountains, and statuary, and paintings, but it must be said that they did not destroy these priceless works for the mere sake of destroying them. The statues symbolized royalty. It was not a Venus that was the object of their hatred — the Venus was their wrong, in stone.

OF THE COMMUNE.

There is much to be said about these Parisian mobs, and whoever knows of the sufferings of the people, even under the mildest form of royalty, cannot wholly condemn. The many laboring for the few; the man with a hungry wife and pallid children does not care much for the art that his oppressors delight in. He looks at immortal work through eyes dimmed with suffering and half blinded with tears, and it is not singular that in his rage he strikes blindly.

At this time Napoleon had fought an unprovoked war, and to perpetuate his dynasty had dragged from their wretched homes thousands of the youth of France, and had been driven back by the Prussians in utter and entire humiliation. Had he crushed Prussia, the glory of the achievement would have atoned in some degree for its cost; but to bear the burden of defeat in shame and humiliation was too much, and though a Republic followed, the Commune was not satisfied. It would not trust the Republic. It looked upon the Republic as a partial change — it wanted a radical one; and, with the childishness peculiar to the French, they commenced the work of reconstruction by destroying what was their own, and which would delight them as much under the Republic of the future as it had their oppressors in the Monarchies of the past.

English, American or German people would have done differently. If these wonderful works reminded them too much of their sufferings to be pleasant, they would have been sold to other nations, and the proceeds devoted to the payment of the national debt.

It is well for the world that so much of the Louvre was preserved, for there are other nations than France that have an interest in it. Art has no nationality — it is the property of the world.

The Communists ruined many of the finest works in the lower part of the building, but fortunately their ravages were confined to a small space. More important matters occupied their attention, and the Louvre was virtually spared. It was set on fire, however, and the magnificent library of ninety thousand volumes was entirely destroyed, and many works of art were injured, but the troops of the Republic arrived in time to arrest the progress of the flames, and the building was preserved.

The first floor of the building is devoted wholly to ancient sculpture, and a wilderness there is of it. Too much of it, in fact, unless one has time for its study. You stop a moment to admire a Psyche; you have only time to glance at the Caryatides in the hall in which Henri IV. celebrated his marriage with Margaret of Valois; you pass through the Salle du Gladiateur, containing the Borghese Gladiator, the famous work made familiar through copies of it; you look down a long hall filled with wonderful statues and see at the farther end the outline of a figure whose very pose is a poem. The room is hung in crimson velvet, and the light, soft and subdued, makes the figure seem almost that of a living, breathing being. At this distance the effect is wonderful. There was great genius in making the sculpture; there was almost as much in placing it.

There is a long vista of beautiful statues lining the way on either side to the crimson chamber, which, with its gentle lights and shades, makes the picture perfect, and as one feels the delight of the scene wonder ceases at the ravings of artists and lovers of art over the Venus of Milo.

There, in the center of the crimson room, stands the armless figure whose perfection of form and face has never been equaled. It stands alone, with nothing near to distract the mind by divided attention, and as the lover of the beautiful looks upon the wondrous beauty of that speechless yet speaking statue, admiration ripens into adoration.

Even Tibbitts and the faro bankeress stood still and silent before it for full twenty minutes, and no greater compliment was ever paid a work of art. It interested even them.

The figure compels feeling. You do not feel that you are enjoying rare sculpture, but your sympathies go out to the beautiful form before you, not in cold marble but in life — real life, with all the tender qualities belonging in nature to such a perfect face and figure.

This may be gush, but there is something about this block of marble that is fascinating beyond expression. In it art has conquered material. The marble lives and breathes. It is marble, but it is marble endowed with life. Or, rather it is not marble, it is life resembling marble. It is a dream caught and materialized. If it is not nature, it is more than nature. It is a poet's idea of what nature should be.

Whether it be the face with the wonderful features that almost speak, or the form so graceful in pose, or the combination of both, cannot be said; but the effect is produced, and no one can withstand the silent appeal made by this creation of an unequaled genius. It is something of which one cannot tire. The oftener it is seen the greater the impression. It can never be forgotten, nor can it be described. It cannot be reproduced, either in marble or oil. There are innumerable copies of it the world over, but to feel and realize the absolute perfection of the work the original must be seen. No copy can do it justice.

The great trouble with the Louvre is there is too much of it. If one could live to the age of Methusaleh it would all be very well, but unfortunately life is short. You wish you had not so much to see, for you want to see it all, and the very wealth is bewildering. Recollection becomes confusing and mixed.

Of course every one selects some one picture or statue which impresses him to the point of carrying away a memory thereof. We had among us a young American physician who stood in the orthodox pose before the Gladiator. Having studied anatomy, muscles and things of that nature were just in his way. He stood for full twenty minutes wrapped in what he desired us to understand as ecstacy, and then delivered himself thus:—

"A——! This is the very actuality of the ideality of individuality."

It was a very pretty speech, and the fact that he had lain awake all the night before arranging it, and that he pulled us all around to the Gladiator to get his chance of firing it off did not detract from its merit. No one knew what it meant, but the words were mouth filling, and it did as well as though it had some glimmer of meaning. There is nothing in art like good sounding words.

From the ground-floor you ascend a broad stair-case, exquisitely carved. You come into another wilderness, only this is in canvas, instead of marble. Every school in the world is represented here, for when the French potentate was not able to buy he could always sieze. You don't stop to inquire how the collection was made; it is here, and to an American, or any other foreigner, that is sufficient. We come to enjoy the pictures, and we don't care whether they were purchased or taken by force. There are, as I said, one hundred and forty of these salons, and you must go through them all. There are galleries devoted to the French school, ancient and modern, the Italian school, the German, Dutch, Flemish, and

Spanish, and you come away feeling a sort of satisfaction that it has been done ; but no man living, in the time one usually has in Paris, can get a good idea of what is there gathered. Four miles of art is rather too much for one short effort. It is bewildering in its very profusion. One may be fond of art, but not educated to the point of taking so much of it in

TIBBITTS AND THE FARO BANKERESS ENJOYING ART.

systematically. Nevertheless, days spent in collections like the Louvre are too good to miss. Some of it will stick to you if you cannot carry it all away.

Tibbitts and the faro bankeress were delighted. Tibbitts, with an eye to speculation, made elaborate calculation as to the cost of the entire collection, and wondered whether or not a good thing could not be made by buying it all up and exhibiting it in New York.

That was the delight he got out of it.

The faro bankeress protested that she had never enjoyed art so much, and had never before known the delight that was in it. From several of the female figures she had got ideas of lace that were entirely new to her, and she had found and fixed in her mind a design for a fancy dress for Lulu, which she should have made the next day. She wondered if she could borrow the picture to show to the modiste. She had no idea that the ladies of ancient days dressed in such good taste, or that they had such wonderful material to dress with. Some of the costumes she had studied were altogether too sweet for anything.

And that was the delight she got out of it.

CHAPTER XXII.

THE Palais-Royal is the Parisian Mecca for all Americans. Its brilliant shops, glittering with diamonds and precious stones, are so many shrines at which Americans are most devout worshipers. They go there day after day, admiring the bewildering display, and the admiration excited by the wily shopkeeper by his skill in arranging his costly wares leads to purchases that would not otherwise have been made. There is a fascination about a shop window literally filled with diamonds, arranged by a Frenchman, that is irresistible, and with hundreds of such windows extending all the way around the immense court, there is no escaping its power. What a Parisian shopkeeper doesn't know about display isn't worth knowing. All Paris is arranged solely for the eye. They ignore the other senses to a very great degree.

With all its present wealth and beauty the Palais-Royal has witnessed some very exciting scenes.

It was built by Cardinal Richelieu for his residence, and he built it extremely well, little dreaming of the scenes of carnival, riot, quarrels, and bloodshed that were to be enacted there long after he had vacated it forever.

In 1663, when it was finished, it was called the Palais-Cardinal, but having been presented by Richelieu to Louis XIII., whose widow, Anne of Austria, with her two sons, Louis XIV. and Philippe d' Orléans, lived there, it was called the Palais-Royal.

Louis, on coming into possession of the Palais, presented it to his brother Philippe, during whose occupancy it was the scene of the most horrible orgies the world ever saw. The royal profligate gathered about him a host whose tastes were as depraved as his own, and with these he led a life of wild debauchery.

Later on, Philippe Egalité, exceeding the excesses of his grandfather, Philippe d'Orléans, made the Palais-Royal the scene of wilder disorders than had ever been seen there before, as bad as it had been. He was so reckless that his princely income was not enough to keep him

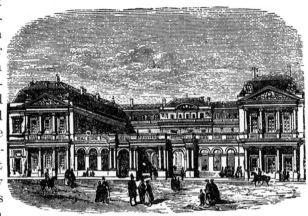

PALAIS-ROYAL.

in ready money. In fact his coffers were well nigh exhausted when he conceived the idea of deriving a revenue from some of the property that surrounded the Palais, which up to that time had been used simply for ornamentation. So he caused a number of shops to be erected around the garden adjoining the Palais, and from the rents paid for these was enabled to keep up his former manner of life until that (to him) memorable morning in November, 1793, when he took a walk to the Place de la Concorde, up a short flight of stairs, and for once in his life laid his head on a hard pillow. The deadly guillotine did its work, and the riotous life of Philippe Egalité came to a sudden end.

At that time the upper rooms of the vast galleries, now converted into handsome restaurants, were devoted to gaming, and it was no child's play, then, either. Here the excitable nobles, fascinated by the green cloth, lived in a constant whirl of excitement. The stakes ran high. Fortunes were made and lost in a night, and the Seine never did so good a business in the way of suicide. While these elegantly furnished and brilliantly lighted salons witnessed the demonstrative joy of the lucky winner or the gloomy despondency of the unhappy loser, scenes of an entirely different nature, and far more terrible in their results were being enacted in the cafés below.

In these cafés met the leaders of the people who were organizing for the destruction of the thoughtless revelers above their heads. It was the old story over again. The *canaille*, as the nobles termed the people, were groaning under the loads imposed upon them. The life-blood of the French people was being drained by the parasites of royalty — it was waste on the one hand and starvation on the other. Every gold piece that passed upon the tables above represented so much unpaid for sweat from the many below. Absolute power had, as it always does, run into unbridled license, and unbridled license had made the people desperate. They might not succeed, but they could no more than die, and the life they had was not worth the having.

It was in these cafés that Camille Desmoulins organized the people, and with such arms as they could seize on that memorable morning in July, marched upon the Bastille. They did not need arms. That mob, so led, could have torn down the hoary old wrong with their bare hands. There was not a man or woman in the throng that surged out of the Palais that morning who had not some especial reason for its destruction. Confined within its walls had died their brothers and fathers. To them it was royalty, and to royalty they owed every woe that afflicted them.

Desperate, determined men they were, crazed with excitement, and caring for nothing. They reached the Bastille and hurled themselves against its stubborn sides. Again and again were they beaten back by the garrison within, but each repulse only served to more determined efforts, and finally on the 14th of July the Bastille was swept from the face of the earth. Nothing was left of it but the terrible memories of the bloody past.

In 1801–7 the first Napoleon assembled the Tribunate in the Palais-Royal, and in 1815, Lucien Bonaparte made it his residence during the "One Hundred Days." From 1815 to 1830 it was again in the possession of Orleans family, and Louis Philippe occupied it until his ascension to the throne. Eighteen

years later, during the Revolution of February, which finally
resulted in the Presidency of Louis Napoleon and subsequently
his election by *plébiscite* as Emperor, the royal apartments

VISION OF THE COMMUNE.

were completely wrecked. The mob, wild with excitement,
went through the Palais like a whirlwind, destroying anything

and everything it could lay its hands upon. Of all the magnificent paintings,.the exquisite statues, the marvelous collections of fine glass and porcelain, with which the royal apartments were adorned, nothing escaped their fury. Almost the entire building was destroyed.

Napoleon III., who did so much to beautify Paris, restored the Palais to its original condition, and it continued so, being the residence of Prince Napoleon, cousin of the Emperor and son of Jeróme Napoleon, until the outbreak of the war in 1870. Then in 1871, on the 22d of May, the Communists took a hand at it, and sad work they made. Almost the entire south wing was destroyed by fire, and the other portions were badly damaged.

Now it is bright and gay with its magnificent display of diamonds, its pleasant little park with fountains and statues, its long spacious galleries that form unequaled promenades, and its restaurants celebrated the world over.

The galleries, four in number, extend entirely around the square park, which is two hundred and fifty-seven yards long and one hundred and ten wide. The Galerie d' Orléans, on the south side, is the most showy. It is three hundred and twenty feet long and one hundred and six feet wide, flanked with shops, containing fine goods of all descriptions. The roof is glass covered, and when lighted up at night, presents a dazzling appearance. It was on this site that, previous to 1830, stood the disreputable shops that gave the locality such an unsavory reputation.

The other galleries, though not so fine in construction, are just as attractive, and their wide pavements, shaded by the high balcony that forms a part of the second story, are thronged day and night with strangers, to whom these windows, ablaze with the light of precious stones, are always a delight. It is a pleasure to saunter slowly along and admire the beauties that increase every minute.

Nowhere in the world can be found so great a collection of gems in so small a space as in these four galleries. The fronts of the stores consist of a huge plate glass window and a small door. Although disproportionate in size, the window suffices to show the goods, and the door is plenty large enough for any one who wishes to enter. The Frenchman has a natural love for the beautiful, and the French jeweler shows his taste in the arrangement of his window. A large space, covered with diamonds, set and unset, of fine gold jewelry, artistic designs in rubies, pearls, opals, or emeralds, is in itself a beautiful sight, but when they are all arranged so as to show them all to the best advantage, then the effect is marvelous.

But there can be too much of a good thing. As a whole day spent among the wonders of the Louvre fatigues the mind and body, so the constant succession of dazzling windows in the Palais-Royal becomes after a while tiresome, and the pretty little park is sought for rest and refreshment. There the scene changes again, and a new and interesting phase of the Palais-Royal's attractions is seen. Under the long rows of trees that fringe the busy galleries are

MOTHER AND BONNE — PALAIS-ROYAL.

groups of women enjoying the cool breeze that just moves the branches above them, and tempers the heat that elsewhere is oppressive. They have some little trifle of fancy work in their hands, and as they languidly ply the needle they talk. It may be too warm to knit. It is never too warm to gossip.

Closely imitating these are the bonnes, or nurse girls, old and young, who chatter away like magpies, while their charges are amusing themselves making pictures in the sand. The

22

youngsters romp and roll about with all the pleasure of childhood. They don't care whether the Palais-Royal ever saw

THE YOUTHFUL BONNE.

bloodsheds and riots or not. It
makes a good playground for
them, and that is all they want.

Then the concerts that are
given there during the afternoons
are enjoyable, and they always
attract large audiences. The entire space on the south side is
occupied by all kinds and conditions of people, and like all
French assemblages, it is quiet
and orderly. The music, if not
of a high classical standard, is
good, and the people enjoy it.
Given a little white table in the
open air, some light Offenbachian
music and a glass of wine, and the Frenchman is happy.

The restaurants in the Palais-Royal form another by no

THE AGED BONNE.

means unimportant feature, for the
average American is no less fond of
a good dinner than the French *bon
vivant*, and in these pleasant places
he can find the perfection of good
living. The skill of French cooks is
acknowledged everywhere. Here he
is on his native heath, and is seen,
or tasted rather, to his best advantage.

The clerk or bookkeeper whose
salary is not in keeping with his
tastes, takes his modest dinner in
one of the second-floor restaurants,

where he gets a small bottle of claret and a well cooked, well
served meal for two francs. The place is clean, the surroundings cheerful, and though there are none of those delicate
trifles the French cook delights in making, there is an abundance of hunger-satisfying viands prepared in a most appetizing

manner, and they are to him better than the delicacies that grace a more elaborate table.

The more pretentious man, or the one having more money, goes to more pretentious places, and takes a dinner of several courses for five francs. There is a pleasing variety of soup, fish and entrées, with a dessert, and, if desired, coffee and cognac afterward, all prepared in good style, and well served.

But the thoroughly good liver goes to none of these. He knows the places, there in the Palais-Royal, where cooking has been reduced to a science; where the finest cooks in Paris bend their best energies to the concoction of dishes that Epicurus himself would have delighted in; where fine pictures and elegant surroundings appeal to the sense of sight, while the sense of taste is being catered to. He hies himself there and revels in the delights of a perfect dinner.

As the Parisian, man, woman, or child, will never sit indoors when the open air is possible, the Palais is always full. As a park it is delightful; the shops are just as attractive to the citizen as to the stranger, for the windows change contents every day, and the variety is such that something new and attractive can be seen at any time. It is a small world by itself, and it is no wonder that every American finds him or herself within it every day.

It is always a good thing to get hold of a good modern legend, a story that, while it may not be as gray-headed as those of the time of the gods and goddesses the ancients wrote of, has still attained a respectable age — a middle-aged legend, as it were. Such an one I have unearthed, and write it down for the benefit of coming generations.

It was during the terrible days of the Commune, Mademoiselle Therese, a beauty of the Faubourg St. Antoine, was loved by a Monsieur Adolph, the son of a rich baker in that quarter. That is to say, the baker was rich — but I am anticipating. Mademoiselle was a dressmaker of ravishing beauty. She could have married far above her condition on account of this ravishing beauty, but she was as wise as she was beautiful. She said to herself, " I could marry, by virtue of my face and figure, a grand gentleman, but — what then? I am not accomplished. I could learn to be a fine lady, it is true; but when

Monsieur should tire of me, as he inevitably would, I should lead a very uncomfortable life. I am a daughter of France — I do not wish to lead an uncomfortable life. Adolph is not handsome; he is only five feet four; he has bandy legs; his hair is bad, and his nose is a pug; but his papa has much ducats, and he is so much in love with me that he will take me without a *dot*, and on his papa's money we shall do business. I shall manage the business, we will make much more money, and found a family of our own, of which I shall be the head! Who knows? My sons will be gentlemen, and my daughters shall marry into the best families. Clearly, I shall marry Adolph."

She had one other suitor whom she favored somewhat, because he was a handsome fellow of some aristocratic connections, but he lacked the money of Adolph's father, being the heir of an impoverished house that had barely enough to live on in a sort of scrimped gentility. He was the son of a widow whose husband died with nothing, leaving her with just what she inherited from her own family, which was little enough, the Lord knows.

In some speculations at this time, Adolph's father, to use the language of the ancients, went up the spout. He lost every sou he had and in his chagrin laid down and died, which precluded the possibility of his acquiring another fortune.

Mademoiselle Therese found herself in this predicament:—

She was solemnly engaged to Adolph.

Adolph was bandy-legged, five feet four inches in height, with a pug nose and sandy hair.

Adolph possessed the additional drawback of not having a sou to bless himself or herself with.

It was a terrible situation.

At this precise time Henri, her other suitor, had come into improved circumstances. An uncle had died leaving him something, not as much as she had expected with Adolph, but yet something. In addition to this the handsome young fellow had served gallantly in the war, had attained the rank of Lieutenant, and was well up in the military.

He came to her with his improved prospects and once more tendered her his hand.

She thought it over and decided to accept him. "It is my duty. I adored Adolph, despite his legs, and hair, and nose, but I have a duty I owe to France. How can I bring up children for France on nothing and encumbered with a five-foot four husband with sandy hair, a pug nose, and bandy legs? Clearly it is my duty to marry Henri."

But how to get rid of Adolph? It would never do to jilt him, for it would ruin her reputation, and then she had a regard for his feelings.

"It would drive him to madness should he lose me, and once mad he would become a burden to France. I will spare his feelings."

By this time the Commune was in possession of Paris, and the National troops were besieging the city. Henri was with the National troops, while Adolph was a bitter Communist, as were all the Parisians who had lost their money.

Women are proverbially fickle, and French women especially. Therese was not only a woman, but she was a French woman. Therefore, there could be no question as to her fickleness. She had pondered long and seriously over the situation, and was troubled. Matrimony is a very serious matter, and she finally came to the conclusion that she could not marry Henri. She loved him to distraction, but he had not enough money. Without a rich husband she should still have to depend upon her needle for a living, and if she had to needle her way through life she preferred to do it for herself alone. This interesting female found herself engaged to two men, and determined to marry neither. But she was equal to the emergency.

"I have it," said Therese to herself. "I will extricate myself from this dilemma. I will not marry Henri. I cannot. It is a duty I owe to myself to have money, and a great deal of it. Henri has not enough, and yet I have promised to marry him. Adolph has none, and yet I have promised to marry him, though I cannot blame myself for this. When I promised him he had money. But I will marry neither, and will spare the feelings of both. No daughter of France ever wounds the feelings of those who love her. Love must be respected, even though it cannot be returned. I see my way out of these woods."

A terrible struggle was impending. The citizens and soldiers

could not help coming in collision the next day. Adolph,
armed as the Communists were, called upon her, on the afternoon preceding the final struggle.

She sat calmly, frozen with despair.

"Love of my life," said she, bursting into tears, "you,
to-morrow, rush upon death; I — I shall survive — would that
I might die with you. What will become of me?"

"I may not die," said Adolph, "but if I do it will be for
La Belle France."

And he drew himself up to his full height, which was, as I
have stated, five feet four. All Frenchmen draw themselves
up to their full height when they say "*La Belle France.*"

"I have come, my darling, to bid you farewell. To-morrow
we are to be attacked —"

"Yes, I know it, Adolph, and as much as I adore you, I
adore France more. I am a daughter of France. Fight!
Be a hero! All Frenchmen may be heroes. And listen!
There will lead the enemy to-morrow an officer whom you
must recognize. He is six feet tall, with a black mustache,
dressed in the uniform of the Tenth. He will have a cockade
on the left side of his hat. He must die! He is an aristocrat!
He is brave, and being an aristocrat and brave, clearly he must
die that France may live! Shoot him as you would an enemy
of France! To a hero — a French hero — I can say no more!"

"He dies — I swear it!" ejaculated Adolph, drawing him
self once more up to his full height.

"And now, my heart's beloved, go; and meet whatever
fate may be in reserve for you like a man — like a Frenchman.
But stay! you have a watch, shirt-studs, cuff-buttons, and
some money. Should you fall, this portable property would
be seized by the enemy, and be used against France. That
would be deplorable. In this holy cause one should think of
everything. Leave them with me, and when you return — oh,
my beloved, you must return! Else I shall die!"

And Adolph took his personal effects, and gave them to
her, and with a passionate embrace was about to leave her.

"Stay a moment, my darling. You must not go into battle
without a charm to keep the bullets from you. Here!" and
she twisted a ribbon, a very red one, into a bow, and pinned
it in the front of his cap. "Now go and be a hero!"

He gave her a passionate embrace, she sank to the floor in a fainting fit, and he rushed out with a gesture.

As soon as the door was shut, she rose very calmly, and inventoried the property.

"It is not much, but it is better than nothing. I am a daughter of France. I will be content with what is sent me; but I think the chain is oroide, and I know the shirt studs are snide."

A few moments later Henri entered. She received him with evident signs of pleasure.

"Therese," said the handsome young fellow, "I know that you love me. We attack the *canaille* to-morrow. I come to bid you farewell. I may never see you again!"

"Henri! I love you! But fight like a hero for France!"

"Adorable! Rapture! This is peaches! I will fight; I will be a hero — I am in the hero line just now. You have given me a new heart. Oh, Therese!"

And then there was more kissing and embracing, which was all very nice.

Then Henri rose and said he must go. Mars could not wait upon Venus. France called him.

"Must you go? Alas! But, Henri, should you fall, what would become of me?"

"Die," said Henri, "and follow me to the next world."

Therese said to herself, "Not much, I thank you. I know a trick worth two of that. I prefer to live." But she said audibly:

"I cannot die, for I shall live to avenge you and France. But should you die on the field, the horrible Commune will take your watch, your chain, your personal effects, to continue this sacrilegious strife. Leave them with me."

Henri emptied his pockets, and took off his watch and everything on his person that had value, even to his cuff buttons, and then Therese said:

"You have your money in the hands of Duclos, the Notary. Give me an order for that, for he is affected toward the Commune. France before everything. When you return we will destroy the paper. Should you fall, I will spend it to avenge you."

Then Henri wrote the order for the money, and the prudent girl had up the concierge, who witnessed it, to make it all legal like, and then with one passionate embrace she bade him farewell.

"Stay, but for a moment, my heart's beloved," she said. "Foremost on the barricade to-morrow you will see a young man who is an enemy of France. There isn't much of him, but what there is, is pizen. You will know him — he is only five feet four high, has sandy hair and a pug nose, and very bandy legs. He ought to dance well, for he is put up on elliptic springs. He wears a red bow in his cap in front. He must die, for he is an enemy to France. Swear that he shall not live."

"I swear. He is as good as dead now. You may bet your sweet life he populates a trench to-morrow night. He shall count one in the census of the hereafter."

"Thanks — for France. And now, my beloved, go! Be a hero. But stay, wear this for my sake."

And she pinned very securely upon the left side of his hat, a cockade, and they embraced once more, and he left the room, leaving her in a swoon.

"Poor thing!" said he to himself, as he took one last look at her, curled up gracefully on the floor, "shall I leave her thus? Yes; she could not endure a second parting."

And he went. Then she immediately got up and inventoried his property, and put the order for his money in her bosom, which all French women do, though I can't say that that is a very safe place — in France. And she was pleased to find that his jewelry, though not extensive, was all genuine, and she said her prayers and went to bed, with the calmness of one who had done her whole duty.

The next day the assault was made and things worked about as Therese had calculated. Adolph had but one objective point and that was the man with a cockade, and Henri carried a carbine for the fellow with the red bow. They saw each other at precisely the same moment, both fired the same moment, and both fell mortally wounded. Having each noticed a peculiar mark upon the other's hat they used what life was left in them to crawl to each other.

"Who put that ribbon in your cap?" gasped Henri.

"Therese! And who that cockade in yours?"

"Therese! And she took my effects?"

"And mine. *Perfide!* But we die for France all the same?"

"Precisely."

And they both went into the hereafter. Therese waited quietly and with great resignation till the troubles were over, and then real-ized upon her trust funds. Shortly after she purchased a café in a good drinking quar-ter and grew wealthy. She married a rich banker, whose place of busi-ness was just over her's, and they waxed very rich.

"What kind of a banker was he?" I in-quired of a gen-tleman who in-distinctly mas-tered some of the English language.

"He eez some thing vat you

"WHO PUT THAT RIBBON IN YOUR CAP?"

in L' Amerique would call — vat eez eet? — *oui*, a faro banker."

I do not vouch for the truth of this legend, though I have every reason to believe it to be true. I was personally in a café presided over by a woman whom I firmly believe could manage just such a scheme. True or not, it shows what the women of France will do for their beloved country.

CHAPTER XXIII.

FRENCH DRINKING.

The French are the most temperate people on the globe. Why this is so is not easily explained, for it would be naturally supposed that so excitable a people ought, in the very nature of things, to be intemperate. They have no fixed code of morals, as the Saxon people have, and they make no pretense of anything of the kind. They are intemperate enough, heaven knows, in their politics, and apparently so, to a stranger who does not understand French, in their conversation; but in the matter of drinking they don't do enough of it to injure an English baby, and an American is lost in amazement at the little stimulant they get on with.

There are drinkers of the deadly absinthe, and occasionally indulgers in the more immediate but less fearful brandy, but they are rare. The absinthe drinkers are, as a rule, literary men, reformers, and the long-haired visionaries who have a notion that in stimulants there is inspiration, and the reckless ones who hold that the more they get out of life in ten minutes the more they enjoy. They are the men who invite the guillotine, and walk to the scaffold with great alacrity, and shout "Vive La France," in the most picturesque and absurd manner. The devotee of absinthe drinks it as a part of his social system, and generally dies of softening of the brain at about thirty-five. He thinks he has a good time, but he does not.

There are low people who stupefy themselves with cheap brandy, but they are not common. The Frenchman does not take kindly to the fierce stimulant so common across the channel, and the amount of raw whisky consumed each day by the average whisky-drinking American would fill him with astonishment. He cannot comprehend it at all, and regards such a man as a brute. Possibly he is not very much out of the way. I, for one, quite agree with him.

And when it comes to wine he is very moderate. There is very little alcohol in the red wine he drinks, so little that Tibbitts, after taking a glass of it, remarked that he had known water in America that was more exhilarating. And that wine, mild as it is, he dilutes fully one-half with water, and sips it very slowly. In an evening he consumes not more than a pint of it, getting out of that pint about as much stimu- lation as is held in one drink of American sod-corn whisky.

But it suffices him. He sits and laughs and talks just as well over this mild swash as the American does over his fiery, bowel-burning, stomach-destroying, brain-shriveling liquor, and a great deal more, for he enjoys himself, and the American does not. At least, so I have been informed.

The use of wine is universal. It is in the bed-room in the morning, on the table at twelve o'clock breakfast, it is taken at dinner at six o'clock, and during the evening till bed-time.

The water of Paris is very bad; at least, so all Parisians tell you, though I cannot see why it should be. I tasted it several times, and I saw no especial difference between Paris water and any other, except, as they do not use ice, it does get rather insipid in the Summer, when the thermometer reaches ninety-five. But there is a superstition prevalent that it is unhealthy, and hence it is never used as a beverage unless it is qualified. The Frenchman drops a lump of sugar in it when he takes it raw, though, as a rule, wine is used as a corrective.

Tibbitts had a bottle of cognac in his room to mix with the water. He insisted that he thought too much of his mother and her happiness to endanger his life by taking the water, bad as it was, clear, and the wine of the country did not agree with him. He wanted to get back to America, he did, that his friends might have the benefit of his foreign experience.

An American in London remarked, that in all the time he spent in that city he met but one cordial Englishman, and he was a Dublin man. So with me in Paris. In all the time I spent there I saw very few drunken Frenchmen, and they were to a man from either London or New York, and I made very thorough search. The sobriety of the people is something wonderful.

I saw plenty of men exhilarated; I heard more laughter

THE CORRECTIVE USED BY MR. TIBBITTS.

than I ever heard in twice the time in any other country: but drunkenness, the drunkenness that maunders, and is idiotic, or the drunkenness that tends to destroying property or life, I saw none of. In the Jardin Mabille, where in England or America drunkenness would be co-extensive with the attendance, at the students' balls, at the Chateau Rouge or at even the less pretentious places, there was hilarity in plenty, but no vinous or spirituous excess. The same condition of affairs obtains in Switzerland and Germany. I don't want any man to say this is not so, for I assert that drunkenness is comparatively unknown in the two countries where wine and beer are the staple drinks of the people of all classes. I am aware that the same statement has been made hundreds of times before and disputed a thousand times, and therefore I was at pains to get at the truth of the matter.

The use of wine in France is universal. It is drank by the commonest laborer and the most aristocratic citizen. You go nowhere that you do not see it — it is everywhere present, and is the one drink of the country. The fruitful vineyards of France make it almost as cheap as water, and the pampered wives and daughters of the ancient nobility who bathed in wine were not guilty of a very frightful extravagance after all.

What a Frenchman satisfies his appetite with for drink is

something astonishing. The middle-aged man in America who

THE COCO SELLER.

would deliberately ask for the root-beer of his youth would be
laughed at as a milk-sop. In America even the lemonade

drinker is not looked upon with favor, although that is admissible.

But in Paris you shall see a sturdy man walking the streets with an immense can upon his back with cups attached, and men of all ages stop him. He draws from the can a cup full of a liquid. He drinks it and pays for it. What do you suppose this liquid is? Merely a decoction of herbs and Spanish licorice, and coco, as harmless as mother's milk, and a great deal more insipid. Of mother's milk I cannot speak, for it is a long time since I have tasted it. I wish to heaven that the gap between the present and the mother's milk period were less. But the Frenchman patronizes the coco seller, and his Chinese pagoda arrangement is always well patronized.

There is no drunkenness. It may be that the Frenchman does not want to get drunk, but I am convinced that the nature of the regular beverage of the country is to be credited with this delightful exemption from the great curse that devastates other countries. I am compelled to this conclusion, for I have noticed that the French in America and England, where spirituous liquors are the rule, come to be as frightful drunkards as anybody; and, per contra, I know scores of Americans in Paris who at home drank whisky habitually, and in consequence rarely went to bed sober — so seldom that when it did happen their wives needed an introduction to them — I know scores of these men here who have fallen into the French habit, and drink nothing but wine, and are as sober as the French themselves. They are getting to be so good that some of them have felt justified in taking on other sins to keep them down to the true American average. They have discovered that they can get on very well with wine, and do not crave the fiery liquid they considered so necessary at home.

I made a point of investigating this very thoroughly, for in days past I have seen some drunkenness and the effects thereof. I have seen the dead bodies of women murdered by drunken husbands; I have seen the best men in America go down to disgraceful graves; I have seen fortunes wrecked, prospects blighted; and I have perused a great many pages of statistics. There are crimes on the calendar not resulting from rum, but, were rum eliminated, the catalogue would be so reduced as to make it hardly worth the compiling. Directly or indirectly, rum is chargeable with a good ninety per cent. of the woes that afflict our country.

The moral to all this is — but come to think of it I am not here to point out morals. I have made a true statement, and each one may extract from it any moral he chooses. This is all there is of it : The French drink all the wine they want, and the French are a sober people. It hasn't much to do with foreign travel ; but to see thousands of men sitting and drinking without a fight, an angry word, a broken head, or a black eye, was so delightful an experience that I felt it must go upon paper.

CHAPTER XXIV.

The Parisian family, unless it be one of the bloated aristo-
crats and pampered children of luxury, do not occupy separate
houses, as families do in American cities. Rents are somewhat
too high to permit that luxury, and besides they never were
used to it, and it would n't suit them at all. They have been
accustomed to living up stairs for so many generations that I
doubt if a genuine Parisian of the middle classes could be
happy on or near the ground floor.

The first floor, and, for that matter, the second and third,
in the heart of the city, are devoted to business purposes.
Above the third floors the residences begin, and they continue
to the very top. As a rule, each floor constitutes a dwelling
by itself, with halls, parlor or drawing-room, dining and sleeping rooms and kitchen, all compactly and very conveniently
arranged. True, some of these apartments are small, not large
enough to swing a cat in; but, as Mr. Dick Swiveler wisely
observed, "You don't want to swing a cat, you know." The
French housekeeper finds a kitchen five feet wide and six feet
long quite large enough for the preparation of the food for the
family, and the sleeping rooms, being only used for sleeping,
may be very comfortable, if they are only large enough to
hold a bed and the other necessary furniture.

The entrance to these buildings is on the ground floor, and
is a wide gateway with a diminutive suite of apartments on
one side, which is habited by the concierge, or, as the English
call it, the porter. This personage, usually a woman, receives
all messages from the different flats above her, answers all
calls and gives all the information concerning the various
families inhabiting it. It is she who cleans the main stair·

(352)

case which goes to the top of the house, and has charge of the buildings.

At night, say at eleven, the great doors guarding this common entrance are shut, and whoever desires to enter thereafter finds a bell-pull, the other end of which is at the head of the concierge's bed. She doesn't bother herself to get up and see who it is, but she merely pulls a wire, the bolt of the great door is withdrawn, you enter, and shutting the door after you — it fastens with a spring lock — go to your floor, and enter your own house.

Tibbitts likes this idea very much. He says that when you come home late at night, and not precisely in the condition to be accurate about things, there isn't any nonsense about finding a key first, and then going through the more delicate operations of finding a keyhole and getting the key in right side up. "All you have to do is to catch on that bell-pull, and the more unsteady you are, the better, for you lean back upon it, and your whole weight takes it." And he further remarked that there wasn't a concierge in Paris who wouldn't know his ring before he had been in the house a week.

The principal business of the concierge and her entire family is to keep the stairs clean. I once held that the Philadelphia servant girl would die were the supply of water to run out so that she could not wash sidewalks and marble steps, but she has a worthy rival in the Parisian. The stairs leading to the top of the buildings are kept sloppy all the time with the perpetual cleaning. Indeed so constantly is this going on that no time is given to enjoy the luxury of clean stairs. Not only the stairs are cleansed, but the very sides of the building are washed and scrubbed once in so many years, by law. If Paris only took as much pains with its inside as it does with its outside! But it doesn't.

Once inside the houses, the first thing that strikes an American is the total absence of carpets; that is, carpets as we have them. The floors are of wood in many patterns, and in the center there may or may not be a rug, which covers, perhaps, two-thirds of the room. A room carpeted the entire surface is very rare, and I must say that therein the French housekeeper does better than the American. These rugs are

23

taken up very frequently, it being no trouble, and are kept clean and free of dust, something impossible when they are fastened to the floor, as is the custom across the water.

In the Summer they are taken out of the way entirely, and the bright waxed floor is deliciously cool, and in the Winter the rug, always in warm colors, forms a pleasing contrast to the wood on the edges. The French idea is better than ours.

The French housekeeper is perfection in her way. She allows nothing to go to waste. There is not a penny's worth more purchased than can be used, and the ending of the day sees the ending of what was bought for the day. If there are ten to sit down to the table there is soup made for just ten — not enough for twenty and the remainder to the slop bucket — and there is just meat enough to make ten portions, and no more. There is butter for ten and vegetables for ten. By the way, very little butter is used. Wine is provided *ad libitum*, and even that, cheap as it is, is carefully poured from the half or two-thirds emptied bottles into others and carefully husbanded till the next meal brings it out.

There is nothing of meanness in this — only the good sense not to waste. The French housewife, very properly, sees no use in throwing away food any more than she does money. Consequently, despite the much higher cost of provisions, a French house gets on in better style than an American, and at a much less expenditure.

The skill of the French cook is proverbial, and his reputation is deserved. One of the craft once said that with a pair of cavalry boots, a handful of grass and plenty of salt and pepper, he could make soup for a regiment, and I believe him. They use more vegetables than we do, and use them infinitely better. Out of the despised carrot, which seldom makes its appearance on American tables, they make a delicious dish, and their treatment of potatoes, tomatoes, and the whole race of salad-making vegetables, is something akin to miraculous. They use oil in profusion, and no matter what the raw material is that comes under the hands of a French cook, there is a taste and relish about the product that is satisfying as well as gratifying. The Frenchman at his table aims at all the senses. To begin with it is garnished with flowers, and, second, the dishes gratify hunger, and, thirdly, they gratify the taste. Then, as an appropriate finish, they will have the most cheerful conversation, and for the time all care and trouble is banished and the feeding time is the good time of the household. A Frenchman may come to his house ever so much depressed, but he has a thoroughly enjoyable time at his dinner. He may rise from the table and blow his brains out, but at the table no one would ever know or dream that he ever had a trouble.

Among the middle classes, and indeed the better, the lady of the house does the marketing in person. It is too important a matter to be entrusted to a servant, for they are exceedingly particular as to the quality, and equally so as to the price of the supplies. French market-people, especially the women, are the shrewdest and the most unscrupulous in the world, and it requires much care and skill not to be imposed upon. I went one morning with my landlady to see a French market.

The first thing desired was a lobster. One was selected and then commenced the bargaining.

"How much?" demanded the Madame.

"Five francs," was the answer, "and very cheap it is. Observe, Madame, its size, and its condition. Oh, I have nothing but the best. Shall I put it into your basket?"

"No, it is too much!"

"Too much! Madame, you would starve me. Well, then, you are an old customer (she had never seen Madame before), I will give it to you—I would no one else—for four and a half. It is ruin, but I can't keep them over."

"I will give you two francs."

"Two francs! You jest, Madame. Two francs for this king of lobsters—this emperor! Ah no! but I will say four —and little Jean shall go without shoes."

"Two francs."

"Say three and a half—my landlord can do without his rent till times are better."

Precisely as the two franc offer was being accepted, a young man drove up in a stylish coupe.

"How much for that lobster?"

"Ten francs, Monsieur le Colonel," replied the dame with-out a blush.

"Wrap it up and put it in my carriage," was the reply, and it was done.

"Why did you ask him ten francs when you only asked me five to begin with, and intended to take two?" demanded my landlady, purely that I might hear the answer.

"Eh? Oh, the young man has plenty of money — it is for his little woman, I suppose. We poor must live, and I must make my profit. But here is one just like it — rather better. Shall I say three francs?"

"Two."

"Well, it must be so. But I lose money."

The old dame made a good hundred per cent. as it was.

As it was in lobsters so it was in everything. The price offered in every instance was about two-fifths of the price asked and even then it was not certain but that too much was not paid. But when a French market woman and a French housekeeper come together there is not going to be very much swindling. Both know their business and whoever gets the best in the encounter may congratulate herself upon possessing a great deal of acumen.

The servants in French families are now tolerably attentive and obliging, but their bearing depends very much upon the political condition of the country. Every Frenchman is a pol-itician, and they have all the shades of politics down to the humblest, and the lower orders, as elsewhere, take their poli-tics from their superiors. The retainers in the families of the old nobility are Monarchists to a man, and hate the Republic with a hatred that the dispossessed nobility themselves do not feel. The waiters at the cafés and those who entered domestic service latterly are all virulent Republicans, disagreeably so. Especially was this true just after the downfall of the Third Napoleon, and after the Commune. A lady of my acquaint-ance, who got out of Paris just before the Commune, returned and rearranged her household after order was restored Her daughter had engaged servants, and the good old lady rang for one.

"Are you one of the new servants?" she asked, as a strange man answered her summons.

"No, Madame. I am in your employment, but no servant. Since the Republic, there are no servants. Address me, please, as 'citizen!'"

And she was compelled to do it, or go without service. The man considered himself the equal of his mistress in all particulars, and would be counted nothing less.

Fuel is very costly in France, and consequently very little used. In Paris the climate is mild, and very little is needed. But the same economy is observed in this as in everything. Twigs of trees and the smallest bushes, cut in uniform lengths, are used for firing, and for cooking the use of charcoal is almost universal.

As the shops furnish food as cheaply as it can be prepared at home, it is only in families that cooking is done. The washing among this class is done altogether at the public wash-houses in the Seine. These are immense boats anchored close to the bank and partitioned off into spaces just wide enough for a woman to work comfortably. For two sous, the woman has the use of tubs and hot and cold water *ad libitum*. She takes her bundle of soiled goods, and her own soap, and washes them, using a heavy wooden paddle to drive the soap through the fabric, instead of the pounder and washboard, and, wringing them out, carries them home wet. A few sous' worth of charcoal suffices to iron them, and the same fire cooks her little dinner, and so two very important birds are killed with one stone. The shop girls, whose attics will not admit of a fire, have no other way of washing their clothes, and so the public wash-houses are always full.

The eating of the day commences with a very slight breakfast in your room at any hour you choose. The said breakfast consists of exactly one cup of coffee or chocolate — it is measured accurately, there is exactly one cup in the little pot — two rolls and an infinitesimal portion of fresh butter. You bid good-bye to salted butter when you leave the steamer. On this you exist till twelve, or thereabouts, when you have a breakfast as is a breakfast. There are eggs and one or two varieties of meat, and wine *ad libitum*, ending with sweets.

This over, at six you have the meal of the day, the dinner,
consisting of five or six courses, commencing with the everlast-

IN ANY OF THE PARKS.

ing soup, and ending with black coffee. Wine constitutes the
drink of this meal, as at the breakfast.

It takes an American some little time to get used to this
light breakfast, but when accustomed to it he is entirely satis-

fied with it. If he has nothing to do it is certainly better than the heavy breakfast of his own country, and unless he has the most violent bodily labor to perform, it is better than to go to business with an overloaded stomach. Anyhow, whether you like it or not, it is all you can get, and a wise man always manages to like what is inevitable. One very soon gets to liking this very strange innovation upon one's established habits.

The French woman esteems tidiness and cleanliness above everything on earth, that is, outward tidiness. If rumor be true, they are not so particular as to internal economy, but the outside of the platter must be as white as the driven snow. An English or American woman will walk the sloppy streets and drag her skirts in the mud and filth till they are not only uncomfortable but are absolutely indecent in appearance. All this could be avoided by merely lifting the skirts, but the notion of delicacy, the fear of exposing an ankle, prevents this. That is the Anglo-Saxon notion of delicacy. The French woman has other views. Her ankles are not sacred, but her skirts are. She will not have soiled skirts, she will not have petticoats with the filth of the streets upon them, and so when she comes to a vile spot, she lifts her skirts and passes over without carrying any of the filth with her. It matters not if her ankles are exposed. That she expects. But she does this skirt-lifting with such a grace and such a manner that to an American even it is the most natural thing in the world. The French woman hoists her skirts in a way that makes it apparent to the most critical observer that it is not done to show neatly turned ankles, but to save her person from filth. It is a necessity with her, from her stand-point, and is consequently accepted as such. She has no objection to exposing a shapely ankle, but whether the ankle be shapely or not, no Parisian woman will ever, under any circumstances, be untidy. She has a passion for neatness, and a very pleasant passion it is. Would that she were as correct in her other passions.

Every woman in Paris, or for that matter everywhere in France, works. This is the secret of French prosperity. This explains the ease with which the French people recovered from the extravagance of the Empire, the frightful cost of the war with Prussia, and the enormous indemnity exacted by the merciless Bismarck. It is the universality of labor, and the knowing how to live well upon next to nothing. A French

THE NO-LEGGED BEGGAR WOMAN—BOULEVARD DES CAPUCINES.

wife not only does the house keeping for her family, but she takes care of the shop. She sells the goods which her husband makes. Say he is a trunkmaker — he is in the shop on the floor above, or the floor below, as the case may be, working for dear life, but in the salesroom sits Madame, his wife, or

Mademoiselle, his daughter, who sells the goods, takes the money, keeps the books, buys the materials, and runs the business end of the concern.

But this is not all. Customers do not come in every minute, and Madame has time upon her hands. She does not waste it. There are her children, too young to work, but they must be clothed, and if there are no children there are a few sous to be earned by knitting, or fancy needlework. And so all this spare time is put in by Madame, sewing or knitting, either for her own family or for a market. Not a minute goes to waste. Wherever you see a French woman you see her doing some thing. The nurse-maid, who takes her charges out for an airing, has work in her hands, and she works. In the gardens in the Palais-Royal you shall see hundreds of nurse-maids whose charges are playing under the beautiful trees, knitting industriously, one eye on the work and the other on the children, and in every shop you enter you see the same thing.

Wages are very low, but with this absolute economy of time and the more absolute economy in the matter of living, the French workingman manages to get on better, on an average, than those in the same station in any other country in the world. French industry and French thrift make anything in the way of living possible. There is nothing like it.

Transportation is very cheap in Paris and exceedingly good. The omnibusses are large and the street cars likewise, and have the delight of holding as many people on the top as on the inside. And then they are never overcrowded. You are entitled to and get a seat. When the seats are all taken the sign "Complet," is displayed, and no more passengers are admitted. A ride on the top of a French omnibus in good weather is a delight.

The Frenchman tries to imitate the English and Americans in the matters of sport, but it is a sorry failure. The young French sport gets himself up in remarkable sporting costumes, and goes out gunning, and always returns with game. Does he shoot it? Alas! It can be bought, and — he buys it. But he brings in his hare or his birds, or whatever can be bought that has been freshly killed, and proudly displays it to his friends and talks loudly of the pleasures of field sports.

Fishing in the Seine is another amusement, though I never met anybody who had ever caught a fish. There are more lines in the Seine any hour of the day than there are fish, but

HOW THE FRENCH SPORT KILLS GAME.

they all fish just the same. The docks are lined with men and boys at all hours, and all standing as gravely and patiently as though they made their living by it. The sight of a fish would astonish them.

Bloss, my old showman friend, arrived last night from Switzerland. There are a number of bears kept at Berne, the property of the city, one of which, some years ago, killed an

FISHING IN THE SEINE.

English officer who fell into his den. That bear—but Bloss may tell his own story.

"Wat I wantid wuz that bear. I wantid that identical bear, the very one that squoze the Britisher. Ef I cood hev

got that bear it wood hev bin the biggest thing in the annals
of the show biznis.   So I went to Berne and saw the President

INSIDE A PARISIAN OMNIBUS.

of the Swiss Republic.   I offered him fust two hundred dollars
for it, pervided he would write a certifikit on parchment and
put the seal of the Republic onto it that it wuz the identical

animile. Ye see, ef he hed done this I should hev put it onto the bills this way :—

That there may be no doubt in the minds of a too-oft deceived public, deceived by audacious pretenders who advertise what they know they cannot perform, that this is the identical ferocious bear that did actually kill an unfortunate British officer in the presence of his newly-made bride (he wasn't married at all, but you can't awaken no interest without the pathetic) — who was powerless to extricate him from the tenacious grasp of the ferocious brute, the most dangerous of the species, the certificate of the President of the Swiss Republic, with the broad seal of the Republic attached, will be exhibited at each and every entertainment, all reports to the contrary notwithstanding, and positively without any extra charge. This statement is made to counteract the envious and malicious reports of would-be rivals, who seek to make up by slander and misrepresentation, what they lack in enterprise and resource.

THE SHOWMAN SHOWN THE DOOR.

I should hev hed a copy — a fac-similer — uv the certifikit printed, in two colors, and I shood hev hed the certifikit itself

hung out afore the big tent, and it would hev bin wuth a heap
uv money to me.

"Did you succeed?"

"Succeed! Why the bloated aristocrat refoozed to hev
anything to say to me, and directed a servant to show me out.
A pretty Republic that is, where the President won't hear a
common biznis proposishen! And then I went to the Mayor
uv the city, and when my proposishen wuz translated to him,
he remarked that he wuzn't in the bear biznis, and he hed me
showed out. I shood like to be a voter in Berne at one elec-
shun. But I shel hev the bear that killed the offiser jes the
same. That is, I shel advertise that one uv the bears I yoose
that eat the children in the Elijah act is the identikle one. I
don't like to deceeve the public — I hed ruther deal strate with
'em, but I must git my expenses out uv that trip to Berne
somehow, and I shel hev the President's certifikit all the same.
Yes, and blast me ef I don't add the Mayor's to it to make
ashoorence doubly shoor. I ain't agoin' to Berne for nothin',
nor am I goin' to lose an ijee. Ijees are too skase to waste one."

"Did you enjoy this trip to the land of Tell?"

The sound of the word "Tell," was sufficient to tap the
old gentleman once more, and he went off into a narrative
that flowed smoothly as cider from a barrel.

"The land uv Tell! I shel never forgit Tell — Willyum,
the Swiss wat shot a apple offen his boy's head. It wuz way
back in 1844, when I was runnin' my great aggregashun in the
West. We had a minstrel sideshow in the afternoon, and a
regler theater for a sideshow in the evenin'. Our leadin' man
wuz Mortimer de Lacy, from the principal European and Noo
York theaters — his real name was Tubbs; he wuz the son uv
a ginooine Injun physician, which hed stands about the country suthin' like a circus — who wuz very fond uv playin' Tell.
De Lacy wuz one uv the most yooseful men I ever hed. He
rid the six hoss act, the "Rooshun Courier uv Moscow," and
did the stone-breakin' act, where he bends over on his arms and
hez stuns broken on his breast with sledges, and he did the
cannon ball act, and in the afternoon wuz the interlocootor in
the minstrel show, playin' the triangle — anybody kin play the
triangle, and he alluz sed he wood give anything ef he cood

manage a banjo or even a accordeon so ez to git up in the perfesh — and in the evenin' he did the classical in high tragedy. The afternoon minstrel show wuz for the country people, but the play in the evenin' wuz to ketch the more refined towns folks. Well, one day De Lacy cum to me, and sez he:—

"'Guvnor, I hev a idear.'

"'Spit it out,' sez I. 'Idears is wuth money in our biznis.'

"'I kin make Tell more realistic. You know the way we do the shootin' uv the apple off the boy's head is to shoot an arrer into the wings and the boy comes runnin' out with a split apple in his hand.'

"'Yes, that's the way it alluz hez bin done. It's a tradishn uv the stage.'

"'I perpose to hev the boy stand on the stage in full view uv the awjence, and to shoot the apple off his head under their very eyes. It's a big thing.'

"'Big thing! I should say so. But you can't shoot an apple with an arrer. You couldn't hit the side of a barn.'

"'Very good, but this is my idear. We only play Tell at night. We stretch a wire across the stage jes the height of the boy, and the wire runs through the apple on the boy's head. Then I hev a loop fixed onto the arrer, and when I shoot it runs along the wire — see? — and knocks the apple into smithereens. It's a big notion.'

"It occurred to me that it wood be a good piece of biznis and I agreed to it. My youngest boy, Sam, alluz played the boy, and De Lacy and I fixed the riggin' and hed it all right. To make it more realistic De Lacy hed a very broad-headed arrer made so that the awjence should see it wuz reel, and everythin' wuz ready. When that scene come on, the boy come out walkin' very keerful — we hed the apple fixed tight upon his head so that ef he walked in a strate line it wooden't be moved, and he wuz placed. After the speeches De Lacy sprung the bow, and let the arrer drive with all the force it hed."

"It must have been a thrilling scene."

"Thrillin'! Yoo bet! But we didn't repeat it. Bekaze yoo see the wire slackened, and the arrer struck Sam on the top uv the head and scalped him as clean as a Camanche Injun cood hev done it, and he howled and jumped onter De Lacy and the wire tore down the two wings it wuz hitched onter, and De Lacy in gittin' rid uv him tore down the rest uv the wings, and they clinched and rolled down onto the stage, and the awjence got up and howled, and the peeple all rushed on, and there wuz about ez lively a scene ez I ever witnessed in a long and varied experience. It wuz picteresk and lurid. I rung the curtain down and separated 'em. It wuz a good idear, but it didn't jes work, owin' to defective machinery."

"But it turned out pretty well, after all. The smart man is he who turns wat to others wood be a misfortoon to account.

THE TELL CATASTROPHE.

I hed the scalp tanned with the hair outside, and ez soon ez Sam's bald head healed up I exhibited him in a blue rounda-bout, with brass buttons — I bought the soot cheap uv a bell

boy at a hotel in Cincinnati — ez the son uv the Rev. Melchiza-
dek Smith, a missionary for thirty years among the Injuns,
who wuz scalped at the time his father wuz barbariously killed,
and I hed a life uv the Rev. Smith writ, and an account of the
massacre, and Sam sold it after he hed bin exhibited. It did
very well till he got too big for that biznis."

"But Sam is doin' very well. He is now an end man in a
minstrel show, and he does the Lancashire clog, and does
mighty well in the wench biznis, and he hez a partner in the
brother biznis, the De Montmorencies, I beleeve they wuz,
the last time I heerd uv 'em He will git on — he hez a great
deal uv talent and kin turn his hand to almost anything."

ZOOLOGICAL ROOM — BRITISH MUSEUM.

24

CHAPTER XXV.

IRELAND.

" 'Tis the most distressful country that ever yet was seen,
They're hanging men and women there for the wearin' of the green."

FROM France the gay, France the prosperous, France the delightful, to Ireland the sad, Ireland the poor, Ireland the oppressed, is a tremendous jump. Contrasts are necessary, and my readers are going to have all they want of them.

CORK HARBOR.

Cork is a lovely city; that is, it would be a lovely city were it a city at all. Nature intended Cork for a great city, but man stepped in and thwarted Nature. It is situated on the most magnificent site for a city there is in all Europe. A

(370)

wonderfully beautiful river, with water enough to float any vessel, flows through it; and at the mouth of that river, twelve miles below, is one of the great harbors of the world. Queenstown — I wonder that any Irishman ever consented to call it Queenstown — is the nearest port to the great western hemisphere, and Cork should be the center of all the trade from America.

It is twenty-four hours nearer New York than Liverpool, and should be the final landing-place of the American lines, instead of being simply a point to be touched.

QUEENSTOWN.

Cork is a sleepy city of perhaps seventy thousand population, made up of the handsomest men and most beautiful women and children on the face of the globe. You shall see more feminine beauty on the streets of Cork in an hour than you can anywhere else in a week. Homely women there are none — beautiful women are so plenty that it really becomes monotonous. One rather gets to wishing that he could see an occasional pair of English feet, for the sake of variety.

The city itself is beautiful, as are all the cities of Ireland; but it is a sad city, as are all the cities of Ireland. It is not prosperous, and cannot be, for it is under English domination, and England will not permit prosperity in Ireland. It is only the attachment which an Irishman has for his own country that makes anybody stay there. With every natural advantage, with every facility for manufacturing, for trade and commerce, with the best harbor in the world, and the nearest point for American trade, it has no manufactures to speak of, and no trade whatever. Its population has decreased thirty thousand within fifteen years, and its trade is slowly but surely dwindling to nothingness.

The river Lea is a wonderfully beautiful stream, and Cork, which occupies both sides of it, is a wonderfully beautiful city, and would be an enjoyable city but for the feeling of sadness that comes to an American the moment he sees the empty warehouses, the empty dwellings, and the signs of decay that are everywhere.

There are churches everywhere, and churches with a history. Here is the church of Shandon, of whose chimes Father Prout wrote ·

> "The bells of Shandon
> That sound so grand on
> The pleasant waters of the river Lea.'

Here is climate, soil, situation — everything to make a great controlling city; here are a people with industry, intelligence, brains, and all the requisites to make a great controlling city; but, despite all these points in its favor, Cork has decreased year by year, and is to-day absolutely nothing. The city has lost population every year; its business is leaving it, its warehouses are empty, its streets are deserted, its quays are silent — it is nothing.

What is the reason for this? It is all summed up in one word — landlordism. There is no man in the world, not excepting the Frenchman, who will work longer or harder than the Irishman. There is no race of men who are better merchants or more enterprising dealers, and there is no reason, but one, why Cork should not be one of the largest and richest cities of the world. That reason is, English ownership of Irish soil.

Irish landlordism is condensed villainy. It is the very top and summit of oppression, cruelty, brutality and terror.

It was conceived in lust and greed, born of fraud, and perpetuated by force.

It does not recognize manhood, womanhood or childhood. Its cold hand is upon every cradle in Ireland. Its victims are the five millions of people in Ireland who cannot get away, and the instruments used to hold them are bayonets and ball cartridges.

It is a ghoul that would invade grave-yards were there any profit to be gotten out of grave-yards. It is the coldest-blooded, cruelest infamy that the world has ever seen, and that any race of people was ever fated to groan under.

Irish landlordism is legal brigandage — it is an organized hell.

Wesley said that African slavery was the sum of all villainies. Irish landlordism comprises all the villainies that the devil ever invented, with African slavery thrown in. Irish landlordism makes African slavery a virtue by comparison. For when a negro slave got too old to work, he was given some place in which to live, and sufficient food to keep him in some sort of life, and clothes enough to shield him from the elements.

The Irish tenant, when he becomes old and cannot work, is thrown out upon the roadside, with his wife and his children, to die and rot. He has created lands with his own hands, which he is not allowed to occupy ; he has grown crops which he is not allowed to eat ; he has labored as no other man in the world has labored, without being permitted to enjoy the fruits of his labor. The virtue of his wife and daughter are in the keeping of the villain, who by virtue of bayonets, controls his land. In short, to sum it all up in one word, the Irishman is a serf, a slave.

In a country that makes a boast of its freedom, he is the suffering victim of men who claim to be Christians ; he is the robbed, outraged sufferer of a few men who are as unfeeling as the bayonets that keep him down, as merciless and cruel as tigers.

From the above feeble utterances my readers will, I hope, get the idea that I do not like Irish landlordism. I hope some day to get sufficient command of words to make my meaning apparent. I really would like to make it understood just how I feel about it.

To see Ireland you must not do as the regular tourist always does, follow the regular routes of tourists' travel. You may go all over Ireland, in one way, and you will not see a particle of suffering, or any discontent. At Glengariff, for instance, the most charming spot on the earth, you are lodged in as fine a hotel as there is anywhere; the people are all well dressed and well fed, and the visitor wonders why there should be any discontent.

This is a part of the English Government's policy. On these lines of travel, which the tourist for pleasure always takes, the misery is kept out of sight, and the mouths of the people who serve you are sealed. The American lady traveling through that country don't like to see naked women and squalid poverty, for it would make her uncomfortable. None of it is shown her, and she wonders at the discontent of the Irish.

But just take a boat at Glengariff, leave the splendid hotel, and be rowed two miles across the bay, and you begin to see Ireland, the real Ireland. You then know why Ireland is agitated; you then see the real reason why an Englishman is hated with an intensity that would find expression in a rifle shot, if rifles were permitted to be owned and used.

We took a train for Fermoy, a distance of perhaps fifty miles from Cork. In Fermoy, a tolerably prosperous village for Ireland, the women did not only have no shoes or stockings, but they had scarcely anything else to wear.

"This is nothing," said the wise Mr. Redpath, who was with us; "these people are fairly prosperous — for Ireland. I shall show you something worth while before night."

It puzzled me somewhat to understand how anybody could be worse off than to be walking in cold mud without any protection whatever for the feet, but I found it at Mitchells-town, at the foot of the Galtee mountains.

The Irish jaunting-car, being the most inconvenient and detestable vehicle on earth, deserves a description. It should be known in order to be avoided. A jaunting-car is simply a two-wheeled vehicle with the body that supports the seat reversed. Instead of sitting so as to look forward, you are on the side; the seat runs the wrong way—which is character-istic of almost everything in Ireland. The driver sits looking toward the horse, the passengers sit backing each other, and the concern is so balanced that you must hold on a rail with a death-grip, or be flung off upon the road by every jolt. As

AN IRISH WOMAN AND HER DAUGHTER ON THE ROAD TO CHURCH.

detestable as it is, it is the national Irish vehicle, and you ride on the car, or go afoot.

On one of these atrocious conveyances, we left Mitchells-town at nine o'clock in the morning, in a soaking rain-storm.

the cold, misty drizzle going through our heavy overcoats, and almost penetrating the very marrow. The road wound along past well cultivated fields, over picturesque streams, now up gentle declivities that gave us, or would have given us had the day been clear and fine, an admirable view of the valley that lay spread at the foot of the Galtee Mountains. But on that day the picture was not a cheering one. The sun refused to shine, the rain was cold, and the whole prospect was bleak and desolate. Then our driver was a loquacious fellow, who had at his tongue's end hundreds of instances of the oppression of landlords and the terrible sufferings of the poor, evicted tenants. He talked fast, and, his whole heart being in the subject, he talked well, oftentimes emphasizing his stories by pointing to bare-footed, bare-legged and bare-headed women, who went trudging along the cold, wet road, with no protection from the frightful inclemency of the weather but a light shawl thrown over the ragged dress that scarcely covered their bodies. These women, whom he pointed out as evicted tenants, were not the rough, degraded-looking beggars that are commonly supposed to overrun Ireland, and make the tourist's life one of continual annoyance. They were bright, intelligent and handsome, and, notwithstanding the horrors of their situation, comparatively cheerful. But it was an unnatural cheerfulness, for it was noticeable that there were lines about the mouth and around the eyes that told only too plainly their story of want and suffering.

Even with these living evidences, we could hardly believe the stories of cruelties committed by the landlords and their agents, which our driver kept pouring into our ears. We could not realize that they could be true. They seemed so absolutely barbarous that we utterly refused to accept them, and did not, till, having gone about nine miles from Mitchellstown, we stopped at a little roadside cabin, as they called it, although we would have more properly denominated it a hovel.

At the invitation of our guide we alighted, shook the rain off from our great coats, and entered the place to inquire for Michael Duggan, who worked the little holding back of it. He was not at home, but his wife, a comely, buxom woman of about forty years, asked us to be seated, at the same time offering a small stool on which one of the girls of the family had been sitting near the fire, taking care of an infant.

While our guide was inquiring for Mr. Duggan, we made an inspection of the house, where a man, his wife and seven children lived. There was the one principal room in which we were standing, which was about ten by twelve feet, and eight feet high. There was no floor, except the original earth. There was only one opening for a window, and that had never known a pane of glass. In one end of the room there was a dingy, smoky fireplace, around which were huddled three or

A COUNTY CORK CABIN.

four children, scantily dressed in loose cotton slips that came to just below the knee. At the other end of the room a brood of chickens disported themselves in a pile of furze, while every few minutes a huge porker would push his nose in at the open door, only to be driven away by one of the children.

The family was very interesting. The mother was tall, well formed, and of an exceedingly pleasant appearance, while the children, shy at the sight of so many strangers, were sturdy, healthful and *clean*. They were bright and intelligent, and under any other circumstances and mode of life would grow up to be eminently representative citizens.

On the return of Mr. Duggan from the fields, we went with him up the Galtee Mountains, he explaining on the way that he was very comfortably fixed compared with his neighbors. He said that his grandfather had taken the little holding he occupied, when it was full of stones and rocks, and was next to worthless. He paid a rent of three shillings an acre for it. During his lifetime the land was partially reclaimed, the rocks and boulders were taken out of a part

INTERIOR OF A BETTER CLASS CABIN, COUNTY CORK.

of one field, and the rent was advanced to seven shillings. His father further improved it and raised some little crops, and the rent went up to twenty shillings. When the present tenant succeeded to it, it was in comparatively good shape, and with the improvements he had made, building the house, or rather hovel, the value of the land had increased enough in the mind of the landlord to justify him in placing the rent at two pounds.

That tract of land in America, if one were to go to the few districts where such abominably bad land can be found, would be thought extremely high if it were sold at a dollar, or four shillings an acre.

"Well, how in the world can you raise enough on such a holding to pay such an exorbitant rent?"

ROYAL IRISH CONSTABULARY.

"I can't do it. I've tried my best, but it is absolutely impossible."

"Suppose you don't pay the rent, then what?"

"I'll be thrown out in the road, with my family and the little furniture we have gotten together."

"In case you refuse to be thrown out of the house you have built, and off the land you and your fathers before you made from utterly worthless fields of rocks?"

"Then those fellows would come down upon me."

As he spoke he pointed to a flying squadron of a hundred and fifty men, who were riding back to Mitchellstown after having evicted a number of tenants who had been unable to

INTERIOR OF A CABIN IN KILLALEEN.

pay the back rent. They were a fine looking body of men, well mounted and well armed, each one carrying a loaded carbine, while at his side was dangling a sword bayonet.

But our business in hand was not speculating upon results so much as to see the actual conditions that led to and still sustains the agitation. So we plodded on, through the drenching rain that was coming down in torrents, up the bleak and desolate hill side.

Along the side of the road were high stone fences, from four to seven feet wide at the top, rather good fences for so poor a country.

"Why, you see," said Mr. Duggan in reply to an inquiry as to how they found time to make such solid substantial fences, "those stones were every one taken from that field there, and having no other place to put them we made a fence, and our rent was raised on us for doing it, worse the luck."

We looked into the field whence these stones were taken. It was as uninviting a piece of ground as can be imagined, still full of huge boulders, rocks, weeds and the never-dying heather. It was not capable of supporting a sparrow, yet for the slight improvement that had been made, the rent had been raised. Great inducement that for a man to work!

Seeing a little low, thatched cabin just off the road, we asked in all simplicity, if it had any history, for by this time it was beginning to dawn upon us that almost everything in that vicinity had some story connected with it. But we were totally unprepared for the reply.

A QUIVER FULL.

"No, there's no history about it. It is simply the dwelling place of a family of people who are daily expecting to be evicted because they can't pay the rent, the father having been unable, through sickness, to work all of the season."

The idea that human beings, made in God's image, having the power to think, to reason and to act, could live, even exist, in such a hovel as that was so incredible that we insisted upon going over and seeing how it was done.

Wading through mud and slush coming over our shoe-tops, we bent our heads and entered. The room, if so it could, by a stretch of the imagination, be called, was so low that we could not stand erect. The cold bare earth that constituted the floor was damp and slippery as the rain came trickling down through the broken thatch and formed little pools on the ground. Near a suggestion of a fire, were huddled a woman and four children, the eldest not more than eight years of age. As we entered they all arose. We were horrified to see that they were as usual without stockings or shoes, and their clothing was so torn and ragged that it afforded no warmth whatever. The mother and her little girls were blue with cold. Their features were pinched with hunger. Their whole appearance indicated the want and suffering they had been patiently enduring for years.

Over in one corner of the room was what they called a bed. It consisted of four posts driven into the ground. On stringers were laid a few rough boards; on these boards were dried leaves and heather, covered by a few old potato sacks. There was where this family of six persons slept. There was no window in the house, the only light and ventilation being furnished by the door and the cracks in the thatched roof.

It was too horrible and we went out again into the rain — there we could at least get a breath of fresh air. We asked our guide how these people managed to keep the breath of life in them. He said they lived as their neighbors did, on potatoes and "stirabout."

"What is 'stirabout'?"

"It is a sort of a mush made of Indian meal and skimmed milk. They have that occasionally, for a little luxury, or when the potatoes are so scarce that they think they must husband them."

"You don't mean to say that these people actually live on that fare? that they have nothing else? They at least have meat with their potatoes?"

"God bless you, sir," and the honest man's eyes filled with tears, "they never know the taste of meat. There has not been a bit of meat in my house since last Christmas, when we were fortunate enough to get a bit of pig's head. But up here they don't even have that."

Surely this must have been an exceptional case. It was impossible that even in that country there could be more than one or two instances of such utter and abject woe and misery.

But Mr. Duggan told us to the contrary. He said that the house we had just left was only a fair sample of what was to be seen all over the Galtee Mountains. To be convinced, we trudged painfully through the rain for seven long hours.

We toiled through fields that in America would not be accepted as a gift. Here, if the exorbitant rent charged for them could not be paid, the holders were evicted. We went through roads so wretchedly bad that teams could not travel over them. Yet taxes had to be paid by those who had holdings on either side. We saw fields that had been reclaimed from the original state, had been made productive, and had been the cause of the eviction of the holder because he could not pay the rent which the improvements brought upon him. He had been thrown off the land and it was rapidly going to waste again. Large patches of heather, which is worse than the American farmer's bane, the Canada thistle, were growing over it, choking all other forms of vegetation. It would only take another season to make the land so worthless that three years of hard work would be required to put it back to the condition it was in when the holder had been compelled to leave it, after having devoted the best years of his life to reclaiming and making it productive.

After seven hours of such sights as these, which cannot be described, we were wet, weary and mad. We had seen enough for one day, and were ready to go back. All during the long drive to Mitchellstown not a word was said. The subject was too terrible to discuss.

CHAPTER XXVI.

BANTRY.

THE village of Bantry, in County Cork, some forty miles from Cork, is owned and controlled by My Lord Bantry, who is, or, at least, ought to be, one of the richest men in Ireland. Whether he is or not depends entirely upon how expensively he lives in Paris, and how much extravagance he commits there and in London. He certainly screws enough money out of the unfortunates born upon the land stolen from them by English Kings and given to him, to make him a richer man

A STREET IN AN IRISH VILLAGE.

than Rothschild, if he has taken care of it. But I don't suppose he has. Probably the magnificent estate, robbed from the people, is mortgaged to its full value, and he supports himself by keeping his so-called tenants down to a point, in food, shelter, and clothes, that a Camanche Indian would turn up his nose at. Indeed, were the most degraded Piute compelled to accept life on the terms that My Lord Bantry imposes upon the men he robs, he would paint his face, sing his death song, go out and kill somebody, and die with great pleasure.

Bantry is a pleasant village; that is, some of its streets are pleasant, and it has the most beautiful bay on the coast. Sailing across the most lovely body of water I have ever seen, is the famous watering place, Glengariff, which is the most delicious spot of land in the world. And Bantry itself has much in its favor, all marred by the abject poverty of nine-tenths of its inhabitants.

Leaving the main street, which is, like all the streets of Irish villages, made up of small stores, or shops, as they are called, you walk up a rather steep hill, pass through a crooked street, and you find yourself in the midst of the regulation Irish cabins.

Miserable

BLARNEY CASTLE.

structures of stones piled one upon the other, not even daubed with plaster, with no windows, as a rule, though the more pretentious ones have a single pane of glass in the wall somewhere. However, as that pane is almost invariably broken, its principal use is the extra ventilation it affords.

The cabin is the same size as those on farms, say from ten to twelve feet wide by fifteen or sixteen in length. In the country, however, they do have the space above, to the thatched roof, but land is more valuable in the villages, and My Lord Bantry's expenses in London and Paris are enormous.

25

He must get more money out of the villagers, and he makes two stories out of the wretched hovel, and by crowding in two families makes double rent. The first floor is not above five feet six inches in height, and the upper is a good foot shorter. In neither floor can an ordinary man stand upright.

We went up the miserable stairs in one of them, and gained the still more miserable den above. It was more like a coffin than a room, and the idea of a coffin was brought forcibly to the mind as you glanced at the wretched occupants. On a miserable bed of dried leaves, covered with potato sacks on the one side, was the emaciated form of a man dying of starvation and consumption. He had about forty-eight hours of life in him. Upon my word I felt happy to see he was so near death. For having an excellent reputation, having always been a good man, he is certain to go, after death, where there would not be the slightest possible chance of meeting My Lord Bantry or his agent. In the other corner was a flat stone, upon which a consumptive fire of peat was burning, the smoke filling the room. Huddled around this fire were five children, under the watchful eye of a very comely woman. The children were barefooted and stocking-less, and clad in the most deplorable rags, while the mother, also bare footed, was clothed in the regular cotton slip, without a particle of underclothing of any kind or description. And into that garret, poor as it was, came other women, not clothed sufficiently to be decent, to boil their potatoes at the wretched fire. They have a practice of exchanging fires in this way, that none shall be wasted.

"What do you pay for this apartment?"

"Ten-pence a week, sor!"

"Are you in arrears for rent?"

"Yis sor. He (pointing to her husband) has been sick, sor, for months, sor, and cud not worruk."

"What will you do if he dies?"

"We shall be put out, sor."

This with no burst of anguish, with no special tone of anger or manifestation of emotion. To be "put out" is the common lot of the Irish laborer, and Irish wife, and they expect it.

And within a mile of that wretched spot, of that dying man and starving children, My Lord Bantry has a most beautiful castle, luxurious furniture, filled with pampered

FREE SPEECH IN IRELAND—INTERDICTING A LAND LEAGUE MEETING.

flunkies, his stable crowded with the most wonderful horses, and his table groaning under the weight of the luxuries of every clime

Surely, not for ten pence a week will he tear this woman from the side of her dead husband, and throw her, with her helpless children, out into the cold and wet street?

Yes, but he will, though!

For this family is but one of many thousands on the land which a bad King stole from the people who owned it. Were this the only case he might relent; but should he do it in this case he would have to do it for others, and ten pence a week from thousands aggregates a very large sum, and My Lord Bantry's expenses are very high, for it costs money to run a castle, and there is his house in London, his house in Paris, and his house in Rome, and his houses the Lord knows where; and then his yacht is rather expensive, as his officers and men must be paid, to say nothing of the larder and wines necessary to entertain his friends; and then there is the terrible expense of entertaining his friends from London during the shooting season, and occasional losses at play, and all that.

Clearly, the Widow Flanagan, must either pay her rent or be pitched out into the street to make room for some other widow who can pay, for a while at least, and when she can't pay there are others who can.

It is needless to add that there is in Bantry Bay a splendid English gunboat armed as in time of war, with burnished guns, with bombs of all sort of explosive power, rifled guns, which would knock poor Bantry into a cocked hat in ten minutes, with fine looking marines, armed to the teeth, which, with the military on shore, would make it very warm for the widow Flanagan and her friends, should they presume to interfere with My Lord's land agent, and the bailiffs and the soldiers behind them. The widow has nothing to do but to bow her head and submit, and pray that some relief may come to her from somewhere. But where is it to come from? Not from My Lord, for, as I said, he has his private expenses to meet; not from his agent, for he was selected for his especial fondness for pitching women and children into the street; not from England, for England looks upon every country it has anything to do with as either to be plundered or traded with; not from the peasantry about them, for they are in the same boat with the widow.

What becomes of her finally, I don't know. I am altogether too soft-hearted to stay any length of time where such
things are to be seen every hour.

A pathetic little scene took place in the widow's loft, which
illustrates something of Irish character. As I said the husband
and father was lying upon his wretched pallet, dying of consumption. The
youngest but one
of the children
was the most beau-
tiful child I have
ever seen, a sweet
little fairy, with
long curly, blonde
hair and black
eyes, built from
the ground up,
and with a face
that a painter
would walk miles
to sketch. She
was a delicious lit-
tle dream, a dainty
bit of humanity.
True, she had
nothing but rags
upon her delight-
ful little figure,
and true it was

IN A BOG VILLAGE.

that her sweet little face was smeared with dirt, and her little
hands were as grimy as grimy could be, and her little shapely
bare legs were very red and somewhat pimply. But why
not? Clothes cannot be had for the children when the father
works for ten pence a day and is sick half the time, and nickel-
plated bath-tubs and scented soap are not to be expected in the
top of a cabin in which you cannot stand upright; and how
can a child's face be kept clean where there is no chimney, and
where the room is so thick with peat smoke that you may
almost cut it with a knife, and a child that never had a pair of

shoes and stockings could hardly be expected to have white legs and feet.   The cold prevents that.

In our party was an American gentleman, who was blessed with an abundance of boys, but no girls, and he and his wife had been contemplating the adoption of a girl.   Here was an opportunity to secure not only a girl, but just the kind of a girl that he would have given half his estate to be the father of.   And so he opened negotiations.

An Irishman who knew him, explained to the father and mother that the gentleman was a man of means, that his wife was an excellent, good woman, and that the child would be adopted regularly under the laws of the State in which he lived, and would be educated, and would rank equally with his own children in the matter of inheritance, and all that.   In short, Norah would be reared a lady.

Then the American struck in.   She, the mother, might select a girl to accompany the child across the Atlantic, and the girl selected should go into his family as the child's nurse, and the child should be reared in the religion of its parents.

The father and mother consulted long and anxiously.   It was a terrible struggle.   On the one hand was the child's advantage; on the other, paternal and maternal love.

Finally a conclusion was arrived at.

" God help me," said the mother, " you shall have her.   I know you will be good to her."

Then the arrangements were pushed very briskly, and, with regular American business-like vehemence.   The girl selected to act as nurse was the mother's sister, a comely girl of twenty. The American took the child, and rushed out to the haberdasher's, and purchased an outfit for her.   He put shoes and stockings on her, which was a novel experience, and a pretty little dress, and a little hat with a feather in it, and a little sash, and all that sort of thing; and he procured shoes and stockings for the elder girl, and a tidy dress, and a hat and shawl, and so forth.   And then he brought them back, instructing the mother that he should leave with them for Cork the next morning at eleven, and that the girl and the child should be dressed and ready to depart.

The next morning came, and the American went for his

child. She was dressed, though very awkwardly The mother
had never had any experience in dressing children, and it was
a wonder that she did not get the dress wrong side up. But
there she was, and the mother wailed as one who was parting
with everything that was dear to her, and the father lay and
moaned, looking from Norah to the American. Time was up.
The mother took the baby in her arms, and gave it the final
embrace, and the long, loving kiss; the father took her in his

"DROP THE CHILD!"

arms, and kissed her; the other children looked on astounded,
while the girl stood weeping.

"Good-bye!" said the American; "I will take good care of
the baby," and, taking her from the mother's arms, he started
for the door. There was a shriek -- the woman darted to him
just as he was closing the door, and snatched the baby from him.

"Drop the child!" said the father. "You can't have her
for all the money there is in Ameriky."

"No, sor!" ejaculated the mother, half way between fainting and hysterics. "I can't part wid her!"

And she commenced undressing the baby.

"Take back yer beautiful clothes — give me back the rags
that was on her — but ye can't have the child!"

And the girl — she commenced undressing, too; for she
did not want to obtain clothes under false pretenses. But the
American stopped the disrobing.

"It's bad for the child," he said, "but somehow I can't
blame you. You are welcome to the clothes, though."

And he left as fast as he could, and I noticed he was busy
with his handkerchief about his eyes for some minutes. And
I am sorry to say he indulged in a very profane soliloquy, till
he got out of the street, and his objurgations were not leveled
at the father and mother.

What became of the clothes I know not, but I presume
that, when the husband died and went where landlords cease
from troubling and the weary are at rest, the widow pawned
them to pay the rent, and save the dead body of her husband
from being pitched into the street with herself and children;
and that when My Lord Bantry saw her name on the list, as
paid, he remarked:

"Ah! the Widow Flanagan has paid her rent. I thought
she would! What is necessary with these Irish, is to be firm
with them. By the way, is she paying enough?"

And after ascertaining that the wine had been properly
frappéd, he went to his dinner, and the gunboat, and the royal
constabulary felt relieved.

It is a pleasant thing for all concerned to have the Widow
Flanagan pay her rent promptly, and make no fuss about it,
except, of course, for the Widow Flanagan. But she, being
an Irish widow, is not to be considered. But if there is a God
of justice and mercy, there will come a time when she will be
considered, and then it will be made very warm for My Lord
Bantry, his agent, the captain of the gunboat, the officers of
the soldiery, and the whole brood of oppressors. There is a
Court at which the Widow Flanagan can appear on equal
terms with her landlord, but it is not in Ireland.

If I ever leaned toward the doctrines taught by the Univer-

salists, a contemplation of the system of Bantryism has entirely
and completely convinced me that they are erroneous.   If

NATURE'S LOOKING GLASS.

there is not a lake of fire and brimstone, a very wide and very
deep, and very hot one there ought to be, and when the

British House of Lords meet there, there will always be a quorum. And My Lord will lift up his eyes to the widow Flanagan and beg for a drop of water to cool his parched tongue. But he won't get it. He don't deserve it.

It is impossible to make an American comprehend the width, depth and breadth of Irish misery until he has seen it with his own eyes. No other man's eyes are good for anything in this matter, for the reason that nothing parallel exists this side of the water. And besides this the writers for the stage and of general literature have most woefully misrepresented the Irish man and woman, and very much to his and her disadvantage.

THE IRISHMAN OF THE STAGE AND NOVEL.

The Irishman of the stage and novel is always a rollicking, happy-go-lucky sort of a reckless fellow, with a short-tailed coat, red vest and corduroy trowsers, woolen stockings and stout brogans; with a bottle of whisky peeping out of his pocket, a blackthorn shillelah in his fist; always ready for a dance, or a fight, or for love-making, or any other pleasant employment. There is always on his head a rather bad hat, worn jauntily, however, and though he may be occasionally rather short of food, he manages always to get enough to be fat, sleek, and rosy. And then he always has a laugh on his face, a joke on his lips, and he goes through life with a perpetual "Hurroo."

And Katy—she is always presented to us clad in a short woolen gown, her shapely legs enclosed in warm red stockings; and she had a bright red handkerchief about her neck, with good, comfortable shoes, and a coquettish straw hat — a buxom girl, who can dance down any lad within ten miles, and can " hurroo " as well as Pat, and a little better.

The Irish priest is always represented to us as a fat, sleek, jolly fellow, who is constantly giving his people good advice but who nevertheless is always ready to sing " The Cruiskeen Lawn," in a " rich, mellow voice," before a splendid fire in the house of his parishioners, with a glass of poteen in one hand and a pipe in the other, the company joining jollily in the cho-

rus. He is supposed to live in luxury from the superstition of his people, and to have about as rosy a life as any man on earth.

All these are lies.

The Irishman is the saddest man on the surface of the globe. You may travel a week and never see a smile or hear a laugh. Utter and abject misery, starvation and help-lessness, are not con-ducive of merriment.

THE EVICTED IRISHMAN.

The Irishman has not only no short-tailed coat, but he con-siders himself fortunate if he has any coat at all. He has what by courtesy may be called trowsers, but the vest is a myth. He has no comfortable woolen stockings, nor is he possessed of the regulation stage shoes. He does not sing, dance or laugh, for he has no place to sing, laugh and dance in. He is a mov-ing pyramid of rags. A man who cuts bog all day from day-light to dark, whose diet consists of a few potatoes twice a day, is not much in the humor for dancing all night, even were there a place for him to dance in. And as for jollity, a man with a land agent watching him like a hawk to see how much he is improving his land, with the charitable intent of raising the rent, if by any possibility he can screw more out of him, is not in the mood to laugh, sing, dance or "hurroo." One might as well think of laughing at a funeral. Ireland is one perpetual funeral. The ghastly procession is constantly passing.

There is unquestionably a vast fund of humor in the Irishman, which would be delightful could it have proper vent. You hear faint tones of it, as it is; but it is in the minor key, and very sad. It always has a flavor of rack-rent in it, a taste of starvation, a suggestion of eviction and death, by

cold and hunger, on the road-side. It isn't cheerful. I had much rather have the Irishman silent, than to hear this remnant of jocularity w h i c h i s always streaked with blood.

The Irish girl is always comely, and, properly clothed and fed, would be beautiful; still she is comely. Irish landlordism has not been sufficient to destroy her beauty, although it has done its best. But she has no gown of woolen stuff

TO MARKET AND BACK FOR SIXPENCE.   — a cotton slip, without underclothing of any kind, makes up her costume. The comfortable stockings and stout shoes, and the red kerchief about her neck, are so many libels upon Irish landlordism. Were My Lord's agent to see such clothing upon a girl, he would immediately raise the rent upon her father, and confiscate those clothes. And he would keep on raising the rent till he was certain that shoes and stockings would be forever impossible. Neither does she dance Pat down at rustic balls, for a most excellent reason — there are no balls; and, besides, when she has cut and dried a donkey load of peat, and walked beside that donkey, barefooted in the cold mud, twelve miles and back again, and sold that peat for a sixpence, she is not very much in the humor for dancing down any one. On the contrary, she is mighty glad to get into her wretched bed of dried leaves, and pull over her the potato sack which constitutes her sole covering, and, soothed to sleep by the gruntings of the pigs in the wretched cabin, forget landlords and rent, and go off into the land of happiness, which to her is America. She finds in sleep surcease of sorrow, and, besides, it refreshes her to the degree of walking barefooted through the mud twenty four miles on the morrow, to sell another load of peat for sixpence, that she may pay more money to My Lord Bantry, whose town-house in London, and whose mistresses in Paris, require a great deal of money. Champagne and the delicacies of the season are always expensive; and My Lord's appetite, and the appetite of his wife and mistresses, and his children, legitimate and illegitimate, are delicate. Clearly, Katy is in no

THE REAL IRISH GIRL.

humor for dancing. She has her share to contribute to all these objects. And so she eats her meal of potato or stirabout —she never has both at once—and goes into sleep and dreams.

As to the priest, there never was a wilder delusion than exists in the minds of the American people concerning him. I was at the houses, or rather lodgings, of a great many of them, but one example will suffice.

Half-way between Kenmare and Killarney, in a wild, desolate country, lives one of these parish priests who are supposed to inhabit luxurious houses, and to live gorgeously, and to be perpetually singing the "Cruiskeen Lawn," with a pipe in one hand and a glass of poteen in the other.

He is a magnificent man. In face and figure he is the exact picture of the lamented Salmon P. Chase, one of the greatest of Americans; and I venture the assertion that had he chosen any other profession, and come to America, where genius and intellect mean something, and where great ability finds great rewards, he would have been one of the most eminent of men.

A SMALL, BUT WELL-TO-DO FARMER—COUNTY CORK.

A man of great learning, of wonderful intuitions, of cool and clear judgment, of great nerve and unbounded heart, he would, were he to come to America, and drop his priestly robes be president of a great railroad corporation, or a senator, or anything else he chose to be.

But what is he in Ireland? His apartments consist of a bed-room, just large enough to hold a very poor bed, and a study, in a better class farm-house, and for which he pays rent, the same as everybody else does. His floor is uncarpeted, and the entire furniture of his rooms, leaving out his library, would not invoice ten dollars. His Parish is one of the wildest and bleakest in Ireland, and is twenty-five miles long and eighteen wide.

Now, understand that this man is the lawyer, the friend, the guide and director in temporal as well as spiritual matters of the entire population of this district. If a husband and wife quarrel it is his duty to hear and decide. If a tenant gets into trouble with his landlord he is the go-between to arrange it. In short every trouble, great and small, in the Parish is referred to him, and he must act. He is their lawyer as well as their priest. He is their everything. He supplies to them the intelligence that the most infernal Government on earth has denied them.

But this is a small part of his duties. He has to conduct services at all the chapels in this stretch of country. He has to watch over the morals of all the people. But this is not all. No matter at what hour of night, no matter what the condition of the weather, the summons to the bedside of a dying man to administer the last sacraments of the church must be obeyed. It may be that to do this requires a ride on horseback of twenty miles in a blinding storm, but it must be done. Every child must be christened, every death-bed must be soothed, every sorrow mitigated by the only comfort this suffering people have — faith in their church.

What do you suppose this magnificent man gets for all this? The largest income he ever received in his life was one hundred pounds, which, reduced to American money, amounts to exactly four hundred and eighty-one dollars. And out of this he has to pay his rent, his food, his clothing, the keeping of his horse, and all that remained goes in charity to the suffering sick — every cent of it.

When the father dies his nephews and neices will not find good picking from what is left, I assure you.

"Why do you," I asked, "a man capable of doing so much in the world, stay and do this enormous work, for nothing?"

"I was called to it," was the answer, "what would these poor people do without me?"

That was all. Here is a man capable of anything, who deliberately sacrifices a career, sacrifices comfort, sacrifices the life he was fitted for, sinks his identity, foregoes fame, reputation, everything, for the sake of a suffering people!

"I was called to it — what would these poor people do without me!"

I am a very vigorous Protestant, and have no especial love for the Catholic Church, but I shall esteem myself especially fortunate if I can make a record in this world that will give me a place in the next within gun shot of where this man will be placed. I am not capable of making the sacrifices for my fellows that he is doing — I wish to Heaven I was. I found by actual demonstration why the Irish so love their priests. They would be in a still worse way, if possible, without them.

Ignorance of the real condition of the farming Irish is almost as common among the better class of Irishmen, I mean the dwellers in the cities, as it is among Americans. At one of the fine hotels in Glengariff, a watering place, I made the acquaintance of an Irish lady, a resident of Cork. Her husband is a wealthy citizen, a thorough Irishman, a Land Leaguer and all that, and she is a more ardent Land Leaguer than her husband. She is a more than usually intelligent lady, with a warm heart, and she realized, she thought, the wrongs Ireland was suffering, and was doing, she supposed, all she could to aid the oppressed people.

Now in Glengariff suffering is not permitted to be seen. The hotels are magnificent, the servants well-clothed and well fed, and it is so arranged that the people in rags are seldom seen in that vicinity.

But two miles across the bay and you may see all the misery you can endure. I had been over there and had gone through a dozen or more cabins, and on my return I expressed myself to the lady in as strong terms as my command of language permitted.

"Are you not exaggerating?" asked she. "I have never seen such misery as you describe. It cannot be."

"Because you have never sought it out. But it is there. Fifteen minutes in a boat will take you to it. Will you go over now, and see for yourself if I have exaggerated?"

She went. It was a lovely morning; the waters were smiling, and the Glengariff shore, with its beautiful buildings, its long hedges of fuchsias along the winding street, the background a mountain of flowers, was a fairy scene. From this side the mountains on the opposite in the delicate brown of Autumn, were beautiful. Distance showed you only the beauties of Nature; it mercifully hid the squalid poverty the mountains contained.

We landed and began the ascent. The land was, as everywhere, bog and rock, with here and there a spot reclaimed, which smiled in green. We approached one of the regular hovels.

"How far have we to go before we come to one of the houses you spoke of?"

"We are at one now."

The woman stood petrified.

"Do people live in such places?"

"Madam, that cabin holds a man, his wife, six children, the wife's father and brother, pigs, calves and poultry. But you must see for yourself that I did not exaggerate. Come in with me."

The lady entered, wading pluckily through the slush and mud that surrounded the cabin, and saw all and more than I had told her. There was the cold earth floor, wet and slippery, the two wretched beds on which these people slept, the pigs, the calves and the poultry, which must be sheltered and grown and fattened, not for their eating, but that My Lord may have his rent. There was the flat stone in one corner, with the smoky peat fire, no chimney to carry away the smoke; there were the half-ragged men, the half-naked women and children, shoeless, stockingless, skirtless, less everything; in short, there were all the horrors of absolute destitution, without one single redeeming feature

"Take me out of this place," she gasped.

It was not a pleasant sight for a lady delicately nurtured and daintily kept, whose hands had never been in cold water and upon whose face cold wind had never blown. These people were of her own blood, her own race, almost her own kin. She said never a word on the way back, but that afternoon she left Glengariff for Cork. But before she went, a boat went over the bay, and a dozen families had at least one square meal, and more money than they had ever seen before.

It is to be hoped that they ate the provisions, but the money — that went to My Lord's agent for rent, beyond a doubt. And if My Lord's agent was certain that he could depend upon the lady from Cork as a permanent almoner, he would ascertain to a penny just how much she intended to give, and raise the rent to that amount.

26

My Lord's agent is as ravenous and insatiable as a grave-yard — he takes all that comes.

The lady from Cork is spending her entire time and a great deal of money in the interest of her people. It requires actual sight to understand the condition of the Irish.

SKETCHES IN GALWAY.

CHAPTER XXVII.

AN IRISH MASS MEETING.

Mr. Charles Stewart Parnell, lately in Kilmainhaim Jail for the crime of lifting up his voice in behalf of an oppressed people, represents Cork in the British Parliament, and his constituents determined to give him a reception.

In Catholic countries political demonstrations take place on Sunday, always, the Catholic having attended services in the morning, devoting the rest of the day to recreation and public business. And besides this reason for Sunday demonstrations in any country under British rule, the citizen does not have time enough on any other day to make any demonstrations, political or otherwise. He has to earn his two meals of potatoes a day, and his landlord has a mortgage upon the remainder of his time. Sunday is his only day, and it is a blessed thing for him that the Church of England stands between him and his landlord. Were not labor on the Sabbath illegal, My Lord would raise his rent to the point of making Sunday labor necessary.

I had always supposed that America was the country for demonstrations of a public nature, and indeed we do get up some monsters in this way, but the Irish, in 1881, did things, compared with which our largest are but pigmies.

Early in the morning the city began filling with people. They came singly and in pairs, and in processions. They came from down the river, from up the river, from the east, west, north and south; they came in steamboats, by rail, on horses and donkeys, in wagons and donkey carts, and on foot. By nine o'clock Cork was swarming with people, literally swarming.

Then came the most wonderful procession I ever saw or ever expect to see. The trades and occupations of the city were in bodies with emblems, flags and banners; the Land Leagues of the entire south of Ireland were there with appropriate banners, and then came a swarming, seething, boiling mass of humanity, without order, without form or coherence. There were men, women and children, on foot, and in all sorts and descriptions of vehicles, and bestriding every animal that permits its back to be crossed   There were women with children in their arms, men carrying their boys to save them from being crushed in the press; there were old men, young men and boys, maids and matrons of all ages, all sorts and conditions of people, in all sorts of garments; men and women shod, men and women barefooted, and all in one inextricable jam.

If there was an idea in the way of a banner that was not in that procession it escaped my notice; and if there was a form or manner of decoration that was not in the seemingly endless mass of humanity that I did not notice, it was because there was so much of it that one pair of eyes could not take it all in.

The procession was fully ten miles long, and there were in it not less than one hundred thousand people. I know that mass meetings are always exaggerated, but there were actually that number in that monster procession on that Sunday.

A very great deal is said about the intemperance of the Irish people. In all this vast throng, this hive of human beings, there were but three drunken men. Also, much is said about their tendency to brawls. There was not a single fight. The procession was wild in enthusiasm, wild in cheering and handkerchief-shaking, but there was not a blackened eye nor a broken head. I never saw one-fourth the number of Americans together that did not eventuate in a score or two of fights. Ireland certainly behaved herself remarkably well on that occasion.

There was one curious scene. A young man in Cork in the early days of the Land League had been suspected of playing into the hands of the government, for gain. Since the movement became overwhelmingly popular, he shifted his course and tried to curry favor with the Leaguers, but without success. They did not trust him. A carriage was set apart for the use of the prominent Americans then in the city, and he, by sheer impudence, forced himself upon them. He managed to get himself seated upon the box of the carriage, making himself exceedingly conspicuous.

It was a kind of conspicuosity which the young Irishmen did not like. They remembered his betrayal of the cause a few months before, and they believed his present zeal was for effect and not honest. They would not have him foist himself upon their American friends. There was no violence, no obstreperousness. Ten of them, five upon each side, formed beside the carriage, and they kept step as soldiers do, only instead of the regular "Left!" "Left!" the words were "Come down!" "Come down!" He tried to reason with them; he said all sorts of pretty things to them; he assured them of his entire and utter devotion to the cause; but to every word he uttered there came the one response, "Come down!" "Come down!" He came. He might have resisted force, but the moral suasion in the simple words "Come down!" was too much for him. He descended from the carriage and slunk away in the crowd, and we saw no more of him. Immediately the young men fell into rank, and the procession swept on. It was their way of punishing one who was seeking for himself instead of for the mass.

And that enormous mass of people paraded the streets all day, and in the evening, in the fields outside the city, they waited patiently and listened to speeches from the leaders of the people, every sentence bringing a quick response.

As grand as was the demonstration, it was no mere man worship that was at the bottom of it. It was not so much in honor of their leader; it was a protest of a great people against a system which has already driven out from the country two-thirds of the entire population, and which would drive out the remainder were there means enough left to take them. It was the wail of a starving people, a naked people, a robbed, outraged and oppressed people. It was a protest against bayonet rule, a protest against carbines and ball cartridges, an appeal for the right to live upon the ground upon which they

were born. Had they arms probably they would make this
protest in another form, and there never was a cause in which

AFFIXING NOTICE OF EVICTION UNDER PROTECTION OF THE POLICE.

arms could be taken up so justly, but unfortunately they have
not. The British government allows the Irishman to bear
nothing more deadly than the spade, and all the arms that are

in Ireland are used to compel him to use that implement for British greed.

I was present at an eviction near Skibbereen. An eviction is a very simple thing. The landlord desires to possess himself of the land which a tenant holds, having been born upon it, his father and his grandfather for many generations back. When the land passed into the hands of the present alleged owners it was worthless, but several generations have toiled upon it, until it has been "reclaimed," as they term it, and made into good soil, which will yield crops. The landlord has raised the rent regularly, keeping the tenant and his family down to the potato and stirabout point, until it is impossible for him to pay. There is no question of a desire to pay —paying is a physical impossibility, unless the tenant has a son in America, and even in that case the rent is raised to the point of

EVICTION.

absorbing the boy's wages. Just as the crop is ripening the landlord gets out a process of eviction, a bailiff, backed by thirty constabularly, go to the house, the warrant is served, the tenant knows exactly what is to happen, and he goes out without a word. But the mother, not so well versed in English law, does make a protest. As wretched as the cabin is, as poor as are her surroundings, it is the only home she has. In this wretched cabin her children were born, this is her home, and no woman relinquishes that without a protest. But she might as well whistle against the north wind. There is no pity nor mercy in these beasts, to say nothing of justice.

First the poor furniture is pitched out into the road, then the children are thrown out after the furniture, and then the woman is hustled out, the door is nailed up, and the family are by the roadside in the cold or rain. Pat or Mick, as the case may be, is offered another farm, farther up the mountain, a piece of land, bog and rock, which he may go on and convert

THE EVICTION WE SAW.

into smiling fields only to be evicted from that when his landlord sees fit, or he may die by the roadside.

In the village of Kenmare, there were thirteen families one cold wet morning, out on the roadside, men, women and children, some of the latter being only two months old, their only protection being blankets made of potato sacks stretched upon four sticks driven into the cold clay, and their only bed, leaves, which were wet with the rain. The mothers were boiling their potatoes, contributed by neighbors almost as poor as themselves, in pots suspended from extemporized tripods, the fuel being leaves and twigs.

What became of them? I do not know. I presume some of the children died from exposure, but that was nothing to

EVICTED — SCENE IN GALWAY.

the landlord or his agent. They were too young to work, and really stood in the way of the mother and father paying their rent.   Possibly the father working in the mines in Wales, got money enough before the children were all dead to enable them to get into some kind of a shelter.

FARMING IN COUNTY MAYO.

It is only necessary for me to say that they were there, and there because they could not pay an unmerciful rent unmercifully exacted and relentlessly pursued.

An English landlord's agent would levy upon a child's coffin for arrearages of rent, and the British government would give him thirty soldiers to protect the bailiff in serving the process. They wish it distinctly understood that rent must be paid though the heavens fall. Rent is My Lord's living and the agent's also. Where mercy is shown to one tenant others might expect it, and so the rule must be inexorable.

"Boycotting" is a system devised by Mr. James Redpath, of America. It is this: The landlord, when he has made up his mind that he wants to rob a tenant of the land he once owned, and which he has, does not evict him in the Spring. He waits till the tenant has dug up the ground, planted it and tended it, and it is ready for the harvest. He wants to steal the crops as well as the land, and so just before harvest he gets out his process, and accompanied by the everlasting thirty constables, armed with carbines, he makes his descent. The process is served, the tenant and his family are pitched out into the street, and the place taken possession of.

Prior to the Land League, the villain had no difficulty in employing labor to secure the crop, thus giving the agent his percentage of the robbery, and enabling My Lord to indulge in fresh extravagances in London or Paris, or wherever he might be. But the Land League steps in now, and My Lord's agent cannot find a man who will put a sickle into the ground. No matter what price he offers, or how sorely the laborer needs work, or how cheaply he would be glad to work for any one else, he will not work for this man at any price. Consequently the crops rot on the ground, and if the robbed tenant gets no benefit from his labor, My Lord in Paris, and his agent at home, do not.

I was in one cottage over the bay from Glengariff, in a cabin in which three men were sitting listlessly, waiting for work. They had nothing to eat but the everlasting potatoes, and would have given their lives, almost, for something to do that would keep the pot boiling, even though there was nothing but potatoes in it.

Enter My Lord's agent.

"Come, men, I want you for a few days."

"Yis, sor, what is it?"

"I want you on Captain ———'s place. I will give you two shillings a day."

Ten pence a day is good wages.

"Is it on Mickey Doolan's farrum?"

"Yes."

"We don't want wurruk. We're rich, and are enjoyin' ourselves."

Mickey Doolan was the evicted tenant, and had the agent offered them a thousand pounds an hour he could not have got a stroke from one of them.

This is boycotting. The process was first tried upon a Captain Boycott, hence the term. It was an invention of Mr. James Redpath, as I said, and a very clever one it is.

To prevent the evicted tenant from taking another farm, and reclaiming it for the benefit of My Lord and his agent, the Land League makes him the princely allowance of three shillings a week, on which he supports his family, and it finds him some sort of a shelter. My Lord and his agent have the privilege of getting in the crops themselves, else they rot in the field.

There is no violence, no shooting or mobbing — only passive resistance. The British government cannot compel a man to labor, and there is left the Irish the blessed boon of dying from starvation. Possibly the government will make labor compulsory — it would not be worse than most of the laws for the government of the unhappy island now in force. But so far the Irishman need not labor for an unjust landlord unless he chooses to, and that means he need not labor for any of them.

There is no such thing as a just landlord in Ireland. Ireland is a cow to be milked, and just enough potatoes are given her to make the milk.

You hear a great deal in America about shooting landlords. How many landlords have been shot? It is much to the discredit of the Irish race that more have not been; but the melancholy fact is, only a very few have been put out of the way by buck-shot. When I look over the meagre list I blush for the Irish. It is something in the way of an offset to know that they are not permitted to have arms, and it may be plead in extenuation that the police and soldiery are all pervading;

but, nevertheless, it does seem as though a few more might be picked off. If they cannot have fire-arms, there are at least pitch-forks and stones. Clearly, the Irish are not so public-spirited as they should be.

One was shot, some years ago, and a great to-do was made about it. In this case, as in most of the others, it was not a question of rent. My Lord had visited his estates to see how

MY LORD'S AGENT.

much more money could be screwed out of his tenants, and his lecherous eye happened to rest upon a very beautiful girl, the eldest daughter of a widow with seven children. Now, this beautiful girl was betrothed to a nice sort of a boy, who, having been in America, knew a thing or two. My Lord, through his agent, who is always a pimp as well as a brigand, ordered Kitty to come to the castle. Kitty, knowing very well what that meant, refused.

"Very good," says the agent, "your mother is in arrears for rent, and you had better see My Lord, or I shall be compelled to evict her."

Kitty knew what that meant, also. It meant that her gray-haired mother, her six helpless brothers and sisters, would be pitched out by the roadside, to die of starvation and exposure; and so Kitty, without saying a word to her mother or any one

else, went to the castle, and was kept there three days, till My
Lord was tired of her, when she was permitted to go.

THE KIND OF A GIRL MY LORD WANTS.

She went to her lover, like an honest girl, and told him she
would not marry him, but refused to give any reason.

Finally, the truth was wrenched out of her, and Mike went
and found a shot-gun that had escaped the watchful eye of the

royal constabulary, and he got powder, and shot, and old nails, and he lay behind a hedge under a tree for several days. Finally, one day My Lord came riding by, all so gay, and that gun went off, and "subsequent events interested him no more." There was a hole, a blessed hole, clear through him, and he never was so good a man before, because there was less of him.

Then Mike went to Kitty and told her to be of good cheer, and not be cast down; that the little difference between him and My Lord had been happily settled, and that they would be married as soon as possible. And they were married, and ı had the pleasure of taking in my hand the very hand that fired the blessed shot, and of seeing the wife to avenge whose cruel wrongs the shot was fired.

"Vengeance is mine!" is written. In these cases it is well to facilitate the vengeance a trifle by means of a shot-gun. I object to keeping such a man as My Lord out of fire and brimstone a minute. Give the devil his due, and never let the note he holds go to protest.

An immense reward was offered for information leading to the conviction of the noble man who fired the shot, but, though every man, woman and child in a radius of twenty miles knew exactly who did it, no one was found base enough to lodge information against him.

You see the Irish all have daughters and they are all comely, and if shooting lords for such crimes comes to be a rule, the lords will turn their lecherous eyes elsewhere. There are worse things in the world than shot-guns. That particular one should be wreathed with flowers, and hung up in the church of that Parish. There is much moral suasion in a shot-gun loaded with rusty nails.

I entered one cabin in the Galtees which rather eclipsed anything in the way of misery that I had seen. It was the smallest and the most wretched of any I had investigated, and there was a refinement of wretchedness about the whole arrangement that to an American would seem impossible. The children were the thinnest that I had ever seen. It was poverty condensed — it was wretchedness boiled down. It was the very essence of misery.

"What rent do you pay for this place?"

"Three pounds a year, sor!"

Then with an inflection in my voice that had something of sarcasm, I suppose, in it, I asked:—

"Is that all?"

"Oh, no sor, I pay a pound a year, poor rate!"

THE WOMAN WHO PAID THE POOR RATE.

Think of it! To pay a poor rate implies that somebody is poorer than the payer. Here was a family living in a pig style, and paying fifteen dollars a year for the privilege, who, with a starving and almost naked family, was compelled in addition to this monstrous rental to contribute an additional five dollars per year for the support of the poor!

This would be humorous were it not ghastly. Had she intended it as a joke it would have been a good one, but unfortunately it was no joke. The British government is not jocular. The wretched woman was actually paying a tax to support the poor! What must be the condition of the poor if such as she were paying to support them?

I was in the postoffice at Cork, when a middle-aged woman came in and received a letter. She opened it and read it, or rather read a few lines. The letter dropped to the floor, and she staggered and would have fallen but for the friendly wall against which she leaned.

"What is the matter?"

"Oh, sor, Patsey is dead—*and who'll pay the rint!*"

Here it was again! Patsey was her son, a boy of nineteen, who by the aid of an uncle who had fortunately escaped from the clutches of the British government, years ago, had been taken to America. He had found employment and had been regularly sending money to his mother to pay the rent of the miserable cabin she existed in. She had not heard from him for six weeks and had been worried about him. This letter was from his room-mate, and it conveyed the intelligence that he had been sick for six weeks, and that his sickness had terminated in death. Poor Patsey was dead and buried.

What kind of an infamy is it that will not permit a mother to mourn the death of her first born without connecting it with "rint?" This one could not, for as dearly as she loved Patsey, there were six others just as dear to her, to whom Patsey was the life. It was Patsey in America who shielded the others from starvation. What kind of an infernalism is it that grips the hearts of women, that lays its icy iron finger upon the tenderest chords in a mother's heart?

"Patsey's dead — who'll pay the rint!"

Death and rent! A most proper combination. Rent *is* death.

Tibbitts is here, but I am sorry to say that that not altogether exemplary young man is paying a great deal more attention to Irish whisky than he is to Irish troubles.

He came in very much intoxicated last night at twelve o'clock, and I reproved him for the condition he was in.

"It's my (hic) mother that did it," he replied. "My mother in Oshkosh."

"Your mother, you — well, that is too much!"

"True, 'shoor you. She wrote me a long letter, which I got this mornin'. (Hic.) R'ligious letter, and a mighty (hic) good one. (Hic.) Great woman, mother. She said man in state of nature (hic) was wicked as sparks fly upward. Struck me (hic) as true. What was duty? To get out of state of nature. (Hic.) Man full of Irish whisky is not in state (hic) nature — entirely unnatural. Ergo — man drunk not bein' in state of nature, not sinner. See? Logic. Have too much regard (hic) for mother's feelings to be in state of nature. Never will be, so long as the old (hic) man comes down."

27

I don't think he ever will be. Clearly, it is my duty to have the young man sent home as soon as possible.

While I am informed that Irish whisky is less destructive of the tissues than English gin or British brandy, or the vile compound they call ale, it will intoxicate, and I do not accept Mr. Tibbitt's logic. His getting outside of whisky does not enable him to get outside of himself.

On the Quay Galway

A Claddagh boy making twine.

Conemara Women.

CHAPTER XXVIII.

IT is very difficult to make an American understand the Irish question, for the simple reason we have nothing parallel to it in our own country; for which every American should thank his Heavenly Father, who cast his lines in such pleasant places.

Whenever you speak to an American about the woes and wrongs of Ireland he at once says, "Why does the Irish farmer sign a lease which he knows he cannot live to?" "If he don't like the country and the laws, why don't he get out of it?" "Why is it, the country being under one government, that the English farmer and the North of Ireland farmer are prosperous, while the South of Ireland farmer is in a state of discontent?"

The trouble with the man who asks these questions is, he doesn't know anything about the subject. He measures everybody's grain in his half-bushel. He supposes that under English government, as in America, there is one law which obtains everywhere, and under which all men are equal.

I shall try to make it plain how a farmer in one part of Ireland may be prosperous, and in another poorer than the pigs he fattens.

To understand this matter it is necessary to go back some hundreds of years. All grievances took root a long way back — the world has got too wise to commence or tolerate any new ones.

Originally Ireland was an independent kingdom; in fact, five independent kingdoms. Under the kings were the clans. The Clan O'Connor, for instance, held a certain amount of land — not each man an owner in fee simple, but in common.

(419)

That is to say, the ownership of the soil was in the clan as a community, each family of the clan holding its land forever, and that land was distributed among them as the best interests of the clan dictated. The chief of the clan was elected, and he was their general, their counsellor, their judge, their

AT WORK IN THE BOG.

advisor, philosopher, guide and friend. He was the father of the clan.

To support the dignity of his position, and to bear the expenses of the post of honor put upon him, a tribute was paid to him, based upon the land held — so much per acre. It was very light, for the chief farmed land, as did the clansmen; and there was, for the time, a fair degree of prosperity in the island — as much as could be expected for that day and generation. At least everybody had all they could eat, drink and wear.

The English wanted Ireland, and England did with Ireland as it has done with every country it ever desired to possess. She simply measured bayonets, and, finding her bayonet the strongest, took possession. This work was begun by Henry II., but received a great impetus from Henry VIII., the brute who was so handy at decapitating his wives, and it was followed up vigorously by succeeding kings and queens.

The country was conquered, the chieftains were expelled, the land was divided up among the favorites of the English kings, and the people found themselves tenants at will of a foreign proprietary, instead of being actually owners in fee simple of their own land.

England never does an injustice by halves. She is very moderate in the matter of mercy and justice, and things of that nature, but when it comes to robbery and spoliation she knows no middle way. When Elizabeth determined upon occupying Ireland, the orders were to spare neither man, woman nor child.

The chiefs were driven out, and the land of the clans was distributed among the favorites of the English court. Sir Walter Raleigh had forty-two thousand acres given him from the estate of the Munster Geraldines, and a proclamation was made through England, inviting "younger brothers of good families" to undertake the planting of the land from which the Irish — the owners and occupiers of the soil — had been killed or driven off, and the repopulation of the country, "none of the native Irish to be admitted."

Under this invitation, which the English robbers were not slow to accept, scores of estates were given to the dissolute nobility of England, who were willing enough to take possession of land which they got for nothing, and which would give them means to dodge the primal curse of labor. What they wanted was to live as they wanted, by the sweat of other men's brows, and British bayonets gave the means.

It is not possible to detail the outrages perpetrated upon this unfortunate people by the kings and queens of England, but let it suffice to say that a wholesale system of spoliation, robbery, and even extirpation, was inaugurated and most relentlessly and rigorously pursued. Man, woman and child, and even the animals that could not be driven off and sold, were destroyed.

There never was, in the history of the world, a record so

SOME OF THE DUKE OF LEINSTER'S KILDARE TENANTS.

black with infamy, so red with blood, or so scarlet with injustice.

This is the way England obtained possession of Ireland. This is the title by which My Lord This, and My Lord That, holds the lands he exacts rent for to-day. This is his deed to the property upon which five millions of people are eating two meals of potatoes a day, that he may gamble and keep mistresses in London and Paris.

"Why does he sign a lease, the conditions of which he cannot fulfil?"

There are no leases. It is not as it is in America, where the tenant and the landlord come together, and bargain and wrangle over the terms, and when an agreement is arrived at both are bound by the terms thereof. There is no lease, no writing, no courts, except for the landlord. The tenant is born upon the ground which British brute force, the only principle there is in British government, robbed him of. The new landlord enforced upon him by the pikes of Elizabeth's banditti, said to him, "The rent of this land will be one shilling an acre." He could go nowhere else. He knew no other country, and so he bowed his head and built with his own hands a cabin — in the subjugation the old homes were entirely destroyed — and went to work upon land, forty acres of which, in its natural state, would not pasture a goat.

Before it had any value whatever the bog had to be cut off, the stones dug out — in short, the land had to be made. They call it "reclaiming."

The tenant has no lease. He is purely and simply in the power of the landlord. Whatever rent the landlord chooses to exact, that is the rent he must pay. He is a tenant at will — and the will is the will of his landlord, the English robber who lives in luxury in London and Paris, and permits himself to be fleeced by sharpers, who, differing from the English, use finesse instead of force. In brute force the English cannot be excelled; when it comes to decent robbery, the kind of robbery where the victim has some sort of compensation in the knowing that it was accomplished by superior acumen, the English are babies.

The tenant — the robbed farmer — for his own sake is compelled to go on and reclaim the land; he must raise something, for he has children who must be fed; and so he digs out the rocks, and cuts the bog, and makes good, arable land out of what was a barren and dreary waste.

What happens to him then? Why, My Lord in Paris has a subordinate watching his tenant. There is nothing so mean that there is not something meaner. Cruel as My Lord is, he has a crueller man under him. And that is My Lord's agent. He comes to the miserable holding, and he notices that Pat has reclaimed an acre more this year. Immediately he says to Pat, "Your rent next year, my fine fellow, will be advanced."

What can Pat do? Nothing. He can't get off the land, for the merciless exactions of My Lord, who is living in Paris and London, have left him nothing; he cannot get away; he has no title to possession a minute; he can be evicted from his holding at any time, for any one of a thousand causes; there are no courts he can appeal to, as in America, for the magistrates are all landlords. And so he bows his head, and meekly goes on

TENANT FARMER, COUNTY MEATH.

and reclaims more land, only to have the rent raised for every acre made valuable by the labor of his own hands; until, finally, it comes to a point where he has reclaimed the entire holding, and My Lord's agent comes to the conclusion that it is better for him and My Lord — their interests are identical — to convert the farm into a sheep-walk, and Pat is evicted — which is to say, he is thrown out upon the roadside to starve, with his wife and children; and the cabin he has built is torn down.

Does he get anything for the making of the land? Not a halfpenny. All the labor bestowed upon that land, originally his, goes to My Lord, whose mistresses in London and Paris need it. They must have their silks and velvets, they must have their wines and carriages, and horses and servants — and Pat must pay for it.

It must be understood that there is no such thing as leases in the South and West of Ireland — the landlord dictates the terms, and the tenant must accept them. He has no alternative. He cannot get away; he has nothing to get away with. As to the difference between the farmer of the North and South of Ireland, it is not true that the farmer of the North is a wonderfully prosperous man, but it is true that he is better off than the farmer of the South. Why? Because there is not one law governing the whole country. The "custom" that governs one section does not govern the other.

Now, please, get this infamy in your mind, and try to comprehend it. The British government actually drove the Irish, which is to say the native owners of the soil, out of the North of Ireland into the South. The phrase "To hell or Connaught" had its origin in this. It was to Connaught that these people were condemned to go, the alternative being death.

Of course no American can understand why anybody should go to any place that he does not want to go, America being a free country. But the American must understand that England is not a free country; that the corrupt and vicious nobility of England wanted ground upon which they could commit piracy, and that they had the entire power of the British government behind it. The English bayonet is a rare persuader, especially when it has the stolid cruelty and the iron will of a Cromwell behind it. Let a man like Oliver Cromwell breathe upon a bayonet, and you may reasonably expect to see a baby impaled upon it in a minute. To have satisfied his ambition, and what he, in a mistaken way, considered his duty, he would have burned his mother.

It was considered necessary to have an English garrison in the land. To accomplish this the Irish were driven out of the

North of Ireland, and when I say driven out, I mean driven out. They were forced to go, man, woman and child, into the wilds of Connaught.

Then the land vacated by this exodus, at the end of a bayonet — British rule always means bayonet, British statesmanship begins and ends with a bayonet, that being the only thing in the world that does not think — this land was divided up among the dissolute villains who infested the British Court, and for whom, they being the alleged sons of nobles, something must be done.

IN A DISCONTENTED DISTRICT.

But a condition was attached to these grants of stolen lands. No native Irishman was to have a holding there. It was considered necessary that there should be in Ireland a garrison of what they chose to call "loyal" citizens, to hold the robbed and outraged Irish who had been driven into the South in check. Therefore the North of Ireland was given to the dissolute younger sons of dissolute English Lords, upon condition that their tenants should be English or Scotch, and in all cases Protestants.

To get English or Scotch farmers to join in this wholesale brigandage, there had to be some inducement held out. They were not compelled to come upon the ground, and they made their bargain with the Lords. They insisted upon fixity of tenure, a low rent and free sale, which is to say they would not enter upon these stolen lands except upon a low rent, and if they made improvements they should have the benefit thereof, and if they chose to quit the lands they should have the right to sell the improvements they had made, and that the improvements should be a part of the value of the lands, and their interest therein should be an interest in law and equity.

This was agreed to, and on these conditions the Nortn of Ireland was settled by English and Scotch Protestants; the

PROTECTING A GENTLEMAN FARMER.

"custom" known as "Ulster custom" was established, and is law to-day.

But "Ulster custom" does not extend over the entire island. While the farmer in Ulster has fair rent, fixity of tenure and free sale, the farmer of Cork and Tipperary has nothing of the kind. He is a simple tenant at will. He holds a farm at the will of his landlord; his life is in the hands of a dissolute scoundrel who has no brains, backed by a dissolute scoundrel in the form of an agent who has brains, and both of these scoundrels are backed by the bayonets of the most infamous government on the face of the earth.

"Ulster custom" gives the tenant some rights. "Cork custom" is quite another thing. "Ulster custom" was a bribe. "Cork custom" is robbery. It is a system of wholesale confiscation of labor, of body and soul.

The farmer of Cork and Tipperary has nothing to say about

himself, his wife or his children.   If the son of the thief who
stole his land loses money at bacaret in Paris, he telegraphs
the other thief, his agent, that he wants money, and the
secondary thief, who has a percentage in the robbery, goes
about among the tenants, and raises the rent.   And that is
all there is about it.   The tenant farmer has no lease.   He
lives upon the land at the pleasure of his landlord, and the
measure of the rent he pays is the measure of the landlord's
vices and the agent's expectations.

Each county has its own "custom," and the poor, robbed
slave lives under that custom.   The North of Ireland farmer
comes nearer to keeping body and soul together than the South
of Ireland farmer, because the villain robbers who expelled the
Irish from the North of Ireland had to make a custom more
favorable to get the Scotch and English to go there to keep
the Catholic Irish in check, and they would not have gone to
the country except for some advantage.   An English lord will
do anything mean for the love of it—the Scotch are altogether
too acute to do a mean thing without being paid for it.

An instance, not a very large one, but enough to illustrate
the power of the landlord over his victim, the tenant, occurred
upon the estate of My Lord Leitrim, who is this minute where
I hope never to go if there is a hereafter.

This worthy descendant of a very unworthy race had an
industrious tenant, whose farm he had been long coveting.
But somehow he did not dare to take it by force, with the feeling there was in the country at the time, and so he sought a
legal pretext.   An Irish tenant is not permitted by the paternal
government, under which he starves and goes naked, to make
any improvements without the consent of the landlord.   He
cannot build an addition to his cabin (this condition is unnecessary, for he could n't if he would), he cannot dig a ditch or do
anything.   This is the law, but it has never been enforced, for
in the very nature of things the tenant would not do more than
was profitable to himself for the improvement of the land is
the enrichment of the landlord, who religiously raises the rent
with every improvement made.

This tenant needed a ditch preparatory to the reclamation
of a bog farther back, and he had been putting in all his spare

time for two years digging it. He did not suppose that My Lord would object to his reclaiming the bog.

One Saturday Mike was working in the ditch up to his

THE FILLING OF THE DITCH.

knees in water when My Lord came riding by. He saw his opportunity. He knew the law.

"What are you doing?" he asked.

"Making the drain, sor," replied Pat, proudly, for it was a big thing he had undertaken.

"Who gave you permission to make a ditch on my land?" demanded My Lord. "My fine fellow, you have that dirt all back by Monday morning, or out you go."

Mike saw the trap he had fallen into. Before striking a spade he should have gone to My Lord's agent, and got permission. But he was in for it, for he know that My Lord had a legal excuse to rob him of his years of labor.

But the next morning he went to the chapel, and interviewed the priest. The priest asked:—

"If you get that earth back by Monday morning, will you hold the land?"

"Unless the ould—that is—My Lord doesn't kape his worrud."

"We'll try whether he does!" said the father.

And so the sermon that morning was a very short one, and mostly devoted to Mike's case. At its conclusion the father asked every man in the parish to come at once with his spade and put that earth back. They came—thousands of them—and they wrought with a will, and long before Monday morning the drain was filled up as nicely as possible; and when My Lord came riding by again to see the drain, and give orders for the eviction of Mike, he found that his cruel alternative had been fulfilled, as if by faries.

An Irishman in Corduroy knee-breeches, with a spade in his hand and a short clay pipe in his mouth, would not make a very happy stage fairy, but he was a very serviceable fairy to Mike.

Had Mike not been so assisted he would have been evicted, and there would have been no appeal from it. He couldn't employ counsel to fight his battle, for he had nothing with which to pay counsel, and the Justice would be a landlord anyhow, who had other Mikes to evict, and so Mike would have never gone into court at all, but would have accepted his fate in silence.

A cheerful state of affairs, surely.

And speaking of the possibility of paying rent, I remember a young man on the Galtees, insufficiently clad (that was nothing new), working for dear life in a soaking rain.

"How many hours do you work?" I asked.

"From daylight to dark, sor," was his answer, first peering around before speaking, to be sure that no one heard him. In free Britain it is dangerous for him to talk even of so small a matter as wages.

"And what are your wages?"

"Ten pence a day, sor."

"Are you satisfied to work for so many hours for so little money?"

"Troth, sor, it wuld be betther for my ould mother if I cud get that the year around."

Ten pence is about nineteen cents; and understand he was not boarded. Out of that pittance he had to furnish his own food and his own bed. And yet he would have been thankful to the man who would have given him steady work at that price.

To know something of what landlordism really is, and how it all came about, read the following little history of the Barony of Farney:

In 1606 Lord Essex, who had "obtained" a grant of the Barony of Farney, leased it to Evar McMahon, at a yearly rent of two hundred and fifty pounds. And this was a mighty comfortable rent, for, understand, under the *Crown* grants the one receiving it was only

READY FOR EMIGRATION.

charged for arable land, the bog and mountain land adjacent, then esteemed worthless, being thrown in.

McMahon sub-let it to poorer men, and they so improved it that, fourteen years later, the same land was let for one thousand five hundred pounds, and in 1636 thirty-eight tenants were compelled to pay a rental of two thousand and twenty-three pounds.

Under the strong hands of the original owners, the robbed peasantry, who found themselves tenants on their own lands, this piece of property was mounting up in value very rapidly.

The Earl of Essex died in 1636 A. D. "His" estate went to his sisters. There is in English families always somebody to inherit, and in case there should not be, the Crown steps in and takes it, that the proceeds of the robbery may not go out of the race. The two sisters married and had children, of course, and in 1690, when the two came together to divide their plunder, it was found that the rentals had risen to twenty-six hundred and twenty-six pounds. Then the rents began to be put up so as to produce something like.

The two daughters had children to be educated and provided for, marriages were getting to be common in the family, and the debts of the youngsters had to be paid. And so in 1769 this estate, which started so modestly at two hundred and fifty pounds, yielded eight thousand pounds.

How? Easily enough. The land in this stolen estate, as I said, was nine-tenths of it bog and stone, and only the arable land, some twenty-five hundred acres, was set down in the lease, all the bog and mountain adjacent for miles around being thrown in. By judiciously evicting the tenants from the arable land and converting it into cattle and sheep walks, and compelling the tenants to go upon the bog and stone land, which they were compelled to reclaim and drain, the original twenty-five hundred acres of arable land silently grew into twenty-four thousand six hundred acres, and fifty-seven families had multiplied to a population of twenty-three thousand eight hundred!

Can there be any way of making a great estate so delightful as this? It is a pleasant thing to have a government steal land and give it to you, and then protect you with bayonets while you are compelling the original owners to improve it for you.

Bear in mind this fact. The plunderers never put a penny upon this land. They never dug a ditch, dug out a stone, or cut a square foot of bog. The cabins the tenantry lived in they built themselves, and every improvement, great and small, they made themselves.

And this process of swindling, robbing, confiscation, spoliation and plunder went on until this estate, which commenced at two hundred and fifty-nine pounds in 1606, now yields the enormous revenue of sixty thousand pounds, or three hundred thousand dollars per annum!

Which is to say, the laborers on this estate have been yearly robbed of their labor, and starved and frozen, that one family in England may live in wasteful luxury. This is all there is of it.

About the same time that Essex got his grant, Sir Walter Raleigh got a grant of forty-two thousand acres (exclusive of bog and waste) from the plunder of the Earl of Desmond's estates. There lived in London at the time a young lawyer named Boyle, who was probably the worst man then

OLD BUT TOLERABLY CHEERFUL.

living. He had been a horse thief, a forger, and murder had been charged to him. Raleigh was in prison and wanted money, and Boyle offered him one thousand five hundred pounds for his grant, which Raleigh accepted. Boyle paid him five hundred pounds on account, and promptly swindled him out of the balance.

Boyle being serviceable to the court (such men always are), was created Earl of Cork, and got from James I. patents for his plunder. Then he proceeded to marry his children into noble English families, the Duke of Devonshire being one of the descendants. One small portion of the estate now yields His Grace an annual income of thirty thousand pounds, being only a part of the land for which his ancestor, the horse-thief, forger and murderer, paid five hundred pounds.

His Grace, the Duke, is not content with the land. Under

28

some clause in the patent given by the pedantic **James** to the criminal Boyle, he claims the right to the fisheries in the Blackwater, and the Irish Appellate Court, an English land-lord's institution, as are all the courts, sustain the claim, and he levies tribute upon every fish drawn from the waters.

If it were very certain that there is no hereafter, and if a man had no more heart than an exploded bomb shell, it would be a very good thing to be a duke, with a forger and horse-thief for an ancestor. The duke was very judicious in the selection of a father.

The English landlord found after a while that sheep and cattle raising was more profitable than diversified farming, and with that calm, sublime disregard of the rights of the people which is characteristic of the ruling classes in England, eviction became fashionable. The policy pretty much all over Ireland was to clean out the population and consolidate a thousand small farms into one large one.

Between the years 1841 and 1861, twenty years, there were destroyed in Ireland two hundred and seventy thousand cabins, representing a population of one million three hundred thousand, all driven to the workhouse, to exile or death.

The process was a very simple one. A process of eviction was served, the tenant and his family would be pitched out into the road, and the cottage be leveled to the ground. This was originally done with crowbars, but crowbars were too slow. A mechanical genius, who was a landlord and had a great deal of eviction to do, invented a machine to facilitate the process. It was an elaborate arrangement of ropes, and pulleys, and iron dogs, and all that sort of thing, which could be run up beside a cabin and tear the miserable structure down in a few minutes and save a great deal in the way of labor.

This is the only labor-saving machine Irish landlordism has ever produced.

Any system that does not permit the marriage of two persons of sound bodies and minds and of the proper age, is an infamy that should be wiped out at no matter what cost, and no matter what means.

I was walking down a street in Bantry, when I came to a little grocery store, with a ladder projecting over the wretched

sidewalk. My Lord Bantry, who owns, or professes to, every
foot of the ground in the village, is not willing to put the sidewalks in good order. His tenants, who pay him ground rent,

AFTER A WHOLESALE EVICTION.

built their own homes and are expected to build the sidewalks
and keep them in order if they want them. Otherwise they

may walk in the mud.   My Lord Bantry has his carriage,
but he never drives through the village.   He does not like to
see distress.

THE "FIRSHT FAYMALE PAINTHER IN OIRLAND!"

This grocery was the
property of
an old lady
of seventy,
and perched
on the ladder
was a girl of
about seven
teen — her
grand child.
She was using a paint
brush as vigorously, if not
as skillfully,
as any male
painter that
ever lived.

We halted
a minute and
greeted her.
Unclosing a
pair of very
rosy lips and showing a magnificent row of teeth (it might
have been a pride in the teeth that made her open her mouth
so wide, but, if so, it was pardonable!), she exclaimed:

"I am the firsht faymale painther in Oirland! Have ye a
job ye can give me?"

And she laughed a very cheery laugh at the little pleasantry.

There was with us a boatman whom we had employed for
a sail on the bay.   As we passed, he looked back with a pleased
expression.

"Nancy, there, on the ladther, is my gurl."

We congratulated him on his good fortune, for Nancy was

THE BOATMAN AND NANCY.

a bright, handsome, buxom, cheery girl, who was just the kind
that such a man should marry.

"You are to marry her?"

"Yes, some time."

"Why not now?"

"Marry her now! What on? She has her grandmudther
to care for, I have my fadther and mudther, and there is but
little boating to do, and the rint is to pay jist the same. I
have lived in Ameriky, and want to get back, but I won't go
widout Nancy, and God knows whin I shall git enough to go
wid her."

"Why don't you marry her and take the chances."

"Niver! I'll niver marry a gurl and bring childher into
the world to go through what we have had to. I've seen
enough of it. My fadther has been upon the place all his life
and his fadther afore him. They made the land they wuz
born upon, and the rint has bin raised rigularly, lavin us jist
what we could git to eat, and now at sixty-five and bad wid
the rheumatiz, so that he can't work half the time, he has
nothing. I went away to sea, and got to Ameriky, but I had
to kim back to take care of him and my mudther, and it's all I
kin do to keep 'em from bein' evicted. An Amerikin gev me
the boat, which he had built for the season, and if it wuzn't
for wat I make out of it we would all be in the workhouse.
I'll never marry Nancy till I kin find some way to git to
Ameriky, and some way there to make a dacint livin'. I will
niver marry and settle here, to see Nancy and her childher kim
up as I kim up, and me livin' as my fadther and mudther is
livin'."

"And Nancy?"

"It's hard on the poor gurl, for there are any quantity uv
the byes who wants to marry her, but she, with her grandmudther on her hands, knows all about it, and she has sense
enough to wait for something to toorn up. It will come, we
hope, some day; but it's weary waitin'."

And so the two, who in any other country would be wedded
and have a cottage of their own, with plenty to eat, and drink,
and wear, two who owe the world by this time at least three
chubby urchins, the girls like their mother and the boys like
their father, are kept apart by this more than inhuman system

of landlordism, which is the bottom, top and sides of Irish

misery. Others who never knew what it was to live better, would marry and would add to the eternal roll of paupers that make up the population of Ireland; but a residence in God's country unfitted this man for that. He discovered that man's natural inheritance was not rags, and filth and starvation, and he determined not to marry till he could get, somehow, to the country where

OLD AND NOT CHEERFUL.

that crowning achievement of the devil's most astute prime minister, a landlord, is unknown.

But the poor fellow will have to wait a long time. He is like a bear chained to a post — he can neither fight nor run. My Lord has a mortgage on him, and My Lord's agent will never let up on him so long as there is a penny to be squeezed out of him. What to My Lord is Nancy and her woes or her hopes? He would be willing she should marry and multiply and replenish the earth, for it would give him more muscle to enslave in time, or rather, the young lord who is riding by on his gaily caparisoned pony, with two flunkies after him, would, when he came into the estate, have the children of the boatman and Nancy to fleece, as the present lord fleeces Nancy and the boatman. But as for his having any care for the welfare of Nancy and the boatman, that is preposterous. The cost of the trappings of the young lord's pony would make them comfortable, but he would be a bold man who would suggest such a thing to him.

CHAPTER XXIX.

ENGLAND, IRELAND, SCOTLAND — ROYALTY AND NOBILITY.

THIS will be found to be a mixed chapter, but I respectfully desire every American to read it very carefully, and to give it some thought after reading it. In America, where one man is as good as another, we have so much that is good that we do not appreciate the blessings we enjoy; we do not realize how much a free government is worth. I am going to put upon paper some few governmental facts, to the end of showing my countrymen what a good government is worth to them, and what a bad government costs the people who groan under it.

In a late number of that especial organ of king-worshipers, the London *Illustrated News*, there is a beautiful engraving, entitled "The Princess of Wales and Her Daughter, in the Garden of Sandringham." It is a lovely picture. The garden itself is a study, with its wonderful shrubbery, and flowers, and statuary; a garden that falls but little short of being a Paradise. And the Princess of Wales and her six or eight daughters are just as lovely — by the way, as the British Parliament gives every child born in the royal family a princely estate and an enormous allowance to start with, the royal family all have large families — the Princess herself is arrayed in gorgeous morning costume, with a hat trimmed with ostrich feathers, with a parasol with silken fringe upon it a foot deep, and everything comporting. The children are likewise gorgeously arrayed, and one of them is teaching a pug dog how to sit up, the said pug costing the British people at least an hundred guineas. The entire party are in as jolly a state as can be imagined.

Now I like such scenes as this immensely. I like to see comfort and even luxury. Had the husband of this fortunate woman and the father of these happy children been, early in life, a shoemaker, a tailor, a lawyer, a merchant, or anything under heaven, and had by his own labor and his own skill accumulated the means for all this luxury, I should insist upon his right to enjoy it because he had earned it, and had given the world something for it. But how did this woman get it? Why is she with a parasol with silken fringe a foot deep, her children in silks and satins, while just as good children, and just as good women, in Ireland, are shoeless, stockingless and almost naked! What title has she to the gardens at Sandringham, and by what right does she starve the peasantry of Ireland that she may thus disport herself and her children?

Simply this: She is the wife a dissolute middle-aged man, whose stupid mother was the niece of a stupid uncle, who was the son or brother or something or other of the worst kind of a man in the world, who happened to be the son of a king who was half a lunatic and half an idiot — the same who attempted by hireling soldiery to subjugate America — who became a king because he was the descendant of a race of pirates, who by arms wrested from the people of the countries they invaded, all their rights, and assumed to own the land.

Have these people from first to last ever added one penny to the wealth of the world? Is there any one thing they have ever done to push forward the progress of the nations? Not a thing. On the contrary, they have been the dead weights; they have been the blocks in the way. They simply live, and eat, and drink, and wear and disport themselves in the gardens at Sandringham and an hundred other gardens; they have castles, and servants, and special trains, and all that sort of thing, and hundreds of Guinea pug dogs; and to support all this, with the horde of nobility hanging upon them, and their retainers, the men of Ireland are starving, and the women of Ireland are going shoeless, stockingless, and well nigh naked.

I am not especially cruel in my nature, but were the royal family of England to invite the royal family of Prussia, and the Czar of Russia, and the King of Italy, and the Sultan of Turkey, and all the kings of the world, with all their nobles, to an excursion on the German ocean, and were the ships all to go down to the bottom of the sea, and make an end of the whole business at once, I should thank Heaven more fervently than I ever did before in my life. Royalty is larceny in the first degree. It is larceny all the way down, according to the amount of the spoil.

THE PROPER END OF ROYALTY.

I did not confine my observations of land troubles to Ireland alone, though it is in Ireland that there is the worst condition of affairs, for the reason that there is a vital difference between the ruling classes of England and the entire Irish people, in race and religion, and that makes a great deal more difference in the British Empire than anywhere else on the footstool.

But the English or Scotch farmer has not so happy a time of it as he might have, and England will have just as violent a land agitation as Ireland within a very few years. The average Englishman has a vast veneration for royalty and nobility, and all that sort of thing, for he ascribes to the "system" what he himself has done to make Britain great, but his wife and children are nearer to him than Her Majesty or My Lord, and he is beginning to ask why he is yearly getting worse off, while Her Majesty and My Lord are living even more luxuriously and expensively than ever?

When a strong, vigorous race of men get to asking themselves this question, it is high time that Her Majesty and My Lord begin to look out for themselves. The French peasantry and the French artisans made it very warm for the "Divine Righters" several times, and finally they have a republic that will endure; not the best republic in the world, but a very good attempt at one; as good as we could expect from Frenchmen.

Farming in England doesn't pay much better than in Ireland, and the reason for it, as in Ireland, is summed up in the one word, rent. In Bedfordshire, Lincolnshire, Nottinghamshire, and Cambridgeshire, there are hundreds upon hundreds of farms vacant, and doing nothing, the reason being the insecurity of tenant farmers and the rottenness of land ownership. It all comes from the fact that in England as in Ireland, the fee simple of the land is in the hands of the few, and that the few owners regard the tenants as so many cows to be milked for their infernal extravagancies, and that they are so stupid that they cannot be made to understand that there is a point beyond which the tenant cannot go, and that when that point is reached something must break.

One farm I saw was a good piece of land of two hundred and eighty acres. It lies as dead as Julius Cæsar, and is growing up to thistles. Why? Because the rent is four hundred pounds a year, or two thousand dollars. It has been screwed up to that point by successive owners, till the closest

labor and the most starving economy will not pay the rent.
It would not pay it anywhere on the globe.

In Nottinghamshire the "Noble" proprietors are having
their farms left upon their hands for the same reasons, and
they are attempting to farm them by their agents, practically
evicting the skilled labor which was born upon the soil and is
best fitted to cultivate it.

These owners are those whose debts compel them to get
something out of their land. They either attempt to farm

MEATH LADS AT CROSSAKEEL.

them themselves, or they make leases at a rent just low enough
to induce their tenants to continue.

But there is another class that is not so merciful — or rather
who are not compelled to be just, and the English nobleman is
never just except upon compulsion. These are the drones
who are actually rich, and have an income from some plunder
outside of their lands. They will not make leases at all, for
fear of losing the game! They want this beautiful land to
grow up into shelter for hares and birds and all that sort of
thing, for the sake of the pleasure of shooting in the season.
The distress of the evicted tenant — eviction by reason of exor-

bitant rent is as certain as eviction for non-payment — is nothing to them. They must have their preserves of game; they must have their sport.

The process is the same in England as it is in Ireland. The landlord puts his estates in the hands of an agent, selecting for the purpose a man with a heart of flint and a face of brass, one who knows no mercy, and who would not do a kind act were he paid for it.

The tenant appeals to him for a reduction, but he might as well ask mercy of a tiger. Then in his despair goes to the landlord.

"My good sir," says the landlord, beaming upon him benevolently, "I know nothing about these things. The matter is entirely in the hands of Mr. Smithson, my agent. Go to him."

"But I have been to him and he will do nothing."

"Really I regret it. But Mr. Smithson knows all about it — I don't. If he, with a knowledge of the situation — that is what he is there for — can do nothing, I cannot. I am not to be expected to know anything about it, nor can I meddle with business that is his."

And the poor devil of a tenant, with the prospect of starving on the land or emigrating from the only place on earth which to him is a home, goes away sadly, and My Lord or the Rev., as the case may be, drops his agent a note, saying:—"Jobson was here to get a reduction of his rent. He will stay, and can be made to pay. Be firm with him."

Then the agent tells Jobson that lowering the rent is out of the question — and Jobson stays, for he does not want to leave. He buys his artificial manures and his fertilizers from the agent, for he can get credit nowhere else, the agent has a handsome commission from the manufacturer, and so between the agent and the landlord, the manufacturer and the usurer, and the rest of them, Jobson works fourteen hours a day only in the end to either lie down and die or by the help of friends get away to America.

I know one tenant who, dissatisfied with an agent's apology for serious and unreasonable raising of his rent, determined to see the duke himself. At the interview His Grace said he really knew nothing about the matter; he had put the re-valuing into the hands of the most eminent man recommended to him; and, in short, if the tenant did not feel comfortable, it was open to him to leave and let another man come in at the new terms. Now this was the cruel truth, but only part of the truth. The tenant could not quit without tremendous sacrifice of his property—to say nothing of his home-love and other feelings. So he answered, "Your Grace, I cannot leave without ruinous loss; I have farmed well for many years; I can get nothing else at my time of life; and hence your power to oppress me."

All England is dotted with unoccupied farms, and these blotches upon the fair face of nature are becoming more frequent every year.

There are in England about five hundred packs of hounds, numbering about eighty each, or forty thousand in all. The hunting horses number about one hundred and fifteen thousand, and the yearly cost of

A MAYO FARMER.

these hunting establishments is estimated at more than forty-five million dollars.

These estimates do not include the original cost of the establishments, it is merely the annual expense. The first cost goes up into hundreds of thousands, for enormous prices are paid for good hunters and the better breeds of hounds.

And this hunting is no joke to the farmer. The horsemen and the hounds go across the country, and it matters little to them what damage is done to crops, grounds and animals. The tenant has no rights that the landlord is bound to respect, and he must submit to whatever burdens are imposed upon him.

It may be necessary to keep up the "good old English customs," and to encourage "manly sports," but are not the stomachs of the tenants and the stomachs of the tenant's children worthy of some consideration? And then if killing game is a sport to be encouraged to keep up English manliness, why not give the tenantry, who, after all, do the fighting, a shy at it? Why keep all the good things for the nobility? John Hodge could improve his markmanship and his manhood by having an occasional shot at a deer, or a hare, and the deer or hare would not be an unacceptable addition to his remarkably short commons at table. But were John to presume to be seen with a gun in his hand he would be shot at by a burly game keeper, and if not killed would be arrested, tried, convicted and transported. What is My Lord's amusement is John Hodge's crime.

Inasmuch as the British government is for one class only, that class takes mighty good care of itself. Men in favor with the ruling classes are pensioned for life, and in many cases the pension goes beyond life, and is handed down to descendants on more pleas than is comprehensible. The army, the navy, the law departments, the State departments, the — well, if there is a department in the English government that is not like a comet, the pension tail ten times as long as the department nucleus, I have not found it.

The list of pensioners set in very small type, two columns to the page, occupy twenty-two large pages. And this enormous list is made up not of the common soldiers and sailors, but entirely of what are called gentlemen pensioners — men who were foisted into office as the younger sons of the nobility, or "sisters, cousins and aunts," and after a few years of loafing about the government offices retired upon life pensions.

A fair sample of these pensions is that of the Duke of Schomberg. The duke was killed at the battle of the Boyne, in the year 1690, and a pension of six thousand pounds or thirty thousand dollars per annum was given his heirs. It is estimated that this family, the heirs of a foreign mercenary, has received from the British government the enormous sum of six hundred and eighty thousand pounds, or in American money three million four hundred thousand dollars! And this for his being a favorite of William of Orange, a Dutch King!

Rev. J. Smith, whoever he may be, served at the Lord knows what, twenty-three years, at a yearly salary of three hundred and sixty-four pounds, and was retired at fifty-six years of age with the comfortable pension for life of two hundred and thirty-one pounds annually! And so on you go, wading through twenty-two closely printed pages, two columns to the page, of just such cases, the yearly allowance for these excres-cencies footing up for the year 1879 the enormous sum of one million three hundred and thirteen thousand two hundred and fifty-eight pounds! It is a good thing to be the favorite of a duke.

MAYO PEASANTRY.

The Royal family have a remarkably soft thing of it. Her Royal Highness, the Princess Royal, receives a yearly allow-ance of eight thou-sand pounds, the Prince of Wales re-ceives the snug sum of forty thousand pounds, which he manages to squander in questionable ways (this does not include the grants Parlia-ment has made at divers and sundry times to pay his debts), the Princess of Wales ten thousand pounds, Prince Alfred ten thousand pounds from his marriage and fifteen thousand pounds from his majority — twenty-five thousand pounds in all — Prince Arthur fifteen thousand pounds, Princess Alice six thousand pounds, Princess Louise, she of Canada, six thousand pounds, Princess Mary five thousand pounds, Prince Leopold fifteen thousand pounds, Princess Augusta three thousand pounds, Duke of Cambridge twelve thousand pounds, and in addition the last mentioned fraud has princely pay as field marshal, general, colonel, and no one knows what else.

Whoever chooses may figure up what all this costs the people of Great Britain. I have not the patience.

And bear in mind the fact that this does not represent any portion of what these absorbers take out of the people. This is merely pin money for the female leeches and pocket money for the male! In addition to this they have enormous estates all over England, Ireland, Scotland and Wales; they have offices beyond number, with a salary attached to each, and they have allowances for everything under heaven. If the tax-payer breathes it costs him something, for the nobility have revenues based upon everything.

The Royal household is a curiosity. There's the Lord Steward, who draws two thousand pounds a year; the Lord Treasurer and Comptroller, nine hundred pounds each; Master of the Household, twenty one hundred and fifty-eight pounds; Secretary of the Board of Green Cloth, whatever that may be, three hundred pounds; Paymaster, five hundred pounds; Lord Chamberlain, two thousand pounds; Keeper of the Privy Purse, two thousand pounds; Assistant Keeper of the Privy Purse, one thousand pounds. It takes two men to keep the privy purse, and it is large enough to require it. Then there are eight Lords in waiting, who get for waiting seven hundred and two pounds each, and there are grooms in waiting, grooms of the privy chamber, extra grooms in waiting, four gentlemen ushers, one "Black Rod," whatever he may do I don't know, but for being a "Black Rod" he gets two thousand pounds a year. Then there's a clerk of the closet, mistress of the robes, ladies of the bed-chamber, and bed-chamber women, maids of honor, and poet laureate, and examiner of plays.

The poet laureate gets five hundred pounds a year for writing a very bad ode in praise of Her Majesty on each birth-day, which must be a very bitter pill for him, he being actually a poet. But he does not give the worth of the money, for there is absolutely nothing in the Queen of England to praise. Mr. Tennyson has a very hard place.

The Master of the Horse receives two thousand five hundred pounds, the Master of the Buck-hounds one thousand seven hundred pounds, Hereditary Grand Falconer one thousand two hundred pounds, (by the way kings don't falcon any more), then there are eight Equerries in Ordinary at seven hundred pounds each, which is certainly cheap; five Pages of Honor at one hundred and twenty pounds each, and a Master of the Tennis Court, which is a sort of a ten pins, I suppose, at one hundred and thirty-two pounds.

These, understand, are only a few of the people belonging to the Royal household. There are over a thousand persons, male and female, attached thereto, all receiving magnificent salaries, for real or imaginary services to Her Majesty.

The Queen receives, exclusive of the vast income of her estates, for the running of her household and pen

INHABITANTS OF A BOG VILLAGE.

sions for the dead-beats who get too old to show themselves, the enormous sum of four hundred and seven thousand pounds, or, in American money, two million thirty-five thousand dollars per annum! And this represents but a portion of the swindle, as constantly allowances are being made and annuities granted which do not show upon paper, and can only be reached by the most ferret-like acuteness and perseverance.

Ninety per cent. of all this mummery, for which the people of England have to pay in good hard cash, is the most absurd and utter nonsense. Like falconry and all that business, it has gone out of date. In the old times kings kept buck-hounds and flew falcons, and such offices were necessary, that is, if kings were ever necessary, which I deny, but it has all gone, never to return. But the offices remain—and the salaries. They are kept up to make places for illegitimate children of lords, for poor relations of royalty and nobility, and for favorites whose fathers or themselves have done dirty work for the government.

In the name of all that's good, what does the Queen of England want of eight ladies of the bed-chamber, and thirteen women of the bed-chamber? Can't she unhook her dress and corset, untie the fastenings of her skirts, peel off her clothes, draw on her woolen night-cap over her foolish old head, and turn in the same as other women? What does she want of all these people about her? I can understand that it would take that number and more to make the ancient nuisance presentable in the morning, but why tax the people of Great Britain forty-four thousand pounds a year for this service?

And then when it is taken into account that the entire royal family have each all this humbuggery, to a less extent, it can be figured up what a very expensive thing royalty is, and how wise the American people were to bundle the whole business off the continent at the time they did.

One thousand people at salaries ranging from one hundred to ten thousand dollars a year, to take care of one rickety old woman, who is mortal the same as is the humblest of those ground into the dust by her and hers, and who has no more title to the place she occupies than a theif has to your watch.

Ireland swarms with soldiers, and, for that matter, every nook and corner of the British Empire is scarlet with military. Royalty and nobility, having no reason for existence, have to be maintained by brute force. Royalty and nobility do not pay for this expenditure; a subjugated people pay for their own debasement. To every pound of the expenditure in the British Empire, sixteen shillings four and one-eighth pence go to the war debt and the support of the army, leaving three shillings seven and seven-eighth pence for all other purposes whatsoever. Military power is the basis of despotism everywhere. Germany groans under it; Russia sweats under it; and wherever a king is tolerated you will find bayonets and artillery in most uncomfortable plenty. Some day, let it be hoped, the kings and nobles will experience the delight of looking down the muzzles of these arms themselves.

Up to the time of the disestablishment of the Irish Church, the Irish were compelled to support the archbishops and bishops of a church whose religion is as foreign to them as Buddhism, paying therefor the sum of one hundred and two thousand eight hundred and twenty-five pounds per annum, and to other attaches, for curacies and all that business, a vast amount more. This immense amount of money was a tax yearly upon a starved and overworked people, to keep in luxurious idleness a parcel of drones whose only functions in life were to eat, sleep and hunt; who were of no earthly use to the people who supported them, either in a temporal or a spiritual way. There is one English church at Glengariff, in a parish in which there are only six Protestants, the rector, his wife, two children, and two servants. The rector has as fine a house as there is in the country-side, the cost of which and its support is a burden on a people struggling for their daily bread.

Pauperism is a certain consequence of royalty and nobility. The Queen of England cannot have one thousand men and women about her person under pay without taking bread from the mouths of many people, and the luxury of a noble must find an echo in the other extreme, the workhouse.

The number of adult paupers in England and Wales in 1880, exclusive of vagrants, was seven hundred and eleven thousand seven hundred and twelve and the cost to the labor of the country to relieve them footed up eight millions eight hundred and nineteen thousand six hundred and seventy-eight pounds.

This does not include Ireland and Scotland, but England, the most prosperous part of the British Empire. The English writers on political economy ascribe this appalling pauperism to every cause but the right one. Wipe out royalty, nobility, and landlordism, and give the people a chance to earn their bread, and this army would be reduced to almost nothing.

Crime goes on hand in hand with pauperism. In 1879 the United Kingdom had the enormous number of one million four hundred and ninety thousand four hundred and thirty-nine committals for crime. This does not include the cases of

drunkenness or kindred offences which come before magistrates
and are summarily disposed of.

DUBLIN.

The principal business of the aristocracy of England is to
make places for themselves and their sons and nephews. No

matter how large the plunder of the tenantry, the landed aristocracy must have government employment for their surplus children, for they cannot all stay on the acres originally stolen from the people. And so British arms conquer other lands, or British diplomacy, which is a lie backed by a man-of-war, "acquires" it, and immediately a full staff of officials is sent out, all under magnificent salaries, to stay just long enough to be retired upon a fat pension. If possible, the expense of governing the "acquired" possession is squeezed out of the unfortunate natives; if not, the home government makes up the deficiency.

Cyprus, an island made almost barren by years of Turkish misrule and oppression, is now in the hands of the English, with a commander-in chief at fifteen thousand pounds a year, and a complete staff, the cost of which is not less than seventy thousand pounds per annum, to say nothing about the armament necessary to be kept there.

The island of Maritius, a speck in the Indian Ocean, thirty-six miles long and twenty miles broad, furnishes sinecures for the scions of English nobility to the tune of eleven thousand six hundred pounds per year, and three little islands off the Malayan Peninsula are governed by a parcel of "Sirs" and "Hons." at an annual cost of twenty-one thousand two hundred and ten pounds.

These are only samples. England has such harbors of refuge for her surplus nobility everywhere, and the cost of supporting these locusts is a crushing tax upon the labor of the country. The items of pauperism and crime are easily accounted for.

Some of her stolen dependencies, however, are made to pay very well. The total receipts from British India for the year 1879, (customs, taxes, etc.), were sixty-five million one hundred and ninety-nine thousand six hundred and sixty-two pounds, while the expenditures for the same year were sixty-three million one hundred and sixty-five thousand three hundred and fifty-six pounds. India is so worked as to support a vast army of officials and leave a balance of two million pounds for profit besides. But the real profit is much larger. The manufacturers and merchants of England compel the down-trodden natives to buy their goods at their own prices, and a never failing stream of wealth flows from India to England. India was a successful piece of brigandage, and has always paid very well.

Other steals have been successful — in fact they all have been. These younger sons, legitimate and illegitimate, have to be supported some how, by the labor of the country, and to transfer even a portion of their cost to the people of other countries is a saving of just that much from the people at home. But where is the necessity of supporting them at all? What necessity is there for their existence?

The peers of the realm number four hundred and eighty-seven, and of this number four hundred and two own, or at least get rent for, fourteen million one hundred and twenty-nine thousand nine hundred and thirty-one acres of land, which bring them a rental annually of eleven million six hundred and seventy-nine thousand eight hundred and thirty-nine pounds. In addition to this enormous income the most of them have appointments of various kinds, all of which make the position of peer a very comfortable one.

They have a very pleasant life of it. They all have a castle on their estates in the country, and in the season guests made up of the same class, with a few poets, novelists and painters to supply the intellect and make variety, indulge in all sorts of festivities, and in town, in the season, their houses are constantly filled, at no matter what expense. Then they each have a membership in all the clubs, and between their country houses, and their town houses, and their clubs, they take pleasure and cultivate gout till death, which has no more respect for them than it has for their oppressed tenants, takes them to a place where there is no difference between a duke and a laborer.

Gout, by the way, is the fashionable English disease, and a nobleman or a squire of an old family would rather have it than not. It is a sort of mark of gentility, about as essential to his position as his family tree, and no matter how they suffer under it, they bear it with fortitude as one of the evils incident to their rank — an evil that emphasizes their dignity. When Dickens sent Sir Leicester Deadlock into the next world *via* the family gout, he did not satirize at all. The starved Irish never have the gout, nor do the working people who clamor for some measure of right. The Jack Cades never were so afflicted; only your noble, who toils not, neither does he spin, who goes to bed every night full of every flesh that exists, every wine that is pressed, to say nothing of more potent beverages. It is an accompaniment of "gentle birth," and very liberal living — living so liberal as to be only possible by those who have other people's unrequited labor to live upon.

An Englishman dearly loves a lord. There is a cringing servility, a hat-off reverence for noble birth, in England, that to an American is about the most disgusting thing he sees. My Lord may be a thin-haired, weak-legged, half-witted being, capable of nothing under heaven but billiards and horses, loaded to the guards with vices, and only not possessing all of them because of his lack of ability to master them. He may be the most infernal cumberer of the earth in existence, but if he is of noble birth, if he has the proper handle to his name, he is bowed to, deferred to in every possible way. A London tradesman had rather be swindled by a nobleman than paid honestly by a common man, and for one to have permission to put over his door, "Plumber (for instance) to His Royal Highness the Prince of Wales," is to put him in the seventh heaven of ecstacy. The farm population of England show outward deference, but they don't feel it, and the Irish have so intimate an acquaintance with them that they refuse even lip service and ignore the "hat-off" requirement altogether. This lack of respect for the nobility in Ireland is considered one of the most alarming signs of the times.

I saw a sample of this bowing to royalty, in Scotland. I happened to be doing Holyrood Castle at the same time His Majesty Kalakeau, King of the Sandwich Islands, was in Edinburgh. Now King K. may be a very good man, but in appearance he is an ordinary looking man of half negro blood, and not a very remarkable mulatto at that. Our Fred Douglas would cut up into a thousand of him.

He is a sort of a two-for-a-penny king; but he is a king for all that, and so all the dignitaries of Edinburgh, the mayor, the principal citizens, a duke or two, and a half dozen right honorables showed him the city, and escorted him, and lunched him, and banquetted him. They brought him to Holyrood, and the entire lot of them formed in two ranks, and, with hats in hand, bowed reverently as this king of a few thousand breechless, semi-civilized savages, passed to his carriage. And they glared ferociously upon the few Americans who, not just

THEY GLARED FEROCIOUSLY UPON THE AMERICANS.

au fait in such matters, and not knowing precisely who the distinguished colored man was, stood with their hats on their heads, inasmuch as it was raining. Had it been the King of the Fijis, and had it been raining hot pitchforks, these snobs would have stood with uncovered and bowed heads, simply because he was a king. To these people, "there is a divinity which doth hedge a king," no matter what kind of a king it is. They do the same thing for that venerable old stupidity, Victoria Guelph, precisely as they did it for that amiable imbecility, Albert, her husband, and are doing it every day for those embryo locusts, their children. Burns wrote:—

> "Rank is but the guinea's stamp,
> A man's a man for a' that."

But this class of Scotch have forgotten Burns. Possibly they never understood him. But Burns was wrong. Kalakeau may be a man, but the snobs who toadied to him so meekly, are not, and never can be.

"Look upon that picture, and then upon this!" I have shown how the English oppressor lives. Let us go, by actual figures, taken from official sources, for a few actual facts as to the Irish tenant. The Parish of Glencolumbkille, in County Donegal, is a fair sample of the west coast. In this parish there are eight hundred families. In the famine of 1880, seven hundred of these families were on the relief list, and on to the end of the famine (if famine may be said to ever end in Ireland), four hundred families had absolutely nothing but what the relief committees gave them.

The committees were able to give each of these families per head per week seven pounds of Indian meal, costing five pence farthing, up to about five dollars and fifty cents per year.

These people all said that if they got half as much more, ten and one-half pounds, it would be as much as they would use in times of plenty.

Your pencil and figures will show you that this would be equivalent in good years, to an expenditure per head for food for every individual, of one pound thirteen shillings and sixpence a year, or for the average family of say four and one-half, seven pounds thirteen shillings and sixpence per year.

This is the cost of food for the average family per year when the times are good.

When potatoes are cheaper than Indian meal potatoes are eaten, but one or the other constitutes the sole food of the people. As the cost is always about the same, the figures are not changed in either case.

To this you want to add about three pounds a year for "luxuries." Luxury in an Irish cabin means an ounce of tobacco a week for the man of the house, and the remainder of the three pounds goes for tea. I admit this is an extravagance, this tobacco and tea, and I doubt not that a commission will be appointed by Parliament to devise ways and means to extinguish the dudheen of the man and abolish the teapot of the woman. This three pounds a year, thus squandered, would enable the landlords to have a great many more comforts than they now enjoy. I presume the Earl of Cork could build another yacht on what his tenantry squander in tea and tobacco.

Add to this one pound for clothing (an extravagant estimate) for each member of the family, and you have the entire cost of the existence of the Donegal family, twelve pounds three shillings six and three-quarters pence, or, in American money, fifty-seven dollars and sixty-one cents!

The clothing provided by this pound a year means for the man of the house a pair of brogans, which he must have to work at all, a couple of shirts, a pair of corduroy trowsers, and a second-hand coat of some kind. The women and children wear no shoes or stockings, and their clothing I have described before. Of bed-clothing they have nothing to speak of. A few potato sacks, or gunny bags, or anything else that contributes anything of warmth, makes up that item.

The Queen and the Princess of Wales sleep on down and under silk, and the Queen has one thousand people about her person. My Lord has his yacht in the harbor, and the humblest seaman on board sleeps under woolen and has meat three times a day.

Some day there will be a Board of Equalization from whose decision there will be no appeal. Then I would rather be the Donegal peasant's wife than the Queen. Despite the fact that she sent one hundred pounds to the starving Irish, she won't need silken covering to keep her warm.

To pay the rent and provide this fifty-eight dollars for food and clothing consumes the entire time of every member of the household. The land will not pay it — it is impossible to get it off the soil. So the man of the house plants his crops and leaves them for the women and children to care for, and he goes off to England or Wales, and works in mines, or in harvest fields in the season, or at anything to make some little money to fill the insatiable maw of the landlord, and to keep absolute starvation from the house.

Then the boy in America sends his stipend, which helps — provided his remittances can be kept from the lynx-eyed agent, who would raise the rent in a minute if he knew that remittances were coming.

But the work of caring for the crops is not all the women

and children do. They knit and sew, every minute of the
spare time they have from field work, making thereby from

BOG VILLAGE, COUNTY ROSCOMMON.

two to three cents a day. This knitting is done for dealers
who furnish the material and pay for the work, and to get the

material journeys of twenty to forty miles, and the same distance back again to deliver the finished work, have to be performed.

In brief, there is not a moment to be lost, nor an opportunity wasted to make a penny. The penny not earned makes the difference between enough food to sustain life, bare as life is of everything that makes it desirable, and absolute pinching, merciless hunger. No matter at what sacrifice, the penny must be earned and religiously applied either for rent or food. Clothing is always a secondary consideration — a place to stay in and food to keep life in the body, these are the first.

What is the amount paid the drones of England in the form of pensions? How much does the Queen receive? How much do the little Princes and Princesses cost the Nation? How much the Dukes and Dukelings, the Right Honorables and the Generals and Colonels, and the Secretaries and all that? "Look upon this picture and then upon that!" A nobility rioting in extravagance — a whole people starving!

And yet there are those who believe the people of Great Britain have no grievances, but should settle down contentedly and in quiet!

If there is an American who does not hate royalty, nobility, and aristocracy, in no matter what form they come to view, he either wants to be an aristocrat himself, or is grossly ignorant of what this triplet of infamy means. If there is an American who does not sympathize with the common people of England, Ireland, Scotland and Wales, he is either a heartless man or does not know the condition of the laboring classes of that unhappy Empire. And if there is an American who reads these pages, and does not from this time out, make politics just as much a part of his business as planting his crops, that American does not know what is good for him. Government is the most important matter on this earth. Good or bad government makes the difference between nobility-ridden England and free America.

CHAPTER XXX.

FROM Ireland with its woes, Ireland with its oppressions, through England, the world's oppressor, to Paris, and from Paris to Switzerland — that was the route our party took; not so much because it was consecutive or in order, but because the whim so to do seized us. We were out to see, and to us all countries that were to be seen were alike of interest. We spent a few more days in Paris — everybody wants to spend a few more days in Paris — and then turned our reluctant faces southward.

A dismal, gloomy night; the fine, penetrating rain, cold and disagreeable, that chills the very marrow, half hides the dimly burning gas-lights, and makes the streets utterly forlorn. The belated pedestrian bends his head to the blast and hurries along, eager to reach the cozy room where the gloom that pervades everything out of doors cannot penetrate. The cabs roll along the stony pavements with a dead, metallic sound that adds to the general dreariness.

Everything and everybody is depressed.

So it was when the train drew out of the dimly lighted station in Paris, and plunged into the unfathomable gloom and darkness of the country beyond.

Wonderful invention — this railroad! and never so wonderful as at night. The mariner has his compass to guide him — the engine-driver has the rail. You go to sleep, or try to, in Paris; you wake in Switzerland. It makes reality of the magic carpet in the "Arabian Night's Tales."

Though the coarse, stuffy compartment afforded no pleasure, the dull roar of the train as it sped on through the driving storm lulled the senses, gave our memory full sway; gradually the rain ceased its pattering against the window pane, the sky broke into a rosy blue, the brilliant sunlight streamed out in the night over the beautiful white city, and Paris, the frivolous empress of the world, held out to the mind its multitudinous

COMPARTMENT IN A FRENCH CAR.

attractions and unlimited pleasures. We saw again, reflected in the memory of the last six weeks, the long, wide boulevards, with their cheerful cafés filled with beautifully dressed women and leisure-loving men. There was the constant, ever-changing streams of humanity surging on to some end, each in his own way. There were the lights, the flowers, the gaities of the beautiful city, where the attainment of happiness and pleasure seems to be the chief aim of existence. The Louvre with its infinity of beauties, the Palais Royal with its bewildering jewels, the Place de Concorde with' its historic memories, the Champ Elysées dazzling bright, with its arch-crowned vista of brilliant equipages, the Bois du Boulogne with its flower-lined walls and flower-lined lakes. There was rare relief, ever present to us, in all its glory, all its pleasure, all its gaiety. Days passed into weeks, and weeks into months, of perfect enjoyment that came to an end only when the guard in gruff tones hustled us out of the car at Macon, to change for the train going to Geneva. The transition was sudden and decidedly unpleasant.

There were eight of us in the compartment all that night — a Frenchman and four small daughters, on their way to Geneva, Tibbitts and ourselves. Tibbitts, who could not speak a word of French, except "*Der bock*," which means in English "two beers," and "*Combien?*" which is "how much," entered into a cheerful conversation with the Frenchman, who could not speak a word of English. It was vastly entertaining. Tibbitts would make a beautiful remark in English, to which the Frenchman would reply, "Oui, Monsieur." Then the Frenchman would make an elaborate observation on something or other in French, to which Tibbitts would reply, "Oui, Monsieur," and so on all night.

It was not pleasant for those trying to sleep, but it seemed to amuse the two participants.

At Macon, in the morning, the Frenchman followed Tibbitts around the platform, attempting by gesture and a volley of Parisian French, to make something known to him.

Tibbitts came to me alarmed.

"What is 'Oui Monsieur' in English?"

"It means simply 'Yes, sir,' or 'Certainly, sir.'"

"Did you know what that Frenchman was saying last night?"

"Not a word."

"I said 'Oui, Monsieur' to everything he said. Suppose he

asked me to lend him a hundred francs! I am in a fix about it. I can't go back on my word, and if he asked me that I certainly promised to do it, and if I have to do it I shall have to borrow it of you."

Mr. Tibbitts' fears were unfounded. A hotel-porter who could master a trifle of English, came between them, and found that the Frenchman had been so impressed with the urbanity of my Oshkosh friend as to ask him in the night to take care of his four children to Geneva, that he might return by the next train to Paris, and Tibbitts had said "Oui, Monsieur" to the proposition, and he had the babies on his hands all the way.

They were lively children, and made the poor fellow much

THEY WERE LIVELY CHILDREN.

trouble. and Tibbitts heaved a prodigious sigh of relief when he turned them over to their waiting guardian at Geneva. He immediately asked for the French word for "No," and vowed solemnly to ever after use that word when in conversation with Frenchmen on railroads or elsewhere.

The day broke dull and cheerless, but as soon as the sun came up the clouds were driven away, and the whole country was bright and beautiful. The road passes through some of the best wine districts of France, and nearly all of the little towns through which the train whirls with only a long shriek of the whistle, are devoted to the handling of wine, although in most of them there is a church or two and some monuments, just enough to make it a show place.

A town on this side of the water is no town at all if it does not have at least two or three places that were either old or historical, or both. Thus at Tournus, a little town of six thousand inhabitants, there is an Abbey church that was begun in 960, and not completed until late in the twelfth century. It isn't much of a church, but it attracts visitors to the town, and so adds to its revenue. It pays to have show places.

From Macon to Culoz the line passes through lovely vineyards that lie spread out almost as far as the eye can reach, over gently undulating hills and dales that are watered by pretty little streams, clear and pure, having their source way off in the mountains, dimly discernible in the distance. Soon after passing Culoz the country assumes a more picturesque appearance, the vine-clad hills giving way to rugged mountains that tower high above the fertile valley, through which the train has been rushing for the past two or three hours. Swift, deep streams, fed by mountain springs, come tumbling down the sides of the high cliffs and lose themselves in the mass of foliage that skirts the base of the range, which hourly grows more and more imposing. We are whirled through long tunnels, over high bridges, and are treated to magnificent prospects. Green mountain sides crowned with the ruins of old castles that in days long gone by had been the terror of the neighborhood, picturesque towns nestling in cozy nooks flit by as the train speeds rapidly on, until, early in the forenoon, we arrive at Geneva, the **Mecca** of all strangers who contemplate an Alpine or Swiss tour.

The day was perfect. A cool breeze from lovely Lake Leman tempered the heat that otherwise would have been oppressive; the sky was without a cloud and as the pure air was gratefully inhaled by long delightful breaths, there was a sense of joyousness and happiness that was heavenly. Near at hand a long range of high mountains stretched out into the country and

30

lost itself in the range that skirts the shores of the long irregular lake.   Far off in the distance, between the dimly outlined
peaks of another range, Mont Blanc rears its grand white head
high among the clouds, its aged covering of pure white,

THE LAKE AND CITY OF GENEVA.

glistening and glinting in the sunlight.   It is an impressive
scene, full of strange fascinating beauty.

Grandly the view changes.   A light fleecy cloud floats
languidly past the summit, casting a weird shadow on the spot-
less white.   That delicate lace-like cloud, beautiful in form and
color, is followed by another, darker and more threatening.
Another and another comes, each darker and more forbidding,
until suddenly the whole is overcast.   Mont Blanc is enveloped
in a sable mantle from which, presently, issues a low rumbling
noise that foretells in unmistakable language what is to come.
Now long jagged flashes of lightning rend the gloomy masses
of fast scudding clouds, that turned the bright day into darkness, the wind sweeps down from the mountain with a wail
half human; the rain comes down in torrents, not in fitful
gusts but in a steady, angry stream.   The placid waters of the
lake, only a moment before laughing in the bright sunlight, are
lashed to a fury, as the storm increases in violence.   Terrific
peals of thunder that seem to shake the earth, break directly
overhead and then go rolling and rumbling away up the valley,
until they exhaust themselves and die away with one final
crash.   All the elements seem to combine to produce a grand

spectacle that strikes the beholder with awe-tempered admiration.

As quickly as it came the storm died away, and in a short time all nature smiled again and seemed to feel better after the display of its ability in getting up grand sights on short notice. The sun came out with renewed splendor and tinged Mont Blanc forty miles away, with a rosy hue, that lasted all the afternoon, long until the other and less pretentious peaks had become mere outlines in the twilight that presaged the coming night. And then even the King of Peaks began to fade. Gradually but constantly the pink tints turned lighter until it was ashen. Then it became darker and darker until at length its massive proportions faded entirely away and were lost in the darkness that had come so gradually that its presence was hardly felt.

Geneva is a curious old city, one of the links that connect the dead past with the terribly active and quite distinct present. Its memories are of monks and opposers of monks ; its present is of watches and music boxes. However, the Genevan has been shrewd enough to carefully preserve the dust of the past, out of which, combined with its delightful situation, it gathers many shekels from the horde of tourists who sweep over Europe every year. Everybody must and does see Geneva. It is the capital of the smallest canton in Switzerland but one, the entire territory being but fifteen miles long by as many square, a large portion of this being taken up by the lake. Its population is less than fifty thousand, but, nevertheless, it is the largest city in Switzerland, and one which has the most of historical interest attached to it.

The land is so nearly perpendicular in Switzerland that large cities are impossible.

So small was the canton of Geneva that Voltaire said of it : " When I shake my wig, I powder the whole Republic," and when some commotion occurred in the little Republic the Emperor Paul said of it : "It is a tempest in a glass of water."

But, small as it is, it has played its part, and a very important one it has been, in the history of the world. Here lived John Calvin, or Jean Caulvin, who originated that cheerful form of religious faith known as Calvinism. As he preached, and, to the credit of his powers of endurance be it said, practiced, it made a good heaven necessary in the next world, to compensate somewhat for what his disciples had to endure in this. He eliminated from life everything that was pleasant, everything that was cheerful, everything that was pleasurable, and brought mankind into a sort of religious straight-jacket, that made any swerving from a straight line impossible.

During Calvin's reign, for his rule was almost absolute, Geneva was a safe place to live in (if you believed with Calvin, or pretended to believe hard enough), but it would hardly suit a Parisian. Theaters were considered the especially wide gateways to perdition, and everything that savored of amusement was strictly prohibited. As his was a stern and gloomy religion, which made the business of this life a constant preparation for the next, and the reward for all this sort of penance a continuance of the same in the next, his doctrines found more ardent support in Scotland than in France.

In opposing the Catholic Church, as the Catholic Church was in that day, Calvin, with Luther, did a great work, but Calvin, after all, simply wanted the people to exchange one form of spiritual despotism for another. The chief benefit arising to the world was that, in moving the people out of Romanism he taught them that they *could* move, and, so instructed, they lost but little time in moving out from the perpetual thunder-cloud he put over them.

For many years he was supreme in Geneva in temporal as well as spiritual matters. As a Liberal who hates authority invariably becomes in time the worst bigot, so Calvin, who commenced as a champion of liberty of conscience, came to executing and banishing all who differed with him on points of religious belief. He wanted everybody to believe as their conscience taught them, provided it taught them his belief. Castellio, one of his oldest supporters, differed with him on the doctrine of predestination, and Calvin promptly banished him. Servetus, a Spaniard, wrote a treatise on the doctrine of the Trinity. He was arrested by Calvin in 1553, and was promptly tried, found guilty of not believing as the great reformer did, and was condemned to the stake, and was burned, Calvin standing by to make it impressive.

Tibbitts told an old Boston story of a confirmed joker who was dying. A friend called upon him one morning, and finding his feet warm sought to encourage him.

"Barnes, you ain't going to die. No man ever died with warm feet."

"One did."

"Who?"

"John Rogers!"

Servetus died with warm feet, and his ashes were scattered to the four winds. He and Calvin differed about the exact meaning of some passages of scripture and as it had not been revised at that date, Calvin made himself the authority. As he had supreme power and could do as he pleased he succeeded in having a tolerable degree of unanimity. After the burning of Servetus there were but few who desired to argue with Calvin.

I have observed that burning and otherwise killing for the up-building of the kingdom of the Prince of Peace has been common in all ages, and that the sect that does the most of it is always the one that happens to be in power. The Jesuits have published a sort of Catholic "Fox's Book of Martyrs," which sets forth with ghastly wood engravings the histories of the persecutions of Catholics by Protestants. The burning of Servetus by Calvin is the subject of one of the illustrations, though the editor carefully omits the fact that Servetus was not a Catholic at all.

Rosseau, the great Socialist, was born here, and here he wrote the works that have consigned his memory to infamy or glory, according as the reader believes. He was a man of wonderful genius, one of the foremost writers of the world, but he was as fantastic as any other Frenchman, and his doctrines were based upon a condition of things which only a dreamy poet could imagine as possible. He was a Socialist, a latitudinarian, and one of the kind of "world reformers" who hold that everything that is, is wrong, and that to destroy anything is to better the condition of the world.

It is a curious commentary upon French morals that after he had been the lover, (with all that the word implies) of a dozen or more of French titled women who affected men of letters, and while living openly with his cook, who bore him five illegitimate children, a French college invited him to write a treatise upon the "Effect of Science and Art Upon Morals," which invitation he most cheerfully accepted. He was the reverse of Calvin, but like Calvin, he left his impress upon the thought of the little city.

Geneva is a pleasant place to come to, and, but for the extortionate hotels, would be a place that one would be loth to leave. Swiss hotel keepers have got swindling down to so fine a point that further progress in that direction is impossible. There is a legend afloat that hotel keepers from all over Europe come to Geneva to learn the business, and that lectures on the art of swindling travelers are given regularly by the managers of Geneva hotels; in short, that Geneva is a sort of hotel college, but I don't know as to its truth. Any hotel keeper here, however, is competent to fill a professorship — in such an institution.

You are charged for candles, a franc each. You never use a candle, except during the minute necessary to disrobe for your bed, but you are charged a franc for it just the same. The more conscientious hotel manager wants to satisfy you with a new candle every night, and so he has a little machine, something like a pencil sharpener, with which he tapers off the top of the burned candle, making it look as though it had never been lighted, and charges you right over again for it.

Tibbitts exasperated his landlord by putting his candle in his pocket every morning, and from the front of the hotel giving it to the first poor person who passed. But the landlord smiled grimly, in French, when he saw the little trick, and promptly instructed his clerk to charge Monsieur Tibbitts two francs a day for broken glass.

You are to depart to-morrow morning, and you charge the clerk with great distinctness to have your bill made out before you retire. You want to go over the items and see that everything is correct. The clerk, with great suavity, assures you that it shall be done. but it is n't. You come for it and find the office closed. The next morning you arise betimes and make the same request; you say you want your bill immediately, to which the same answer is given with an apology for its not having been done the night before. You get through your breakfast — it is not yet done. Minutes fly, the carriage is at the door to take you to your train, and just as the last minute possible to catch the train is on you, it comes — as long as your arm, written in French, which you can't understand if you had time to, but which now is utterly impossible. You glance at the grand total — it is a grand total — and you pay it, objurgating because it is a trifle over twice what it should be.

Then comes the long array of servants, the chambermaid, the boots, the elevator boy, the head waiter, the table waiter, and so on, all of whom expect and plumply demand recognition, and you think you are done. But you are not.

Just as you are getting into the carriage, a chambermaid, not the one who had charge of your room, but her sister, appears with one of your silk handkerchiefs.

"Monsieur forgot the handkerchief."

She extends the handkerchief with one hand, holding out the other for a franc. You give it to her of course, knowing all the time that your own chambermaid abstracted it and gave it to her for the purpose of wringing the last possible drop of blood out of you, and that this wretch has done the same kind office for your chambermaid, to be practised upon another victim who leaves to-morrow.

I presume the landlord compels a division of these swindles, for as they all lay awake nights to devise ways and means to wrench money from tourists it is not likely they would let so easy a source of revenue escape them.

Here everybody takes gratuities, even excelling the English in the practice.

There is a story which comes in here by way of illustration. An old lady had a case in court which was going slowly. She desired more speed, and asked an old man, who was supposed to know everything, how she could accelerate the matter.

"Give your lawyer twenty francs."

"What! will the grave and great man take twenty francs? Would he not throw the money in my face and feel so insulted that he would throw up my case?"

"He might, but I can tell you how to know whether he

will take the gratuity or not. When you come into his pres‧ence observe his mouth. If it runs up and down his face don't offer it to him, for he would not take it. But if his mouth runs across his face offer it with confidence. Every man in Switzerland whose mouth is cut crosswise the face will accept a gratuity."

It so happened that in sailing up the lake the question of piracy came up,—it grew out of a discussion of the charges at the various hotels—when Tibbitts broke in with that calm confidence that distinguishes the young man:—

"I have been giving the matter of piracy most serious consideration, its rise, decline and fall. Formerly piracy was everywhere on the high seas. Adventurous spirits manned vessels which were built, armed and sent out by wealthy corporations, their business being to capture merchant vessels, cut the throats of the male passengers and crew and confiscate the property. In those halcyon days money was gold and silver, and the pirates after capturing a rich prize sailed their vessels to some point on the Spanish main, where there was a convenient cove, captured a Spanish village, murdered the men, and made such love to the women that they very soon preferred the picturesque villains to their virtuous but common-place and insipid (because honest) husbands. And there they lived; gaily dancing fandangos and boleros, under the shade of palms, to the soft pleasings of the lute, till the money was spent (by the way I never could see how they spent money in such places after they had killed all the shop-keepers and saloon men) and then they sailed sweetly out to be a scourge of the seas once more.

"It was a pleasant thing to be a pirate in those days.

"The first blow this industry received was the invention of sight draft, by which money could be transmitted. The pirate who seized drafts couldn't forge the names necessary to their collection, to say nothing of the risk of presenting himself at a bank in London to collect them.

"The second and severest blow was the introduction and general use of dollar jewelry. Dollar jewelry has done more for the suppression of piracy than the Christian religion. Imagine a pirate captain parading the crew of a captured ship to despoil their persons before inviting them to walk the plank, the hungry sharks about the vessel in joyful — not jawful — anticipation. Imagine his disgust at tearing out a pair of ear-drops from a lady's ears of the size of hickory nuts, that ought to be worth thousands, and finding them Parisian imitation stones set in oroide gold. Such experiences were heart-breaking. Who would cut a throat for oroide gold with imitation stones?

" A score of daring spirits once organized a piratical party for a steamer on Lake Erie. We proposed to take passage Sundays, when there were excursions; to murder the excursionists, and throw their bodies over to the catfish, the nearest approach we have to sharks on the lakes. Our first attempt was our last. There was an excursion from Indiana, the party numbering eight hundred. We had a contract with a gentleman named Moses for their clothes, so much a dozen for stockings, shirts, and so on, as they run; and the money and jewelry we proposed to divide among the party, each one disposing of his share of the plunder as he pleased.

"It was a disgusting failure. We discovered that the passengers had spent all their money in purchasing round tickets for the excursion, they had brought their lunches with them in baskets, and there wasn't a single piece of anything but dollar jewelry among them; and as for their clothes — Mr. Moses was on board, and he looked over the lot and begged us not to inaugurate our slaughter, as "'selp him, he vouldn't gif tventy-fife tollar for all as it stood." We stood idly by, endured the excursion ourselves, and were even reduced to the ineffable chagrin of paying for our own dinners and refreshments. The dashing captain actually begged his dinner of an old lady in spectacles.

" That was the last effort at piracy on the lakes, and it is about the same on the high seas. Drafts and dollar jewelry have tamed the adventurous spirit of the buccaneer, and driven them all into keeping hotels in Switzerland, the captains as proprietors, the second officers as head-porters, and the crew as waiters, chambermaids, etc. They are doing as well, probably, as before, and by similar methods, though piracy has lost its picturesqueness. Your pirate, instead of wearing a broad hat and a picturesque sash, and all that, is clad in sober broadcloth, with a white necktie; his cutlass is transformed into a pen, the deck of his vessel is the floor of the corridor of his hotel. But he preys upon mankind the same as of old. It is the method only that is changed. Dollar jewelry don't affect them, except in cases where the landlord has to seize baggage for his bill. Sometimes he comes to grief then, but not often."

"YOUR HOTEL IS A SWINDLE, SIR!"

One of the most amusing things connected with the hotels is the final talk that ensues when the traveler has paid his bill, and is buttoning up his coat for departure.

"Your hotel is a swindle, sir, and I will never darken its doors again. I will take especial pains to inform my friends, sir. This bill is an outrage, sir, an outrage! and my friends shall know of it!"

"*Oui*, Monsieur," says the landlord, bowing gracefully and grimacing as expressively as a monkey.

The plundered guest tells everybody not to go to the National, but by all means go to the Beau Rivage, not knowing, poor soul, that the very minute he was abusing, justly abusing, the proprietor of the National, another man just like him was abusing the proprietor of the Beau Rivage, and that, while he is sending guests to the Beau Rivage, the swindled Beau Rivager is sending his friends to the National.

"Ze zentleman ees offend," smirkingly remarked the land-lord of the National, after one of these scenes; "vera goot. He sents all hees frients to ze Beau Rivage. The proprietor of ze Beau Rivage ees my frère — vat yoo call 'im, eh? — bruz-zer. Ve ees in partnersheep."

And so it is. All the hotel men are in partnership, and, besides this powerful leverage, they know that so many come every year, anyhow; that those flayed at the National this year will go to be fleeced at the Beau Rivage next, and so on around.

Despite this modified piracy, Geneva is a pleasant and hospitable place to visit, and one difficult to leave. It is a thoroughly enjoyable old city, and life there was very full. There is just enough quaintness in its queer, rambling streets to make one wish to be constantly exploring them, hoping, yet fearing, that he would get lost. It was an especial delight to go across the river and prowl among the steep, narrow streets that end finally against a dead wall; to scale high hills, with old fashioned houses forming alleys so narrow that two people could scarcely pass. We loved to plunge into dark, forbidding passages, groping our way along under houses, until, when least expected, we found ourselves in a bright, well-paved street in another portion of the town.

And then the long rambles on the lake shore, especially at night, when, far off in the distance could be seen the twinkling lights of the city on both sides of the lake, connected by a tiny belt of light across the bridge that connected the old with the new.

And the concerts at the Jardin du Lac, a pleasant garden with trees and flowers and fountains, on the south bank of the lake, where a fine orchestra furnishes exquisite music during the soft, balmy Summer evenings. Ah! those were indeed days and nights of rare enjoyment.

Geneva is divided into two sections; one as distinct from the other as an Indiana cabin is from the cathedral at Cologne. On the one side of the river it is the same as the freshly built and lively looking streets of a new American city. You see the modern cornice on the roofs and over the windows, the elegant plate glass fronts to the shops, the massive buildings for the factories, the orthodox basement dwellings in the main part of the city, and the modern villas with ample grounds farther out.

This is the new part, the part created by the latter day Swiss, who were compelled by the reconstruction of Paris to modernize and wipe out the old to make room for the new. There is less of reverence in a dollar than in anything else in the world. The owner of a historical old rookery didn't care a straw for the associations connected with his premises; what he wanted was rent, and so the quaint old piles were demolished and new buildings, modeled after the new Paris, went up in their stead. The uncomfortable old streets were widened into something like boulevards, the beautifully smooth and clean asphalt pavement took the place of the wretched old bowlders, and everything that was old, no matter whether its savor was of the Puritanic Calvin, or the antedating monk, was bundled out of the way with as little reverence as a Cromwellian soldier displayed in cleaning out an English or Irish monastery.

But the other side of the river has escaped the hand of the vandal, and whoever hungers for the uncomfortable past can find all he wants of it. The streets are as wretched as the most exacting could desire, and the houses run up as many stories as you choose, and the old notion of a building being so high that you have to look twice to get to the top of it, is well nigh realized. Very like the conductor who was boasting of the speed of his train:

"Thunder," says he, "we passed Millgrove so fast that the station master had to call out the telegraph operator to help him ketch a glance at us."

There are passages so tortuous and cavernous, built for no earthly purpose that any one can divine now-a-days, buildings like small Alps, with the quaintest windows, the most absurd staircases, and the most inconvenient arrangements, shops in passages so dark as to require artificial light in mid-day, and human habitations in these underground burrows.

Old Geneva, like Old Paris, has a musty smell and ancient flavor that is delightful, if you do not have to live in it.

On the other side you are oppressed with watches and music boxes, the manufacture of which support the city. In the matter of watches Geneva is not so absolute as she was, for the inventive Yankee makes a better watch than the Genevan hand-worker. We do not make so many kinds or so curious specimens of horology, but for substantial wear and constant use, the American watch is conceded even by the Genevan to be the best.

But in music boxes and every species of musical machinery, Geneva has no rival. At your hotel the doors of some of the grand halls reel off snatches of opera as they swing upon their hinges, the caraffe from which you pour your water at table sings an air as the water gurgles from its mouth, and you shall see beautiful trees with gorgeous birds hopping from limb to limb, and all singing deliciously and naturally. Snuff boxes, tobacco boxes, cigar cases, everything of the kind has a musical attachment, that discusses sweet melody whenever opened. In short, there is such a wealth of melody, and it comes to you from such unexpected quarters, that one gets rather tired of it, and wishes he could go somewhere to get out from under it.

A perpetual concert is rather too much of a good thing. And they get prices for these goods, too. My friend, the faro bankeress, who has about as much of an idea of music as a pig has of the Greek Testament, paid five thousand dollars for a tree with singing birds, because, I presume, the price was five thousand dollars. Had it been fifty dollars I doubt if she would have taken it.

It didn't matter to her. Her husband's establishment could win that amount any night, and it pleased her to astonish the manufacturers of these airy nothings, with her profuseness of expenditure. I saw a duplicate sold to a man who knew something about these things for one thousand dollars. These sellers of whims know their customers at sight.

CHAPTER XXXI.

SOME one remarked to the Rev. Mr. Henry Ward Beecher, before he had the little difference with Mr. Theodore Tilton, and was editing the *Independent*, "Mr. Beecher, I like your paper. You had a religious article in the last number. Now I think it is the correct thing for a church paper to have, occasionally, a religious article." So, in a record of travels, I think it entirely proper to say something, occasionally, about the country the traveler explores.

The lake, at one end of which sits the beautiful though much mixed Geneva, is known abroad as Lake Geneva, but here as Lake Leman, the name given it by the Romans who once occupied this country, as they did every other country they could reach and conquer. The inlet to the lake is the River Rhone, and so, likewise, is its outlet; which is to say, the lake is simply a widening of the river, a huge goitre, as it were, on the lovely neck of that beautiful stream.

The Rhone collects the waters that fall on the south side of the chain of mountains, as the Rhine does the water drainage of the north side, and is created originally, and fed as it goes, by the glaciers that adorn the mountain sides, and support Switzerland by attracting tourists.

At the top of the mountains there is snow, soft, regular snow, which slides down fissures, and which, as it gets down the slides, changes from snow to ice. It melts slowly all the Summer, the water seeking the bottom of the field of ice, but its thickness being constantly maintained by fresh supplies of snow from the top.

(478)

This water brings out of the mountains all sorts of material, rocks and earth, which fill the streams that come down the mountain side in swiftly flowing streams which lose themselves in the river in the valley below.

The Rhone flows past Sion, Martigny, Bex, and other points, till it falls into Lake Leman, as beautiful an inland body of water as there is in Europe, and almost as beautiful as some of the American lakes.

Before and at its entrance into the lake, the water of the Rhone is as muddy as the Mississippi at St. Louis. It is about the color of cheap restaurant coffee, but the lake acts as a great settling bed. or filter, or both; and by the time the water finds itself in its new location it becomes the most pure and limpid of any in Europe. The water in the lake, which was so muddy and discolored in the river above, becomes so pure and limpid that the fish may be seen disporting themselves in its lowest depths, and the minute pebbles on the bottom are distinctly to be seen.

Geneva is at the lower point of the lake, and the Rhone, which was buried in it at the upper end, is resurrected at Geneva, and issues therefrom in a stream of fearful rapidity. The waters spring out from the lake with a fall that would be called rapids in America, and rush through the city actually singing as if with joy at its deliverance. It rushes out as if it spurned all impediments of shore that kept it into a well behaved and quiet lake, and as if anxious to get the freedom of rushing through the valleys, over rocks, and tumbling around generally in a free and easy way till it runs its race and loses itself forever in the common sepulchre of all rivers, the great sea.

Laundrying is done in Geneva as it is in Paris. Anchored in the river are large boats arranged for wash houses. In these floating temples are furnaces which supply hot water, and plank tables at which the washerwomen do their work. The garment is taken and swashed in the hot water of the floating laundry, then they are religiously and conscientiously soaped, and placed upon these thick tables, and pounded with a wooden paddle till the soap and water is driven completely through them. Then they are rinsed in the swift running water of the Rhone, and pounded more, and rinsed and rinsed again, till they come out as white as the snow from which comes the water.

These nymphs of the paddle and soap-kettle are industrious workers, with strong muscular arms that seem capable of doing any kind of work, as indeed they are. It is no small matter to carry down to the river the enormous bundles of superlatively filthy clothes, and after the soaping and beating and wringing, carrying them home wet and heavy. But possibly there are no more pounds to carry home than they brought. There is added weight in the water they hold, but

GROUP OF SWISS GIRLS.

the dirt is gone down the river to form bars below and impede navigation. Possibly the loss of the dirt balances the increased weight of the water. It is a stand-off.

These women earn a good living, for there is any quantity of laundrying to do, not from the citizens, but from the horde of tourists who throng the city and make Geneva their headquarters for the Alpine tour, and who here lay in a fresh stock of linen.

The Genevan, like all other men of French or partially French extraction, is a tremendous worker, and this includes the female as well as the male. The male Genevan is up with the lark, or whatever bird in Switzerland has the disagreeable habit of early rising, and his labor continues as long as he can see, and even after. And he works, not in a perfunctory sort of way, but tackles his business as though he was doing it for the simple liking of it. He is a most persistent and rapid worker.

I was exploring the old part of the city one night, and in groping through the narrow, half-underground passages, I came upon a baker's shop. As I wanted to get at the secret of the delicious bread for which the French are famous, I investigated. It was a scorching night, but nevertheless there was a

THE SWEAT OF OTHER MEN'S BROWS.

roaring oven, heated seven times hotter than any furnace I had ever read of, except one. In front of this furnace, were the mixing and kneading troughs, and at them, in a space of not more than twenty feet square, were a score or more of men naked to the waist, with perspiration pouring from every pore, at work at the stiff and tenacious dough. They would lift a mass of it half as large as their bodies, and slap it about, and pull it out, and compress it, and elongate it, and torture it in all sorts of shapes, and in every way possible for dough to be tortured. It was as hard manual labor as I had ever seen performed.

31

And finally after the dough had been tormented a sufficient length of time it was formed into rolls, five or six feet long, and not more than six inches in diameter, and placed in the oven, from whence it emerged the most deliciously crisp bread that ever was eaten, and entirely different from the heavy, soggy English bread which has dyspepsia in every crumb of it.

The secret of this light, delicious crustiness is not only in the form in which it is baked, but also in the thoroughness of the kneading. It is worked over and over, till it is as smooth as silk all the way through, and as light as a feather. Such bread needs no butter (and, by the way, very little is used) and may be eaten with gustatory delight anywhere, and at any time.

Still, a person who has to eat bread had better not go and see it made, on the same principle that a wise old boarder of experience never ventures near the kitchen. "Where igno-rance is bliss," etc. The industry and conscientious persever-ance of the kneaders cannot be too highly commended, but the consumer of their product had better remain in ignorance of the perspiration. I prefer not to live upon the sweat of other men's brows. There are seasonings more to my taste.

One of the very pleasant things in Switzerland, and France as well, is the perfect system of roads everywhere, and the care taken to shade the roads. The road-beds are marvels of excellence, and well would it be for America could we find it in our people to pay some little attention to this important matter. Whatever else may be slighted the roads are not. In making a comparison between Swiss roadways and American, I take into consideration the fact, that Switzerland is old and America new, and that the present Swiss road represents the labor of hundreds, or, for that matter, thousands of years, while the average age of the American road is not sixty years. Still, we might, and should, with our enterprise come nearer to continental roads than we do.

Everywhere in Switzerland the earth on the roadway is removed to the depth of four or more feet, and pounded stone, gravel and sand are deposited in its stead, gutters on the side are carefully made ; till you have, to travel over, a beautifully rounded way which never can be wet, and never anything but solid and smooth. Along the entire length there are, beside the road, small piles of broken stone, and at regular distances are men with tools, whose business is to keep them clean and in perfect order. Whenever a depression, no matter how slight, appears, it is instantly filled, as skillfully as a tailor puts a patch in your trowsers; thus keeping them, everywhere and always, smooth, uniform and clean.

The bridges are solid masonry, and on the edge of declivities and dangerous places are solid walls of stone. Not a point, either for safety or comfort, is overlooked.

They are rather costly to make, to begin with, and it costs something to keep them in order, but it pays, after all. Enormous loads are hauled over these smooth roads, and the wear and tear upon horses, vehicles and harness is reduced to well-nigh nothing, to say nothing of the comfort and pleasure. Bad weather makes no difference with their inland traffic, for just as great a burden can be hauled in wet weather as in dry, nor does frost affect them.

I would that every American farmer, in the month, say, of March, could see these roads, could view the enormous loads piled upon the enormous wagons, and see with what ease they are moved. Then his mind should go back to his own country, and there should come up a recollection of the last March, when he was lashing and swearing at his poor horses, who were doing their level best to pull him, in an empty wagon, through the rivers of mud we call roads. A Swiss horse would commit suicide were he taken to Illinois in Winter or Spring.

It would pay America to imitate Switzerland in this particular. Our half-made roads should be at once abolished, and the money spread out over ten miles, which the first thaw obliterates, should be used in making one mile of permanent road, and that mile should be extended just as fast as the people can bear the burden. The Swiss are not so fast as we are, but their work, when once done, stays. There is scarcely any section of America where material of some sort is not attainable to make better roads than the wretched apologies we have for them. Whoever makes himself the apostle of good roads in America will have many generations to rise up and call him blessed.

Next to the perfection of the roads comes the delightful shade that is over them. This has been done, not spasmodically and at the whim of the people residing along the roads, but it is a government matter, and as much care is taken of it as of the roads. On either hand are lines of beautiful trees, forming a most delightful arch over the road, and the shade is as grateful to the horses as to the riders. A long vista of trees, whose branches form an arch over the roadway is not only a comfort, but it gratifies all the senses. A Swiss tree-bordered road is one of the most delightful sights in the country.

We cannot, of course, compel the planting of trees by the roadside, by law, but if the farmers of America could be made to understand the beauty and comfort there is in it, they would do it of their own free will and accord. New England has shaded roads, and some scattering parts of other sections, but it should be made general. It would add several per cent. to the value of every farm, to say nothing of the perpetual gratification it would afford. We have the best shade trees in the world, and the cost of transplanting is comparatively nothing.

Road shading should be systematically pushed in America, and the sooner it is commenced the better.

At Geneva you get the first glimpse of the Alpenstock people, male and female. They are a queer lot. They appear to you at the hotels clad as follows: The men with a sort of blouse bound by an enormous belt, for which there is no earthly use, short knee breeches with woolen stockings reaching above the knee, and the most utterly absurd shoes that ever annoyed the human foot. The soles of these shoes are an inch thick; they project beyond the uppers, and are studded with nails, as if the wearer had joined an exploring party which would require eight years of his life, and make necessary one pair of shoes that should exist all that time, inasmuch as he would be far beyond the reach of that important adjunct of civilization, a cobbler. Then he has a broad-brimmed hat, with a clout about it, hanging down behind, and a vast assortment of baskets, flasks and glasses, and all sorts of appliances, provisions enough to join Livingstone or Stanley for the exploration of the interior of Africa.

The women are either misses of seventeen or mature women of thirty-eight. They have the same outfit of material and differ from the males only in the matter of dress. Everything that savors of femininity is religiously eliminated (even the

THE ALPINE GUIDE.

bustle is sacrificed), heavy underclothing is worn, a most ungraceful skirt, the most barbarous English shoes appear on feet never too small, and their entire hideousness is made painfully visible, inasmuch as the straight skirt never reaches below the ankle.

The Alpenstock is a staff perhaps seven feet long, of ash, very stout, with a hook upon one end and a spike in the other.

In this hideous garb, in a stern sort of a way, as though they were leading a forlorn hope and never expected to escape with their lives, but were doing it as a sort of sacrificial duty, they ride out to the foot of the Alps somewhere, as safely and in as much luxury as though they were in rocking chairs in their own homes, and coming to the hotel thereat they purchase another lot of climbing apparatus, and hire all sorts of donkeys and mules and guides, and after a day or so commence the ascent. They go up roads that are so plain as to need no guides, on donkeys or mules, over paths that could be walked as well, and tiring half way up, stop and rest and never go farther, but return, with their mouths full of lies. Every mother's son and daughter of them claim to have made the full ascent of the peak essayed, and having read themselves up, talk as glibly about it as though they had lived upon the mountains all their lives, and knew every glacier as familiarly as they do their bedrooms.

And then when they come down they are stared at by the last arrivals, and laughed at by the old ones, and they go to a shop around the corner, and pay several francs to have the name and date of the ascent of the mountains in the neighborhood burned in upon their Alpenstocks, which they cart all over Europe, and finally hang up in their homes as "souvenirs."

There ought to be an Alpenstock shop in New York, where all this could be done. It would save a deal of annoyance to a great many people and do just as well.

Did I ascend any of these mountains? I did not. Some of my party did, but I preferred not to essay it. The heat was intense, the paths are not good, and lifting one's self by sheer strength up sixteen thousand feet is not the thing to do, especially when you may read it, see it in engravings, and even make the ascent yourself — with a telescope — at the cost of a franc. I did it by telescope, and have never regretted it. I could buy an Alpenstock just the same, and have burned in it, "Mont Blanc, July 20, 1881," just as well. And, as they all lie about it, anyhow, why not, if you are going to lie, commence lying at the beginning, and save labor? If tongue work is to do it, why not use your tongue, and save your legs? Were I to lie at all, I would sooner lie from the door of the hotel than half way up the mountain.

But I will not lie at all. I did go up Mt. Blanc, perhaps five hundred feet, to the very foot of one of the glaciers, and saw and touched it. That did me. I had seen all that was to be seen, and I was glad enough to get back. I was willing that anybody who chose should do the remaining fifteen thousand feet; five hundred was quite enough for me.

A NON-PROFESSIONAL LADY TOURIST.

It is a most amusing thing to see a woman with this absurd gown, actually glorying in looking hideous, with her ghastly blue spectacles, Alpenstock in hand, ride up to a hotel on a mule, and march boldly into the grand hall, after one of these fraudulent excursions. She speaks of the topmost peaks as though she had been there; she talks of chasms in the glaciers, of the risks she ran because the ropes were not exactly right; she abuses her guide, and says he was the worst she ever had, as though she had been climbing Alps from the time she left off short dresses; and when her little stock is run out, she goes to her room, and reads up her guide-books and such local

printed matter as is attainable, and commences again. She
buys Alpine flowers at the market in the village, and sends
them home as gathered on the mountains; she has all sorts of
carved work which she swears she purchased from the Alpine
dwellers who make it (there are factories of these "souvenirs"
all over Switzerland); and she loads herself with all sorts of
rubbish, all of which her people at home will preserve and
cherish as carefully as though the lies she told about it were
truths.   There are enthusiasts who make it the business of
their lives to explore the Alps, and as they alone take the risk,
they do no harm if they do no good. But the average amateur
climber is about as absurd a being as is permitted to exist, and
inasmuch as there are thousands of them, one may imagine
what an offense they are.

You meet all sorts of queer people in Europe, and as many
in Switzerland as anywhere, unless it be Paris, which is a common sink for all the world. I met in Geneva a very curious
specimen, whose career is worth a place in history.

He was the son of one of the most wealthy men of New
York. His father had made some millions of dollars in trade
and judicious real-estate investments, and brought up his family
as all rich New Yorkers do. The young man had gone through
college, and had graduated by the skin of his teeth. He had
learned much of boating and base ball, and was one of the best
billiard players in his set. Out of college with a lot of knowledge that he could make no use of, for he had nothing to do in
life, he became a club man in New York, and commenced the
pursuit of pleasure. It was all well enough for a time Yacht-
ing occupied him for two seasons, horses took his attention for
two more. He once, in desperation, made a trip in a wagon
from New York to Montreal, just to put in a Summer, with
three companions, he footing all the bills. Horses palling on
his taste, he entered upon a life of general and miscellaneous
dissipation, and finally that tired him and he was without an
aim in life.

He had hunted pleasure and now pleasure was hunting him.

In despair he took to travel, and for five years he rambled
from one capital to another, seeing everything and being bored
by everything.

Here he was living at the best hotel, in the best style; he

kept a servant or two, and had oceans of friends, as every man has who has money, but life to him was a curse. He had nothing to do.

"Why don't you go up the Alps?" I said to him.

"Bless your innocent soul I have been up the Alps a dozen times. There isn't a dangerous place that I haven't attempted, nor anything that is regular that I haven't done. It don't pay."

He had seen all the theaters, all the stock places were as familiar to him as the alphabet, and as for the dissipations he had so tired of them that he was a saint. He was virtuous from necessity.

One morning I asked him to go with me to inspect a machine shop which was one of the lions of the place. For sheer want of something else to do, he put on his coat and went. I was very much interested in some of the processes which were new to me, but my friend yawned through the whole of it, in the same *ennuied* way that was manifest since I knew him. Finally we came before a machine known in machinery as a shaper. It was a powerful tool, which went backward and forward, cutting at each forward movement a thin thread of iron. The work it was doing was cutting a slot in a shaft of iron. The shaft, before it went into the shaper, was a round piece of iron. Delancy looked at it with the first expression of interest I had ever seen in his face.

The man at the machine had nothing to do after the shaft was put into the "chucks" but to sit and read a novel, the machine doing all the work with regularity and accuracy.

"Do you forge this shaft originally?" he asked the man.

"Certainly, sir."

"How long does it take you to cut this slot in it?"

"About four hours."

"Then why don't you have the piece of iron forged with this slot made down to within say a quarter-inch and save nine-tenths of this time?"

"We never did it that way," was the reply of the man; "it won't do."

"But it will do," said Delancy. "That shaft can be forged, to begin with, something as it should come out, and it's a cussed waste of time to do it in this way."

The foreman assured him that it could be done in no other way. The workmen corroborated the foreman, but Delancy was not satisfied.

That evening in his room he had a dictionary of mechanics, and was intent upon the parts relating to forging. He called my attention to it, and swore great oaths that the machinists were a set of asses, and that they hadn't a process which he could not better.

The next morning he was up at six and had an early breakfast and was at the shop driving the workmen mad with his persistent inquiries. At dinner he talked of nothing but machines and machinery, and the evening he devoted to whittling curiously shaped things out of wood.

Suddenly he disappeared. One morning I went to the shops again, and who should I see in a greasy suit of overalls, with his gold eye-glasses, but a man who looked like my friend Delancy, at a lathe.

It was a curious transformation, and about the most incongruous spectacle I had ever seen. Here was a man with gold eye-glasses, a diamond ring, thin white hands, patent leather boots, with greasy overalls. It was an earnest mechanic engrafted upon a Broadway exquisite.

"Do my eyes deceive me?"

"They do not. It is I, Delancy. Not the old Delancy, but an entirely new one. I have now something to live for."

"Why have you quit the hotel?"

"Because I want to associate with my fellows. I am living with them. I have been admitted as one of them, and they all know me as well as though I had been born one of them, which I wish to Heaven I had. I can eat something now, and their beer — well, with a lot of good fellows it lays all over the champagne I have always paid for. You see I have made up my mind to demonstrate to these ignoramuses that a piece of iron can be forged to any shape, with any depression in it desirable, and that these men at the lathes and shapers waste ninety per cent. of their time. We have got to have machinery, and we want it cheap. I have something to live for. I shall be a machinist."

The man had actually bribed the master of the works to

accept him as an apprentice, and he had made an exceedingly good one. He was at the works at the regular hour, and stayed as late as the latest. And he developed wonderful genius in the way of mechanics, and was in a fair way to arrive at a high position in the business.

The workmen idolized him. He delighted to go with them evenings to the cafés they frequented, to be a little king among them; he helped the sick and unfortunate; he took some interest in their concerns, and they in turn did everything possible to acquaint him with the practical part of the trade.

"They are a much better lot," he said, "than the leeches who used to hang upon me."

He invited me to dine with him one day, and the amount of coarse food he could consume — this man who had not had an appetite for twenty years — was something wonderful.

For the first time in his life, he declared, he was absolutely happy. He had something to do.

Before he had been in the shop a week he showed the master how the iron bar could be forged to the shape required, and how two-thirds of the time at the machine could be saved, and he succeeded in having his system introduced.

He vows that he will stick to it till he has learned his trade, then go home to New York and start the most perfect machine shop on the continent, and that, moreover, he will be perfectly happy therein. He is not *ennuied* any more, for he has found something to do. There are others who would do well to follow his example.

CHAPTER XXXII.

On a clear bright day, the hot air tempered by a gentle breeze wafted down from the ice-covered mountains, with others we left Geneva, to cross the mountains and visit Mont Blanc, that patriarch of the Alps. The blue waters of Lake Geneva danced and sparkled in the sunlight as our steamer sped along towards Nyon.

At last we were skimming over the surface of that wonderful body of water whose peans have for hundreds of years been sung by the poets, in prose and verse, of all countries. Rosseau, Voltaire, Byron, Goethe have revelled in the delights of its tranquil beauty and celebrated its charms in immortal words. And it is indeed a fitting theme for a poet's song. To-day its deep blue surface is broken into a myriad of ripples. Here and there, sailing slowly along, are large barges with the graceful lateen sails that are seldom seen except upon the Mediterranean. The shores are lined with rich foliage, the cedar of Lebanon mingling its sweet odor with that of the chestnut, the walnut and the magnolia, the whole enlivened with pretty villas and picturesque hamlets.

Though more beautiful, Lake Geneva has a peculiarity that is enjoyed by Lake Constance. It is subject to a change of level. At places, where the bed of the lake is narrow, the water occasionally rises several feet above the ordinary level, and remains so for half an hour or more, this too without any previous warning of what was about to occur. Another peculiarity is that hidden springs oftentimes break forth from the bed of the lake and form a current so swift that it is impossible, almost, to stem the tide. These springs are very dangerous to oarsmen and are nearly as badly feared by the fishermen as the waterspouts that frequently occur.

Here, as everywhere, we had all sorts of people with us. We had a widower, and a widow with a daughter, and the widower had been making love to the widow all the way from London, which the widow accepted more than kindly. Indeed, the attentions of the ancient beau had become so marked, that to the mind of any widow of experience, it was only a question of time as to a proposal direct, which she was waiting for impatiently.

Among others on the boat was the Young Man who Knows Everything, who has studied everything, and who has that rasping memory that enables him to retain everything he ever

THE YOUNG MAN WITH HIS INOPPORTUNE REMARKS.

read, as well as every thought that ever passed through his mind, and the self-sufficiency that impels him to thrust his own talk at you, at no matter how inopportune a time, and no matter how inapplicable it may be to whatever is being discussed. He will discuss a question with you to-day, and when in his bed at night he will remember something that he should have said at the time, and break in upon you a week after with the omitted remark, with no preface, no explanation, taking it for granted that any discussion you ever had with him was of sufficient importance to take full possession of your mind and occupy it forever and forever. He had had an argument with the widower the night before at the hotel in Geneva, upon the authority of the Old Testament, which the widower, as was natural, forgot in an hour. Our widow and widower were sitting near the stern, in loving proximity, discussing quietly the loneliness of their situation. The young man was waiting very close, entirely oblivious of what they were saying, and only anxious to fire off his charge.

"Ah, Mrs. Redding," said the widower, "when one has once tasted the sweets of congenial companionship—"

In broke the young man:

"It was the old dispensation, and is not binding on us to-day at all. Therefore you need n't do everything that Moses put upon the Jews; but, Mr. Thompson, you can just bet your sweet life that you are perfectly safe in not doing anything that he said the Jews should not do."

The widower looked daggers, and the widow broadswords. As handsome a proposal as was ever to be made was nipped in the bud — an opportunity for the widow was lost which might never be regained. Who could tell? Possibly his passion might cool off. The fish was hooked but not landed, and this insufferable argument-monger was the cause of it.

"Blast your Moses," uttered the irate widower. "Madam, if there is any part of this boat safe from the intrusion of young men who dabble in Moses, let us find it."

And they went off, leaving the young man not at all abashed. He merely turned to an amused spectator, with the remark:

"That man's face proves the correctness of the Darwinian theory. In time his descendants may become men. I was about to enlighten him on an important subject, but he would not."

There never was a boat loaded with tourists which did not have on its deck the man who was doing Europe on insufficient capital. He spent money freely in London, Paris nearly finished him, and he commenced traveling on credit in Switzerland. His method was very simple: he borrowed a hundred francs of every man he thought simple enough to lend it to him. It was always the same story, he had drawn on his peo-

ple at home and would have the money at the next stopping place *but one.* Then he always slipped away from his victim at the *next* stopping place and was seen no more. We had him, but he did not succeed. There were too many old travelers in the party.

Geneva, on a plateau above the level of the lake, with its picturesque background of rugged mountains, gradually melts into a solid mass of buildings, bridges and parks as we go up the lake, past the mammoth hotels, with their beautifully arranged lawns and gardens. On the

"WOULD YOU OBLIGE ME WITH A HUNDRED FRANCS TILL SATURDAY?"

left, in an immense pleasure park, is the Rothschild villa, a country seat as beautiful as the surroundings. For miles the left bank of the lake is lined with summer residences, nestling among the lovely groves of fragrant trees.

On the right bank, a range of hills, starting way up the lake, rises gradually higher and higher until it culminates, apparently, in Mt. Blanc, fifty-six miles away. These mountains, rugged and severe, slope gradually down to the bank of the lake, which is lined with well cultivated farms.

The lake is a study. Its bright blue waters are as clear as crystal, the small white pebbles on the bottom being plainly discernable. As the sharp prow cleaves the water and throws it off on either side, the hue is changed into a dark green, making a charming contrast with the unruffled water beyond, which retains its peculiar blue.

Long before Nyon is reached, the white buildings of Geneva have faded away in a mild rose colored haze, through which the dim outlines of the mountains can just be seen.

After an hour's run, full of beauty, Nyon, a favorite resting

place for tourists, is reached, and the steamer stops long enough
to take on three or four mountain climbers, who, with Alpenstocks in hand and knapsacks on back, are going on a pedestrian expedition on the other side of the lake.

The sharp pointed roofs of Nyon's houses, its quaint streets,
pretentious hotels and historic buildings make it a favorite
resort all Summer long.

The faro bankeress was of the party, she and her husband.
The husband looked listlessly into the blue water, and enjoyed
the succession of beautiful views, and studied nature in all its
aspects, with a party of kindred spirits, in the hot cabin below,
over a game of euchre, with a rapid succession of orders for
cognac and water. That's all he saw of Lake Leman. He
played moodily, as though the time taken from his magnificent
game at home was so much wasted. Green cloth was more to
him than emerald water, and he never desired to see an elevation greater than a roulette ball.

His wife made the acquaintance of, and fastened herself to,
a party of actual tourists, and to them she discoursed volubly
of the prices of silk stockings in Paris, and of dress making and
millinery and kindred topics. There was one young girl who
really had the eye of a hawk for the actually beautiful, who
would go into raptures as some wonderfully beautiful view
dawned upon us, and who felt an enthusiasm which she must
share with somebody. And so she would pull the faro bankeress by the sleeve, and interrupt her flow of talk.

"And then you see these stockings are—"

"Oh, Mrs. ——, do look at that mountain with the cataract
rushing down its side!"

A hasty glance at the wonderful work of nature.

"Oh, yes, my dear—it's *nice*. But them stockings. Why,
in New York, at any first-class store—"

And so forth, and so on.

Tibbitts was gorgeously arrayed in a Parisian suit, with
trowsers very wide at the bottom, and cuffs of preposterous
length and width. He discussed all sorts of abstruse questions
with grave German professors, neither understanding a word
of what the other was saying, and so he passed for a very
wise young man. More men would be so esteemed if they

would always talk in language which nobody can understand. I remember of being wonderfully impressed with the profundity of a New England metaphysical talker, but alas! when his six syllabled words were translated into common

"SEE ME UNMASK THIS JEW."

English, I wondered at the stupidity of his commonplaces.

But poor Tibbitts was finally conquered. There was a Jew on board who was selling the "art work" of the country. He spoke all languages, as the Continental Jews all can. Tibbitts admired a little ivory carving.

"What is the price of it?"

"My tear sir ze work of art vill be given avay for ze

32

redeecoolus sum oof two huntret francs. It gost me dwice dot."

Then Tibbitts winked a wink of intelligence to the rest of us, as if he should say, "See me unmask this Jew."

"I will give you five francs for it."

"Fife francs? Fadder Abraham, but you laugh at me! I vill dake—but no, mine friend, dis ees a bat season—you dake him."

Then the laugh was not with Tibbitts. The "ivory carv_ing" was the basest kind of an imitation, and would be dear at a half franc. And Tibbitts retired sullenly to the cabin below, and all the way up his American friends amused themselves by asking to see his rare ivory carving.

There is so much that is beautiful on this side that time slips away without notice, so that when Thonon is reached it scarcely seems possible that it has taken an hour to make the run across the lake from Nyon.

At the entrance to Thonon, the channel is very tortuous, and once, near the landing, you may seek in vain for the entrance or the way out. There is a little lake all by itself, hemmed in on every side, apparently, by mountain and forest.

Surrounded by mountains, Thonon nestles at the foot of a vineyard-covered hill, up the sides of which low houses, with their queer, overhanging roofs, line narrow, angular streets that seem to be too steep for any practical use.

High up the side of the hill is a picturesque terrace, with pretty, vine-clad houses on the site of the old ducal palaces destroyed by the Bernese in 1536, from which a beautiful view of the lake and surrounding country is obtained.

At one time this little place was the residence of the Counts and Dukes of Savoy, it still being the capital of the Savoyard Province of Chamblais. The vineyards in this neighborhood produce the fine white wines that are celebrated the world over.

Touching for a few minutes at Evian, a favorite resort for wealthy people from the south of France, with its pretty hotels, charming oak shaded promenades, the boat sped rapidly on toward Auchy, crossing the lake again. Looking up the lake the mountain ranges, towering high above, change their form and color with every revolution of the wheel. Just ahead of us on the right, a great peak, starting abruptly from the water's edge, shoots straight up into the air for a thousand or two feet. All about us are the green covered hills, forming a rare frame for the picture of the sun-lit lake, dotted here and there with a lateen sail, and the slowly drifting smoke of a pleasure steamer that skirts along the shores. At this point a long detour is made around a huge hill that juts out into the water, completely shutting out the view on the right. As we passed round it, an exclamation of surprise and wonder involuntarily burst forth at the sight of the Tête Noire, which lay before us, with its lofty peaks crowned with eternal snow.

On we go, past pretty little villages, any one of which would be a most delightful place to spend the Summer; past vineyards, with their luscious fruit ripening in the sun, until, just above Chillon, we come to the Castle of Chillon, made famous by Byron.

> " Chillon, thy prison is a holy place,
>   And thy sad floor an altar, for 'twas trod —
> Until his very steps have left a trace,
>   Worn, as if the cold pavement were a sod —
> By Bonivard ! May none those marks efface,
>   For they appeal from tyranny to God."

This ancient castle, built as far back as A. D. 830, stands in a picturesque position on a barren rock some twenty yards from the shore, with which it is connected by a wooden bridge. Its history is full of romance, from the time Louis le Debonnaire incarcerated within its gloomy walls — from which but the sky, the Alps, and Lake Leman, could be seen — the Abbot Wala of Corvey, for instigating his sons to rebellion, down to the reigns of the Counts of Savoy, who used it as a military prison. The walls of its dingy dungeons are literally covered with names of persons who have visited them, among others being those of Byron, Victor Hugo, George Sands, and Eugene Sue.

Here in Republican Switzerland the traces only of monarchy remain, for which the Swiss should perpetually thank heaven. Everywhere else in Europe the monster actually lives — here only its ghost survives. It is here a remembrance to be shuddered at, not a living reality. But they had it here

once. There was a time, and the Castle of Chillon is a silent
testimony to it, when a duke or a king, who claimed to be of
better clay than ordinary mortals, could seize a man and
immure him within its gloomy walls, just as Victoria, by the
accident of birth, Mistress of Britain, may order the arrest of
an Irishman who opens his mouth the wrong way. Kilmain-
ham is the Irish Chillon, and there are within its walls men
whose hair is turning gray, not in a single night, but turning
gray just as surely.

The ancient tyrants who lorded it over Switzerland were
not one whit worse than the tyrants who now lord it over
Europe. Royalty is royalty, the same in all ages, because
based upon the same infernal heresy. It is the absolute rule
of a class, backed by organized force.

Switzerland, America and France have repudiated it, and
the rest of the civilized world will. But what oceans of blood
must flow before all this is accomplished.

In order to be a complete and very radical Republican one
needs to visit a few just such places as the Castle of Chillon,
that the true inwardness of monarchy may be realized.

As the castle, so full of historical interest, fades away, the
boat rounds the head of the lake, where the river Rhone
pours its gray glacial waters into the brilliant blue of the lake,
making a clearly defined mark of gray and blue at least a
quarter of a mile from the shore. Then Vernayaz is reached
and we disembark for our trip across the Alps.

As the boat glides up to the dock, the ancient castle, built
in the twelfth century, is pointed out. Its walls and towers
are very massive, and bid fair to stand as long as the city
endures. Near the castle is a chateau, where, at one time,
Joseph Bonaparte lived. It is now the property of the Mora-
vians, and all its former grandeur is sunk in the abysses of a
boys' school.

Just opposite the town the Jura mountains have entirely
changed in appearance, and are full of strange, fantastic peaks
and crags, while Mt. Blanc, always visible, presents different
faces as the boat changes its course, always, however, grand
and fascinating.

SWISS TIMBER VILLAGE.

CHAPTER XXXIII.

A SHORT drive over one of those wonderfully hard, smooth roads that make carriage traveling in Switzerland so delight-ful, and we are at the hotel at the Gorge du Trient, whence, early in the morning, we are to begin the ascent of the moun-tains. The time before dinner is occupied in an exploration of the wildly picturesque gorge, with its winding foot-bridge built alongside the cliffs, over yawning chasms, around jutting bowlders that rise to such a height that the sky seems like a strip of blue ribbon suspended high above our heads. At the bottom of the gorge a mountain torrent, springing from some unknown nook way up in the mountain, comes rushing and tumbling down over the jagged rocks, foaming and whirl-ing, and dashing its spray high in the air, as it hurries along to join the Rhone.

The slender bridge, at times hanging apparently without any support over deep pools of water, seems too fragile to bear the weight of a person, and one treads lightly, lest the frail structure give way, and he be precipitated into the unfathom-able abyss below. The gorge is about three-quarters of a mile long, and is wierdly picturesque.

After dinner, some rash member of the party suggested that we do a little mountain climbing. Then a wager was immediately laid that no one had the courage and endurance to go to the summit of a high peak near by. Of course the challenge was accepted, and the whole party, there were three ladies and five gentlemen, all started to accomplish the easy feat. It looked easy. The path zigzagged up the hill, and

(502)

was provided with resting places at stated intervals. Nothing could be more delightful than to skip merrily along, like chamois, clear to the summit. It was all very well for the

THE SLENDER BRIDGE.

first few hundred feet, and we laughed and vowed that mountain climbing was not such a terrible affair, after all. But at the first resting place two of the gentlemen and one of the

ladies announced that they were subject to heart disease, and
dare not go any farther. They *could* do it, but it was a duty

A BIT OF CLIMBING.

they owed to their families and the world at large not to
tempt death.

At the next resting place one of the ladies discovered that

she had turned her ankle, and she went back. She danced as briskly as usual, however, at the hotel that evening.

Another of the gentlemen thought it his duty to assist her down to the hotel. This left but three, who silently lifted themselves up step by step to the next resting place. From this the view was something unutterably grand. The valley sweeping out to the lake, the mountains on the other side, with the clouds kissing their summits, the fleecy white, pink-tinged by the setting sun, forming a beautiful contrast to the forbidding black of the rocks, and the dark green of the mountain foliage. One of the gentlemen looked up to the dizzy height still before him, and remarked that he had seen as much grandeur as he could take in at one time, and down hill he went.

The other and last smiled a contemptuous smile as he disappeared on the zigzag path, and setting his teeth, turned his footsteps upward. He reached the summit, and waving a small American flag (which he always carried about his person), took in the wonderful view, and slowly but majestically descended.

I will not say which of the eight persevered and made the ascent. It is a fault, a common fault, in travelers, this boasting of their own achievements, and because one has a command of type and presses I do not see why he should use those facilities to record his own performances. If any one else of the party publishes an account of the excursion I shall see my name in this connection, but never will I write it.

But I — or rather, that is, the one who did persevere to the summit, was rewarded with a sight that amply repaid me — or him — for my, or his labor. There at his feet, bathed in the light of the sinking sun, was the valley of the Rhone, brilliant with its covering of green, relieved by the silvery river meandering through its center. To the right, crossing and cutting off the valley, are the Bernese Alps, their snow-covered peaks glistening in the sunlight. It was a magnificent view, giving us a good idea of the glories of nature that were to be entered upon on the morrow.

When the Gorge du Trient was organized, nature must have been laboring under an attack of cholera morbus.

At some remote period in the history of the earth there

was a solid mountain, but some glacier, or earthquake, or other irresistible force, cleft it in twain, and the ever present water, nature's slow but exceedingly certain worker, poured into the chasm to finish what the first rude force commenced.

There is a great plenty of water stored away in these mountains, and it has been pouring through this rent in the bosom of the earth, wearing away a few feet here and a few feet there, augmenting in volume as the space for it increased, until it has become a wild, resistless torrent, which does n't dance, but rushes through the rocks, till after its brief attack of delirium tremens it loses itself in the Rhone and finally in Lake Geneva, and becomes as quiet and well-behaved as you could wish.

The scenic artist who painted "The Devil's Glen" in the Black Crook, had doubtless visited this gorge. If devils ever came together in convention, and wanted a place, the horrible wildness of which should be absolutely satanic, they could find it here.

The rocks on either hand are nearly five hundred feet high, and the ravine twists and turns in every direction, the sides approaching each other so nearly at every turn at their summit that the gorge seems to be but an immense vaulted cavern with an entirely irresponsible torrent of water gyrating through it.

It drops itself down sheer precipices, in places thirty feet, and everywhere *rushes*, it never dances, but rushes with an ugly, wicked, vindictive rush, a cruel rush, a resistless force, as if it wanted to catch something in its merciless grasp, and toss it against rocks, grasp it when it came back, and hurl it down a dizzy fall of cruel, jagged rocks, and shoot it way up the side of the gorge, on other rocks, and finally release it when pounded to a jelly, in the river below.

This water is well-behaved enough when it reaches the river. but up here in the gorge it is the wildest, most cruel, most devilish and wicked water I ever saw.

Niagara impresses one with its calm, resistless strength, Minnehaha is beautiful enough to induce one, almost, to go over it, but this torrent in the gorge has strength only. It is a fiendish, impish body of water.

It is not utilized. Its only use is to support a very good

hotel, the venerable party who takes a franc for admission to it, and several shops devoted to selling "souvenirs" to tourists. These are the only wheels this water power turns. About one hundred people make a comfortable living from the gorge, and they no doubt esteem it highly.

Of course the gorge has its legend. Every well regulated gorge in Switzerland as well as every other country in Europe has a legend, done in the most atrocious English, and execrably printed, which you can purchase of the local guide for what is equivalant to ten cents American money. I doubt not that Switzerland has a legend-factory running somewhere, which turns them out to order. People go several times, you see, and they want a new legend every time.

This legend accounts for the formation of the gorge, and I spent an entire night getting it into understandable English. It runs thus:—

Way back in the dark ages, when the devil was in the habit of coming in person to transact his business with men — and women — there was no gorge at all. The mountain was shaped not as it is now, but was a respectable mountain, with a properly conducted stream dancing down its side. This stream turned two mills, one owned by a very nice miller, named Balthazar, and the other by a very wicked miller, named Caspar.

Balthazar had the respect and esteem of his fellow-men, while Caspar was universally detested. He was a griping, grasping man, who took double toll, and was as avaricious as a grave-yard. Balthazar, on the other hand, was beloved by everybody, because he was good; and, because he was good, he was very poor. Caspar had succeeded in buying up his notes, and he held a claim on his mill, which he desired to get out of the way, as he wanted no competition. But Balthazar kept right along, for he had friends somewhere who advanced money to him, so that he could keep up the interest and defy the enemy.

Caspar tried every way to get rid of his competitor, but he could not, and he chafed under it. He dwelt upon it so long that it became a mania with him. How to crush Balthazar and have the sole privilege of plundering the people was the thought with him by day and night.

One Spring he bought more of Balthazar's paper, but, to his chagrin, Balthazar came around promptly and paid it, the day it was due, and Caspar found himself foiled again.

And so that night when he was pacing his room and fretting and fuming about his disappointment, he remarked to himself mentally — a very dangerous thing in those days — that he would give his soul to be relieved of this popular rival.

No sooner thought than done. The archdemon appeared in person, and Caspar did not seem to be surprised.

"Are you in earnest, Herr Caspar?"

"Indeed I am. That man is poison to me. I must get rid of him and his mill."

"Very right. You can do it, but you know the terms?"

"Certainly. You remove the mill, you ruin Balthazar, and after a time I become yours, I sign an article of agreement, writing my name in my own blood. That's the regular thing, I believe!"

"You are right, old man, right as a trivet. Sign here."

And he produced the document which he had with him. It stipulated that Balthazar's mill was to be utterly destroyed, and Caspar's not injured, and that things should be so fixed that Caspar's would be the only respectable water-power possible on the mountain.

As a consideration for this friendly service, Caspar was, after twenty years of milling with no competition, to yield himself gracefully to the demon, body and soul.

Caspar whipped off his coat, cut his arm for blood, and signed.

The devil disappeared in a clap of thunder, leaving a perceptible odor of brimstone in the room, and Caspar went calmly to bed.

The next morning he heard that an immense stream of water had burst out of the mountain below his mill, and that it had swept poor Balthazar's property entirely away — that not a vestige of it was left. He smiled grimly, doubled the size of his toll-dish, and went about his business.

Twenty years later, to the minute, the devil appeared and demanded his pay. But he did not know Caspar, who had been thinking the matter over for some two years, and being hale and hearty, had no idea of going at all, and especially of going where he had rashly ticketed himself. He had consulted an abbott of rare power in such cases, and the abbott had shown him how to evade the contract. The writer of the legend does not state just what this was, but it was sufficient.

Caspar declined to fulfil his contract, and the devil saw he was foiled. He recognized the superior power of the abbott, but he couldn't help himself. He merely lashed his tail around, and smiling sarcastically, remarked :

" Very good, my fine fellow, you have won the first point in this game, but I shall proceed to show you that there are things over which the abbott has no control. Good night."

He sailed out into the night, Caspar jeering him. He jeered too soon. For just then there came a horrible darkness, with terrible thunder and flashes of frightful lightning, and the mountain was rent in twain, and Caspar's mill with himself and his live stock all went down into the chasm, and the Gorge du Trient was made.

Caspar's body was found in the river below, with ugly marks about the throat, with the debris of his mill. There was not a splinter left of anything.

This is the legend. I don't believe it, for several reasons.

If the devil had sufficient knowledge of the intention of men in advance to bring with him a contract all drawn up, (which must have cost him some trouble unless he kept them printed in blank) he would also have known that Caspar would outwit him in the end.

If he had the power to catch Caspar by destroying his mill by splitting the mountain, he had the same power before, and was just as sure of the miller before as after this exhibition of his power.

Going through all this rigmarole of signing and making contracts would be totally unnecessary. Satan is supposed to be cunning. What sense was there in laying traps for Caspar when Caspar was doing his level best to get to him anyhow? Had he let him alone, Caspar would have come to him of his own accord.

And then splitting a mountain to catch one miller would be something like firing a columbiad at a cock sparrow. It would be a great waste of ammunition. He could safely have depended upon Caspar's own toll-dish.

He may have made the gorge knowing it would be used, as time rolled on, by guides and hotel-keepers, but the legend of the miller will not do.

However, it is the legend of the place, and so I have to give it. The only lesson I can draw from it is not a good one. The virtuous Balthazar lost his property just the same as the wicked Caspar, and as he probably starved to death immediately, while Caspar had a good time for twenty years, his virtue counted him nothing, so far as this world goes. I have found that out, however, in my own experience.

In every country in the world that has rocks, there is some frightfully high one from which a great many years ago a maiden leaped. Indian maidens were addicted to this in America, and so were maidens in Switzerland.

You are compelled to climb to the very top of the mountain on one side of the gorge to see the place where a maiden threw herself over. The guide said she was crossed in love by her parents, while our landlord had it that she was deserted by her lover. Thus you had two stories at the price of one, and could believe which you chose.

Tibbitts looked calmly down the frightful chasm.

"The maiden leaped from this spot?"

"Yes, sare."

"How under Heaven did she *ever* get back!"

"She did not get back."

"Did she hurt herself?"

"Hurt hairselluf! It ees five huntret veet to ze bottom. How could she fall five huntret veet and not hurt hairselluf?"

"Five hundred feet! Well, I should say it was rather risky. What did the old folks do about it?"

He wanted to know all the circumstances, but the information of guides on such subjects always ends with the blood-curdling tragedy. They know nothing of what happened after the girl took the fatal plunge.

The road from Vernayaz leads through a number of pretty Swiss villages, whose peculiarly built stone houses contrast strangely with the pretentious edifices of the towns and cities

we had just left. The one narrow street through which the
carriages passed is filled with queerly dressed people, to whom

WHERE THE MAIDEN LEAPED FROM.

the passing of a tourist party is about the only event that
relieves the dull routine of their monotonous lives.

Near Martigny we pass an old dilapidated castle, that,

seven hundred years ago, was the stronghold of Peter of
Savoy, who ruled with an iron hand the people in the
neighboring Cantons.

Now we leave the valley of the Rhone and begin in earnest
the ascent of the mountains.

It is hard to realize that horses and carriage can make their
way over these great towering mountains. Apparently they
are inaccessible as the clouds that float lazily above them.
But we bowl along the hard white road at a rattling pace, and
are soon at an elevation from which the villages in the valley
below look like toy towns. The road is a continuous letter Z,
winding up the side of the mountain, each tack bringing us
higher and higher.

The air is clear and dry, so that at each turn in the road a
wonderful view is afforded. Across the valley are seen well
cultivated farms, with men and women hard at work in the
harvest fields. Further down is a grove, the green foliage
standing out in bold relief from the golden fields of grain
that surround it, while above towers an old ruined church, its
cold, gray color softened and subdued by the ivy that nearly
covers it.

There is an exhilaration as we mount higher and higher.
All thoughts of worldly cares are thrown to the winds and we
revel in the delights of this new and wonderful experience.
We almost envy the Swiss peasant as he cuts the sweet-
smelling grass high up the mountain side. We are tempted
to stop and visit some of these ugly chalets, with their stone-
anchored roofs, which looked like miniature bee-hives from the
valley below. We want to do almost anything to give vent
to the superabundant supply of animal spirits this clear and
bracing air produces.

We were subjected, however, to many grievous disappoint-
ments. We expected the moment we struck the Alps to see
the graceful chamois, leaping from crag to crag, the Alpine
hunter, dressed in knee breeches, with a peaked hat and parti-
colored ribbons wound around his stockings. We kept sharp
lookout for the Swiss maidens with their broad-brimmed hats
and picturesque short dresses, and above all we hungered for a
sight of a Swiss chalet, one of those delightfully beautiful and

picturesque houses, all angles and gables, and things of that nature, which we all have admired at Long Branch and other watering places in America.

We saw no chamois, either leaping from crag to crag, or in any other business. If there are any chamois they manage to keep themselves in very strict seclusion.

There being no chamois, it follows, as a matter of course, that there are no Alpine hunters after them, for the Alpine Swiss don't go about posing in picturesque garments for the benefit of tourists. Not he. He keeps himself busy in his shop, making carvings of wood, which he sells to the tourists, and he isn't picturesque

THE CHAMOIS.

TAKING THE CATTLE TO THE MOUNTAINS.

either. He wears shocking bad clothes, just about the same

33

that poor people wear the world over, and poverty is scarcely ever picturesque.

The smiling Swiss maiden is also a myth. Those we met on the roads were anything but pretty, anything but smiling, and anything but pleasant to look at. They were, as a rule, short, dumpy young ladies, with either bare feet or feet in wooden shoes, carrying enormous loads, their mothers following them, also carrying a heavy load of grass or wood, and she and the mother were generally ornamented with immense goitres which hung down from their necks in particularly disagreeable prominence.

This disease is fearfully prevalent in these mountains, almost every other woman of age having it. I don't remember seeing a man with it, nor a very young woman, but it is almost the rule in some sections, in women of forty and over.

Physicians do not pretend to cure it, and so it hangs and grows, and the neck swells and swells, till the goitre becomes an immense bag.

It is a singular dispensation. Why should it be the exclusive property of women? It doesn't make much difference how a man looks, and the Swiss women, worked to death as they are, have little enough beauty at best, and with all these disadvantages to hang a goitre upon their necks is burdening them a trifle too much. Still, so much do they love their mountains, that they would stay among them if their necks should enlarge to the degree of requiring wheelbarrows to carry them comfortably.

The Swiss chalet is another disappointment. We expected to see the mountains dotted all over with those beautiful houses, all gables and dormer windows, picturesquely painted in all sorts of gay colors, such as we see in the theaters.

Such a house with a pretty peasant girl in short dress, with gay colored stockings, and a simple but very sweet broad straw hat, and a few dozens of chamois leaping from crag to crag, would make a very pretty picture and one worth going a long way to see.

As we were disappointed in the chamois and the maidens, so were we in the Swiss houses. There is everything in them but beauty. They are just about as beautiful as a western grain elevator or a Quaker meeting-house. There is enough timber in them — each stick crossing the other in a most unnecessary way, and there are gables, and dormer windows and all that, but they are put together in a most unsatisfactory way, if beauty is what you are after. They are absolutely shapeless. The roof is burdened with layers of stone to keep it on in the high winds that prevail, and they are invariably weather - beat-en, dingy, and altogether un-satisfactory.

In one end of these un-couth dwel-lings the fami-ly reside, and the work is done, and in the other the cattle are stab-led, in what in America we use as a barn. The cattle, the pigs and the poultry are all stabled con-venient, only a

OUTSIDE THE CHALET.

thin wall separating them from the women and children.

It must be confessed that the residence end of the hideous building is kept very clean, and very nicely, for your Swiss housewife is a good one, but the proximity to the stock would not be considered pleasant in any other country. They cannot plead lack of land for thus crowding together, for these moun-tains are immense, and very sparsely settled. It is so arranged probably for convenience.

Inasmuch as the traveler through Switzerland is always dis-appointed in the matter of chamois, picturesquely clad and pretty girls and Swiss chalets, I insist that the government should furnish them. It is a matter for national action. The government should breed chamois, and train them to skip from crag to crag, it should maintain a force of chamois hunters, such as we see in pictures and at the theater, to hunt them, and it should have pretty girls dressed as we were led to expect to see them, at regular intervals, even if it should import them from Paris, and it should build on each Alpine pass at least a dozen chalets of the regulation style.

Then tourists would be satisfied and invest more liberally

INSIDE THE CHALET.

in wood carvings and music boxes, and would be more content with having got the full worth of their money.

The principal industry on the mountains is cheese, and selling refreshments to travelers. The travelers stop and drink wine every time possible, for the purpose of improving their taste in wines, which affords a very respectable revenue to the inhabitants along the roads.

The cattle in the Spring are driven to the very summits of such of the mountains as are not tipped with snow, in the little valleys of which a very sweet grass is found, which makes a cheese almost as good as the imitations that are produced in various sections of America. The people live upon a tolerably bad cheese, very bad bread, and still worse wine, and when one looks at the almost absolute sterility of the soil, the wonder is how they get enough of that to sustain life.

But they do. It takes very little to sustain a mountain family in this country. The women don't wear gaiters with high heels at ten dollars a pair — wooden shoes, a pair of which lasts for several generations, does them, if indeed they do not go barefooted, which in the Summer is the prevailing fashion. Their clothing is substantial, though very coarse, and if they don't go to theaters or operas, or have any of the expenses of a more luxurious civilization, they get on very well, and seem to be happy. As it is a day's journey down a mountain to a village where there is anything to buy, they don't buy very much; and as their little land furnishes all they can eat, drink and wear, they are just as rich as Rothschild, every bit. It isn't what you want that makes you rich, it is what you don't want. The mountain Swiss don't want anything, and they have it. Therefore they are rich. Their government does n't bother them with taxes to any extent; they don't require daily newspapers or magazines, or anything of that kind, and so they live on the next thing to nothing a long time, and die at the end of it, when they have just as much as anybody.

As quiet and stagnant as is the life of a Swiss family, don't make the mistake of supposing them to be either unintelligent or stupid. They are well educated, and in every one of these ugly houses there are books, and books that are used. They keep themselves posted in everything that is going on in the world outside, their intelligence being a month or such a matter behind the rest of the world, but they get it, and they understand it when they do get it.

A sturdy race they are, and the world knows and appreciates them. There is scarcely a battle-field in Europe upon which they have not bled, and though subjected to the stigma of being hirelings and mercenaries, they have never proved false to the side they hired to. They do not scrutinize the cause they fight for very closely, unless it be their own, but when once enlisted they can be depended upon to the death.

Thousands of them are coming to the United States, and I wish every one of them could be multiplied by a hundred. They make excellent Americans, and we can't have too many of them.

CHAPTER XXXIV.

It is just in the midst of the hay harvest, and men, women and children are all cutting, raking and carrying from the mountain side to the vale below.

All this work is done by hand. There can be no such thing as a team on these mountains — one would as soon think of driving a team up the side of a wall.

The Swiss woman takes an active part in tne duties of the field, and an immense amount of work she is capable of. While the men are cutting the grass, she fills a huge sheet with that which has dried, forming a bundle about eight feet square and two or three feet high. This she balances upon her head and carries it down the steep mountain side to their curiously constructed barns, which have the side of the hill for one end.

Women in this region do the most of the outdoor work, and do every kind. The Swiss maid or matron isn't lolling about parlors or spending her time over her dressing bureau. She plows, or rather digs, for on these steep mountain sides plowing is an impossibility, for so steep are they that should the team be plowing transversely the upper horse would fall and crush his mate on the lower side. They dig up the ground with a heavy mattock, a tool heavier than I would care to wield, and the women are just as expert at it as the men. Muscular parties are these Swiss women, and their lives are anything but easy. In such a country every one must labor to procure the common necessaries of life — men, women and children. It is a good thing, however, to have so much that is kindly in nature as to make a living sure if those wanting the living are willing to work for it.

Tibbitts observed these stout, sturdy women as they came zig-zagging down the mountain, carrying these enormous burdens as patiently as mules and quite as surely. There was

AN ALPINE HOMESTEAD.

a lapse of five minutes, during which time he never spoke a word, which was something so unusual as to cause remark.

"I was thinking," said Tibbitts, "that could polygamy be

introduced into Switzerland, I should emigrate to this country and become a William Tell. I should secure a large tract of this land and go into a general marrying business. I should

"I SHOULD WAKE THEM UP CHEERILY WITH AN ALPINE HORN."

take to my bosom say fifty of these maidens — nay I would n't object to widows, not even those with goitres, for I have noticed that the goitre, no matter how large, does not interfere with an elderly woman's capacity for carrying hay down the mountain. Indeed, a goitre, skillfully managed, may be helpful. For if arranged so as to hang on the upper side of the woman it would assist materially in preserving her equilibrium. With fifty of these wives the labor problem is solved. I should wake them up early in the morning cheerily with an Alpine horn (after taking one myself), and after the frugal meal of black bread and cheese, I should have them skip merrily up the mountains and cut the sweet smelling grass, and rake it and turn it, like so many Maud Mullers, and tie it up in bundles and carry it down to the modest chalet, where I would be to see that other wives stored it safely away for use in the long Alpine Winter.

"I should at once purchase cows, with the dowry of my fifty wives, and establish a cheese factory, making the fragrant Limberger for the Germans in America, and the smooth Neuchatel for more delicate appetites, and all the other varieties. To carry on the business successfully would take me much to Geneva, and, in pursuit of a better market, to Paris, where, as the proprietors of the Jardin Mabille are large consumers of the products of the Swiss dairies, I should be thrown largely into society that would prevent life from becoming too monotonous.

"And while I was away, my fifty wives would rise early in the gladsome morn and labor cheerily, singing the while the simple carols of their native mountains till dewy eve, and sleep sweetly, gaining strength for a larger day's work on the morrow.

"There is some sense in marrying a Swiss woman, for she can do something toward supporting you. An American woman expects to be supported; she expects to have luxurious surroundings, and all that sort of thing, which the man labors for. I like this scheme the best. But, unfortunately, one is not sufficient to support a man, and, as polygamy is unlawful, I shall not marry in Switzerland. One could not be made useful, and when I marry for ornament, I shall require something more ornamental."

And Tibbitts relapsed into moody silence, disgusted with life because the Swiss government would not permit him to marry enough women to insure him a comfortable living.

At Geneva we took a courier. A courier is a man who professes to speak seven languages, but in reality speaks one well, generally the German, and two, English and French, very badly. He is invariably the champion liar of the universe. There isn't a lying club on the Pacific coast of which the humblest and most recent courier would not at once be unanimously elected perpetual president. He lies, not from necessity growing out of his situation, but because to him it is a luxury. He revels in it, and is never so happy in it as when he has accomplished a gorgeous lie — one of those picturesque lies that the listener is compelled to accept, though he knows it to be false.

He approaches a lie with the feverish anxiety that always accompanies an expected pleasure ; rapturizes over the performance, and is unhappy till he can bring forth another. He has been in all countries; he has been in the service of every notable on earth, from the Shah of Persia down; and he is with you at the absurd price of forty-five dollars a month only, because he has to wait a month for a Russian Prince, who would never take a step without him.

You feel from the beginning that you are under obligations to this gorgeous being ; you are ashamed of yourself when you hand him the miserable pittance he condescends to accept for his services; and you would no more think of asking him to account for any moneys put into his hands than you would of offering a tip to the Queen of England.

The courier is a man who professes to know all the hotels, all the roads, all the manners and customs, everything of the country through which you pass; and he takes charge of a party for a stipulated price per month, pledging himself to use his wonderful gifts entirely for your benefit.

At the beginning, while you are engaging him, he warns you that to travel through any country is to expose yourself to swindles, and extortions and impositions of all kinds, from an exorbitant hotel bill up the whole gamut to the swindle in works of art — the only protection against which is a good courier.

"Am I dot man? I vill not say. But ask the Prince Petrowski, the Duke of Magenta, the Earl of Strathcommon. Dose are my references."

These personages being a long way off, you don't ask them at all; but you engage him and flatter yourself that from this time on your pocket is safe and your comfort is assured.

The courier is your servant for one day, and your master all the rest of the time he is with you.

The second day he comes to you with a smile.

" I have you feexed goot. Dot rascal landlord knows me, and he vouldn't dare try a schwindle mit any barty oof mine."

" What do you pay for the rooms?"

" Ten francs — only ten francs!"

"But we had better rooms day before yesterday for six!"

"Not in dees blace. Het you pin alone you would hef baid feefteen."

This was all a lie. The courier is known to all the land-lords, and the landlords allow him a very snug commission on all parties he brings into their sheep fold to be sheared.

This matter of commission goes into everything you touch. Your courier will not permit you to purchase anything without him — he places himself between you and everything, from a picture to a tooth pick. He buys for you, the goods are sent to your hotel, you give the courier the money to pay it, which he does, bringing back a receipt for the money which he has really paid, less the commission, all of which was added to the price of the goods at the beginning.

In order that you may not escape him in material things, he reduces you to abject helplessness in things not material. He bears down upon you in such a way that you comprehend the fact that you can do nothing without him. For instance, you see a beautiful spring by the roadside; the water as pure and sweet as water can be, which actually invites you to drink. Now, should you ask the courier if that is good water, he doubtless would say yes; but should you spring from the carriage and attempt to drink without permission, he jumps also and holds you back.

" Dot vater ees boison," he says. "I vill show you de vater vot you may trink mit safety."

Likewise in the matter of wines. At one resting place on the mountains, Tibbitts was ferocious for a bottle of the delightful white wine you get everywhere, and called for a bottle without consulting the courier. Promptly the man countermanded the order.

"Mr. Teebbeets, de vine here ish pat mit de stomach. Ve vell vait till ve get to de next blace."

Tibbitts was furious, for he was arid.

"Look here, my friend," he said, "I am not carrying your stomach around with me. The one I am endangering I have had a proprietary interest in for twenty-six years, and if I don't know its capacity, its powers of endurance, and all that, I don't know who does. You take care of your stomach and let mine alone. *Mademoiselle, apportez moi* ze — that is — d — n it — *botteille* — bottle — *du vin* — that is, fetch back that bottle and be mighty quick about it."

And a minute later he was pouring it out, and as he swallowed it, he remarked to himself, "Injure the stomach, indeed! A man who has swallowed enough sod-corn whisky in Oshkosh to float the Great Eastern, to be afraid of this thin drink. If it were aquafortis now —"

The courier was mortally offended, and sulked all the afternoon. If Tibbitts could order a bottle of wine without his permission, he might possibly buy a Swiss carving in Chamonix when we arrived there, without consulting him, and then where would be the commission?

After the rest and the wine, and the bad bread and the tolerably bad cheese, we proceeded on our journey. From that time on it was a succession of wonderful views, a panorama sometimes beautiful, sometimes awesome, sometimes soothing, and sometimes frightful. But no matter which it was, it was never insipid. There was a positive character to each view, something that you must observe, whether or no, and something that seen left an impression that many years will not efface.

The Pass Tête Noir is an experience that will last a life time.

We made a sharp turn in the road at one point, and a view burst upon us that was worth a journey across the Atlantic to see. We were hanging over a chasm full six thousand feet deep — that is, to the first impediment to a full and satisfactory fall. Should you go down that six thousand feet you would

strike upon a ledge and bound off a number of thousand feet
more before you finally came to the bottom. Across this
yawning gulf was a mountain, the twin of the one on whose

ON THE ROAD TO CHAMONIX.

sides we were hanging, covered with evergreen trees to a
certain way up to the top, which was crowned with the pure

white of the eternal snow and ice. There were a thousand shades of color as the eye commenced at the level we were on and traveled up to the top, all brought out gloriously by the sunlight of noon-day.

One of the party took in the whole view and very properly went into a rapture.

"Is there anything under heaven so magnificent as this combination of colors!" she exclaimed, holding her breath in an ecstacy.

Then up spoke the faro bankeress as she took it all in at a glance:

"What a dress it would make, could one only have them colors brought out in silk!"

The scenery, always grand and imposing, changes with every bend in the road, and always gives a view better than the preceding one. We are now at an altitude where the fragrant spruce lines the narrow roadway, and covers the hillside with everlasting green. Way over there, where the cold gray of the rocks is hidden under a mantle of green, on which the sun and clouds make ever-changing pictures, is a bright, flashing stream, dancing and sparkling in the sunlight, as it falls tumultuously from rock to rock, now losing itself in a chasm hundreds of feet deep, then springing out again further down, until at length it worries and frets itself over the crags and cliffs till it reaches the valley, and flows tranquilly and smoothly along to the lake. It typifies life, with its early struggles, its constant striving for the rest and quiet that comes at last.

Now we approach the summit of the mountains. All around, as far as the eye can reach, is nothing but a series of rough, jagged crags, the peaks of the irregular range of mountains. Not the forest-covered hills we have been riding through, but vast piles of everlasting snow, which even the fierce and angry sun is unable to make any impression upon.

But we were not permitted to take all the enjoyment possible out of the wondrous views. There never was a party that did not have a professor in it, who knows all about everything, and who considers it his mission to instruct everybody else. Add to this, a courier who knows all the stock show points, professionally, and life becomes a burden. Some peak would come to our view higher and grander than any we had encountered. And then the courier:

"Ladies unt shentlemen, dot ish —"

The Professor, who had charge of Tibbitts:

"Lemuel, particularly note that mountain peak. It is —"

"Of course it is," said Tibbitts "What am I here for, anyhow? What did I sail across the Atlantic, and come to Switzerland for? Why do you and that other weazened monkey interrupt me when I am contemplating nature, by calling my attention to it, and asking me to note it? Havn't I got eyes? Don't I know the difference between a Western prairie and an Alpine peak? And as for the names of the places, havn't I got a guide book, and can't I read? Am I a baby in my A B Abs? Curious you can't let a fellow alone."

The faro bankeress was asleep, she had been for many miles, and her husband was asking her why they charged a franc for a little bit of ice, at the last hotel, when the mountains were all covered with it.

The road, which, up to this time, had been comparatively pleasant, now assumed a more dangerous look to those who have only known wide paved streets. It winds along the very edge of precipices, where a single balk would send us all tumbling down three or four thousand feet. At places it is cut out of the side of the hill, so that on one side there is a solid wall of rock rising high above our heads, while on the other is a sheer descent of thousands of feet. As we rattle around the sharp curves there is an involuntary clutching at the seats, for it seems certain that the carriage cannot keep the road. But the Swiss voiturier is an expert driver, and his horses are sure footed, so there is not the slightest danger, perilous though it may seem.

After a brief rest at the summit, the brakes are put on, one of the three horses is taken from the front, and down we go on the other side of the mountain it took us all day to ascend.

If the journey so far was attended with any danger, fancied or real, the fact was driven out of our minds by the nature of the road we were descending. It was frightful. From the carriage we could look down into a valley miles and miles away, and the road was so narrow that the slightest slip would have sent us into that valley in short order. The view was grand, but the ride was fearful. We were all charmed when we reached the valley and were enabled to look up at the dizzy heights that had given us such a scare.

From this on to the hotel at Tête Noir, there was a constant succession of tunnels, high bridges over deep crevasses, and sharp curves around jutting crags that almost blocked the road.

At the "half-way house," as it is called, the view is beautiful; three or four waterfalls tumbling down the mountain sides, and falling into the mad stream that goes careering wildly over the rocks and bowlders.

Then another long ride through a rough and barren country, indicating the approach to the glacier region, and then at a sudden turn in the road, Mont Blanc looms up high above the great peaks by which it is surrounded. We speed rapidly over the floor-like road, and at six o'clock in the evening, after having been on the road since seven in the morning, we are in Chamonix, the little village at the foot of Mt. Blanc, that lives entirely on tourists.

Of course the great point of interest is Mt. Blanc, the highest point of the central chain of the Swiss and Italian High Alps.

There it is—fifteen thousand seven hundred and thirty-one feet high, covered with a great mass of ice and snow that has been accumulating for ages.

There stands the patriarch of the Alps, crowned with the centuries, and still smiling grimly at Time.

It stands alone in its fearful beauty. Of all the European mountains, it impresses the mind with the power of the forces, the source of which are hidden to man, and which it is not given to man to comprehend. One feels his own insignificance as he gazes on this wonderful peak, and, no matter what his creed, feels a profound reverence for whatever power he believes created it.

Around it are other peaks that elsewhere would be considered very high, but compared with this giant they are pigmies. Mt. Blanc is not to be described. Descriptions and pictures can convey no idea of it. One must stand under the shadow of that eternal snow, must feel the presence of the grand old mountain, to fully appreciate it.

From the streets of Chamonix the sides seem to be as smooth as a frozen pond, as the sun glistens on the ice and snow; but viewed through the powerful telescope great crags are seen. Wide chasms, no one knows how deep, yawn on every side. Blank, inaccessible walls shoot straight up in the air, hundreds of feet. There are impassible glaciers and great gullies where, centuries ago, a great landslide occurred. All this can be seen through the telescope, but not till one attempts the ascent can he realize the nature of Mt. Blanc's formation. Then he finds his path beset with dangers he never dreamed of. He sees the glaciers, which by the glass seemed only rough places, are full of deep crevices hundreds of feet wide. He hears the rumbling of wild streams of water far down in the ice, as they swirl and swish round and round in the cavities formed by the everlasting action of the water against the flinty ice. He comes upon solid mountains of ice, around or over which it is next to impossible to go. He finds bridges of ice, where one misstep would launch him down a crevice, so far that his body could never be recovered. In short, he finds that Mt. Blanc is only smooth and safe and pleasant when seen at a distance through a telescope.

34

CHAPTER XXXV.

GOING UP THE MOUNTAIN.

I CANNOT see why any one should desire to ascend Mt. Blanc It is a trip of great danger, is very fatiguing, and, it is said, even when the summit is reached the view is unsatisfactory, on account of the great distance from all objects save the jagged peaks of the big mountain. Yet there are quite a number of ascents made every year.

Why? Because the innocents who do it dearly love to start out, the males with their knee breeches and horrible spiked

THE PRESUMED CHAMOIS HUNTER.

shoes, and the females with their hideous dresses, and after the ascent is either made, or not made, it is a pleasant thing to be photographed in groups in these costumes. Thousands of these photographs are taken, for home consumption.

Everybody likes to be photographed in the act of doing what they can't do. The stupid man who never looks into a book always wants to be taken with one elbow upon a pile of books, and his fore finger thoughtfully upon his forehead, as though he were devising a plan for the payment of the national debt; the young sprout who buys a double-barreled shot-gun, which is destined never to take animal life, always rushes to be photographed in complete sporting costume, shot-gun, game-bag, dog and all; and where was there ever a militia officer who did not want to be photographed in full uniform, as though he had served with credit through the great rebellion?

So these Alpine climbers, these Mt. Blanc ascenders, would no more leave Chamounix without being photographed in costume than they would leave their letters of credit behind them.

Photography is an unconscious liar. It is as unreliable as history.

Mt. Blanc was first ascended in 1786; then in 1787; again in 1825. Since then the trip has been made several times, two ladies, even, having gone to the very summit.

The guides and souvenir dealers in Chamonix are full of stories of the dangers incurred in making the trip. They say that some forty or fifty years ago a couple of guides made a misstep, and were hurled down a chasm. An attempt was made to recover the bodies but without success. They were never found as a whole. Some thirty or forty years afterward, portions of their clothing, with a few bones, were found in a glacier, having been gradually worked from the place they were killed, by the slow but continual motion of the ice. They didn't show us the shoes nor the bones, so we did not feel obliged to believe the story.

Accidents! There have been enough of them to deter any sane man or woman from attempting the perilous ascent. The scientists who ascend these dizzy heights, which a goat hardly dares essay, may be excused, for the real scientist is bound by his profession to risk his life any time to establish or demolish

a theory, but there can be no excuse for the mere sight seer to
attempt it.   Some years ago four English clergymen attempted

THE FATE OF TWO ENGLISHMEN.

the ascent.   When near the top, toiling up a precipice of ice,
the rope to which they were attached broke, and two of them

slid down the smooth descent to a precipice, and plunged into a chasm thousands upon thousands of feet deep, and were never more seen. In these ascents every care must be used, for every step is only one step from death. A fall of three thousand feet may be an easy way to die, provided one wants to die, but people are not, as a rule, anxious for so sudden a parting with things sublunary. Imagine the feelings of a man in the instant after the rope breaks and he feels himself nearing the chasm, with nothing on earth to save him!

It is now a well established fact that these immense glaciers,

A FREQUENT ACCIDENT.

between ten and twenty miles long, and from one to three miles wide, and oftentimes five hundred feet thick, are continually moving, though of course very slowly, averaging from one hundred to as high as five hundred feet per annum. The Mer de Glace, near Chamonix, which is twelve miles long and nearly a mile wide, is said to have moved a foot a day during the past year.

This glacier, the Mer de Glace, is one of the most beautiful of the four hundred that are to be found in the Alps near Mt.

Blanc. De Saussure, the Genevese naturalist, speaking of its surface, said that it "resembles a sea suddenly frozen, not during a tempest, but when the wind has subsided, and the waves, although still high, have become blunted and rounded. These great waves are intersected by transverse crevasses, the interior of which appears blue, while the ice is white on the surface."

The journey from Chamonix to Montavert, where the best

view on the "Sea of Ice" can be had, is very tiresome, and not unattended with danger, but the sight is well worth the time and trouble. Twelve miles of solid ice in the most fantastic shapes, "a sea suddenly frozen," is a sight never to be forgotten.

A very little mountain climbing goes a great way. We tried

THE MER DE GLACE.

it and know whereof we speak. The courier was to blame for it.

Couriers make men do more foolish things than any other agency in the world. We had been out to visit a gorge some six or seven miles from Chamonix, and had been delighted with the ravine, with its foaming stream tearing along way down the valley. We had walked for an hour or more on a rickety old foot-bridge, hundreds of feet above the bottom of the gorge, we had crept along wooden galleries fastened to the sides of the precipices, the tops of which were well-nigh out of sight, and the bottoms scarcely discernable. Galleries that creaked and shook, and swayed under our weight, secured to the rocks with rusty irons, renewed no one knew when, and suggesting at every step the probability of giving way, and

A SLIP TOWARDS THE EDGE.

letting you down thousands of feet upon jagged rocks, and bounding from one to another till your corpse finally struck water, a torrent as wild and uncontrollable as Niagara. The gallery did not go down and we had gone to the end and admired the waterfall, and then on our way back to Chamonix that courier insisted upon our going up the Glacier des Bossons.

In vain we demurred, and told him we could see the Glacier from the road quite well enough. He insisted. It was an easy path clear up, and the view was something marvelous. Our whole visit to Europe would be a failure if we missed this view.

There was no help for it and we went. The ladies were provided with mules, while the gentlemen, under the guidance of the courier, struck out across lots.

For the first quarter of an hour it was all right. There was a good path, and the hill was not very steep. We crossed a number of little brooks that had their source in the glaciers above, and emptied into the Arve in the valley below. The woods through which we passed were huge pine trees, among which the narrow path wound its tortuous course. Occasionally there would be a little clearing and then we could get a glimpse of the valley and the mountains towering high above us.

The higher we ascended the more precipitous became the path.

CREVASSES.

We found huge bowlders obstructing our way, and soon had to begin climbing in real earnest, oftentimes using both hands and feet. At length we reached a narrow ledge that led directly to the little house at the foot of the glacier, whither we were going. This ledge was like a backbone, with only a tiny path two or three feet wide. On the right, was a sharp descent of several hundred feet to the woods through which we passed. Beyond these woods could be seen bright spots of green and yellow, where harvesting was in progress. Further down was the Chamonix valley, its broad acres divided by the silvery Arve, that starts from the Mer de Glace, and empties into the Rhone, just below Geneva.

On the left there is a descent of some five or six hundred feet to the ice crags of the glacier. It requires steady nerves and a sure foot to walk along this dizzy path, for a stumble or fall would be attended with fatal results.

And right here was where the infernal persistency of the courier got in its worst work. One of the party was a gentleman of full habit, who weighs, perhaps, two hundred and twenty-five pounds, one of that kind whose head becomes dizzy when at any elevation, who hardly dares to look out of a third-story window, one of those who have an almost uncontrollable desire to spring off any elevation they may be so unfortunate as to be placed upon. He came panting like a second Falstaff to this narrow ledge, the edge of which was not more than three feet wide, and the descent on either side was hundreds of feet. It was a place that nothing but a goat or a born Alpine climber should ever think of essaying, and here was a fleshy party, with a dizzy head, never sure-footed in anything but his morals, with an impulse to jump down a chasm, either to the right or to the left!

THE MORAINE.

He did not desire to jump, he could not go forward, and to go backward was just as impossible. He thought of his pleasant home across the Atlantic, he thought of his wife and family, his creditors, and all who had an interest in him, and shut his eyes and sat down, clinging desperately to the few bushes that were within reach.

Another of the party, who had skipped very like a goat over the ridge, and had gained the porch of the little tavern, saw his danger, and called the courier. The party were all amused at the predicament of the fleshy man except the fleshy man himself. To him it was no joke. He was anchored in the fix described by the colored clergyman. "On de one side, bredern, is perdition, and on de oder damnation."

But the courier, good for something, acted promptly. He seized a loaf of bread and a bottle of wine, and rushed down the path. He bade the victim of an attempt to do something he couldn't do, to eat of the loaf and drink all he could of

THE DILEMMA—WHICH SIDE TO FALL.

wine (which he did, especially the latter), shut his eyes, grab his hand, and run; adding cheerfully:—

"Geep your eysh shut dight—oof yoo opens dem at all yoo are gone—and run mit me."

In this way the poor man was brought to the little tavern, where he sat in gloomy silence while the rest of the party essayed the glacier.

I may add here that he made the descent safely. There is another path, a mile or two longer, but entirely safe. He didn't mind the mile or two.

The Glacier des Bossons, while not so imposing as the Mer de Glace, has a great many wonderful points. Here at the beginning of this dangerous ledge is one of the best places to study it. The surface, rough and jagged, with sharp peaks and crags from three to twenty feet high, is partially covered with slate, rocks and debris, while beneath this, bright and sparkling, is the pure, solid ice, with its greenish-blue tint.

Just opposite us, resting on the ice, is an immense bowlder that must weigh at least twenty tons, while all about are smaller stones, varying in weight from one hundred pounds to four or five tons. These immense stones became detached from the mountain, ages ago, by the continued pressure of the solid ice, expanded by the heat and contracted again by the cold, and have grad-

ROCKS POLISHED BY OLD GLACIERS.

ually been carried down the mountain on the bosom of this imperceptibly moving field of ice.

The warm sun, which beats down upon us with terrible effect, gradually melts exposed portions of the snow and ice, and tiny rivulets are seen trickling along in the crevasses and depressions. They come together at the foot of the glacier, and, after a fall of about sixty feet, they wander off down the woods to join the Arve.

As we stand there enjoying the beautiful view down the Chamonix Valley, the courier breaks in and says it is time to go on. Day dreaming is over, and, with no kindly feelings toward him, we push on up the steep and narrow ledge.

At the Pavilion, a little one-story house, we obtained a fine view of the glacier. We also obtained some fine wine and bread. At this height the air is so rarified that a little wine is all that one can drink. But after the long, hard walk through the intense heat, it is very refreshing, and revives one's drooping spirits wonderfully.

Leaving the Pavilion, a narrow foot-path, cut out of the side of the mountain, leads to a long flight of steps, at the bottom of which we reach the ice. There a long scramble over its slippery surface, to the entrance of the cavern. Imagine a solid wall of clear, transparent ice. Into this by means of picks and spades a cave eighty-five yards long, eight feet wide and seven feet high has been dug. As you go in, the little lights flickering along the side seem to say, "Who enters here leaves hope behind." But we push on through the dripping water at the entrance, and finally find ourselves walking on ice that is hard and dry, while the atmosphere is cold enough to make an overcoat comfortable.

From the end of the cavern the view is like a glimpse of fairyland. Away down the dimly lighted tunnel, the tiny lights reflected against the crystalline blue, can be seen the smooth surface of the ice, gradually growing bluer and bluer until, at the very entrance, where the sunlight pours down upon it, it becomes nearly transparent, forming a dazzling frame to the bright picture of the glacier, the forest-covered mountain and brilliant sky beyond.

As we are about to emerge from the cavern the guide shows us a hole in the side, where we can see, some distance off, a subterranean stream, that has forced a channel through the ice. Here we can hear most distinctly the glacier mills in full operation. There is one, very large, near this spot, said to be sixteen hundred feet deep. It was formed by the action of huge stones moved by the water against the ice, making, during the ages the glacier has been in existence, a deep round well in the ice. This low, rumbling noise we hear is the water rushing into that well with terrific force, and working the stones against its sides.

But we are aweary of mountain climbing and glacier exploring, and it is with a sigh of relief that we retrace our steps, take another glass of wine at the Pavilion, and, after a short rest, descend the mountain by an easy path. A short drive, and we are in Chamonix, some of the party telling marvelous stories of our hair-breadth escapes during our perilous ascent of Mt. Blanc. Of course they didn't go up Mt. Blanc, but the glacier gave them all the experience in mountain climbing they wanted. It satisfied them just as well as though they had scaled the great peak.

As a matter of course all these people purchased Alpenstocks, which they had marked "Mt. Blanc, July 22, 1861," and were all photographed in Alpine climbing costume, which the enterprising photographer leases you for a consideration.

And these photographs went home with the Alpenstocks, and are to-day being displayed upon center-tables and in albums, while the fraudulent Alpenstock has the post of honor in libraries.

Also we did n't see any chamois, nor any chamois hunters, nor any sweet Swiss maidens in picturesque costumes. Like the fever and ague in the West, "there ain't none of it here, but there's any quantity of it over in the next county."

That evening, in the hotel, Tibbitts became indignant. He noticed for the first time that the sheets and pillow cases on his bed were marked with the name of the hotel in indelible ink.

"What is this for?" he demanded.

"To keep guests of the house from carrying them off, I suppose."

"Then the prevailing impression is that everybody in the world is a thief? The idea is that I, Tibbitts, am going to snake off these sheets and cram them in my valise and tote them all over the continent, and finally take them to Oshkosh for my mother's use!

"It is my opinion, and I say it deliberately, that the vices of one-half of mankind keep the other half of mankind busy. It is the wickedness of man that makes courts necessary, and sheriffs and policemen, and all that sort of thing. But for vice we could dispense with nine-tenths of the churches and ministry, and we could let up on standing armies. All the locksmiths and the time wasted upon marking these sheets and pillow cases could have been devoted to the multiplication of the wealth of the world. Think of the number of hotels in the world, and the number of sheets and pillow cases in them, and the quantity of indelible ink and the time spent in using it, just to keep them from being stolen! The grand aggregate is appalling. And then add to that all the rest of the precautions, and mighty expensive they are, that have to be taken to keep the property you have, and it amounts to the absorption of fully a half of the industry of the world.

"I have made up my mind what I am going to do. I am going home, and shall immediately organize societies for the promotion of common honesty. I shall have to pay for the marking of these sheets and pillow-cases in my bill to-morrow. In self-defense these societies must be organized, and this sort of thing done away. Had the time employed in marking these sheets been used in making cheese, we should not have to pay such prices for it in America. Vice is an expensive luxury — it eats two ways; it consumes the time of the vicer, and the time of another man to watch him. It must be crushed out!"

And Tibbitts went to bed full of projects for the suppression of vice and for the eventual universality of virtue.

We had at the hotel, of course, the everlasting talker — that man is ubiquitous, and as frequent as sin. The class was represented with us by a commission merchant from Milwaukee.

One evening the discussion happened to turn upon the tariff question, and overflowing its banks, as conversation always does, meandered off into a variety of channels.

One gentleman asked Jones, the Milwaukee man, why wheat could be manufactured into flour at Minneapolis, and not at points further East.

And this question set Jones running, and he answered:

"That question is easily answered. I'll illustrate it. You know Filkins & Beaver, of Buffalo? No? I have always known 'em — ever since I have been in the business. I have sold 'em many a thousand bushel of wheat since I have been in Milwaukee, and many a thousand barrel of flour for 'em when I was in Toronto. Ef there is anything about wheat and flour that they don't know, you just want to go and tell 'em, you do, and they are the whitest men in the business. They have been longer in it than any two men livin'. They have the immense Eagle mill in Buffalo, and the Excelsior in Lockport, down on the second dock, the best water-power in Lockport, and that's saying a good deal, for the fall there is immense — it is the water-power that has made Lockport. Take that away and there wouldn't be anything of that city at all, and the people there are enterprising enough to use it, they are. Filkins & Beaver, take all their mills together, must flour one hundred thousand bushels of wheat a day, and that's no small business, and don't you forget it. It takes good heads to run such a business, y' bet yer. They know me mighty well, I tell ye, for I have done business with 'em for nigh onto thirty years, and every time I go to Buffalo, and I have to go there once a month, I have to stop with either one or the other of 'em. They wouldn't any more let me go to a hotel than they'd let me sleep on·the street.

"Both of 'em came from the same village in England and both went back and married the girls they were engaged to afore they left, and then brought 'em to Buffalo, and settled down to work. They worked themselves, they did, y' bet yer. First they bought the little Eagle mill, that hadn't only two run of stone, and they did the whole work with their own hands, they made a great deal of money for they were close operators, and kept the run of the markets, and they enlarged the Eagle till it kivered all the ground they had, and then they built the Continental, and that was too small for 'em, and then they went to Lockport and bought a water-power there, and built the Excelsior, and another one at Wellsville, and I don't know where all.

In glided the Young Man who Knows Everything,

as chirpy as possible, and he broke into Jones' narration without as much as saying "by your leave."

"Jones, there's no use in trying it. You can't cover up bad actions with loud professions. You can't smother the scent of a skunk by singing 'Old Hundred.'"

"What in blazes has bad actions and skunks to do with —"

He might as well have talked to an Atlantic gale. The young man ambled off serenely and attacked another party with the same cheerfulness with which he assailed Jones, who resumed his narrative:

"As I was saying when that blasted — well, then they bought a propeller, the old Ada, and they paid for it in cash. They always pay cash for everything. There ain't none of their paper afloat, and they have the prettiest bank balance of any concern in Buffalo.

"I always have a good time with 'em, no matter which I stay with. Sometimes I go to Filkins' and sometimes to Beaver's. Filkins' wife is a rather high-falutin sort of a woman, and when Filkins got rich she made him go and buy a lot on Eagle street — no cheap lot, bet yer — one hundred feet front, and the Lord knows how deep, and she made him build the best house on it there is in Buffalo. She has conservatories, and a carriage, and velvet carpets, pianos, and bath rooms, and silver, and everything bang up, and when they dine the old man has to sit down in a dress coat, with a nigger behind him. Oh, it's nifty, y' bet yer.

"But old Beaver he'd never do anything of the kind. He stuck to the little frame cottage he built for himself down on Swan street, and he sets down to his dinner in his shirt sleeves, and eats off'n stone ware, and has no wines like Filkins, and swears he wouldn't trade his toby of ale for all the wines that ever were imported. And his wife only keeps one hired gal, and does the heft of the work about the house herself. You kin see her any time with her sleeves rolled up and her apern on, bustlin' about in jist the same old way, and they have their friends on Sunday to take pot-luck with 'em, and I ain't sure after all but that Beaver is right. He swears he will never build a new house till he has thirty grand-children, and then only one jist large enough to accommodate and hold 'em all at one table Christmas day. He laughs at Filkins with his fine airs, though they are the best friends in the world. You could n't get a word of difference between 'em for any one of their mills, or for all of 'em together.

"I remember in 1865 I was in Buffalo, and one of their propellers — it was the Jeannette, I believe — no, it was the Ariel, had just —"

One by one the party had slipped out of the smoking-room at the beginning of the new chapter of the experience of Filkins & Beaver, the termination of which no man could foretell. I took advantage of his raising his glass to his lips to get away myself. I presume he finished the story to the waiter, for the next day when I casually remarked that Jones was coming he looked frightened, and quietly slipped out of the room.

But no one of the party ever learned why wheat could not be advantageously floured east of Minneapolis.

33

CHAPTER XXXVI.

The scenery from Chamonix to Geneva, by the way of Sallanches, St. Martin, Cluses and Bonneville is magnificent. Leaving Chamonix the road winds down the beautiful valley with the Glacier des Bossons, overshadowed by Mont Blanc, on the right, while on the left are the pretty hamlets and fruit-ful farms that relieve the barren, rugged mountains on either side.

The road, which is a marvel of smoothness, as are all the roads in Switzerland, crosses and recrosses the river Arve, until, after passing through a long tunnel, hewn through a massive rock, it strikes another valley and makes a wide sweep around the horseshoe-shaped mountain, giving a splendid view up and down the valley. Far across this valley is a long high range of mountains down which at different places great cata-racts of water come tumbling, dashing the spray high in air.

Here we pass through the pretty village of St. Gervais, with its celebrated baths. Then a long straight drive for an hour or more, and with an extra crack of the whip the carriage whirls into Sallanches, where the horses are changed, while the weary, hot and dusty travelers rest and refresh themselves.

At St. Gervais is one celebrated bathing establishment con-ducted by an Englishman and patronized almost entirely by English and Americans, the principal treatment being for rheu-matism and kindred diseases, and especially for the alcoholic habit. It is claimed that the most inveterate drunkard can be cured by the use of these waters, and therefore it is continually full of men who have burned life's candle at both ends, and who need rest from their vices, and moral, as well as physical recuperation.

Tibbitts determined to stay a week and test the efficacy of the waters.

"I should n't need it if I could have the regular Oshkosh sod-corn, but a foundation of vile English brandy, and the edifice built up and topped off with French cognac is too much for me. I will test the waters."

The fact that a half-dozen very wild Americans of his own age and tastes were at the establishment was really what induced him to stay, but he repeated over and again, that what he wanted was to stay a while in a place where rum was impossible. He wanted to get away from it.

We left him, and the next week I received a letter, the following being an extract therefrom:—

"I did not go over to the Cure at once, for the day you left I met a young American, troubled as I was, who decided to go with me. Slosson (he is from St. Louis) and I, having met the proprietor of the Cure and taken a fancy to him, determined to do him a good turn, and to that end we would not go to his establishment till we had got ourselves into a condition that would make a cure creditable. I am always ready to make sacrifices for those I love.

"We then went over to the establishment to get out of the way of rum.

"We had been in the house perhaps five minutes, when the proprietor took us one side and remarked, casually, that while he would not advise any one in the establishment to drink, if one must, he could furnish much better liquor than could be had in the village. And it was injurious to those taking the baths to walk much either before or after.

"It is a good thing to get out of the way of rum.

"The bar man was an American who could mix a cocktail, and so we drank to the old flag and went to our dinner. The wine at the place is excellent.

"After dinner we walked up to the village with an American to whom I was introduced, and he took us to a very comfortable place where the cognac was good, very good, and we sampled it several times.

"If there is a place on earth where the alcohol appetite can be cured it is here.

"On the way down the main street of the village we stopped in another place like the first one, for the purpose of seeing whether there was any difference in cognac.

"There are superior facilities for getting away from rum at this place.

"There is a museum in the village which has a smoking room attached, which we visited that evening. The cognac was better than at the first place.

"To have the vile stuff out of reach is a great help to the struggling victim of strong drink.

"What we would call a drug store in America was the next place we visited, to have some prescriptions filled, and the proprietor, an English-

THE PATH TO THE VILLAGE.

man, insisted upon our tasting some very old brandy he kept for medicinal purposes.

"There is no place in the world where you are so safe from the destroyer as here.

" Returning to the Cure we thought it unfair not to patronize it. We did — twice.

" St. Gervais offers inducements for those really trying to reform.

" We went to our room and sat down to a quiet game of poker. It was suggested that it would be dry work, and a bottle of cognac was ordered, and if I remember, there wasn't enough left to make a cocktail for a flea. The very smell was gone.

"For absolute absence of temptation to drink, St. Gervais is the place. I will write you concerning the water when I have tasted some.

"P. S.—I forgot to mention that another thing you come here for is to get regular sleep, and plenty of it, in the early part of the night. Having resolved upon this, we played poker till three in the morning.

" If you have a friend who desires to reform, by all means advise him to come to St. Gervais. There is no such place on the continent for reform. A man in the next room, with acute inflammatory rheumatism, actually complained of us this morning. He said he couldn't sleep with us near him. We sent word to him that there were other hotels, but that we couldn't peril our chances of reform by moving. We were determined to persevere till we had made new men of ourselves. We were very positive, and would not move.

"We could hear the rheumatic gentleman swear, through the wall, but we sat there reforming all the same, and smiling at his irascibility. Why will such men come to places intended as reformatories ? What is a man with rheumatism, inflammatory or otherwise, to five men trying to mend their ways ? I think we played an hour longer than we would, for the pleasure of hearing him profane.

" St. Gervais is a good place to come to to get away from rum, but it is of no account for rheumatism. This man thought so, for he left the house in the morning. I will write you about the baths to-morrow. I have no doubt they are good. It is said they do away with the rum appetite."

From Sallanches the road is through a most beautiful country. As we approach St. Martin the carriage is stopped, so that we can have one last look at the dazzling peaks of Mt. Blanc. They are at the very head of the valley, and although twelve miles away, in a straight line, they loom up so magnificently that they seem only a short distance from where we stand. It is a sight never to be forgotten.

The valley now assumes a more barren appearance, with but little to interest one. An occasional waterfall, a handsome hedge or two, relieves the dull monotony of the ride, till Bonneville, a picturesque town, the capital of the province, is reached. There we have dinner, and then on towards Geneva, passing the two ruined towers of the ancient castle of Fancingny, after which the province was named. Crossing the long substantial bridge of the Foron river, we come to Anne-masse, and then rush through a number of pretty little villages, reaching the suburbs of Geneva, and, after having been on the

MONT BLANC AND THE VALLEY OF CHAMONIX FROM SALLANCHES.

road since seven o'clock, finally draw up at the hotel on the lake, a thoroughly tired, hot and dusty party.

This is the especial part of Switzerland where beggary is

reduced to a science. Your carriage is going at a very rapid rate, but in advance you notice one of those ugly Swiss cottages. The mother is in the door, holding well in hand four children, ranging in age from five to ten, boys and girls. As you get opposite the door, she looses her hold upon them, and then commences the chase. These children, trained as they are, can keep up with a carriage at a seven-mile-an-hour pace, and, bare-headed and bare-footed, they do it, two on each side. They make no appeal; they say nothing, either by word or look; they simply run by the side of the carriage, as though it were a race intended as a test of the endurance of Swiss children against Swiss horses. After ten minutes of this, you begin to feel some concern for the children, and you ask the courier what they want.

"Vat dey vant? Oof you vants to kit rid mit dem, fling 'em some sous. Dey vill run into Zhenave oof you ton't."

And so, merely to get them out of your sight, knowing that they dare not go home to their mother without something; a shower of sous fall in the dust, which the children gather, and return to the cottage to wait for the next coach. Sometimes they catch one on the return trip, which is good luck.

It is the most systematic begging I have yet encountered. The strong point in it is the not asking. There is no professional whine, no story; nothing but a sturdy assault upon your sympathies. They make the legs take the place of the tongue. It is very well done, and, as carriages loaded with tourists pass every half hour, it must pay well. I presume the rent of these cottages is fixed with reference to their facilities for begging. An advertisement of one of them reads as follows, I suppose:

FOR RENT—An eligible begging station, on the route from Chamonix to Geneva. Regular diligence route, and the favorite route for carriages of rich English and Americans. There are no hills near, the course in each direction is level for miles, permitting children to run a long distance without exhaustion. Especially recommended for very young children. Half hour after dining station, which ensures good nature on the part of passengers. The most certain and profitable location on the route. Owner will take a percentage of the collections for rent, or will rent for a certainty.

The journey by cars from Geneva to Interlaken is delight-

ful.   The road follows the left bank of Lake Geneva until Lausanne is reached.   Now and then a break in the woods gives a
glimpse of the blue waters of the lake, with the mountains
beyond, then a long, dark tunnel shuts off every view, but only
for a few minutes.   Then we enter a country that is magnificent in its quiet beauty.   The hillsides are cultivated to the
summit.   Rich vineyards with their luscious grapes fast ripening in the sun, fine farms with the variegated fields hide from
sight the cold gray stone that makes the Chamonix valley so
desolate.

After passing Lausanne, Lake Leman is left behind and we
go nearly due north to Friburg, a beautiful town situated on a
rocky eminence and nearly surrounded by the River Sarine.

Friburg, like every Swiss city, has its organ and legend.
The organ is one of the finest of Europe, and is played every
afternoon and evening, provided the admissions amount to
twenty francs.   If there is not the vast amount of four dollars
in the house the curtain does not go up, or rather, there is no
performance.   However, there are generally enough tourists
present to justify the performance, and the listener is well
rewarded for the expenditure of time.

In front of the council house is an immense lime tree, partly
supported by stone pillars.   It has its legend.   It is said that a
young man of Friburg—a participant in the great victory of
Morat, in the year 1476, was sent after the battle to convey
the glad news to his townsmen.   He arrived, breathless and
exhausted, so much so that he had just strength left to gasp
the word "Victory!" and expired.   There was in his lifeless
hand a lime twig which the citizens planted, and it grew to be
the patriarch of trees it now is, and it is guarded with as much
care as though the legend were actually true.

How many in our late war ran from battle-fields, who
might have had lime twigs in their hands if they had waited
long enough to get them.   But they did not.   They were in
too great a hurry to reach Canada, from which they will all
(1882) return to claim pensions under the arrearages of pensions
act.

It would have been well for the country if all of this class
had imitated the example of the young man of Friburg, and

expired. The citizens could well have afforded the time to plant the twigs in their hands.

Only a short stop is made here, and then to Berne, one of the most interesting cities in Switzerland.

Berne is the city of bears, and were it located in Wisconsin would be called Bearville. A bear was its origin. Berthold DeZahringen, some centuries ago, killed a tremendous bear on the ground now occupied by the pretty city, and founded a town in commemoration of the event, and so the bear became as common in Berne as the lion is in England, or the eagle in America. There is bear everywhere. The public decorations are in the form of bears, the flags have bears on them, the bread is stamped with bears, the pot you drink your beer out of is in form a bear; the children's toys are all bears, and the city keeps two bear-pits, in which a dozen, more or less, fine specimens are kept. Not many years ago an English officer, who, with his lately wedded bride, were doing Switzerland, fell into one of these pits, and after a desperate struggle with the ferocious brutes, was literally torn to pieces in the sight of his agonized wife. I could not learn who it was the heart-broken wife married the next year, or whether she married well or not.

It is a quaint and curious old city, and well worth a day or two. The situation is particularly beautiful, and as it has preserved the peculiar characteristics of the long ago, it is an instructive place.

In the older section the streets have no sidewalks, the ground floors being made into arcades, with the houses above supported upon arches, under which you walk. It is always well for an American to visit the older portions of these cities, that he may more fervently thank heaven that his lot was cast in a new country, where there is no ancient and inconvenient rubbish to worry him. There is more of convenience in any one modern American house than there is in all of the old part Berne, or, for that matter, of any ancient city. They do well to look at, but that is all the use they should be put to. I have a profound sympathy for the people condemned to live in them.

Berne is the capital of the little Republic, and here its Congress meets. Its sessions last a month, as a rule, and then

Congress adjourns, and the members go home. The country is too poor to have much to steal, and consequently a short session is sufficient.

I was shaved in Berne, and, speaking of shaving and barbers generally, I want to say all I have to say on that subject at once.

There is no barber like the American barber, and no such comfort anywhere in barbers as we enjoy at home. Tourists have complained of the straight chairs, the dull razors, and all that sort of thing, and with some reason, though it is not as bad as represented. I have never known of any one being absolutely killed by an European barber, either at sight or sixty days.

It is true that you do not have the luxurious reclining chair, nor the soothing manipulations of a deft artist, nor the delightful hair dressing, and all that. In England you are seated in a common, straight-backed chair, a napkin is adjusted closely about your neck, a dab of soap, three strokes of a bad razor, and you are permitted to staunch the blood and wash off the soap yourself. If you desire your hair dressed, as a very clumsy brushing is called, it is "tuppence extra."

In France the operation is the same, only the barber, being always a statesman, talks you to the verge of madness. He knows that you do not understand a word of his language, but he talks on cheerfully just the same, till he is through, and really believes he has entertained you.

The German barber does not talk you to death, for he is by nature phlegmatic. He stays by you longer, however, and leaves less of your face to carry away than either the English or French torturer. He wants to earn his money, and he does.

The Swiss is less airy than the Frenchman, and more active than the German, for, very likely, he is of both nationalities. He is more careful, likewise. When his razor enters the flesh, he does not slice the whole side of the face off, for his time is not occupied with talk, as is the Frenchman, nor is he so heavy as the German. No, indeed! When he sees that his razor has cut through the skin, and is entering the flesh, he stops right there, and calls your attention to the fact that he has stopped, and claims some credit for not carving off a half pound or more.

French, German, and Swiss allow you to wash your own face, and comb your own hair, and otherwise fix yourself, but the Swiss is the best of the three.

But even in Switzerland, it is better for the tourist if he has his own shaving material, and does it himself. He may cut and scar himself, but he will have some skin left, and may console himself that the cutting was the result of his own lack of skill, and not that of another.

The continental barber has much to learn in the

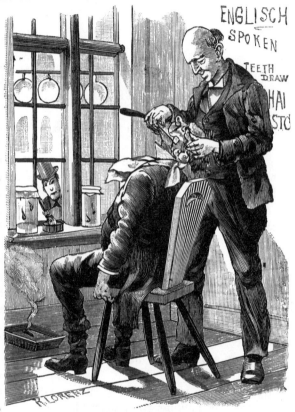

THE CONSCIENTIOUS BARBER.

matter of shaving. The English barbers say they would like to adopt the American system, but their English customers will not. I understand it. Their fathers were scarified, and why should they not be? It would be un-English to change. And so they go on with the same straight-backed chairs, the same clumsy contrivances, and they will so go on, till the end of time. The last Englishman will be so shaved, when he might have had comfort and luxury all his life.

CHAPTER XXXVII.

From Berne to Thun the scenery is less bold and rugged, although the horizon is always filled with great peaks that are to be seen from every quarter.

At Thun we take steamer across Lake Thun, one of the most beautiful of all the Swiss lakes. It is not so large as Lake Geneva, and is not fringed with such enormous mountain chains, but it abounds with unexpected views of rare beauty, resembling very much our own picturesque Lake George.

As the steamer skirts the north bank of the lake, which is a succession of vineyards, we suddenly come upon a magnificent view of the Jungfrau, almost as impressive as Mt. Blanc. From that time on the great range gradually unfolds itself like the views of a panorama, until at length we have all the highest peaks in full sight.

At Därlingen we leave the steamer, and, after a short wait, see a peculiar looking train dash through the tunnel, at the head of the lake, and then come puffing noisily into the station. This is the celebrated Bödeli railway, the second shortest in the world. It runs from Därlingen to Interlaken, a distance of a mile and a half. Its cars are especially adapted to sight seeing, being constructed in two stories, so that every one can have an outside seat, to fully enjoy the picturesque scenery between the two stations.

The one main street of Interlaken is chiefly devoted to hotels. especially the upper portion of it, for from this location one has the best view of the celebrated Jungfrau, that stands head and shoulders above the high Silberhorn on the right and the Schneehorn on the left. Further down, the street is occupied with tempting stores filled with Swiss wood carvings. From this time on nothing can be seen but wood carving, save perhaps an occasional bit of chamois horn.

It is a quaint old town, full of odd nooks and corners, that would afford interesting study for weeks at a time. While there are no particular attractions, Interlaken is a favorite resort of tourists, and is always full of strangers, who enjoy the mild, equable climate and find pleasure in resting.

THE JUNGFRAU, FROM INTERLAKEN.

The broad walnut-lined Höheweg, a beautiful avenue, leads down across an old-fashioned, massive stone bridge to a street set aside for markets. Here, during the forenoon, is a miniature Petticoat Lane, only the people are all clean, picturesquely dressed and decent. There are no rum shops, reeking with the vile odors of stale liquors and still staler tobacco smoke; there are no intoxicated men and women. Everything is quiet, orderly and well conducted. But the variety of articles offered for sale is something astonishing. Here an enterprising woman, as stiff and formal as the high white cap she wears, has a small stock of dry goods spread out on the pavement for the inspection of the picturesquely dressed peasants, who trade their milk and farm products for clothing material. A little further on you will find a complete assortment of boots and shoes, of all kinds and conditions. There a man has a hat store and a junk shop combined. At any place, almost, you can buy specimens of Swiss skill in carving. These stores or exchanges are all on the street, along which it is difficult to thread one's way, so crowded is it with buyers and sellers.

These narrow, crooked streets are lined with houses built the Lord only knows how long ago. The long beams that cross each other in the front of the houses are carved and cut in every conceivable shape. Sometimes the artist was a little ambitious and attempted very elaborate work, not always successfully, however, for the heads and figures that adorn the fronts of some of them are grotesque to a degree.

Interlaken is the starting point for most of the mountaineering parties that visit the Bernese Oberland, the chief point of interest centering about the Jungfrau, which is forty-one hundred and sixty-seven feet high. The ascent of this mountain, which, though very fatiguing, is not dangerous, was first made in 1811, and between that time and 1856 it was only accomplished five times. Since the latter date, however, it has been made very frequently. We did not attempt to explore the icy regions, so far above the clouds, being perfectly content with our experience at Mont Blanc.

Interlaken is the great distributing point for the vast quantities of carved goods made in this vicinity. There are a number of large factories in the city, but the greater part of the work is done in the little towns near there. The displays made in the large stores are wonderful, some of the pieces being the work of genius. While every possible subject is treated, the carvers have a passion for bears, the heraldic emblem of some of the Cantons. You will see bears of every conceivable size, and in every attitude. Whole parties of them, playing billiards or cards, or dancing a quadrille; bears standing, sitting, lying down; bears everywhere and doing everything. Some of this work is wonderfully well done, the lines and spaces being so delicately cut that it seems as though a breath would break them.

On the way from Interlaken to Brienz we passed through little villages, whose one street is filled with wood carving establishments, and almost every house between the two places

has a small factory for the manufacture of these pretty trifles. At Brienz we went through a very large factory and saw the patient Swiss chipping away tirelessly at the huge piece of

wood that was soon to be a medallion portrait. It is an art
that requires great skill and delicacy of touch to produce fine
work. In this factory there were some four hundred or five
hundred men employed, and the work they turned out was
marvelously beautiful. In fact one cannot sufficiently admire

THE HOME OF THE CARVER.

the wood carving of the region. The patient workers do
everything artistic in the material, and it is artistic. Land-
scapes, portraits, hunting scenes, animals, angels, scriptural
subjects, everything that is done on canvas or in marble, is
done in wood, and many of the pieces are purchased by crowned
heads, and at a very high price.

The artists in wood are, however, very poorly paid, even
for Switzerland. In America their wages would be considered

as close to starvation as possible, without touching it.   Think of a man capable of doing the most artistic work laboring at four francs a day, or eighty cents!   This is as high as any, except an occasional phenomenal genius, gets, and they appear to be content with it.   For this miserable sum they work so long as they can see, commencing at daylight and ending at dark.

True, living is very cheap, and such as it is it ought to be. The wretched beer of the region is only about a cent a glass, and the black bread of the country costs next to nothing, and so the artist works all day and at night sits himself in his little café, and with his cheap wine and cheaper beer, plays cards contentedly, and enjoys himself thoroughly.

After all he is as well as though he got ten dollars a day. He couldn't drink any more wine than he does, and neither would additional pay enlarge his capacity for black bread, and what does he want of anything more?   It isn't what you want — it's what you don't want that makes you rich.   Even in little wood carving Brienz, romance gets in.

We saw on the street, there is only one in Brienz, a young man whose demoralized clothing, fiery eyes and unsteady steps, all bore evidence to the terrible fact of dissipation.   He was the first drunken man of the genus loafer we had struck in Switzerland.   The Young Man who Knows Everything looked at him and promptly remarked:—

"That young man has wisdom.   He is cultivating a vice. When he wants to economize he has a basis for economy. Suppose he had always lived a perfectly correct life, and some emergency should come to him that demanded economy, what would he have to economize on?   Every man should so live that he can, if he must, better himself.   I admire that young man, for he leaves himself room for development."

The landlord gave us his history.   The young man was ruined by prosperity.   He was an industrious and very skillful carver, and had attained sixty cents a day with an immediate prospect of a raise of twenty cents, which is the summit of a legitimate Brienz ambition.

He was engaged to be married to the daughter of a poor Swiss farmer, who had three cows and a goat or two, and there

36

was no reason under heaven why he should not have been happy. He had health, strength, skill; Josepha was beautiful, and there was nothing to prevent his marrying her, and settling down quietly to watch the development of her goitre, and passing a long and happy life.

But evil was hanging over them. An uncle of Rudolph's, who was a cook in Paris, died without issue, and left his entire estate, sixty-eight dollars and fifty cents, to his nephew, our Rudolph, in Brienz.

Immediately Rudolph grew cold towards Josepha. He did not meet her on the little bridge after his work; he did not take her to fairs where the two drank beer lovingly out of the same mug; he did not always have some little present for her; in short, he avoided her. To use the strong though not elegant English of

FEMALE COSTUMES IN APPENZELL.

the wild and untamed West, he "shook" her.

Josepha noticed this change, and wept in her enforced solitude. With true womanly instinct she felt what was coming. There was now an inseparable bar between them. Could she, a plain country girl, with no dowry to speak of, hope to wed a man with a fortune of sixty-eight dollars and fifty cents?

And so she wept her lost love, her first love, which never comes again. One may love twice, but the second love has not the twang, the flavor, as it were, of the first. It is the difference of a meal on an empty stomach and the tail end of a feast.

They met and Josepha made one appeal to him. He answered her briefly, brutally:

"I did love you, Josepha," he said, "and could love you

again, were it possible. But you must remember, my girl, that circumstances have changed; I am a man of fortune—you are the daughter of a poor farmer with but three cows, and those to be divided among ten children. And the price of cheese is sadly going down, and must still go down, owing to the competition of the factory system in America, where they can imitate even our most penetrating Limburger, and sell it cheaper here than we can produce it. It is no use to talk of buying our own product, all people buy where they can buy the cheapest. That is political economy.

"Had you an uncle, a cook in Paris, and liable to die, with sixty-eight dollars and fifty cents, the aspect of things would be changed. But you have no such uncle, and really, Josepha, you cannot expect me, in my altered condition, to so throw myself away. No indeed. But I wish you well. Forget me, if you can, and marry some one in your own sphere, and be happy. You would not want to wed me, and see me miserable! Life would then be a burden to both. Be ye not unequally yoked."

Josepha, weeping, turned away, for despite her love, she realized the truth of what he said. And Rudolph, whistling an air, gaily went into the café, and sought to drown his feelings in wine.

He knew he had done a very mean thing, but he felt it to be impossible for a youth of his prospects to marry a penniless girl.

Reveling in his wealth he pursued his mad career and came to grief, as such men always do. He quit work, he dressed extravagantly, and finally he made an unlucky investment in stocks, which swept off every sou he had. His sixty-eight dollars and fifty cents were irrevocably gone, and Rudolph the Gay found himself without money, with an expensive appetite for wine and an extreme disposition to do no work of any kind.

One morning he heard a wild rumor that a brother of Josepha in America had made a strike in oil and had sent Josepha five hundred dollars. Then his feelings toward that young lady changed. He went to her and remarked that he forgave her for her treatment of him; that the cloud that had come between them and obscured their happiness had passed away, and that there was no reason now why they should not realize the dreams of their youth and wed.

It was now Josepha's turn. She remarked that sentiment was all well enough, but that there was something in viewing matters from a mere worldly standpoint. Love was sweet, but fortunately the stock of the article in the world was not limited. It was not to be expected in her altered condition that she should unite her fortunes with those of a penniless man. She quite agreed with what he (Rudolph) had said to her on a former occasion, "Be ye not unequally yoked." She (Josepha) had now five hundred dollars. He (Rudolph) had not a sou. Had he (Rudolph) five hundred dollars, and had he the good habits of his youth when he was an humble worker in wood, she would wed him gladly, but as he (Rudolph) was, in the language of the world, short of that amount, and as she (Josepha) had any quantity of coin, she rather thought she wouldn't. She should always regard him in the light of a friend, and should weep with great regularity when she thought of their severed loves, but there was a young farmer up the mountain who had twelve cows, and with her capital could double the stock, and she believed that her best show was with him.

And so Rudolph, penniless, loveless, and with an appetite which, like jealousy, makes the meat it feeds on, is a mere cumberer on the earth about Brienz, the wreck we saw.

And Josepha, she married the young grazier, and has two children and one of the largest goitres in the neighborhood, and the two have prospered to the point of seriously contemplating the starting of a small inn, near a convenient waterfall, that they may fleece strangers, which is a more lucrative business in Switzerland than cheese-making or wood-carving.

In the evening we were rowed across the Lake of Brienz to the Giessbach, the regular sight of the locality. The lake is twenty feet higher than Lake Thun, from which it is separated by a narrow strip of low land only two miles wide. It is thought that at one time the two lakes were joined. Lake Brienz is from five hundred to nine hundred feet deep, its water being of a very dark blue.

The Giessbach consists of seven falls, the highest being one

thousand one hundred and forty-seven feet above the lake.
The water comes from a lake in the summit of the mountain,
and tumbles from rock to rock
till it finds its level in the lake
below.   All the seven are visible at once, and the sight is
one of the most delightful in
all Switzerland.   Opposite the
falls, on the other side of the
enormous chasm, is a magnificent hotel, as a matter of
course, where you are charged
very reasonably — not more
than twice what the same
accommodations would cost
you in a first-class hotel anywhere else.   For this reason-
ableness you try to feel very
thankful.   One has to see the
Giessbach, anyhow; and, as
there is but one place to stop,
the proprietor's facilities for
swindling are unlimited.   A
mere double charge may be
classed as reasonable, there;
especially as the sight is worth
almost any expenditure.

OUR PARTY AT THE GIESSBACH.

It was nearly dark when we
reached the Geissbach shore,
so that we had but an imperfect view of the lovely falls,
as we climbed up the steep
path leading to the terrace,
three hundred and nine feet
above the lake.   But even in the half twilight they were
wondrously beautiful, as they dashed from rock to rock, hundreds of feet apart.

As it grew darker, the green foliage on each side threw out
the silvery cascades, dancing from one to the other, in bold
relief.   Gradually darkness completely enveloped them, and

we could see nothing but the dark, gloomy mass of mountains down whose side for a thousand feet the water fell, from one pool to another.

The terrace on which the hotel stands was brilliantly lighted, and was filled with tourists who were spending some little time here, visiting the many beautiful spots that make the Giessbach one of the favorite resorts in Switzerland.

Suddenly, about nine o'clock, a rocket flew skyward, from a point on the mountain opposite us. Then one went up from the terrace, and while we were admiring its flight high in air, the lights about the hotel and on the terrace were extinguished and we were left in utter darkness. A long drawn "Oh-h-h" involuntarily burst forth as the lowest cascade suddenly stood before us, a brilliant, beautiful sheet of water, of a delicate light blue tint. Then simultaneously the other cascades above shone forth in all their splendor. The scene was wonderful. It was fairy land.

Bengal lights of different colors were arranged back of the sheets of water, so that each cascade was brilliantly lighted, producing an effect exquisitely and indescribably beautiful.

Gradually the lights under the water went out, the gas at hotel was relighted, and we were rowed back to Brienz with a picture of wondrous beauty printed indelibly on our minds.

Tibbitts, who has rejoined the party after his attempt at reformation at the St. Gervais baths, (by the way his personal appearance is not a good advertisement for the waters,) got an idea at Giessbach, which he developed thus:

"I have at last got my fortune made. What is wanted in Switzerland is more waterfalls, with legends, more mineral springs, and more ruins, secular and sacred. As soon as I get back to New York I am going to organize a company for a Waterfall, Ruin and Spring Company."

"But all the eligible waterfalls are taken."

"Very true, and to get one we should have to pay too large a price. This is the very essence of my idea — I am going to create a waterfall. What is a waterfall, anyway? Nothing more than water pouring over a rock or other material. All that is necessary to a waterfall is an elevation and water. Turn on the water, and it can't help falling, and there you are.

"How shall we get water? Easily enough. A side of a precipice, with a notch in it big enough for a hotel, can be bought anywhere along the Lake of Brienz for almost nothing. What is more easy than to construct a reservoir on the top, put a ninety-horse power engine in at the lake, and pump the water to the reservoir on the summit, and when visitors are there turn it on, and give them the best waterfall in all Switzerland.

PEASANTS OF EASTERN SWITZERLAND.

"Keep the water on till after they all go to bed, and for an hour or so after, so the roar 'll soothe them to sleep; and if any rich Americans choose to stay up all night, and buy wine, keep it on all night. We must have nothing mean about our waterfall.

"There are a great many advantages in this over the natural article. The water can be turned off while the lights are being placed behind the sheet for illuminations, and the flow can be regulated so as to suit every taste. If the party is made up of young ladies who delight in the soft and beautiful, we can make a Minnehaha of it; if it is strong men and old maids who hunger for the grand, why, whack on more steam, and we can have a Niagara.

"About a mile or so away I am going to have a castle in ruins—ruins aint expensive where there is so much rock—and I can have any newspaper man write me a proper legend of it for ten dollars. This for the history crank. For the more devout we want the ruins of an ancient church, which was destroyed by whoever you choose This will fetch all those who are on their way to the Holy Land. They don't spend as much money for wine as the other classes, but we can make it up in charges for board and guides. The ruins must be so built as to make a guide necessary, and so extensive that two days will be necessary to get the proper views of them, and to study their history understandingly.

NEAR BRIENZ.

"But this speculation will not be complete without mineral springs in the valley below. This is the easiest thing of the lot. You will build a reservoir and chuck into it a few barrels of salt, and a few bushels of rusty iron filings with sulphuric acid, a ton or so of sulphur (we must be liberal with sulphur for it is cheap), and any other articles that smell — asafoetida isn't bad — get it so thundering strong that it would drive a yellow dog out of a tanyard, and have it cure anything, from original sin to corns. We want a gorgeous cure, and a corps of distinguished physicians, and an analysis of the water, and all that, and we can just rope in the money. We commence them at the falls, we deplete them at the ruined castle, and dig into them at the ruined church, and finally finish them at the medicinal springs. We want a bank at the latter place, and, if the law permits it, a faro bank. Anyhow, we can get a Swiss hotel man, and if every blessed tourist doesn't have to draw more money before he gets out, then the race has lost its cunning.

"I am going to be the president of this company, with a brother-in-law I have in Wisconsin for treasurer. There's money lying around loose, and this scheme will corral all of it I shall ever want."

Tibbitts talked of his joint-stock Waterfall, Ruin and Medicinal Spring Company all the way into Lucerne.

CHAPTER XXXVIII.

THE road from Brienz to Lucerne, over the Brünig Pass, follows the valley of Meiringen for a long distance, and gives some very pretty views of Lake Brienz, the River Aare, and a number of cascades in the mountains across the valley. As the ascent of the pass begins the road is frequently overshadowed by hanging rocks, which seem about to topple over every minute.

As we wind around the mountains occasional glimpses are obtained of the valley far below, and then, after having gone over the summit of the pass, we have a long almost level stretch along the side of the mountain, from which we have a magnificent view of the valley of Sarnea, with its pretty little lakes and rivers, its long, straight, white roads, and its queer little towns.

Two hours later we come in sight of Pilatus rearing its lofty head high above Lake Lucerne, as though it were the guardian of that beautiful body of water. Then a long drive on the banks of the lake, where the road is cut out of the solid rocks, and in a short time we rattle over the rough stones of a pavement, across the Reuss River and are in Lucerne.

This city, which is to Switzerland what Saratoga is to America, is prettily built at the head of Lake Lucerne, or, as the Swiss call it, the Vierwaldstätter See, which resembles somewhat in shape a Roman cross, Lucerne being at the head. It is situated in an ampitheater, if the term might be so applied, facing the snow capped Alps of Uri and Engelberg, with Rigi on one side and Pilatus on the other. Around it are massive walls and watch towers, built in 1385, and still in a good state of preservation.

The hotels are nearly all located on the Schwéizerhof Quays, which occupies the site of an arm of the lake that was filled up some fourteen years ago. From any one of these mammoth hotels magnificent views may be obtained on any clear day. Directly in front is the lake; to the right the Rigi group, with its hotel-crowned summit; in the center the Reuss-stock chain, and to the extreme right Pilatus. All of these mountains are full of points of interest, and are annually visited by thousands of tourists, who make up their parties at Lucerne· The sail across the lake to any part of the town on its borders,

LION OF LUCERNE.

makes a delightful excursion that is always new and interesting.

The show sight here is the celebrated Lion of Lucerne, which photographs and pictures have made famous the world over. It is an immense figure, cut in the side of a great rock, about a quarter of a mile from the quay, in memory of the twenty-six officers and seven hundred soldiers who were massacred in the Tuileries, Paris, on the tenth of August, 1792, when the Commune obtained control of the government, and compelled King Louis to fly for his life. An immense lion, twenty eight feet in length, lies dying in a grotto, transfixed with a broken lance. Under one paw, as though he would shelter it even in death, is the Bourbon lily. On either side of the lion are the names of the officers, and an inscription. The idea is a simple one, but the work was done by a master hand, (the Danish sculptor Thorwalsden being the artist) and is very impressive.

As a rule, people thrill when they look upon this famous
Lion of Lucerne, but I declined to do anything of the kind.
The death of these Swiss, in Paris, was a purely commercial
matter.   They were the hirelings of an infamous despot, who
was crushing the life out of the French people by their aid.
I have no sympathy for king. queen or noble, and when one
dies I have a hosanna to sing immediately.   And I cannot
imagine anything more disgraceful than a man, Swiss, or of
any other nationality, who would sell himself to a despot.
These fellows, who fell in defense of Louis, had but one mer t:
they sold their blood, bones and sinews, and they carried out
their contract.   They were simply honest butchers, who contracted to do certain work for a lecherous French king, and
did it.   But the monument at Lucerne to these hirelings is an
insult to humanity, and all the good I got out of it, was the
contemplation of a wondrously carved lion, and the drawback
to that satisfaction was the frightful fact that the men, to
whose memory it stands, never should have had any monument
erected at all.   This inscription is the only one they deserved:

"Sacred to the memory of some hundreds of hired soldiery, who fought
for pay only, had too much animal courage to run, and who died to carry
out a contract."

As a work of art, Thorwalsden's lion is worth seeing—as a
piece of sentiment, excuse me.   I have seen too many soldiers
in Europe who sell their sinews for pay, and I have seen too
many starving people who are kept poor to support them.   I
do not like any soldiers but volunteers, and whenever the people get the upper hand of the other kind, I want to contribute
for a monument to the people, not to their oppressors.

Aside from the bridges, whose only merit is their age, and
one or two rather scantily furnished churches, there is but little
of interest in Lucerne.

The Glacier Mills are an attraction, and are well
worth seeing.   There is no humbug about nature.   You climb
a hill after looking at the lion, and you come to a garden in
which are a series of the great pits known as Glacier Mills.

These are simply great holes in solid rock thirty or forty
feet deep, and about the same in diameter.   In the ages gone
by when this country was covered with glaciers, the action of
water wore holes in the rock, great stones lost themselves in

these cavities, the water came in and the stones, weighing many tons, revolved by the action of the water, wore away the rock and enlarged the pit at every revolution.

This work went on for ages. The water forced itself into the pit, the great rock revolved, by its action enlarging the cavity at every revolution, until finally the glacier disappeared and the rocks were at rest.

And here they are to-day, round as marbles, lying at the bottom of the pits they made, so many evidences of the irresistible forces of nature.

In this enclosure there are, perhaps, twenty of them, varying in depth from thirty to fifty feet, and about the same distance across.

Tibbitts believed they were artificial, and said he should dig a few for his Hotel and Ruin Company, but he is entirely mistaken. The glacier mills are genuine and the same forces are at work to-day under every ice-field, and doing the work precisely as this was done. However, there is no reason why he should not manufacture a few — tourists would take them just the same, and be just as well satisfied. He claims that with nitro-glycerine he can do in five hours the work that requires centuries to accomplish with water and rock, which demonstrates the supremacy of mind over matter.

Mont Pilatus, just out of Lucerne, is something you must see whether you want to or not. It isn't a very remarkable mountain, but the astute hotel keeper and the more rapacious hackman, has made it necessary for you to spend more money than you want to, by seeing Mont Pilatus. It is a proper mountain to see, nothing extraordinary, as a mountain, but you are compelled to go anyhow, and you do. And this is why you go.

There has to be a legend for every point of sufficient interest to attract a traveler, and so Pilatus has its legend. You are told gravely that after Pontius Pilate washed his hands of the blood of our Savior, and saw him go to his death, instead of saving him as he might have done, he was struck with remorse, returned to Rome, and pursued by a feeling which he could not get rid of, made his way to this mountain in Switzer-land, and lived in a cave therein, a recluse, expiating by a life

of solitude the crime he had been guilty of in shedding innocent blood.

And they show you gravely and without a blush, a pond
in the top of the mountain, where, after he became an old
man, he ended the life that was a burden to him, by
drowning himself therein, and they tell you of the earthquakes and things of unpleasant nature that followed his

THE END OF PONTIUS PILATE.

demise. The Arch Enemy of mankind was on hand in person
to seize him, and when he had struck the water he was taken
bodily by His Satanic Majesty and whisked away to the lower
regions.

Did all this happen? Possibly. I was not there, and
therefore cannot say positively that it did not I wish to be
truthful and reasonable. But I will venture my opinion that

Pilate never came to Switzerland; that after his term expired as Governor of Judea he stole all he could lay his hands upon and went back to Rome, and went over to the new Emperor or Consul, or whatever they called the official who had the giving out of patronage, and got a new appointment somewhere else. That is what became of Pontius Pilate.

However, Mt. Pilatus is well worth seeing, and the legend is a very effective one, and the guide who tells it to you always gets several francs in addition to his original swindle.

You must have legends, and as people believe them it is the same as though they were true

An imaginative friend of mine was once standing upon the railroad platform at Forest, Ohio, in the war years, probably the most lonesome and desolate station in the world. There were twenty passengers with him for a train that was so far behind that no one could guess as to when it would arrive.

He had cut a little switch from a tree near the platform, and as he flourished it ostentatiously, some one asked him where he got it.

With a quickness of invention — a fertility of lying that was simply admirable — he said it was the tip of the flag-staff of Fort Donelson!

Now this was nothing but a little switch cut within twenty feet of where they were standing, but immediately all the passengers came up and took it in their hands and examined it critically, and commented on it, as though it were something of actual importance. It was, to them. The battle was discussed, the merits of Grant as a soldier were discussed, and the whole war was with its causes and consequences, reviewed. And all this because a prompt liar, in an impulsive way, located a Forest switch as the tip of the flag-staff of Donelson.

We believed it, and handled the switch reverently. The tourist to Pilatus swallows the legend of Pilate, and it does him just as much good as though it were true.

The moral to all this is, the wise man swallows what is set before him and asks no questions for his stomach's sake.

Never go into the kitchen in which your hash is made. Be ignorant and happy.

By this time we were ready for another mountaineering

expedition, especially as in this instance the ascent could be made in a comfortable railway car. To reach Vitznau, where

LUCERNE-RIGI-RAIL—VITZNAU AS SEEN FROM THE EICHBERG.

the railway station is, we took a sail of about an hour and a half, through beautiful scenery. As we steam out from Lucerne, the city is seen to its best advantage, its long walnut-shaded quay, its massive hotels, churches, walls and towers, standing up from the water and thrown into relief by the dark green forests on the mountains behind it.

LUCERNE-RIGI-RAIL—VIEW FROM THE KANZELI.

Soon after Lucerne fades away we see the cross-like formation of the lake, one arm, known as Lake Küssnach, stretching way to the north, while on the other side is Lake Alpnach. Far ahead of us is the Bay of Buosch and Lake of Uri, forming the foot of the cross. At the head of Lake Küssnach can be seen the town of that name. Here, in the central part of the cross, the view is particularly impressive; the Rigi, on the left, with its wooded slopes shining in the sunlight, contrasting strangely with the mist and clouds that envelope Pilatus, on the other side of the lake. As we see the clouds lowering around the high peak of Mt. Pilate, the legend told by Antonio, the guide in Sir Walter Scott's "Anne of Gierestein," comes vividly to mind. I have given my readers my notion of the legend of Pilatus—now they have it exactly as the guide books give it. You pay your money and you take your choice. Here it is in guide book talk:

'The wicked Pontius Pilate, Proconsul of Judea, here found the termi nation of his impious life; having, after spending years in the recesses of the mountain which bears his name, at length, in remorse and despair rather than in penitence, plunged into the dismal lake that occupies the summit Whether water refused to do the executioner's duty upon such a wretch, or whether, his body being drowned, his vexed spirit continued to haunt the place where he committed suicide, no one pretended to say. But a form was often seen to emerge from the gloomy waters, and go through the action of washing his hands, and when he did so dark clouds of mist gathered, first round the bosom of the Infernal Lake (such it had been styled of old), and then wrapping the whole upper part of the mountain in darkness, presaged a tempest or hurricane, which was sure to follow in a short space. The evil spirit was peculiarly exasperated at the audacity of such strangers as ascended the mountain to gaze at his place of punishment, and, in consequence, the magistrates of Lucerne had prohibited any one from approaching Mt. Pilate, under severe penalties."

It is perhaps needless to say that the prohibition has been long removed, and that every season a great many tourists ascend the grand old peak, to see the Infernal Lake on its summit. All do it who can afford to pay for it.

And speaking of these miracles and appearances, and all that sort of thing, they don't take place any more. Pilate hasn't appeared in person to any tourists for hundreds of years. His appearance is something that used to happen, but doesn't any more.

Tibbitts remarked that when he got his hotel done, he would have Pilate appear, actually washing his hands, no matter what it cost him. He intended to have a lot of fresh miracles. He

37

would treat his patrons decently, and not palm off upon them a lot of old legends. He could get a man to do the Pilate business for thirty dollars a month, and he wouldn't be mean enough to stop at so small an expense as that.

Passing Weggis, a pretty village nestling at the foot of the Rigi, Vitznau is reached, and there we disembark for our ride up the mountain. The Rigi has long been a favorite resort for tourists, and as far back as 1868 an attempt was made to assist them in reaching the summit with less fatigue and greater comfort and security. In that year, one Riggenbach, of Olten, and an engineer of Aaron, named Olivier Zschokke, after having experimented for years on the subject, published

a pamphlet, in which they declared that it was possible to construct a railway from Vitznau to the summit of the Rigi.

The treatise attracted a great deal of attention, and the following year the two engineers applied for aid

THE OLD WAY OF ASCENDING THE RIGI.

from the Government of Lucerne to carry out the scheme they had devised. This aid was granted, and in two years the road was finished to Stoffel, over half the distance, and two years later to the very summit of the mountain.

The new system consists of two rails of standard gauge, such as are used on ordinary railways, firmly fixed on sleepers, which are solidly secured to the rock by every device known, to insure their solidity. Then a third rail, supplied with cogs, is placed between the other two, and on this the cogged driving wheel of the engine of a new construction propels the engine up the hill. Engines of a special pattern were built, for as the ascent is often at an angle of twenty-five degrees, ordinary locomotives would not do. The boiler in the new

NIGHT ASCENT OF THE RIGI IN THE OLD TIMES.

engine is perpendicular and the rear is slightly elevated. The tread-wheels are connected with the cog wheel in the center of the engine in such a manner that each wheel bears its proportion of the weight. The road has been a complete success from the start, not a single accident having ever occurred.

The sensation after the car leaves level ground at the station in Vitznau and begins to climb steadily up the mountain is peculiar. The ground seems to melt away, and yet is always replaced. As we mount higher and higher, the view becomes more extensive. Now we can see the little town we have just left on the pretty little bay, at the foot of the mountains. Beyond it the lake stretches out to the mountains that seem to come to its very edge. Then the road passes through a tunnel, a marvel of engineering skill, for going through there the ascent is at a rise of twenty-five degrees.

Emerging from this tunnel, the train speeds across a bridge, over a yawning chasm, whose sides are lined with stunted trees and great bowlders, that are washed by a large stream which takes its rise higher up the mountain.

From this point the view is grand. Pilate, towering above the lake, is clearly seen on the right; just below is Weggis, and further on the bright buildings of Lucerne shine in the sunlight, while the lake, with its different arms, looks like "a painted sea." All around and above are the huge red rocks of the Rigi. There are two or three stations along the route, but we push steadily on, the views becoming grander and grander with each successive step, until the summit is reached, and then the panorama is complete. You see the Alps in the eastern part of Switzerland, the massive pile of the Loudi, all the western mountains of Schwyz, and to the north the cantons of Zug, Zurich and Lucerne spread out like a map at our feet. Way down the valley can be seen eleven different lakes, with little clumps of houses, the villages on the shores of the "Vierwaldstätter See."

Passing by the great hotels that flourish here so high above the world, we go to the great bluff which is so prominently seen from Lucerne, and there the view is magnificent. As far as the eye can reach on the south are the countless peaks of the Alps, covered with snow the year around. Near at hand are beautiful valleys with winding rivers and straight, thread like roads.

As we stand there, lost in wonder at the overpowering

magnificence of the scene, the sun, which up to this time had been shining brightly, was obscured by clouds, and we were treated to a thunder storm which raged with terrific fury for half an hour or more. Then the sun broke forth again in all his splendor and we saw the clouds disappear beneath his powerful rays.

Sunrise as seen from the Rigi Kulm is said to be one of the most magnificent sights imaginable. One enthusiastic German writer gives a very glowing account of it, which has been literally translated and is sold in all the bookstores in Lucerne. The

RAILWAY UP THE RIGI.

translation is so good (?) that it should be universally read. A portion of it is reproduced:

"The starlight night far expanded and aromatic with the herbs of the Alps and the meadow ground, now begins to assume a gray and hazy veil. Their mists arise from the top of the feathered pines, an airy crowd of ghost-like silent shapes approaching the light, that with a feebly pale glimmering dawns in the East. It is a strange beginning, a gentle breath of the morning air greets us from the rocky walls in the deep, and brings confused noises from below. That is a signal for all who did not like to ascend so high, without beholding the sunrise. Meanwhile the day breaks out bright and clear; a golden stripe, getting broader and broader, covers the mountains of St. Gall; the peaks of snow change their colors, indifferently white at first, then yellowish, and at last they turn a lovely pink. The new-born day illuminates them. Now, a general suspense! One bright flash — and the first ray of the sun shoots forth. A loud and general "oh" bursts out. The public feels grateful, be it a ray of the rising sun, or a rocket burnt off and dying away in the distance, with an illuminating tail of fire, and, after the refulgent globe, giving life to our little planet, has

THE RIGI RAILWAY.

fully risen, the crowd of people drop off one by one to their various occupations."

The ride down, while full of surprising views, is not so interesting as the ascent, for one is familiar with every turn, and has not that feeling of novelty that impresses him while going up.

Going back to Lucerne we are treated to a magnificent sunset, old Sol sinking behind the mountains with a grand blaze of glory that tinges the peaks all around the horizon with a brilliant golden outline.

On the eastern border of this wondrously beautiful lake is

a chapel, built, it is said, upon the spot where Tell leaped from

THE RAILWAY UP THE MOUNTAIN.

the boat of Gesler, the Austrian tyrant, while on his way to prison, and shot him. It is a pretty little structure, at the water's edge, and is every year visited by thousands of people who come to enthuse over the alleged Swiss patriot.

I should have enthused with the rest, only ever since I have been in Switzerland I have been investigating Tell, and to my profound grief I find that like Sairy Gamp's Mrs. Harris, "There ain't no sich a person," and never was.

When I say to my profound grief, I mean it. In my boyhood — alas, that was mány a year ago — I had several pet heroes among men and things. Tell shooting the arrow off

his boy's head and saving another arrow to shoot Gesler had he harmed his son, was one of them; Jackson and his cotton bales at New Orleans was another; the maelstrom, sucking down whales and ships, as depicted in the school geographies, was another; and then came Wellington with his "Up guards and at 'em," at Waterloo, the quiet

TELL'S CHAPEL, LAKE OF LUCERNE.

but heroic General Taylor at Monterey with his "A little more grape, Captain Bragg!" with others too tedious to mention. Among my especial hatreds was the cruel King Richard, of England, who slaughtered the infant princes in the tower.

Alas for history and geography! One by one these idols were dismounted. Later geographical investigation proves that there is no maelstrom on the coast of Norway; that the statement was founded upon a few rather ugly currents that swirl and eddy among some islands, but which are yet perfectly safe for vessels of light draft.

I had scarcely recovered from this before it came to light that Jackson's riflemen did not rest their unerring pieces upon cotton bales. When one thinks of it, it would be rather risky to fire flint-lock rifles over such inflammable material as cotton, to say nothing of the confession of that Brobindignagian fraud, Vincent Nolte, who confessed that all there was of the cotton story was this: He was moving a few bales of cotton he had in New Orleans up the country for safety, when it was feared the British would burn the city, and one of his mule teams, with two bales upon the wagon, was passing where some Tennesseeans were throwing up an earthwork. The wild backwoodsmen, in sheer mischief, upset the wagon, cut the mules loose, and buried the two bales and the wagon under the earth. Then, as he sued the government, per custom, for the price of five hundred bales, it was said that the battle was fought behind cotton, and the pictures show it.

For Wellington to have said "Up guards and at them!" would be to presume that Wellington was in the extreme front with the guards, and Taylor, to have made his exclamation, must have been sitting on his horse beside Captain Bragg, something generals never do.

But I said, though all these are gone, I have my Tell left me. Alas! Swiss and German investigators have proved conclusively that there never was such a man as Tell; that Gesler is quite as much of a fiction, and that the whole business of the apple on the son's head, the leap from the boat, and all the rest of it, is a poetic legend, the counterpart of which may be found in the literature of all old people. There is no mention either of Tell or Gesler in any authentic history.

But I thank heaven my objects of dislike are proved to be just as much fictions as the others. For up comes an English essayist who proves that Richard III. did not smother the infant princes, that he was not a cruel, humpbacked tyrant, but was the wisest and best king England had ever had, and that his untimely taking off was one of the greatest misfortunes that ever befell that country.

So these investigators have reduced humanity to a sort of average dead level, with no Mt. Blancs of goodness and no Jungfraus of badness.

Tibbitts was very indignant when I told him this about Tell. He remarked that he preferred not to believe the investigators; he preferred to believe in Tell. He didn't care a straw for the investigators, he defied them. Suppose Tell didn't shoot the apple? What then? Tell shooting the apple made a picturesque picture, and it pleased him. He protested against reducing all mankind to the drawing of molasses and the hewing of calico. He wanted heroes and heroines, and if they didn't appear in real life the poet gave them to us, and it did just as well.

By this time Tibbitts got wound up. "How does any one know that there was no Tell? I demand proof. You can't prove that there was *not* such a man, and that he did *not* do the feats ascribed to him. Very well! I assert there *was* such a man; that there was a Gesler; that Gesler put his hat on a pole in the market place, and required everybody to bow to it, and Tell refused; and then Gesler insisted that he should shoot an apple from his boy's head, and he did it. You have no proof that this is not so. I have proof that it is. I can show you the market place, and an apple. That the feat is possible every schoolboy knows, for have we not all seen Buffalo Bill do the same thing in the theaters? And, then, if it were not precisely true, it should have been. We want such incidents to keep alive a love of country, a healthy spirit of patriotism, and a wholesome hatred of tyrants who go about putting caps upon poles and requiring people to bow to them. Admitting it to be a fable, we want more such fables. What difference does it make if it is a fable? Does it not inculcate a great principle just the same? And inculcating a great principle is the main thing. I hold to Tell with all the simple faith I had in childhood, and even more. For in childhood Tell was merely a romantic and highly colored sensation — now he has grown to the sublime dimensions of a moral necessity."

And in spite of the bald facts staring him in the face, he went into ecstacies in the chapel, and spoke of it as a "shrine," and remarked that it would be better for the world had it had more Tells, and said everything that everybody says.

The Young Man who Knows Everything ambled in at this point with the remark that worms were made for sparrows, and the sparrows know it. It is a beautiful provision of nature that the strong eat the weak. If intellect and strength won't provide a living, what is the use of intellect and strength. A man might as well be a fool as anything else, if he can't live on his mental endowments.

Which, as it had no earthly application to the subject under discussion, was characteristic, very. But it satisfied him.

But you had better not express any doubt as to Tell to any of the Swiss, especially in this region. They believe in him as firmly as Americans do in Washington, and in the apple as steadily as we do in the hatchet. There was a book published in Berne, proving Tell to be a myth, and it was suppressed by the government, and all the copies in circulation siezed and burned.

Tell is a national pride, and besides, the legend brings tourists into the country, and keeps them longer after they come, which is a matter of national profit. And so, between pride and profit, they keep up the fiction, and will, to the end of time.

However, I still believe in Washington's hatchet, and in Franklin's eating bread in the streets of Philadelphia. I am going to cling to something of my youth. But I suppose somebody will disembowel these legends in the course of time, and life thereafter will be as monotonous as a mill-pond—all on a dead level.

CHAPTER XXXIX.

Leaving Lucerne, Mont Pilatus and the Rigi behind us, we speed rapidly on through pleasant valleys and fragrant meadows. The country loses its high, mountainous nature, and becomes a level, well-farmed district, extremely pleasant after three weeks of nothing but huge mountains, steep passes and rugged hills. Mountain scenery is all very well in its way, but one can have too much of it. A little is quite sufficient.

Zurich is a beautiful city, lying around the head of the lake of the same name. The old portion dates back to the twelfth century, and contains many interesting relics of that period. But around the old part there has grown up a fine modern city, whose solid substantial buildings, of fine architecture, contrast strangely with the old houses and churches that were built centuries ago.

Its location could not be more beautiful. In front is the clear pale-green lake, from which the limpid Limmat emerges and divides the city into two parts. Its shores are lined with picturesque villas, peeping out from among the orchards and vineyards that clothe the banks, clear to the foot of the snow clad Alps which form a strong background, being so far away that they are soft and subdued in the hazy air that partly obscures them from view.

The pride of Zurich is her schools, indeed all of German Switzerland is proud to recognize this place as its educational center. For centuries it has enjoyed this distinction, and its University, founded in 1832, is maintaining in these years the reputation of the city.

Where German is spoken three things are always found, music, wine and beer. Bacchus, Gambrinus and Orpheus go

hand in hand, and they engross the German mind about
equally. Zurich has more music to the square foot than any
of the Swiss cities, and the other two members of the trinity
are by no means neglected.

The Tonhalle is a spacious building finely decorated with
rare plants and flowers, and brilliantly lighted with gas jets

TIBBITTS IN A CONCERT HALL, ZURICH.

springing from artificial palm trees. Here the good citizens
of Zurich spend an evening of perfect enjoyment. An orchestra of seventy pieces, each performer a trained musician,
renders a programme of classical and popular music, in the
most perfect manner. The vast audience, composed of ladies
and gentlemen of the best standing, sit around the little
round tables sipping their light wine or beer, listening to the

music and, during the intervals, chatting and laughing and thoroughly enjoying themselves. There is a something about such an evening that is irresistable. The perfect order that prevails, the exquisite music, the brilliancy of the room, all combined to make it a perfect delight. Night after night — the programme is never twice alike — the Tonhalle is crowded with the wealth and fashion of Zurich, people of refinement and culture, who can fully appreciate and enjoy the delightful music.

There is one custom which obtains all over Germany, and especially in Zurich, which is a German city in reality, which custom I would could be transplanted in all its native vigor to America; and that is the carrying of the family relation into amusement as well as business.

A Zuricher doesn't eat his supper in silence, his mind full of his business, and after, without a word, put on his hat and overcoat, and with some indistinct reference to a lodge or a council meeting, or "the office," walk off to a club or beer place, and spend the evening convivially, only to return in the middle of the night, and roll into his bed without knowing or caring whether his wife and children have had a pleasant evening or no.

Not he! On the contrary, he consults his wife at lunch as to whether she prefers a dinner at home or at the gardens. The programmes of the various places are consulted, and it is decided, we will say, that the Tonhalle affords the most ponderous inducement; and so the whole family — father, mother, children, and grandchildren and grandparents, if such there be — go together and dine to the soft pleasings of the lute, or, rather, to the music of a magnificent orchestra.

For, be it known, at all these musical resorts there are superb restaurants, where splendid repasts are served at a very low price, so that in the matter of expense it makes no difference whether a family dines at home or at the public gardens.

The whole family sit and chat over their dinner in the jolliest way, listening to, enjoying and discussing the music, and after the dinner there is the long evening over the delightful light wines for the ladies and children, and the heavier beer for the adults; there are cigars for the males, and confections for the women and children, and so on, until the hour comes for home.

These concerts are made up of all kinds of music, from the weightiest classical to the most simple and popular, but the simple and popular is rendered with as much painstaking conscientiousness as the highest. They do "Way down upon the Swanee River" as conscientiously as a selection from Wagner, and as the performance lasts four hours or more there is variety enough to suit every taste.

And then, after it is over, the whole family go home, pleased with their simple enjoyment, and they go home together. The husband does not stop on the way; his enjoyment is with his family, and in his family.

There is no more pleasant sight in Europe than a Swiss or German family around one of these tables, enjoying drinking, music, smoking, and conversation, all at once. Happy people! They have the rare art of gratifying all the senses at once, at less cost than an American can any one singly. The whole cost of an evening in the Tonhalle for a man and his entire family is less than many an American of very moderate means spends upon himself alone, and they get ten times as much out of it as we do.

Tibbitts insisted the first night he was with a German family at one of these places, that he should certainly marry a German girl and settle in Switzerland. When you can dine a large family for a dollar, wine, music and cigars included, was his remark, there is some inducement for having a family. He could afford, if the price of land kept up in Wisconsin, to have an indefinite number of children.

And the Young Man who Knows Everything, who felt the influence of the heady wine he had drank, added, with great gravity: "Better a dinner of herbs on a house-top with a brawling woman, than to dwell with a stalled ox in the tents of wickedness." It was his time for a quotation.

From Zurich through Basle, or Bale, we come to Strasburg, one of the most interesting cities in Europe.

In this old city of Strasburg, founded by the Romans hundreds of years ago, we get a better idea of old architecture than in any city yet visited. Its narrow, crooked streets, with high, many-storied roofs, tell the story of its age in unmis-

takable language. The unique wood carving that embellishes
the facades of so many of the old wooden buildings look
strange and out of place in this matter-of-fact age, but in
years gone by they gave to Strasburg the name of "the most
beautiful city."

Approaching the city we pass a number of strong fortifications, which were in active use during the Franco-Prussian
war. Strasburg, two miles from the Rhine, has always been
a strategical point, and played a very important part in the
struggle of 1870–71, the siege, which lasted from the thirteenth
of August till the twenty-seventh of September, being one of
the marked episodes of the war.

Once in the city the tourist turns first to the cathedral,
which stands nearly in the center of the city. Unfortunately
for the general effect, it is located in a neighborhood of
narrow streets and ugly high-roofed houses that entirely
surround the massive pile, and the first impression is rather
disappointing. But this feeling soon wears off. There is a
certain majesty about the noble building that compels admiration, while the cloud-cleaving spire, wondrously graceful, is a
marvel of strength and grace. It is a fascinating structure.
The more one studies its beautiful proportions, and the wonderful decorations which so profusely embellish it, the more he is
struck with wonder at the genius of the architect and the skill
of the patient builders.

The present cathedral was begun some time during the
twelfth century, on the site of one destroyed by fire, said to
have been built during the sixth century. Tradition says that
the site of the present cathedral has been devoted to worship
from the remotest times; that there was a sacred wood in the
midst of which the Celts built their Druidical Dolmen. After
the Romans conquered Gaul, they founded a fortified town,
where Strasburg now stands, and in place of the Dolmen they
dedicated a temple to Hercules and Mars. Old chronicles
record that in the fourth century St. Armand built a church on
the ruins of an old Roman temple, the previous existence of
which is authenticated by the finding of several brass statues of
Hercules and Mars, during the excavations for the foundations
of the first cathedral.

From the beginning of the work on the present cathedral

down to 1870 it has been terribly unfortunate, having been
burned, struck by lightning, shaken by earthquakes, and in
1870 it suffered terribly by the cannon balls of the German
besiegers.   In the first part of the siege of Strasburg, the Ger-

PRINCIPAL ENTRANCE TO STRASBURG CATHEDRAL.

mans tried to force the surrender by the bombardment and
partial destruction of the inner town.   In the night of the 23d
of August began for the frightened inhabitants the real time
of terror; however, that night the rising conflagrations, for
instance in St. Thomas' Church, were quickly put out.   But in

38

the following night the new church, the library of the town, the museum of painting, and many of the finest houses, became a heap of ruins, and under the hail of shells all efforts to extinguish the fire were useless. For the cathedral the night from the 25th to the 26th of August was the worst. Towards midnight the flames broke out from the roof perforated by shells, and increased by the melting copper they rose to a fearful height beside the pyramid of the spire. The sight of this grand volume of flames, rising above the town, was indescribable and tinged the whole sky with its glowing reflection. And the guns went on thundering, and shattering parts of the stone ornaments which adorned the front and sides of the cathedral. The whole roof came down and the fire died out for want of fuel.

The following morning the interior was covered with ruins, and through the holes in the vault of the nave one could see the blue sky. The beautiful organ built by Silbermann was pierced by a shell, and the magnificent painted windows were in great part spoiled. On the 4th of September two shells hit the crown of the cathedral and hurled the stone masses to incredible distance; on the 15th a shot came even into the point below the cross, which was bent on one side, and had its threatened fall only prevented by the iron bars of the lightning conductor which held it.

After the entrance of the Germans into the reconquered town, the difficult and dangerous work of restoration of the point of the spire was begun at once and happily ended a few months after. They have now obliterated all traces of the ruin and devastation of that dreadful time.

This is war, and what was this war all about? Why, Louis Napoleon, who stole France and kept the French enslaved by amusing one-half of them that he might rob the other half, had to appeal to French patriotism and plunge France into a war to cover his Imperial thefts. On the other hand, the Kaiser William, and the iron-handed Bismarck, who had been grinding the people of Germany for years to prepare for war, were not slow to accept the challenge. What they wanted was to have more territory to plunder. There was no bad blood between the French and German people; it was the self-constituted rulers of the two peoples, who, for their own glory, set them to butchering each other. And so at it they went.

These kings and emperors respect neither God nor man, and so they sent their bombs hurtling through this wonderful temple dedicated to God.

Nothing to the gunners inspired by royalty was the delicate tracery, the genius-inspired proportions, the almost breathing statues, the wonderfully beautiful spire, that crystallized dream; nothing to them the magnificent organ, attuned to the sweetest worship of the Most High, nothing the recollections of the centuries that clustered about it, nothing the art treasures it held. It was Strasburg, and Strasburg must fall.

And they counted God's images in the doomed city even less than they did God's temple. And so they sent shells crashing through the homes of Strasburg, and men were killed in its streets, women in the houses, and children in their cradles. It made no difference to the white-bearded William, the iron-handed Bismarck, or the sensual Napoleon. It was their fight, but they bore none of the suffering. The Kaiser actually had the impudence to order a thanksgiving for the slaughter of ten thousand Frenchmen, and Louis Napoleon would have done the same had he been in condition.

I have expressed my opinion of kings before. The more one sees of them and their work the less love he has for them. Soldiers and thin soup for the people in Germany, soldiers and starvation in Ireland. That's what royalty and nobility mean everywhere — brute force and suffering.

The façade of the great cathedral is by Erwin, of Steinbach, the most famous architect of the middle ages, and is a marvel of beauty, its massive proportions being toned down and improved by the innumerable figures, statues, and a fine rose window, forty-two feet in diameter, that adorn it.

Entering the cathedral, one is greatly impressed with the harmonious effect produced by the massive yet graceful columns from which spring the light arches that form the ceiling. The proportions are admirable, the height being ninety-nine feet, the width forty-five yards, and the length one hundred and twenty-one yards.

The pulpit, a fine specimen of stone carving, dates back to

1485, and affords a good idea of the style of art that flourished in Germany at that time.

Next to the cathedral itself, which demands a great deal of study, the great astronomical clock attracts the most attention.

PIG MARKET, STRASBURG.

It was constructed during the years 1838–42, by a Strasburg clockmaker named Schwilgue, and is a wonderful piece of mechanism. The exterior, handsomely decorated with exquisite carvings and paintings, shows a perpetual calendar, with the feasts that vary, according to their connection with Easter or Advent Sunday. The dial, which is thirty feet in circumference, is subject to a revolution in three hundred and sixty-five or three hundred and sixty-six days, and indicates the suppression of the circular bi-sextile days. There is also a complete planetarium, representing the mean tropical revolutions of each of the planets visible to the naked eye, the phases of the moon, and the eclipses of the sun and moon calculated forever.

Then with the same mechanism a number of figures are made to go through certain motions at stated intervals. At noon the twelve apostles appear before the Savior, who raises his hands to bless them, during which time a cock flaps his wings, and crows three times. A figure of Death stands in the midst of figures representing the four ages, childhood striking the first quarter of the hour, youth the second, manhood the third, and old age the last. Just before each quarter is struck, one of the two genii seated above this perpetual calendar strikes a note of warning. When the hour is struck by Death, the second of these genii turns over the hour glass he holds in his hand. It is a wonderful piece of mechanism.

As with everything else of public interest around this section, where in olden times imagination ran riot, this clock has its legend. It is said that, long ages ago, a mechanic of Strasburg labored and studied for years for the accomplishment of some purpose that he kept secret from all his neighbors. Even his only child, a lovely girl who was sought in marriage by a prospective mayor of the city, and by a handsome young clockmaker, was not allowed to enter the room where this mysterious work was being carried on.

In the course of time the elder suitor was made mayor, and then proposed for the hand of the beautiful girl, who, loving the young man, refused him. Soon after this, the old mechanic showed to the astonished citizens of Strasburg, who up to this time had ridiculed him as an insane person, the wonderful clock he had constructed. He at once became very popular, much to the disgust of the mayor who had been rejected by his daughter.

The clockmaker's fame spread all over the country, and the citizens of Basel, a neighboring city, attempted to buy the wonderful piece of mechanism. But the corporation of Strasburg would not part with it, and caused a chapel to be built in the cathedral for its reception. Then the citizens of Basel offered a large sum of money if the master would construct them a similar clock, and he accepted their offer.

This would never do. The wonderful clock was the principal glory of Strasburg, and people were coming from all parts of the then civilized world to see it. If Basel should have a clock like it or superior to it, it would divide the trade as well as the glory, and Strasburg, instead of standing alone as the possessor of such a piece of mechanism, would have a rival. Should Basel get a clock, the citizen thereof would cock his hat upon one side of his head and say, to a Strasburger, "You need n't put on airs about your old clock, with its twelve apostles, and all that. We see your twelve apostles and go you a Judas Iscariot better. You have a rooster it is true, we admit that, but we have one with all the latest improvements. He flaps his wings better than yours, and his crow is three times as loud. Come over to Basel and see a really good clock."

To prevent this the City Council of Strasburg, at the suggestion of the mayor who had never got over being rejected by the clock-maker's daughter, determined to put out the old gentleman's eyes, which they rightly judged would prevent him from making any more clocks, and Strasburg would still have the glory of owning the most wonderful one in the world. This was assented to and the poor man was asked if there was anything he wanted before the sentence was executed. He asked to have the terrible operation performed in front of his noble work. When taken before it, he gazed at it fondly, and secretly slipped out of place two or three important springs. Just as the torture was completed the works in the clock began to whirr, it struck thirteen times and then ceased to work. The glory of Strasburg was destroyed. The artisan lost his sight, the city its clock, the mayor his love — in short, it was a dead loss all around, as it always is when fair dealing is departed from.

Years after the young clockmaker married his old blind

friend's daughter, and after many years of hard, steady work, succeeded in repairing and improving the clock, which was the predecessor of the one now in the cathedral.

This is the legend of the clock.

In the Protestant church of St. Thomas is one of the finest monuments in Europe. It was erected by Louis XV. in honor of Marshal Saxe.

In front of a high tablet, upon which there is a long inscription, is a figure of the Marshal, heroic size, dressed in military uniform. He is descending a short flight of steps leading to a coffin, the lid of which Death holds open for his reception. A female figure, representing France, attempts to detain the Marshal and ward off Death. On the left, Hercules in a mournful attitude leans upon his club. Commemorating the Marshal's victories in the Flemish war are the Austrian eagle, the Dutch lion and the English lion.

The whole work is exquisitely done, the figures of France and Death being wonderful specimens of carving in marble. The artist, Pigalle, was occupied twenty years in the execution of this masterpiece.

There are several other things of interest in the old church of St. Thomas, besides the memorial of the great marshal, though they are of the ghastly order, and more curious than pleasing.

A great many years ago there lived in Strasburg a lunatic whose very soul was bound up in this old church. His soul being devoted to it, he determined to throw in his body, and so he starved himself to death that he might leave the corporation more money. He left all his fortune to the church, and the least it could do was to give him a tomb, which it did, and then carved upon it his emaciated form, taking him after death, that nothing should be lacking in ghastliness. When religion or vanity, or a compound of both, is freakish, it is very freakish.

The most repulsive sight in all Europe is within these venerable walls. The Duke of Nassau wanted immortality, and so his remains — he was killed in battle — are carefully preserved in a glass case, hermetically sealed, clad in the very garments he wore when death struck him. And after he was killed his little daughter, aged thirteen, died, and the family had her poor remains, clad in the silks and tinsel of the period, disposed of in the same way.

And there they are to this day, as beautiful a commentary on human hopes and human ambitions as one would wish to see.

The Duke of Nassau was a mighty man in his day, and he hoped to be remembered of men for all time. What is he now? The flesh has melted from his bones, the very bones are crumbling into dust, the garments in which he was clad are disappearing, and all there is of him is a grinning, ghastly skeleton, and the daughter is the same in the same way; the flesh has disappeared from her bones, the little finger, once-so plump and taper, is now a bone which time has eaten away to almost nothing; the ring of gold which she wore in life is still there, but it hangs on a time-wasted bone, the flesh having melted from under it.

It is a ghastly commentary. The duke undertook a fight with Time with a certainty of Time's winning. The philosopher draws a moral from his poor remains, the loose-minded make jokes over them. Could he hear the comments on his once august body he would get up and walk out of that church, and go and bury himself somewhere in some cemetery, that he might, as he should, be forgotten once for all. The duke should have realized the fact before he had himself put in this glass case, that so far as earth goes, everything ends with death, and that efforts that men have made to perpetuate their memory have been invariably failures. The kings who built the pyramids, solid as they are, are scarcely remembered.

It was in a famous beer house in Strasburg that we met an American who was not of the regulation kind, and who, consequently, was a sweet boon.

He came into the place with a slouching gait, though his manner was by no means deprecatory or humble. There was nothing in him to distinguish him from the regular tramp, except that his rum-illuminated face carried on its surface more intelligence and less brutality than the usual tramp shows, and he evidently had some idea of not bidding eternal good-bye to his respectability. Instead of the greasy wrap about the throat of the regular tramp, he had a paper collar, which he had unquestionably picked up somewhere and turned, and his coat was buttoned up carefully to conceal the painfully evident absence of a shirt, a deceit the confirmed tramp would scorn to practice. And then he wore a tall hat, and had made attempts to brush it, and his carriage, when he knew he was observed, was bold and defiant, and not cringing or slouching.

He sat down at the table with us, and commenced conversation with some remarks about the weather, some original remarks concerning the state of trade, and from that he glided with a grace that was to be commended into a disquisition as to the effect upon the commerce of the world of the building of a ship-canal across the Isthmus, and likewise the effect it would have upon the climate of the United States, ending his conversation with the request of the loan of a dollar.

"How happens it," I asked, "that a man informed as you are, with your evident education and your general information, should be borrowing dollars in this way?"

"Excuse me, sir," said he; "I have not borrowed dollars, to yet, though I hope to. You have, as yet, made no response as my modest appeal. But why am I thus? Can you tell? Can I tell? Who is responsible for what happens to him? Who can control tastes? Who can analyze that subtle and unknown thing we call mind?"

"But who are you, anyhow?"

"I am a graduate of Harvard, sir, and a son of one of the once wealthiest men in Boston."

"Why this condition of things, then?"

"My dear sir, I was born fortunately—you would say unfortunately—I say fortunately. I had tastes, appetites, and a philosophical mind. While a student I indulged those tastes to the top of my bent. I was the best billiard player, the most constant and steady drinker, the hardest rider, and, in fact, the most confirmed pleasure seeker in the college. I utterly refused to do anything that did not please me. I learned much, for the pursuit of knowledge afforded me a delight, but I would learn nothing the getting of which did not afford me pleasure.

"At the close of my college career, the world was before me. The question was, what should I do? What should be the plan of my life? Should I go into business, and make a great fortune? Should I go into literature, and make myself an imperishable name? Should I go into politics, and control the destinies of nations?

"Fortunately philosophy came to my aid. What earthly good would all this do me? What good of piling up money? What good of making a name, and what earthly use was there in controlling the destiny of nations? I could do something for myself, and what I did for myself I got the good of, but why worry about making a name, or why labor to make money which I could not take with me?

"I could see no good in any of it, and so I followed the impulses of my nature, feeling that if nature was no guide then was I lost, indeed.

"I sang, I drank, I yachted, I did everything till my money was gone, and here I am."

"Would it not have been better for you had you followed a more reputable career?"

"I don't see it. I could have done anything that I wanted to, but to what purpose? Sir, the world is coming to an end, shortly. The approach of various planets to the earth, the frequency of comets, the changes so common now that have been totally unknown, all conspire to a very sudden ending of the planet on which we live and move. Within my life-time, doubtless, there will be a collapse. We shall either get away from the sun or get into it, or some erratic planet will come bouncing into us, and the entire universe will go to eternal smash. The earth will either melt or freeze solid, or it will be dispersed into infinitesimal fragments.

"Now, sir, let me ask you what encouragement there is for a man to worry himself about making a fortune with this terrible condition of things staring him in the face? What good would the ownership of the New York Central Railroad be when there is a certainty that the entire structure, road-bed, depots, rolling stock and everything will be utterly destroyed within my life-time? Under such circumstances who would care to own a city, or to possess in fee simple the cattle on a thousand hills? What is beef going to be worth then?

"And then reputation. When the earth melts and the sky

is rolled up like a scroll, where is your Shakespeare? Where is Milton, Byron, Burns, and the long list of men who have written that their names may be everlasting? The dust of Shakespeare will be mingled with that of the organ grinder across the street, and the pyramids will be of no more account than the dirt-heap on the other side, which the Street Commissioner never moves away. The libraries will all be destroyed, and in the general annihilation, clergymen, scholars, capitalists, life insurance agents, presidents, emperors, book agents and tramps will all stand upon a common level. One fragment of me may assume the character of an aerolite and astonish the natives of another planet, and another fragment may go to feed the sun and thus furnish heat for the shivering tramp on Mars, and mingled with me may be the iron that is now in the system of Vanderbilt.

"Therefore I have no desire for a name or money. Things are not sufficiently permanent to be desirable for an ambitious man.

"But speaking of the great cataclysm that is imminent, I did not hear any response to my application for a loan of a dollar to relieve my hunger. That is permanent, and will be till the universal smash-up."

I gave the man a franc.

"It is little but it will do, it will assuage the pangs of hunger. A philosopher needs but little. Thank you. Farewell forever. In the smash that is to come, let us hope that our fragments may come together, and that we may sail through space in company."

And he departed. He did not go to a restaurant, but he went, as straight as the bird flies, to the nearest brandy shop from which he emerged in a minute with his face illuminated. He did not live by bread alone.

Strasburg is rich in antiquity, rich in the quaintest old houses on the continent, houses that commence inland from the sidewalk, each story projecting above the one under it, the fronts filled full of carving of the quaintest and most curious description. These houses, some of them, count the years of their being by the hundreds, and Strasburg, sleepy old town that it is, either keeps them because she is too lazy to pull them down, or because she really treasures them because of their age.

An American looking at them feels that time has gone backward with him, and that he has awakened in the four-teenth century.

Here you see the genuine Alsatian costume. The women are, as a rule, fine-looking, some of them pretty, and the style of dress fits their peculiar style of beauty. They wear immense bows of wide black ribbon, which stands up at the back of the head, and flares out at the sides like the wings of a wind-mill. This admits of no hat or any other head-gear, and its effect, though odd at first sight, is rather pleasing. However, any-thing looks well on a pretty woman, and the women of Alsace are all comely. They wear their gowns short, that the effect of shapely ankles and trim feet may not be lost, and altogether they are good specimens of feminity.

The peculiarity of the old houses in Strasburg, already spoken of, is greatly intensified by the huge storks' nests that crown the large awkward chimneys of many of the houses. All Summer long, the great white storks live in Strasburg, until the cold weather drives them further south. Their nests are built on the tops of chimneys, of rough sticks and straw, and are very clumsy-looking affairs. But when there is a white stork standing in them, solemn and grave, on one leg, the other drawn closely under him, the effect is extremely ludicrous.

The stork is a peculiarly Strasburgian institution. It is considered a bad omen if a stork leaves a house, in the chimney of which he has once built his nest, and misfortune is certain, so they believe, to follow any one who mistreats or offends a stork.

There are thousands of legends about them, in brief the stork figures in everything Strasburgian. It is said that about a week before their departure in the Autumn, all the storks meet in a meadow outside of the city and hold solemn council, the oldest acting as chairman, and all talking and discussing things the same as men do, in their own language. It is not said that they come to blows in their debates, as American Congressmen do, but that is doubtless because they know only French and German usages. The stork is a well behaved bird.

CHAPTER XL.

BADEN BADEN AND THINGS THEREIN.

AT one time Baden Baden was one of the most famous gambling places in the world, but it is now simply a fashionable watering place, very like Saratoga. It is beautifully situated in the valley of the Oos, at the entrance to the Black Forest. During the time the gambling rooms flourished, great pains were taken to make it as attractive as possible. Long, wide avenues were laid out and planted with beautiful trees, picturesque drives were made, and all the natural advantages were improved a thousand fold, so that to-day it is one of the most beautiful spots imaginable.

The buildings, formerly the scenes of fashionable riot and dissipation, were built in the most elaborate manner and most lavishly decorated with beautiful frescoes by most eminent artists.

Nature made Baden Baden a natural pleasure and health resort, and wherever men and women go for pleasure or health you may be sure of meeting vice in almost every form. The pleasure seekers must be perpetually stimulated, and those who haunt mineral springs to recover health, generally lost by persistent following of vicious practices, come expecting the waters to build them up to the resumption of the vices that brought them down. Consequently they gamble.

A few years ago Baden Baden was the head centre of gambling for the world. The Frenchman, Englishman, German, Russian, American, Turk, and, for that matter, men of all nations came here to drink the waters, take the baths and gamble. Following in the train of the rich invalids came the professional gamblers, hawks following pigeons everywhere.

The government gave the exclusive right to manage a

gambling house to one company, or rather one man.   Origin-

THE GREAT HALL.

ally a Frenchman named Benezet had it, paying some forty

thousand dollars a year for the privilege of plucking fools, and when he died, leaving an immense fortune, his son-in-law, Dupressoir, continued the business. The money received by the government for this privilege was appropriated to the beautifying of the city and the other mineral water resorts in the Grand Duchy.

The gambling was done in an immense building which is now the "Conversation-haus," and, if its walls could speak, many a tale, comic and tragic, they could tell.

You are assailed with all sorts of legends concerning it There was a lady, of what nationality was never known, a woman who commenced gambling at the age of thirty-six, who always came to the rooms closely veiled, whose face was never seen. She played so much money invariably, leaving the rooms when she had lost or won her limit. It was never ascertained where she lodged, even. For twenty years she came to the rooms twice each day, staking a Napoleon (four dollars) on each turn of the wheel till she had lost or won fifty, and when that loss or that winning was accomplished she glided out, only to reappear the next day.

There is a wild legend prevalent that this mysterious being's lover had lost his fortune at the tables, and had blown his brains out as a fitting finish to his folly, and that there was an irresistible impulse that brought her to the scene of his death, and kept her there all her life.

What interested Tibbitts the most in this legend was the statement that the lover lost all his money, and then blew out his brains.

"Any man, or alleged man," said Tibbitts, "who would lose a fortune at such a game as they played here, must have great faith in his marksmanship, to try to hit his brains, no matter how short the range."

The Young Man who Knows Everything wanted Tibbitts to make plain the point to the remark, and then the Professor had to go on and explain that what Mr. Tibbitts intended was that a man who would gamble at all must have an infinitesimal brain, so small, indeed, as to make it safe from the best marksman. The young man pondered over it a minute, and expressed himself satisfied.

There is another story of a woman, an old and haggard woman, who came every day and staked a Napoleon. She would not play unless there should be in the room a child, a young, fresh child; and she used to take the baby, and put her Napoleon in its little hand, and have it place it on the black or red, as the child's whim dictated. And it is said that she generally won. Like all the rest of the

THE YOUNG MAN WANTED TIBBITTS TO MAKE PLAIN THE POINT.

mysterious beings of the gambling hall, this eccentric old lady disappeared one day, and was never seen again.

It made little difference to her successors. The croupier,

that calm, impassive man, raked in the Napoleons, or raked them out, the wheel revolved, and the life or death of one habitué of the place made no more difference than a footprint on the sands of the sea.

German students who, by extravagant living, encumbered themselves with debt, and who were afraid to apply at home for more money, came hither to make enough at gambling to restore themselves. They never did it. M. Benezet was not paying forty thousand dollars a year rent for the privilege of running a game at which improvident and extravagant young men could make up their folly — not he. His game was to take what they had left, without knowing or caring what became of them afterward.

The most common legend of them all is of the young man who walked calmly into the room with one hundred Napoleons, all he had left, and staked one piece after another, and lost invariably. Finally there was but one left. Turning to his friend, he remarked calmly, "This is my life I am wagering." He put it upon the black, the wheel revolved, he lost.

Without a word this calm young man went out, and hung himself with his handkerchief to a tree, where his inanimate body was found the next morning.

This young man is very plenty in Baden-Baden, though not much more so than the same kind of a fellow who, staking his last gold piece, draws a pistol from his pocket, and shoots himself at the table, the croupier paying no attention to it, and going on with the game as though it was a regular part of it, and an everyday occurrence.

Tibbitts frowned upon this legend severely, holding it to be unworthy of credence. "The young man," said Tibbitts, "would have gone out and pawned his revolver for ten dollars, and taken another hack at it."

And then this young man with a lively imagination went on to show that no matter how desperate the situation there is always a chance to get out. His story was to this effect:

A young New Yorker had gone to Paris with some thousands of dollars given him by his indulgent father, that he might see the world and study the languages. He studied French with a young grisette whose acquaintance he had

39

made, and a very pleasant life he lived, till one morning the two discovered that they hadn't a dollar between them left, that he had spent in three months with his syren what was sufficient to have supported him decently for three years. He dared not send home for more money, he could not leave his friend (that's what they call it), and they had not enough to buy another meal.

The pawn shops were resorted to, till everything they had was gone and starvation stared them in the face.

They wept over it, and finally came to a conclusion. They loved each other dearly, they could not live apart, and so they decided to die together. She rushed out and pawned her last pair of stockings to purchase charcoal; they closed all the cracks in the room and lighted the coal, that its fumes might kill them in the regular Parisian style.

The girl died, but life was left in the young man. He rose and broke a window with a boot — no, he had pawned his boots — but with something, anyhow, and let in fresh air, which saved his life.

Then he turned and looked at the poor girl on the bed, her long hair flung negligently over the pillow, her face not wasted by disease, but plump and fresh as in life.

"Poor Fifine," he sighed in agony; "how beautiful she is, and how I loved her and how she loved me! I shall never love again. From this time out my life, should I live, will be a desert waste. Should I live? Alas! I cannot, will not live. Why did I spring from that couch and break open the window? I cannot live without her; I will die with her."

He commenced closing the window and looking for more charcoal, when something occurred to him.

"Come to think, I won't die with her. Dying with her wouldn't do her any good, and if I live, she, my love, will perpetually have something to look down upon."

He merely walked down and reported a case of suicide, and after the investigation claimed the body as the next best friend, which was all right.

Then he sold the body to a medical college for dissection, for sixty dollars, and bought a second-class ticket and went home to New York and told his mother he had been robbed of his money, and got her to intercede with the irate father, and is, I believe, living in comparative luxury to-day."

"How could he have got out on the street, if he had pawned all his clothes and his boots?" queried the Young Man who Knows Everything.

Tibbitts answered with asperity that there were so-called men everywhere in the world who perpetually strewed the salt of fact over the flowery fields of fancy. "You are the young man, I believe, who made me miserable the other day, by unearthing the fact that there never was a William Tell."

The Professor, after thinking the tale over awhile, said that such a thing might have happened in Oshkosh, but never in Paris. In Paris the young woman would have lived and sold the body of the young man and started a café on the proceeds.

Then the young man remarked that revenge was a fool's luxury, and that the New Testament precept about turning the other cheek, was not only sound in religion, but was the highest good sense, as religion always is. To nurse a hatred is more expensive than to keep a horse in feed or a fine watch in repair.

The gambling came to an end finally, and the romance of Baden Baden with it. A decree withdrew the privilege of the establishment, another prohibited the establishing of other places, and on one fateful night in 1872, at twelve o'clock, the bankers turned off their lights, and Baden Baden as a gambling resort was no more.

The old gambling house is now called the Conversationhaus and is used for concerts and balls, and is the favorite rendezvous for the fashionable world, especially during the time the band plays, in the morning, afternoon and evening. Then the wealth and fashion residing in Baden and representing all nationalities promenades the beautiful avenues, or, making little parties, sips beer and laughs and flirts to its hearts' content.

Near the Conversationhaus is the "Trinkhalle," where invalids, and those who wish to be thought invalids, drink the famous mineral waters that have made Baden celebrated all over the world. The rooms are magnificently furnished, and on the arcade in front of the building are some fine frescoes illustrating different legends of the Black Forest.

The peculiar waters of Baden Baden come from a great
many springs in the hill-sides, and are conducted to the various
bathing places in pipes, and they are as hot as you want them.

IN FRONT OF THE KURSAAL, AT BADEN.

One of the springs is known as Hell Spring, because of the
temperature of the water, one would suppose, but the Badenese
have another reason for its name. Of course they have a
legend for it, which runs thus:

A great many centuries ago an irascible and very wicked old man who possessed the ground on which the spring is, had, as a matter of course, a beautiful and supernaturally good daughter. By the way, I never could understand why excessively wicked men in legends always had so sweet a lot of daughters, but I suppose it is necessary in order to have legends.

This daughter was beloved by the son of a neighboring noble who was at feud with her father, and, as a matter of course, the old man opposed the match. The present hot spring was then as cold as ice and a most delicious water for drinking, of which the old man was very fond, which statement proves the legend to be false. No German noble in this or any other period of the world's history ever knew whether the water on his estate was good for drinking or not. He may have tested it for other purposes, but never for a beverage. He prefers wine or beer.

One day going down to his pet spring he found his girl there, and with her her lover. He was enraged, and when the young man told him he loved his daughter and would wed her, he exclaimed with a horrible oath:

"Wed her! You may wed her when this spring is as hot as hell, and when that happens I will drink to your nuptials in its waters!"

No sooner said than done. The spring changed from its lovely greenish blue to a sulphurous and salty color. Great jets of gas with an unpleasant smell issued, and the water boiled up quite as hot as the place the profane old man had indicated as a standard. And Satan himself, with tail and hoofs, and everything complete, appeared, from where none of the three could determine, and politely handed him a goblet of the boiling water.

He had sworn an oath, and there was no going back upon it. So he took the goblet and swallowed the contents and rolled over in agony and died, as I should suppose any one would.

The young man married the girl, and I doubt not his descendants are interested in the bath houses supplied from the springs.

It isn't much of a legend, indeed with a little practice I

believe I could write a better one myself, but it is as they gave
it to me.

THE SWIMMING BATH.

The grand bathing houses are on a scale of magnificence

that is truly wonderful, and one almost feels like shamming illness simply to enjoy their luxury. Nothing that money can buy, and in Europe as in America, it will buy almost anything, has been spared to make them as attractive to the eye and the other senses as possible. They make up Baden's stock in trade, and Baden is too good a merchant not to have attractive wares for sale.

One of the favorite excursions from Baden is up the hill to the south of the city to the old castle, the walls of which are said to have been built in the third century, when the Romans constructed fortifications here. From the twelfth century till the completion of the new castle nearer the city, the old Schloss was the residence of the Margraves of the Duchy.

The road leading to the castle winds up the Battert, giving some beautiful views of the valley, with Baden, rich with its luxuriant foliage, nestling at the foot of the Black Mountains, whose dark profile stretches away off far to the north.

Before reaching the steep portion of the ascent, the ladies of the party were provided with donkeys.

The Professor, whose age and avoirdupois rendered steep-hill climbing a matter of great difficulty, determined that he would ride.

A diminutive donkey, scarcely larger than a good sized Newfoundland dog, was assigned to him, and a most ludicrous sight it was as the party made its start up the hill.

A gentleman six feet in height, with very long legs and a remarkably protuberant abdomen, arrayed in a very ill-fitting coat, light trowsers, a tall hat, and enormous spectacles, with an immense cotton umbrella under one arm, is not a sight to inspire respect, even when it is traveling as infantry.

But take that figure and put it astride of a donkey so small that the rider's legs have to be drawn up to keep the feet off the ground, and have that donkey a perverse and mischievous animal (most of them answer to this description), and it is about as ludicrous a sight as was ever vouchsafed to mortal ken.

Each donkey is led or driven, as the case may be, by a boy, and the German boy has all the elements of mischief in him that any other boy possesses. And so when this especial boy saw that the entire party were laughing at the Professor, he wisely determined to gain popularity by adding to the merriment. And so he would wink at the people following, and twist the donkey's tail, and the intelligent animal, knowing what was expected of him, would kick up his heels, and the Professor, one hand busy with the bridle and the other with the umbrella under his arm, would objurgate as much as a Professor dared.

THE DONKEY ENJOYED IT HUGELY.

The donkey enjoyed it hugely, for he kicked up his heels with delight, and pranced from one side of the road to the other in an ecstacy of pleasure.

The portly gentleman did n't seem to think it very funny, although at last he was compelled to join in the general laugh that went up at his expense.

Finally he beat the boy and the donkey both. When the donkey would kick up behind he simply dropped both feet to the ground and brought him to anchor; and when he attempted a shy to one side, one foot on the ground held him to his business; and catching the boy at the trick he took him by the arm, and, with a grip that long years of flagellating boys had perfected, pulled him up in front of him, and everything was pleasant again.

THE LICHTENTHAL AVENUE—BADEN.

As we toiled up the long hill the gathering clouds presaged a rain storm. Then they broke, and as we reached the old ruin the sun came out with great brilliancy, and gave us a magnificent view up and down the broad, fertile valley.

But, unexpectedly, before we had time to go through the various rooms of the castle the rain began to fall in torrents,

which was uncomfortable, the roof having long years ago
succumbed to time, which has no more respect for a margrave's
castle than it has for a laborer's hut.   Time is no aristocrat.

We sought shelter in a room that had been fitted up as a
restaurant, and then we were treated to a genuine storm right
from the Black Forest. The wind howled around the open

PROMENADE IN BADEN-BADEN.

spaces of the ruined walls, the rain dashed against the window
panes in fitful gusts, while above all other sounds could be
heard the creaking and moaning of the trees all around us, as
they were bent and swayed by the storm   It required but a
little stretch of the imagination to fill the room with gallant
knights, and to believe it was the din and clatter of battle we
heard without.

We were sitting on the ground on which knights and ladies
in the centuries past had sat and feasted.   There was not an
inch of space within a half mile of us that had not its story.
Mailed knights in that very room had

> "Carved their meat in gloves of steel,
> And drank red wine with their visors down."

And possibly their spirits were hovering over us. If they
were, we did not know it; they did not materialize.   Instead
of the mailed knights and beardless pages and fair ladies of
the middle ages, there was a party of Americans in tall hats
and short coats, ladies in the latest possible Parisian walking
dresses, and instead of the glorious game of war it was a
simple game of euchre, which the men played with the same

earnestness that characterizes them at home in their business, and the ladies with that utter disregard of rule that characterizes feminine card playing everywhere. It is needless to

CHARCOAL BURNERS IN THE BLACK FOREST.

observe that in the matter of wine the example of the old knights was followed, only we had no visors.

A party of Americans playing cards in the castle of a

warlike king! Well! well! There are steamboats on Loch Katrine; there will be a railroad to Jerusalem, and the holy places will yet be illuminated with the electric light. There is no room to-day for sentiment.

This castle was built, originally, by the Romans, and fell into the hands of the Margrave of Baden in 1112. It was necessary in that day to have these strongholds, from which the margraves could issue and make war upon their neighbors, that being their principal business. It was continued as a residence for the Baden potentates till 1689, when Louis XV. of France demolished it, leaving it, less the ivy that has grown over it, as it is to-day.

Its principal use now is to give employment to the donkeys to get to it, and the selling of wine and refreshments to the tourists who hunger after the delightful view it affords.

The new Friedrichsbad is an imposing edifice built against the hillside upon which the springs are located. The exterior is a fine specimen of the Renaissance style of architecture, and is embellished with a great many fine statues, busts and medallions.

The interior is a marvel of completeness and elegance, being finer in all its details than any similar bathing establishment in the world. The wood work is all massive and elegant; the walls and ceilings are artistically frescoed; the bath tubs, large swimming baths, are cut out of solid marble, and are so arranged that the bather can go from one to another, securing any desired temperature without inconvenience.

The water comes from springs on the hillsides, at a temperature of 144° Fahrenheit, and is conveyed by pipes throughout the building, the pipes being so arranged that the water is gradually cooled. In this way one is enabled to bathe in any kind of water he desires. The yield is upwards of one hundred gallons a minute, and are said to be among the most efficacious mineral springs known, the solid ingredients, chiefly chloride of sodium, amounting only to three per cent.

In this magnificent structure, there are the common bath tubs, hewn out of solid blocks of marble and completely let into the floor, with steps leading down to them; large hip baths, supplied with a continual stream of mineral water; an electric bathroom for inhaling the thermal water; baths for the cold water treatment and the cold shower baths; vapor baths, hot air baths, swimming baths of different degrees of temperature, supplied also with shower baths the temperature of whose water can be regulated by the bather, and vapor baths in boxes.

After taking as many of these as he desires, and having been rubbed in a room lurid with hot air, the bather is conducted to a large room where he is enveloped in a warm bath cloak. Then he is taken to a large, luxuriously furnished room where he lies down for half or three-quarters of an hour.

When he emerges from the building, he feels like a new man — or says he does, which is the same thing.

When The Young Man who Knows Everything made that remark, Tibbitts replied promptly that he most earnestly hoped the change would be permanent. "My young friend, if you feel symptoms of getting back to your original self, take more baths."

Baden merits all the good things said of it. It is a delicious spot, and if one had nothing to do in life but enjoy it, I know of no place where, with money, he could get more out of it. Its people are hospitable, and its physicians will humor you to any disease you choose. If there is nothing the matter with you, they will prescribe just as cheerfully as though you had all the ills that human flesh is heir to, and will pocket their fees with a grace unexcelled. They have had vast experience with hypochondriacs, and know all about it.

CHAPTER XLI.

THERE is hardly a man, woman or child in the world who has not heard of Heidelberg, and who does not know something of this famous little city of students, wine, beer, castle and casks. It is a place better known, probably, than any in Europe of its size and non-political importance, and it entertains more sight-seers than any other. It is well worth the attention given it.

Heidelberg is beautifully situated on the River Neckar, about twelve miles from its junction with the Rhine, and a more delightful spot for establishing the seat of a palatial residence does not exist in all Germany.

On the one side is a high range of hills, on the other the beautiful Neckar, the opposite bank of which is covered to the tops of the lovely hills with terraced vineyards.

The very first thing the tourist has to see is the old Schloss, founded by the Count Palatine Rudolph I., about the beginning of the fourteenth century. It has passed through remarkable events. Various princes and electors improved and fortified the original structure of Rudolph, until, in 1720, when Elector Carl Theador rebuilt it, it covered a vast extent of territory.

Situated on a spur of the Königestuhl, it is surrounded on three sides by beautiful woods, while on the fourth the River Neckar flows past the town down a wondrously beautiful valley, and loses itself in the Rhine, twelve miles below. The outside walls are plain and unpretending, being designed entirely for defense. But inside, the façades are embellished with fine carvings, allegorical figures, the window arches having medallions of eminent men of ancient times. In niches around

(622)

the front, facing the entrance, are statues of the sixteen Counts Palatine. This front is thought to be the most magnificent, architecturally, of any of the four, combining, as it does, four

HEIDELBERG CASTLE, INSIDE THE COURT.

different styles: Doric, Tuscan, Ionic and Corinthian. It certainly is very imposing, and before it was battered and disfigured by cannon balls, during the war of 1693, it must have been a wonderfully fine piece of work.

The regular thing to do at Heidelberg is to go through the

great, gloomy subterranean passages that wind in and out under the massive pile. It is not a cheerful trip, but it gives one a good idea of the solidity of ancient masonry, and of the security of their old dungeons.

The Grand Balcony is a wide, well-built terrace on the river side of the castle. From this point the view is magnificent, the whole Neckar valley being spread out like a map, below us. Then we go on through great rooms, whose ivy-covered walls once resounded with song and merry jest, to the huge tower at the eastern angle of the castle. This old tower is, or was, rather, a monster, being ninety-three feet in diameter, with walls twenty-one feet thick. In 1689, when the French General, Melac, was obliged to surrender the castle and town to the Germans, he blew up the fortifications and set the castle on fire. The attempt to demolish the tower was only a partial success. The walls were so thick and so well built that the explosion only detached about a half of it, which fell, a solid mass, into the moat, where it is to-day, as solid as it was two centuries ago, though now its rough sides are covered with shrubs and ivy.

The best view of the castle in its entirety is from the Great Terrace, quite a little distance from the garden that surrounds the grand old ruin. From this height is seen the beautiful valley, with the town spread out in irregular shape on the banks of the Neckar. Across a deep ravine, beautifully clothed with green, is the ruined castle, standing out in bold relief, the ruined tower, the dismantled walls, the grand promenade making a picture of rare beauty.

The castle is decidedly the finest structure of the kind in Europe, beautiful in its location, beautiful in its design, and beautiful even in its ruin.

Like most things that are interesting in these old countries, it is, however, a remembrance of the days when force was the only law, when the sword and the spear were the only arbiters, and he who had command of the most of them was the ruler.

It has had many masters. In 1685 Louis XIV., of France, set up a claim to the country and invaded it. Of course he had no earthly right to it, any more than the then occupant, but that didn't matter. They didn't split hairs in those days.

When a king wanted an adjoining country he simply figured up how many cut-throats he had and how many cut-throats the king had that he proposed to go for, and if he had more cut-throats than the other king, why he went for him.

And so Count Melac, Louis's chief cut-throat, assailed Heidelberg, and the city and castle capitulated to him. He occupied it during the Winter of 1688, but as the German armies were approaching in too great force to suit his notions, in March, 1689, he evacuated the place, having first blown up the fortifications and burned the town, and made what havoc he could. Four years later the French finished the destruction, then the Germans rebuilt it in part, but, as if fate had a spite against it, it was struck by lightning shortly after and was abandoned as a fortress and palace, and so it stands to-day.

Ruin as it is, it is the most wonderful combination of nature and art I have ever seen or ever expect to. The old kings who built it had good eyes for effect as well as defense. The mountain is three hundred and thirty feet above the river, and it is a precipice inaccessible except by winding paths, which, when fortified, an hundred men might hold against ten thousand. This before the days of rifled guns. Our present artillery would knock the place as it was into a cocked hat in an hour. But in those smooth-bore days it was a place of strength, and could only be taken by a systematic siege.

We are much obliged to the French for one piece of vandalism When they evacuated it the last time they tried to blow up the principal round tower. They placed a frightful amount of powder in it, and it exploded, but so well had the work been built that it merely broke off about a third of it, which toppled over into the moat and still lies there as it fell. The walls at the point where the break is, are twenty feet thick, and are as solid as a rock. There was no shoddy in this work. There needed to be no shoddy, for the work cost the Rhine robbers who built it nothing. They confiscated the quarries for the stone, and then drafted a sufficient force of men from all parts of their dominions to do the work, feeding them upon black bread and sour wine, which they seized also, making the building of almost any kind of a castle a very cheap affair.

It is a curious place — this reminiscence of the past. There
40

are miles of halls, of passages, secret and open; there are
drawbridges and turrets, and posts for warders; there is the
enormous terrace, overlooking the beautiful Neckar and the
vine-clad hills on the opposite bank; there is the wonderful
court in the interior, the walls facing inward, rich in statuary
and wondrous carving, grandly even though a ruin.

Imagine this vast structure when it was itself, filled with
knights and ladies, on the night of some festival! Think of it,
with lights gleaming from every window, the terrace filled
with happy dancers, and the immense court full of pleasure-
seekers!

GREAT CASK—HEIDELBERG CASTLE.

There have been high jinks in the old Schloss. It must have
been a wonderful place for everyone except the wretched
peasantry — whose unrequited labor built it, whose unrequited labor supported it, and whose bodies
defended it.

It is well that it is in ruins. Its walls are royal, and, the
fact is, I hate everything that savors of royalty.

In the castle is the famous tun of Heidelberg. This famous
cask is twenty-six feet high and thirty-two feet long, and it
holds, or rather held, for it has not been filled for several years,

eight hundred hogsheads of wine, or two hundred and thirty-six thousand bottles. There is a platform on the top of it, upon which a cotillion can be comfortably danced.

The University at Heidelberg has in course of preparation for future beer drinking some eight hundred students, from all the countries of the world. I suppose they do pay some attention to studies, that they do attend lectures and recitations, and all that sort of thing; but all I saw them do was to drink beer, which they do in a way that no other class of young men in the world can. It is a large thing in Heidelberg to be able to drink more beer than any one else.

Smoking divides the honors with beer, although, as one student can smoke about as much as another, there is not that opportunity for display of talent that there is in beer drinking

The students are all in societies or clubs, and each club wears a cap of a peculiar color. You go into one of the innumerable beer halls, and you see at one table students with blue caps, at another with red, and another with yellow, and so on. They never mix, and each society is at deadly feud with all the others. They sit, and sit, and sit, at these tables, drinking beer out of mugs, and smoking enormous pipes, mostly meerschaum, which they are at great pains to color.

As a red-capped student is supposed to be at mortal feud with all the other colored caps, duels are as common as beer — and I can't say more than that. But a duel in Heidelberg is not a remarkably sanguinary affair. It is about as harmless as a French duel. They don't fight with revolvers at ten paces, or shot-guns at thirty, or sabres, or anything of that sort; and instead of trying to kill each other, every possible precaution is taken not to kill at all. The weapons are rapiers, very sharp, and ugly enough, if the duelist really meant business; but both contestants are so swaddled in cloths, so wrapped in cotton defences, that any harm, aside from a cut in the face, is impossible. They fence and thrust, and do all sorts of things, the object being to inflict a wound upon the face; and the student receiving the wound is very proud of it, and if his flesh is healthy enough to heal without a scar, he tears it open. The scars he must have, for they are testimonials, as it were, of his bravery.

So you see on the streets of Heidelberg any number of students with their faces scarred and seamed, horribly disfigured, but not one of them would sell a scar for anything earthly.

Their beer-drinking proclivities I have referred to. Tibbitts had a letter to one of the red-capped students, who immediately introduced him to his club, and the result was — beer. The quantity that Lemuel could consume nettled his friend, and an attempt was made to put him under the table. The Professor, who believes that there is a devil in every drop of beer, warned Tibbitts against joining the party.

"They will get you intoxicated," said the good old man.

"Will they? Perhaps they will. But, Professor, a young man of good physique, a son of nature, who has lived in Oshkosh, need not fear any man who comes of the effete civilization of Germany. Don't fear the result of this encounter. I shall do credit to the old flag. To my beloved country I dedicate my stomach. I will fetch them all."

And so Tibbitts sat down with them, and he drank as often as they did for a half hour, then he urged the drinking, and he called for larger mugs.

There was consternation among the students. Tibbitts' friend was the President of the club, and a mighty man among the beer drinkers; indeed, he owed his official position to his prowess in this line, and here was a fresh American urging him to deeper and deeper draughts.

The contest waxed warm. One by one the feebler men dropped out until only two remained — Tibbitts and the President. Tibbitts was cool and collected, the President was hot and flurried.

Tibbitts made the President understand that he wanted larger mugs. He explained that he was thirsty, and that the time consumed in bringing the small mugs (they held nearly a quart) was so much waste, and that the effect of one quencher died out before another could be brought. What he wanted was a mug that held some beer. He was not a baby, but a man.

And so mugs were brought about twice the size of those they had been using. Tibbitts touched his opponent's mug in good-fellowship, after the custom, and putting his lips to it drank it off at one pull, and tapped on the table to have it re-filled, to the delight of the other colored caps, and the dismay of the reds. The President smiled in a sickly sort of way and drank. He finished the mug, and leering wildly around the room, made a feeble attempt to get his pipe to his mouth, reeled and fell prostrate. He was vanquished, and his friends bore him senseless from the floor.

"The idea of a mere German attempting to drink with a man who was weaned on Oshkosh whisky," said Tibbitts, con-

MR. TIBBITTS AND THE STUDENTS.

temptuously. "I am now just in humor to tackle the Vice-President, Secretary and Treasurer of this Club, all at once."

He did not, however, for they were all gone. But the honor of America was saved — according to the notion of Tibbitts.

A curious place is the famous restaurant on Haupstrasse, which for many years has been the resort of the University student. Here he sits and drinks his beer at a table that is literally covered with the names of students carved in the solid oak. Many of the names there engraved are now known the world over, though when they were cut there, many decades ago, the youthful carvers were great in literature, science or art, only in the dreams of their early manhood.

A RHINE STEAMER.

CHAPTER XLII.

AN INLAND GERMAN CITY — MANNHEIM.

It was comfort to get out of the beaten routes of tourists, and find yourself in a city where you do not hear English, and where the sight-seer with the inevitable guide book and field-glass, does not display himself. It was a relief to get into a city that had not been half Anglicised and Americanized by the constant stream of tourists that pour over Europe every Summer, where you could see Germany and the Germans, pure and

MANNHEIM.

simple. Such a place is Mannheim, at the confluence of the Rhine and Neckar, twelve miles below Heidelberg.

Mannheim is a delicious old city, once the seat of the grand Dukes of Baden, but now the seat of what is a great deal better than grand dukes, much merchandising and manufacturing. It is the only city in Europe that is laid out like Philadelphia, in regular squares.

The principal pride of the Mannheimers is their theàter, and the Mannheimers have every reason to be proud of it, for, in addition to its being one of the best conducted in Europe, it is

(631)

where Schiller and other great German poets won their first successes.

The Germans amuse themselves at public cost whenever possible. For instance, this beautiful theater, which contains costumes and stage sets for all the standard operas, is supported by the city government. There is a small fee for admission, (I believe the most expensive seat in the house is a trifle less than a dollar, and ranging down from that to ten cents), but the deficiency is put upon the tax duplicate and paid the same as other taxes.

Nowhere in Europe are better performances given, either operatic or dramatic. The principal characters are assigned to artists of the very highest order, the orchestra is made up of picked musicians, every one a soloist, and the chorus is not that mass of associated howlers that drive us mad in America; but the members are trained singers, as well as actors.

For the presentation of Wagner's "Lohengrin" there was an orchestra of fifty-eight in number, a chorus of two hundred and fifty, and as many more supernumeraries. Nowhere is the detail of a presentation so carefully and conscientiously worked out, and nowhere an opera more satisfactorily given than in this little German city of less than fifty thousand.

The singers enter into a contract with the Direction for a term of years, and if they sing or act the full term they may go elsewhere, but they are pensioned by the city for life. Their salaries are very small, but the resultant pension is so comfortable a thing that they never break their engagements and never do slovenly work.

The Sunday night we reached Mannheim, Wagner's "Lohengrin" was given, the performance commencing at half-past five in the afternoon and continuing till eleven at night. It was not as in American opera houses. There wasn't a note omitted, a song, or line of text cut; the entire opera as it came from the composer was given with a degree of conscientious care that the American party had never heard before.

Tibbitts was in a state of surprise all the time. First going to an opera, not a matinee, in daylight; and then another custom that was as novel and strange as the hour at which the performance began. After entering the vestibule we passed through a long hallway lined with shelves; on these shelves the gentlemen placed their hats, overcoats, canes and umbrellas, and then passed into the auditorium without getting any check for the articles so left.

"Imagine," said Tibbitts, "an American theater with a free cloak room in the lobby! How many hats, coats and walking sticks would be left by the time the entertainment was over? Think of such a thing in New York, or even Oshkosh! Why, in Oshkosh the boys out of one such audience would supply themselves with overcoats, hats and umbrellas for a year. It is a temptation even to me, as well as I have been brought up."

TIBBITTS IN THE CLOAK ROOM.

The opera of Lohengrin is extremely difficult to render, but in this little German town of only forty-seven thousand inhabitants, it was done in a manner that would surprise the grand opera goers of New York, or even Paris or London. The stage settings were magnificent, every detail being most carefully and faithfully attended to.

Wagner's music, to be fully appreciated and enjoyed, must be heard under the most favorable circumstances — at the Mannheim Court Theater, for instance. There is an individuality about it, an expression of thought by sound, that has never been equalled by any other composer. And when performed by such a company as that at Mannheim it rises to the sublime. Every member of that great company from the star down to the most humble member of the orchestra, was a thorough artist, and having had the very best training they interpreted the divine work of the great master in the same spirit in which it was conceived. It was a rare performance.

Tannhauser was the next opera, and performed as carefully as Lohengrin. It was enjoyed by the entire party except Tibbitts. He is not musical or asthetic. And so when the Young Man who Knows Everything went into raptures over the wonderful orchestra, Tibbitts spoke of it contemptuously as "sound factory." And he jeered at the procession of pilgrims who, in the opera, are returning, to delicious music, from Rome, where they had been for their sins. "Yes, that's the way of it. They load up with iniquity and go to Rome, if they are Catholics, or somewhere else if they are of other beliefs. Then they come back as good as new and entirely ready to take another load."

He criticised other points in the opera. Tannhauser was in despair at having committed the unpardonable sin of heathen worship. "You see how it is. Other sinners who had merely committed murders and sins like that, made a pilgrimage to Rome and were absolved, but Tannhauser knew better. Religious power forgives everything except joining the opposition shop." And he was particularly severe upon Tannhauser for confessing his sin to his love. "For," he continued, "had he kept it to himself it would have been just as well. But I suppose it had to be. Had Tannhauser kept his counsel and married the girl, the opera would have closed at the second act."

Mannheim is a purely commercial and manufacturing town. It enjoys a most picturesque situation. It's streets are regular and handsome, and in the outskirts of the city are numerous pretty parks, which add greatly to the beauty of the place.

When, in 1821, the Elector, Charles Philip had ecclesiastical differences with the Protestant citizens of Heidelberg, where up to that time he had his court, he transferred the seat to Mannheim, which from that time became an important place. The town was founded in 1606, and destroyed by the French eighty-three years later.

During the residence there of Charles Philip, the spacious castle, which occupies the entire southwestern portion of the town, was built, and though it suffered partial destruction in 1795, it has been restored, and with the lovely grounds surrounding it, forms one of the most attractive spots in Mannheim.

In appearance Mannheim is quite modern, though some of its buildings bear the impress of the hand of time. But as a rule, its wealthy citizens, with the enterprise and go-ahead activity that characterizes a mercantile people, have erected solid substantial buildings of the most approved modern style, which gives the city the look of wealth and business success it possesses.

The theater, next to the castle, is probably the oldest building in the town. It was constructed during the last century, and restored in 1854.

The people of Mannheim are industrious, hard-working Germans, full of enterprise and business tact. During business hours they are always on duty, but, with the purely German characteristic, as soon as business is over they devote themselves to innocent amusement with as much gusto as they do to their work during the day. And the German citizen is not selfish in his enjoyments. He wants his whole family to partake of them with him. So in the evening, in the parks where the bands play, you will see him surrounded by his whole family, wife, daughters and sons, sipping beer, chatting with friends, and enjoying the music. They are a social lot of people, these Germans, and know full well how to get all the pleasure there is in life.

They differ materially from the French and the English. The French are full of life and vivacity that spur them up to an unusual state of activity all the time. They must have a constant excitement, and noise, and show, or they are miserable. He is the most generous man in speech and the closest man in action in the world. He is effusive. He will, on a steamer, embrace you at parting, and insist upon your making his house your home when you visit Paris. He will swear that he will devote his whole time to you, that he will take it as a mortal affront if you do not command him, and all that. But don't take too much stock in it. He doubtless means it while he is saying it, but when he reaches Paris, and you find him there, it is quite another thing. You are not necessary to his happiness any more, and in the most adroit and suave way he gets rid of you, and forever.

Very like people the world over, however. The man who applauds a virtuous sentiment the most vehemently at a theater is the very fellow who will go home and kick his wife, and the

wildest approver of patriotic sentiments is the very man who
goes to Canada to avoid a draft, or jumps the bounty for a
thousand dollars. The Frenchman makes the best outward
show of any one in the world, but his goodness is very thin.
It will not bear the solid weight of actual use.

The Englishman delights in what he is pleased to think
dignity, but what is really overweening conceit. He is pom-
pous, dull and heavy. If he does a good thing, he does it in
such a way as to make it an offense.

The German is neither the one nor the other. He goes
through life tranquilly, in perfect content with himself, always
making the best of his opportunities, and in a perfectly rational
way getting all the enjoyment he possibly can.

He does not profess to be your friend unless he is so in good
faith, and when he invites you to his house he always means it.
He is rather careful about his friendships, for as he never falsi-
fies in this, he needs to be, but when once said it is done. A
rare good man to meet is your German. He has his peculiarities, but he is good and solid all the way through.

In Mannheim, as in all German communities, the absurd
American fashion of treating is most sternly discountenanced
and tabooed. The true German will not have it at all, at any
price. Your friend asks you to join him in a bottle of wine,
and you accept, but that does not mean that he pays for your
drink. Not at all. He desires you to join him because you
are his friend, because he likes your society, and because he
wants to talk to you and have you talk to him. And when
the bottle, or three, as a German says, is consumed each pays
for what he has had and they go their way.

Consequently the bar-room beat so common in America is
an unknown institution in Germany, and the beery, bloated
pimpled faces hanging around public places waiting for invi-
tations are never seen.

Mr. Tibbitts most heartily approved of this custom. He
remarked that the American system of treating came very
nearly ruining him. In Oshkosh he had a very large circle of
close friends, who loved him dearly. They were very fond of
him, why, he would not say, because he was a modest man. It
might have been that they admired his physical graces, or

possibly his intellectual endowments — men have tastes that cannot be accounted for. I met one gentleman on this trip who admired the Young Man who Knows Everything; that is, he said he rather liked him.

He was studying law in Oshkosh, and after wrestling all the forenoon with his studies he was, naturally, mentally as well as physically exhausted.

"I tell you," said Mr. Tibbitts, "when a young and enthusiastic student at law has been poring all day over the pages of Walter Scott, or Dickens, or Thackeray, with only an occasional intermission at a beer-shop across the street, without feeling something like a squeezed lemon, he is a strong man indeed. I am physically fragile, and my active mental nature makes fearful drains upon my body.

"And so on my way to my boarding house for dinner I was accustomed to stop over a minute at the Spread Eagle Hotel, to take one solitary cock-tail, which I really needed as a bracer, as it were, to the system; something that would encourage nature to the point of taking in a full meal, a meal that would hold me up to the work of the afternoon.

"Now here is where the infernalism of the American system comes in. There would be at the bar every day at the same hour seven fellows, all good, jolly men, all particular friends of mine, who came there, as I did, for just one drink. Now, understand, I went in there for one drink, which I felt I needed, and one drink only. But seeing the other seven in classical poses about the bar, I could do no less than to ask them to join me, which in the freshness of youth and the first blush of a strong manhood, they always did promptly. After a minute of joyous conversation, Snedeker would wink at the barkeeper, who would set before us another. More talk, a little more cheerful than before, and Wilson would insist upon all drinking with him. Still more talk, and Adams would consider it an offense if we did not take just one more with him.

"By this time any one of us would have taken something with anybody, for good sense, that faithful though easily overcome sentinel over our passions, had been driven out, and we were on the high road to inebriety. And there we would stand, and stand, taking 'just another one,' till we had forgotten all about dinner and everything pertaining to life, except of that article contained in the bottles before us.

"I have known these incidents to cover a great space of time and much territory. I have gone into the Spread Eagle for just one cock-tail, and in consequence of the infernal American system of treating, have found myself a day or two later in St. Louis, paying a most recklessly incurred hotel bill from money obtained by pawning my watch and overcoat. And once I extended the excursion as far as New Orleans, and probably would have gone on through Mexico if delirium tremens had not kindly put in an estopper.

"If we did in America as they do in Germany I should have gone in and taken one cock-tail and gone to my dinner and returned to my studies, and gone home to my supper and have been a good and useful citizen."

And Tibbitts having got fairly launched upon the wide ocean of drinking continued :

"Americans are fools in their way of drinking. All other peoples have a defined idea of what they want to accomplish with stimulants, but the American has not. Your Englishman wants to get stupid drunk; he wants forgetfulness, which I can't blame him for. Were I living in England I should want forgetfulness in large doses. I don't blame an Englishman, condemned to London climate and London customs, for drinking. The Frenchman and German drink just enough to produce the requisite hilarity, the general good feeling which light stimulants in moderation produces, and then they quit. An American does nothing of the sort. He drinks through all the stages, the slightly exhilerant, the mild hilarious, the boisterous idiotic, the brutally quarrelsome, the pitiful maudlin, and then slips off his chair harmless because helpless.

"Why, I have heard a nine-tenths drunken man rouse up his companion by shaking him, with the appeal: 'Jimmy, rouse up! Can't you *stand* another one?'

"Just think of it! In this fellow's case there was no pleasure to be had from the drinking of 'another one.' His poor, outraged stomach rebelled against it, the very smell of it was death, and the taste worse than death, and yet he was asked if he could not endure 'another one!' He was asked if his abused system could not be further outraged. And he did manage to stagger up to the bar and swallow another dose of poison, which was the last straw that broke the camel's back. His indignant stomach deposited it on the floor with great promptness. A moment's rest, and he did take 'another one,' and subsided into a miserable sleep.

"I have seen so much of the infernalism of the American treating system that I could deliver a wonderful lecture upon that and kindred temperance subjects."

"Why don't you lecture on temperance?" asked one of the party.

"Alas! I am not a reformed drunkard," was Tibbitts reply.

Then up spoke the Young Man who Knows Everything.

"My dear sir, all you have to do is to reform."

Tibbitts disdained to answer this, and walked moodily away.

MAYENCE.

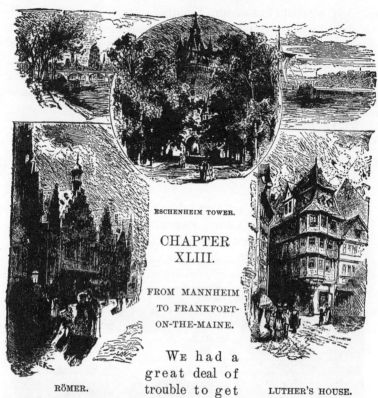

ESCHENHEIM TOWER.

CHAPTER XLIII.

FROM MANNHEIM
TO FRANKFORT-
ON-THE-MAINE.

We had a
great deal of
trouble to get

RÖMER.

LUTHER'S HOUSE.

out of Mannheim. All German railroad officials are in uniform,
and the regulations are about as strict in the railroad service
as in the military. The train we were compelled to take left at
six o'clock in the morning, and we were at the station promptly.
That is, we had four of five minutes in which to get our tickets,
see to our baggage and go on. We hurried to the little window in the ticket-office, but it was down. Through the window we could see the official in an ordinary coat, and we
knocked on the glass. He did not open it, but sat there, nerv-
ously consulting his watch. The minutes were rushing on,
tumbling over each other with frightful rapidity. But still he
did not open the window, and we were ticketless, and the train
was within a minute of departure.

What was the matter? Why simply this: The ticket agent

(640)

had sent his uniform coat out to be brushed and the boy had not returned with it. He would no more think of selling a ticket except with that blue coat on, buttoned up to the chin, and with every button there, than he would have thought of cutting off his right hand. It mattered not that passengers were waiting, it mattered not that the engine was whistling its last warning notes, that coat was not brushed and on the official's back, and no tickets could be sold till it was.

Fortunately the boy came with the coat, the official got it on somehow, the train waited two or three minutes, tickets were sold hurriedly and we did get away.

What would have happened if the boy had not come back with the coat at all, no one can answer.

Certainly no one would have got tickets till he got his coat, and we should all have missed our train.

Red-tape is a great institution, and nowhere do you see more of it than in Germany. But we got away finally to Frankfort.

Contrasting strangely with Mannheim's straight streets and quiet unpretentious business blocks, is the very peculiar city of Frankfort, where within a stone's throw of each other are streets so entirely different, that in one you may imagine yourself on Broadway, while in the other you may with equal propriety consider yourself set back five or six hundred years.

New Frankfort is the newest city I know of. It is more fresh and recent than Broadway. It is very like Broadway, except that its buildings are less garish, and more solidly built.

The line between the old and the new is only a street, and the old is the oldest in Europe, as the new is the newest. The contrast is wonderful. It is the fourteenth century and the nineteenth shaking hands across the chasm of time. It is the mediæval knight and the London exquisite side by side. The same may be seen in all European cities, but nowhere so striking as in Frankfort.

Approaching the city you see the old watch towers high on the hills that surround the environs of Frankfort, those remaining monuments of the reign of force, when the people, ruled mercilessly by the nobles, erected these towers from which the usurpers watched each other. Germany is not yet free from

41

this kind of rule; it has merely taken a different form. Gun-powder changed the form of force, but not its spirit. These once impregnable fortresses would not stand a minute be-fore the artillery of the present, and so they are abandoned. But in their stead are the regiments we saw in Mann-heim and every-where else, each one a fortress of flesh and blood. Ger-many will get rid of the whole of it one of these days, and the million of men employed to support that one unmitiga-ted curse of the world, royalty, will be added to the pro-ductive power of the country instead of living upon it.

STREET ON THE RÖMERBERG.

As we leave the fine station and enter the wide " An-lagen," or public grounds, that com-pletely encircle the city and are lined with handsome buildings, it is hard to realize that the city of Frankfort dates from the time of Charlemagne, and that it has for centuries played an important part in the history of Germany. From the year 1152 the German emperors were chosen in Frankfort.

The Kaiser-strasse leads directly to the center of the city, and is lined with magnificent business blocks and dwellings. The street is wide and well kept, the buildings are all of the modern style of architecture, built of cut stone, and they present a fresh and attractive appearance.

Speaking of buildings in European cities, it would be fortunate for us of America if we could imitate them ever so slightly. In London I visited a steam fire engine house, and was amused at the clumsiness of the apparatus, and the slowness in general of the entire concern. The horses, for instance, were stabled around a corner! In New York the horses are in the same room with the engine, fastened so they may be unhitched by electricity, the men sleep in their clothes above, and everything is arranged so that in one second the engine is on the street, and on its way to the fire on a run.

"How long does it take you to get out upon the street?" I asked.

"From seven to ten minutes."

"Why, in America we get out in two and one-half seconds."

"Y-a-a-s, and so would we, *if we built tinder boxes.*"

There he had me and had me badly. There is no necessity for rapid and extensive fire departments in Europe, for the houses are not mere lumber yards, as with us. When a man wants to build in a European city he has to get a license. His plans are submitted to the authorities, and, if approved, a proper authority stands over the work and sees that it is properly built. You are not permitted to run up a fire trap in the midst of valuable property; you are not permitted to build a showy sham that may be burned to the ground in ten minutes. Nothing of the sort. Your walls must be solid, your staircases of stone, and open, not of pine with the space under them for coal-oil depositories, there must be so many escapes from the building, the roof must be metal or slate, and the walls must be so built that a fire cannot get beyond the room in which it originates, and the only damage that can possibly result is the destruction of the contents of the room, and such damage as smoke and water may inflict. When a fire occurs in one room in a house, the people in the other rooms keep on as usual. It does not annoy them, for the fire cannot spread.

FRANKFORT-ON-THE-MAINE—THE JEWS' STREET.

No one dreads to occupy a room on the fourth floor of a European hotel, for the idea of fire never occurs to one. They seldom have fires, and when one occurs it is counted a misdemeanor on the part of the owner of the premises.

This all comes of solid and substantial buildings, to begin with. As a matter of course, a house costs something at the start, but when you get through you have a house for all time. The modern buildings in Frankfort will be standing and in good repair centuries hence. I wish I could live to verify this assertion, but I suppose I shall not.

Going on through the Kossmarkt, where there is a fine monument to Gutenberg, we came to the Zeil, a very beautiful street, and then, turning to the right, found ourselves in the celebrated Judengasse, or Jews' street, one of the most dingy, wretched, forlorn quarters that can well be imagined.

The street is narrow, dirty, and squalid. The houses are high structures in the last stages of decay, many of them having great props to keep them from falling. The inmates of these apologies for houses are as dirty and squalid as the street itself. There are little pawn shops, dirty shops where old clothes are sold, an occasional tenement house, and very many liquor stores. It is the very acme of squalor and is in great contrast with the elegance of the Zeil, only a block or two away.

A dirty, squalid, beggarly-looking street is Judengasse, but who knows what wealth is hidden behind all this apparent poverty? The Jew of to-day is no less acute than the Jew of the fourteenth century. He has all the wisdom of his ancestors in money getting, with the added experience of time. He can no longer be hauled up by a mailed knight, and compelled to disgorge; but in the stead of the robber, by the strong hand, there is the tax-gatherer; and, in his passion for the accumulation of wealth and disinclination to part with it, the Frankfort Israelite hates the one as heartily as his ancestor did the other. The American Israelite lives as bravely and ostentatiously as any man, and even more so, but the habit in the old European cities is to conceal wealth, to live meanly, and to find enjoyment, not in the using of money but its accumulation.

This street has always been set apart for Jews, and down to the year 1806 it was closed every evening, and on Sundays and holidays, throughout the entire day, and no one of its inhabitants were allowed in any other part of the city, under heavy penalty. Until the time of the Prince Primate, in 1806, no Jew was ever allowed to enter the Römerberg, or market place in front of the town hall. It is said that while the persecutions of the Jews from the twelfth to the seventeenth century throughout the continent was merciless, it continued longer in Germany than any other country, coming down, in Frankfort, even to the present century.

Notwithstanding the abridgement of their rights, a great many of the Jews attained wealth and distinction. The house is still pointed out in Judengasse where the Rothschilds, the founders of the present great banking house, lived during those troubulous times.

It is the same old story. The Jews, despised, persecuted and outraged in every way, bore everything patiently, waiting for the time for their revenge. And their revenge has come in every country. In the olden days, in all the countries of Europe, the Jew had no rights which any other nationality or blood was bound to respect. He was outside of the law. He was taxed at the caprice of every prince and power. He had no chance in any court where a Christian was opposed to him, and when they differed among themselves, it was made a pretext to rob him. The most absurd laws were made against them, and it really seemed as though the native rulers and their subjects laid awake nights to invent ways to oppress them.

All this has changed. With a power of endurance simply wonderful, they bowed their heads to their oppressors, and, as all oppressed people do, substituted cunning for brute strength, and trained minds for lusty thews and sinews. They won in the end.

The despised family of Rothschild, once compelled by the haughty citizens to confine themselves to one quarter of the city, is now its boast. The Frankforter takes more pride to-day in the fact that the city was the home of the Rothschilds, than it does in the fact that it was for centuries the seat of government of the German Empire. The Jew in Europe, while yet under something of a ban, is not the despised creature he was. The world has learned to respect him.

There is not a calling in Europe that a Jew is not at the

very head and front of. He has composed all the great operas, the sons and daughters of Judea are the great actors and singers of the world; in law and divinity, and learning of all kinds, they stand at the head, and in finance they are the world's creditors. A convention of Jew bankers could be called together who could shake every throne in Europe.

Kings and nobles don't pull the teeth of Jews any more to extract loans. On the contrary, they come into the presence of these great financiers with hat in hand and humble step. The Jew holds the forceps now, and it is the noble's teeth that are pulled. How, in the absence of all law, hated, despised and contemned, and persecuted, they could amass wealth, is a mystery, but they did it.

When persecution in one State got too warm for them they always had enough wealth to get away to another, and they always found a prince who needed money badly enough to give them protection, for a time, at least, and these same princes were wont to become silent partners with the Jews in the work of eating up their own subjects with usury, which held until the Jews got the upper hand, when the prince always made a raid upon them, paying his debts to them in this way, and they flitted.

Finally they got some measure of rights, when they made themselves felt. The hatred of Jews continues in Germany and Russia, for the reason that their superior energy and acuteness has made them the masters of the trade of those countries. There is no business that they do not control. A great people are the descendants of Abraham, Isaac and Jacob. They live where all others die, they wax rich where others starve. It is so in Europe, it is so in America, it is so everywhere. There is no village so small that it has not its Jew, precisely as in America. The Jew with his goods is the first man in a new town — he progresses a little faster than progress. He was in the front or in the rear of the armies going southward; he was at the western end of every rail laid on the Pacific Road; he is essentially the pioneer in money and trade. They are a wonderful people.

The Jew of the fifteenth century and the Jew of to-day are practically the same. They use different methods, but the underlying principle that moves them remains unchanged. We had two of them in the cars coming to Frankfort, an elderly Israelite with the regular nose, and his nephew, who was the exact picture of his uncle. The old man was giving the boy sage counsel:

"Vot is necessary for a peesnis man, Abram, is berseverance more ash anyting else. Berseverance is vot vins, every dime. Ven I livet in Shalesfille, shust back mit Vicksberg, (I vas in clodink), der vash Cohen and Lilienthal both in groceries. Cohen vas doin der besht peesness and it made Lilienthal mat. Lilienthal mate a special ding oof mackarel and Cohen unterselt him. Den Lilienthal put down sugar but Cohen unterselt him. Lilienthal put rice down mit almosht nottin, unt Cohen almosht gif it avay. Cohen het de peesnis, and no matter how much Lilienthal sanded hees sugar and vatered hees vishkey Cohen alvays beet him. Dot Cohen vas a goot peesnis man.

"But Lilienthal vash de most berseverin man ash ever vash, and he vash pound to beat Cohen anyhow, and so vun day he notist dot Cohen het a fery fine delivery mule. So Lilienthal he sait to Cohen:

"'Shake, dit you efer dink dot oof dot mule oof yours hed dot wart off his hint leg he wood pring you more ash dwice vot he vood now?'

"'Dot wart? It don't look vell. But how ish dot wart to be got off? Der hint leg oof a helty mule isn't der pesht blace to go foolin round.'

"Lilienthal vas a most berseverin' man. He sait:

"'It's der easiest ting vot efer vos. You come up behint dot mule mit a red hot iron and burn off der wart. De mule is vort a huntret tollars more ash he vas.'

"Cohen triet it der next tay, unt hish funeral vash der piggest vot dey efer hat in Shalesfille. Lilienthal attented it hisself in two carriages, an' he vent right along and did all de peesness, and at a goot brofit, vor he hedn't no gompetishun. Lilienthal vosh a berseverin' man, Abram. Der ain't notting in peesness like berseverance. Remember dot."

In a historic point of view, very interesting is the Römer, or Council Hall, erected about the year 1406. It faces the Römerberg, and its three pointed gables give it a picturesque appearance. In the principal hall on the second floor are "Portraits of the Emperors," beginning with Charlemagne (768-

"DER HINT LEG OOF A HELTY MULE ISN'T DER PESHT BLACE TO GO FOOLIN' ROUNT."

814), and Conrad I. (911-918), and coming down to Ferdinand III. (1637-1658). It was in this room the new emperor dined with the electors and then showed himself to the people assembled in the market place in front. Adjoining this room is a smaller one, in which the electors used to meet to consult on the choice of an emperor. It is still preserved in the style of the olden days.

Of course Frankfort has fine churches and a cathedral, but there is no especial merit in them.

Near the monument erected on the Friedberger Thor by Frederick William II. to the memory of the Hessians who fell in 1792, during the attack on Frankfort, is a small circular building which contains one of the most beautiful as well as most celebrated works of art in Germany, if not in Europe.

A wealthy banker, named Bethman, purchased from the artist, Dannecker, of Stuttgart, his masterpiece, the exquisite "Ariadne on the Panther," and erected this building for its exhibition. In one part of the room is a recess, separated from the room by a crimson curtain. The ceiling is of glass, across which is stretched some heavy crimson cloth stuff. This filters the light, soft and subdued upon the group, producing a most beautiful effect. The figure of Ariadne, nearly life-size, is half sitting, half reclining on the back of the panther, one elbow resting on the animal's head. The position is one of grace itself, and the modeling is perfect. As the soft light is shed upon the pure white marble, one can almost believe that it is the figure of a living, breathing woman before him. The effect is greatly heightened by the arrangement of the pedestal which allows the statue to be slowly revolved, thus giving the peculiar light and shade effect to every part. It is truly a most marvelous piece of statuary, and is worthy the admiration and praise bestowed upon it by the most eminent critics.

During the sixteenth and seventeenth centuries, Frankfort derived the most of her importance from the great fairs that were held there annually. Merchants came from all parts of the country, with their stuffs, and made the old city, for the time being, a great commercial center, a position its excellent location especially adapted it for. But later, these fairs lost their prestige, and finally died away altogether, though occasionally they have an industrial exposition. But they are nothing compared to the fairs of the olden time.

While we were in Frankfort an Industrial Exposition was in progress which, of course, we visited, and spent at least two hours very pleasantly, wandering around the different buildings and the beautiful grounds. The display was about equal to an ordinary State Fair in Western America. The most enjoyable portion of it all was the ride back to the depot, through the floral gardens, with their magnificent flowers and plants and shrubs, and along the broad Anlagen, with their handsome residences and well kept lawns.

COLOGNE CATHEDRAL.

CHAPTER XLIV.

WHAT a flood of anticipations came trooping through the mind at the mere thought of a sail "Down the Rhine." Down that famous old river, every mile the scene of a legend; the river in whose praise poets have sung for ages; whose every turn reveals a castle or fortress that has figured for centuries in story and song! What visions of wooded banks, vine-clad hills, and ivy-covered ruins! What pure, unalloyed pleasure a trip "Down the Rhine" must be!

And it is. Poets may have written what seemed to be over-wrought praises of its marvelous beauty; writers may have gone into ecstacies over its beauty, its grandeur and its sublimity, but they have none of them exaggerated. It is all that has been said of it, and more.

We were whirled into the fortified city of Mayence, a place that has long been an important strategical point, early in the afternoon of a lovely day in August. The sun was shining brightly, the river was clear and limpid, and everything was propitious. Favorable, indeed, began our trip down the Rhine.

Sailing down the river, past the grim fortifications on both sides, we pass between two islands, and soon reach the pretty little town of Biebrich, where, in A. D. 840, Louis the Pious, son and successor of Charlemagne, died.

The river at this point begins to assume a bolder and more picturesque appearance than it did near Mayence, and as we approach Eltville we get the first glimpse of a ruined castle, built in 1330, by Baldwin, Archbishop of Treves, who was then Governor of Mayence. It stands high up the bank, and is almost hidden from view by the trees that surround it. Just beyond, back of a low-lying island, is the town of Erbach, near which are some old abbey's ruins.

(652)

From here the river is dotted with little islands whose irregular shape and diversified surface adds a new charm to the scene; while over on the right bank, in a commanding position, surrounded by fruitful vineyards, is the celebrated Schloss Johannisberg, built in 1716 on the site of an old Benedictine monastery founded in 1106. Around this old castle, which is in good repair, are the vineyards from which come the famous Johannisberger wines, the favorite of all Rhine wines. From this point all along the river to the "Siebengeberger" or "Seven Mountains," the vineyards that clothe the banks of the river are famous for their exquisite wines.

A few minutes further on and on the same bank Rüdesheim comes into sight, flanked by the massive Brömserburg, a massive castle, with ivy-grown walls, that towers high above the little town below it. This is another famous wine-producing district, its fame having been handed down from as far back as the twelfth century. The castle, a three-storied rectangular building, was erected in the twelfth century, and has but recently been restored.

With a graceful sweep that reveals new beauties every minute, we came in sight of Bingen, "fair Bingen on the Rhine," just where the River Nahe empties into the noble stream. High above it, on a thickly wooded eminence, on the site of an ancient Roman fortress, is the Castle Klopp, with its frowning battlements and forbidding towers.

No one can see what there is about Bingen to make it famous. It never would have been famous but for the Hon. Mrs. Norton, an English poetess, who found the name to be properly accented, and of the right number of syllables for use in a poem, which she wrote. It will be known so long as the platform is infested with readers and there are school exhibitions.

"A soldier of the legion lay dying in Algiers,
There was lack of woman's nursing, there was dearth of woman's tears."

That's the way it commences, and the burden to each stanza is:—

"For I was born in Bingen—fair Bingen on the Rhine."

It is a most absurd poem. There must necessarily be a lack of woman's tears around a shot soldier in a foreign land,

for no government on earth could afford its soldiers any such
luxury. How, possibly, could a government send out a com-
plement of wives, sisters, cousins and aunts to nurse and weep
over each wounded individual? And then this soldier, mortally wounded, instead of dying properly, goes on through
nearly two hundred lines to send messages to everybody he
ever knew in Bingen, ending each message with:

'Fair Bingen on the Rhine."

"And so, as the boat approached Bingen, all the excursionists, especially the sweet girls from the seminaries, who
were on their Summer vacation, murmured softly:

" For I was born at Bingen—fair Bingen on the Rhine."

And one young divinity student, with long hair, and a high
forehead, and long, narrow white hands, deliberately recited
the whole poem with what he firmly believed to be "expression," which consisted in ending each sentence with the upward
inflection. The ineffable nuisance had spent the night in
committing the drivel to memory, and he spared us never a
line.

The school-girls all said, "How nice!" Tibbitts went below
and amused himself with a bottle of wine, and the majority of
the other passengers walked forward where they could smoke.

And then the real worry of life began. The dozen or more
young men with high foreheads, who did hear the "reader"
through, sought you out, and collared you, and said: "Did you
hear Mr. ——— read Bingen? He thinks he can read, but he
can't. Now this is the proper way to read that poem."

And he went right on, and read it to you as he thought it
should be done. There were thirteen of them.

Scarcely has this view faded from sight before we pass the
ruined towers of a castle erected in 1210, and destroyed by the
French in 1689. Just opposite this ruin is the famous Mouse
Tower, a small, circular tower, built of massive stone. It takes
its name from the legend of Hatto, Archbishop of Mayence.
The legend runs that during a great famine in the land thereabouts, the poor people were sorely distressed for corn, and
vainly besought Archbishop Hatto, who had graneries full of
the previous year's crop, to aid them in their time of want. At
length he promised that to all who should be at his barn on a

certain morning he would give corn. Of course the poor
people flocked thither, and when the barn was full he locked
the doors, and, despite their piteous cries for mercy, set the
barn on fire, and laughed at their cries, comparing them to
mice that had come to carry away his corn.

DEATH OF ARCHBISHOP HATTO.

That night he had troubled dreams, as was proper, and in
the morning his servants told him to fly, for his grounds were
being filled with rats who had eaten all the corn he had saved.
He hastily quitted his castle and sought refuge in the castle on
the island, thinking that the steep rocks and swift water would

prevent the rats from finding him there. But they swarmed over the island by millions and the cruel Archbishop died a terrible lingering death.

This is a good solid legend, with meat in it. There is a great moral lesson inculcated, and every legend should inculcate a moral. It contains, I thought, a solemn warning to American grain operators.

But Tibbitts found a great many flaws in it, and said he did not consider it a good legend at all. It was full of improbabilities. Hatto made a corner on corn. Very good. He had some purpose in it. Very good. That purpose could have been nothing but a speculative desire to run up the price of his corn and sell out at an advance. Very good. To whom could he sell the corn at a profit? Only to the starving people. Now what an ass he must have been to corner the corn and then go and burn up his customers, the people to whom he could have sold the corn at any price! Mr. Tibbitts insisted that that wouldn't wash.

He doubted the rat story also. He knew all about grain operators. He knew many of them in Chicago who frequently saw rats, and snakes, and all that sort of thing. Probably Archbishop Hatto had been drinking, and fancied these things. But it was well enough. One must have legends and it wouldn't do to go any more closely into particulars about legends, than it does to be too critical as to the character of candidates for Congress. He should accept Hatto, corn, rats and all. It was a very pretty story — for children. It would teach them not to burn people.

At this point the Rhine makes a sudden bend and the channel becomes very narrow. Formerly the passage was very dangerous, and in the olden times it was a favorite spot for the robber knights who had their strongholds on the banks thereabouts, to stop trading vessels on their way up and down the river to request the payment of tolls.

The merchants always paid the tolls. Sir Hugo, or Sir Bruno, or Sir whoever he might be, did not need a Custom House to collect his imposts. He merely had a score or more of cut-throats, fellows who would kill a man for sixpence, or its equivalent in the money of the day, and in default of the sixpence would do it for the sheer love of the thing, and the trader found it much better to give what was asked than to go to the bottom of the Rhine with a slit in his windpipe. But I have no idea that he lost anything. He counted this in his expense account, the same as the merchant of to-day does his insurance and bad debts, and he took it out of his customers, and they in turn took it out of the people. All of these things come out of the ground at the end. It is the tiller of the soil who finally pays for the soldier, the robber, the judge and jury, the gin-mill and the faro bank. And Tibbitts referred at once to a remark he had previously made, that it was vice, not virtue, that cost the world, that to wipe out the gin-mills was to do away with the police, the courts, and with the hangman, and everything else connected with what is called justice, that is so expensive. Armies are supported to sustain kings and courts, liquor makes police and justices' courts necessary, and while everybody seems to pay a tax, none of them do it but the tiller of the soil, for they all charge up these expenses on what they do till it gets down to him. What he would do would be to do away with vice. Virtue is very cheap—so cheap that he wondered more people did not encourage it.

The banks now assume a more rugged appearance, and on each eminence is a castle or a ruin. We pass by in rapid succession a number of very picturesque views, in each one of which these ancient fortresses play an important part. Those old robbers knew well where to build, and they built exceeding well.

After passing Lorch we came to the pretty stream of the Wisper, which empties into the Rhine at this point. On the left bank of the stream is a rugged cliff, towering high in the air, called the "Devil's Ladder," which, of course, has its legend.

Near Lorch there lived a knight who, after losing his wife, became sullen and morose, and would have nothing to do with any one but his daughter, a lovely girl, just budding into womanhood. He refused to grant hospitality to any one who asked it. One stormy night a knight in distress applied for shelter and rest and was gruffly refused. The next morning when old Sibo, the knight, inquired for his daughter, he was

42

told that she had been seen early in the morning with two
sprites going up the impassable crag across the river. The
distracted father hastened after and could see his daughter on
the very summit of the crag. Almost crazed with grief he in
vain besought the sprites to return her to him. But they only
laughed and jeered at him. Finally, after a long time had
passed, a young knight who had long loved the maid returned
from the wars, and hearing the rather awkward situation his
early love was in, hastily repaired to the foot of the crag
determined to rescue her. But it was in vain. There was no
way of making the ascent. He was about giving up in
despair when a little figure suddenly appeared before him,
and asked him why he was so despondent. On learning his
love for the girl she told him to come again at the same time
the following evening. The young knight returned promptly,
as young men in love always do, and was surprised to find a
ladder reaching from the foot to the top of the crag. He
hastily mounted to the summit, and there in an enchanted
garden he found the object of his search, and soon restored her
to her father, who henceforth was most lavish with his hospitality. The maiden and the brave young knight were united
in marriage and lived a long and happy life. The ladder
remained on the rock for many years, and was called the
Devil's Ladder. It fell away in the course of time, but the
name has ever since been applied to the great rugged cliff.

It is a thousand pities that some of these ladders and things
don't remain, simply to give us faith in the legends. If there
was just one round of the ladder left, if one could only be
shown the holes in the rock in which he was fastened, it would
be something, but there is nothing of the kind. You have to
take it all on faith, and that is sometimes wrenching.

All the way along the river, from here to beyond Coblenz,
the Rhine is a succession of constantly changing views as the
boat winds its way around the tortuous channel, every one
more beautiful and picturesque than its predecessor. There are
castles on high hills on the right bank, some close to the river,
others further inland, just discernable through the trees. On
the left bank are pretty villas and more castles, and occasionally an island is passed that has on it a ruined watch tower

built hundreds of years ago, when might was right in this romantic country.

Just before approaching the pretty village of St. Goar, on the left hand of the Rhine, the imposing rocks of the Lurlie rise over four hundred feet above the river. Here the current is very swift, and many are the tales told of bold adventurous knights who have lost their lives under the shadow of this famous rock.

Of course the Lurlieberg, as the rock is called, has its legend, as has every well regulated rock on the river. A rock without an appropriate legend would be no rock at all. The knights and ladies, and witches and devils, of the olden time, existed, apparently, solely in the interest of the booksellers of Mayence, and the other cities of to-day. The legend of the Lurlie runs something like this:

The rock known as the Lurlie was the resort of a water-nymph, who was about as capricious as other nymphs. She was a young lady who could live under water as well as above it; in fact, her permanent residence was under the Rhine. Her regular recreation was to come out of the wet, and sit on a rock, and comb her long, yellow hair (she was a natural blonde, as all entrancers are), and sing, accompanying herself on a golden lute.

Of course all the young men in the vicinity fell desperately in love with her, and they went for her. But while the nymph would sing and pose for them so as to set them crazy, their boats were all dashed to pieces upon the rock, whereat the nymph would laugh, and comb her hair, and sing, and entice other young fellows to their doom. She was kindly only to fishermen, and the one item to her credit is that she never did them harm, but always good. That was probably because they were old men, and unimpressible.

The son of a count in the vicinity, fell in love with her, and despite the warnings he had received, determined to conquer her. He ordered his boat, and commanded the men to steer for the fatal rock. There was no nymph on it at first, but after a minute or two she appeared more radiantly beautiful than ever. The foolish young man attempted to climb the rock, but he fell into the seething waves and was never more seen.

Then his father swore vengeance and sent valiant men to seize her and burn her as a witch. The result might have been anticipated. The nymph sang a song to the waves and plunged into them, laughing, the same waves upsetting the boat which held the soldiers, and she descended to her cave under the water, while her pursuers thought themselves lucky to escape with their lives.

At another time a maiden loved a young man who was to go to Palestine to fight the Saracens. During his absence she was so persecuted by the other young men that she retired to a convent near the Lurlie, and waited for her lover. At last she saw a boat approaching filled with men, and among them, gorgeously attired, was her young man. Unfortunately to get to where she was the boat had to come very near the rock, the water-demons raised the whirlpool, the beautiful nymph presiding with a mocking smile, and they seized the doomed craft and hurled it against the rock, and down it went, and all on board were lost. The hapless maid plunged into the seething waves after her lover, and as she went under the flood, the nymph of the Lurlie appeared on the surface, beautiful as ever, but with the laugh that was frightfully harsh and discordant. She could not bear to see earthly young maids happy.

That same night she was on the rock as usual, combing her hair, and other young men got into her toils, till there was a scarcity of eligible suitors in the neighborhood.

She was a dangerous person, this young nymph of Lurlie.

Passing Coblenz, a beautiful city, picturesquely situated at the confluence of the Mosel and the Rhine, we soon came to the Siebengebergen, "Seven Mountains," the rugged banks gradually tone down, and between Bonn and Cologne the scenery is not so interesting, because of the grandeur of that which has preceded it. Still it is not altogether devoid of interest, though it is of a quieter and less imposing kind. After a five hours' ride through such magnificence, one is quite willing to take it in a little milder form, and we were thoroughly content when we landed in Cologne, the great cathedral city.

Was there ever a steamboat, or stage, or rail car, or any other place where people are thrown together in such a way that they can not escape, that that unmitigated nuisance, that nuisance without any compensating features, the knowing young man, the young man who knows everything that a young man should be ashamed to have it known that he does know, is not present? There is a tremendous crop of these weeds every year. Lightning strikes innocent cows and beautiful houses, but it never hits one of these fellows, which argues a great waste of electricity. Good men and beautiful women die of fevers and such complaints, but these insects never have anything of the kind. A row of shanties never burns, but stately buildings go down or up in smoke daily.

They are an exasperating set. They do not seem to know that it is rather discreditable than otherwise for a man not in the trade to actually *know* all about wines and liquors, and things of that nature. But when a young fellow is weak enough to profess this disreputable knowledge when he has it not, he ought to be immediately taken out and killed. To see the old wine tasters and the ancient beer drinkers, who do actually know all about these things, smile and wink at the vaporings of these young simpletons, is a piteous sight. But, heaven help them, they go on just the same. Panoplied in egotism, they do not know they are asses, and therefore enjoy themselves. It is a delightful thing to be an egotist. An egotist pities the people who do not enjoy him.

We had him on our steamer down the Rhine. He was six feet high, with a moustache, and a billy-cock hat, and pointed shoes, and short coat, and all that, and he talked to everybody.

"Know Ned Stokes? Should say so! Knew him before he killed Jim Fisk. Used to meet him at Harry Felter's, and many a hot old time I've had with him. Last time I met Ned was in Chicago, and we were both so blind drunk we didn't know whether we were in Illinois or Louisiana."

He rattled on about wines, and salads, and so on, and then a bottle of wine that he had ordered came up. He took a little of it in his mouth, and rinsed it, and passed the bottle under his nose, backward and forward, and sniffed critically, and then remarked sagely that it would do, but that it was not quite up to the mark, and that it was difficult to get good wine even in the Rhine country.

From this he glided off to beer, criticising the various varieties, with the air of a man who had lived a long life in sampling beverages and doing everything else of that kind, and he branched out in cheerful conversation about celebrities in the various walks of life.

"D'ye ever meet Ned Sothern? Poor Ned! There was Ned and Billy Florence, and we used to have high old times before poor Ned went under. I remember—"

Tibbitts moved uneasily in his chair, which portended something.

"Then there was Uncle John Brougham, and Lester Wallack"—and he went glibly through all the noted actors and actresses as though he had been a boon companion and bosom friend of all of them for years.

Then he took a short excursion into the realm of sport. He knew every pugilist who had ever fought, every rower, every pedestrian, and all the crack shots and base ball players, and he had the dates of their various performances down to a dot. He reeled off this interesting matter, toying the while with corks from champagne bottles, pausing a moment in his narrations, to give the history of each one.

He not only knew all these people, but he never by any means used family names. He did not say, "Mr. Fechter," it was "Charley," "Old Charley," and when he spoke of women it was not "Miss Rose Eytinge," it was "Rosy." And he kept on talking of clubs, and horses, and yachts, and fishing, and gunning, and cards, and women, and racing, and "events" of that sort, till Tibbitts pounced down upon him as a cat does upon a mouse.

"May I ask what part of the Great Republic you are from?" asked Tibbitts.

"I hail from Kokomo, Indiana, but I spend most of my time East."

"Your business?"

"Business, ah, I am in hardware."

"I see—you have a branch house in New York. Do you know Billy Vanderbilt? No? You ought to know him. Take Billy Vanderbilt and Russ Sage, and Cy Field, and little Gouldy, and you just more than have an everlasting team.

And there's Chet Arthur; who'd ever spose that Chet would ever have got to be President? Some men have all the luck. And there's Jack Sherman, of Ohio, why Jack and I — but never mind. I don't let on all I know. But I tell you, when Jack and his brother Cump — he's the general of the armies now, and his other brother Charley, is a judge. Poor Scotty, of Philadelphia, the president of the Pennsylvania Road, he's gone. He couldn't stand the racket, and he went under. But Hughy Jewett, of the Erie, he's another kind of a rooster, he is. He is in with Gus Belmont, and they two, with Jim Keene and Dave Mills, of San Francisco — well you ought to just see them punish wine after they have taken the boys in and done for 'em. They are up to everything, they are. I remember one night — "

"Where are you from?" asked the knowing young man, gasping in astonishment at this array of names and the familiarity with which they were used.

"Me! Oh, I'm from Oshkosh; but I have a branch house in New York too. I go down just once a year to sell live stock, and I pick up more names in the week I stay there than an ordinary man can remember, and I remember all their given names, and I can reel them off just as fast as any Indiana young man I ever met, and I know them just as well. Only I prefer financiers and statesmen to horse men, actors and prize fighters. I am very select. Next year I shall not know anybody under a senator. You may just as well know big men, really great men, as merely notorious ones. Now there's 'Lyss Grant and Bob Schenck, and Rufe Ingalls, and Black Jack Logan, you ought to just sit down with them at a game of poker! That's where you have sport, and as for fishing, Bill Wheeler, till he got spoiled by being Vice-President, he could everlastingly handle a rod, and the way he'd yank 'em out was a caution. He was no slouch. Many a time I've — "

The wise young man from Kokomo, Indiana, Who Knew Everybody, could not endure the reminiscences of the Oshkosh young man, and he beat a precipitate retreat and we saw him no more. Tibbitts drew a sigh of relief and remarked that he had never strained his imagination so frightfully in all his life.

CHAPTER XLV.

COLOGNE, ITS CATHEDRAL AND OTHER THINGS.

THERE may be altogether too much of even cathedrals. After going through those in London, then tackling those in Northern France and wandering through those in Paris, going out of your way to see a dozen more or less in Southern France, then taking by the way the big and little ones in Switzerland, one gets, as it were, somewhat tired of cathedrals, and wishes the necessities of travel did not compel him to see more of them.

To a certain extent they are all alike. It is true they are all built in different styles, but there is a striking family resemblance, and they are so alike that after you have seen a dozen or two you will not be very much interested in those to follow. The interiors are all alike, and the "objects of interest" are the same. They have the same style of pictures, there is always a "Descent from the Cross" by an old master, and there is a well-selected assortment of saints, also by old masters, and the interiors are always dim and sombre, and have the precise kind of light that aggravates the always too faithful picture of a saint undergoing martyrdom, or dead just after martyrdom.

Mr. Tibbitts discoursed at length upon the general gloominess of religious institutions. Inasmuch as the builders of churches put in their time and money for the good of mankind, he wondered why they didn't have the knowledge of human nature, and the good sense of those engaged in wicked pursuits.

"Cathedrals in Europe," said he, "and even the churches in our own beloved country, are always the darkest, gloomiest places that human ingenuity can possibly devise. I remember the one my grandmother used to compel me to attend when I was a boy of six. The interior, even to the pews, and their furnishings were of a dark and dismal color, the hen-coop pulpit was dark, the trimmings about it were dark, the windows were narrow and very high up The ceiling was dark, and **to**

(664)

add to the prevailing gloominess, there were outside green blinds over the windows that admitted just enough light to make the gloom of the interior felt. And then the domine was a sallow man with gray hair, brushed back from his forehead; and he dressed in a black frock coat buttoned up to his chin. He was the least cheerful picture in the church.

"The seats in the pews were very high, and slanted slightly forward, as did the backs; and as the feet of a six-year-old child wouldn't touch the floor, it was the most distressing thing in life to sit there. And then the music! The worthy old gentleman in the pulpit, in a voice as harsh as a saw mill, would grind out a most doleful hymn, which was always sung to most doleful music. And that was followed by a sermon three hours long, on the doctrine of foreordination! Cheerful, for a boy of six, who, when dragged into that gloom on a bright June morning, looked longingly out upon the bright, green fields, on which the soft sunlight was falling like a benison from a good Creator; and who, to get to the church, had to cross a beautiful brook with trout, which knew no Sunday, swimming in the clear waters, every ripple of which was an invitation to him.

"Now the wicked people are a great deal more wise than this. A wicked place is always made attractive. There never was such a lie written as " Vice is a monster of such hideous mien." Vice is not hideous; it is that which follows vice that is hideous. Champagne is as beautiful as can be; its effects are hideous. It isn't the getting drunk that is hideous; it is the resultant headache the next morning. A bar-room is always made light and pleasant; there is silverware, and curious glass, and chandeliers, and warm fires, and everything pleasant and cheerful. Your merchant, who is worldly if not wicked, makes his place as pleasant as possible, and even the butcher dresses his meats in sprigs of evergreen. If I ever go into the ministry, I shall do away with gloom, and have my place as pleasant as light and flowers can make it. As religion is the best thing in the world, I don't see why it should be made the gloomiest. As for these pictures — bah!"

Then we went through the cathedral. We did it as a duty.

There's another trouble about cathedrals, and that is the " restoration" that is going on perpetually and constantly.

They were all commenced some hundreds of years ago, they were very slow in building, and by the time the last part was done the first part had decayed, and had to be restored. Go wherever you may in a cathedral, you shall see a large part of it disfigured with scaffolds, with workmen on them, and building material around, giving one the idea they are yet unfinished.

It is said by scoffers and sneerers that the reason why it took several centuries to finish a cathedral was to prolong the time for pulling money out of the faithful, and that the perpetual restorations that are going on are for the same purpose, but of course that is a slander. Boss Tweed might do such a thing, but not those filled with zeal for cathedrals.

Cologne has many points of interest, but the principal one is its grand cathedral, the fourth largest in Christendom; St. Peter's at Rome standing first, the cathedral at Milan second, St. Paul's in London third, Cologne fourth.

Though it may not be so huge in its dimensions as the other three, it certainly cannot be excelled in beauty of design or artistic excellence in construction. It is cruciform in shape, with a total length of one hundred and forty-eight yards, and sixty-seven yards breadth. Its walls are one hundred and fifty feet high, the roof two hundred and one feet, and the tower over the transept three hundred and fifty-seven feet, and the two towers over the west façade two hundred and fifty feet high.

Tibbitts didn't think much of the architect. The tower over the transept, he insisted, should have been an inch, or an inch and a half, wider at the top.

These figures, however, give but a faint idea of the immensity of the structure, whose imposing appearance is greatly heightened by the elaborate galleries, turrets, flying buttresses and cornices that adorn every portion of the walls and towers.

The history of this cathedral, which has been building since 1248, is somewhat interesting to those who take any interest in cathedrals. The foundation stone was laid on the twenty-fourth of August, 1248, by Archbishop Conrad, of Hechstaden, but it was a number of years before anything more was done. In 1322 the choir was finished and consecrated. In 1388 the nave was fitted up for use, and in 1447 the bells were placed in the south tower. From that time the interest in the work gradually died out, and it seemed as though the original design would never be carried out. In 1796 the French took off the lead roof that had been placed over the decaying building, and converted it into a hay magazine.

It was not till 1823 that anything was done to restore the church. In that year the work of renovation commenced, and a few years later a talented architect named Zwirner, sug. gested the completion of the building according to the original designs. The idea was enthusiastically taken up, and in 1842 the work was begun, and has been steadily continued, until now only a few finishing touches remain to be given.

The architect who first designed this structure, undoubtedly the finest Gothic edifice in the world, is not definitely known, though it is commonly supposed to be Meister Gerard, of Riehl, a small village near Cologne. The imaginative people there had to have a legend about the cathedral, which is as follows:

Archbishop St. Engelbert conceived the idea of building, on the site of an old Roman church, the most magnificent cathedral the world ever saw. He called to him a young architect and told him to prepare plans in accordance with this idea. The young man, delighted with this opportunity of distinguishing himself and making his name famous forever, worked night and day to design a building that would meet the requirements of the Archbishop. But there was one part he could not master. He became almost insane over his disappointment, and was about to give up, when one night he dreamed he saw the missing portion sketched on the wall of his chamber. Thoroughly awakened, he sprang from his bed to make a copy of it. But it had disappeared, and in the room stood Satan with an illuminated parchment in his hand. This contained the long sought plan. Satan, doing the regular thing, offered it to the despairing architect on condition that he should have his soul and that of the first person who entered the cathedral. The young man was distracted. He wanted the plan, and told Satan he might have his soul; but he could not barter away the salvation of another. Satan smiled, returned the parchment to his bosom, and was about to go away, when the young man acceded to his terms.

The devil knew his business. He knew that the architect's ambition would not let him stop for a soul or two, as he had mortgaged his own, and that he would get him finally. He has gone on that principle ever since and has always won.

The plans were then made out, and work on the beautiful edifice was pushed rapidly forward, and at length was so far

LEGEND OF THE CATHEDRAL—COLOGNE.

completed that a date was set for the consecration. Then the architect realized the position he was in. Not only was his own soul everlastingly lost, but that of an innocent person. This so preyed upon his mind that the people noticed his agitation and besought the Archbishop to ascertain the cause. The unhappy man finally told the good father the whole circumstance, much to the latter's horror. He was advised to make his peace with God, while the Archbishop determined to sacrifice a woman of ill-repute who was in prison awaiting sentence, by making her the first to enter the church.

When the day for consecration came, a long box containing, as was supposed, the poor woman, was carried to the cathedral, the door was opened, the lid of the box was taken off, and the unfortunate victim crawled on her knees into the church, the attendants sprinkling holy water all the time.

As she entered there was a terrific noise. Satan appeared, broke the neck of the unfortunate in the box, flying off, presumably, with her soul. He then flew to the architect's house and broke his neck. As Satan disappeared from the church, the woman arose from the box, went into the building to pray, while the servants carried from the dome the carcass of a pig, which had been enveloped in a woman's gown, and sacrificed.

This legend will not do, any more than the other legends you hear about these places. Satan could not have been fooled with a pig. It is no compliment to him. To suppose that he did not see the woman enter the church is to give him credit for very little intelligence and a most singular neglect of his own business; and the attempt to try to swindle him with so clumsy a contrivance is too absurd. And then why should Satan be perpetually swindled? The contract was a fair one, and should have been carried out in good faith.

It may be remarked, in passing, that Satan does not, now-a-days, appear to those having charge of government buildings in the United States, making offers of plans and other assistance, that he may get them in the end. He is too acute for that. Why should he go to the trouble of helping them, when he knows perfectly well that he will get them, anyhow? He doesn't waste his time that way any longer.

The interior of the cathedral is large and very impressive, the fifty-six pillars which support the roof being of huge but graceful dimensions, giving a pleasing aspect to the whole. The stained glass windows are particularly fine, being among the best in Europe.

The various chapels that surround the nave are all handsomely decorated with statues, frescoes, and fine altars, done in the highest style of art. The wood carving representing The Passion in the altar of St. Clara is especially good, as is also the tapestry on the walls back of the choir stalls, illustrative of the Nicene creed and the seven sacraments. This tapestry was worked by the ladies of Cologne, and is a fine specimen of that style of art.

From the cathedral the visitor naturally turns to the other churches, but a hasty inspection of them is all that is required, for, after the cathedral, everything else loses its interest. There are some very imposing edifices, which, if they did not suffer so by comparison with the cathedral, would be considered fine specimens of early architecture. For instance, the Gross St. Martin, consecrated in 1172, which is a massive building, with an imposing tower surrounded by four corner turrets.

The still older church, St. Maria im Capital, consecrated in 1049, is in the shape of a cross, built in the Romanesque style. The interior is decorated with modern frescoes that are very badly done, being of light and gaudy colors, that do away entirely with the idea that they adorn a place of worship. Other churches of interest are, St. Peter's and St. Cecilia, the former of the sixteenth and the latter of the tenth and twelfth century; St. Gereon, dedicated to the three hundred and eighteen martyrs of the Theban legion, with their Captain Gereon, who perished on the site of the church during the the persecutions of the Christians under Diocletian.

On the substructure of an ancient Roman stronghold stands the Rath-house, a picturesque building erected in different centuries, beginning with the fourteenth. Here the meetings of Hanseatic League were held in the fourteenth century.

From the Rath-house the visitor turns to the markets, passing through narrow, dirty streets, with high overlapping houses, to the monument of Frederick William III., a huge equestrian statue of the King. Here is the Heumarkt, and a busy sight it is. As far as the eye can reach is a vast concourse of people, buying and selling all manner of things. The women, with their white caps and peculiar dresses, flit hither and yon, talking, laughing and jesting with men, who are arrayed in costumes that suggest the old Rheinish peasants, made familiar by the painters of the old Rheinish school.

Time was when Cologne, founded by the Ubii, when Agrippa compelled them to migrate from the right to the left bank of the Rhine, was a power in that land. At the end of the fifteenth century she was the wealthiest and most influential city in Germany. Not only was it great in commerce, but it was the center of German art, both in architecture and painting, as may be seen yet by the elegant buildings, designed and erected in those olden days, that are yet standing, and in the pictures of that age that are still preserved.

Cologne's great troubles were internal dissensions, which finally led to the banishment of the Protestants in 1608. It was due more than to any other one cause, to these discords that caused the city to gradually decline in power as early as the middle of the sixteenth century. Later on she lost nearly all her importance and continued in a state of lethargy until the Prussians obtained control in 1815, since which time her trade and commerce have been steadily improving, making her to-day one of the chiefest commercial cities in Germany.

In the old church of St. Ursula are the alleged bones of eleven thousand virgins. The legend is that this sainted woman, a Scotch princess, was returning from a pilgrimage to Rome with eleven thousand virgins in her train, and they were set upon by the barbarous Huns and all slain. There can be no doubt as to the truth of the legend (if you want to believe it), for you are shown, through gratings, bones enough to stock a cemetery.

I have no opinion about it. Possibly St. Ursula was skillful enough to corner that number of virgins; but would the Huns have slain them all? That makes us pause. It was a great many years ago, and I am glad the legend has it (for I wish to believe all the legends I can) that the virgins came from a country far distant from Cologne. Could a saint, be she ever so devout, find that number in Cologne now? It is not for me to say. Possibly they are all gone on pilgrimages. Let us take the legend down at one gulp, and forget the fact that among these bones are the remains of any number of males, and likewise any number of animals.

In this same church you are shown one of the identical jars in which water was miraculously turned into wine at the marriage in Cana, and various other relics, such as the teeth of saints, and cheerful things of that nature, in which I really could take no especial interest. After the eleven thousand skeletons of virgins, anything else in the way of relics seemed tame. If they had saved the teeth of eleven thousand saints, it would have been something like ; but isolated teeth, single teeth at that, make too small a show. The teeth were doubt- less genuine, but there were too few of them.

Cologne is probably the best known city in Europe. Leav- ing out the wonderful cathedral, and the bones of the virgins and the history that clings to it, giving it a musty and ancient flavor, it is the place where cologne water was invented, and where is the American school-girl who does not know all about that? She may know nothing about the cathedral, but she knows all about that especial perfume. A man named Farina invented it several generations ago, and every male child born since in the families of perfumers has been christened Farina. There are at least fifty places where the "original" is sold. Here you get the genuine, and though you shall have it much better in any little drug store, in any Western village in Amer- ica, you buy a flask of it in Cologne, at one of the originals. It is the thing to do. Our party all supplied themselves, though I noticed that the most of them threw the flasks away, from the train on the way to Brussels. It was genu- ine, but cologne by any other name would smell as sweet.

Home ! There are other countries to see, but, first, home. Three thousand miles away lies a land fairer than any yet visited, a country more pleasing. We are glad that our time is expended, for we go home ! Six months of absence is quite enough, and the thought of returning makes the blood course quicker in one's veins. And yet never was time more profitably spent than in these rambles through strange countries, for the experience put us in condition to appreciate our own. An American has no idea how good America is, till he sees Europe. He does not know how good a government he has, till he lives for a time under others. It requires a glimpse of oppressed Ireland or king-ridden Prussia, to make one prop- erly appreciate a Republic. We have no palaces, but we have no soldiers. We have no cathedrals, but we have no paupers. We have no ruins, and shall never have, for under our system the ephemeral structures of to-day will be replaced to-morrow with what will be eternal. Every American should go abroad once at least, that he may, with sufficient fervor, thank the fates that cast his lines in pleasant places. And so, glad that we have been abroad, but much gladder to get back, we turn our faces westward. Our exile is ended.

THE END.